Their eyes met. Joh... twenties, dashingly ... , with wavy blond hair and a kindly eye. Selina was lucky, she thought — though the young man stirred nothing very deep within her.

What he saw, however, was something he would never forget — a young woman with the most hauntingly beautiful eyes he had ever encountered. The rest of her face was handsome enough but those eyes held him entranced. It was not love at first sight, for he was not so shallow as that. Indeed, in those first few moments he was so struck by her beauty, he almost forgot she was a person and so gazed at her more as one might examine a beautiful work of art.

'I live at Lanfear,' she explained. 'I am Miss Visick's cousin. My name is Johanna Rosewarne.'

A Notorious Woman

Malcolm Ross

HEADLINE

ISBN 0 7472 3250 4

Printed and bound in Great Britain by
Collins, Glasgow

HEADLINE BOOK PUBLISHING PLC
Headline House
79 Great Titchfield Street
London W1P 7FN

A Notorious Woman

PART ONE

STILL LIFE

Chapter One

Somewhere high on Trigonning Hill a vixen yapped at the frost; the year was turning. A chill breeze keened back and forth through the loose lights of the decaying window, like the drone of some ancient piper, playing to no one. A cold slab of moonlight lay across the threadbare carpet and climbed up the antique counterpane, where it came to gentle rest upon the sleeping form of the young woman. In the deep dark of the passageway beyond, a nervous hand strayed forward, touched the door, edged its opening wider, wider . . . until a creaking of the hinge made it freeze.

The young woman stirred in her sleep, turned on her back, breathed easy again.

Raw eyes in the pitch-dark passage roamed greedily where the hands that now stayed the door and its jamb longed to follow. Such a pretty creature – in sleep so gentle . . . such a shame, such a waste!

'Mr Visick! What ever are you doing?'

John Visick, lord of Wheal Venton mine, master of Lanfear House – and, indeed, lord and master of his questioner – put a finger to his lips, closed the door, this time without a squeak, and tiptoed toward her. His excitement, or the evidence of it, died in those few steps; it did not revive when he embraced her bony frame. 'Mrs Visick, my dear, you will take a chill.'

'But what were you doing there?'

He steered her back toward the carpeted regions of the house, explaining as they went that he had thought he heard voices.

'Voices?'

3

'And laughter.'

'Laughter?'

He laughed, as if to show her what the word meant. 'Is my speech so defective, my dear, that you must confirm my every word?'

'But how could there be laughter — at this hour?' The way he nudged her into their chamber and prodded her toward the bed was most disagreeable. 'And in Johanna's room of all places.'

'That was my thought, too, ma'am. My very thought.' He ran his hand down the washboard of her ribs, rested at the awkward protrusion of her hip, and shivered. 'Fortunately it was just the wind. Must get some putty for those lights or they'll drop out in the next gale.' He kissed her on the neck. 'You are cold, my dear. We both need a little warming.'

Theresa Visick lay back and sighed. 'Be as quick as you can,' she begged. 'How we shall survive tomorrow, I do not know.'

Their two heads lay side by side, a universe apart. She stared at the ceiling, conjuring one after another of the coming day's disasters; he closed his eyes, buried his face in her pillow, and, such is the magic of desire, fleshed her bones with those young, supple, enticing curves that still called to him through the dark labyrinth of the house. Then he was quick, indeed.

In her chill little room that was not quite a servant's garret and not quite 'family', either, Johanna slept on. Outside, in the now-waning moonlight, the vixen trotted over the hilltop to bark in some more likely parish.

Dawn awakened a different John Visick: he scrubbed off sin like the rime of sleep and clad himself in the Bible black of righteousness. There was no giveaway gleam in his eyes as he muttered his solemn, everyday, 'Morning, maid,' to Johanna. As always, she was first at the breakfast table — having already been about the house for her usual hour, plus, on this day of days, an extra one beside.

She glanced up briefly from the list she was compiling. 'Good morning, Uncle John. I hope you slept well?'

The question merited its customary grunt as he settled behind his curtain of newsprint.

4

'The nights are certainly turning chill,' she added, at the same time writing: *7 pm — Jessy to put the warming pan through Dr Moore's sheets.*

'What? What? What's that? Chill?' Mrs Visick, a bundle of frayed nerves and sleep-starved bones, came bustling into the breakfast room and flopped, already exhausted, into her chair. 'How you can stuff yourself like that, I don't know,' she snapped at Johanna.

The young woman greeted her aunt and hoped she, too, had slept well.

'Sleep!' the woman echoed. Then, to the maidservant, 'I can't touch a thing. Just a piece of dry toast.'

'You'll wither away, Mrs Visick,' her husband warned mechanically. 'You'll slip between the floorboards.'

When the maid brought the toast, her mistress said, as if complaining, 'Perhaps I could manage a peach. A small peach?'

The maid nodded and left them; before the door was quite closed, her mistress added, 'Bring two if they are *very* small.'

Johanna spread the last of her dole of marmalade and popped it in her mouth. *Willie to see to Dr Moore's boots before he does the lamps,* she wrote.

'Well, here's a fine breakfast,' Theresa Visick commented. 'Nothing but reading and writing about me!'

'Bring your household accounts, my dear,' her husband advised jovially. 'Then we shall complete the academy.' He smiled at his niece (his *wife's* niece, actually, as he often reminded himself) to see her smile in return.

But Johanna was too long in this house to be drawn in like that. Her smile was ambiguous enough for her aunt to read into it: *How little these men understand!* The older woman, however, was in no mood to be patronized. 'Speaking of the accounts . . .' she said to Johanna.

'We have been rather busy on other things,' her niece reminded her.

'You needn't speak as if the entire burden of it has fallen to you,' Mrs Visick responded. 'I've had my share.'

Johanna smiled inwardly. Her aunt's 'share' had consisted of one, single question: What shall Selina wear for the visit of Dr Anthony Moore? Even her uncle, though he knew full well the importance of this occasion, had been forced to joke about it in the end. 'The Corn Laws are repealed,' he said, 'and ruin faces the countryside. America takes up arms against Mexico. In India, our army is decimating the Sikhs. The Irish potato crop is set to fail yet again. The world groans under matters of great moment, yet what is it frets our sleep and wears our nerves to a ravelling? *What shall Selina wear?* Great gods and little fishes!'

The basic decision had been easy enough: Selina would wear the dress her mother had worn to such good effect in 1823 (for had it not led almost directly to her marriage in 1825 and the birth of Selina herself in 1826?) It was of a fine cream-coloured wool woven with a pink silk stripe and printed in a dainty floral pattern of yellow, red, green, blue, and a purple that had faded rather pleasantly, as if it had known the way mid-century taste would go.

The impossibly difficult question had been: How to alter it? Should it be left plain or should a flounce be added? Two dresses in the last *Ladies Journal* had sported a flounce about eight inches above the pavement-sweeping hem. It was a question of fashion, and no one down here, at the far end of England, was quite, quite sure what fashion, at present, decreed.

But fashion was not all. There was also a question concerning the front of the bodice. Should the point of it be stitched down? The answer reached beyond *la mode* into realms of morality, for, if the bodice were left free, it would suggest (to a person of discrimination) that Selina possessed a watch of her own, that being where the fob pocket was usually concealed. And, if matters proceeded toward a satisfactory climax, Dr Moore might offer the girl a chaste embrace − and thus discover its absence. Might he not then think her somewhat dishonest, pretending to possess that which she lacked? And might he not consider it symptomatic of a deeper fault within her?

Questions fashionable, questions moral − and also questions practical. For example, if the sleeves were made detachable, she could wear that lovely mantle of shot silk and taffeta with black net gloves for calling, while for evening she could wear the long silk shawl with matching sleeves. Then it would be a dress for all occasions. But might

6

dear Dr Moore consider that to reveal a somewhat cheese-paring character? Or would he applaud their common sense and thrift?

The arguments had worn Mrs Visick to a frazzle — which she considered her 'fair share' of the burden of Dr Moore's visit.

Next to arrive at the breakfast table was Terence Visick, the oldest of Johanna's cousins. In fact, at twenty-six he was three years her senior; but he behaved as if she were still the sad little orphan whom fate had wished upon this household more than ten years ago.

'*Bonjour, ma chère cousine!*' he cried. 'Any kipper today?'

'*Bonjour, cher cousin.* Fresh herring,' she told him.

'Good egg!'

All dishes were 'good egg!' to Terence — except, oddly enough, egg itself, in any of its forms.

As the only son, and heir to half the Visick-Trahearne partnership in the Wheal Venton mines, he put in a grudging two days a week at the office and spent the rest of the time repairing his status as a gentleman. Today he was off to fish a private reach in the Pendarves estate.

'Who's going to rouse the belle of the ball?' he asked cheerily.

'Rouse?' his mother asked.

The two youngest of the family, Deirdre and Ethna, eighteen and sixteen respectively, tried to slip unnoticed into their places. Their father lowered his paper until his eyes just met theirs. 'Are you sitting comfortably?' he asked in an ominous tone.

'Thank you, Papa,' came the terrified replies.

'Bottoms not cold?'

'No, Papa.' They almost fell over each other to assure him.

'Because I can warm them for you.'

'We're sorry, Papa . . .'

'It's Selina, you see. She won't get up.'

'Ah!' Terence said. 'Say what you will about us Visicks — you can't fault us on our sense of loyalty!' He winked at Johanna.

'And you're not too old to thrash, sir,' his father growled at him.

'Who is these days,' the youth answered amiably. 'If you're looking for a bottom to warm, Pater, Selina's probably expecting you upstairs. Anyway — she's refusing to get up.' He engulfed a huge spoon of thick, claggy porridge.

Mr Visick rose hastily, but his wife was ahead of him. 'Leave this to me, Mr Visick, my dear,' she said firmly.

Their eyes met, he yielded after a struggle. 'With every confidence, ma'am. I shall return shortly before one o'clock.' He departed for the mine office in Helston.

Mrs Visick turned to her son. 'Now, why is she refusing to get up?'

'Cold water,' he advised.

'I'll give her cold water! Your father's not the only one who can sting her bottom.' She turned to Johanna. 'I don't suppose you know anything of this?'

Johanna thought she did, but not in terms her aunt might understand.

'Then I shall sting her bottom,' Mrs Visick repeated and went in search of the key to the cupboard where her husband always kept a large stock of fresh withies.

'Let me talk to her, Aunt,' her niece begged as she followed her out. 'Please?'

'You!' The woman was scornful but she offered no actual resistance.

Selina had locked her door against the world but she had forgotten there was another way in from the old nursery; that second door was actually in a curtained alcove where hung all her petticoats and chemises. The key to this alternative entrance was discovered after one or two attempts, which alerted Selina to the invasion. As a result, when Johanna pulled open the door, gritting her teeth against its complaining hinges, she found her cousin, still in her nightdress, busy trying to wedge a chair under its handle.

'That wouldn't have worked, anyway,' she said. 'It opens outwards.'

Selina burst into tears and rushed back to her bed; but, Johanna noticed, she peeped out furtively to see whether her mother and the birch were at hand.

Johanna pulled up a chair and sat beside her cousin. While she waited she looked about her. The contrast with her own bedroom could hardly have been greater; not that it bothered her much. Sometimes, in the depth of winter, when the wind howled around Lanfear and fought its way in through every crack and cranny, she envied Selina this spacious chamber with its sheltered aspect and evening fire. But on a late-summer's morning, like today's, it seemed uncomfortably large and unwelcoming. All in all she preferred her own smaller and much simpler room − 'Luxurious for a governess, but far too good for a servant,' as Mr Visick had commented when nursery days were done and the room became available for life's semi-fortunates.

Selina stirred at last; snivelling up an ocean of salt as she croaked, 'Thank heavens it's only you. I couldn't bear any of the others. Oh, Jo, you are lucky!'

'And then there were two,' Johanna replied.

'I don't see how anyone could say that of me. I think I must be the most miserable girl alive.'

Johanna waited.

'I mean,' Selina went on, 'you'll never be married, never have to go through all this.'

'All what? What is so terrible?'

'All ... everything! It's not just today, you know. Today's only a tiny bit of it. It's just ... everything.'

Johanna was at a loss. Like the rest of the family she had assumed this was some minor tantrum that a few well-chosen words might cure; but now it began to sound serious. 'Everything?' she echoed. 'It must start somewhere. Tell me where it begins.'

'In the cradle, I suppose.' Selina closed her eyes, turned on her side and curled herself up in a tight little ball. 'Oh, I wish I could lie here like this for ever and ever. It begins the moment they say congratulations, it's a dear little baby girl. Or it begins when we start learning our Accomplishments. It begins when we go to the County Ball and let half Cornwall's eligible manhood push us around the floor − trying us out. How do we converse? Is our breath sweet? Our rosebud cheeks − how did we get them? It begins when we are yoked to...' She ran out of breath. 'Oh,' she concluded, 'it begins, it begins, it begins, but it never ends.'

'But it's always been like that,' Johanna said. 'How could it be otherwise? And after all' − she brightened, remembering the comfort she had half-prepared while forcing her entrance – 'Dr Moore did ask you for *two* dances.'

'Oh hush about that!'

'No other girl was so favoured.'

'Stop it, stop it!'

'Not Desirée Curwen, not Felicity Beckerleg, not even Bathsheba Strike – and everyone said they'd be the queens of the ball.'

Selina vanished beneath her sheets and screamed.

Johanna eased down the counterpane. 'Get up and let me brush out your hair. You'll feel so much better for it.'

'How would *you* know?' Selina sneered.

'Well, even with my little mop I never feel right until I've taken out all its tangles.'

Selina thrashed like an eel on a line, turning herself over until she faced away from Johanna. 'Damn you!' she said. 'Damn everybody!'

'Selina!'

'You're so *humble*. So *cheerful,* always. Why don't you claw our eyes out? I know I would.'

'I'm sure I'm most grateful to my aunt and uncle. It would have been cruel to bring me up as one of you when I could never expect half your advantages.'

With slow deliberation, Selina turned to face her cousin. 'You truly mean it, I think,' she said.

'I could certainly never expect the sort of match they are preparing for you.'

Wearily Selina closed her eyes and let her head fall back to the pillow. 'I knew no one could understand it,' she said.

'I'll try,' Johanna promised. 'Get up and let me brush your hair and you tell me all about it.' She tugged gently at the sheet.

For a moment Selina resisted and then just lay there passively while Johanna pulled back all the bedding. She did not stir, however, until her cousin took up a feather from the mattress and began trying to push it into her ear; then she giggled and sought to bury her ear in her shoulder. 'Ogre!' she cried.

'Ogress,' Johanna corrected.

'Schoolmarm!' Then, in one of her mercurial changes of

mood, she became all at once serious. 'That's what you should be, you know. That's what I'd do if I were you. I wouldn't tolerate this house a day longer. I'd get a position as a teacher somewhere – in Normandy, perhaps. Or a governess in a nice family.'

Johanna nodded toward the dressing table.

Selina allowed herself to be guided across the room. 'Why don't you, Jo? Be a governess?'

Johanna's smile, reflected in the looking glass, answered for her, saying she thought her cousin's words the very height of fancy.

'I was never more earnest in my life,' the other protested. A crafty look crept into her eyes. 'I know. Why don't *you* make eyes at dear Dr Moore when he comes, and bewitch him. And then they'll be so angry they'll turn you off from here.'

'And then?'

'And then I'll come with you and we can both go and be governesses or teachers somewhere and never have to bother with . . .' She caught sight of Johanna's smile and her mood darkened at once. 'Give me that!' She snatched the brush away and began ruining all the good work in a hasty assault on her tangled locks. 'You always win in the end, don't you,' she said angrily.

Johanna just sat there patiently, holding out her hand, waiting for the brush to be returned – which it was, soon enough.

Selina became contrite again. 'But wouldn't it be sublime?' she asked. 'We could just please ourselves.'

'And whoever employed us,' Johanna pointed out, resuming her brushing.

'Oh . . . yes. That hadn't struck me.' Selina grew thoughtful. 'I suppose a husband is an employer of a kind,' she said at last.

'What would you like for breakfast?' Johanna thought it time to ask.

'Oh, how could you! I shan't eat for a week.'

'Then when you're dressed, why don't we go for a walk to the top of Trigonning Hill and spread our parasols and sit in the sunshine and pretend that one o'clock is years and years away?'

11

Selina clasped her cousin's hand to her cheek. 'Oh, I do so wish I had been a kinder person,' she said mournfully. 'But I'm not, you see. And now I'm going to be found out.'

'You can tell me all about it when we're on our walk. There!' Johanna extricated her hand. 'It's a glorious day and everything will look very different, I'm sure. I'll send Rose to dress you, shall I? Will you unbolt the door if I do?'

She left the way she had come, via the old nursery.

'Well?' Mrs Visick snapped the moment she saw Johanna.

'She is still a little vaporous, Aunt Theresa. Her mood is fragile.'

'Fragile, indeed? I'll teach her to have moods! What does a girl her age need to have moods for − and on such a day as this.'

'If I may suggest?'

'Well?'

'I believe that sunshine and fresh air and . . .' Johanna tried to think of a kindly way of saying 'escape from this house,' but could not. 'I think if she and I took a brief constitutional to the top of Trigonning, she might return calm and refreshed.'

'On an empty stomach? I'll wager she'll eat no breakfast.'

'I'll ask cook to make us some sandwiches.'

'Make *her* some sandwiches, you mean, surely.' Her aunt, annoyed at finding no harsher solution, and fearful of doing nothing, threw up her hands and flounced away. 'On your head be it,' she added vaguely. 'And don't stay up there all morning.'

'I'll set all the servants to their tasks before I go,' Johanna promised.

For two young women, nominally of the same family, they made an odd pair − the daughters of a rich squire and of a poor parson, one would have guessed, for the Visicks were careful enough not to dress their poor niece as a servant. Their way to the summit of the hill led between hedges, burgeoning with life in the full vigour of late summer. Cow parsley, woodbine, coltsfoot, and yarrow spilled in flowery profusion from tenuous footholds in the earth between the hedging stones. The fields and hedgerow ended a quarter of the way up the western slope of

Trigonning; from there on it was the haunt of ling and gorse and a dry, sedgy grass that was slippery underfoot. They spoke in disjointed trivialities, for the slope was too steep and their long dresses too cumbersome for sustained converse.

At last they gained the long ridge of the summit, or, rather, a shallow, sandy pit just beneath the brow on its sunward side. That cavity was Terence's sole contribution to the world of archaeology; he had abandoned it when it yielded up its entire treasure – a George III penny. They spread their parasols and sat a while in silence, gazing out over the busy waters of the bay. The rare intimacy of their earlier conversation now seemed to elude them; each could feel the other straining for the words that might restore it.

'Fancy being a miner out there under all that water!' Selina shuddered. 'I should dread every moment.'

'Yes, but I often envy the people on all those boats,' Johanna confessed. 'Always travelling. Always moving on. Even their arrivals are only temporary.'

Selina agreed. 'Never stuck anywhere for long.' After a pause she added, as if it followed naturally from the advantages of the nautical life, 'I wish it were midnight already and this day over and done with.'

She looked nervously at Johanna, who merely shook her head in bewilderment.

'If someone asked you to marry him, Jo, what would you say?' Selina went on.

'It would depend who did the asking.'

'Pick the nicest man you know. I'm not seeking to pry, but what would you say?'

Johanna laughed. 'I'd say yes, of course.'

'Without a qualm?'

'What about?'

'Well ... oh dear.' Selina screwed up her eyes. 'I mean ... d'you feel *ready?* D'you think you could manage it all? The house ... servants .. the *lord and master* – could you manage *him?* That's what frightens me. I wish we lived in the days when marriages were properly arranged and there wasn't any nonsense about needing to be in love as well, don't you?'

Johanna looked at her in surprise. 'But why?'

'So that I could call him *Mister* Ponsonby, or whatever his name was and he'd call me *Mrs* Ponsonby, and we'd say cold, cold things to each other at breakfast and snap at one another all through supper but in between we'd be perfectly free.'

Johanna thought a moment and then said, 'And after supper?'

'Have our own bedrooms,' Selina said at once.

'But what would such a marriage be for?' Johanna objected.

'It would stop all this nonsense. No more suitors. No more yes-papa, no-papa, and please can I have? No more chaperones. No more being controlled by glances and coughs and shivers of the fan. Oh bliss!' She lay back among the ling and closed her eyes. Then she remembered Johanna's original question and added, 'That's what it would be *for* – to escape! I wish there were some way of doing it without having to marry, that's all.'

After a while Johanna said, 'I wonder if men go through such torments.'

'I shouldn't imagine so for a minute,' Selina replied. 'Who knows?'

'Have you never asked? What d'you talk about when you dance with them?'

Selina laughed. 'Certainly nothing so interesting as that. One talks about the Four Safe Topics – the Season, the Music, the Charm of the host and hostess . . .' she lapsed into moody silence.

'And the fourth?' Johanna prompted after a while.

Her cousin shrugged. 'Actually, there's only one topic – Boredom. That's what one is *really* talking about.' She gave a shrill, almost despairing laugh. 'What a pair! Here's you would rather marry than anything, I suppose. And here's me would give all my prospects to anyone who could take them off me – simply not to have to walk back home and prepare myself to be meet and fitting in the eyes of the great and wonderful Dr Anthony Moore.'

'Heavens, what can be so dreadful in him?'

'He'll want to . . . touch me, and kiss me, and hold me in his arms . . .' she shivered. 'And I shall just be so maladroit and gauche, I know it. And he'll murmur at me and I shan't

14

know what to reply. And he'll ask me things and even though I know the answer I'll forget it. I just *know* it's going to be awful.'

Johanna tried to think of something comforting that would not also sound hopelessly anodyne.

'How do people kiss?' Selina asked. 'D'you know anything about it? No, I don't suppose you do. I don't know why I let you drag me up here at all.'

It so happened that Johanna did, indeed, know quite a bit about the pastime of kissing. She had kissed cousin Terence, once, in an experimental moment. She had kissed young Isaak Meagor, off the farm below Lanfear, more than once. She had kissed Willie Kemp, the junior excise officer, while his superior was searching for smuggled brandy – quite recently, that was. And she had been kissed by the parson, the last but one; he had caressed her bosom too – but that was before the scandal between him and Mrs Bolsover. However, she wasn't about to reveal any of this to Selina. 'I imagine,' she said, 'it's one of those things where you just know what to do when the moment comes.'

'You would!' Selina gazed at her coldly. 'What if Dr Moore should prefer you to me? He's rich enough not to let any thought of a dowry worry him unduly. Promise me you won't do anything to encourage it?'

Johanna shook her head pityingly. 'Dear Selina, you'll worry yourself to no purpose, so that all your worst fears will come true. You'll *make* them come true. But you have nothing to fear, honestly.'

'You see – you wriggle out of it. You won't promise.'

'What? What is there to promise? That I shan't make eyes at Dr Moore? As if I would! When did you ever see me making eyes at anybody?'

'So why won't you promise?'

'Because it's so absurd. I mean, even to make such a promise would be like admitting its possibility. If you asked me to promise not to cast you down that mineshaft over there, I should also refuse – and for the same reason. It's just too absurd.' After a pause, she said in a more conciliatory tone, 'Would you like a sandwich now?'

The question galvanized Selina. She sat bolt upright and gave out a great cry of rage, which was also a cry of terror and of frustration. 'You're no better than anyone!' she howled. The tears began to stream down her face. 'I thought you might ... I mean, I hoped you of all people ... Oh God! Who can help me? Who can help me now?' And she rose to her feet and began to stumble off down the hillside.

Johanna scrambled up and set off after her. She was used to her cousin's mercurial changes of mood but even for her this was something out of the ordinary. Selina became aware she was being followed. She halted and spun around. 'Don't you dare!' she yelled. 'Just stay up here and be useless where it can't hurt anyone. If you come after me, I'll make you sorry you were ever born.'

Still Johanna took a step toward her but it provoked only a fresh paroxysm of rage. 'I don't want you,' she shrieked. 'Can't you get that into your thick skull? You are not wanted. You've never been wanted — anywhere! Why don't you go and cast *yourself* down a mineshaft?'

And she turned and stormed away.

The peace that closed in around Johanna was only bliss. Time was when such an exchange would have plunged her into gloom for days, but now it was just water off an eider's back. She turned and walked the few paces to the very crest of the hill, which, at over six hundred feet, was the highest for several miles. From here you could actually see the geography of the far west of Cornwall, from the Atlantic on the northern coast, some eight miles off, to the Channel shore, a mile or two southwards. She stood there and turned a slow, full circle, breathing great drafts of the western breeze, fresh off three thousand miles of ocean. From here all human works and feelings were set in their true proportions.

The great tin mines whose belching chimneys described a mighty arc from Godolphin in the north, round through Wheal Vor, Pallas Consols, Carnmeal, and the legendary Wheal Fortune to the east, seemed mere toys. In their satanic workings they had maimed and broken generations of Cornishmen — and women, too, for most of the surface work was done by the bal maidens; but from here they seemed no more than playthings, scattered by a greedy and impatient child, careless of the landscape's charm. The fields, too, were shrunk to a patchwork quilt, an incompetent

16

creation designed by a horde of squabbling beginners. At various moments in history the run of the hedges and lanes must have made sense to *someone* but those reasons had long vanished, leaving nothing beyond a perverse but fertile confusion of arable, pasture, and croft. Here and there was the occasional intrusion of a remnant woodland covert where the gentry preserved their game.

Johanna let the familiarity of it all reclaim her and bring its peace. Most of her days she lived from moment to moment, from room to room; it was easier so. But the spirit also needs that longer perspective, both of space and of time. Poor Selina! She always behaved as if two quite different girls were at war within her, one arrogantly certain of her maturity, the other a frightened child desperate for reassurance; each begged you to side with her and was resentful if you did not. If a real Selina existed at all, she was prisoner to both. People said, 'She'll be different when she grows up — she'll soon settle.' But Johanna, who knew her better than anyone, having been the butt of her venom so often, now doubted it. Five years hence they'd probably be saying, 'She'll be different when she has her next baby — that'll soon settle her.'

Far off across the peninsula a hoot from a train on the Hayle Railway brought Johanna out of her reverie. Half past eleven. She ought to be going back to Lanfear, to supervise the preparations for the guest of guests. She folded Selina's sandwiches back into their paper and placed the bundle in a rabbit hole — a gift to a fox or a piskey. Then she turned for home. The day was so fine, however, that she could not deny herself the pleasure of going the long road around, between Balwest and Greatwork and on by way of Trevithan. She picked her way down the hillside, singing 'As I went a-strolling one morning in May,' in her clear but uncertain soprano; and it seemed to her she had little enough to complain of. If she could honestly pity someone with as many advantages and prospects as Selina, then she must be among the most rather than the least fortunate of people.

At Trevithan she faced a choice of paths. The carriageway went around Lanfear, almost three fourths of a circle, approaching the house from the west; or there was a shorter bridleway over the fields that would bring her in through the kitchen garden, to the east of the house. It all depended on which pump they were using to fork out Greatwork; if it were the one on this side of the hill, the stream would be too high for her to cross. She had just decided to risk it when she heard a gig approaching down the lane behind her and a man's voice crying, 'Hoa there! Hoa-back sir!'

'Young lady?' he called, catching her half-way across the stile and unable to turn and face him. 'Pardon my presumption, but if I go out of my way once more, they'll think it worth their while to set up tolls at every junction. Pray tell me, does *any* road hereabouts lead to Lanfear House? I'm a stranger to this district, you see.'

Johanna froze. This young man could be none other than Dr Anthony Moore himself — almost two hours earlier than expected. How like a bachelor! But what could she do? If she directed him truly, he would arrive within five minutes and discover a house in turmoil. If she misdirected him, he would find out soon enough and then how would she face him every day for the next two weeks?

'Young lady?' he prompted hesitantly.

'Pardon me, sir,' she explained. 'My dress is caught in a bramble here. It will only take a moment.' She bent and pretended to fiddle with it, giving herself time to think.

'Are you by any chance Dr Moore?' she asked. 'From Plymouth?'

'Why yes.' He gave a small, surprised laugh. 'You know of me, then? Am I so close to my goal?'

'You are not expected until one o'clock,' she told him as she stood up and faced him at last.

Their eyes met. She saw a young man in his mid-twenties, dashingly handsome, with wavy blond hair and a kindly eye. Selina was lucky, she thought — though the young man stirred nothing very deep within her.

What he saw, however, was something he would never forget — a young woman with the most hauntingly beautiful eyes he had ever encountered. The rest of her face was handsome enough but those eyes held him entranced. It was not love at first sight, for he was not so shallow as that. Indeed, in those first few moments he was so struck by her beauty, he almost forgot she was a person and so gazed at her more as one might examine a beautiful work of art.

'I live at Lanfear,' she explained. 'I am Miss Visick's cousin. My name is Johanna Rosewarne.'

His gaze fell as he recollected himself. 'Ah. The truth is I thought I'd get no farther than Truro yesterday, Miss Rosewarne. In fact, the road was so good I pressed on to Helston. Will it matter, my turning up early?'

'Not if you have cures for heart attacks in your bag,' she told him.

'Oh. Like that?' he sighed, consulted his watch, and then looked vaguely about him. 'How to kill two hours? Is there a good prospect from yonder hill? Has it a name?'

'Trigonning Hill, they call it.'

'I presume one may walk to its crest?'

'You could drive as far as Balwest Farm and leave your gig there. They'd bring it round this afternoon.'

'And you are bound for Lanfear House, Miss Rosewarne? May I not take you at least part-way there?'

Curiosity got the better of her. 'If I may ride with you to Balwest, sir, that will then be my shortest way. I'll accompany you to the hilltop and you'll see the path I take to Lanfear.'

He jumped down to hand her up into the gig. 'So be it.' And, smiling to himself, he gathered up the reins.

Chapter Two

The first thing Johanna pointed out to Dr Moore was Lanfear House itself. Then, moving wider: 'Most of this nearby land is in Germoe parish. That's Land's End in the distance.'

'I can see St Michael's Mount!' He appeared surprised. 'But it's so exactly like all the engravings. One almost forgets it's a real place.' He turned seaward, bringing her into his field of view again. 'And there is Mount's Bay, eh?'

She nodded contentedly, as if she part-owned it. 'I think the waters are never the same two days on end. Indeed, they can change five times in the hour.'

'And so many ships.'

'One can usually see five or six sails.' She glanced at him shyly. 'Sometimes, when I'm sewing at my window, I watch them pass and I try to imagine all the lives going on out there. Every creek and inlet has its little lobster catchers, so I might actually know some of them. Or their families, anyway. And then every tide one can see fishermen putting out from Newlyn, Penzance, Porthleven ... Mullion.' Her finger traced the rim of the bay, turning her full circle toward him again.

He gave only a token glance at the sea. She found his attention discomforting − yet not unpleasing.

'That fellow,' he remarked, with another brief dart toward the sea, 'He's no fisherman.'

'A lugger,' she agreed. 'They go from port to port all along the coast, from as far away as Bristol.'

He smiled. 'As far away as Bristol!'

'Yes. They come all down the north coast to Hayle, then

around Land's End to Penzance and Falmouth, and so on, back to England again.'

'Then they must also go "as far away as Plymouth,"' he pointed out with gentle mockery.

'Everywhere seems far away down here.' She scanned the horizon. 'That big one out there – the three-master, almost hull down. She's an ocean-going trader. Oh, and look! There's another, wearing towards us. D'you know, some of them haven't sighted land since the Cape or the Horn? And we're the first thing they see – Cornwall. A revenue man told me a seaman told him they forget what the colour green is like. Isn't it a marvel?'

'A marvel,' he echoed, turning his eyes inland. 'And these are the famous tin mines. What a devastation they have caused!'

'It's bread in the belly, though.' She sighed. 'Without them the destitution of the poor would be unimaginable.'

He put his hand to his midriff and laughed. 'I wish you hadn't said that, Miss Rosewarne.'

'Oh, are you hungry, Dr Moore?' She stooped and produced Selina's sandwiches – to his utter amazement.

'Do you sleep in a bottle?' he asked. 'Have I only two wishes to go? Because I hope you'd warn me. There's one wish I'd . . . well, I'd sooner die than make it my fourth.'

She laughed and explained, passing lightly over the true state of her cousin's nerves. 'You will be kindly?' she urged. 'This visit of yours means so very much to her – and you know how easy it is to put one's foot wrong in . . . when one is . . .'

'Ah.' He returned his gaze to the sea.

'Why do you say that?'

He tugged briefly at his lower lip. 'I have no idea of Lanfear House – what it will be like – what you and your family are like.'

'Nothing very remarkable, I'm sure. Miss Visick is, or can be, a little highly strung.'

'What can one learn of anyone or anything in one evening? And at a ball, too. Such artificial circumstances.'

'Indeed.'

'I hope I don't compromise you, Miss Rosewarne – bringing you up here alone?'

She laughed. 'Oh, we are chaperoned, have no fear. I imagine at least a dozen pairs of eyes are upon us at this moment, Dr Moore. Besides, it is unlikely I shall marry into any circle where such compromising counts for much ... if, indeed ... well, you were saying you know nothing of us?'

'Yes. All I know is that Miss Visick struck me as the most interesting young lady there. Therefore I rashly asked her for two dances ... received this invitation ... and ...' He appeared not to know how to finish the thought.

'Is there anything amiss in that?' she asked.

'No, not at all. Well ... perhaps ... in this sense: expectations may have been raised that I did not intend to rouse. I regard this visit merely as a chance to know Miss Visick — in fact, to know all of you — better. Not to cement any lasting ... you know?'

She smiled. 'Are you seeking my advice?'

He nodded. 'I see you are *of* the family and yet a little apart from it.'

'Then if I were you, I should find the earliest opportunity to tell Miss Visick what you have just told me.'

'I don't wish to sound conceited but ... it will not disappoint her?'

Johanna shook her head. 'And now I really must go.' Briefly she took off her bonnet to retie its ribbon.

He stared at her in frank amazement. She felt she ought to explain. 'When I was sixteen ...'

'But your eyes are such an astonishing blue!' he said. 'And yet your hair is black as a raven's wing. Oh, do forgive such personal remarks — but the combination is so rare. I had no idea.'

Did he think her eyebrows were painted then? 'It's not uncommon here — and very common, they say, in Brittany.' Or was he just rather unobservant?

'Celtic, eh?'

Doctors shouldn't be unobservant. She went on, 'Old Joel Rogers — well, you don't know him of course, but he sells strewing sand from door to door — he told me the old folks used to call colouring like mine "candle and ray" because those who are ... those who have it, possess supernatural powers of ...' She hesitated. Joel Rogers had actually said, 'supernatural powers of attraction.' She moved her hands

22

awkwardly. 'Supernatural powers ... of some kind. Silly talk.'

'As a moth to a taper, maid,' Rogers had said, combing her hair with his fingers as if he could not believe its intensity until he saw it against his own weatherbeaten skin. 'Candle and ray.'

'I really must be going now,' she repeated, replacing her bonnet and tucking her short hair in all around the brim. 'I need hardly remind you we have a very important visitor arriving today – and I'm sure the house is falling apart down there. I only hope he has the courtesy to arrive a little late.'

The doctor laughed. 'You were going to tell me something about when you were sixteen?'

'Oh' – she shrugged awkwardly, still half-turned to leave – 'Mrs Visick somehow acquired the notion that hair of my particular colouring is extraordinarily susceptible to headlice and ringworm and things – to spare me the indignity of which she ...' Johanna smiled and snipped the air with her fingers.

He struggled vainly to find a polite way of saying stuff and nonsense. 'I shall disabuse her of any such notion at the earliest opportunity,' he promised.

'Not on my account, please.'

'You don't mind? No, why should you, come to think of it.'

She turned her gaze to the south, to the wide waters of the bay. 'I was unhappy at the time, of course. For a day or two.'

'No more than that?'

'And then I realized what that new little face, staring back at me out of every wretched looking glass ... what it reminded me of: a pageboy I once saw in an engraving. My father, God rest his soul, used to subscribe to the *Art Journal*. And I remembered an engraving he once showed me. A portrait by Veronese of some Florentine grandee with this young pageboy at his side. "In those days," he explained to me, "painters weren't the gods they like to think they are today. If they wanted to show their scorn for a rich, jumped-up patron like this grandee, they had to be very subtle about it. Just look what old Veronese's done".'

23

Johanna moved her hands as if the journal were before her still. He watched her, fascinated at a gift for recall that was so total, so loving. ' "First look at our grandee himself. Slightly coarse, perhaps? Or then again perhaps not. The feeling vanishes and returns and vanishes once more — very subtle. Much too subtle for a grand fellow like that even to notice, consumed by self-love as he is. But now look at this pageboy! It's as if Veronese were saying, *See! I can indeed paint the look of wisdom, if I wish. I can depict true grandeur of soul. If you doubt me, study this young lad.* And so there he stands, the humble little servant whose nobility mocks a master who, for his part, will never twig what's happening!" ' She laughed at a cunning so deep it could ring down the centuries like that. Then she turned to him apologetically. 'Of course, the only similarity between me and the page was the style of the hair. I shouldn't wish you to think ... I mean ...'

He eyed her shrewdly. 'The only similarity, Miss Rosewarne? If the pageboy knew what Veronese had done, then there is at least one more. Isn't there?' After a silence he prompted her: 'D'you suppose the lad did know?'

She gave him a reluctant grin. 'Yes!'

He took a step toward her. 'And now I hardly need an explanation of why you were not at the ball.'

She turned and walked from him, down the path to Lanfear House. 'Ten past one would be politely tardy,' she called back over her shoulder. 'Oh — and we haven't met ... when we finally do meet ... if you see what I mean.' As she went back down the hill she could not help thinking what a pleasant young man he was and how lucky Selina would be if his liking for her ripened into love.

If she herself ever married — and if she could take her pick of husbands — she would pick Dr Anthony Moore. Or someone very like him.

Chapter Three

From the very first the expectations of the Visick household pressed so heavily upon poor Dr Moore that his chance never came to tell Selina what he had confessed at once to Johanna. And the supposed object of his love was so prickly whenever the conversation came within a million miles of that topic, he began to despair — just as the family, for its part, began to despair of his proposal. By the start of the second week they were resigned to accepting that the 'usual thing' had happened.

The rituals of courtship, which had served well enough in the age of the frankly arranged marriage, were quite inadequate to modern puposes; for lately there had arisen the somewhat novel notion (due, no doubt, to a recent flood of 'novels' upon the subject) that love should play some small part in the process. The 'usual thing,' then, was that young people who became enamoured of each other in, say, the hothouse of a County Ball, found that the tender buds of love were soon nipped in the frosts of a two-week visit. There was then nothing to do but pass the time in as civil a manner as possible and part friends. And so it was as friends that the three young people, Dr Moore, Selina, and their chaperone, Johanna, set out for a picnic at Praa Sands one afternoon early in the second week of his visit. Any day now it would be in order for him to receive an urgent summons home; a sense of finality hung over the occasion.

Theresa Visick was naturally heartbroken that so much planning and preparation should have come to naught. But a mother who wears her heart on her sleeve — especially when it is in that condition — is soon an object of ridicule;

her nubile daughter, moreover, would drop several points in the race. So Theresa smiled till she ached and was in every way the gracious, carefree hostess. God and the household alone knew what fires were banked as she stood beneath the Doric porticoes of Lanfear House and waved the youngsters out of sight.

It was a sunny, breezy day, blowing in from the south-west. Far out toward the Atlantic hung clouds that threatened rain; but they dissolved into air as they approached the Land's End peninsula, leaving nothing but scattered, fleecy white nimbus to temper the sun from time to time.

'It's a disgrace to be driving there,' Johanna commented. 'It's not above two miles, even by these twisting lanes.'

'What about the picnic things?' Selina asked, reasonably enough.

'Jenkins could have driven down with them. Still, it gives us more time on the sands. Shall we go the Pentreath way and come back past Pengersick?'

'That's quite a steep downhill at Pentreath . . . with three of us up?'

They looked at Dr Moore.

'The brakes are quite good,' he observed. 'You'll have to tell me the way, though. Every one of your lanes looks the same to me.'

They soon reached the main road, a mile-long, gentle, downhill run into the broad, shallow valley whose meeting with the sea formed the sands of Praa. At Germoe crossroads they passed a gang of men felling the last of an ancient stand of oak — a timber for which the mines had an insatiable appetite.

'As soon as one gets this side of Truro,' Moore commented, 'one sees nothing but tree stumps everywhere. It's like the descriptions one reads of pioneer lands in Canada and America.'

The two women agreed that, even in their short memories, the landscape had improved enormously — though they should not like to see all the trees removed. Johanna added, 'My mother told me Cornwall used to be like fairy-tale country, all dark and grim and shadowed with trees.'

'Everything decaying and dank.' Selina shivered.

'Yes, that's the trouble with forests,' Moore told them solemnly. 'The real Robin Hood died of the rheumatics, I'll wager.'

The game amused them all the way to the Pentreath turn. When they came to the steep part of the lane he whistled and said, 'I see what you mean. Pray it's dry.' He hauled at the brakes with all his might and they just managed it without a slide. There were a few close shaves, though, which made it necessary for the women to cling to him tightly and throw their weight behind his; manfully, he raised no objection. They were quite breathless when they arrived at the foot of the hill. There a spring gave rise to a brief but vigorous stream that ran down toward the beach. They tethered the pony by its banks, giving water and a little grazing to keep him content; the shady overhang of willow and ash would keep him and the picnic cool, too. Then they strolled the last furlong, down to the lobstermen's cottages, where the road levelled out onto the grassy dunes above the beach. There the stream ran out upon the sand, all the way down to the sea, which was at three-quarters tide.

Moore gave a cry of delight and raced down to the water's edge, where he began trying to bounce the flat, rounded pebbles across the choppy water in the game called ducks and drakes. Selina was about to join him when her cousin held her back. 'You remember what you told me — when we walked up Trigonning last week?'

'Yes.'

'Try to find some way of telling *him*. Here and now — today.'

Selina's eyes went wide in surprise. 'D'you think I could?'

'Trust me. Find different words if you like, but make him understand.'

'Oh!' She closed her eyes. 'I've thought of nothing else all week.' A thought came to her rescue. 'But actually there's no need now. He's obviously not going to ask me to marry him.'

'But that's exactly why you should tell him. I promise you, you'll be pleasantly surprised. I promise.'

'Well . . .' She was still dubious. 'We'll see.'

They went down onto the sand; he was already coming back to join them.

'Oh dear,' Selina called out.

'What's the matter?' he asked.

'Well, at low tide you can walk around the end of this stream. The sand sort of swallows it up half way.'

At the present water, however, they were forced to hop from one precarious stepping stone to the next. Moore went first, and then developed a gentlemanly curiosity in the shape of Rinsey Head, whose sheer cliffs marked the eastern end of the sands, a hazy mile away. This allowed the women to lift their skirts and make the hazardous crossing in privacy. As soon as they were over, Johanna said, 'You two go on. I could never resist this.' And she peeled off her gloves, picked up a boulder, big as a nine-inch egg, and hurled it into the bed of the stream, leaping back to avoid the splash.

'Oh, that looks fun.' Moore picked up an even larger boulder and hurled it after hers. The splash soused him neatly down one side, from shoulder to foot – a narrow line, as if from a dribbling hose.

Johanna laughed. 'There's a knack to it. Go on – I'll catch you up before long.' She took out her handkerchief and gave his wet jacket a token dab or two. 'Remember what you told me that day up Trigonning?' she asked under her breath.

'Mm-hmm.' He eyed her warily. He had told her so much, he recalled – too much, perhaps.

'Tell Miss Visick. You'll . . .'

'Tell her? But I've been trying to do nothing else for the past week!'

'I think she'll listen today. Try, anyway. I think you might be very pleasantly surprised.'

'Aren't you coming?' Selina called from some way off.

Tony trotted to join her.

They walked side by side, close but not touching. The sand was coarse and slithery, making each step a small labour. 'Johanna and Terence once built quite a large reservoir down here,' Selina explained. The moment they were out of earshot she went on, 'What d'you think of her, by the way?'

He coughed. 'I hardly think that a ... well ...'

'Oh come on, Dr Moore.' There was more than a hint of weariness in her voice.

'I beg your pardon?'

'Jo has organized this so that we may put our cards on the table. I saw her talking to you just know — telling you the same as she just told me, I'm sure. So — what d'you say?'

He smiled. 'I say ladies first.'

She sighed. 'We all know why you're paying us this visit. And you and I both realize it hasn't worked — greatly to our mutual relief, I suspect.'

'Oh.' The surprise was merely social.

'But ...' She turned round and stared at her cousin. 'Jo is absolutely right!' she murmured to herself. She returned to him with a smile. 'Don't you see — the chance it now gives us? Oh yes — this a rare opportunity.'

'Opportunity?' He began to feel a slight alarm.

'We can really, really talk. Have you ever done that? I haven't. Those ghastly, ghastly conversations we had at the Ball! Look — you'll be gone soon and we'll probably never meet again. There's no need to guard our words, to flatter, to reach for the conventional ... the safe remark.'

'I see.' He grew thoughtful.

She waited for him to take up her original question — what did he think of Johanna? When he did not, she intoned, giving each syllable precisely equal weight: 'What a char-ming view I think Corn-wall's so pret-ty at this time of year don't you?'

After a while he said, 'There may be dangers in frankness, Miss Visick. Untutored frankness between young women and young men.'

'Indeed?'

'We may rail against society and chafe at its restrictions. And yet they do arise out of certain practical considerations. Much wisdom has gone into the making of them.'

'Really?' Selina replied.

'The innocence of children — which is often so wickedly knowing — is really appropriate only to ... well, to the years of childhood.'

'I hope I did not mean to babble at you, Dr Moore.'

29

'The choice of words is yours, Miss Visick, but . . .'

'I did not realize that, as one grows older, the great pageant of life must reduce itself to the Four Safe Topics.'

'By the great pageant of life you mean . . .'

'I mean our hopes, our ambitions, our feelings.'

'Ah!'

'What d'you mean: *ah?*'

'You bring me back to my point when you talk of feelings. I presume you do not refer to superficial feelings – like our feelings at struggling over this excessively yielding sand?'

'I'm sorry our beach is not to your liking. Perhaps we should . . .'

'No, no. That was just an example. Forget I said that. But you know what I mean. Or perhaps not?'

Selina masked a smile. 'You mean our emotions, Dr Moore. You think it's bad form, do you?'

This accusation of shallowness stung him. 'More than bad form, Miss Visick. It is dangerous.'

'Hah!'

'Believe me, I know this – not simply as a man of the world but as a doctor, too.'

'To all people, at all times? And in all places and circumstances?' She looked about them with amused contempt.

But he retained his solemnity. 'Indeed. When I mentioned children just now, I did not intend it as a rebuke, and I'm sorry if you read that into it. I make a distinction between being child*ish* and child*like,* you see. Women have a child*like* innocence and beauty that is their greatest charm. But just as children can pass in a moment from the angelic to the savage – because they do not understand the source of their emotions and therefore cannot control them – so, too, can a woman. Indeed, so, too, can a man. The difference is that a man, or a gentleman, is *supposed* to understand such a transformation and is therefore obliged to strive with all his might to avoid those circumstances in which . . . oh dear! This has beome impossibly pompous. Just tell me you know what I mean?' He smiled to recruit her agreement.

But she saw that he had exposed the chink in his armour.

'You mean, despite the gentleman's true feeling at that moment?'

'Y-e-s.' The agreement was reluctant.

'Voilà!'

'And what may you mean by that?'

'I think if any explanation is due, Dr Moore, you are the one who owes it.'

'But I've just . . .'

'Are you seriously maintaining that you and I, walking in perfect though chaperoned seclusion along this strand — I agree, it is tiresome, by the way . . . shall we rest awhile on that bit of driftwood? — anyway, that you and I may not talk of anything of the slightest interest or importance for fear that we should turn into beasts?'

'You always go to extremes,' he snapped. 'Of course, you know I think no such thing.'

'Do I? But what ground have you . . .'

'The point is that, once those rules are relaxed, once a general spirit of laxity is allowed to creep in — and it would always creep in at the edges in exactly the manner you are now proposing — then who knows where it might end?'

'Ah! Here we have it at last! You and I are to discuss the weather, the scenery, and doh-re-mi, not for our own sakes — because, of course, the idea that *we* might turn into ravening beasts is too obviously absurd. We do so entirely in order to help young gentlemen and ladies yet unborn to pass the evening safely at the Duchess of Devonshire's ball in eighteen *sixty*-seven! What wonderful logic!'

He sat in miserable silence at her side.

'You make me afraid to toss pebbles into the sea,' she added.

'Why?' he was forced to ask.

'For fear that the gravitational disturbance should drag the moon out of her course.'

After a further silence she became aware that he was shivering at her side. Uncontrolled fury? Tears? She turned to him at the moment he burst into laughter.

She laughed, too.

'I tried.' He tipped back his hat and sought the Recording Angel somewhere above. 'I truly did try.'

'I win?' she asked. 'I mean, common sense wins?'

He shrugged. 'What does common sense wish to know, Miss Visick?'

'Selina.'

'Oh − I say!'

'Yes, Anthony − or is it Tony?'

'Tony,' he said, not really meaning to concede the intimacy. 'I did not realize you intended ... I mean, d'you think this is altogether wise, Miss ... er?'

'Is it patriotic?' She stressed the words as if correcting him. 'Or is it slender? Or blue?'

'I'm afraid I don't quite ... er.'

'I mean all these questions are equally meaningless to me. Wise? What is wise? In what way could I possibly judge it? All I know is that we, you and I, would probably make better friends than ever we would ... anything else. Or d'you think that's not possible. A man and a woman cannot ever really be just friends?'

After a moment's reflection he replied in a more relaxed tone, 'I wonder? I have often thought of it ... that is to say, I often used to think of it.'

'But not so much of late?'

'No.' He turned to her. 'And it had not struck me until this moment.' He smiled mischievously and added, 'Selina.'

She relaxed, too, shedding her rather bright prickliness. 'That's better. Well, let's not try answering the question out of the depths of our ignorance.'

'What other question then?' His manner suggested it would be all right as long as one viewed it as a kind of game.

And so, as if it were, indeed, a kind of game, she rose and resumed their walk, slowly, casually. And − slowly, casually − she asked, 'Why are you looking for a wife?'

He gave a single, whispered laugh, as if she had punched him. 'I say.'

'No, no, Tony dear!' Her tone was half-teasing, half-warning. 'We have traversed that tunnel and come out the other side. Honesty can no longer do us much harm. And time is short. So − have you actually given the matter any thought? Or are you wanting a wife because you're now − what? Past twenty-five? And all the world knows a man should marry by thirty. Is it no deeper than that?'

He nodded gravely, accepting the conditional rebuke. 'I *thought* I had pondered it all out,' he told her, 'but you suddenly make me aware how shallow my conclusions were. So let me try again, out loud this time. You see, I took my training in medicine very seriously.'

He relapsed into silence, grappling with some way of conveying those momentous years in a few brief sentences.

'Papa says you walked off with all the prizes,' she prompted.

'Three, actually.'

'But the three highest in the land.'

'Matter of opinion,' he mumbled. 'Anyway, the point is, those studies absorbed my every minute. I had no time for anything else. And it was the same when I took up practice in Plymouth.' There was a further pause and then he gave an apologetic shrug. 'I can find no way of conveying the excitement ... the utter ... absorbing ...'

'Ah, Tony! You come very close to understanding my difficulty when you say that.'

'In what way?'

'You see, I feel there must be an excitement like that, for me, out there.' She pointed vaguely inland. 'Waiting.' She took his arm, as if softening a blow before she added: 'But I don't think it has anything to do with marriage – not in my case.'

He made no immediate reply.

'You're shocked,' she challenged.

'Not at all. Worried, perhaps, but not shocked. You see, the world being what it is, a woman really needs the protection of a man. However strong-minded and independent she may be, there are occasions when she must have ... perhaps *protection* is the wrong word – but there are occasions when she must have the *agency* of a man. Dealing with money. Dealing with the law. Acquiring property – or even managing it. Of course, a very wealthy heiress, especially if she's widowed ... well, for her it's different. She simply employs men to act for her.' He smiled shyly. 'Not wishing to pry, Selina, but ... er?'

She laughed. 'There is certainly no fortune like that in the offing.' Her amusement died as she added, 'Nor any prospect of earning it, I'm afraid.'

'Ah, well, that's the other point I was going to make. The excitement I spoke about, you see ... it came from applying everything I'd learned at medical school. If I'd been a rotten scholar ... well, it's the difference between the terror an incompetent lion tamer must surely feel compared with the pleasure felt by one who knows his job well. You see what I mean? It isn't simply money. It's the thrill of putting all one's training into practice. Plus, of course, not being afraid to do it.'

'And what am I trained for?' Selina asked bitterly. 'Hardly to manage a household even.' She turned and looked at Johanna. 'She's the one who can do all that. Without training, too — she just seems to have it at her fingertips. She's the one you should marry, you know.'

When he made no reply she turned to him — and was surprised to find him standing there, eyes closed, smiling and shaking his head ironically. 'Ah!' she said, knowing she had at last touched a nerve.

He opened his eyes then, and nodded.

'I did wonder,' Selina went on, 'You've masked it pretty well, I must say. Does Jo herself know?'

'No,' he murmured, 'I don't believe it myself, either. I don't trust it. Love at first sight is ... absurd. I don't trust it.'

Selina held her peace.

He could not leave it alone, though. 'Do you and she ... has she ever mentioned me?'

'She wouldn't dream of discussing such things with me.'

'Oh.' After a pause he added, 'I find it hard to ... er, ascertain her position in the household.'

'A superior abigail,' Selina replied evenly, watching closely for his reaction.

He turned to her in surprise, not at the news but at her frankness.

She grinned. 'And I'm sure you *ascertained* the fact within the first five minutes.'

'Do you really have no idea what her opinion of me might be?'

'I can find out soon enough.'

'Oh, well ... I'm not sure ...' Then, more confidently, he went on, 'Why would you do such a thing?'

She chuckled. 'You mean I don't strike you as one given over to charitable gestures like that? You're quite right, Tony. I don't have many illusions about myself, either, but ...'

'Oh, but I didn't mean that. I think you're too hard there.'

The interruption was so immediate, and so heartfelt, it penetrated the shell of her rather brittle self-deprecation. She turned and walked on.

He beckoned Johanna to join them but she pretended to misunderstand and merely waved back. He caught up with Selina. 'Come now,' he told her jovially. 'You must tell me one good thing about yourself, too. Show me you can be balanced in your judgement.'

She did not take him up. 'Preparing for your visit — that's what opened my eyes, you know. Ever since I can remember, the talk has been, "When you're married ... when you have a home and family of your own ..." and so on. But it's always been in a comforting sort of nowhere. A long way off. Fairy-tale country ...'

'And suddenly it began to seem very close?'

'I thought of it again, just now, when we were talking about Cornwall and the ancient forests. When you're a child and you read about Little Red Riding Hood, you're afraid, of course, but it's a comforting sort of fear. Playtime fear. But when you find yourself in a real forest, and you know there might be real wolves trotting in the shadows ... d'you know what I mean?'

'Wolves?' he queried. 'Are we menfolk really as terrifying as that?'

'All right — not terror but apprehension. Don't quibble.'

He raised his hands in a gesture of surrender. 'But we come back to that basic objection — if you have no great fortune, and no especial training ... well, it's a hard furrow to plough, Selina.'

Her smile suggested he had paid her a compliment. Turning once more, she called out, 'Johanna — come on!' as if her cousin were a recalcitrant child.

They stood their ground and waited. Johanna barely heard the cry, but the windmilling arms, beckoning her, were unambiguous. She started the long, arduous slog across the yielding sand. Now, however, Tony kept his eyes on Selina. 'Have I perhaps been a little hasty?' he mused aloud.

'In what way?' She did not look at him.

'You make me ashamed of my earlier ... I mean, I had no idea we could talk together like *this*. You're quite a surprise.'

'I didn't really finish what I started to say. I didn't mean to babble' − she smiled at him as she produced the word − 'about forests and wolves and things. What I was going to say, Tony, was that the thought of your visit, and your reason for it and so on − made me examine myself rather more deeply than ... no ... for the first time, to be honest.'

'Was it so very dreadful?' His jocular tone showed that he did not suppose it was.

'If one does an indifferent little watercolour for one's private diary, one can be indulgent of its shortcomings. But if someone comes along, suddenly, and tells you a prominent collector will be calling, with a view to acquiring the wretched thing − well, it's suddenly not the same picture at all, is it.'

'Indulgence may still be in order, though, don't you think?'

'I'll tell you what I think. I think I'd like to take a sponge and wash me away and start it all again.'

He stared at her, forcing her to turn to him at last. She fixed him with an unblinking gaze, and he saw a would-be hardness there within her. But behind it all he caught a fleeting glimpse of a vulnerability that cried out to his sympathy. 'You are wrong,' he murmured. 'You must be wrong.'

She turned slowly from him, disappointed, as if she had expected some quite different response. Her eyes sought Johanna and could not immediately find her.

'May I help?' he felt impelled to add, not having the first practical notion in mind.

She softened at that and turned to him briefly again. 'Perhaps,' she said gently. Then she caught sight of her cousin, walking on the firmer ground among the dunes, just above the beach. 'Sensible girl,' she said. 'Let's go up there and meet her.'

As they waited for Johanna to cover the last hundred yards or so, he asked quietly, 'Will you really find out what she thinks of me?'

'Of course,' Selina said — as if that were only the first step.

Chapter Four

That evening, Johanna retired to her room as usual, taking some needlework with her. She sat at the window to catch the last of the light, saving her allowance of candle for reading later. The silk thread wove itself in and out of the cloth almost of its own accord, so accustomed were her fingers to the work by now. She watched the pattern grow with an abstracted interest, while her true thoughts turned to Dr Moore and Selina.

Something strange had happened between them that afternoon, down at Praa. At first, when she caught up with them, it appeared they had, after all, decided to 'give it a try,' or however one might express it — especially as they were calling each other Tony and Selina all of a sudden. Yet it had soon become clear that they were, if anything, even farther from romance than before; they chatted and smiled at each other like . . . well, it sounded absurd, but like old friends.

Unfortunately, the doctor seemed to take this new understanding with Selina as a sort of licence to turn his attention toward her, Johanna. Even now, in the safety of her own room, she could not feel easy. Not that she found his attention unwelcome — far from it. It was the aftermath she feared. Her cousin might take it all calmly (for the moment, anyway — one never knew what way she'd turn next) but her aunt would never forgive her. It was one thing to accept the inevitable — that the spark of love had somehow died between the County Ball and now; but to see her late sister's child, the undowered orphan of the family, walk off with the prize instead . . . no, that would make her life here absolutely intolerable.

On the other hand, Johanna could not help reflecting that if Dr Moore were serious in his interest, and if, in the usual

way of things, it led to a proposal and an engagement ...
well, her aunt could do precious little about it. She began to
daydream.

Wouldn't it be marvellous if she woke up to discover she
was, after all, in love with him! Everything would become so
simple. She wondered, in fact, that it had not already
happened. Objectively he had all the qualities of which a
young girl might dream – or ought to dream: handsome,
charming, esteemed, with a good income that was quite
independent of his professional earnings ... and well connected, they said. Why did she feel merely warm about it all?
Why did she not burn for him?

Perhaps love – real love – was like that? A great, warm,
banked up fire that glowed for ages, a lifetime. And all that
burning passion people spoke of, perhaps that was just a
spark, painfully brilliant one moment, extinct the next. She
was sure they could be the most tremendous friends.
Perhaps that was the true inclination of her heart, made for
solid friendship rather than the flights and excesses of
passion? Suppose she did marry him and they never fell in
love – just enjoyed a deep and lifelong friendship together
– made a home, raised a family, and cherished their
friendship. Would that be so terrible? Especially when the
alternative was so bleak.

She sighed. There lay the trouble, of course. Aunt
Theresa's plan was for her own children to go off and marry
well while the orphan cousin stayed at 'home' and took care
of the parents in their old age. She never said as much, or not
in so many words, but she had reared Johanna in the firm
expectation that she would never marry or leave this house.
So if Dr Moore were fully sixty years of age, bald, toothless,
and wooden legged, he would still seem attractive to her.

There was a swish of silk along the passageway outside.
Not one of the servants; Aunt Theresa, probably. Johanna
rested her work and waited for the door to be flung open.
Instead there was a hesitant little knock and Selina's voice
saying, 'Jo? May I come in?'

'Of course,' she called out, darting another few stitches.

A moment later her cousin was framed in the gloom of the
doorway. 'What are you doing?' she asked hesitantly. 'How
can you possibly see?'

Johanna laid down her work again. 'I was just about to finish. Come and sit in the window seat and watch the sunset.'

'But the sun went down ages ago.' Selina closed the door carefully and crossed the narrow room.

'You can still see the colours. It went from pink to green just now. Soon it'll go purple.'

'I think I'll be an artist,' Selina said as she settled herself comfortably, not even glancing at the sky. 'So this is where you do all that beautiful needlework. I can't remember the last time I was in here.'

'When it was a nursery, probably.' Johanna tidied her workbox and returned it to its place in the cupboard.

Her cousin watched her as if every action deserved some special amazement. 'D'you actually like it here, Jo?' she asked at length.

'It would be ungrateful not to.'

'Well said!' Selina gave her an ironic pat on the arm. 'Now tell me truly.'

'I like it here as much as you do, I think.'

Selina laughed.

'What happened this afternoon?' Johanna risked asking.

'I found a friend.' There was a defiant edge to the statement, daring Johanna to see something faintly comic in its simplicity. When the challenge was declined she added, 'And that friend found one, too.'

'It has obviously pleased you.'

'Ah, you've noticed a change in me, then?'

Johanna began to wish she had work to distract her; she was not used to this intense kind of talk from her cousin. 'I suppose so.'

'No fits and tantrums. They were never really me, in fact.'

'I knew that.'

'Oh, did you!' Selina bridled, revealing a touch of her old self for an instant.

'Yes. You always peeped out between your fingers to see what effect it was having.'

Selina teetered on the edge of that former personality before rescuing herself with a laugh. 'I shall be a reformed character now, you'll see.'

'*And* an artist! Busy days ahead.'

'And lots of other things beside. Yes, very busy. But that's not what I wanted to talk about. Tell me what you think of Tony.'

'Dr Moore?'

Selina gave a mischievous grin. 'Yes, I anticipate, perhaps. Anyway, do tell me.'

'He is certainly a most handsome young man.'

'Yes?'

'And charming and . . . attentive?'

'Attentive! He positively hangs on every word you say.'

'Oh, Selina!' Johanna looked apprehensively toward the door. More than once she had been aware that her uncle listened at the keyhole — though she could hardly tell her cousin as much.

'I'm not teasing, Jo. He'd marry you tomorrow if you'd have him. What d'you say to that?'

'I'd say it would be wicked and ungrateful of me even to think of such a possibility — when we all know why he's paying us this visit.'

Selina stared at her in open disbelief. Then the light of understanding dawned. 'You think I'm testing you! That's it, isn't it! And if you show the slightest interest in him, I'll go running directly to Mama and peach on you.'

'As if you'd do such a thing!' Johanna's challenge was sarcastic.

'Mind you . . .' Selina gave a thoughtful smile. 'If I did, they'd turn you out of this house on the instant. You wouldn't see another sunrise through those' — she peered at the window for the first time and continued, in a different tone — 'disgraceful lights. Don't you positively freeze here in winter?' She shivered theatrically. 'Come to my room and we'll light the lamp. I can't make out your expression any longer and it unnerves me.'

Johanna made no move. That playful threat worried her. 'Why would you think of doing such a thing?' she asked. 'Going and telling your mother, I mean?'

'Oh, they'd turn you out and that would force poor Tony to do something about it. Just think of the time it would save!'

'I hope this is some sort of jest,' Johanna responded. 'I think we will go to your room. You're not the only one who needs to see the other's expression.'

The two women glided through the dark, winding passages of the old house. Johanna brought along a stocking that needed darning. 'Where is Dr Moore, anyway?' she asked.

'Losing gallantly at billiards to Father.'

'And my aunt?'

'She's reading *Sybil* to Ethna and Deirdre, poor things.'

Selina lit the oil lamp. Johanna sat at the table and began to work on the stocking. 'Oh, put that horrid stuff away,' her cousin said.

'You'd best have something handy, too,' Johanna warned. 'In case your mother tires of her reading.'

Selina gave a strangled cry of futile rage, but she fished out her own needlework and put it where she could snatch it up quickly should the need arise; it was a rather botched panel for a firescreen. She looked at it fondly. 'I could be an artist,' she said, as if the discovery were slightly surprising. Then she turned to Johanna with eager anticipation. 'Now!'

'Now what?'

'How are we going to manage it? We need a plan.'

Johanna shot her a glance of alarm but said nothing.

'Poor Tony, you see — he's so torn between ... well, three things, really. First, there's the cry of his heart, then there's his idea of social duty, and finally the fact that he can't truly believe he's in love with you. He distrusts strong and sudden feelings like that.'

'Sensible man.'

'Perhaps, but that doesn't help us. The fact remains that while he's torn apart, he won't actually do anything.'

Johanna leaned forward and whispered. 'Are you saying we should conspire to ...' In the event she could not say it.

'To make him propose to you. Yes! He's a man of honour and once he's blurted it out, he'll never go back on it. Good lord, I thought that was understood.'

'Keep your voice down, for the love of heaven. It's not understood by me.'

Selina stared at her cousin in frank disbelief. 'You mean you ... are saying you want to go on living here?'

'Not necessarily.' Johanna gave an awkward shrug. 'But I couldn't take advantage . . .'

'Not necessarily!' Selina echoed. 'Honestly, Jo, you are beyond comprehension sometimes.'

'It's easy for you to sneer but I owe a duty to your mother and father. Their charity was all that stood between me and the workhouse when my parents . . .'

'Stuff and nonsense! They took you in because the tongues in Helston would never have ceased wagging if they had not. Charity, indeed! And the moment they realized what a competent and trustworthy little housekeeper you are, they decided to keep you at it for life.'

Johanna maintained an awkward silence.

'I hope you don't still imagine I'm testing you?' Selina pressed.

'No.' She abandoned that first line of defence with reluctance.

'So it's not a question of what you owe them. I think you've repaid the cost of your upbringing many times over. Now you must think what you owe yourself.'

Johanna put down her work. 'I'd feel happier if I knew why you're taking such an interest, Selina. In my happiness, I mean. I'm not used to it.'

'You want a selfish reason, eh?' Selina smiled.

The other tried to think of a polite way to say it would be more convincing.

'The only attraction of marriage for me' − Selina spoke quite seriously now − 'is that it would give me some independence. Well, you know all the arguments as well as I do. If I were in your shoes, I'm sure I'd have done nothing but scheme about marriage for years. It's your only way out, you know.'

'And yours. It's the only way out for any girl, surely.'

'Perhaps not.'

A bewildered Johanna waited for her cousin to explain. It was an unusual struggle between cunning and honesty. 'If I tell you, it might spoil it,' Selina said at last.

'Any secret would be safe with me.'

Selina shook her head. 'It's not that kind of secret. It involves you. In fact, you're at the centre of it, you and Tony. On the other hand, if I don't tell you . . . well, we

43

could all end up misunderstanding each other in the most damaging way.' She chuckled. 'I mean, if you thought I was acting out of pure altruism and a desire to secure your happiness!'

Johanna laughed at the very idea — a response that made up Selina's mind for her. 'I'm sure you *would* be happy with Tony,' she said. 'In fact, if you weren't, the whole scheme would collapse. What I really want, you see, is to be free — free of this house, free of this dreadful obligation to cease burdening my poor, dear parents and ensnare a husband at all costs. But what is freedom if it exists only during those brief months while I flit from one prison to another?'

'Home? A prison?'

'Perhaps not to you, my dear. That's why it could all work so well, you see?'

Johanna shook her head. 'I'm afraid I don't.'

'Well, surely this house *is* a prison to you? You can't deny that, if you don't marry, you'll be here at forty, wheeling your aunt and uncle out into the conservatory every day to ripen in the sun. So I should think you'd be jolly grateful to anyone who helped you escape such a fate.' She smoothed her sleeve contentedly. 'And there's no need to ask whether Tony would be grateful. So, when you and he have an establishment of your own somewhere — in Plymouth, I presume — there'd probably be a teeny weeny little room in it for me?'

'For life?' Johanna was aghast.

'Hah!' Selina laughed. 'Oh, Jo — what a very practical girl you are! At least you don't throw up your hands and say an outright no!'

Johanna swallowed hard.

Selina reached across and squeezed her arm. 'I'm the one who says no — not for life. But perhaps for a year or two — just while I see what's possible and what's not.'

'And if nothing turns out to be possible?'

Selina tossed her head in annoyance. 'I shan't even think of that yet.'

Johanna's eyes narrowed. 'Have you discussed any of this with Tony . . . with Dr Moore?'

'Of course not!' She was shocked. 'He's just like any other man. If ever you try to talk about anything serious,

44

feelings and that, they have this bolt-hole. They turn all pompous and preach at you. A gentleman's duty is to save a lady from the excesses of her own heart.' She softened, enough to give a small chuckle. 'To think that I spent all those weeks since the County Ball in mortal terror of him. You remember?'

Johanna smiled. 'I seem to, yes.'

'And then five minutes after I met him, I realized he felt the same about me. And you, too, actually.'

'Nonsense!'

'It's true. He's afraid of all women. I think every man is. That's why they invent this alleged duty to protect us from ourselves. What they're really doing is protecting *them*selves, and from us. They do it to evade the necessity of discovering what we really are.'

For the first time Johanna felt the beginnings of understanding. It evaporated almost at once among the certainties that had been drilled into her since childhood; but just for a moment she glimpsed ... not another truth, but the *possibility* of another truth. 'And what are we, really?' she asked with genuine interest.

'How do I know? That's what I want to find out. It might take' – she grinned – 'two years, in fact.'

Johanna laughed. But her cousin grew serious again. 'It's as if I've been walking up and down a particular street all my life and passing this little side alley. And everyone's always told me, "Oh, that's a dead end." And then one day I take a few, tentative little steps down it, and I find it's not a dead end at all. Isn't it exciting?'

Johanna nodded in mystified agreement.

Selina now had the bit between her teeth. 'But suppose I were calf-sick in love with some man. Mooning about the place, picking at my food ... sighing. What could I ever learn then? Love? It seems to me it's the worst prison of all. I'm glad I'm never going to fall for it. I shall be free. You watch – really free!'

'Free to manipulate people?' Johanna asked.

The other frowned.

'Well, you're certainly trying to manipulate Dr Moore and me. You can't deny that.'

'But I do deny it, Jo. When you help two people to do

45

something that — in their heart of hearts — they really do want to do anyway . . . well, that's not manipulation.'

'And suppose that — in their heart of hearts, as you say — suppose they don't want it? Or one of them doesn't?'

Selina smiled at her, eyes brimming with tender sympathy. 'But you do, my dear. Honestly. You may not realize it yet, but you do want it.'

Chapter Five

A sense of oppression hung over the following morning. It came to a head when Mrs Visick asked the young people what they intended doing that day. Dr Moore was writing a letter at the time, so the question was directed at Selina, who turned to her cousin and snapped. 'Well?'

'Well what?' Johanna replied in some surprise.

'I suppose it's for you to say.'

'I can't imagine why.' Johanna looked nervously at her aunt, who agreed that she, too, could not see why, and waited for an explanation.

'I'll spare your blushes, cousin dear.' Selina spoke with acid sweetness as she swept her mother into the drawing room.

But Johanna got a foot in the door. There was a token struggle before Selina capitulated. 'Very well, if you insist,' she said carelessly.

'Please,' Johanna responded. 'I don't know what you may intend, Selina, but if it has any bearing on our conversation of yesterday evening, then I beg you will say no more.'

'What is going on?' Mrs Visick asked testily. Then, realizing that surprise had reversed her sense of priority, she turned to Johanna and added, 'The impertinence of it! She shall say whatever she likes.'

Johanna ignored her. 'Please, Selina?' she repeated, more urgently.

Her cousin, unobserved by her mother, gave a wink. 'I've kept silent long enough,' she said coldly. 'It's time the truth came out. Sit down, Mama.'

'No!' Johanna commanded, equally firmly.

Mrs Visick sat down and stared defiantly at her niece. 'The very idea!' she said.

'Aunt Theresa, I beg you − do not stay. Do not listen. If you stay and . . .'

'How dare you!' the woman thundered. 'You forget yourself strangely, young miss.'

'And you may forget all future peace of mind if you ignore my warning now.'

Selina saw that her mother's confidence was dented enough, at least, to cause her to turn and ask if this were some silly prank they had devised. Hastily, then, she blurted it out: 'Dr Moore is in love with Johanna! So now!'

Johanna wished she were a thousand miles away. She stood there, consumed with anger and dread, waiting for her aunt to erupt.

It did not take long. 'W h a a a a t!' The word began in her boots and finished somewhere near the ceiling. She stared at her daughter, who somehow produced a tear and caused it to tremble on her eyelid. Then she turned to Johanna and drew a breath through nostrils like cannon mouths. 'Is this true?' she asked in an ominously subdued monotone.

'It was none of my doing,' Johanna started to explain.

'By heavens, it is true! Listen to the baggage!'

'How did I know he would arrive by the back lanes?' Johanna protested.

The moment the words were out, she saw it was a mistake. She had assumed that Selina knew all about the accidental meeting, but, of course, as she now realized, Dr Moore would not have breathed a word of it.

Selina was quick, though. 'That's how you did it!' she crowed. 'Oh, Mama! The devious snake! She must have seen − when we were up on Trigonning, that day he came, you remember? Yes − it's quite clear now. She must have seen him on the road from Carleen. So she sent me home and went on to forestall me. You viper!' Another merry wink belied the words, unseen by the mother, of course.

'Is this true, Johanna?' her aunt asked. 'I find this hard to believe − even of you.'

Johanna rose and went to the door. 'There is no point in

going on,' she told them. 'You wouldn't believe me in any case.'

Mrs Visick showed a surprising turn of speed, springing to her feet and reaching the door just ahead of her niece. But Selina cried out, 'Let her go!' The pain sounded so genuine that her mother returned to her at once.

Pausing only to put on her hat and gloves, Johanna went outdoors. Her first steps down the path were made unreal, or supernaturally real, by her sense of the occasion, for this was almost certainly the last aimless walk, the last walk-for-walking's-sake, she would ever take from Lanfear House. At the garden gate she hesitated; here the path divided – right toward Trigonning, left to Godolphin. Today, being in no mood for the godlike view, she turned left.

Godolphin Hill, a sentinel outpost less than a mile to the north of Trigonning, affords a glimpse into the secret places of west Cornwall – its valleys and streams, its pastures and dells, its villages, copses, and lanes – all of which it obscures from the grander summit to its south. If this really were Johanna's last day at Lanfear, here was the Cornwall to which she would be saying farewell.

Her way to it led through a wasteland of rock and mud, a bedlam of mine tailings smeared across the land, collectively known as Greatwork. Yet once that was behind her, once she stood upon the emerald turf that carpeted the ancient warrens of Godolphin Manor, she felt her mood lighten and the old secluded promise of the place stole over her.

How much she had learned over the years – just standing here and observing: dozens of lives had been hers for the sharing, not all of them human. She had discovered the runs of foxes and the knolls where the corncrakes would nest. She knew where the rising air would support the quartering of buzzards. The crannies where vipers would lurk, the basking stones of lizards, the favourite nooks of hares . . . she had learned these things as any schoolchild learns the way to school, not even realizing it was knowledge. Yet the little human dramas were what chiefly lured her here. Often they had helped to set her own unhappiness in true proportion.

Down there, in Rocky Lane, was where the letter carrier

would always pause for a gossip, never for one moment supposing his voice would carry too. And *such* information! And there in Trescowe fields was where Joel Barnicoat set his snares — in the obvious delusion that the hedge which concealed him from the farmhouse rendered him invisible to all the world besides. A half mile farther on, at Oak Tree farm, Mrs Jones would tip her household refuse in an old section of open-cast mine; and within the hour Sarah Blight would be out there, sorting through it all, looking for letters or anything else with a tale to tell. Old Sarah thought Gabriel Jones should have married her instead, and given her child a name. And, while on that particular subject, when Tommy Williams broke off his engagement to his cousin up Polladras last year, and married Susan Verrigo instead (and in haste), Johanna was less surprised than most.

And now, or soon, she'd be bidding farewell to it all. She tried to rekindle her anger against Selina, but found she could not. Indeed, she had to admit there was something thrilling, almost magnificent, in what her cousin had done. It was so final, so irrevocable. Her actual plan was quite absurd, of course; yet could she, just by pursuing it with that same blind ruthlessness, make it happen nonetheless? Probably not, Johanna decided; for though, at the moment, Dr Moore might be lost in his romantic delusions, nothing would sober him down better than to see the object of his supposed affections branded a traitress and deceiver. All he needed do was to mumble, 'Sorry, my mistake,' and what price Selina's clever plans then?

Johanna wondered she could be so calm about it. For most of her life she'd had little choice but to accept her situation — to accept that life would often serve her poorly and there'd be little enough she could do about it. It had made her more than slightly fatalistic, she knew that. But this unexpected calm went beyond mere fatalism. Indeed, there was almost an eagerness within her, as if some long-dormant part of her were stirring at last, having waited only for an event as final and irrevocable as this to unfold.

Was that why she hadn't stayed to argue? She could certainly have told her aunt something of Selina's absurd hopes. The woman may not have believed her, or not entirely, but at least it would have given her pause for thought. In fact, Johanna realized, her walking out like that had left the field to Selina, making it almost certain that her plan – or that part of it which called for Johanna's expulsion from Lanfear – would come to pass.

A voice called out from half-way down the hill behind her, 'You have a fascination with high places, Miss Rosewarne.'

Her spirit quickened; it was Tony Moore, of course, striding easily over the rabbit-cropped turf. She gave him a hesitant wave and returned to her scrutiny of the landscape.

'Oh, but it's all quite different from here,' he remarked as he drew closer. 'Compared with the view from the larger hill, I mean.'

'I suppose the house is in uproar?' she asked.

He came to a halt beside her, a yard or so between them, and, folding his arms, stared intently at the scene. 'It's like the way children draw,' he said at last. 'Some of those fields down there seem to be standing almost vertically. D'you see?'

She waited for him to answer her question.

He gave a little laugh. 'I expect they'd all be surprised to realize how much you know about their lives.' He nodded toward the hamlets and the isolated farmhouses. 'If you come here often, that is?' He turned to her then. His eyebrows were raised but they asked a deeper, less posable, question.

'My aunt and cousin ... have you spoken to them?'

He nodded, unconcerned. 'I could not bear the pretence a moment longer.'

She frowned. It was not quite the expected answer. 'I mean, did they not speak to you?'

'I told them I had packed my things and would be leaving before noon.'

'But Selina ... I mean, didn't she ...?'

'I also told them my reasons – and now I've come to tell you, too. Or can you guess?' He smiled expectantly and then almost at once said, 'No, that's a coward's way to go about it.'

By now Johanna was beginning to wonder whether she had

not perhaps dreamed the argument with her aunt and cousin.
'You say you told ... but weren't they distressed or ...'

'They were when I had finished.'

'No, I mean before. When you came down from writing
your letter ... I mean, how did they seem?'

He shrugged. 'Perfectly calm. Normal. Why do you
ask?'

Johanna thought of a number of answers before she said,
'No, pray continue. What were you about to tell me?'

He stared out across the landscape for a while before he
said, more to himself than her, 'I can't even begin.' He
faced her then. 'I came up here with a million thoughts
flying in my mind, things I wished to tell you ... but really
there's only one. They all boil down to one. I want to bring
you happiness, Miss Rosewarne. I want to try and make
you happy. That's all.'

She smiled at him. 'Oh dear.'

He pulled a face. 'Is the mere thought of it so dreadful,
then?'

'No, of course not, but is that what you told my aunt?'

He nodded. 'Never mind them. What about you?'

'Please, I must know. Everything hinges on ... I mean,
what did she say? Was Selina there?'

'They were polite, of course. And very cold. Positively
frigid, in fact − not that one can blame them. I'm afraid I
haven't behaved too ...'

'What, even Selina? But yesterday, down at Praa ...'

'I know. But she seems to have changed completely. Not
that I'm in any position to cast stones, mind, but she is, well
− mercurial, don't you think?'

'She pretends to be. I used to believe she was. But no
longer. Oh, for all I know, she's mad.'

He eyed her uncertainly. 'May I ask what you and she
discussed last night? I assure you it's no idle curiosity.'

'It made no sense to me,' Johanna told him guardedly.

'Perhaps, if you told me, then?' he offered.

'Or if *you* told me?'

'What? I'll tell you anything, just as long as you'll give
me an answer.'

'Tell me what you and she discussed on the beach − since
it must, in some way, have led to the things she said to me.'

'Oh.' He pulled a face. 'I meant I'd tell you anything as long as you answered me *first*. Still . . .'

'Why did the pair of you start all formal and polite at Pentreath and end up like old friends only half an hour later at Pengersick?'

'Ah, I suppose the short answer is that she put an end to the awkwardness between us. You know what about, I'm sure. She said we'd be far better friends, she and I, than suitor and . . . what's the object of suitor? Anyway, you know what I mean. She was right, too. She pointed out that the fact I no longer sought any romantic association with her – while she had never sought any such thing with me – gave us the chance to be true friends without the slightest suspicion of an ulterior motive.'

'It doesn't sound like Selina at all.'

'Well, those aren't her exact words. I'm giving you the gist of quite a long discussion.'

'And did she mention freedom at all?'

'From the demands of that sort of emotion? Yes.'

'No, I mean freedom from the necessity of marrying – of being always under the protection of a man?'

He frowned at the effort of recall. 'Yes, I suppose she did.'

'And are you aware how she proposes to acquire that freedom?'

The edge to her question made him look at her sharply. 'You seem to imply that I ought to be, Miss Rosewarne.'

'We both ought to be, Dr Moore. We would be part of it.'

He chewed his lip abstractedly. 'I see,' he said at last.

'Not quite what you had in mind, I expect?' she prompted.

He smiled. 'If it were the price of setting a ring upon your finger, my dear, I'd accept the entire family.' But then he closed his eyes and shook his head, as if he had done something foolish. 'There now! That is precisely what I wished *not* to say.'

'Then tell me,' she said gently.

'My intention was, well, somehow to convey my feelings – my feelings toward you, which you must know are – oh, I've imagined myself in love before but it was never anything like this . . .' He fell silent. The tips of his ears, or of the one Johanna could see, turned bright red. 'I know I must seem

53

absurd,' he continued. 'I still find it so incredible myself.'

She reached forward and touched his arm. 'No,' she murmured.

He looked at her in amazement. 'Truly?'

'Truly.'

'But I was not going to press you to any response − or no direct response to that. Indeed, that is still my intention. All I hope for is that you will not say me an outright no?'

'You are quite sure that in no circumstances would you renew your suit with my cousin?'

'Not if she were the last . . . no, that sounds awful. I don't mean that. Anyway, I am quite sure.'

'Then, of course I will not say an outright no.'

'But?' He tried to encourage her with his eyes. 'You give me no positive indication . . .'

'Come, let us walk home,' she said, taking his arm and thereby turning the suggestion into one he could not refuse. 'You must try to understand how hard this is for me. I am not a very emotional woman − at least, I do not think I am. Perhaps I was once. I seem to remember . . .' Her voice tailed off. 'But no matter. The circumstances of my up-bringing have made it necessary for me to quell any sudden show of . . . I mean, I envy Selina, who is always so spontaneous, both in her affection and her anger. There is a point where the suppression of one's feelings ceases to be mere prudence and becomes a habit. And then it etches its way into one's very soul.' After a pause she added, 'It is hard for me even to say this much.' She gave his arm an encouraging squeeze and hoped it was enough.

At length he responded. 'In a way it leads me to what I *was* going to suggest. I should be impossibly conceited if I imagined that you felt toward me even a hundredth part of my feelings for you. So what I wanted − what I hoped − was that we might devise some way in which we could meet on social terms and so learn to know each other better. In other words, if there were only some small glow of warmth toward me, we could provide it with the opportunity to . . .'

She felt all the muscles of his arm grow tense with frustration. 'I understand,' she assured him.

He laughed. 'Why, when I try to talk seriously with women, do I turn so pompous and long-winded? It happened yesterday with Selina. Anyway – once I realized what your situation here is … I mean, that you can expect no financial support from your relations – once I realized …'

'They have many calls upon their purse.' She felt she ought still to defend the Visicks.

He shrugged awkwardly. 'Leaving aside all question of blame, the fact remains that if you leave this place, you will have to make your own way in the world. Now nothing would delight me more, and nothing would be easier, than to arrange an allowance' – he felt the objections bubbling up inside her but before she could speak he went on – 'but, of course, it's out of the question. You must not feel under the slightest obligation toward me until I have convinced you that, merely by accepting my suit, you place me under obligations I could never discharge. So I racked my brains for some way out of this impasse and then, last night, it suddenly struck me. I have the answer. I've had it all along. That was the letter I wrote this morning – but I shall not send it unless you agree.'

His hand went to his pocket.

'No, you tell me,' she said.

'Very well. I live in Windsor Terrace, in the more salubrious part of Plymouth, overlooking the Promenade upon the Hoe.'

'Where Drake played bowls while the Armada drew near.'

'So legend has it. Well, five doors down from me live a charming couple. Charles Dugdale and his wife Eleanor, who have two lovely little daughters of seven and nine. Also three sons, who are, I don't know, older. The eldest must be eighteen. But the two girls, Amelia and Felicity, need a good governess. If you took the position – they are people of the highest respectability – we could learn to know each other better without the slightest risk to your reputation.'

They had reached the edge of the warren. Half hidden under some ragged outgrowth of ling she saw the whitened skull of a rabbit. A memory stirred. 'Look at that,' she said. 'A crocus grew out through one of the eye things – what d'you call them? – sockets, this spring. I kept coming here to see if it was really true.'

'Shall I send that letter?' he asked.

She turned to him and lifted her face toward his. Her eyelids shut out the day. Her lips parted loosely. Her breathing came in shivers. 'Of course,' she whispered.

Nothing happened.

She opened her eyes and found him staring at her, not daring to believe. His hand rose and touched her cheek. 'How can you be so dear to me?' he murmured. 'From the moment I saw you until now ... I have not ... wavered in ...' His voice tailed off. He yielded to the incoherence, the disorientation he had kept at bay these last centuries of days.

She stood on tiptoe and shut her eyes once more. His lips closed against hers, softly at first, then hungrily.

Chapter Six

While Johanna and Tony were standing on Godolphin Hill, making decisions that were to alter their lives, a second drama was taking place less than a mile away — but many fathoms beneath their feet. Although these two events were as yet unconnected, a chain of circumstance was soon to bind them inextricably together. Indeed, its first link already existed, for the locus of this other drama was the Fifty Fathom West at Wheal Venton, one of the mines owned by John Visick of Lanfear and his partner, Walter Trahearne of Nineveh House.

Say 'mine' to most people and they think of a hole sunk through a deep, horizontal slab of rock until it strikes a layer of valuable mineral — which is also more or less horizontal. In Cornwall, things are different. You could describe the whole of the county's geology and never once use the word 'horizontal', so violently have the rocks been folded and faulted and tilted and twisted. In fact, the strata lie, for the most part, between forty-five degrees and vertical. A typical mineral lode, therefore, begins as a streak of tolerant vegetation across the landscape and dips steeply downward into the hot, wet bowels of the earth.

The earliest mines, whose fabulous quality brought Phoenician traders to Cornwall long before Caesar and his legions saw Kent, were shallow workings at grass level. Over the next two thousand years, increasing boldness and desperation drove the miners ever wider and deeper in their search for metal; but always they were limited by the level at which a mine could drain itself. The trick was to find the lowest free-draining point in the surrounding countryside —

the sea itself, if it were close enough — and from it drive a horizontal tunnel, or adit, into the workings, which would thus drain by gravity into rivers or sea. A few extra fathoms, no more, could be gained by forking out from a sump into the adit, using buckets and a horse-driven whim. And that was where progress in Cornish mining had been halted for centuries before the coming of the steam engine — an event still within the living memory of many who now worked at Wheal Venton. Thanks to a gleaming, hissing, coal-devouring monster from Messrs Boulton and Watt, whose fifty-four-inch cylinder could lift up to twelve tons of water at a stroke, and at six strokes a minute, they had now reached sixty fathoms below the adit.

Over the coming decades the various working levels in that vast tilting sheet of ore would join up, leaving nothing but air to hold apart the two sloping faces of the surrounding rock — the 'gozan' as miners call it. Up around Redruth, where the gozan was granite, it was quite safe to leave vast stretches unsupported in this way. Nearer by, from Pallas Consols southward, where the gozan was the more friable elvanstone, islands of unmined rock, known as 'horses,' were needed every few fathoms. But here at Wheal Venton, where granite and elvan gozans mingled, there was more opinion than fact in the argument.

The mine captain, Enion Hosking, was a conservative to the marrow. He had come up in the early days of steam, when centuries-old constraints seemed to have been abolished overnight. In that first rapture of delving deep below the adit, corners had been cut and risks taken that could only be called criminal. Anyone with the remotest knowledge of mining could name half a dozen pretty lodes that could no longer be worked because the greed and ignorance of that earlier generation had left them unsafe. Captain Hosking was determined that no successor should curse his memory as he now cursed that of captains Curnow and Blight, who, for the sake of a few bushels of ore, had doubled the hazards of this working for all future miners.

'I say he stays,' he said. 'The way he'm planned now.'

'That's well enough for you, Cap'n,' Eli Watson grumbled. 'You haven't tributed for that bunch.'

'No more have you, neither,' the captain pointed out.

'That horse was excluded from the tribute.'

'Well, no one never told I.'

'You shouldn't ought to need no telling. Everyone do know. While I'm cap'n at this here mine, there'll be a horse at every sixth fathom, up and down, and forth and back. Every sixth fathom. Now you can measure six fathom so well as me — and that's all the telling you should need. 'Tis all you'll get, anyhow.'

Hal Penrose had managed to stay out of the argument so far — not an easy thing for him to do, especially standing fifty fathoms below grass, wet and half naked and with the sweat running off him in rivers. But Eli Watson turned to him, as Captain Hosking's assistant. 'Four hundred bushel of ore,' he said in disgust. 'With the prettiest bunches we seen at Wheal Venton in twenty year. He in't right, neither right nor fair.'

''Tis the way of the plan, Eli,' Hal said.

Captain Hosking heard the reluctance in his voice and gave an angry snort.

Eli went on, 'What difference is he going to make if that horse is moved two fathom further west? Or up or down?'

Hal, uncomfortable at being singled out as a potential supporter in what looked like becoming a campaign to overturn the captain's decision, glanced at his superior. He meant no more than to give him the courtesy of answering but Captain Hosking took it as a gesture of unspoken support for Eli Watson. The scowl deepened; the ridges and knots of his frown were sharply etched by the flickering light of their three candles. 'I'll tell 'ee what difference he do make, boy. S'pose I do let 'ee take out that horse, and then eight feet further on you go and find the bunches are twice so pretty as what they are now. Then you'll be standing here again and saying let's put in a timber horse and take the whole bloody lot. Don't tell me. I know! I've heard this all afore — scores o'times. That's why no one can go in the Three Fathom East now. Nor the Six Fathom East, neither. 'Cos your father and John Trebilcock done that very thing there, and Cap'n Blight was soft enough to let them.'

He nodded twice, firmly; the second was aimed at Hal, who hoping to defuse what could become an explosive wrangle, said, 'How about this, then? Leave the horse where it's planned, and if the bunches look prettier on the other side of it, then nothing's lost. But if they pinch out to nothing, why then we could leave a dead horse and go back and take the live one.'

Eli looked as if he might just about agree to that, for, like all tributers, he lived from day to day and it was almost a physical pain to him to leave a pretty bunch of tin staring at him, unmined.

But Captain Hosking almost had a fit. 'Why, damm 'ee, Penrose, if you aren't more trouble nor fifty tributers! You can't never abide nothing what I do say, can 'ee.'

'One horse!' Hal protested. 'One horse will be a fathom or so out of place. Now where's the danger in that?'

'The horse do stay,' the captain barked as he turned and stalked away. Then a further thought struck him and he came back, walking straight to the tributer. 'And I shall measure him,' he said menacingly. 'And if you durst take so much as an inch, you'll be off this pitch and that's the end of your tributing days. You'll be back on tutwork and picking halvans.' He put a finger almost against the man's nose. 'One inch!'

Eli Watson did not stir. His eyes, filled with the cold anger of righteousness, dwelled steadily on the captain's.

Hosking, now doubly furious, turned again on his heel and stormed off. 'Come on, Penrose,' he cried. 'We're wasting time and money here.'

Hal stayed long enough to say, 'One day, Eli, I'll do that man a mischief.'

The tributer gave him a companionable punch on the arm. 'I'm first. Tell he to keep his helmet on. They backs are troublesome.'

The 'backs' were the ceilings of the workings, where most of the ore was won. Tributers preferred to drill and blast upward through the lode, letting gravity do what would be heavy labour if they worked downward instead; but it meant that large stretches of overhead rock were always in a precarious condition. So it was no idle threat that Eli Watson made.

'See here, Penrose,' the captain said when Hal caught up with him. 'I do look to 'ee for more support than that . . .'

'I believe there was a misunderstanding,' Hal muttered tersely.

'Don't interrupt, dam 'ee! If you weren't kin to the Trahearnes, why, I'd not have 'ee here one day longer, and that's a fact.'

Hal counted a silence of five, so as not to be accused of interrupting again, but before he could speak the captain burst out with, 'And you do make silence the worst opposition of all, dam 'ee.'

Hal clenched his fists but still, somehow, managed to hold his peace.

It infuriated the captain still further. 'Now you've done it!' he roared. 'I shall send directly for Mr Trahearne and Mr Visick and I shall tell them – if you don't go, I will. And that's a fact, now.'

They had reached the sump of the pumping shaft, a vile cauldron of water polluted by the wastes of the mine and its workers. Hal, goaded beyond endurance at last, turned and shouted, 'Then I shall save you the trouble, sir!'

And, seizing the startled captain by the scruff of his collar and the seat of his pants, he hurled him into the water.

The only trouble with this magnificent gesture, he thought as he made his way back up to grass, was that folk would say their argument had really been about the captain's daughter Jemima. Even Hal himself could not deny there'd be some truth in that. *Damn all women,* he said to himself, not for the first time.

It was a day of astonishments for poor Theresa Visick. First there had been her daughter's almost unbelievable news about Dr Moore and Johanna. Then came Selina's audacious plan to pretend they were taking it all quite calmly – until dead of night, when they would chastise Johanna and banish her to stay with the Trahearnes at Nineveh House, over near Hayle. The treacherous Dr Moore would never find her there – 'Which,' as the girl explained cheerfully to her mother, 'will leave the field open to me once more.'

Theresa was not entirely convinced. 'We must send for your father and ask his opinion,' she said.

And that had produced an even greater surprise, for her husband had replied by note, saying that Hal Penrose had

61

caused a disturbance at Wheal Venton and he was required there most urgently.

'As if anything could possibly be more urgent than this!' Theresa exclaimed angrily.

Selina rubbed salt in it. 'Hal Penrose!' she said. 'Another orphan taken in by kindly relations — and now biting the hand that fed him!'

'Charity!' her mother responded. But anger robbed her of invention. All she could think of to say was, 'It's supposed to begin at home.'

'And should never go out of doors,' Selina responded.

'How true! How true! Oh yes, our ungrateful little viper must go. No doubt of it. I think you're right. Whip her thoroughly and send her to the Trahearnes. Oh, *why* will your father not come when called?'

And she sent the lad out again with a yet more peremptory demand.

On their way back to the house Johanna and Tony had reached the identical conclusion. Honour and duty made it impossible for them to remain at Lanfear a moment longer than was necessary.

'I shall stay at the Angel in Helston tonight,' he said, 'and take the mail coach to Plymouth tomorrow.'

His purpose in saying this was somehow to coax her into joining him.

'But your pony and trap?' she objected.

'Oh, I'll pay someone to bring it after me,' he replied. And then he had a better idea. 'Why not you? Surely you know some respectable lady who would accompany you and be glad of the journey?'

She shook her head. 'I want to be gone tonight. I'll stay only to take my leave of my uncle and then I'll go. I do have some friends here who will give me shelter for a while. Miss Grylls, I'm sure, will oblige.' She gave him a smile that turned him upside down. 'Those neighbours you mentioned, the Dugdales? With the two little girls?'

He nodded.

'Ask if they still need a governess. Then you can send for me, *poste restante,* to Helston.'

'Oh, my dearest, dearest Miss Rosewarne — do you truly mean it? Is it possible that . . .'

She held up a warning finger. 'I can make no promises, Dr Moore. Please do not read more into this than is there. I am not so impulsive as my haste must make me seem, but I am driven by necessity, I have little choice.'

'Of course, of course.' He seemed contrite, but his smile said he realized it was feminine modesty that spoke, not her heart.

'I must go and pack. And so must you, indeed.'

'Ah.' Her words brought their present situation home to him. 'Then — we shall not meet again until . . . Plymouth?'

She offered her lips for a parting kiss. 'Plymouth,' she murmured.

He was so grateful, so overwhelmed by the power of his feelings for her. She wondered if she would ever feel so strongly about him — or, indeed, about anyone or anything.

Chapter Seven

The master of the house did not come home until after six that evening. It took him some time to understand how a drama involving his wife and daughter could, for once, be of greater consequence than the crisis that had filled his own day.

'You do not understand, Mrs Visick, my dear,' he complained. 'The bullying wretch threw poor Hosking into the sump! Yes, just threw him in — in full fig!'

'The clothing will probably dry in the fullness of time, Mr Visick,' she replied coldly. 'What, meanwhile, of your daughter's ...'

'Eh? Yes, yes. Quite. Poor child. But it's the ingratitude of the fellow, don't you know. Old Trahearne is outraged. All his charity to that great lump of a nephew ... all simply thrown back.'

'And what of the viper we have nurtured in our own bosom, sir?' she interrupted shrilly. 'Our own niece. Our own charity. Thrown back, you say? She has *hurled* it back in our very teeth.'

Through it all, Selina lay curled upon the sofa, sobbing with obtrusive reticence.

Visick could take no more of it. Annoyed at having his best tale in years capped by some incomprehensible female nonsense, he said, 'Eh, eh, what? Where's Dr Moore? Ask him to come and explain it to me. I'm sure there's some quite elementary cause for ...'

'Oh, it's elementary, all right,' his wife sneered. 'Not to say element*al!* Our angelic niece has ... she has ... that is to say, she must have ... *seduced* the doctor. Or — since the

64

man is obviously quite insensible to honour — he is the one who . . .'

'Mama!' Selina looked up in alarm; such slander had no part in her plan.

'My dear, you are surely overwrought?' Visick patted the air about her as if the dreadful words might still be scooped up and stuffed back into her mouth. 'I insist that the doctor be sent for. He will surely . . .'

'By all means.' Theresa produced Tony's letter of apology like a small trump, the first of a good handful. 'Send to Helston by all means.'

'Helston?' His eyes scanned the letter. It was brief without being curt, apologetic without grovelling. 'Nothing here about . . . ermmmerm.' He glanced across at Selina as he cleared his throat.

'Oh, you are both so taken in by that baggage! Butter wouldn't melt in her mouth. I ask you — what other explanation could there possibly be? She has seduced him?'

'The ways of love, Mrs Visick, are not . . .'

'Love!' she exploded contemptuously. 'Where might that little waif have learned the first thing about love?'

'It becomes impossible to discuss the matter if I am not permitted to finish a single sentence,' he responded coldly.

'Discuss away, then!' His wife threw up her hands in sarcastic resignation. 'The conclusion will be the same. The baggage must be turned out. This act of charity *ends* at home!'

Visick glanced toward his daughter, who was now awkwardly poised between sob and eavesdrop. 'Not with the girl here,' he murmured. 'It is far too delicate a . . .'

'She knows full well what we're talking about.'

Visick was shocked. 'My dear, was that wise?'

Selina sprang to her feet. 'Papa is right,' she told her mother firmly. 'The matter has now come to a head. Only you and he can properly decide what's for the best. It would be quite unseemly for me to play any further part here.'

Visick's encouraging nod quashed all further protest; but his wife could not disguise her disappointment, for she had been rather counting on the girl's support. Without it she doubted her ability to make Visick feel that the decision to expel Johanna was truly his own.

'Come, sit down, my dear,' he cajoled, the moment they were alone. 'We should indeed be monsters to reach so dire a decision in this flurry of accusation and denial. Tell me calmly now, from the beginning . . .'

The thought that his beautiful Sleeping Venus might have been awakened by another was hard enough to bear. But the notion that she had woken of her own accord and then spread the relish for . . . No! He thrust the pictures from his mind.

'What opportunity have they had?' he asked with kindly sarcasm.

'All they might need,' she answered stoutly. 'Their rooms were not ten miles apart.'

She forbore to add that he himself should know how easy was the path at dead of night.

Visick smiled tolerantly. But his mind's eye saw Johanna turning in her bed, whose every inch was the heart of his mental landscape. He could see her moving to its edge, raising the covers on the untenanted side, smiling at the handsome young . . .

He shook his head with a curiously birdlike gesture. 'You think I should not have heard it?' he asked. 'I who can hear the mice as they breathe?'

'Out of doors, then.' Theresa was uneager to question his nocturnal hearing — indeed, his nocturnal anything.

'But Selina has been with them every instant.' He packed away the whole absurd notion and started another tack, one that would touch him less and his wife more: 'We have to consider the future, my dear. Long after this little storm is over, we . . .'

'*Little* storm!'

'Very well — big storm. Hurricane. Tornado. But even the greatest of storms will blow itself out. And then we must face the certainties that will have survived it — that our daughters *will* marry, our son *will* set up his own establishment. And what then? You and me, alone in this house. To lay out hard cash to a stranger to perform those services that obligation and kinship compel upon Johanna, *un*paid, would be profligate indeed.' He warmed to his theme. 'Not to say a dereliction of our duty as her guardians and mentors. Providence is surely testing *us* here as well as

66

her? Do we dare to play Pontius Pilate?'

Theresa was about to point out that they could certainly afford a housekeeper's mite ... that the pollution of their daughters was too great a risk to run ... that the idea of entrusting their old age to a wanton ... but she caught a familiar gleam in her husband's eye and realized that nothing, neither appeal nor argument, would sway him. A desperate plan began to shape itself in her mind. She raised an inquiring eyebrow, ostensibly encouraging him to continue.

'Yes,' he asserted. 'Even if we grant that your dreadful suspicions are justified to the smallest detail, is it not our duty to bring her back to a proper sense of her wickedness — to heap upon her conscience one further reason to live out her years in useful dedication to us, and thus repay us in the only coin she may find in her slender little purse?'

A happier picture effaced the one that had so appalled him earlier. Now he sat in his bath chair while Johanna leaned over him, tucking in his blankets. He thought of her artless, fragrant, eternally young body. He thought of an old man's privileges ...

He swallowed hard.

Theresa took the plunge. 'Selina was not with them when they met on the day of his arrival. Nor this morning when they held their assignation in Godolphin Warren. Oh yes — you may return your eyes to their sockets, Mr Visick. Johanna and the good doctor spent the entire morning together up there — unaccompanied. What music they made I leave you to conjecture!'

The barriers in his mind yielded. He saw Johanna naked, green spears of grass erect between her gently parted thighs ... A red mist of fury rose to blot it out.

Theresa saw the effect of her words and went on remorselessly. 'I will not commit our declining years to the care of such a wanton.'

'Wanton,' Visick echoed. The smile of her lips ... the laughter ... 'She must be taught a severe lesson. You are right, as ever, my dear.'

Rolling over and over on the velvet turf ... the sun flashing on those pale curves ...

'She must be chastised.'

67

'Chastised, yes.' He nodded in hearty but only half-comprehending agreement.

The curves of her . . .

'You must chastise her, Visick, as you were forced to do on the very day she first entered this house and accepted our charity . . . and so many times more in the months that followed.'

He stared at her, not daring to believe what he imagined he was hearing.

'Upon the bare posteriors!' She confirmed it for him.

He licked his lips. 'But do you not think she is . . . well, a little too . . .' He faltered, seeking some form of words that would enfeeble this most natural objection.

'Too old?' She took him up. 'Too big? Too strong? Well then, what of it? She must be tied down first. You shall strap her to the frame of her bed.' She watched him carefully, giving him time to overcome a slight problem with his breathing; then she hammered all three nails home. 'Strap her down. Expose her posteriors. And go at her with fresh young birch until the claret flows.'

Visick mastered himself at last. 'It would certainly restore her to a sense of shame,' he said gravely. 'But see here, my dear, perhaps we could ask the parish beadle to . . . no, no — that would be cowardice. I shall detest every minute but I think I know my own duty and I hope I may be spared to do it.'

And he went to choose the supplest and most stinging of the birches from his wife's cupboard. 'A whip for a horse,' he said. 'A rod for a fool's back. Proverbs Twenty-six.'

Alone in the drawing room, Theresa smiled. 'The father may chastise you with whips,' she murmured. 'I will chastise you with scorpions.' She caught sight of herself in the looking glass and added, 'Kings Twelve.'

But there were to be neither whips nor scorpions — nor even straps and birches — for at that very moment Selina was helping Johanna carry almost all her worldly possessions down to the turnpike at Ashton. They had almost reached it when they found their way barred by a gentleman on horseback. Twilight was so far advanced that it took the girls a second or two to recognize him. 'Oh, it's only Terence,' Selina said wearily.

'Well, well, well,' he challenged, taking in the situation. 'No lantern? Where might you be off to? And what's in the bags? The good doctor's torso? Couldn't bear the sanctimonious young sap a moment longer, eh? Can't say I blame you.'

'Such a wag!' his sister sneered. 'Listen if you so much as breathe a word of this . . .'

'Yes?' he encouraged with mock patience when she found herself unable to complete the threat.

Johanna assumed charge. Dropping her bag she went to his side. 'Hoo boy!' She patted the horse, who had taken a nervous sidestep. 'Terence isn't going to breathe a word,' she said softly. 'Are you? Terence knows the value of a secret kept.'

She put her gloved index finger on his kneecap and walked a bipedal hand up his thigh, saying, 'One step, two step – and tickle you under there!'

'Why you hoyden!' he exclaimed, not knowing whether to laugh proudly or be angry. 'You were listening!'

'I was trying to go to sleep,' she corrected.

'You never said a word about it.'

'That's what I mean about secrets being safe. That's all one need do, you see – never say a word about them.'

He gave an uncertain little laugh. 'What's afoot? Where are you going?'

'To Helston.'

'No . . . I didn't mean that.'

'I'm leaving, Terence. I'm going for good.'

It took him some moments to absorb. 'No good-byes?'

'Oh, I'll see you again.' She chuckled and repeating the farewell in its standard Cornish form, 'See 'gin boy!' she rapped the horse's flank. 'Gee up!'

Still in a daze, he resumed his homeward trot.

'Am I right?' she called after him. 'About secrets?'

'Yes,' he promised.

'What was all that?' asked a bewildered Selina as they turned again toward the main road.

'D'you really need to ask?'

'Terence? He did . . . but not . . . I mean surely not . . . with *you?*'

Johanna laughed at the very idea.

69

'One of the maids? Oh do tell me — which one?' Her voice grew all conspiratorial.

'Ah, who can say?'

'Jenny?'

Johanna gave a short, sharp, indrawn sigh — an ambiguous Cornish usage that stands for 'yes', 'my, my!' or 'do you say so? — I'm sorry to hear it', or any one of a dozen such tags, depending on circumstances.

'Meg, then?'

Another sigh-in.

'*All* of them?' Selina was aghast.

Johanna laughed.

They reached the main road. Not a vehicle was in sight. 'Let's go on toward the Lion and Lamb,' Selina suggested. 'We might meet someone coming up from Rinsey.'

They walked on in silence. Then Selina returned to the new fascination. 'Did they talk? What did he say to her? The girl must be mad. Did you overhear?'

'It was private,' Johanna objected — rather foolishly.

'Then you did overhear them! Go on, it stopped being private the moment you spied on them. What did he say to her? Pleeease?'

'Nothing. Honestly. He said all the things you'd expect. If you just made it up out of your own fancy, you'd get most of it.'

Selina was about to redouble her plea when she realized what her cousin was inviting her to do. She smiled. 'He told her how pretty she was, and all that, I suppose? Little angel? Sweet ringlets? Delicate brow? Such kind and gentle eyes . . . pierced his heart . . . made him her slave . . .'

'He hasn't quite your talent with words,' Johanna objected.

'No, that's true. Did he talk about her . . . well, her other charms? Didn't he talk about what they were doing? Lord, I wish I'd known. I'd have crept up and watched. I'll bet he kept a candle going.'

When Johanna said nothing Selina dropped her burden in surprise. 'You did, didn't you! You crept up and watched. Oh, Jo — I wish I could see your face.' Then a memory struck her and she laughed. 'And to think I accused you of knowing nothing about *kissing!* You slyboots!'

'I think I can hear a cart coming up from Rinsey,' Johanna said. 'We'd best step out.'

'What did she look like?' Selina asked, breathless at her side. 'The expression on her face? Was she ... did it look painful?'

Johanna thought it over. 'Not painful,' she confessed. 'Decidedly not that.'

'Well, what then? Did she say anything at all. Why did she let him do it?'

'I thought it was pain.' The words did not come easily to Johanna. 'It sounded like pain ...'

'But?'

'I think it was a sweetness almost too painful to bear.'

So awesome a thought held Selina in thrall for a while. 'They must love each other very much,' she said at length.

'I don't imagine there's anything of that in it.'

'But there must be.'

Reluctantly Johanna insisted. 'It appears not to be necessary.'

'How did you feel, watching it?'

'Like a traitor.'

'No! You know what I mean. How did you *feel?*'

'Like a traitor.'

Selina sighed, 'Oh, I wish I could have been there. Is it still going on between them? Perhaps I could sleep in your room now you've gone?'

The cart from Rinsey had been a false hope, but there was undoubtedly a vehicle coming up from Germoe, behind them. They stopped and waited.

'Why so interested, anyway?' Johanna asked.

'Well, isn't it the best way to learn anything? Let others take the risk and suffer the pain while you just look on? Don't say you weren't grateful for it.'

Johanna chuckled. 'Oh yes! If ever I'm tempted to folly – in a servant's garret – between coarse linsey blankets – half dead with fatigue – a smoky candle at my ear – and plagued by a man who has no true feelings for me at all ... oh, yes! Then I'll remember that scene with all due gratitude.'

Chapter Eight

It was a local carrier, Willy Rodda, who brought Johanna into Helston. 'You going Harvest Fair, are 'ee maid?' he wanted to know.

'Yes, that's right, Mr Rodda.' She had forgotten the fair, but it gave a convenient explanation.

He was onto it at once. 'How are you carrying all they bags then?'

'It's only one bag, and a little valise. I shall probably be staying for a day or two.'

He leaned to one side, letting the light of a gig lamp fall upon her entire stock of worldly goods. 'A day or two,' he echoed, as if struggling to believe it.

'And then I might go on,' Johanna admitted. 'There comes a time to spread one's wings.'

He glanced at her and grinned. 'Well, that's a marvel.'

'Hundreds do it every day.'

He drew in his breath at the truth of it. 'You'll go teaching, I dare say?'

'Yes, privately, in a family, you know.'

'Up Truro.'

She smiled into the dark; now he had his teeth into it, there'd be no letting go. 'Truro's a bit close home,' she pointed out. 'If I'm going to fly, I'll alight somewhat farther off.'

'Up Lunnon?'

She felt his interest wane as her presumed destination vanished over his personal horizon. 'Who knows?' she commented.

'I speck they Visicks give 'ee their blessing?' he asked.

'Time will tell.'

He looked at her shrewdly and nodded. ''Tin't like taking a orphan off the parish — your own kin. 'Tin't the same obligation.'

'It's an obligation none the less. Tell me — what's in the fair this year? Is it a big one? They have a fine night for a change.'

''Tis better'n last year. They got naphtha fires like daylight all up Coinagehall Street, and a waxworks with a peepshow, and a dead mermaid, and wrestling, and a German band — and there's a fellow there selling spectacles. Scores and scores of them. That's what I'm going for. He's surely got one pair there'll do my old eyes.'

After a silence he went on. 'Funny thing, you leaving Lanfear today — just this very day.'

'Is it? I don't follow?'

'You haven't heard, then — the amazements at Wheal Venton? I'd have thought Lanfear was upside-down with it.'

'Mr Visick was rather late coming home. What's been happening then?'

They must be in Breage by now. She tried to work out exactly what part of the long, straggling village they had reached but the lamplit windows were few and too widely scattered. Then came the noise of singing from the pub, the Queen's Arms; the church clock struck seven, momentarily drowning it; from these two sounds she was able to fix their whereabouts. 'You're sticking to the toll road,' she commented.

'I'm paid up to Michaelmas.'

Of course, he would be. 'Sorry — you were telling me about Wheal Venton?'

He smacked his lips. 'I speck you do know that-there Hal Penrose?'

'I know of him.' People often assumed she and Hal would be the greatest of friends, not just because they were both orphans taken in by relatives but also because their families were partners in business. In fact, she hadn't set eyes on him for eight years or more — and on that occasion they had taken an intense and equal dislike to each other. 'The Visicks and the Trahearnes don't meet socially very often,' she explained. 'I mean, not as

73

families. Nineveh House is so far away from Lanfear.'

Rodda chuckled. 'He's closer than Penzance, I tell 'ee that. But that's a thing I often remarked, now – north-coast folks and south-coast folks, they don't scarcely mix. 'Tis like two Cornwalls.'

'Anyway, what about Mr Penrose?'

'Well, I calculate he's saying farewell to Nineveh at this very hour – just like you and Lanfear. I shouldn't suppose he's too welcome there now. Would you know he to look at, at all?'

'Probably not. He was about sixteen when last we met.'

'Why, he's grown up some since that. Like a great bull he is now. Got an eye for the ladies, too. They do call he Nineveh Bull. I seen he lift up a four-hundredweight sack of corn and toss it on his shoulder like 'twas no more'n feathers. So I reckon what they say he done – well, I reckon that's the truth now. They do say he got hisself in some argument with that-there old Captain Hosking – Enion Hosking. He do live up Crowntown. His missus, now, was second cousin to your father, I believe.'

'Yes, I know who you mean. They say he's a great stickler for doing things properly underground.'

'That's the fellow. Well, he got in some argument with Nineveh Bull, over his daughter, they say. The Bull and she was walking out one time. Anyway – down Wheal Venton this afternoon – the Bull just picked he up by the collar and cast'n in the sump.'

'Never!'

Rodda laughed. 'That's worse nor any duck pond. Worse nor a pig midden. Oh, there was sparks, I can tell 'ee.'

Johanna remembered young Hal climbing to the top of a tree in just a few seconds, swinging his way up, strong and easy-limbed. He was always a very *physical* person. He'd spent most of that day chasing her – but only to pull her pigtails, which he considered the most exquisite sport. That must have been just before the time her aunt cut all her hair off. An odious boy. And it sounded as if he'd grown up to become an equally odious young man.

'I'm sure they turned him off at Wheal Venton, then,' she commented.

'He turned hisself off. How he never come to blows with

74

that-there Cap'n Hosking afore now, that's a mystery. Hosking always thought he were a spy, see? Keeping a weather eye on things for the Trahearnes. He's tried scores of times to goad he up to a fight. Specially after ... well, that business with the daughter, Jemima.'

He clearly wanted her to take him up on this hint; but she was not interested. 'Where will he find work now?' she wondered. 'Knowing the way the mineral lords all stick together.'

'There is one place,' Rodda said guardedly.

'Oh, you mean Wheal Vor. Yes, I suppose he could try there.'

Wheal Vor, one of the richest mines in the world, lay not far from Godolphin, between Greatwork and Pallas Consols. It had once belonged to the Gundry brothers, local bankers who had gone bust early in the century. Their affairs had then been handled by a Helston solicitor, Humphry Grylls. According to the mineral lords, Grylls and his cronies had stolen Wheal Vor from the Gundry estate, leaving the rest of it worthless; according to others, however, and especiallly the tin miners themselves, Grylls had saved the venture from hopeless mismanagement and had provided continuous employment for hundreds who would otherwise have starved. The legal action between the two parties had lasted most of the century, even though Grylls himself had died some ten years ago. Whatever the truth of the matter, Wheal Vor was probably the only mine at which Hal Penrose might now hope to find work.

Not that Johanna cared twopence either way.

'A rum business.' Rodda was still testing the water. 'How that old court case do go on and on.'

'And the bitterness. Thank heavens I don't have to take sides. In fact, I'm hoping to be able to stay with Miss Grylls tonight.'

He laughed. 'That's what you do call a foot in both camps.'

'Or in neither. Can we go in by way of Cross Street?'

'We should have to do that anyway, 'cos of the fair, see?'

But when they arrived at Miss Grylls's house there was a shock awaiting Johanna: Her friend was visiting a cousin in Taunton and was not expected back for at least two more weeks. The house was shrouded and the servants were on board wages.

What now? Johanna stood uncertainly at the kerbside while Willy Rodda lifted her bags back upon his cart. 'There's Mrs Hillier, old Widow Hillier, up Meneage Street, two along from we. I know for a fact she got a room. Tenpence with breakfast, six without.' When Johanna did not immediately respond he added, ''Course, if you do know some other place . . .'

She stepped back to let through a passer-by, a woman, deeply veiled in mourning. It was so dark they almost collided, for the only light in Cross Street, apart from the glow of the gig lamps, was that reflected off the sky from the naphtha fires up in Coinagehall Street.

'I just don't know,' Johanna said, not wishing to seem churlish — but also not wanting to spend even sixpence if she might avoid it.

The veiled woman heard her voice and turned to stare at her. 'Miss Rosewarne?' she asked.

The accent gave her away at once. It was Lady Nina Brookes, wife of Colonel Brookes, a friend of the Visicks. They had dined at Lanfear a couple of times.

'Lady Nina?' she replied. 'How d'you do?'

'Is that some sort of a quandary I see you standing in?'

The joviality of the question, the smile in the voice — both in strong contrast to her veil and mourning — emboldened Johanna to explain.

'Then aren't you the lucky one,' Lady Nina said cheerfully. 'Your bed's already airing.'

'Oh, but I couldn't . . .' Johanna started to say.

The other ignored her. 'Is that you, Rodda?'

'None else, your ladyship.'

'Then take her things along to my house. She and I will walk.' As the cart pulled away, she linked arms with Johanna and went on, 'So you've taken wing at last, eh? I wondered how long it would be. I'm surprised you didn't do it sooner. Still — now you've crossed this particular Rubicon, I expect you're surprised it's taken so long, too.'

To her amazement Johanna realized it was true. She hadn't thought about it at all — well, she'd hardly had time. And yet, in the first few seconds, this remarkable woman had seen it. 'Why yes!' she laughed.

'Talking of surprises, are you surprised to see me in these weeds?' Lady Nina asked.

Johanna stopped laughing abruptly. 'Yes, I'm sorry. But I hadn't heard . . .'

Now it was her companion who laughed. 'No need. He had a good innings, dear old Brookesy — many a good innings — and he died with that certain smile on his face. He's not complaining up there.'

Johanna did not know what to say to that.

The other laughed again. 'And nor am I down here, by God! Now it's my turn for a good innings. You're not shocked, I hope?'

'No.'

'Not that it would make any difference. I felt sure the news of it hadn't reached Lanfear. I've received no cards of condolence from that quarter at all.'

'Oh, well, you see, Lady Nina, the whole house has been in such a turmoil over the visit of Dr Moore, who was to . . . well . . .'

'Ah yes, I heard about that. Poor Brookesy died on me in Venice. I've only been back two days. But that all started before we left — the County Ball, wasn't it?'

'That's right.'

'And did it all go off as planned?'

Johanna sighed. 'Not really. Not at all, in fact.'

'And here you are, running away all of a sudden, eh! Well, well. It grows more *intriguing* by the minute. Where are you running to? Not Plymouth, by any chance?'

'I don't know. I'm not sure.'

'Hmm. Best stay here awhile, then. In any case, I shan't let you go until you've told me all. I'm sure you've not eaten?'

'I was thinking of going to the fair.'

Lady Nina let go her arm and stepped out. 'We'll do both, my dear. Why not! I want to see the wrestling, don't you?'

They turned in at her gateway.

Liston Court was a splendid Regency mansion, distanced from Cross Street by a grand carriage sweep; the name was spuriously derived from Hen-Liston, the old Cornish name for Helston, in an attempt to suggest that it replaced an ancient manor — when, in fact, all it had replaced was fifty

77

cottages and their attendant pigsties. Johanna was shown up to the grandest bedroom she had ever seen in her life; but the maid who helped her with her toilette was no stranger. Indeed, she and Margaret Tyzack had both attended the dame school in Joppa, near Hayle, before her parents had died.

'Well now!' Margaret said as she hooked the buttons on Johanna's dress. 'That's a proper turn of the wheel!'

'Not for long, Maggie,' Johanna assured her. 'I'm too close home. What news of the others I used to know at Joppa?'

It was a commonplace enough recital — this one married, that one in service, those two emigrated, and another one dead.

'When were you last back there?' Johanna asked. 'Did you go to Venice with Lady Nina?'

'No. Oh, no. I only now come from there, this evening. 'Course, the one talk on everyone's lips is Hal Penrose. What they say up Lanfear, then?'

'I didn't wait to hear. Willy Rodda told me all about it on the way in. What are they saying over at Joppa?'

Of course, Joppa was only a mile or so from Nineveh House. She had known the two at such wildly different stages of her life that the connection did not come readily to her.

'They're all on his side, of course,' Margaret replied.

'Captain Hosking's?'

'No! Hal's side. All the women, anyway. He should ought to of done it years ago, they say.'

'Yes, come to think of it, I once heard someone say he had the patience of a saint not to.'

Margaret laughed. 'If he has, 'tis the only saintly thing about him! 'Course, you do know he fairly well I s'pose?' There was a strange wistfulness in the question.

'Hal Penrose? I've not seen him for years. I can't say I liked him, though.'

The girl laughed. 'You'd like he well enough now, and that's a fact. All the girls round home . . .'

'Why d'you say that?'

Lady Nina entered the room at that moment; she had exchanged a day dress of black taffeta for a common sort of morning dress in black serge — a precaution, no doubt, against the ravages of the fair. 'Come on,' she urged. 'I'm ravenous.'

Margaret gave Johanna a few unnecessary pats and preens — just long enough to hold her while she said, 'Because he's the most handsomest young devil ever you seen, that's why.'

Chapter Nine

Dinner consisted of steak and kidney pudding followed by the most delicious plum duff.

'Don't let it raise your hopes,' Lady Nina warned. 'We only eat like this when I've done without luncheon. I must try and shed this excess now there's no call for it.' She put her fists to her hips and pushed hard.

Johanna's bewilderment must have shown for her hostess went on to explain amiably, 'Old Brookesy liked what he called "good handles." As to all this avoirdupois, black is flattering but I shall look a sight when I can get back into colours. Why that smile?'

'The only people who ever talk about losing fat are the ones who don't need to shed a pound. You never hear Mrs Trebilcock say a word about it. I wish I could gain a bit, I know that.'

'Oh well, enough said. We'll fatten you in no time. Beginning now.' She rang a little silver handbell that stood on the table before her. 'Cook may warm up some treacle for the pudding,' she told the footman who answered.

'Er . . . Lady Nina,' Johanna ventured.

'If you're going to stay here, you'd better call me just Nina. We're practically the same age as it is. What are you — twenty-seven?'

'Almost. In fact, I'm twenty-four.'

'Really? It must be all those years of domestic responsibility. I'm twenty-nine.' She grinned and added, '. . . and so I shall remain for several years yet. Anyway, what were you about to say?'

'Well — Nina — you talk as if it's been arranged for me to stay here . . .'

'Oh dear – d'you want an *arrangement?* An actual, formal arrangement?'

'No, that's not it at all. I mean, I can't just sponge ... don't you see?'

Nina took a mouthful of pie and chewed as if judging it for a medal; she stared at her fingertips. 'You're quite right,' she said soberly. 'That's my Irish blood, you see. What matter the morrow? The man who made time made it aplenty. The moment I recognized you just now, out there in the street, I thought here's old Providence, at it again. I'm a great believer in Providence, aren't you?'

'I go to church,' Johanna replied, wishing she could put her finger on whatever it was about this woman that made her feel so... lacking. Everything Nina said gave her the feeling she was missing half of it.

Her hostess laughed. 'I suppose I mean chance, not Providence – though chance is a great provider, mind. Tell me, how much money have you? In all the world, now, what's your portion?' She turned her pale, intense gaze upon poor Johanna – and added, 'D'you know we have almost the same colour eyes, and yet your hair could hardly be blacker nor mine more fair.'

'Four pounds, thirteen shillings and fourpence,' Johanna admitted.

'God, then you have two pounds, thirteen and four more than I had when Providence pushed Brookesy in my direction.' She smiled as if she had won a small skirmish. 'So when I saw your face in the light of the gig lamp out there – when you found Miss Grylls not home and yourself all alonio – I knew just what was going through your mind.'

Johanna smiled gratefully. 'I'm sure your kindness will be rewarded ...' she began.

'Oh, it's no charity. I haven't a charitable corpuscle about me. Or I hope not. If I find one, I'll shed it with these handles.' Again that laugh. 'No, it's what I said: Providence. Isn't this the way of it – you have certain needs; I have certain needs. Yours are acute; mine are more what you might call of an extended nature. But they answer each other. For the moment, at least.' She eyed Johanna shrewdly. 'Cards on the table?'

Johanna shrugged uncomfortably and smiled.

'What you need is a roof above you, a bit more flesh on those bones, a modest income you can call your own, good advice, and the chance to meet the right sort of a fellow. And from what you've told me, I don't think it's Dr Anthony Moore.'

'But I haven't told you anything,' Johanna protested.

'Exactly. So there you are. Now — as to my needs. Thanks to dear old Brookesy, I have a grand little house here and more than enough pelf. I'm no spendthrift — as you'll soon discover. But I'm no miser, either. I can squeeze a full guinea out of any old shilling, so I can. What's more, I earned every penny of it, take my word. So now I mean to enjoy it without so much as a qualm. But — and at last we come to you, dear — I don't want my pleasure tainted with scandal. And, you know yourself now, when a vivacious young widow lives alone, the tongues of her neighbours will furnish an entire population of gentlemen for every empty room.' She leaned back and challenged Johanna. 'Now d'you see it?'

'You want a companion.'

Why had she made such a rigmarole of it?

Nina reached forward and touched her cheek in a brief display of affection. 'I want you,' she said.

'But why?'

The hand fell. 'Oh Jo!' She sighed. 'I shall call you Jo, unless you object? No? Good. Well Jo, I could tell you that you have just the requisite degree of gravity about you. I could lyricize your spotless reputation — with a fa-la-la. And, to be sure, 'twould all be the God's truth. But a lie none the less. I would not hire you as a funeral undertaker would hire his mutes — for their solemn mien. The fact is, let me tell you now, and this really is cards on the table: The moment I first saw you, when the colonel and I came a-calling at Lanfear — or the moment I became aware of your true situation in that house — I felt a certain powerful kinship with you . . . a degree of sisterhood, even. And *that,* or so I believe, is the Providence which put you in my path this night.'

She laughed then, as if she had come safely through an ordeal. 'Enough of that. We'll gulp our puddings and go. They start the wrestling in half an hour, you know.'

And for the rest of the meal she made no further reference to her offer, nor to anything else that she had mentioned in making it.

When they rose, she took Johanna's hand and squeezed it warmly. 'You are a very *good* person, Jo. D'you know that? I suppose the Visicks can take some of the credit for it – after all, they gave you so many opportunities for practising!'

Johanna chuckled. 'Such nonsense,' she dared to say.

Nina gave her hand another squeeze and let go. 'One thing you've *not* had much chance to practise is accepting compliments. Well, we can change that, too.'

'I don't know about this so-called *good*ness,' Johanna replied. 'Almost any horse will be good if the bearing rein is pulled tight enough.'

'Well, well.' Nina stepped back and assessed her, as if she were a newcomer. 'Let us slacken this bearing rein a notch or two and see what our pretty young filly might be good for. As long as it's not on the back stretch, eh!' She turned to the footman who was helping them into their coats and said, 'We'll walk, Fisher. You may tell the groom to go off.'

She threw a common shawl over her head; no one would take her for a lady at all. Then they stepped out into the dark.

Nina took Johanna's arm. 'I hope you'll let your hair grow now,' she said.

'I think I will,' Johanna replied. 'Wasn't your father an earl?'

'He was – and, indeed, still is. You have to be a lot worse than him before they take it all back. Anyway, it's too late now. We can trace ourselves back by eight different pedigrees to Charlemagne, you know. Indeed, we often used to do it – wondering where all the money vanished to on the way!' A quick-fire laugh changed the subject slightly. 'I suppose, now I'm a widow, I should really call myself Nina, Lady Brookes. But doesn't it strike a chill in the heart!'

'Does it?'

'It does in mine. How many dowagers do you know who are the right side of sixty? Anyway, it's only a courtesy title. I suppose I may do what I like with it.'

When they reached the road, Nina turned them right, toward Church Street, which led to the top end of the town.

'Isn't the wrestling down at the green?' Johanna asked.

'Yes, but I want to see all the stalls and shows on the way. We've got time. Look — you'd think the whole town was on fire!'

As they picked their way in the dark, Johanna said, 'I don't understand all that business about titles and courtesy titles. I looked it up in Mr Visick's encyclopedia before that first time you and Colonel Brookes called, but it's all . . .'

'You didn't! What ever for?'

'To put an end to Mrs Visick's vapours. She almost died wondering whether to call you Your Grace and things like that.'

Nina let out a peal of delighted, slightly malicious laughter. 'And then didn't she go and call me Lady Brookes, which is the biggest bloomer possible.'

'I remember reading that, but I've forgotten all the reasons.'

'It's very simple. All the children of all the aristocracy are commoners. My father's Earl of Coolderry, but I'm a commoner. Our titles are only by courtesy. Mind you — try calling us mister or miss and you'll soon see where the courtesy finishes! Anyway, the eldest son of an earl is Lord . . . whatever is the family's second title. Like my eldest brother is Lord Bulloghe, because our second title is Baron Bulloghe — the family title before whoever got made the first earl. I used to know them all once. Thomas someone. God, he had the sharpest, cruellest eyes! I used to hide the candle flame every time I walked past his portrait. Where was I?'

They turned into Church Street, where there was some rudimentary lighting, supplemented by the ever-strengthening glow from the main street above.

'Shall we walk this side?' Johanna suggested. 'The stream seems to have overflowed its channel over there.'

'I said it would happen — the minute they laid a proper granite course for the water — I said the people would throw dead dogs and offal in it and this would happen. I know what I meant to ask you — what about Selina Visick and young Dr Moore? Has it truly all come to nothing?'

'I don't suppose it was ever . . .' Johanna sighed and tried to think how on earth to explain what had happened.

'. . . possible?' Nina suggested.

'Selina is . . . was . . . oh dear, if you knew her, you'd understand.'

'She seemed to nurse very little liking for you — that day we called.'

'She's changed a lot lately. It was she who helped me escape this evening.'

'Escape! Goodness, how exciting! Must we batten our windows tonight? Will they send the beadle after you like some runaway apprentice?'

'I don't know,' Johanna admitted.

'Of course they won't,' Nina asserted scornfully. 'When they hear where you are they'll claim we're all old friends and it's been arranged for months. Hah! The power of a title — even a courtesy one! Oh, we shall do great things with it, you'll see. But tell me more about Selina? Is she not inconsolable?'

'Not at all. She's extremely relieved, in fact.'

'Really? Really! But what does she want, then? I don't quite follow any of this.'

'You wouldn't believe it if I told you,' Johanna said.

Nina laughed.

Then, when Johanna volunteered nothing further, she prompted, 'Well?'

'I'm not making it up,' Johanna warned. 'She wanted — I mean she wants, she still wants — her scheme is for me to marry Doctor Moore and then to make room for her in the household.'

'But how very in-*tri*-guing!' Nina said after a short pause.

'I said you wouldn't believe it.'

'Oh, but I do. I do. Can't you understand it? I can. She wants to get out from under Mama's vigilant eye without paying the usual forfeit. No demanding husband for Selina, eh?'

'You're right, Nina — you *do* understand. Oh I wish . . .'

'What?'

'I wish I had your experience of people, your quick grasp . . . you know?'

There was a pause before the woman answered; when she

did, it was in a tone Johanna had not heard before — solemn, even slightly wistful. 'Be careful with your wishes when you're young, my dear. Life can be rather cruel.'

Johanna laughed, thinking this lugubrious tone was merely assumed. 'You mean there's some malevolent power just waiting out there to thwart them?'

'No, no, no — to *grant* them.'

There was a burst of laughter from the crowd in Coinagehall Street, which they had almost reached by now. Nina brightened at once. 'Enough of that. You must ask your cousin to call on us quite soon. I think I might like to know her, if what you say is true.'

Chapter Ten

It was the same arrangement as for the Whitsun Fair: the shows were ranked down the north side of Coinagehall Street, while 'stannins,' or stalls, were to the south. All day yesterday the caravans and wagons had come lumbering over the Eastern Turnpike and down the narrow, cobbled street to the heart of the town. The children had skipped from one to the other, waiting with impatience for them to put out their placards and billboards, which they then read off with whoops of glee. The tales they had carried home — to the farmers and fisherfolk of the Lizard, the miners of Breage and Carleen, the 'downsers' of Goonhilly, the 'triggers', or shellfish gatherers, of Gweek and the Helford — now ensured that the town was packed to bursting.

The two young women, eager to reach the wrestling booth down on the green, had to squeeze their way through the slow-milling throng. It caused many a ribald comment from the younger bloods, to each of which Lady Nina gave an equally spirited reply, much to Johanna's amazement and envy. She herself was less keen to watch the wrestling and would rather have lingered among the other attractions of the fair.

Most were old faithfuls, like Lubbock's Menagerie and Dysart's Waxworks. The menagerie always had at least one or two new animals; last year there was a Polish bison — which had started a great argument, for half the town maintained it was just a dyed Hereford bull with old loofahs stuck onto its shoulders. This year it was something even more contentious.

'Look at that!' Johanna said, plucking Nina's sleeve.

Amazing New Attraction, read the top lines of the billboard, the fresh paint contrasting strongly with the faded lines that told of lions, tigers, a giraffe, a crocodile … *The Wild Congo Pygmy — Never Before Caged Alive.*

'Oh, do let's see that?'

'Of course, dear, but after the wrestling. I don't expect he'll run away.'

The waxworks had no new tableaux this year. The Execution of Mary Queen of Scots, the Coiners' Den, the Auto-da-fé, and the Drowning Girl were favourites of old. There was, however, a new booth — a peepshow of live tableaux, which was proving a great favourite among the gentlemen. Three ladies in black stood beside the sentry box from which penny tickets were offered, ostentatiously waving their notebooks and calling out the purchasers' names; Johanna recognized them as pillars of that Methodist chapel whose tall windows stared down opposite, darkened, grim, and affronted.

'Jacob Wills,' called one.

'That's never Jacob Wills, missis,' came a shout from the line of men. 'That's his cousin Isaac.'

Great gales of laughter — for Isaac Wills was a noted local preacher.

'Let's cross to the other side,' Nina said. 'It seems less crowded there.'

On their way Mrs Wearne of Breage recognized Johanna and stopped to tell her she must on no account miss the new marionette show. 'They have a phosphorescent skeleton, my dear, that dances about the stage and it all comes to bits and the bits all dance separately and then all come together again. It's ghastly but you must see it. And the shipwreck, too. It's very good. The screams are so piteous and so real.' All the while she spoke, she glanced around, seeking someone else. She gave no sign of recognizing Lady Nina, though she certainly knew her, too; she must simply have taken her for a servant.

'Is your aunt with you?' she asked at last.

'I came out with Selina,' Johanna answered evenly. 'Dr Moore is also in Helston this evening.'

'Ah!' Understanding spread a knowing smile all over her face and, satisfied, she left them.

'Well done!' Nina said with genuine though slightly surprised admiration. 'I've clearly underestimated you, Jo, my dear — and I don't suppose I'm the only one. Perhaps that's your great strength.'

When they reached the far side of the street, Johanna stared at the faces all about her, hot, excited faces, with gleaming eyes made to seem even wilder by the flares that crowned almost every booth and stall; eyes replete with past excitements, glowing in anticipation of pleasures yet to come; eyes like buttons, like the button-eyes of hawks, searching among the crowd ... for what? For victims, answers, novelties ... joys as yet undreamed of. There was something oppressive, even menacing, in the sight of so much glee, so many varieties of anticipation.

Most of the stalls sold 'niceys and fairings' — ginger-breads, cinnamon comfits, home-made rock, West-of-England almonds in a tooth-hazarding armour of pink and blue sugar; also that great old Cornish standby for all occasions: fuggan cake — currants and raisins compressed by steam hammer (or so you'd swear) and baked in a hard, unleavened dough until, like its cousin the pasty, it would survive the drop down any local mine shaft. The pavement was thronged with youngsters, begging for these sweetmeats — and with adults, for whom they had acquired a somewhat different significance. For when the ardent rustic gives his 'shiner' a twist of niceys, it is as good as inviting her to stroll down Castle Wary lane, on the eastern edge of Helston, and tarry awhile in the bushes there; and when she pops the first of the comfits between her lips, it is as good as her spoken consent to such recreation.

'I adore mint humbugs,' Nina said. 'Don't you? Shall I buy us some?'

Johanna shook her head. 'Not on my account, thanks.' She was staring in fascination at a cheapjack just beyond the humbug stall; he was doing a brisk trade in an elixir that was guaranteed to cure glanders, mastitis, cancer, falling hair, bad breath, and melancholia; it also dealt passing blows at all the common diseases of childhood.

Nina followed her gaze and at once misunderstood, for her eyes strayed past the cheapjack and settled on a handsome, powerfully built young man standing in the half-light beyond. She turned back to Johanna and said, 'There's a cure for all ills, I'm sure.'

Her young companion's shy smile only compounded the misunderstanding.

Nina looked back but the man had vanished into the crowd; Johanna, to judge by her expression, went on seeing him in her mind's eye.

Down the hill was a group of stalls, the 'triggs,' which sold cockles, mussels, queens, and what were locally called wrinkles. There were also oysters from Calamansack Creek on the Helford nearby; they were considered a poor man's sort of shellfish, so Johanna was more than a little surprised when Nina bought half a dozen.

'Try one,' she said, offering the first to her.

'Oh, I couldn't.' Johanna recoiled from the raw, pink, jellylike flesh that quivered on the opened shell, which Nina held menacingly close.

'I don't believe you've ever eaten it,' Nina said sharply, as if she took the refusal personally.

Johanna shook her head.

'Well then, how d'you know? Go on – try. It has the most wonderful effects upon the constitution.'

It was no longer an invitation. Johanna submitted, and was surprised to find the mouthful quite innocuous. 'It tastes like a slightly salty . . . cold . . . sort of nothingness,' she said.

'There you are! You must stop saying no to things you've never tried. It's a bad habit.'

Johanna couldn't think of anything else she had refused but she let the comment pass. She and Nina divided the oysters equally after that. It seemed to please Nina enormously; she took her companion's arm and stepped out purposefully for the green.

But after half a dozen strides she stopped suddenly. 'There he is,' she said under her breath.

'Who?' Johanna asked.

'Over there. I'm sure that's him. Just look at the size of him!'

Johanna saw him then, a tall young man with the broadest shoulders she had ever seen.

'Don't play the innocent,' Nina added. 'I saw you looking

at him back there — not that I blame you. Shall we find out who he is?'

Johanna considered the matter. Despite the man's size and obvious strength there was something lithe and graceful about him. He looked a gentleman — or at least the sort of man you'd like to know. 'Yes,' she replied, never for one moment supposing that Nina would let go her arm and, after taking a couple of skips through the crowd, pluck boldly at the young man's sleeve.

When he turned she cried, 'Well, me oul' bucko,' — with a lot more Irish in her voice than usual — 'that's a powerful steam in your walk. Would you take two frail craft in tow and bring us through to the wrestling?'

Johanna was about to lose herself in shamed embarrassment when Nina turned toward her and said, 'Would you ever come on, Meg. I have him cot.'

'Well, I aren't so sure now . . .' She thickened her native accent until it would pass among any group of bal-maidens.

The brazenness of it! Nina must be mad. Her chance of being recognized, as she had already proved, was small; but even so, it would only take one shopkeeper or servant to twig it and then the fat would be in the fire.

Come to think of it, this boldness put a funny question mark over her supposed fear of scandal, too.

'Here's me friend, Meg Merrilies,' Nina told the fellow. 'And I'm Kathleen. Kathy Bulloghe. And yourself now?'

'Harry . . .' the man said, looking them up and down — with undisguised approval.

'Has it a handle?' Nina asked.

'Harry Bertram,' he said, still staring at Johanna.

His gaze so discomfited her that it took a moment to register what he had said: Harry Bertram!

That could only mean the game was up. He must have recognized that her false name, Meg Merrilies, came from Sir Walter Scott's *Guy Mannering*, for the hero of that tale was, indeed, one 'Harry Bertram.' Nina did not react, so either her neck was made of brass or she had plucked the name out of her general consciousness rather than from any particular reading of the novel. Johanna could not help smiling at the young man's swiftness — for surely Nina had 'cot' him completely by surprise. It occurred to her they might enjoy a gentle game at Nina's expense.

He caught her smile and winked back.

Watching them, and especially watching him, Nina was suddenly and sadly aware that a powerful attraction had flashed between them the moment their eyes met. She turned to Johanna just in time to catch that smile – so shy, so warm, so guileless. Then a second certainty possessed her: No matter what her plans for Johanna might have been – and might still, in the short term, be – and no matter what ties of obligation and friendship she might bind between them, she had already lost her to an emotion that had never known right from wrong, or loyalty from betrayal. Johanna might not understand it as yet – indeed, she seemed to understand remarkably little about herself in any respect whatever – but the spark was struck.

'I'd be honoured to escort two such charming ladies,' he said, offering an arm to each. 'Your face, Miss Merrilies, is familiar. If you'll pardon my saying so. Did you ever live over near Hayle?'

'Indeed I did,' she replied in her normal voice, happy to give up a deception he had penetrated so easily. 'When I was a child.' Come to think of it, there was something familiar about him, too.

'That must be it. Even at that tender age, I'm sure, such beauty was already distinctive. And you, too, Miss Bulloghe. You're not from these parts and yet I feel sure I've seen you somewhere?'

As he spoke he gave Johanna's arm a furtive squeeze, as if to say, 'This is just for form's sake now; you're the one, really.'

Had he given Nina such a squeeze, too, she wondered?

'Sure the wish is father to the thought,' Nina told him vaguely. 'What of it, anyway? The night's before us, not behind. Are you entered in the wrestling, now, Mr Bertram? Or have they paid you to stay out of the challenge!'

Each woman felt his arm go taut. 'I'd best not fight tonight,' he said tersely, as if apologizing to them.

Nina picked it up at once. 'Ah g'wan! What would it take to make you? Not the purse of five guineas, that's clear.'

'It's a game for fools. It's not Cornish wrestling, you know. That was put about in error. Or as a deliberate

mischief. It's a sort of anything-goes scuffle. The only rule is
no biting or kicking — or not where the populace may
observe it. Our huge country lads have no chance against the
scoundrels whose livelihood it is. Against every pound of
sheer muscle they throw a dozen fiendish tricks. A fool's
game, as I say.'

'But even so . . .' Nina stopped and tried to get her hands
to meet around his biceps. She failed. The power of him
made her shiver; her innards felt suddenly hollow.

He played to it, tightening the muscle until her hands
seemed puny.

'Couldn't you just wipe the grins off all those faces!' she
murmured, fluttering her eyelashes at him.

He swallowed hard. 'Not tonight,' he replied, glancing
toward Johanna as if for moral support.

'Pray you don't find one of them's called Gossin,' she
said innocently. Gossin was Harry Bertram's arch-enemy in
Scott's tale.

He laughed and relaxed again. Nina raised inquiring
eyebrows at her companion, who smiled back at her as if she
surely shared the joke, too.

They were at the edge of the crowd around the green by
now. Though it was large, the rising ground made it
unnecessary for them to crush together; in fact, there was
some advantage in standing back a little from the people in
front. The green itself was level, though, and there, with the
darkened valley and hills for a backdrop, 'Lord' George
Dansie had set up his wrestling booth.

Johanna, already regretting the private joke at Nina's
expense, leaned forward and said, 'The eldest son of an earl,
would you say?'

Nina laughed and, shedding half her accent, replied,
'He'd have to be the younger son of a duke or marquis,
actually — I never did finish all that, did I.'

Harry Bertram looked from one to another in perplexity.

The booth stood beyond an unroped 'ring' — a canvas
stage, full fifteen feet square but no more that two feet high.
The whole was backed by a canvas wall on which was the
proclamation, in Egyptian letters four feet tall, Lord George
Dansie's Challengers.

Physically obscuring this piece of provocation, though

they more than made up for it in stance and gesture, was as ugly a row of villains as Johanna had ever set eyes upon. Six in all, not counting Dansie himself, they were not men but man-sized dwarves, muscle-clad homunculi, this one lacking an eye, that one an ear, another his teeth – and all of them totally, gleamingly, horrifyingly bald.

She glanced toward Nina; surely now that she could see the raw – the very raw – material for these so-called wrestling bouts, she would turn at once and leave. The Wild Congo Pygmy was a positive education when set beside this vile-looking crew. But Nina leaned forward and inspected them avidly, as if they were the most fascinating specimens ever.

They stood upon the stage, gazing with contempt at a crowd that outnumbered them by several hundred to one. Dansie had already started his harangue. 'Not that I blame you,' he sneered, 'Cornwall's a poor country for *real* men and Helston the poorest part of it.'

A great angry roar went up at that, but people were loving every minute of it. This was what dignified the carnage to come.

'There's no *real* men left, I hear, between St Austell and America. And I can believe it. On our way here we passed one of your miserable tin mines and what was the sight to greet our eyes? Women! A great sea of women, picking the stone and doing all the work. And where are all your men? says I. Why, underground, my lord, says one of them. What hiding? says I. Have you got them all afeared of 'ee then?'

This time the anger mingled with laughter.

Dansie held up his hand. 'You may laugh but 'tis true, I tell 'ee.' He looked at one of his creatures. 'You, Michael, what did you ask me? Must we fight such women as that, my lord? Shivering like a babby, wasn't 'ee? Oh yes – fine great females with muscles on them like Hercules. Frighted 'ee proper, didn't it, Michael?'

Michael nodded with dutiful vigour, which produced more laughter.

'So I tell 'ee, women of Cornwall, if you do mark these fine boys of mine a-standing here a-shivering and a-shaking, 'tis 'cos they'm afeared of 'ee. Double afeared!' He paused dramatically and stabbed the sky with an upraised finger.

'Double afeared. First that 'tis only the women of Cornwall has got the bowels to take up the Dansie Challenge. And second – that if a woman was to go in the ring with one of my boys, there isn't a man left in Cornwall with sperrit enough to stop her!' Both hands flashed skyward, as if he would gather up the rabble, screw it into a ball, and discard it as trash. 'And *that's* Lord George Dansie's Challenge,' he roared.

After that there was no stemming the flood of takers, though more than half of them were pulled back by their womenfolk and friends. What remained, however, seemed more than a match for the 'boys.' There were young miners, sound yet in wind and limb, with muscles hardened to steel by the long daily climb up and down ladders, by endless hammering at the drill bar as it bit its way into the overhead rock, by lifting the ore, often in more-than-hundredweight slabs, into the skips and drams. There were farmers' sons, great, patient, weatherbeaten lads who could jerk a plough from the claggiest soil, on the steepest hillside, and throw it at the new furrow without so much as a break in stride. There were fishermen with kippered skins, and sinews that could haul even the most miraculous draught of fishes inboard at dead of night and in the teeth of the gale.

Thrusting aside all past experience, the crowd rubbed its hands and sucked its teeth and settled to watch the trouncing of the pros. While Lord George dealt with the challengers, inspecting their fingernails and frisking them for horseshoes, knives, and the like, his women went among the spectators, gathering up their subscriptions. When they were satisfied all had paid, his lordship raised his hands in a further flourish; a vast, expectant silence fell.

The impresario led the first pair forward – the smallest of his boys and one of the largest locals. It looked an impossible contest. The moment Lord George stepped from the 'ring,' one of the women struck the bell a single blow with a hammer.

'Go it, Charley!' went up the roar. But before the bell's reverberations had died, it was all over. Charley lay cold on the canvas.

'That's not wrestling,' Johanna cried angrily.

It had been no more than a flurry of fists, knees, elbows,

and heads. In fact, the pro had finished Charley off by leaping up and butting him under the jaw with his head, gripping him tight by the hair all the while.

'That's how they're all shaven and shorn, see,' the man in front of Nina explained to his sweetheart.

'Very disappointing,' Nina said, but not in the same spirit as Johanna. She hoped for a longer bout, fought almost to exhaustion.

'How can you?' Johanna wanted to ask, but she saw that her friend was now in some kind of elevated state, with eyes only for the ring as she clung to Harry for support.

Harry looked at Johanna and gave a don't-blame-me sort of smile, as if Nina's excitement might somehow be all his fault.

The second bout was plainly rigged. No one recognized the 'local' who walked off with his five-pound prize money after a cautious and lacklustre contest, all groans and yells but no blood at all.

And so it went on — bout after bout in which the pros fought like wildcats and left a trail of smashed lips, missing teeth, cut eyes, and one or two broken bones among the locals.

It brought Nina to the highest pitch of excitement, but the effect on Harry was quite the opposite. His mood grew blacker and blacker until, in the end, Johanna could feel him trembling with barely containable fury. 'Let's go,' she murmured to him. 'This is dreadful.'

But he was past heeding her now. The tiniest thing, she realized, would compel him there to join that slaughter.

The know-all in front supplied it. He turned and noticed Harry, seemingly for the first time. 'Why, boy,' he said, breaking into a broad grin, 'how are 'ee standing back here then? How aren't 'ee up there showing they creatures a true bit o' Cornish mettle?'

'No!' Johanna protested, but it was already too late.

Harry piled his jacket into her arms and followed it with a shirt and undervest. 'Their other trick is to pick your pockets,' he explained grimly.

The effect on Johanna was amazing. His great torso, naked to the waist and looming over her, ceased to be an entity called 'Harry,' ceased almost to be human. She felt it

had turned into some kind of sublime machine, created —
no, *dedicated* — to one sole purpose: the vindication of
Cornwall's honour there that night.

As she hugged his clothing to her, wreathed in the alien,
exciting warmth of him, as she watched him thread his way
among the crowd, she felt the tension curling in her like . . .
like nothing she had ever experienced before.

A new feeling. It was like a sense of dread, even though it
roused her. And it was like a monstrous fear; yet it quickened
her spirit. And it was like something falling, falling, falling
inside her — and yet it buoyed her up. And all these strangely
exciting, shifting, fleeting sensations were held together —
suffused by . . . warmth! An enormous sense of warmth.

She turned toward the contestants in an entirely altered
frame of mind. Was this what had also stirred Nina?

She glanced at her friend, only to find her staring back
with an oddly forlorn expression. The excitement, the
intoxication, the frenzy — all had died. There was only that
disconsolate awareness of something lost, or never quite
grasped.

However, the moment Nina became aware she was
observed, all her gaiety returned. 'Go it, Harry!' she
shouted.

Harry had reached the ringside by now. A stir went
through the crowd as they realized his purpose — and saw
his physique. A stir of a less comfortable kind went among
Lord George and his boys as they saw it too.

But the man in front of Nina turned around and said,
'What did 'ee call 'n then, maid?' He jerked his head toward
the ring.

'Harry,' Nina told him. 'That's Harry Bertram. He's a
particular friend.' Then, seeing the man's expression, she
added, 'Surely, it's Harry?'

'Harry it may be,' the man allowed. 'Though I always
heard tell as Hal were short for Hannibal. But as to Bertram
. . .'

Johanna felt her throat go dry. 'Hannibal?' she repeated.
The man nodded.

Johanna stared at the giant who had now leaped up into
the ring and was beckoning the first of the boys to meet him.
Of course, she thought. *What had shielded her from*

acknowledging it until now — until this had happened to her? 'Hannibal Penrose,' she murmured.

The man pointed at her and grinned. 'She do know,' he assured Nina.

Even the crowd affirmed it now. 'Go at 'n, Bull!' they yelled.

Then: 'Bull, Bull, Bull . . .' the chant began.

'*Do* you know him then?' Nina asked, more intrigued than affronted.

'I do now,' she admitted. 'I mean I recognize him now . . . the Bull.' The name sounded experimental on her lips. 'The Bull of Nineveh.'

And she hugged his clothing tighter, crushing out the man-smell of him until it enveloped her. And she lifted her head and cried to the heavens, 'Go it Hal. Kill them! Kill the lot!'

Chapter Eleven

Hal winced as he eased himself back into his shirt; the congratulations rained down upon him as fast and furious as the blows he had endured before winning the five guineas. People seemed to believe his triumph was like some sort of powder that would rub off on them.

'Black eye, cut lip, and a skinned knuckle or two,' he said ruefully. 'And more bruises by tomorrow than I'll wish to count, I'm sure. Oh, but I'm getting old.'

Johanna smoothed out his shirt, unnecessarily; she just wanted to touch him. She pulled and patted his great body as if she were remoulding it, to restore him and take away his pain. Not that he showed the slightest sign of hurt, she thought. But still, no man could stand up to such a storm of punishment and go unscathed. 'When you picked that last one up,' she said . . .

'By the scut of him!' Nina interrupted gleefully.

'The one he called Michael, was it?' Johanna went on. 'When you picked him up and made ninepins of the other two! Did you hear the roar that went up?'

His smile made her innards spin. 'It's all a bit dreamlike, Jo. It is Jo, isn't it? Johanna Rosewarne of Lanfear?'

The colour rose to her cheeks. She nodded.

'I knew it,' he crowed, turning to Nina as if he expected congratulations. 'Half-way through the fight, when that big fellow rushed me and knocked me flat . . .'

'Oh, dear God, but I thought you were gone then,' Nina said, allowing her eyes to relive the horror of it for him.

'Yes,' Johanna agreed. 'I screamed.'

'That's when it came to me. I suddenly realized who you

99

are.' His smile grew mischievous and his hand crept behind her. 'Are they still there?' he asked. 'Those lovely plaits?'

Johanna shook her head and clutched her bonnet to her.

'Show him,' Nina suggested with a sweet malice that almost challenged Johanna into doing it.

But Hal was saying, 'Have you forgiven me yet?'

She nodded again.

'Then that's your good nature for I've done naught to earn it.' He shrugged on his coat. 'I tell you what − let me take you to dinner. Both of you. What say you ladies?' He fixed Nina with a comic accusation. 'I still have one disguise to penetrate.'

'Have you now!' she countered.

'I believe I have.'

'There's no tax on belief.' She fluttered her eyelashes at him, half parodying (but only half) that sort of provocation. 'And I'm thinking t'would be aisy work for a grand young fella like yourself. I mean p e n e t r a t i n g' − she lingered on the word − 'disguises.'

His laugh was like an acceptance of a further challenge as he took their arms and pointed them up the hill. Again he gave Johanna's elbow a secret squeeze. And again she wondered if he was doing the same for Nina on the other side; but this time her curiosity was not nearly so dispassionate.

'We've already dined,' she objected as they set off.

Nina was scornful. 'Sure what cause is that not to dine again? We hadn't but a pick of loose meat and a peck at an oul' pudding. And anyway, all that shouting and yelling since has it steamed off me entirely. I could eat a haystack a mile off, so I could.'

'And you?' Hal asked Johanna. 'Could you really not eat again? How may I earn your forgiveness for the dreadful things I did all those years ago?'

'Well . . . perhaps I could manage a little,' she had to say. 'The trouble is my stomach's had no training for it.'

'I can believe that! Just take some fruit, or a water ice? They have a new machine at the Angel. And then we'll all join in a brandy.'

'And then?' Nina asked.

'All the fun of the fair.' He grinned at her.

'None but the brave deserves the fair,' she said, off-handedly patting one of her blonde curls.

Johanna was trying to think of other places they might eat. Hal's mention of the Angel reminded her that Tony was staying there.

'All the quality in the district will dine at the Angel,' she said, with a pointed lift of her eyebrows at Nina.

'So we shan't be plagued by *hoi polloi,*' Hal told her.

Nina reinforced the sentiment with a wink at Johanna – who then gave up the struggle. Anyway, she thought, why shouldn't they meet Tony? She had given out no promises there. No real promises. Let him join them at table if he wished.

Actually, in a crowd like this, they could pass within feet of each other and never know it. And with that comforting thought, she dismissed him altogether from her mind.

Their triumphal stroll was halted at the very first of the niceys stalls, run by Mrs Rogers, who was famous for her mint humbugs. 'Have a packet, Mr Penrose,' she called out to him. 'That was some fine old pop-and-towse down on the green.'

'Did you see it?' he asked eagerly.

The glint in his eyes reminded Johanna of the boy he had once been. But what she could no longer recall was why she had taken so violently against him then.

'Everyone seen it,' the woman replied.

'Are those mints hot?' Nina asked.

Mr Rogers, a chubby, flat-faced man with roguish eyes, who was at that moment replenishing the displays from a store of glass jars in their donkey cart, leaned across the counter and winked. 'Hotter'n hell, my lover,' he assured her. 'If you'm off down Castle Wary for a bit o' couranting, now, they mints'll raise the blood to what you might call a good peeching temperature. There now. Ask the missus if you don't believe I.' And he gave his wife's backside a squeeze that made her screech out with laughter, nearly spilling the packet she was then passing to Hal.

They're not selling sweets, at all, Johanna thought, looking at the eager, laughing faces that ringed the stall. *But hints and winks and hopes . . . and new feelings.* She glanced at Hal, who was running an appreciative eye over the complaisant Mrs Rogers.

Nina tilted the bag toward herself, selected a humbug, and offered it — not to Hal, as Johanna had expected, but to her. 'Thank you,' she said in surprise as her tongue negotiated it into the pouch of her cheek.

Hal tilted the bag toward her; she took one and offered it in the same way to Nina, who kissed it before opening her mouth. Their eyes met and they laughed, though Johanna could not have said why.

'Me? Me?' Hal imitated a little boy's petulance.

They each grabbed a humbug and stuffed it in his mouth. Everyone laughed. Then Rogers came foward and stood before him with one fist doubled up. 'Free go?' he begged.

Hal nodded reluctantly. 'Only on this side.' He touched the left half of his stomach.

Rogers struck the hardest blow he could. Johanna gave a little scream but it was drowned in a dozen others. It seemed impossible any man could take such a punch without reeling; but the only observable result was in the striker, not his victim. The poor fellow hopped around, holding his wrist and dramatizing the pain he felt there.

It fascinated Johanna, who was filled with a sudden longing to have a 'free go' at him, herself.

'Did you hit me yet?' Hal asked disingenuously. Then, amid renewed laughter, he swept the two women away on their royal progress toward the Angel. Only then, and for their hearing alone, did he gasp and murmur 'ouch!' — and genuinely, too.

'Lucky old dog,' was Rogers' parting shot.

It suddenly struck Johanna how they must seem — a prizefighter and his pair of molls.

Only yesterday she would rather have died than imagine herself part of such a scene — in fact, never mind yesterday, only an hour ago it would have appalled her. And yet, now it was actually happening, it seemed the most natural thing ever.

Talking of natural things — what about the bushes of Castle Wary? What if, sometime later this evening, Hal suggested she stroll down there with him?

She shrugged the thought aside. Sometimes you had to plan things to make them happen; sometimes you just let life carry you forward. How could she have *planned* to meet

Lady Nina this evening — and all that had followed from that, including this meeting with Hal and the feelings it had awakened in her?

'Where are you staying in Helston?' she asked him.

'But it's Harvest Fair,' he replied. 'I don't really *stay* anywhere.'

'I heard about the altercation down Wheal Venton, so I don't suppose you'll be going back to Nineveh.'

'Altercation!' he laughed at the description.

Nina asked, 'What altercation?' The words exactly coincided so that they had to link fingers and make a wish, sealing it with the name of a poet.

Surreptitiously she tickled his open palm with her little finger before she said, 'Swift!' — not out of any particular admiration for the old Dean of St Pat's but because someone had once told her it made the wish come true more swiftly.

'Sir Walter Scott,' Hal responded solemnly.

Johanna laughed. Nina asked why. Johanna explained. Nina pretended to be half-hurt, half-angry, but the general good humour of the occasion got the better of her.

'Which brings us back to the question of disguises,' Hal remarked.

'No, tell me about the altercation first.'

They had crossed the street and now stood by the entrance to Lubbock's Menagerie. Johanna took another sweet and said, 'Let's go in and see the pygmy.'

Hal reached for his purse but Lubbock himself waved them in with a smile. 'I've wanted someone to take old Dansie down a peg or two for years,' he chortled. 'You're the most welcome visitor in all that time, Mr Penrose.'

'Fame!' Nina said as they went on in.

There was the merest hint of sarcasm in it, which annoyed Johanna. 'It's probably what he was afraid of,' she said.

'The altercation?' Nina reminded him.

The lions and tigers were first; they seemed as mangy and yet as menacing as ever.

'They can't look you in the eye,' Selina had said last year.

Now, peering into *their* eyes, Johanna had the uneasy feeling they were insane. All those caged-up years, compulsively walking up and down and avoiding people's eyes − it had driven them out of their minds.

Hal was trying to explain to Nina about having to leave horses of rock to keep a mine from collapsing, and Nina was asking what it had to do with altercations. Johanna said, 'Surely it was only chance that you fell out over that? Didn't Cap'n Hosking pick a fight with you over some small thing or other almost every day? And hasn't it been going on for years?'

Hal agreed, not quite looking her in the eye.

'And then today,' Johanna told Nina, 'he came to the end of his tether.'

'No!' She turned eagerly to Hal. 'Really?'

He gave a proudly rueful nod.

'And he picked the captain up and tossed him into the sump,' Johanna concluded.

'From the top of the shaft?' Nina asked admiringly.

An attendant told them not to go too close to the camel, which had the unpleasant habit of vomiting on people.

'No.' Hal laughed. 'The shaft bottom is bad enough.'

'But Jo, dear, isn't this simply intriguing?' Nina asked, forgetting her brogue entirely. 'There must surely be something in the air today?'

'Ah, I have you now!' Hal said happily. 'And I see the need for the *noms de plume.*'

'*Noms de guerre,*' Nina corrected him.

He drew breath to reveal her name but she put a finger against his lips − and then, quite unable to stop herself, caressed them with it, lazily, back and forth.

And he, quite unable to stop himself, kissed it.

Then she pushed the fingertip between his lips; and he pushed it out with his tongue.

And Johanna was suddenly engulfed with fury. 'Where's the pygmy?' she barked at the attendant, who nodded in the only possible direction.

The camel belched and sent them scurrying. Johanna's anger died as quickly as it had flared. 'What this poor old lady's hinting at,' she told Hal, 'is that I, too, have burned my boats. This very day I have left Lanfear House for ever.'

'Sweet child,' Nina murmured, taking up the game. Then, turning to Hal, she added, in a tone which suggested that only another adult like himself would understand: 'They *will* make these brave little gestures! But I simply couldn't allow her to face the world − all alone and *so* unready.'

He pulled a rueful face. 'And to think that I almost came in by way of Cross Street, myself,' he commented.

'Oh, as to that − my house has more rooms than ... Well, anyway' − she dropped the playlet and spoke in a normal manner − 'if you need a roof above your head, Mr Penrose, you have it. And some tender beef?'

His eyebrows shot up.

'For that bruise,' she explained.

'Ah.'

She spoke without a trace of archness, not a twinkle of the eye, not a hint of suggestiveness in her tone − which was adroit of her, for it allowed Hal to say, 'You mean it?' − as if she really were offering no more than a spare room.

'Of course. It's a small enough recompense for the pleasure of meeting you − and seeing you put all Cornwall on that odious man.'

The 'pygmy' looked like a circus midget who'd had an accident with a bottle of walnut stain. His cage was about six feet square and some ten or more high. Clad only in a loincloth, he sat on a crude swing whose seat was a log and whose ropes were manilla with bits of willow bark glued to them − a half-hearted imitation of a jungle creeper. He seemed unaware of their presence; in fact, he did nothing but stare vacantly into space.

A nearby hatstand held a number of canes, provided for the express purpose of poking the creature into action − a stimulus denied to the big cats and other lower animals in the show. Nina selected the longest and thrust it through the bars, catching him rather hard − and quite unintentionally − on his left nipple. He must have been daydreaming for he sprang up quickly, forgetting how he was perched, and fell over. He retired to the back of his cage, rubbing himself and muttering angrily.

'Sorry!' Nina shouted after him, pulling an exaggeratedly naughty-girl face at the other two.

He turned his back on them. The muttering went on. It sounded primitive enough until, in the thick of it, they distinctly heard the syllables, 'fuckin' biddy.'

'It's a fraud,' Johanna said.

The other two stared at her and she realized they had never expected it to be otherwise. They went out and resumed their walk up the street.

At one point, when people were pressing their congratulations on Hal, Johanna took Nina aside and said, 'I know I must seem quite the naive to you . . .'

'I'm sorry, my dear. I shouldn't have made my surprise so . . .'

'No, no – not that. But your invitation to Mr Penrose, to pass the night at Liston Court – is that just . . . it's not . . . you don't truly mean it, do you?'

'But of course I do! It's my night for taking in orphans.'

Naturally the thought excited Johanna – and she was hardly the one to tell the daughter of an earl what was socially acceptable and what wasn't – but all the same . . .

'Why d'you ask?' Nina went on (knowing full well, of course).

'But what'll people say?'

'I hope they'll say what I would say of them. It's their house, their lives, their affair. Anyway, does it matter?'

'Of course it does.'

'Why?'

Johanna could find no ready answer to that; you might just as well ask why it would matter if there was no air to breathe or water to drink. Or was it quite a different case? The question had never occurred to her before.

The skeleton dance in the marionette theatre was impressive; the shipwreck less so – the puppetmaster's attempt at a female scream was lamentable. The dead mermaid proved to be a mummified dugong – or so a sailor in the crowd maintained.

At last they reached the Angel. Formerly the town house of the earls of Godolphin, it had passed into the estate of the Duke of Leeds and was now a thriving inn, catering for the better class of citizen. Tonight, though, it was all comers not in rags and more or less sober. As Nina entered she deftly rearranged her shawl so that it looked like the sort of thing a respectable lady might wear on such a night as this. Though the place was crowded, the landlord made room for Hal, who was by now the hero of the town. They sat at a table for twelve, all of whom knew each other, and the newcomers, at least by sight. They congratulated Hal, nodded gravely at Lady Nina, and stared with surprise at Johanna.

Several people came up to their table, mainly to add their congratulations. Those who knew Lady Nina found oblique ways to express their surprise at seeing her there – circumstances being what they were.

'Brookesy's wish,' she explained jovially – being glad of so early an opportunity to stake out the only ground on which she'd mourn her late husband. 'D'you know – looking back, I think he knew he was going. We were in the Piazza San Marco – he died on me in Venice, you know – and there was a funeral party going by. I don't mean when he died, but in the piazza. Anyway, you never heard such a caterwauling nor saw such long faces. "Don't you ever do such a scurvy thing for me, lady," he said. "Champers at the funeral, dancing till three." That was his command. I wouldn't dare disobey him.' She raised her voice and glanced briefly around the room, slightly above people's heads, as if to a floating spirit.

'The colonel liked to be obeyed,' one of their fellow diners confirmed.

She nodded. 'A very military man. Fond of drill. Could stand to attention and drill for hours,' she told Hal, who managed to keep a straight face.

Someone down the table choked on his soup and the conversation turned to other things. Hal and Nina ate heartily. Johanna's appetite perked up and she joined them in the main course. To be sure, gluttony was a sin; but then you had to balance it out over a lifetime.

Later a smaller table became vacant and they moved there to accommodate friends of the larger party. The waiter brought their brandies, which, so he informed them, had come from France that very day, by way of Gunwalloe Creek.

'I remember when I was about fourteen,' Hal told them, 'there was a great storm in Mount's Bay, and the contraband boats couldn't get inshore at all. So they sailed round Land's End to St Ives Bay, and all the smugglers had to arrange special parties to carry the stuff through the night to the usual hiding places. And I was picked to go with

Skewjack Carter. He liked to claim he was descended from the great Harry Carter, King of Prussia Cove, but he wasn't. Anyway, he was a good enough smuggler in his own right.'

'You must have been a strong young lad even then,' Nina commented.

'I'll swear to that!' Johanna smiled accusingly at Hal and rubbed the back of her scalp, as if the flesh were still tender there.

He reached forward and gave her arm what he supposed was a gentle squeeze. 'Anyway, I thought things must be pretty desperate because Skewjack himself was carrying *two* barrels of brandy when we set off. He was a big strong fellow – could have taken on any of Dansie's boys down there tonight. However – the greatest surprise was to see where our path was leading. D'you know the excise officer's house in Lelant, on the corner by the forge?'

'Yes,' Johanna told him.

Nina said, 'I *think* I do.'

Johanna added, 'He's a man called Kelm? Or Chelm? They had a pew behind the Trelawneys ...'

'Yes. Chelm. You're right. I'd forgotten that. He's gone now ...'

'Anyway!' Nina interrupted brusquely.

'Well, our path went directly through Chelm's garden – in by the side gate, out by the back. And when we passed through that back gate, I saw Skewjack had only one barrel to carry. So – here's to the gallant excisemen!'

They laughed and raised their glasses to the toast. Johanna had never touched brandy, or any other spirits, in her life. It burned her mouth and made her eyes water; but she saw how calmly Nina knocked it back and so did her best to seem unconcerned, too. Then the afterglow warmed her and she began to understand the pleasure people saw in it. She took another sip and found it much less fiery.

'The second barrel,' Hal was saying, 'also vanished – in the garden of the district's most senior magistrate. Whereupon we all breathed easy.'

Nina proposed the obvious second toast: 'To magistrates!'

But Hal leaned forward and held down her arm. 'Not to that one.'

'Of course!' Johanna cried. 'It was Trahearne himself — you left the barrel in your own garden!'

Hal turned to her with a smile that kindled a memory. 'I'll drink to the spot where we left it, though,' he said, and then began feeding her clues: 'By the duckpond that old Trahearne affects to call a lake . . . on a little tongue of land that looks like a path but isn't . . . a dead end . . . with the willows arching down . . .'

Johanna remembered it, too: '. . . and where a gawky little giglet in pigtails might think it safe to run from a great tormenting dawbrained lump of a . . .'

Hal put a finger to her lips. Her voice tailed off. 'No gawky little giglet,' he murmured. 'Hush now, and see through my eyes. I shall remember that day until I die. When I found her there, trapped between the water and the thorns, when she turned and faced me, I suddenly realized she was the most beautiful . . . most desirable . . . just . . .' He shrugged. 'I wanted to comb out — or I wanted to see you comb out those plaits. Oh, I was just knocked for six.'

'Much you showed it!' she replied. But her voice was soft and close to breaking.

'I was suddenly afraid of you, afraid of those feelings. I'd never known anything like it. I was in such turmoil. That's why I pulled them and ran away. Oh, Jo, if you only knew how much . . .'

'Hasn't it grown hot in here,' Nina said. She eased off her shawl and rearranged it.

Hal did not take his eyes off Johanna. 'You have it all still?' he asked. 'That beautiful long hair?'

'Let's down this brandy and go,' Nina suggested. 'I have a better one at home.'

As if mesmerized, Johanna raised her fingers to her bonnet strings.

'No, dear,' Nina warned her softly. 'Come on, let's go.'

The knot parted. The strings hung down, crimped and free. The fingers went on to ease back the material.

Moments later the Italian pageboy — as she would always think of it — sat revealed before him. Defiantly, Johanna downed the rest of her brandy and asked, 'Is there a drop more?'

Then at last she turned her eyes back toward Hal. 'I can hardly believe it,' he murmured.

'It was Aunt Theresa's idea,' she explained. 'She supposed that . . .'

But Hal was not even listening. Heedless of Nina's presence he went on, 'I have never seen a woman more lovely, and with less aid.'

Johanna let out the breath she had not even known she was holding. There was a lump in her throat and tears blurred her vision of him. And there they sat, entranced with one another, oblivious of the world.

Nina, feeling *de trop,* looked awkwardly around at the other diners, none of whom was paying them the slightest attention. But her gaze was held by a young, or youngish, man who had just sauntered in at the door.

His eyes scanned the room, seeking a vacant chair. The moment he saw her looking up at him, he froze. His jaw dropped and his eyes widened with shock.

Nina realized he was not looking at her but at Johanna and Hal. Then, with that instinct which has shaped more than half of human history, she knew this could be none other than Dr Anthony Moore — or rather, the ruin of what had once been him. Now she needed no confession from Johanna as to what had been going on at Lanfear House; in that shattered face she saw it all.

But, skilled as she was at summing up a man in under five seconds, she eyed him coolly — knowing that as far as he was concerned, she might as well have been sitting in some other world. Her immediate conclusion was that Johanna was a little fool.

Hal was an exciting man — no doubt of it — probably the most exciting she had ever met. But he had none of the qualities that make a good husband — and at this point in her life, Johanna should be seeking nothing else. Hal was one of life's adventurers. Challenge was what stirred his blood. And anything in long skirts was a challenge. She'd watched him on their way up the street. He couldn't even look at a woman without wondering if she would.

Dr Moore, on the other hand, had fidelity engraved upon

his brow. If he had lately murmured, 'For ever, my dearest Johanna,' then he meant it quite literally. Every particle of him bore the hallmark of 'husband.'

And him so handsome, too — easily a match for the Bull! Was the girl blind?

The ironies of the situation were not lost on her. *Here's me,* she thought, *who could just about do with Hal — for a month or so, anyway; and there's Jo, who should have eyes for none but Anthony Moore until the children were safely in the nursery. And here's all four of us, not six paces apart!*

'Does that man know you?' she asked.

Johanna did not even seem to hear her; but Hal raised a half-interested eyebrow.

'Does he?' she pressed.

'Mmmm?' Johanna turned to her at last.

Nina, seeing the happiness that shone out of those eyes, now regretted her interruption. She was going to point out some innocent stranger across the room when she noticed that Moore had, in any case, vanished from the doorway. 'Obviously not.' She smiled. 'For a moment it looked as if he were about to come over and say hello.'

'Terence Visick?' Johanna suggested. *'Mon cher cousin.'*

'Yes, it could have been. He was only there a second or two.'

Johanna turned back to Hal. 'A little more brandy?'

He began apologizing for his thoughtlessness as a host but Nina repeated that she had better brandy at home. 'I'll chaperone you two youngsters while you dance an hour or two away,' she added. 'Then we'll go where the watch can't harm us.'

Chapter Twelve

The hullabaloo from the fair died down in the small hours.
A short while later the silence awoke Nina. For one confused
moment she thought time had slipped and dear old Brookesy
was there beside her once more. Then she reached across
into the emptiness and gave a little sigh — *triste* rather than
sad. Which of her many kind friends had told her that a
marriage of convenience was a marriage of disasters? She
missed the darling boy more than she would have thought
possible.

She was now so wide awake that sleep, if it returned at all,
would not come soon or easily. She plumped up the warm
goosedown all about her and did what she always did at such
times — thought of the most pleasant things imaginable.
The trick was not to get trapped in a single groove of ideas
but to let her mind flit from one charmed inconsequentiality
to another, like a butterfly passing from flower to flower.

Like Hal passing from woman to woman. Or did he?
True, there was that unmistakable light in his eye. He looked
you up and down and you knew he saw the flesh beneath the
finery. Yet there was a certain reserve there as well; part of
him you could never touch.

There were men like that. She had met quite a few; they'd
be as jovial and warm as you could wish but there was still
that bit they held in reserve. A secret. Even from themselves,
perhaps.

Any other night and he'd have been here in her bed, in the
cold space that had once been warmed by Brooksey. Oh,
he'd caught her invitation — the old come-you. She tried to
imagine him there beside her. The sinewy firmness of his

body. The power of him. A small ripple of pleasure petered out within her, smothered by the same constraint as, no doubt, kept him in his own virtuous bed. Was he awake, too? Thinking of her, wondering, will I chance it or will she cry no on me?

Sure, it wouldn't bother that one a scrap if I did. There's plenty more where I come from.

She moulded the image of him in goosedown and writhed upon him, the way she would if all other things were equal; but again the pleasure died before it could get her in thrall. All other things were not equal; a new star reigned in both their horoscopes now.

What was it about Johanna? The strange power she had, like a hatchling cuckoo, to set aside the even temper of another's life and make her own need paramount? No. It wasn't so blatant as that. She demanded nothing, nor did she beg. There wasn't the hint of a plea even in the most fleeting of her glances. And yet, from the moment Nina had seen her there, marooned in the street, the urge to help had been irresistible.

Had the Visicks felt it once, too? Was this how it always began? The cuckoo hatchling – indeed, a fledgling now – imposing her own imperatives on those unhappy souls who blundered into her life?

'Unhappy' did not seem to describe Nina's present state. Perhaps that was the real measure of Johanna's power. At any other time she'd be lying there, fretting for the creak of a floorboard, desperate for the turn of a door handle, shivering like a filly at stand. But not tonight.

She must see about a perfume for Johanna. Every woman should have her own distinctive . . . and dresses, too. Oh, a good wardrobe would be the crowning of her!

Could anything be done about that hair?

Drat the girl! Think about something else.

Hal. You tried that. What about the other men – since Brooksey? The fella at the consulate, now he knew a thing or two about grief and what it can do to a woman when nothing else could console you. Never a smile out of him, just those great, grand, dark eyes that told you they had wandered on the farthest shores of desolation and returned with messages of mercy for . . . just for you, madame.

113

God, I'd even left Venice before I realized — t'was *me* granting *him* the favour.

And that ship's officer, too. Well, he was different, fair's fair. Ships that pass in the night. He had the right of it, though. That's the way it should always be. No guilt, no remorse . . . no pointing fingers.

Lord, have I done the right thing at all, coming back here to Cornwall? What about Johanna saying you can't have Hal here tonight? There's a terrible cramp of the soul that's abroad in the world when a demure and kindly innocent like her starts laying down the law on that sort of thing. We'll all be looking over our shoulders before we dare smile at a man soon enough.

Never spread her thighs in her life and she's already saying what's right and what's wrong. I wonder, though — maybe she has. And I wonder too — is Hal right for her? I never did give him that beef. I seem to keep coming back to that. No, I mean the genuine sort, for his eye.

Still, was Brooksey right for me? A million would have said not. Oh, Brookesy, me darlin', darlin' man, I would you were here now, lepping onto me like the fireship you were, setting me all alight . . . oh, I've a space that mourns its emptiness of you and your burning.

I wish you'd left me a child.

That Dr Moore, poor man. The look on his face when he saw them!

But never mind that. He's the more likely match. A woman must think of these things, especially one in Johanna's situation. Love's all very well, but . . . maybe I should try to see him before he goes beyond to Plymouth or wherever it is. Plymouth, yes. Not quite far enough away from Hal, but still better than nothing.

There's that cream silk with the little flowers, violets. Johanna would look just grand in that.

Perhaps she's the child I lack . . .

At about the time Nina's meanderings had returned her to the brink of slumber, Hal stirred, turned over, and resettled his head so that the worst of his bruises — quite by chance — was pressed against the knob of his wrist. Moments later he, too, was wide awake.

She never did give me that beef, he thought ruefully. Even that much of a smile made him wince.

Had she waited for him? That's what she meant, no doubt of it — beef. Even now he wondered that he had not gone-a-night-crawling, after so open an invitation. He pictured her easily; those all-promising eyes, the same colour as . . . no — those eyes, brimming with pledges of delight . . . her golden ringlets . . . the elegant neck . . . her strong but delicate shoulders and the swelling curve of her breasts . . .

His hands turned to cups. But even so early in that pleasurable game his mind's eye went blank, his excitement palled; another image, dark, as yet, and all the stronger for it, was biding its time, waiting to claim him.

He held it angrily at bay. Who was the master here? When had he ever bent the knee to any woman — in sincerity, that is? Give them power like that and they'd nail you to the rock.

> *Bind him down upon a rock*
> *And catch his shrieks in cups of gold!*

A *ring* of gold, it should be. Quotations are no better than reach-me-down suits. But seriously, what about it — marriage to Nina.

'The engagement is announced between Nina Lady Brookes, relict of the late Colonel Brookes, et cetera, and Mr Hannibal Penrose, bachelor of this parish . . .'

Man of the world, actually.

It wasn't so impossible. He had the education of a gentleman, and a way of opening doors that remained closed to others. True, he hadn't their income nor their expectations, but she could take care of that. No, it wasn't at all impossible.

Well, dear Nina, the days are fast vanishing when a rich young widow can hold out on her own. These are new times. Almost every day Society has a whole batch of fresh refinements for you. There must be some vast, steam-powered factory, somewhere up there in the Midlands, working all tides, stamping them out by the gross and wholesaling them to the Great British middle classes. Listen now, you know it yourself — a rich young widow had better marry her footman than flaunt the public temptation of her unclaimed person. And if her footman — why not me? I'm not a jealous man, Nina. There wouldn't be any of that nonsense if you . . .

The thought ground to a halt.

Not a jealous man? By heavens, if anyone so much as laid a finger on Johanna, I'd tear him limb from limb.

There it was at last, the thought he could not forever keep at bay — Johanna.

He surrendered to it. The first bleary light of dawn suffused his uncurtained windows. There was no further point in trying to sleep, and no profit in thinking of Nina or . . . all that . . .

It must be love.

No — he'd overworked that word these years gone by.

It must be the kind of love he'd always prided himself on avoiding. Poet's Love, with a capital L. At the first twinge of it he'd always bolted, straight into the arms of the next likely lass. Cat's in the cupboard and can't catch me! Not that there hadn't been one or two close shaves. Joan Ninian, for instance. She could have named him as the father . . .

He murdered the rest of that memory. Nowadays he cringed with shame when he recalled what he had done to Joan Ninian's reputation — or the shreds of it, after the child was born. Still, that was where Love could lead you.

The church clock struck six.

Had he avoided it, though?

He remembered chasing Johanna round the garden at Nineveh and catching her by the lake. He could almost smell the water now — that heavy, torpid scent of decay and summer languor. He saw the willows, dipping down their graceful feathers in curves that seemed to enfold the young girl, his quarry, snaring her for him on that tongue of land. In his mind's eye now he advanced toward her, as he had done on that day, his hand outstretched and the cry of 'Tig, tig, you're it!' on his lips — and again he was seized with a sudden, astonishing, overpowering craving to take her in his arms and cover her with kisses. That face, which only moments ago had been the familiar 'phiz' of a courtesy cousin — whose nose he had often tugged in play, whose cheeks he had tickled with shivery-shaker grass when she would rather read — that face suddenly became the most adorable, beautiful . . . haunting . . .

Later he may have called it Love; at the time his only emotion was panic. Even now it made him sweat again. What choice had he but to spring at her, roaring like a lion, and tug that pigtail till she screamed – and then run laughing away and . . . forget, forget, forget.

How well the strategy had worked – and what a fortress he had built! Between that day and this, he had piled a whole stockade of her sisters . . . three dozen? Ten dozen? More than he could count, anyway. And yet, tonight, one glance from her had been enough to bring him back to the very point at which the long flight from his servitude to her had begun.

The clock struck six – again? It must be a different one.

His uncertainty about the hour was suddenly intolerable. Everything was intolerable. Why should he let her get her hooks into him like this? It was all an illusion, anyway. There was no *real* difference between one woman and another – or nothing that could single out this one as queen of the firmament and set the rest of the world (or the most fascinating half of it) at naught. Who did she imagine she was – telling him what he could do and couldn't do, making him stay away from such a delectable creature as Lady Nina *and* feel the nobler for it? That's how they worked their strange power. They filled you with the bliss of self-congratulation – to be doing things they'd never even asked you to do. But God help the man who failed in such unasked favours! A woman with her hooks well and truly in you could charge the very air with her vague imperatives – and she'd hang you if you blundered.

'Well, I'll show you,' he said defiantly.

He rose, put on one of the colonel's old dressing gowns, and crept out into the corridor, smiling the smile of a man who believes he has carried one small skirmish and may yet win the entire war.

Johanna heard him go by but assumed it was one of the servants. Not that she was a light sleeper, but the morning had already passed her usual hour to rise.

There was something not quite right in that thought – 'her usual hour'.

Come to think of it, *usual* had no meaning now. It referred to life at Lanfear House, which would never be usual for her again. The notion was hard to grasp. She had to tell herself she had written the last grocery order for Mr Kitchen's boy to deliver, counted the Visick-crested silver for the last time, and would never again send that family's linen on its path from new to second-best to servant's attic to charitable cast-off. All the imperatives that had governed her life from the day she had entered that house until yesterday . . . they had all gone.

It suddenly struck her: She did not know what a day *ought* to be like — a real day, an ordinary day, a day in which nothing was preordained. The only sort of day she knew was a Lanfear day.

Surely there had been others — before? But they were childhood days, of little assistance to a young woman suddenly caught up in an exciting world of new freedoms, new friendships . . . Hal Penrose.

And Tony Moore? Her spirit sank at the thought of what she had promised there. Or half promised.

She tried to think of Hal instead — Hal and this astonishing reversal of her feelings about him — but her mind kept slipping back to the discovery that the word *usual* had gone out of her life. It was, she now felt, only the prelude to a much more significant discovery. There was something about her new situation . . . something she had to face before she could allow herself the pleasure of dreaming about Hal.

Or perhaps something in her past?

Or a bit of both?

Her past, then. She cut her mind adrift and let it float back, to settle where it would.

And suddenly there she was on that awful day, the most odious day in her life. She was standing at her father's grave-side in St. Charles's churchyard, too dumb with misery to weep. Her aunt Theresa's hand closed around her arm. For half a second it felt like a gesture of that comfort she so desperately craved; then the grip tightened, thrusting her into the pit of an odious, unfolding truth.

There was a long, angry carriage ride home, *their* home, Lanfear House. While she passed in and out of an exhausted sleep, her benefactors grizzled over what was now to be done with her. The cost of it. The domestic upheaval. The small thanks they'd get. Each word was a dart of new pain to her, though she hadn't understood the full enormity of it until the journey was over, some time in the small hours. Then she stood before her Aunt Theresa, there in the hall, in the dim light of a single candle, waiting for one crumb of real charity.

Had some unwished-for impulse to pity seized the woman then? Of course, that was a later insight. At the time she was just a child, standing there, bewildered and grieving, while Selina, newly awakened and fractious, said she wanted that pretty dress. And then that hateful woman told her, 'Yes, indeed, that dress is much too fine, young madam, the way things are with you now. Take it off this minute!'

The beautiful dress her father had given her — almost the last thing he did before the fever struck him. What else could she do but scream her defiance? And then the hateful woman's hateful husband came and tore it off her, and birched her naked back and bottom until she bled and there was no more voice for her outrage.

And next day she had to mend the torn material and give the dress to Selina, 'I wish you to accept this, cousin dear, as a small recompense to my dear aunt and uncle, whose charity to me will never be properly rewarded.'

She lost count of the number of times he birched her after that. He sought out every tiny trespass and wrote its chastisement, first in his little locked book, then upon her skin. In her innocence she had believed him when he said it hurt him more than it did her — especially when she just lay there, exhausted and shivering with ungovernable violence, while he tried to soothe her, by gentle caresses and kissings of the flesh he had so grossly wounded.

Then Aunt Theresa had caught him at it; the look in that woman's eye had been a whole volume of education. Johanna's hair was cut off but the birching had stopped forthwith.

What would they do now she had gone? In a curious way, she was far more necessary to them than any of their own. Selina and her sisters were encumbrances to be married off as swiftly and advantageously as possible; but she was intended for something more permanent in their lives. Now they, too, would have no *usual* day.

Should she get up and start arranging the household here at Liston Court?

Somehow she didn't think that was what Nina wanted her for.

What then? If not as housekeeper ... what? What did a companion do? Why didn't men have companions?

Perhaps life at Lanfear had deceived her into believing that everyone was only wanted for something, never for themselves. Perhaps Nina only wanted her for herself.

But what was her *self*?

And that, she suddenly realized, was the really important thought — the one that had been hovering in the wings of her awareness ever since she discovered that her usual day no longer existed: The same was true of her usual self!

The Johanna who had endured those dreadful years was a kind of masquerade woman, a strategy for survival rather than a true person. So, just as she now had to discover what a 'real' day was like, she also had to seek out the 'real' Johanna to enjoy it.

It was rather thrilling, at the age of twenty-four and with all of life before you, to discover that your previous self was nothing but an honourable fraud and that, just as your day could now be anything you wanted, so, too, could you. The insight so delighted her that she felt she had to share it at once with Nina — who of all people would surely understand. She rose, put on one of the colonel's dressing gowns, and went in search of her dear friend's room.

Hal opened Nina's door gently, without knocking. The dawn was now sufficiently advanced for him to see her rise on one elbow and clutch the bedclothes around her, 'Mr Penrose!' she exclaimed in the quietest tone that would do.

He waited.

'Well, just standing there is worst of all,' she told him crossly.

He smiled and stepped over her threshold, one pace, no more — sufficient to close the door behind him.

'And?' she asked. Now that an inch or two of stout oak

stood between her and the world she relaxed into a more conversational tone.

'And then there were two,' he said, crossing swiftly through the gloom to her side.

But as he stretched out his hand to raise her sheet, she renewed her clutch upon it and said, 'Oh, no!'

'D'you suppose I'll be the better for being cold?' He chuckled and tugged again at the material.

Her grip tightened but she said nothing.

'You'd like to talk first?' he guessed.

'I'd like to talk.' Even those few words betrayed the shiver in her voice.

'Put the big bolster down the middle of the bed and let me in on the far side. I'll promise not to cross it without your consent. Otherwise I'll die of a chill.'

'You will not — neither die of a chill nor come in by the back door like that. As to consent, you had it eight hours ago. It's shrivelled in the night.'

'Well then . . .' He settled himself complacently on the chair at her bedside. 'Talk on!'

She took up her candle snuffer and poked him sharply with its handle. 'Go you and sit over there. Take the chair into the middle of that carpet.'

He was intrigued enough to comply. Few feminine ploys surprised him any more, but this was something new. 'Dawn is on time I see,' he commented as he reseated himself a half-dozen paces from her.

'Talk to me about Johanna Rosewarne,' she said.

For a brief moment, which seemed an age to both of them, he said nothing. Then he asked, 'What of her?'

'I'm not blind,' she replied. 'That girl has lost her heart to you. I don't know when. Yesterday evening, I think. But perhaps not. When did you last meet her?'

'You heard me — years ago. In any case . . .' He thought better of the rest of the sentence and let it drop.

But she knew what had been on his mind. 'It *is* my affair now,' she told him quietly. 'In some odd way I seem to have elected myself her patroness and protector.'

He saw at once that the trend of her conversation would very soon collide with his own obvious intentions in coming to her room — a meeting of two irreconcilables that would crush his dignity between them. 'Well, she's nothing to me,' he said brusquely. 'I like her, to be sure — which only makes me the sadder if what you say is true.'

'You saw it yourself, man, so don't ask whether I'm telling the truth or no. However, I'm forced to question you again, for I confess that your answer surprises me. Are *you* telling the truth? Are your feelings really as warmly indifferent as you claim.' She smiled thinly. 'You should also understand that, no matter what you may reply, you will not gain the entrée you came here seeking.'

Her tone throughout this announcement put him a second or two ahead of her in its conclusion. He chewed angrily at his lip for a moment and then snapped, 'She is nothing to me. The circumstances of our lives are very similar, which I suppose must give us some more than usual sympathy. Her looks and character would commend her to any man — which must add . . .'

Nina laughed. 'Very well. Spare the cant, Mr Penrose, for those whom it might impress. You have already trespassed too far with me to be anything other than candid.' She paused, giving him the easy exit of anger — which he had wit enough to spurn. 'Good,' she went on in the same calmly reasonable tone. 'Then, since your heart is not engaged, you may throw the full weight of your impartiality into our discussion.'

He stared at her. 'I am not aware of seeking any such discussion, Lady Nina.'

She laughed a little too loudly for her own comfort and had to stifle herself with the flat of her hand. 'I know full well what you're *seeking*, Mr Penrose — just as you know full well that on any other night but this you would not be left shivering on my carpet. But tonight — what little is left of it — tonight there is the vastly more important business of Miss Rosewarne's future to consider.'

'But since I've told you she means nothing to me, how can that interfere with our . . .?'

'Do you know the sort of life she's led?' Nina interrupted.

'I can imagine it.'

'Well I don't have to imagine — I saw it. She has coped with life at Lanfear House by effacing any part of her nature that might . . . Well, in a word she has coped by becoming a species of genteel servant. In a way, I feel I may have done something dreadful to her by removing the necessity to go on being that sort of person. I'm sure she's not aware of it yet, so it may not be too late to mend.'

'Go on,' he urged.

'You see' – Nina picked each word with care – 'she speaks of the chance to go on to Plymouth. This doctor . . . Moore, I believe. You know the story, perhaps?'

'No.' His tone was neutral but she heard how his breathing hardened.

'I don't know how much the Visicks and the Trahearnes talk among themselves.'

'I've heard nothing.' He rubbed his fingers, as if they had grown suddenly cold.

'Oh well, this Dr Moore – who, by all accounts, is a most handsome young man, and gifted, too . . . most highly recommended – anyway, he met Selina at some ball and fell for her. So they say. But when he came to stay at Lanfear House, supposedly to pay his court, he met Miss Rosewarne and . . . well, I suppose you can imagine the rest.'

He pulled his hands apart and sat on them. 'And?' he had to say before she would continue.

'Oh, he's doing the sensible thing now. He'd find it hard to court Miss Rosewarne from Plymouth, so is hoping to arrange for her to take up the position of governess with friends of his. And if, after some suitable interval, she does not utterly reject his suit, why then he will offer her his hand, his name, and his fortune. He is said to be rich.'

'Lucky young woman,' Hal said curtly. His face was black as thunder.

'Very rich,' Nina added. 'Perhaps – as I seem to be the nearest thing she has to a guardian – perhaps I should visit these friends of the good doctor and assure myself of their respectability. And then send her on with my blessing? What do you think, Mr Penrose?'

A dozen answers passed through Hal's mind, not one of them utterable. 'She may do as she pleases,' he said.

Nina was on the point of pressing him again when there came a gentle tapping at her door and an even gentler call of 'Nina?' – spoken little above a whisper.

Hal rose in alarm but Nina, showing her considerable

123

presence of mind, motioned him urgently to resume his seat. Then, in her calmest, sweetest voice, she called out, 'Enter, my dear! Come and join the conference.'

Johanna opened the door, saw Hal, and froze.

'Couldn't you sleep either?' Nina went on easily. 'Come and get into bed here before you catch your death.'

Staring askance at Hal, Johanna skipped across the room and buried herself between the sheets, still clutching the colonel's dressing gown to her. Nina moved over to give her the warm half of the bed. Surreptitiously Johanna slid a leg into the other half and found that it was, indeed, cold. Nina, who had supposed her young friend to be too innocent to leap to such swift conclusions, now revised her opinion. 'Oh? Would you prefer the *cold* half?' she asked pointedly.

'Nina!' Johanna replied with conspiratorial exasperation.

'What?'

'Him!' she whispered.

'Darling,' Nina said tendentiously. She made her next words sound like three separate commands: 'Do. Grow. Up.'

Hal laughed at her coolness. Johanna misunderstood and felt mortified.

'Listen, my precious,' Nina went on, 'there are things one does not put into the hands of children because they would misuse them or break them or hurt themselves. Or worse. But that is no reason for mature, grown-up people like us to chafe under the same constraints. So you just make up your mind, eh? Either you lie there, oohing and ahing and blushing like a schoolgirl, or you may join us in' – she sighed – 'in what I fear is a rather disheartening discussion about the future.'

'Whose future?' Johanna turned toward Hal. 'Yours?'

Nina, seeing that Hal was about to say, 'No yours,' answered quickly: 'Everyone's.'

As if she thought it a game, Johanna lay on her back, closed her eyes, and said, in the most inconsequential tone possible, 'If we went to Paris . . . or Vienna or somewhere . . . Hal could be our brother. We could say we were all brother and sisters. No. Perhaps he'd better be our cousin.'

'I'm sure he's glad to be offered the choice,' Nina interjected.

But before Hal could add his pennyworth, Johanna was bubbling on: 'In a way that's what I came to tell you. I was lying in my room just now, thinking should I get up, should I set the servants to their daily tasks ... go through the laundry — you know. And then it struck me — all that sort of thing belongs to a life that is past. But now' — she sighed, not in the least unhappily — 'I have no idea what to do. I don't truly know who I am, even.'

In the silence that followed, Nina stared at Hal and mouthed the words: 'Too late!'

Chapter Thirteen

Lady Nina found Tony Moore up in the stable yard of the Angel, about to depart for Plymouth. The poor man looked as if he had not slept a wink. Though he had glanced at her briefly last night, he gave no sign of recognition now.

'You do not know me, sir,' she said, handing him her card. 'Pray forgive my importunity. I am a friend of Miss Rosewarne's.'

The transformation that came over him at the mention of Johanna's name was astonishing. The weariness vanished, his eyes lit up. He was a prisoner awaiting reprieve. Then, as the reality of his situation overcame him once more, his eyes fell and all he could say was, 'Oh.' He stared at her with lacklustre interest and asked: 'But how do you know me, Lady Nina?'

'Miss Rosewarne was at my table in the dining hall last night, Dr Moore. I saw you standing at the door.'

He frowned. 'And she told you my name?'

She smiled wanly. 'Your face did that, sir. Look, the town is half asleep. I think we might find the dining hall private enough for a dish of tea and, if I may make even bolder, some conversation?'

She weighed him up as she spoke. A handsome man — and a *good* man, too. Not a trace of divilment in him. And so obviously devoted. Johanna was a fool.

'You have some . . . news?' He hardly dared to say it.

'Not exactly news,' she said mysteriously. 'And not exactly advice. And not exactly cheer. But a pot pourri of all three, perhaps.'

'Then, as this is my erstwhile home, let me presume upon

126

your suggestion and invite you to take tea with me.' He offered her his arm and led her back up the cobbled alleyway to the hotel's side entrance.

His smile was most attractive. If only he were more careless, more cavalier – more like Hal, in fact – he would be devastating. Johanna would be with him now, casting reputation and prudence to the winds and ready to follow him to the ends of the earth. What was it in the female whim, she wondered, that could be so reckless of her own best interests; wherein lurked this incubus of passion that would pass by a good and worthy man, be he never so handsome, and fasten itself instead upon an exciting but negligent, unheeding heart-breaker like Hal? Why in the shaping of a woman's spirit had the Creator set this fuse for the unrighteous to light?

The dining hall was staled with the expired pleasures of Harvest Fair. The physical remains had been swept away but the atmosphere was pervasive. It must have jogged his memory for, the moment he saw her seated – though not at the same table as last night – he said, 'Indeed, I recall you now. But I took you to be Miss Grylls. Is Miss Rosewarne not lodged with her?'

Nina explained. 'The curious thing is, Dr Moore, if one were to tot it up on paper, I have been in Miss Rosewarne's company for less than a day – even if I include the night just passed. I cannot explain it – but then perhaps you are the last person in the world who needs to have it explained – there is something rare in her that engages an almost immediate intimacy of the spirit . . . which cuts through the normal stages of a developing friendship. The moment I saw her standing, so lost and uncertain, outside Miss Grylls's darkened house, I was filled with the most powerful conviction that I had been brought to that place at that hour for no other purpose than to offer her all the assistance at my command.'

He nodded fervently but was too gripped by her words to interrupt.

'Indeed, it is more than a conviction,' she went on. 'It has become a kind of demiurge – a compulsion to help her.' She relaxed her intensity and made a small, self-deprecating gesture. 'This must sound quite absurd to you.'

127

He leaped in at once. 'Oh no, Lady Nina, I do assure you. Every word you say strikes a response.' He tapped his breastbone.

The waiter brought their tea.

When he had gone, Tony could not recover his former intensity. 'I understand you very well,' he said.

She raised the teapot and asked, 'With or without cream?'

He took it with.

'It is almost like love.' Her tone was now entirely conversational. 'I suppose it *is* love. With all my heart I want what is best for Miss Rosewarne. I expect the same goes for you.'

She did not make it a question but he answered, 'From the moment I met her.'

'There you are, then – she does have that quality.' Nina still spoke in everyday tones, as if they were discussing Johanna's skill at needlework or something equally neutral. 'And yet, one cannot help reflecting that her life so far, locked away, one might say, in domestic minutiae, hardly aware of the world beyond the parishes of Breage and Germoe . . . it has provided little training to help her grapple with Life at large.'

He nodded again.

'And great though she is in wit and intelligence, there has been little enough society to nourish them all these years. She has so little basis for her judgment – especially her judgment of people.'

'People like Hal Penrose,' he said.

So he had taken the trouble to discover Hal's name. Not that it would have cost much effort last night. But still . . .

'May I ask your opinion of him?' he went on.

She hesitated; the signs of an internal struggle were plain upon her face. She had intended leading him through precisely this conversation, but now that she found herself in the thick of it she discovered she needed his support. She sighed. 'Yet I, too, have had little enough experience of *this* situation. How far do love's – or friendship's – sanctions run, Dr Moore? Where does well-meaning but unsought assistance shade off into insufferable meddling?'

For a moment his eagerness to be offered a straw, any straw, almost spurred him into giving her the bland assurance she wanted – to say that the bounds were wide and as yet far distant. But his native honesty intervened and he admitted, sadly, 'Saint Peter will probably tell us that on the Day of Judgement. Until then all we can do is follow our most generous instincts.'

He rose still further in her estimation; now more than ever she was certain she was doing the right thing by Johanna. She smiled. 'I see we are of very similar minds, Dr Moore. Forgive what must have seemed a rather self-absorbed preamble, but without it you would have found my next assertion astonishing: I believe that any attachment between Miss Rosewarne and Mr Penrose would be only disastrous. And for both of them. I must add that I like him, too, and cannot ignore his best interests, either.'

'This, ah . . . attachment?' He picked up her word but left the inquiry to hang upon the lift of his eyebrows.

'Puppy love?' she offered. 'Infatuation? They are undoubtedly smitten with each other — I would not offer you the consolation of a lie, Dr Moore. But, when I saw you last night, gazing at the pair of them . . . when I realized who you were . . .'

'But how did you know? Did she . . .'

'When I took her home, after meeting her outside Miss Grylls's dark and shuttered home, she explained the circumstances of her leaving Lanfear House for ever. Naturally, I asked what her plans might be — and she told me of some arrangement you had made for her . . . in Plymouth? From the way she spoke I did not suppose you were driven to it by mere altruism.'

'Plymouth.' He pulled a glum face. 'Little hope of that now!'

She risked giving his arm a light, comforting squeeze. 'In the immediate term I'm afraid you're right. But you are not the man I believe you to be if that is where you draw your double line.'

He was reluctant to agree. 'Affections of this kind are so frail, Lady Nina. And if they are actually discovered to be dying, then hopes for a rally and . . .'

'Do you speak for yourself?' The question was sharp.

'No, of course not. But Miss Rosewarne was scrupulously fair with me. She transformed none of my hopes into expectations.'

'Never mind that.' Nina relaxed again. 'You may leave that with me. For the moment all I need is to be assured *you* will not wilt.'

He drew breath to speak but again she touched his arm. 'And you have assured me. So now I may go to work.'

His grin was so openly conspiratorial she realized he was, in part or in some degree, corruptible. It intrigued her; if he were not destined for Johanna, she would have started to work on it then and there, testing its limits. 'What will you do?' he asked.

'Get as many miles as possible between herself and him. And then ... who can say? A tour of the continent might widen her vision.'

He frowned.

'Oh, poor man!' she cooed. 'Every moment will be a torment. I know that feeling so well.'

'Ignorance is the worst,' he said. 'What is she doing now? Who is she with? Who shares her laughter? Who else is falling under the enchantment of those astonishing eyes? It's not knowing ...'

'I'll write. I promise. Whether we stay here, or travel — whatever we may do — I shall let you know, copiously and frequently. There'll be no need for you to reply. I'll know well enough how each budget of news will be received.'

He grasped her hand and gave it an effusive squeeze. 'I shall hang on every word.' He cleared his throat and, in an altogether different tone, said, 'There are splendid openings for Cornish miners in America these days.'

Nina laughed. 'I came within an ace of telling him that, myself.'

'What held you back?'

'I feel certain that within a week or two the proprietorial classes of Cornwall will have made him ten times more receptive to the idea than he would be now, in the first rosy flush of his rebellion.'

'If he should need assistance with the passage,' Tony said carefully, 'it might come easily from you? And I should happily reimburse the outlay.'

'Why, Dr Moore — there is a buccaneer in you after all!'

His eyes fell as if she had upbraided him but she reached across and gripped his arm, speaking before he could apologize. 'Encourage him – that rover. He is your greatest ally here.'

'I beg your pardon?'

'Pay no attention to what women may *say* – least of all to those righteous dowagers who sit in full, secure possession of their prize. They have either forgotten the way it was with them or they temper their memories with discretion. But if you want the awful truth of the whole business, it is this: No female heart was ever won by goodness alone. No female heart was ever quite so shallow.'

He chuckled. 'Go on.'

'There's nothing to add. I know very well what men think of us – vain, giddy, empty-headed . . .'

'I have never thought such things.'

'There you are! But you would have every right. The way we pretend to admire you for your lofty minds, your nobility of soul, your elevated feelings – could anything be giddier than that?'

'And is it not true?'

'Admire? Yes – admire. That is true. Yet oh, if you but knew how we secretly thrill to the merest suggestion of a flaw in among all that music of the spheres! I felt it myself not a moment since – when you suggested colluding with me to export our little difficulty . . . I most decidedly felt it.'

She held his gaze until he could not doubt her meaning; then he sought to impersonalize it with, 'Like Nelson and his one eye, eh?'

'Like Nelson and his one Emma. His one and only Emma. D'you know what captivated her? His willingness to risk all – his good name, his rank, his prospects . . . everything, even his immortal soul – he was willing to risk it all just to be with her.'

He nodded morosely. 'I always felt rather sorry for Sir William.'

'Exactly. And wasn't he a very *good* man,' she replied with a laugh.

On their way back to the stables it was she who took his arm saying, 'Tell me about Selina Visick.'

'You've met her?' he countered.

'Yes. And I've also heard Miss Rosewarne talking about her. The two impressions were hard to reconcile.'

They walked several paces in silence before he halted, suggesting that what he had to say could not be managed in the few yards that remained.

'I mustn't keep you,' Nina prompted.

'No, no. If Miss Rosewarne is to stay under your wing, it's important for me to answer. I've had plenty of time in which to ponder the whole business. I think Selina is a truly remarkable young woman. I fell for her in a conventional sort of way at the County Ball ... what was your word? Infatuation. That's all it was. But, if I had not chanced to meet Miss Rosewarne on the day of my arrival at Lanfear, I believe I might have developed the profoundest attachment to Selina by now.' He laughed. 'And it would have seemed every bit as hopeless.'

'Why? Is her heart given elsewhere?'

'It is given entirely to Selina Visick. But she makes no secret of it − and I think the object of her donation is not in the least unworthy.'

'Goodness me!'

'We had the most astonishing conversation, which I could not even attempt to summarize. We walked almost the full length of Praa Sands − you know the place, I suppose?'

'Brooksey and I were there several times − usually after we'd visited Lanfear, funnily enough.'

'We set out ... Miss Rosewarne was our very tactful chaperone, holding back some way behind us. Anyway, we set out all formal and frosty but by the time we arrived at Pengersick I felt I'd never come closer to another human being. Not in any romantic sense, you understand, but ... well, I can't put it any other way. Our minds were ...' In his frustration at not finding the words he locked his fingers together and struggled in vain to pull them apart. 'Like that.'

Nina just stared at him.

But he had the bit between his teeth now. 'I believe that life at Lanfear House has been much more baleful for Selina than ever it was for Miss Rosewarne. My irruption upon the family, and the ostensible reason for it, woke her up. In two weeks she achieved as much thinking as most people manage in two years − and she gave me the fruit of it that afternoon. Believe me, she has a most unusual and gifted mind. If you do make this continental journey, take her with you, too. You will be well rewarded, I promise.' He smiled and frowned at the same time. 'I'm sorry. I've lost sight of the fox. What was I supposed to be telling you?'

'About Selina Visick. You haven't strayed at all. In fact, you've told me all I wished to know.'

All and more, she thought glumly.

He gave her his card. 'Do write to me,' he begged.

'Of course.' She passed him back the card together with her little ivory pencil. 'Just scribble PPC on it, there's a good fellow. Helston tongues can make such mountains out of molehills.'

As she walked away she realized that all her certainties were now in ruins. Could it be, she wondered, that what Tony Moore felt for Johanna was far closer to infatuation that he now supposed? Even worse — were these nameless, complex emotions that encircled his image of Selina anything to do with love?

PART TWO

THE TRIBE OF THE BEWITCHERS

Chapter Fourteen

That afternoon, the day being an even Thursday, Lady Nina was At Home to Helston's high society. As bereavement radiates some especial magnetism of its own, four of the ladies who called were also in full mourning; three others had passed the six-month post and graduated into purple. Most of them had heard of Hal's deeds and Johanna's defection; the convolvulus of servants' gossip, which has no more respect for persons or property than the wild woodbine itself, had carried the juice of it along every tendril in town. The persons of property flocked in discreetly inquisitive troupes to drink it all at source.

Johanna had expected to take her usual place at such occasions — somewhat apart, the governess seat, as it were; but Nina, who occupied the wing-back chair beside the fire, placed her in the middle of the sofa opposite. 'Listen and learn,' she advised. 'Among other things, study their costume. We shall be calling in the dressmaker tomorrow.'

Johanna flashed her smile of timid gratitude.

Nina brushed her cheek. 'Look at you,' she said. 'Nervous as a long-tailed cat in a room full of rocking chairs.'

Hal had intended going to seek work at Wheal Vor but somehow the day had slipped by and he was now deputed to assist any other gentlemen callers with passing round the tea and sandwiches and cake. 'I wasn't reared to this life,' he warned.

'Think of it as a different kind of mining,' Nina told him. 'The country is hard. There's only a few ounces of good metal to the ton. And it would take more than your horses of

137

living rock to keep some of the parties apart.'

Mrs Knox was one of the first to arrive, together with her two daughters – Wilhelmina, who had come out several years ago and still lacked a husband, and Grace, who came out last year and whose chances were still put quite high. She had also brought her nephew, Roger Cunningham, from Leeds in Yorkshire – cheerful, energetic, thirtyish, and self-made: Wilhelmina clearly adored him; he barely noticed her, except for an occasional glance her way to receive the tribute of her admiration and allow its few drops to top up his own personal ocean of self-esteem. He was, among many other things, a director of the Leeds and Bradford Railway Company. Or so he said.

Mrs Knox had been born Miss Knox – she had, in fact, married a remote kinsman. Her father, Charles Knox, had founded his own school for 'the sons of gentlemen' in Redruth (the modern term is 'young gentlemen', but the people of that earlier age had been too honest to call them that); the School of Hard Knox, had been its inevitable nickname, and Mrs Knox, who prided herself on her acumen and general *savoir faire,* had never tired of ascribing it to that origin.

After the usual preamble – murmured condolences, observations on the weather, and so on – Mrs Knox nodded toward Hal and said, 'Well, Penrose, we hear you put the county's honour back on the mantelshelf last night. The whole town's a-buzz with it this morning.'

'A mere nine-day wonder, Mrs Knox,' Hal assured her.

'You didn't mistake one of them for poor little Enion Hosking?'

Hal laughed. 'You've heard of that, too?'

'Yes,' she replied meaningfully. 'And that'll be something more than a nine-day wonder – more like a nine-year dead crow hung about your neck, I'm thinking.'

Hal's smile wore thin. 'There's more to engineering than mining,' he told her.

'Engineering, eh?' Cunningham put in. 'Have you thought on railways at all, Mr Penrose? That's the thing of the future, you may be assured.' He winked at the company in general. 'Take it from one who knows, my friends. The bills now before parliament will double our track mileage in the next five years. Think on't.'

'We've a dire need for harbours and roads down here, too, Mr Cunningham,' Hal replied, 'As I'm sure you've noticed.'

'What a fetching costume, Miss Knox,' Nina said.

Such compliments had grown so rare in Wilhelmina's life that she assumed her hostess was addressing her sister. She took advantage of the lull to say what had come into her mind a minute or so earlier. 'You must have been very brave,' she told Hal.

There was an awkward silence. No one wanted to reopen that subject.

'That widow, Mrs Stillwell, made it,' Mrs Knox replied on her daughter's behalf.

'Oh, *this* costume!' Wilhelmina was now all confused.

'We took her an illustration from *The Companion* and she made it all up from that. Very deft, Mrs Stillwell.' She turned to Hal. 'The same as was once housekeeper at Nineveh.'

'I remember her,' he agreed – remembering also the stairs to her room ... the exciting perfume of her. She had been the first. Taught him everything.

'No better than she ought to be, they say,' Nina commented.

'I had not heard she was ill,' Mrs Knox cut in heavily, with a significant glance toward her girls.

The arrival of the formidable Mrs Ramona Troy of Pallas House saved the moment. Her husband, Robert Troy, had died almost ten years ago; it never occurred to anyone to suppose that she might marry again. Johanna had only ever seen her at a distance – which was enough for her, as for most people. Troys and Visicks did not mix. During the last century the two families had fallen out over some question of their mineral demesnes, or setts; and though it had been resolved ages ago, they were still not on social terms. Nina wondered where Johanna's rebellion would place her in Mrs Troy's gallery of the Admissible and the Inadmissible. With her had come her grandson, Hamill Oliver, and her daughter-in-law, Beth Troy, both of whom were about Johanna's age.

'And how is little Morwenna?' Nina asked. 'Not still teething?'

Such were the waves of influence that radiated outward from the Pallas estate, which lay only two or three miles northwest of Helston, that even the baby's teething had left its dint in local consciousness.

Beth Troy laughed, 'Good gracious, no – that was ages ago. But do let me tell you her latest thing. What she does, you see, is . . .'

'She is quite well, I thank you,' Mrs Ramona Troy cut in.

'Yes,' Beth agreed, lowering her eyes and smoothing her dress. 'Very well indeed, thank you.'

'Talking of teeth,' her mother-in-law went on, 'is there to be a memorial of any kind to the dear colonel?'

Everyone wondered what on earth it had to do with teeth – except Nina, who had long since tumbled to the old dowager's trick of imposing a respectful-seeming silence with a non-sequitur like that. 'I have considered it,' she said at once.

'And your conclusion?'

'I have reached none.'

'I see,' Mrs Romana Troy said rather lamely.

Nina was careful not to smile at so minuscule a triumph.

'You could put up a menhir,' Hamill Oliver suggested as he leaned over Johanna to take her plate.

'Put up a men here?' Nina echoed.

'A little more cake?' he asked.

'No, thank you,' was Johanna's ritual reply.

'*Yes,* thank you,' Nina corrected.

Hal was furious at the attention Hamill was paying to Johanna. He stepped forward to take her plate from him. Then he checked. *For heaven's sake!* he told himself. *Look what she's doing to you!* To explain his movement he forced himself to smile at the man – who looked back at him in some alarm, believing it to be the prelude to a request for a place at one of the Pallas mines.

'What was that word you said?' Nina asked.

'A menhir,' Hamill waggled his finger at the butler to indicate that the man should cut a larger slice than that for Johanna.

'Something Olde Cornishey, I've no doubt,' his grandmother commented wearily.

'A rude monolith,' Cunningham interjected, as if quoting a dictionary.

'A single, upright stone,' Hamill explained.

'What a good idea!' Nina turned to Mrs Knox as if she would have the final say. 'You used to know dear Brooksey in his younger days, my dear — what d'you think he'd have made of it?'

The woman shrugged, uncomfortable at being made the arbiter when Mrs Ramona Troy was present. 'I can't say, I'm sure. He wasn't particularly *Cornish,* yet there's something very *fitty* about the notion. I couldn't say what, but . . .'

'Yes, there is. I know what you mean.'

'We had hoped for a window in the church,' Mrs Ramona Troy barked.

'Of course.' Nina's tone implied that a new window for the church went without saying. 'His old regiment is seeing to that. The Duke of Cornwall's. I thought you meant a more personal memorial from me.' She turned to Hamill. 'Where does one buy these menhirs? We could erect one on the front lawn. He'd have loved that.'

'There's no-one making them any more,' Hamill replied with dry solemnity.

'I should think not!' Wilhelmina laughed — alone — until Johanna dutifully supported her. Everyone else knew when Hamill was joking.

'Any farmer'll sell you one,' Beth Troy suggested. 'Scratching stones, they call them, don't they?'

'Get one new from the quarries at Newlyn,' Cunningham proposed. 'I happen to know the overseer there. Owes me a favour. Just give me the nod.'

'Thank you so much, but I think a genuine, well-used stone would be more appropriate to dear old Brookesy,' Nina decided. 'All worn and knobbly and scratched. Johanna, my dear, you're not eating.' She turned to Mrs Ramona Troy. 'We're determined to put some flesh on those bones before winter.'

'Yes, miss!' The dowager rounded on poor Johanna, who squirmed in the spotlight. 'Tell us about this business.'

'There's little enough to tell, Mrs Troy,' she warned.

Every eye turned to the older woman, who allowed the

gathering silence to press the question for her.

Mrs Wellbeck and Mrs Ivey, two recent widows, arrived at that moment, each with a daugher in tow. But Johanna's hope that the interruption might save her was immediately dashed. 'Miss Rosewarne was about to tell us of the goings on at Lanfear House,' Mrs Ramona Troy announced when the mutual condolences were over.

'Oh yes,' Mrs Wellbeck enthused. 'I saw Dr Moore driving out of the Angel yard this morning. Black as thunder at breakfast, or so little Abigail Matthews who serves from the kitchen said. And grinning like an imp come noon. They say someone carried him a message of great cheer.' She smiled archly at Nina and then at Johanna.

Johanna, who had known nothing of Nina's purpose in going out that morning, frowned in bewilderment.

'Talking of cheer,' Mrs Ivey added, 'I saw Mrs Visick and her daughter in Helston just now − on my way here, in fact. The gel, I must say, was bearing up amazingly. Top marks to her!'

Nina took advantage of this interjection to consider her explanation; obviously, to deny there had been a meeting would invest it with a glamour it did not deserve. 'It's kind of you to call it a message of cheer,' she said. 'All I did was invite Dr Moore to join us here for luncheon.' She smiled at Johanna as if she were breaking some unimportant news.

'And he refused you?' Mrs Wellbeck asked, turning at once to see how Johanna took the possibility.

'Refused is too harsh,' Nina replied. 'He hoped to reach St Austell before sundown.'

'Well!' Mrs Ivey exclaimed.

They all admired Johanna's calm dignity − and regretted that courtesy forbade their dwelling on the topic any further, for the moment, at least.

Several new arrivals were announced, including, at last, some extant husbands. The gathering broke up into several smaller groups. The husbands were eager to quiz the encyclopaedic Mr Cunningham about the advisability of putting their capital into railway shares. His advice, to buy, buy, buy, soared above half a dozen lesser conversations. He had it on the direct authority of his great friend and colleague, Mr Hudson, the Railway King himself: railway shares had the touch of Midas.

Hamill Oliver squeezed himself in beside Johanna for a moment, only to say that he didn't want to interrupt his hostess but he knew of two good menhirs that could be hers for the asking; they had been grubbed up during the recent expansion of Wheal Pallas, on the northeastern edge of the Pallas demesne. 'Drive out and look at them tomorrow,' he said. 'I'll meet you. Stay for tea.'

Johanna nodded – and then remembered that the dressmaker was coming. But what did it matter? It would hardly take her all day to measure up for a few simple gowns.

Mrs Wellbeck's daughter told her whatever dress she might choose, it should be trimmed with a deep chrome yellow. Deep chrome yellow was *the* colour for next season. Johanna was much obliged to her.

Mr Cunningham told Hal that if he were seriously interested in an engineering appointment on the railways, 'Cunningham's your man!' Hal was much obliged to him.

The At Home was almost over when the footman announced, 'Mrs John Visick, Miss Visick.'

There was a silence you could touch.

They had heard, of course. The woodbine tendrils could insinuate themselves into Breage and Germoe within hours – any time the occasion demanded.

'Lady Nina!' Theresa cooed. 'What must you think of us! The newspapers have gone unread these weeks and more at home . . .' And so on and so forth.

Selina shook hands with Lady Nina and then turned at once to Johanna, kissing her warmly. 'How did this come about?' she whispered.

'Tell you when there's a chance,' Johanna whispered back.

Selina returned to her hostess and began an urgent, private conversation; but she had barely spoken more than a sentence or two before Nina smiled and patted her reassuringly on the arm. Meanwhile her mother was beaming at Johanna and positively trilling: 'And my dear niece! How are you, my sweet? Is it turning out as well as we all hoped?' She included Nina in the question, too; and then she gave a tinkling little laugh. 'Silly question. It's much too soon to tell. Well, as I said before, you stay here as long as you like − or as long as dear Lady Nina may wish to have you.'

Behind her back Nina winked a didn't-I-tell-you at Johanna, who had to struggle to keep a straight face.

'There was a slight confusion yesterday.' Nina spoke as if she were loyally backing this colossal white lie − greatly to Theresa's relief. 'It was, after all, some months ago that the suggestion first arose. Before the County Ball, I believe.'

'Yes, yes − ideed it was ... but no, there was no confusion ...' Theresa herself was confused by now − but still gushing with gratitude.

'Of course, it must have been before the County Ball,' Nina went on, as if the memory were slowly returning to her, 'because I went on to suggest that Selina, too, might also like to stay with me for a while. D'you remember that?'

And to give Theresa time to absorb this astonishing embroidery of her own lie she turned to the company and said, 'Goodness, don't I sound positively feudal! The way all the wealthy merchants used to send their youngsters to live in the houses of the nobility.'

'What d'you charge, Lady Nina?' someone joked.

When the laughter died she said, 'To take you seriously sir − though I know that was not your intention − there is, indeed, a reward in it for me: the companionship of young and lively minds.'

On which heartwarming note she turned to Theresa Visick and added, 'So, my dear, when are you going to let me have young Selina, eh?'

Chapter Fifteen

Mrs Knox left her lorgnette behind. Johanna discovered only minutes after their carriage had left. She remembered that the younger girl, Grace, had mentioned something about calling at the milliner for chrome yellow ribbons on their way home, so Hal set off in reasonable hope of catching up with them.

Selina had meanwhile deliberately mislaid her gloves — taking care to accompany her mother out to the carriage before discovering her loss. They were the last of the callers to leave.

'I have less than a minute,' she said as she dashed back indoors. 'So tell me — what is all this? It sounds marvellous.'

Johanna explained as briefly as she could; Selina kept turning to Lady Nina for confirmation.

'You come with the highest recommendation, my dear,' Nina told her.

Selina turned toward Johanna in surprise, supposing it was she who had spoken up for her; but Nina said, 'No — from Dr Moore.'

Again she turned to Johanna, this time with a suspicion they were playing a joke on her. Johanna shrugged. 'I myself have only just learned that Lady Nina met Dr Moore.'

'And he spoke most warmly of you,' Nina assured her. 'So much so that I confess I'm surprised things turned out the way they have between you.'

She studied the young woman's reaction closely, for if Selina had had second thoughts about her rejection of the doctor's suit, it would make for such an easy solution to the whole problem. But she seemed completely at a loss; all she could think of was to ask Johanna whether she still intended going to Plymouth.

Johanna turned to their hostess. 'Did he say anything about that?'

Nina shook her head. 'You may take it that he does not expect you to keep that promise.'

'It wasn't really a promise,' she replied uncomfortably.

Nina shrugged. 'Whatever.'

Johanna turned with relief to her cousin. 'We may all be going on a journey, like the Grand Tour,' she said excitedly. 'You, too.'

'Hoo-back!' Nina warned. 'One step at a time, young miss!'

'My mother will never consent to that,' Selina warned sadly.

'We'll lepp that ditch when we reach it.' Nina turned to the doorway, where Theresa was just entering, awkward and diffident – uncertain of a renewed welcome. 'Did you find them, dear?' she asked apologetically.

'Mrs Visick!' Lady Nina stretched her arms and her smile in welcome. 'She hadn't lost them at all. Sure it was just a ruse to bring you back where we may talk without that gaggle of emmets about us. Come and sit by me now and tell me I'm forgiven, for I declare to God you're the last mortal on earth I'd wish to offend.'

For Selina to become part of Lady Nina's household would in any case confer such cachet upon her – especially after so public a rejection of Dr Moore – that Theresa, had she even dared to contemplate the notion, would have moved heaven and earth to bring it about. To be asked to forgive what she so earnestly desired threw her into such confusion that when Nina airily added that they might pay a brief visit to the Eternal City, she almost tripped over her own tongue to agree – especially when her ladyship added that it was 'so important for a yong gel's horizons to be widened before the confines of the domestic round closed about her. And it is so easy, down here in this remote corner of the kingdom, to forget that a wider world exists at all.'

It was arranged, then, that Selina would come to Liston

Court in the early part of the following week.

At that same moment, at the corner of Cross Street, Hal almost ran into Roger Cunningham, who was hurrying back down Church Street. His aunt had discovered her loss the moment the shopkeeper came out to her carriage.

'Eay, that's grand,' he told Hal. 'We can each save the other a half of the errand.' He heaved a deep sigh, making no effort to retrace his steps. 'I declare, I do not know how that household has managed without yours humbly all these years. They fall apart. Women, eh, God bless 'em. They just fall apart.'

'I'll walk on with you if I may,' Hal replied. 'I need the fresh air.'

Cunningham laughed. 'Ah! I think I know what you mean, sir. A very... *colourful* lady, our hostess. Do you, er, lodge there, may I ask?'

'No. It was only because of last night. The nine-day wonder, you know. May I ask you something, sir?'

'Aye, fire away. There's not many questions can stump me.'

'What you said about the need for engineers in the railways – well, could you tell me more? I mean, would there be work down here in Cornwall, for instance?'

Cunningham stopped dead and looked about them as if he expected to find spies in every doorway. 'Why d'you ask that?' he snapped. 'What have you heard?'

'Nothing, I assure you. I ask for myself.'

The other relaxed and broke into a slow smile. 'Sorry. One can't be too careful. Time was when a railroad-survey party could traverse a district and attract nothing but complaints – or the sort of tolerance usually extended to the feebleminded. But now! Just leave one cleft stick with a bit of white paper in the remotest croft and the lanes are choked for miles around with gentlemen waving bills of exchange, desperate to invest money they don't own before the scrip rises to a thousand percent.'

Hal smiled. 'Then I understand your caution.'

'You've no idea, Penrose. That's why, in all my talk of railways down here, I've never mentioned anything nearer than Bristol. People think my work's nothing but a summer's stroll. I know they do. I can see it in their eyes.

But I tell you – there's not one man in a million could accomplish the things I have to tackle day in, day out. But if you're serious...you are serious, I take it?'

'Never more so. I need to work up a little capital. I need to get away from...well, from Cornwall.'

'Survey work is the thing. Now...'

'I've studied surveying,' Hal put in eagerly.

'Now, I was taught by Colonel Dent, who learned the profession direct from Charles Budgen, himself. The majesty of Creation, eh? You can't get much closer to it than on a survey. And you've studied it, you say?'

'Yes. At the institute in Camborne and I've put it into practice down Wheal Venton.'

'Ah...mines.' Cunningham sniffed uncertainly. 'Give me an example.'

Hal described how, when the Six Fathom East and the Six Fathom West were about to unite – having drifted toward each other from two separate shafts half a mile apart – he had convinced a couple of sceptical tributers of the value of the surveyor's art. 'I marked a cross on one face and surveyed back to the shaft, up to grass, over the moor, down the other shaft, and back to the opposing face, where I made the like cross. I told them to drill there and they'd meet.'

'And they did?'

'I was three inches out – not that they noticed.'

Cunningham's eyebrows rose. 'By harry, you're the man for us, Penrose. I myself could have surveyed your mine to within a whisker, of course. But my time's too valuable, you see. I've had to be content, at this stage, to get our falls right to one in two thousand. You're ten times sharper than that.'

Hal did a quick mental calculation and realized the comparison was correct. Had the man just made a lucky guess or did all that swagger conceal quite a sharp brain, after all?

Again Cunningham checked every doorway for spies. 'D'you know a little village called Chacewater – at the head of the Devoran valley? The name derives from the French, you know, meaning the hunting place by the water.'

Hal nodded. 'It's beyond Redruth from here.' He also

knew it marked the present terminus of the railroad but he did not say as much.

'Aye, yon's the one. Well, meet me for luncheon at the Pendarves Arms in Redruth while noon tomorrow. I'm well liked there. Just mention my name if I'm late. I'll show you what the work would involve.'

They shook hands on it. Hal had taken only a few paces back toward Cross Street when Cunningham called after him: 'Not a word to a living soul about any of this, eh? I mean not *anyone*.'

Hal laughed. 'I think I know who you mean.' As he returned to Liston Court he felt as if a weight had been lifted from him.If he could get away from Johanna, he'd forget her within a week. This slavery was intolerable.

And so he set out the following day, telling Nina and Johanna that he was making his postponed visit to Wheal Vor. But by then they couldn't have cared if he were off to Tipperary, for the dressmaker had arrived.

Johanna had never experienced the like of it. In her world a dress was not something cut from a bolt of cloth; it was a garment schemed and patched and revived out of another. In all her days she had only ever seen three 'new' dresses that really deserved the name; all had been made for her aunt, to be sure; even Selina's had been derived from bits of others. But here she was to have four new gowns, and all of them chosen from lengths of cloth Nina kept in her cupboards — actually there in the house! Johanna counted thirty-four different patterns before she gave up.

'Don't feel you have to choose one just because it's there,' Nina told her. 'We can easily pop up to Nicholls's and look out something nicer.'

When she saw how gingerly Johanna handled the materials she began hauling them out with an assertive competence that simply knew a servant was going to tidy it all away afterward.

'Look, here's a lovely white lawn. That'd make a nice tucker. See? With three frills pleated at the neck. Tapering.' She looked at Miss Cousins, the dressmaker, who said, 'Lovely, my lady.'

'And here's a printed cotton. Wouldn't that be nice for next summer? Aren't they sweet little pagodas? I love

Chinese motifs. Full sleeves, very heavily ruched bodice — all lined in white cotton. It would *glow!* Zigzag frills from the hem of the skirt all the way up to your knees — oh, it'd feel like wading through a sea of whipped cream! What d'you think, Miss Cousins? With a very plain neck? Just piping.'

Miss Cousins said, 'Lovely, my lady.'

'Oh, just look at this!' Johanna dared to say as she pulled out a roll of deep-violet barège, a fine tartan weave that incorporated spots of pink rosebuds. 'For a winter dress?' she asked, holding it hesitantly against her.

Nina gave an ecstatic laugh. 'I'd forgotten I had that. I bought it in Plymouth. Oh! The shops in Plymouth, Jo — you've never seen the like. As good as London any day. Don't you agree, Miss Cousins?'

Miss Cousins confirmed that they were lovely.

But Nina wasn't even listening. She gave another cry of delight and said, 'And now I remember why I bought *these!*' She threw open yet another cloth hall of a cupboard and rummaged out several lengths of silk fringe in violet and brown and grey. She gathered them up and held them against the cloth, which Johanna was still clutching to herself. 'Not sheer, my pet. Flounces. Deep flounces. Deep, deep, deep flounces. So! and then these fringes — violet round the bodice, grey round the waist, and brown at the cuffs.'

'Nothing at the neck?'

'Not this neck.' Nina caressed it softly. 'The slightest adornment would be over-adornment, little swan. But you are lucky — today's fashion decrees only the plainest of necks. It was *made* for you, I feel sure.' She returned to the cupboard that had disgorged the fringes. 'And you can have this mantilla. And this cape. And *this* cape — that's for Sundays. Won't you turn all the heads in church! And wasn't Providence marvellous to invent Sundays! I often thought that.'

She frowned as a new idea struck her. 'Talking of churches, we must get them to go sparingly with the red in poor dear Brookesy's window; it would clash horribly. Oh, and we mustn't forget bonnets and gloves — and a little muff. How about this one? No — the moth has been at it. Miss Cousins — here — that's for you.'

'Oh, lovely!' the dressmaker said.

So the morning went — and it carried half the afternoon with it, by which time the number of new gowns had crept from four up to nine, and no one bothered to count the bonnets and gloves and scarves and mittens and sashes and brooches and bags . . . not to mention the unmentionables — the chemises and drawers and petticoats and camisoles and chemisettes . . . oh yes, and her very first pair of *corsets!*

Only then did she remember about Hamill Oliver.

'Don't bother your head about him,' Nina said when she explained. 'Do him good to be left standing. Those Troys think they own the world. Etiquette is for others — not them! When has he ever called here and left cards? Besides, you don't want to burden your acquaintance with him, do you?'

'He seemed very pleasant. I know old Mrs Ramona Troy is arrogant in that way, but he was . . .'

'He'll never amount to anything, you know. You just watch — the Troys are going to go down and down. One sees it happen so often. Old Sir William was the one, by all accounts. Hamill's grandfather. He made that family. One more generation and they'll be unmade again.'

'They had a lawsuit five or six years ago — the poor Troys against the rich Troys.'

Nina smiled complacently. 'That's how it goes. The lawyers will get it all. How did the case go? This is intriguing. I'd not heard of it before now.'

'I didn't really follow it but I think the poor Troys had to abandon the suit for lack of funds.'

Nina chuckled. 'Begod, they must keep them poor, so — or they'll never be free of the worry. D'you suppose it's too late to go out and see little Hamill after all? We could be there in half an hour. Tell him we cast a shoe. Come on! I want to hear more about this.'

Johanna plucked at her sleeve and held it. 'Nina?'

'Yes?' She turned and smiled.

'Thank you. It sounds so inadequate.' Her gaze fell. 'I am inadequate.'

'Of course you aren't!' Nina took both her hands. 'What makes you say such a thing?'

Tears shivered on her eyelids. 'I've had no practice, you

see. No one's ever been. . .' Her voice broke. She stumbled toward Nina and threw her arms about her — mainly to prevent her from seeing her face all uglified like that. 'I don't know how to thank you — how to begin, even.'

Nina held her tight, saying nothing until she had calmed a little; then she murmured, 'Do you think I don't know what loneliness is, too, my dear? Those long watches of the night in a cold, cheerless, half-empty bed? A few mornings ago I saw a fox cross our lawn and I called out to Brookesy to come and see! I forget. I forget. I expect to meet him around every corner. I forget, you see. So what is my gift of the odd rag or two for your back when set against your gifts to me.'

Johanna wondered what gifts they might be but did not feel it the right moment to ask. Nina held her at arm's length and laughed at their folly. 'Just look at us! Here, take this kerchief.'

While Johanna dabbed the fire from her eyes and cheeks Nina went on, 'Did you ever have a sister?'

Johanna nodded. 'She died when I was eight. She was eleven. Roxanne was her name. I think she was the last person I ever really loved — well, except for my parents, of course.'

Nina took the kerchief from her, wet it more, wrung it out, and then put the finishing touches to Johanna's repairs. 'It's curious,' she mused. 'I had a younger sister who died — Clarissa. It's the same sort of feeling though. What do I look like? A sight, I'm sure.'

She passed the cloth to Johanna, who gave her eyes a few perfunctory dabs. 'You're made of sterner stuff than me,' she said, cheerful again. And then, more shyly, 'You are like a sister to me, actually. I've been trying to think what this feeling is like. And that's it. It's been so long.' And as she passed back the kerchief she gave her a timid little kiss — which Nina returned warmly — with a passion that allowed Johanna a glimpse of a kind of loneliness whose depths she had never plumbed.

'Now let's go and tease little Hamill,' Nina said, brisk again. 'Men are such. . .*putty,* aren't they!'

'Not Hal,' Johanna replied. 'I wonder if he got a place at Wheal Vor?'

'If he did,' the other remarked casually, 'he'll prove a great disappointment.'

'To them? I don't...'

'No — to me! I don't give a fig for them. Sorry — I know Miss Grylls is your friend, but I mean he'll greatly disappoint me.'

'But how?' Johanna was amazed at her vehemence.

'Oh...I think that man could really *be* someone. Make his mark. But never if he sticks in this backwater.'

'Cornwall? A backwater?'

Nina gagged herself with the flat of her hand. 'Sorry — I shouldn't be saying these things.'

'Or d'you mean mining is the backwater.'

'Come on — I spoke too rashly. What is it to me, after all?'

She left orders for a grand Lancashire hotpot for their dinner.

Oysters again, Johanna noticed.

Also two bottles of the colonel's best contraband claret were to be brought up and decanted.

When they were on their way out of town, up the steep, winding hill past the church and out through Gwealfolds to the Redruth road, Johanna returned to the topic. 'What would you do if you were Hal?' she asked.

Nina stared at her with a kind of provisional pity, as if she already suspected her answer would not please; she even made Johanna compel her to say it, with: 'If I were Hal? Oh, if I were any man — but especially if I were Hal! D'you really want me to tell you? Would you like to drive, by the way?'

Johanna grinned. 'Yes to both questions!'

Nina passed her the reins and said, 'He's quiet enough but he's apt to shy at gates — if a cow makes a sudden move or something. So — if I were Hal? Well, the first thing I'd do is travel the world a bit. Insufferable as Mr Cunningham may have been he was right about one thing: Put your finger at haphazard upon any portion of the globe and you're touching a desperate need for railway engineers. There's a big smile and an even bigger bag of gold waiting for Hal on every continent. So that's what I'd do.'

'Leave Cornwall?' Johanna felt numb. To have found Hal and then to face the prospect of losing him, all within a few days...

'Only for five or six years, my dear. He'd come back with

enough money to settle, the way a man should. But think what he could command then! He could be a venturer on his own account. Or buy a coastal trader and set up in business from Falmouth or Penzance.'

'He might not make this fortune, though,' Johanna pointed out reasonably enough.

Nina was reasonable, too. 'That's perfectly true. But tell me this — how does his going back to being grass captain at Wheal Vor (and that's the best he can honestly hope for), how does that *increase* his chances? Name me one man who ever got rich that way?'

'Money's not the be-all and end-all.' Johanna leaped with both feet into the rearguard.

Nina laughed, not unkindly. 'But it does buy the most beautiful things, darling. Haven't we spent most of the day draping you in some of them?'

Chapter Sixteen

The Pendarves Arms stood in Station Road, almost opposite what had until recently been the upper terminus of the line connecting Redruth with the north-coast port of Hayle, some eight miles away to the west. It was chiefly a haulage line, carrying tin and copper to the quays and bringing back coal in exchange. Lately its service had been extended a few miles north-eastward into the mining country around Chacewater. Passenger traffic was of the lightest — a few trains each day, except on Fridays, when the market brought the whole countryside into town. On other days, therefore, the public house catered almost exclusively to the carters, porters, and linesmen engaged in the haulage trade. It was not, in Hal's view, the sort of place where one would boast of being 'well liked.'

'I was to meet Mr Cunningham here,' he explained to the landlord.

'Who?' The man ran his eye up and down the slate that recorded his debtors, as if he feared a new name had sneaked in since last he checked. 'Cunning-what?'

'I'll have a half of your own porter,' Hal replied. 'He'll be along in a minute.'

He took the ale outside. The day was gray and overcast, with hardly a breath of wind. Three dogs, sniffing along the base of the wall, worked their way incuriously around his boots and continued onward up the street. Hal tried to imagine a world in which all the landmarks were smells of various kinds; the nearest he could get was the way you knew exactly where you were in a mine when your candle went out and no one else was near — just by listening to the different qualities in the echoes and reverberations.

He strolled up to the station; in a siding opposite the entrance gate they were loading canvas bags filled with semi-refined copper into a covered goods wagon. Half way along the platform on the near side the station master was pruning the old flowered wood out of some rambling roses. He recognized Hal and left off at his approach. 'Quite a sight this year,' he commented, poking the severed shoots into a pile with his toecap.

'I remember them last year.'

'They were better this. And talking of sights — that was some grand old spectacle in Helston the other night, too.'

Hal chuckled. 'Were you there, then?'

'I heard tell about it. And about you and Cap'n Hosking. How are you here in Redruth today, then?'

Surely not hoping any local captain will set you on, was what he meant.

'I'm waiting for Mr Cunningham.'

'Who?' The bewilderment swiftly gave way to a kind of wary resignation. 'Oh, him. He'll be in on the quarter past. He's surveying — or supposed to be — out between Chacewater and Truro.'

'It's no secret, then?'

The man just laughed.

'He's alleged to be somebody quite big in railways, isn't he? Up in Yorkshire, somewhere?'

That laugh again. 'I was told to content him by indulgence — and that's all I do know about Mr Cunningham. And that's all I do *do* about Mr Cunningham, too — I content him by indulgence.' He stared up the line. 'I believe she's coming now.'

A minute or so later the train — or, rather, its plume of smoke — came into view round the bend at Wheal Harmony, a mile or so due north of Redruth. It took a full five minutes to cover the distance, though the gradients were small. It drew up with a screech of its iron brakes and wreathed itself in the usual clouds of fishy-smelling steam. Hal, who had once seen a much lower-pressure cylinder burst at the mine, gave the machine the widest berth as he made his way back up the platform to the brake van, where he assumed Cunningham would be travelling. He emerged from the final bank of vapour to see the man walking toward him, consulting his watch − a vast and impressive hunter on a stout gold chain.

'Mr Cunningham!' he called, uncertain as to whether the man were employer or colleague.

'Penrose!' He caught sight of the empty ale glass. 'I see you've wasted no time. Lord, but I've a thirst whose slaking would float a man of war.'

As they walked back into the street Hal saw the station master tip him a wink. 'Do they serve lunches there?' He nodded toward the inn. 'I saw no dining room.'

'No, my aunt has furnished us with some game pie and a plum pudding, which I left simmering at Chacewater. We'll take a flagon or two of beer and go straight back, eh?'

They timed it nicely for the half-past-noon coal train going up to Chacewater, where they arrived some twenty minutes later.

Before the building of the line, this had been a wild, isolated stretch of moorland in which mining and its attendant trades were the only source of employment − the farming was barely above subsistence level − which meant that the mines had spilled their waste over the landscape with even less regard than usual for its encroachment. Hal, who had supposed the devastation to the east of Trigonning to be as bad as anywhere, now had to revise his opinion. 'Pretty dreadful, eh?' he commented half-apologetically to Cunningham.

'That?' the man asked, giving a tolerantly scornful smile at the whole panorama. 'Eay, lad! Thou should see Castleford and Doncaster if it's wasted land you're seeking.' He nodded approvingly at what looked like a titans' battlefield to their south. 'That's paradise in comparison.'

Two bal maidens, dressed in black − or what had long ago been black − were toiling up a slight incline toward the station, talking what sounded like a foreign tongue, even to Hal, who knew every contortion of the dialect as it was spoken only fifteen miles from here.

'Ah,' Cunningham said, as if he knew them.

Hal raised an inquiring eyebrow.

The other gave a wicked grin. 'Two grand lasses. Would you be interested?'

Hal laughed awkwardly. 'Where's this pudding simmering?'

'All appetites catered for in good time.' He nodded toward a hut in a field beyond the station. 'Seriously – if you are interested. They think the world of me, those two. I gave them both a jolly good *rogering* yesterday, if you'll pardon the pun. It's my impression they'd never known such pleasure was possible. Are you interested?'

'In plum pudding and game pie.'

Cunningham sighed. 'Well, I know I have a monstrously unfair share of that faculty for women – both the appetite, that is, and the means of gratifying it. However...'

The women were level with them by now, no more than a dozen paces away on the far side of a stone hedge, which concealed all but their heads and shoulders.

'Good morrow, my pretties!' Cunningham cried out jovially.

The pair, who had been staring at Hal, transferred their attention to him. 'What a raw, cold day to be sure,' he added – the prelude, of course, to: *Want a little warming?* But before he could reach that dénouement the nearer female, a handsome woman with long dark hair gathered up in two buns, burst out laughing – which set the other off. They covered their mouths in a hint of an apology and hastened away up the lane, still giggling for all they were worth.

Cunningham laughed, too, as he watched them into the distance. 'Such a jolly pair,' he said. 'The dark one's a bit gamey but the other is pure cream. Aiee!'

The fire had gone out some time ago, to judge by the appearance of the plum pudding, which sagged in the cold water, ringed by haloes of congealed lard. 'I'll have that going in no time,' Cunningham said, unabashed. 'The game pie will be as good cold as hot.'

That at least was true. Hal ate ravenously and washed his share down with copious draughts of mild ale. Cunningham ate and drank while he poked the twigs of his fire together and rekindled them.

The drafting table, the hut's only substantial piece of furniture, was littered with scraps of paper, covered with calculations. Not all of them, Hal observed, were 'up to Cocker' – at least, not up to the Cocker who had written the arithmetical textbook from which he had been taught at school. In his day, nine times eight had never made sixty-three . . . nor could the remainder in a long division be larger than the divisor.

Cunningham gathered them up hastily. 'You're staring at a fortune there, Penrose, did you but realize it,' he said. 'I know men who'd give their eye teeth for just one glimpse of these calculations.'

Hal wondered, in that case, why the door had not been locked — but he kept the query to himself. 'I did some reading last night,' he said. 'The old colonel had a wonderful set of Rees's *Cyclopaedia,* you know.'

His companion raised a laconic eyebrow. 'Oh? Are you still at Lady Nina's?'

'Only till tomorrow. Now that I have work on the railway here . . .'

Cunningham was alarmed. 'But I asked you to tell no one.'

'And nor I did. They believe I'm seeking a place at Wheal Vor, whose venturers are in dispute with the rest of the county. It's the only place where I'd be likely . . .'

'Ah, yes — I heard about all that. Our dinner table last night buzzed with little else. See here, Penrose . . . old fellow — I'd esteem it the greatest favour if you'd let no one know you're taking over my survey here. Tell them you have indeed gained your place at Wheal Vor, eh?'

Hal shook his head. 'They'll know within days that I haven't.'

Cunningham saw the truth of it and bit his lip in vexation.

'On the other hand,' Hal went on, 'you must be pretty well in with the directors of the railway here. Why not arrange it to seem they are my employers? Then I could truthfully say I was working for the railway company. But see here, we haven't yet decided that I *am* to take on this work. I know nothing about it beyond what I read in Rees.'

'Rees . . . yes . . .' Cunningham scratched at his chin. 'Published around 1812, wasn't it? Too early, surely, to include anything on railways — well, tramways, yes, I suppose . . .'

'True, but the principle of cuttings and embankments was the same for canals. In fact, railway surveying is easier because canals had the additional constraint of keeping to the contour — or else making very deep cuttings and ending up with a lot of spoil to lose somewhere.'

'Spoil, eh? Now you have it, Penrose. Spoil! The whole nub of our problem is, in fine, how to employ that spoil to the greatest advantage. And I'll tell you what we do.' The man raised a monitorial finger as if he were about to impart the secret of the universe. 'We lose it in the valleys, to build up the embankments, you see. There now!'

'Well I never!' Hal did not bat an eyelid. 'What d'you allow for settlement?'

The other frowned. 'In cash, you mean?'

'No, no. Settlement of the spoil, after you tip it in the valleys it must settle.'

'Oh, that settlement. Ah, well' — he consulted his watch — 'that is a question fraught with difficulty.' He smiled encouragingly at Hal. 'Astute of you to see it, though, old fellow. Yes.' He rubbed his chin thoughtfully, yet again, and repeated, 'Settlement, eh. You'd have some knowledge of that, I suppose? The local geology...that sort of thing?'

'We have to calculate for it when we tip our waste close to our boundaries — so as not to encroach on a neighbour's sett.'

'Quite. Yes, I do see that. And...er, what formula do you use down here, may I ask?'

'The same as you use in Yorkshire, I'm sure.'

Cunningham gave a modest laugh. 'I've devised my own, naturally, which, for local Yorkshire conditions, is vastly more accurate than anything you'd find in a book.'

'What rock have you there?' Hal asked, and went on to name some that he was fairly sure did not occur within fifty miles of that county — indeed, some did not exist at all: 'Ligurian slate? Gray Dolomite? Old Devon sandstone? Icelandic gneiss?'

Cunningham answered warily. 'In various admixtures.'

Hal whistled. 'Well, I take my hat off to you, sir. I'd not like to calculate settlement rates for any one of them — let alone a mixture. Fortunately, down here you've only elvan, blue elvan, and granite to deal with. I expect it's all granite between here and Truro. I assume Truro is our goal?'

Cunningham gave a reluctant nod.

'Well then, the simplest calculations should suffice.'

'Oh. Ah. Er... good. Well, in that case, I dare say I could leave it all quite safely to you?'

Hal accepted the commission without a trace of a smile.

'And now what d'you say to my survey instruments?' Cunningham asked proudly as he threw open a brass-bound military chest.

'Say to them?' Hal had never heard the idiom.

The other began unpacking, lovingly calling out the name of each item. 'Desagulier's level — now she's a rare little beauty.'

'Rare these days,' Hal agreed. It was a splendid piece of which any museum would have been proud. The other instruments, however, were the very latest and all brand new.

'Ramsden's improved theodolite — see how the vernier is now protected?' He lifted out a gleaming mass of polished brass and gave its table a twist or two. 'Look at that movement!'

'I say!' Hal's admiration was genuine; it was, indeed, the finest theodolite he had ever seen.

'And what about this — Everard's cross staff? Collapsible, you see, and yet accurate in rising a perpendicular to a thousandth of an inch.'

It was a telescopic contraption of brass, ebony, and ivory, and it must have cost a small fortune. If a great aristocrat somehow acquired the pastime of surveying his own demesne, these were the instruments he might have commissioned for his own use. 'And Gundry's chains, I see.' Hal nodded toward the only remaining equipment in the chest. (Tolland's *Rudiments of Surveying* and Ellison's *Elementary Surveying Practice; Vol. I — LAND* could hardly be considered 'equipment' for so experienced a man as this, he thought.)

Cunningham pulled the chains out with an air of reverence. 'One hundred links,' he murmured. 'And not a hair of a difference between any pair taken at haphazard.'

'By George!' Hal was checking the magnification of the telescope on the theodolite. He sought and found the two bal maidens, lolling beside a gate a little way up the hill. The dark-haired one was indeed a beauty. 'But I'm surprised you bothered to come down to Cornwall at all, man. With equipment like this, I should think you could have stayed in Yorkshire and measured the lot from your bedroom window.'

Cunningham laughed. 'So!' He waved grandly at the instruments and the landscape beyond the window. 'All yours until you've done.'

Hal was by now ready to strike a hard bargain. It was obvious that, in accepting this surveying commission, poor Cunningham had bitten off far more than he could chew. However, Hal's opening bid of two hundred guineas for the entire survey was accepted without demur, so there was nothing to haggle over. 'Your name will stand as surveyor-in-chief?' Hal suggested.

Cunningham pretended to consider the question. 'I suppose it will have to,' he admitted. 'It will save time.'

'In what way?'

'Well, if they see my name there at the foot of the report, they'll accept it all without question. And as to you – well, for your own sake you'd better tell no one. The local peasantry will know, to be sure, but they're hardly likely to come plaguing you for railway intelligence and speculative advice.'

Hal promised to tell no one, except the two lads he'd hire as assistants. Cunningham was about to object. It was fairly obvious he had been attempting to carry out his survey single-handed – which is like trying to win the Derby without a horse. However, he decided not to risk his ignorance in a direct question. 'You'll start tomorrow?' he asked.

'Today – this very minute. I'll walk the country until the light fails – into Truro by way of Polstrears Moors and back along the southerly road through Killers. Your route must lie somewhere between those two courses. Shall I start where you left off?'

'No, no,' Cunningham replied cheerfully. 'Not the slightest need for that. You'll work better if it all comes from your own genius – which I doubt not. As a matter of fact' – he drew forth that great watch, consulted it, and gave a salacious grin – 'you remember that brace of wenches who passed by a while ago?'

Hal nodded.

'Well, you may not have remarked it, but one of them

laughed in a most peculiar manner? A false laugh, completely assumed, badly executed.'

'A most singular laugh,' Hal agreed.

'In point of fact, 'twas not a laugh at all but a signal I had arranged between us. It means that even now they are awaiting me in the little spinney beside the line, about half a mile back.'

Hal complimented him. 'As a signal to disguise *that* sort of assignation it could hardly have been better chosen,' he said.

With a satisfied smile the other retrieved a polished rosewood cane from the corner of the hut and sauntered away, whistling.

Before Hal left he built the fire properly and kindled it yet again. He would not need to walk all the way to Truro, which lay some six miles away, slightly north of east. His total journey would be less than eight miles. The pudding would be nicely simmered by the time he returned.

No sooner had he gained the road to Polstrears Moors than he ran across the two bal maidens.

'Hello, Penrose,' cried the dark-haired one. 'We've been waiting for you.'

Chapter Seventeen

Johanna and Lady Nina took the long way around, past Yeol Parc and through Coverack Bridges, where the valley of the river Cober was much shallower than on the direct road through Lowertown. Its sides were still steep, however, and a labourer had to leave his hedging and help them up on the Tregathennan side. His strength seemed to fascinate Nina. Johanna, who was still driving, saw that she could not take her eyes off him — crying, 'Well done...good man, yourself . . . oh, you're doing wonders there!' She gave him sixpence for his pains, which was twice what the service would command even from the most generous traveller.

'He put me in mind of young Mikey Hogan at home,' she told Johanna. 'There's a great likeness altogether between us and the Cornish.'

'It must be the Celtic blood.'

Nina chuckled. 'If there's blood in it at all, I'm thinking it's the Spanish.'

'Spanish!'

'From the Armada, you know. Half of it was wrecked off Cornwall, the other half around Scotland, and the rest of it, which must have been another half again, ended up in Ireland. Think of it, Jo — all those dark, handsome young men coming ashore with every tide, half dead, half naked...And the poor women who nursed them back to health — how it must have perturbed their hearts. Think of all those silent and secret romances that were played out here, in our little fishing coves and villages, and in the Highland glens, and on the wild Atlantic shores of Ireland!' She stared around with disgust at the denuded landscape and the reeking mine chimneys. 'And what a dull age we have chosen to live in by comparison!'

Wheal Leander, Hamill Oliver's present home, lay at the northern edge of the Pallas demesne. The young man himself came out into the lane at the sound of their approach. He stood there, arms akimbo — 'Like an excise man,' Johanna commented.

'Like a Troy,' Nina said. 'But you're right — arrogance is the common thread.'

'I'd almost given you up,' he called.

When they were within easier range Nina began to white lie: 'We were unavoidably detained, Mr Oliver . . .'

But he cut her short. 'By a woman with a needle and thread — I know.'

The two ladies exchanged glances of surprise.

He grinned. 'I met Mr Penrose this morning.'

'Ah — on his way to Wheal Vor, no doubt.'

'Er . . . yes, exactly so, Lady Nina. He told me to only half expect you. That's why I left the gate only half open, you see.' He pointed toward the yard entrance.

His tone was so reasonable that Nina did not realize he was joking until Johanna's laugh alerted her.

'The menhirs are lying where we tumbed them at Wheal Pallas,' he explained. 'We may drive round there through Little Tregathennan, back the way you came, or we may walk about half a mile over the croft from here.'

'Oh, let's walk by all means,' Nina replied. 'Have you a handful of oats for this fellow? He did sterling work up the hill at Coverack Bridges.'

A small gate at the foot of the vegetable garden led out to the path across the croft; from there it ran pretty straight among the ling and gorse towards the great outcrop that formed the open mine, or quarry, of Wheal Pallas itself. Hamill went ahead and walked almost crabwise, talking to them obliquely over his shoulder. 'You must have a good eye for horseflesh, lady Nina, That's your Irish blood, of course.'

'Why d'you say so, Mr Oliver?'

'I take it that the fine dappled grey Penrose was riding this morning was one of yours?'

'Ah, yes — a present from dear old Brookesy to me.' She

sighed. 'Our first anniversary, in fact. Good, eh? Nice touch of Arab in him. I hope Penrose hadn't worked him all to a lather?'

'Not at all. He's a fine horseman, indeed.'

'What are the great powers of the county saying about him, have you heard? Will he find any work at all west of the Tamar now?'

'Oddly enough, he stopped and we spoke on that very point. Penrose himself doesn't set his chances very high at Wheal Vor. And for my own part, I suspect that even if he were taken on, he wouldn't last.'

'Why do you say that?' Nina asked.

'Chalk and cheese. Say what you like about Enion Hosking, he'll leave a safe mine to the next generation of tributers. But the way the Grylls faction is stripping out the Great Lode – well, it's not even safe for the present gangs, let alone the ones that may follow. Poor Penrose will see horrors everywhere he looks.'

Nina winked at Johanna.

He saw it. 'I know – spoken like a mineral lord! But it's the truth. They are desperate to get up every last ounce of tin while they yet may – in case the next action goes against them.'

'Ah!' Nina saw her chance. 'While we're on the subject of legal actions, Mr Oliver, what is your Uncle George planning, may I ask?'

He stopped and stared at her in alarm. 'Why – what have you heard?'

'Oh, nothing in particular. But, just as the Wheal Vor case seems to go on and on. . . well, I'm told that the last hearing on the Troy inheritance was fairly inconclusive. Or am I misinformed?'

He moved his head and hands awkwardly, as if trying to marshal too many ideas at once. 'It is complicated,' he said at length, resuming their walk. 'George Troy began an action under an ancient legal process that was abolished about ten years ago. He reopened it under the new system and had to abandon it for lack of funds.'

Nina shivered theatrically but her eye was bright. 'How awesome, Mr Oliver! Each day as you awaken you must wonder if it is your last in possession of the Pallas estate.'

'Now there you are misinformed, Lady Nina. I am not in possession of the Pallas estate. In any case...'

'Your branch of the family then. George Troy's boat might come home any day. I mean, he might suddenly acquire the means to resume his action. Then it would be strictly nett cash for you everywhere. How d'you sleep easy under such a threat? I couldn't bear it, I'm sure. My nails would be down to the quick in a week.'

Hamill inspected his own fingernails and laughed. 'They're safe enough, I believe. There's little fear that Uncle George will somehow 'acquire the means', as you put it. In any case, where breathes the man whose life is so assured he need never fret for the morrow?'

Nina, feeling she had gleaned enough for the present, sought to bury the topic in a platitude. 'Aye,' she sighed briskly. 'I suppose you're wiser than me. Man proposes, God disposes.'

'For the lucky ones,' Hamill observed. 'For the rest of us I think He merely laughs. Now!' He halted and threw out an arm, barring their further progress. 'Look about you. Do you *feel* anything in this place?'

'It's bleak, I'll grant it that,' Nina offered.

But he was staring at Johanna. 'Miss Rosewarne?' he prompted.

She shook her head.

'Look again,' he urged. 'Do you see a mark upon the ground, running away there, and there? Part of a vast circle that, if continued, would enclose Wheal Pallas and much of the valley beyond?'

'An ancient fortification?' Johanna asked, remembering Terence Visick's former enthusiasm for such things.

'An ancient wall, no doubt of it. Let me take you to its centre — the heart of it all.'

'A wall, you say?' Nina's voice was filled with doubt. 'But there's no sign of it now.'

'Indeed not!' There was a triumphant edge to his voice. 'Removed, you see. Every last vestige of it gone!'

'But who would do such a thing? The Troys?'

'Oh no. Where would be our purpose in that?'

'Especially to leave no trace of it behind,' she added pointedly. 'Mineral lords are not usually so tender with our landscape.'

'Exactly,' he said, as if she were supporting his thesis. 'No, they must have been very frightened, don't you think? Those who did it. To remove every last bit.'

Nina gave up.

About a furlong into what he claimed had been the circle he suddenly turned to their left and led them over an expanse of sheep-nibbled ling to a giant column of stone, which had obviously been toppled within the past twelvemonth. 'There's the menhir for you!' he proclaimed, as if its very presence half-proved something. 'It stands – or stood – at the precise centre of our circle. And do you know its name – the name of this circle? *Crows-an-wrea!* The croft of the witch.'

'Ah!' The penny dropped with Nina. 'So you think the local priesthood whipped up the fears of the tribe and they all came out here and demolished the wall – every last stone of it?'

He nodded. 'Futile, of course. There was nothing to the wall as such. Its stones merely marked the line of it.'

'The line of what?'

'Of the Power. It's still there, you know. I've dowsed for it. The most tenacious Power I've ever experienced.' He turned to Johanna. 'I'm surprised you don't feel it, Miss Rosewarne.'

Johanna, who had pricked up her ears at the words *crows-an-wrea,* asked, 'Which is witch?'

Hamill frowned. 'What d'you mean – which is which?'

'No – witch – old woman on a broomstick. That sort of witch.'

'Oh, *wrea.* that's Cornish for witch. Not an old woman on a broomstick, though. Something far more potent and mysterious. It's a Power that lives in this.' He stamped his boots on the peaty soil. 'And in this.' He kicked the fallen menhir. 'And in certain rare women – can't you feel it? I'm surprised.'

'D'you know Joel Rogers?' Johanna asked.

'Delivers strewing sand to the farmers' wives? What of him?'

'He once told me that the old folk used to call people with my colouring – dark hair and pale blue eyes – he said we were called 'candle and ray.' Is that the same, I wonder?'

Hamill laughed. 'Tribe of the witch!' he cried. '*Cendl-an-wrea*, though in your case, Miss Rosewarne, it would be more faithfully rendered as 'Tribe of the bewitcher'! *Cendl* is Cornish for tribe, you see. Candle and ray, indeed! The old language isn't dead, after all. It simply masquerades in the conqueror's orthography.'

Nina seated herself comfortably on the fallen tip of the giant stone. 'Yes,' she said. 'I think this 'rude stone monolith,' as Mr Cunningham affects to call it, suitably re-erected on the lawn at Liston Court, will make a most fitting memorial to dear old Brookesy. What's your price, if I may be so bold? Or would you prefer to deal with my agent?'

'There will be no charge, Lady Nina.' His smile made her feel she had somehow stepped into an obscure trap he had laid for her.

'I must make inquiries,' she said. 'Not every carter in the district will be able to manage something that heavy.'

'I know the very man – a diddicoy in Carleen. Allow me to arrange it. I'll drop him to his keenest price for you, I promise.'

She patted the stone. 'If there's an extra charge for washing off the magic and witchcraft and leaving it all here, I'd not object to paying it.'

He laughed. 'Now there would be a costly task, indeed!'

'Though, on the other hand, I don't know . . .' she mused. 'To wake up one midnight and discover a ring of ghostly village maidens dancing around old Brookesy's rude monolith, all in the frosty moonlight – it wouldn't be too, too dreadfully unfitting.'

'I think you may not be disappointed, Lady Nina,' Hamill told her. 'There is *something* that lingers in such ancient stones. Our rational minds do not care to provide us with an adequate vocabulary to deal with it – spirits, powers, ghosts, forces. . . what are these? Mere stumblings on the path to understanding.'

'Quite,' Nina said. 'It'll be dark soon. We must return.'

'I was sketching the lych gate at Wendron Church this morning. D'you know it?'

'Yes, I believe I do,' Nina replied thoughtfully. 'With the little mortuary above?'

'That's the one. And though I doubt if it ever really was a

mortuary, there is a sort of heavy . . . melancholy, a *douleur,* that hangs about the old stones still. I had to leave before I was finished. That feeling was so overwhelming.'

On their way back to Wheal Leander, Johanna took off her bonnet briefly to shake out her hair. She had slipped a little way behind so that Hamill should not observe her but he turned around at the most inopportune moment and then just stood there, transfixed by what he saw.

'Oh, forgive me,' he exclaimed, recollecting himself at last. 'I was so taken aback . . . unpardonable of me.'

She smiled, trying to put him at his ease once more.

'Actually,' he went on, 'what really startled me was the most astonishing resemblance you bear to a figure in a painting that hangs above the stair at Pallas. Are you interested in art, Miss Rosewarne? Did you know that old Sir William Troy amassed one of the finest private collections of old masters in the country?'

'My father always took the *Art Journal.* He used to read it aloud to me. This painting at Pallas, is it . . .'

'It's a Veronese. A portrait of a rich merchant of Verona and his page boy. I would be honoured to show it to you.' He turned to Nina. 'To you both, of course.'

Johanna was stunned. Of course, there were probably dozens of rich Italian merchants who had themselves painted with their page boys, but still – just imagine if it were the same!

'What say you?' Hamill prompted.

Nina, who had never been farther than the drawing room at Pallas, was delighted to accept for both of them, and settled the appointment for that day week. Johanna was pleased, too, for she knew that if she had accepted the invitation, her excitement would have shown – and Mr Oliver would most probably have misunderstood it. 'That's the day Selina's coming,' she reminded Nina.

'Bring her, too,' Hamill said magnanimously.

As they passed Wheal Leander, he invited them in for 'a dish of tay', but Nina, who did not like negotiating the steep, winding hill by the church after dark, declined.

'Until next week!' he shouted after them.

'Well, what d'you make of him, my dear?' Nina asked as soon as they were out of earshot.

'*Was* there ever a wall out there on that bit of croft?' Johanna asked. 'I looked and looked and saw no. . .'

'Of course there wasn't,' Nina was full of scorn. 'It's all in his fancy. I told you — he's a dreamer.'

'But to be so exact! A circular wall. . . and he showed us the very line of it!'

'Well, that's men for you, dear. They see just what they want to see — as you'll find out soon enough, I fear.'

After a moment's thought Johanna asked, 'In what way. . . I mean how will I find out?'

Nina sighed. 'When Hamill Oliver called you a bewitcher — he turned that rather neatly, incidentally, don't you think? Anyway, when he called you a bewitcher, he spoke the plain truth.'

'Oh, really, Nina!' Johanna protested.

'Truly. Look at the effect you've had on poor Doctor Moore. Not to mention. . .'

'And Hal Penrose? What do you. . .'

'. . . not to mention Hamill Oliver himself.'

'But that's absurd.'

'Didn't you notice?'

'There's something rather sad about him,' Johanna replied. 'That's all I noticed.'

'He is obviously very smitten by you — and all you notice is "something rather sad"!'

'Oh, Nina, don't tell such. . . I mean, it's just not true.'

'Have it your own way.'

After a silence Johanna went on. 'Don't you actually like men, Nina? I can never quite decide.'

'About men?'

'No, about you. I can never make out what you truly think about them.'

'I believe if there were no men, I could still be very happy. However, it's an idle speculation because the creatures do actually exist. They are there. And we are compelled to take note.'

'Compelled?'

'Doesn't it feel like a compulsion to you? Be honest now. This is not a public catechism.' She flashed a winning smile. 'It's only me.'

After a moment of agony Johanna confessed shyly, 'It

does feel like a compulsion with one man — with Hal.'

'Yes — I'm coming to him,' Nina threatened. 'I meant more generally. How many men have you kissed? If, indeed, you've...'

'Half a dozen. Actually, you're right. I think they did see just what they wished to see in me. Yes! Why didn't I realize it before? I never felt they knew me at all. They had a picture of me in their imagination and they were far happier with that than with trying to discover...mind you, I don't think Hal is like this.'

'Very well, let's come to Hal, then,' Nina said with an ominous emphasis. 'Correct me if I'm wrong, but isn't Wendron on the Redruth road out of Helston?'

'Yes. It's less than a mile beyond Coverack Bridges, why?'

'And where is its nearest point to the Wheal Vor road out of Helston?'

Johanna saw at once where the answer led — for there was no 'near point' between the two roads; they diverged steadily from the moment they left Helston. 'Good heavens,' she said.

'Precisely!' Nina grinned fiercely. 'So what was Hal Penrose doing on the road to Redruth?'

Johanna giggled. 'What are you going to do?'

'Let us go to Wendron, since it's not too far from Coverack Bridges, and inquire if a man on a fine dappled grey with a touch of Arab has passed that way since noon, say. And if not, let us give him a surprise — pleasant or not, as the case may be!'

Chapter Eighteen

The curious thing about Wendron is that it hardly exists at all. There is a Wendron Street in Helston; all the fingerboards in the surrounding villages count off the miles to Wendron; the great Wendron Rambuck Fair, which dates back to Celtic times, is held there every year (indeed that must be the origin of the village, for all Celtic festivals are held in godforsaken places out in the middle of nowhere); and yet when travellers actually arrive at Wendron they find it consists of nothing but a church, an alehouse, two or three permanent dwellings, and a sprinkling of cabins for the poor. The highway behaves as if it, too, were seeking more: It makes a wide, semicircular detour around a smallish hill and then, a mere quarter of a mile farther on, finds itself in the much larger hamlet of Trenear − which has no street named after it anywhere, is not mentioned on any fingerboard, and flocks to the Rambuck like everyone else for miles around.

'Well, all I can say,' Nina commented, 'is that the lord of *this* manor, back in the olden days, must have had powerful friends at court.' She surveyed the lot in one brief glance. 'This is no place for two ladies to wait. We'll spring our surprise on Master Penrose at home instead.'

And she turned about and set off again toward Helston, pausing only to get light for the gig lamps at the alehouse. Inquiries there and down in Trenear established that Hal had almost certainly not returned as yet.

'On the subject of surprises,' Johanna commented, 'I wonder what Mrs Ramona Troy is going to make of it − her grandson showing a Visick around Pallas House!'

Nina chuckled. 'Yes, that hadn't struck me. You know these ancient local feuds so much better than I. Well, one thing's certain — it will double the interest of the visit.' After a pause she added, 'Apropos which, we haven't had a chance to talk about it, my precious, but I ought to ask you if *you* object to Selina's coming to stay with us?'

'Object?' Johanna had difficulty with the very idea. 'Me?'

'Well, I can't assure you in one breath that Liston court is now your home, too — and then turn around and behave as if it were still exclusively mine. I ought to have asked you first.'

'But you did! Or anyway we half discussed it.' She wanted to throw her arms about Nina and hug her for the reassurance of it. Instead she said — rather lamely, she felt, 'You're just so good to me.'

Nina went on: 'Don't be so hasty, darling. Think! Suppose now, just suppose, that a friendship were to spring up between Selina and me, a deep friendship — different from yours and mine, of course, because each true friendship is unique — but just suppose. You wouldn't then regret this somewhat heedless welcome you now accord to the idea?'

Johanna merely laughed. 'Good heavens, Nina — what sort of monster do you take me to be? Nothing could please me more. Just think how unpleasant the contrary case would be — if you and she remained on terms no deeper than shallow good nature will carry any two people, while you and I . . . oh, it would be insupportable!' She laughed again, a cajoling giggle. 'Anyway, of course you and she will be friends. The best friends possible.'

'Yes, I think so, too,' Nina agreed contentedly.

They were now headed into the last glimmer of the dying day — a band of paler darkness on the western horizon, much of it obscured by the vast bulk of Tregathennan Hill. A mild, damp autumnal breeze blew steadily from the southwest; its unrelenting evenness somehow managed to strike a deeper chill than a cooler but more gusty wind would have managed. There was never a moment's respite from it; nor, up there on the high moor at Wheal Dream, was there any shelter, either.

'Brrr!' Nina huddled tighter into her clothes. 'At times

174

like this one's very soul leans towards Italy.'

Johanna chuckled.

'Seriously, Jo, what d'you think of it? It's your idea, after all — to travel somewhere warm?'

They were passing a cabin, whose door was open to allow the smoke to escape. A woman squatted before the fire, puffing up the furze wood to a merry blaze, which made the surrounding darkness deeper yet.

'Now there's a task would suit me at this particular moment,' Johanna replied, cupping her gloves around the warm back plate of the gig lamp.

'We could go the Holy Land. It's never cold there.'

'Mmmmm!' Johanna yielded to what she thought was pure fantasy.

'I imagine the Visicks will feel that such a visit would add respectability to what might otherwise seem a most secular jaunt, eh?'

Johanna realized they were talking of everyday possi-bilities, not idle daydreams. 'The Holy Land?' she repeated in tones that Nina had hoped for the first time around.

'Why not? We could sail directly to Ostia, see Rome, Venice, on down to Naples, and then take another boat for Beyrout. Or Joppa or somewhere.'

She could not have picked a more unfortunate name out of her somewhat hazy geography of that region, for the nearest village to Nineveh House was also called Joppa — after biblical precedent, to be sure. A moment later Johanna was wondering how she could have forgotten Hal, even for a moment; and as for an extended tour that would put the greater part of an entire continent between them . . . well, it was unthinkable.

'Would we be safe, travelling alone?' she asked. 'Three females, I mean?'

Nina laughed. 'We are no longer in the Dark Ages, you know.'

'I suppose not.'

'What are you afraid of, Jo? D'you imagine that Uncle Abanazer, the wicked slave trader, will drug you in his remote caravanserai and you'll wake up a prisoner of the harem?'

'How awful!' Johanna shuddered theatrically.

'Yes and no.' Nina laughed. Then she added, 'Anyway, I regret to inform you it doesn't happen any more. The shipping line will arrange it all, including a trustworthy dragoman to meet you at the quayside. And he will manage everything beyond that point — camels, tents, bearers, safe conduct . . . everything. One is probably at less risk in the Orient nowadays than in Piccadilly. So there's absolutely no need to hire a manservant here.'

Johanna was wondering how she could possibly describe what love was like to someone who had either never experienced it or was busy suppressing its memory. 'Well, it would be agreeable,' she said in what she hoped was a suitably grateful tone. 'D'you know — since leaving Lanfear House I've hardly thought of the old place. Just once, that's all — and of course when the two of them called yesterday. But otherwise it's just — pfft! That's rather frightening, don't you think?'

'What brought this up suddenly?' Nina craned forward, seeking the paler ribbon of the road between the dark ramparts of the stone hedges that crowded it on either side.

'When you mentioned Joppa just now, it made me think of Nineveh House, and then Hal, and then me and Lanfear . . .'

Nina mentally kicked herself but said nothing.

'Who's arranging the meals, I wonder? Who's counting the linen in and out? Who's doing the marketing?'

Nina chuckled. 'Yes. I imagine your aunt is just beginning to realize what their petty meanness over the years has now cost them.' She glanced shrewdly at Johanna, whose profile was gilded by the light of the lamp. 'D'you feel the slightest pang?'

'Of conscience?'

'Of anything. Regret, remorse. . . anything?'

Johanna smiled and shook her head. 'Mind you — if we hadn't met . . . I don't know. You make it so very easy, Nina dear, for me not to feel anything of that sort.'

Nina leaned over and kissed her on the cheek. Johanna favoured the spot with the tip of her gloved finger. 'I wish. . .' she began.

'Yes?' Nina prompted when no other words came.

'I wish I had your sort of. . . I wish I could be passionate and impulsive like you, Nina. I do feel things, you know, but I don't seem able to express them. It didn't help to express any sort of feelings at Lanfear House.'

'I can just imagine! On the other hand, some people simply aren't passionate and impulsive, my dear. Perhaps you're among them?'

'I don't know what I'm like. I know what I had to become if I wished to live in any degree of comfort at Lanfear. But I don't think that was really me. I suddenly feel empty.'

Slowly, rather casually, as if she were doing no more than simply pass the journey, Nina asked, 'And how are you proposing to fill that emptiness?'

Before Johanna could tell her she hastened on: 'This is really quite serious, isn't it. The idea had not struck me before, but now you bring it out into the open, I can see these are quite dangerous days for you — days of new freedom, when the old constraints upon you have been lifted. In your ignorance, or at least your uncertainty about what sort of person you truly are, you might fasten upon some quite disastrous course. Has it occurred to you? I wonder.'

Johanna shifted her seat uncomfortably. 'Not in so many words. I mean I could never express it as clearly as that. But I suppose some such fear has been lurking at the back of my mind.' After a moment she added, '*Disastrous* is going a little far, perhaps?'

'Oh, don't you believe it. There are so many disasters open to us women. Our way is beset with them. "When lovely woman stoops to folly, and finds too late that men betray, what charm can soothe her Melancholy, what art can wash her guilt away?" It's still true today, you know.'

'But do all men betray?' Johanna spoke as though she, too, were pursuing the most theoretical sort of discussion.

'All,' Nina assured her.

'Even the Colonel? I don't mean to pry, but...'

'Even he.'

'And didn't you mind?'

Nina sighed. 'Ours was an arranged marriage, you see. If it works, it's far and away the best kind. You begin cool and with your expectations low. And then month by month there are these constant little surprises, as you slowly warm to each other. And your expectations feed on this modest diet and so they, too, gain slowly in strength. In the end it was more...marvellous than either of us deserved or had any right to expect. But the other way − the passionate love match − well, I never knew a love that started hot which did not swiftly cool − or burn itself out in one wild feast of incandescence.'

Johanna held her peace.

'Have I upset you?' Nina asked gently.

'No, not at all. You must be right. At least, it sounds all too true.' She sighed. 'I was just thinking of Selina. She said, or sort of hinted at, something along those lines when we were talking about Doctor Moore's visit − the day he came, in fact. She said she would much prefer an arranged marriage and no nonsense about love.'

'My my,' Nina said admiringly. 'Not a common sentiment among young women today. She sounds extremely mature.'

Johanna laughed. 'Then I must be telling it all wrong. Actually, she was terrified. If maturity is readiness, then she is completely unready. It's awful to be talking about her like this, but I feel I have to tell you since it's through me, really − or something I said − that you've invited her to stay at Liston Court.'

'Go on. I don't think you're being in the least disloyal.'

'It's hard to find the words. She was afraid of ... marriage itself. Of having to be near Tony ... to let him be her ... husband.'

'It's all right, darling. I understand perfectly.' Nina cleared her throat hesitantly. 'And I take it you understand it, too?'

'Well, that's what I was coming to. You see, when she poured out these fears to me, I naturally assumed she was terrified of all that sort of thing. But the other day, when I told her I'd surprised her brother Terence in bed with one of the maidservants, she...'

'Johanna!' Nina's cry even startled the horse and she had to spend a moment or two getting him in hand again.

'What?'

'Nothing.' Nina laughed, more at herself than anything. 'It's just that you never cease to surprise me. Go on. I'm sorry I interrupted. When you told her you saw Terence in bed with a maid — what then? Dear, oh dear!'

'Well, she showed a most unbecoming and unladylike interest in the whole subject and pressed me with questions.'

'Whereas you, of course,' Nina said with gentle irony, 'treated the entire episode in the spirit of some naturalist observing a pair of bugs coupling in an obscure corner of the garden!'

'Not in the least. To start with I was too surprised to be shocked, and then I was too afraid of being discovered to develop any other feelings about it at all.'

'So where does that leave us? Do you share your cousin's terror of the the marriage bed? Or are you indifferent...or what?'

After a silence Johanna replied, 'I think, when the moment arrives, it'll be all right.'

'All right.' Nina's echo of the prophecy blew it away like the most trivial chaff. 'That's all, is it? Well, my dear, I hope it may be so but I'll tell you this — I believe Selina's terrors hold out greater promise for her than your calm anticipation holds out for you.'

The words struck a chill into Johanna's very bones. Like almost everything Nina said, they had the ring of the profoundest truth — something she herself could never have arrived at in a whole lifetime of thinking. She wanted to throw herself upon the rock of that certainty, cling to it, beg Nina to teach her all she had learned. At the very least she simply craved to be told what to do...

'Of course, it all depends on what you really want out of life,' Nina added, to soften her judgement.

What do I want? Johanna wondered. *To be more passionate, more impulsive, more outgoing...more alive.* 'At the moment,' she said, 'what I really want is a nice hot cup of tea.'

Chapter Nineteen

Hal returned to Liston Court in time for dinner.

'We hear you're the grandest man that ever sat a horse,' Nina challenged when the meal was nearly over and he was at his most relaxed.

He laughed. 'Hamill Oliver, eh? Did he call here?'

'No, we called on him,' Johanna explained, remembering how the man's attentions had so angered Hal. Not once since the meal began had he looked at her — not in the eyes, anyway.

He stared at the tablecloth a moment, forcing a smile. 'You'll be weary of it soon enough, Lady Nina,' he told her.

'Of what, pray?'

'There's many an idle gentleman in Cornwall, fretting at the thought of your portion, all unused, and . . .'

'But I am using it, Mr Penrose.'

'. . . and wondering when to start paying his court. But I must say — I think little Oliver's a mite quick off his marks.'

'You do him an injustice, sir. It's my opinion his interest is firmly attached elsewhere. Er — did you know that Miss Rosewarne is of the Tribe of the Bewitchers? A Celtic clan from the days of Tristan and Isolde, if I understood the man aright.'

The smile faded but still he did not look in Johanna's direction. 'So,' he said, 'you also visited Wendron? Not the most populated hamlet in Cornwall.'

'Never mind what *we* were doing there . . .' Nina let the rest of the sentence hang.

'Ah.' He conceded the point. 'Very well. Since it was your horseshoes I wore down, I'd best confess it: I did not go within a dozen miles of Wheal Vor today. I went to Redruth, instead.'

'Upon an errand? An impulse? A whim?'

'An impulse of a kind — though not my own. I have accepted a job for the railway company.'

'Driving a train?' Johanna asked excitedly, for a railway engineer was *the* heroic figure of the age.

'No, no. Not regular work. Just a job.'

'Just a job?' Nina echoed.

'Aye.' He attempted a Yorkshire accent. 'Boot ah'm bound to keep it seeecret, see thee, while ah'm done.'

Despite this caveat, Nina could see he was bursting to tell someone. 'Here's an excellent Barsac,' she assured him, signalling the footman to fill his glass well.

'Shall you have to move to Redruth?' Johanna asked.

'I think not, Miss Rosewarne.' His eyes wandered vaguely near her and moved away again.

'You surely can't go back to Nineveh?'

'No, but I have a good friend, Charley Vose, whose trade would suffer little for helping me...'

'The man who owns the Golden Ram at Goldsithney?' Johanna was surprised. The fellow was notorious throughout the whole of west Cornwall — a crony of criminals, a promoter of dogfights, cockfights, and bareknuckle brawls, a master of smuggling, a womanizer who had worn out three wives...how could anyone call him a good friend?

'Oh, he's not as scarlet as they paint him,' Hal replied. 'And he brews a dashed fine pint of ale. Poor old Charley's the butt of every idle tongue in West Penwith, but he's not done a hundredth part of what he's credited with.'

'Well, his looks certainly match his reputation.'

'There's his trouble, in a word. And I'm sure it's most convenient for the constabulary. When they can't pin a crime to its true author, they may always abandon it, like a foundling, on the doorstep of the Golden Ram, instead.'

'He does little to disabuse the world of the opinion,' Nina commented.

'What sheep ever resented the reputation of a wolf?' he replied. 'Besides, Goldsithney will suit me well while this job lasts. It's but a hop and a skip to the railway, where I may ride gratis to and from Redruth each day.'

'So now we know that the job is on the railway and in Redruth.' Nina commented.

He hesitated. 'In that district,' he admitted.

'It must pay well. You're like a man who lost sixpence and found a shilling. But drink up. You're being left behind.' Again that signal to the footman.

'Shall we see you at all in Helston?' Johanna asked. She wished he would look at her just once.

He sighed, unconvincingly. 'My time will be pretty well taken up, I fear.'

'Oh, then perhaps it doesn't pay so well,' Nina said in a disappointed tone, suspecting that was his weakest flank.

He chuckled to himself. 'It will do for me.'

His hint-dropping secrecy set both women thinking hard — and along more or less the same path. The talk of railways — even before his stab at a Yorkshire voice — instantly reminded them of Mr Cunningham, who had spoken so loudly of all the new lines with bills before parliament. Nina, who would never rush a fence sidelong if there was a clear run at it, said, 'I've been told that that fellow Cunningham. . . you remember? Mrs Knox's nephew?' She paused, forcing him to reply.

He laughed. 'If you're on a fishing expedition, Lady Nina, I'll save you the trouble.'

'Yes?' she prompted when he did not immediately go on.

'When we're private,' he replied, glancing at the footmen and butler.

'That'll be all,' Nina told them. 'Leave the port and brandy.'

The moment the servants had gone she turned to Hal again. 'Well?'

'You were about to tell me something you'd heard,' he reminded her.

'Oh. . .' Nina had forgotten what she had intended saying; she plucked the first notion out of the air: 'I'm told he was seen calling upon Grylls's Bank in Helston today.'

'Today?'

'It made me wonder if there was some investment afoot. I have a shilling or two to spare at the moment. But never mind that. Tell us this deep and deadly secret of yours, do!'

He glanced at each in turn. Johanna felt her insides turn

over. 'It's to go no farther than this table,' he warned.

Both women nodded fervently.

'I am commissioned to survey a new line.' He turned to Nina. 'So there may be investments in the offing. But I doubt our Mr Cunningham was seen in Helston today – because he's the man I met in Redruth. He's the one who's commissioned me.' He chuckled at the memory. 'The poor fellow's been attempting the work on his own. He's got the best surveying tools I've ever seen and he's not been able to put a single mark to paper.'

'Why ever not?'

'I don't think he has the first idea. I never saw a man more out of his depth.'

'This new line. . .' Nina began.

'Yes. It's to run from Truro to. . .to Falmouth.'

'Oh, really?' Nina's interest in the location seemed little more than polite. 'But tell us about Cunningham. Such an all-confident fellow – and you say he's made an almighty hames of his work?'

'He's like that duke who designed his own palace and forgot to put in any staircases. Not that *I'm* complaining! He's paying me right royally to take over the survey – indeed, I'm to do it from scratch, as the racing fraternity say.' He laughed at an unintended joke. 'That's all he's done – scratch about at the starting line.'

Nina's eyes congratulated him. 'Whereas you're sure of running the full course?' She handed him the decanter.

His smile persisted as he helped himself and passed it on to Johanna. 'I'll walk it, Lady Nina. In fact, I walked most of it today. What the poor fellow failed to grasp, you see, was. . .I say, that's a good drop of port.'

'The brandy has its champions, too. Did you ever try them mixed? Angel's Breath, some call it.'

He warded off the suggestion. 'No, thank you. Talking of angels, I've a nag of my own eating its head off in the stable up there. And unless I keep a clear head and steer him towards Goldsithney, he'll take me to Nineveh by long habit.'

'Are you going tonight?' Johanna cried out in disappointment.

'You were telling us about poor Cunningham,' Nina reminded him. 'What was it he failed to realize?'

For a moment Hal could not remember. He shook his head and pushed his glass a token inch or two from him. 'What he didn't realize,' he repeated slowly, and then the memory came: 'Ah yes. What he didn't realize was that the stream has done most of the survey for us. It has carved out a valley, running as the crow flies, almost into Truro. And along the side of that valley we can find a level contour for our line. A Brunel or a Telford could survey it in his head.'

'The Fal?' Johanna asked.

He stared at her uncomprehendingly and said, 'Quite. All we do, you see, to make the flat bed of the track, is level a bit of the hillside...'

'The River Fal,' Johanna repeated.

'Ah! Yes, of course, the River Fal. Anyway, by cutting away the rock on the uphill side and tipping the spoil on the downhill side...well, that's how it's done. And if we come to a stretch where we need more of an embankment, why, all we do is shift the line a few yards uphill, to make the cutting deeper – and there's our extra spoil. Poor Cunningham! No idea!'

'But doesn't the Fal...' Johanna began.

Nina silenced her with a significant raising of an eyebrow. 'Won't you find it strange?' she asked Hal. 'Working out of doors, in full daylight, in all weathers? You'll have to wrap up good and warm.' They worked naked down the mines, which was why they'd never let women go below, or so they said. Her mind's eye had often relished the imagined scene.

Meanwhile Hal was saying, 'Talking of investments, I think I shall put my few shillings into a set of the large-scale Ordnance Survey and a good stock of coal. Nine-tenths of this job will be desk work. I could do it at the bottom of the deepest mine in Cornwall. Or in my room at the Golden Ram, anyway.'

Half an hour later they bade him farewell. They watched the dark swallow him up, until he was no more than a dwindling footfall on the gravel. 'Steady enough for a man who's put away so much,' Nina commented admiringly.

Johanna took her arm and clung to it. 'Oh Nina, would it be a howling disgrace if I ran after him?'

'And did what, my lamb?'

184

'Just...I don't know. Just went as far as the Angel and back with him?'

'He won't thank you,' she warned.

'I wouldn't care. Not even if he whipped me. I can't bear to see him go so coolly. I *know* he's...' The words dried up. 'I just know.'

Nina put an arm around her and squeezed tight. 'Poor darling,' she sighed. 'Go on then.'

'For once in my life let me do a passionate thing?'

'I said − go on.'

She flew up the drive, heedless of the pain of the gravel through her thin cotton soles, and out into the darkened road. She caught up with him at the junction with Church Street, where the water was still overflowing its channel. 'Hal?' she called, stepping warily along the dry isthmus at the foot of the wall.

He turned in surprise. 'What now?' he asked.

She reached the wider footpath and hurled herself at him, making him clasp her for support as her impetus carried him back against the wall. 'Take me with you?' she begged.

He hugged her tight, too astonished to reply. But she could not doubt the yearning in his grasp. 'Anywhere,' she said. 'It doesn't matter. Even to Charley Vose's, I don't mind. Just don't leave me, please?'

Reluctantly he eased his grip. 'Jo,' he murmured.

She buried her head in his chest; if she'd had strength enough she'd have pulled herself inside him. 'Don't say no. Don't say no,' she intoned.

'I must.' He tried to disengage his arms but she clamped them tight beneath her own.

'You feel the same. I know you do. Why couldn't you look at me this evening? And the other night, when you fought all those...the way you looked at me then. What has happened to change you? Is it my hair? I'll grow it. For you. Just say!'

'Oh, Jo.'

'I'll do anything for you Hal. Please let me. I've never felt like this for anyone else. I love you so much. Just ask me − anything. No matter what. Anything. I'll do it. Only just let me be with you.'

At last he used his enormous strength. He pulled his arms

free and put them around her. The moment she felt that, she relaxed, let him ease her head from his chest, turn her face to his. . .let him kiss her with a tenderness that melted every last trace of her misery. 'I knew! I knew,' she murmured in ecstasy.

He went on kissing and fondling her until the storm of her passion settled. Siren voices were urging him to yield, telling him he, too, had never before felt such love, that Johanna was altogether different from any other woman he had ever known, that if he did not change his ways and settle with her, then happiness and he would be strangers forever. But a more practised spirit was also at work, countering every one of these seductions. He had, indeed, felt like this before and had always successfully conquered it. And what had been their names? It would take time and pencil and paper to revive even their memory. On the other hand, if he yielded now, he would never know another moment's independence. This sweet, adorable young angel in his arms, swearing she would 'do anything' for him now, would soon be leading him by the nose, granting and withholding that same 'anything' as her whim and his docility decreed. He steeled himself to reject her.

'Shall we be going?' she whispered.

'You must go back to Liston Court,' he told her quietly. She froze.

'No − listen to me, my darling Jo. You are my darling. I cannot deny it. I love you, but. . .'

She almost passed out with the pleasure of hearing him say it at last. 'And I love you.'

'Please listen!' He was a trifle sharper now. 'As you love me, and as you love your own life and peace of mind − listen. I am not. . .I would be no good for you.'

'Oh, Hal, good and bad − what do they mean? We are as far beyond the reach of good and bad as. . .'

'You don't know me at all. I say I love you − and I truly mean it − but a year from now I'd break your heart. Indeed, it is *because* I love you that I beg you now to turn away − forget me − recover yourself.'

'If I can't be with you, I don't think I want go on living at all,' she said flatly.

It was a threat he had faced before, more than once. But

this time, unlike any previous, he dared not take the usual risk and say it was her choice, not his. 'Then let's make each other miserable,' he responded, equally flatly. Still keeping one arm about her he turned uphill toward the main street and the Angel.

But she held her ground, tugging him back.

'What?' he asked.

'Not miserable,' she said. 'Let's make each other very happy.'

'Oh, Jo...'

'The churchyard's just up there,' she added.

He just stood there, at a loss for words.

'Don't you want to?' she asked.

'More than anything on earth.' He spoke barely above a whisper.

'So?'

Yield! urged the sirens.

'Let me make you a promise,' he said, grasping what he knew was his last, thin lifeline. 'I shall not marry another while you remain free. You see — I bind myself but not you.'

'I am already bound, my darling.'

He shrugged. 'You may yet think better of it.'

'Never!'

'Anyway. I shall not marry before you. And I shall ask you to marry me when I am able to support us both. You must know that I am in no...'

'Oh Hal! My darling, darling man! I have lived these last twelve years on kicks and halfpence. What support do I need? I can conjure a banquet out of the hedgerows if need be...'

'And patch my self-respect with what?'

For one fatal second she hesitated.

He drove the nail home: 'Or would you have me live without it?'

After a long, agonized moment she said, 'You promise you'll wait?'

'I promise.'

'And how do you intend...I mean, you say when you're able to support us...'

'Listen, this is my design. I realize now that I have loved

you since the day I pulled your hair at Nineveh. I fought it, and thought I had vanquished it, only to find it as strong as ever.'

'Me too! That's exactly how I felt — or feel now. In fact, when . . .' she reined in her enthusiasm. 'No. Sorry. You go on.'

'I was going to say that my design in taking up this offer from Cunningham is to amass a small capital — enough to take me to America, say, or one of the other new countries, where I will be able to multiply it much faster than I could at home.'

'And then send for me?'

'Or come back and settle here together. If you will still have me.'

She said nothing.

He folded her in his arms again. 'Well?' he asked.

'Would it be long? How long?'

'I could strike gold or silver almost at once. I know more about geology and mining than ninety-nine out of a hundred of your average fortune seekers.'

She found the bright side of his suggestion. 'Things are different in America. I've read about them. Their womenfolk go with them and endure the same hardships. They're as tough as men, too. I'm like that, you'll see. Send for me very quickly.'

He held her tightly one more time. 'I'm a long way off leaving these shores yet,' he said.

'And we'll see each other often before then?'

'Every possible moment.'

'Promise?'

'Promise.' Gently he eased himself from her.

'We could still go up to the churchyard,' she whispered.

He kissed her again. 'If you were any other woman, Jo, we'd be there now. Take it as a sign of your uniqueness to me that we are not.'

'When shall I see you again?'

'I'll send word.'

'But soon?'

'As soon as possible.'

At the corner she turned back and called after him: 'If I hear nothing after three days, I shall come out to Goldsithney and beset you.'

188

See! he told himself as he strode away up the hill. *The tyranny begins.*

Nina had changed into a chemise and was sitting in her boudoir drinking chocolate. 'Oh, I just had to get out of those corsets,' she told Johanna by way of greeting. 'You wait till you get yours. Did you catch him?'

'Like a plague. Like a fever.' Johanna closed her eyes. 'Like a raging fire. Oh Nina!' She danced a couple of pirouettes.

'I know,' Nina said flatly. 'You're in love.'

'I was in love before. But now I've told him! When the moment came, I could tell him.' She closed her eyes and laughed. 'And he told me.'

Nina said nothing.

Johanna's dance had brought her to Nina's side. 'Have a sip of my chocolate,' she invited. 'It's supposed to sober one up.'

'Oh, I'm not drunk – or not on wine.'

'Sit down, anyway. You're making me feel drunk.'

'I can't. I'm too...' She snatched up Nina's brush and comb. 'Let me do your hair for the night. I need to do something.'

Nina bent her neck obediently. Johanna plied brush and comb for a while and then burst out all over again. 'He asked me to marry him.'

'And you said yes.'

'Of course I did. Aren't you happy for me?'

'What do you propose to live on – if it's not too humdrum and everyday a question?'

'Oh, we're not getting married yet. He'll use the money from this railway job to fund him in America or somewhere. He says he may increase it there many times faster than here. And then he'll send for me. Or come back here and settle.'

Nina's glumness lifted entirely during this speech. Johanna noticed her smiling and asked why.

'Oh, I did not suppose you could be so sensible,' she said happily. Then, struggling to keep the scepticism out of her voice, she added, 'And Mr Penrose has promised to wait until then?'

'He says that while I am single he will not marry. And of

course, while he lives, I shall remain single.'

'Of course,' Nina agreed.

'You needn't say it in that tone. I mean it.'

'And so does he, I'm sure — just as I'm sure that he applies a far higher standard of truth to the affairs of his heart than he does to the affairs of his purse.'

Coldly Johanna laid down the comb and brush; but Nina plucked up her hand and pressed it to her cheek. 'Don't lose all sense of proportion, little swan,' she murmured. 'You have such a strong, intelligent eye for people and the way of the world. Untutored as yet, I grant you, but powerful nonetheless. Do not wilfully blind it. I fear you will need it before many months are out.'

Chapter Twenty

Three days came and went, with no word from Hal. Nina noticed how Johanna contrived to be near the front door around the time of each delivery, how she would ask the maids if they were *sure* there had been no letter for her, and how disconsolate she was at their invariable reply.

'I tell you what, my precious,' she said at length. 'Let us drive over to Falmouth tomorrow morning and see if some obliging boatman will take us up the Fal to Truro?'

Johanna brightened at once.

'Except,' Nina went on, 'well, it is such a contorted, winding sort of a river — we should probably not get the faintest glimpse of the great man himself.'

The words struck a chord in Johanna's memory. 'Yes, I thought that at the time — when he said the river had carved a *straight* line from Truro to Falmouth.'

'Have you ever sailed up it?'

'No, but there was a map of Cornwall hanging in the business room at Lanfear House always. And I don't remember the Fal as being particularly straight.'

Nina, who had privately consulted her own set of maps the very next day, said, 'How astute of you. I wonder if Brookesy ever bought the Ordnance Survey. Shall we go and see?'

They went to the library, where she made a token hunt before discovering them in the most obvious place.

'Well — it's not what any self-respecting engineer would call straight,' she commented when the particular sheets were butted together on the library desk before them.

Johanna laid a ruler roughly north-south, touching both

191

towns. It ran nowhere near the river.

'In any case, that approach to Falmouth would be impossible,' Nina said, putting her finger on the Penryn river, which widens to form Falmouth Harbour immediately north of the town. 'That's a busy navigation. The railway viaduct would have to be at least a hundred and fifty feet high for the masts to go under.'

Johanna stared at the map. In every feature it contradicted what Hal had said. A line along the course he had described would take the form of a backward S. Moreover, it would cut across the estuaries or creeks of seven tributary streams, not to mention the Penryn River.

Nina had an even more practical objection. 'The Daniells at Trelissick would never permit a line through their demesne.' Her finger ran inland, pausing at other noble seats and listing their owners. 'The Sprys, the Devonshires, the Tweedys, the Gossetts – and the Lemons at Carclew – none of them is going to want the beastly thing within a mile of their windows, either. This line – if it exists at all – is going to have to run higher up the Devoran valley, where the countryside is already in ruins.'

'Perhaps if they were given shares?' Johanna suggested.

'Shares?' the other laughed dismissively. 'Shares in what? Where are the profits? Why on earth build a line from Falmouth to Truro when there's a perfectly navigable river to connect them?'

Johanna stared at her, unwilling to accept the obvious conclusion.

'Men are...they can be very devious at times,' Nina added gently.

'But I can't believe it of Hal. It would be such a pointless fib to tell. Especially if he *is* surveying a line somewhere near Truro.'

'Ah!' Nina leaped in. 'So, like me, you doubt that, too?'

'Of course not.' She turned again to the map, seeking any stream that ran more or less as the crow flies toward Truro.

'We exercise a strange sort of power over them,' Nina was saying. 'And they can't really cope with it. Or, rather, they resent having to cope with it. Little Hamill Oliver wraps it up in Celtic twilight. Most of them spin plausible yarns to keep us at bay. And I'm sorry to say that Hal seems no different from the rest.'

'There!' Johanna said, pointing to an unnamed stream that ran from near Chacewater to Calenick, just a mile south of Truro.

Nina abandoned her purpose for the moment and pored over the map with interest. 'Yes,' she said at last. 'The existing line ends at Chacewater, doesn't it? Now if it continued to Calenick and then onward round the hill to Truro, which would permit a gentle downward curve . . . just look where it ends up!' Her finger rested four-square on the docks. 'Now that makes more sense — a line connecting Hayle with Truro and running through the county's richest mining region. There'd be profit in that — for a few lucky shareholders who got in before word of it leaked out.' She glanced at the clock. 'Listen, my dear — immediately after luncheon we'll go up to the bank and you shall see how a clever woman with the right sort of brains, like you, and a lucky one with the right sort of husband, like me, may combine to increase their fortunes.' She took Johanna's arm and, laughing, led her back to the morning room. 'Food for thought, eh? Who needs men? Except, of course, to go out there in the mud and all weathers to make it possible for us — and to feed us their absurdly transparent half-truths about it all.'

'We could go up the Fal, anyway,' Johanna suggested.

'When the warmer weather arrives, perhaps. And — er — what about Goldsithney?'

'I'll allow him a bit longer, I think.'

Nina smiled contentedly. 'And quite right, too. Why should you open your heart and soul to him, and give yourself so unreservedly, if he won't trust you over a simple thing like that?'

Selina arrived at mid-morning on the appointed day. Nina showed her up to her room while Theresa Visick took Johanna aside. 'Oh, my dear, there's such a lot to ask you,' she said breathlessly. 'We simply did not realize how much you contributed toward the smooth running of our little household and I'm sure we never expressed our appreciation properly.'

'I had no right to expect it,' Johanna replied awkwardly.

'All the more reason for us to have shown it. Your Uncle John sends his warmest regards, by the way.'

Johanna considered several replies in which the word 'warmth' had a more savage ring, but her only response was, 'Is there anything in particular you wish to know, Aunt?'

Theresa sighed. 'Yes. I wish. . . ah well, never mind. Tell me, now − little Margaret the scullery maid. She is to receive five or eight pound a year?'

'Five. It is all set down in the red notebook under the cash tray in the safe.'

'I know, dear, but I couldn't quite make out the cypher. And is she to receive her beer on top of that? You didn't make any note of it.'

'That's because − with all the servants − the bargain is for wages, bed, and board, which includes table beer and certain new linen. You may see the terms posted at each hiring fair. If you desire some particular variation, you must make it at the time, otherwise all are bound by it.'

Her aunt's lips moved rapidly as she sought to memorize this intelligence. 'And which maid is to clean the back stairs each morning?' she went on.

'There is a rota pasted behind the scullery door. It shows the daily, weekly, and monthly tasks appointed to each female.'

'I thought as much. So one of those baggages has removed it. They swear black and blue they never saw such a thing.'

'You'll find a copy in the top drawer in the old nursery.'

'Your top drawer, you mean. In your room?'

Johanna gave a noncommittal shrug.

'Talking of which,' her aunt went on hesitantly, 'are you coming back soon − to collect your things?'

'What things?' Johanna was surprised at her own sharpness. She had the uncomfortable feeling that the woman was tempting her into behaving in just such a fashion − offering glimpses of a power she might use; how long it would last once she fell for the bait and walked back inside that old trap was another matter, of course. The only *things* of value she had left behind were her diaries, and they were safely concealed under the floorboards of her old room.

'What things? Why, your pretty clothes, your needle-work, your. . .your writing materials. . .'

'My collection of seashells and pebbles?'

'Indeed.'

When Johanna said nothing further, her aunt repeated, on a dying fall, 'Yes, indeed.'

The other two returned at that moment, laughing gaily. 'Some chocolate?' Nina suggested. 'Give the bell a jangle there, Jo.'

'Oh, Mama,' Selina cried. 'Guess what? Lady Nina is talking of a pilgrimage to the Holy Land.'

'Goodness gracious!' In her surprise Theresa dropped her pocket book.

'With your permission, naturally, Mrs Visick,' Nina added, picking it up and handing it to her. 'I've always thought it so important, before a young gel's horizons shrink to the simple domestic round, she should see something of the world, don't you agree?'

'The orient, though?' Theresa replied dubiously.

'The Holy Land,' her daughter corrected her.

'I'm sure *I* managed without anything so grand.'

'Yes, but suppose when I, or any of us children, suppose when we asked you about Galilee and Canaan and Sodom and Gomorrah and so on — suppose you could have said to us, "I have been there! I have seen it all with my very own eyes!" and then described it to us. Wouldn't that have been. . .'

'I don't remember any of you ever asking such questions. Not once.'

'Terence asked about Sodom and Gomorrah and you didn't know. Nobody did. And anyway *we* knew you hadn't been there. Whereas my children will. . .'

'To have children, my dear — forgive my interruption — but to have children it is widely considered necessary to marry first, in polite society, at least.'

Selina acquired a sudden interest in the plasterwork over-head. 'Yes, Mama.'

'Of course, your wishes are mine, too, Mrs Visick,' Nina said quietly. 'If you dislike the idea of such a pilgrimage, then we shall not go. We shall content ourselves with the usual grand tour — Paris, Vienna, Rome.'

Theresa's eyes grew wider as each new Sodom and Gomorrah was named.

'And Florence, of course. Those Michelangelo sculptures! Oh, what that man didn't know about...have you seen the latest engravings in the *Art Journal?*'

'We do not care to subscribe to such publications, Lady Nina.' She turned a more familiar face toward Johanna and began, 'Your father, on the other hand...' before she remembered her new character. 'Well, what's past is past.'

'Perhaps not, Aunt,' Johanna told her. 'How strange that this should arise just now. When you first cut my hair to this length, you know, it reminded me of a young pageboy in a painting by Veronese that my father showed me — an engraving in that very magazine. And now...'

'I'm sure I fail to see any...'

'And now, last week, when Mr Hamill Oliver saw my hair, he said it reminded him of a pageboy in a painting by Veronese that hangs in Pallas House!'

'Goodness!' Selina exclaimed.

'And today we are all invited there to see it for ourselves. And I shall know if it is, indeed, the same one.'

'We?' Theresa queried. The surprises were coming so thick and fast she felt confused.

'The three of us,' Nina explained. 'But isn't it the most extraordinary thing?'

'And exciting!' Selina said.

'At Pallas House?' her mother asked.

'Yes.' Nina frowned. 'Do you object to that, too?'

The woman shooed away imaginary flies. 'Oh, I don't know. The whole world's gone topsy-turvy of late.' She turned to her daughter. 'Be particularly careful what you say to Mrs Troy.' Her injunction widened to include Johanna. 'Old Mrs Troy, that is. Madame Ramona. She's a terror. If stones had a history she'd wring it out of them.'

'Then I've a menhir or two she may practise on, so,' Nina joked.

Theresa turned to her. 'The Holy Land,' she said. 'I wouldn't wish to question your taste or judgement, Lady Nina, but you're quite sure...I mean, it is...*respectable* these days, is it?'

*   *   *

196

They drove in an open landau and pair, with a retractable hood. Once again Hamill Oliver was waiting for them outside his cottage, Wheal Leander. 'I left the gate fully open this time,' he called out by way of greeting. He held the horses' heads while he added, 'It seems such a mild day and the rain has stopped — I though we might walk over the croft and through the woodlands to the house. But if you'd rather drive . . .'

The women looked doubtfully at each other. 'How tall is the undergrowth?' Nina asked.

'Oh, your dresses will stay quite dry. You saw yourselves how the sheep have nibbled the heather on the croft. And the rides in the woodland are scythed even finer.'

'Then we'll walk so,' Nina decided.

He helped her down, then Selina, and then — with a special flourish — Johanna. 'The Veronese is going to astonish you,' he promised her.

'I'm sure,' she replied, somewhat at a loss.

Nina murmured something to Selina, who laughed and said, 'Yes, always!'

'No secrets now,' Hamill commented as they set off down the garden.

'What, none?' she challenged him. 'Take care how you reply, Mr Oliver. We may put you to the test.'

'I shall submit to it at any time, my lady — as long as you spare me the verdict.'

Laughing, they went out by the narrow gate and onto the croft. He turned and walked backwards, spreading his arms to include all the women. 'The three graces!' he said happily. 'And not an apple in sight for me to bestow.'

'Then we are spared *your* verdict,' Selina commented. 'One all.'

He pretended to take the game seriously. 'Ah, but who wins the point? The one who spares or the one who is spared? Which way was the score before?'

'One love?' Nina suggested.

'Or love one,' Selina added.

Oliver blushed to the roots of his hair and avoided Johanna's eye; the three women dissolved into laughter.

He stared out over the ling and heather, seeking some distraction. 'Ah,' he said at length. 'I meant to tell you. You may prepare a pit for your menhir. There's a carrier called Tyacke or Tague — a whole family of them, in fact — in Carleen. He'll move it for two pounds and erect it for a further thirty shillings, which I thought quite reasonable.'

Nina thought so, too, and the job was set for the coming Friday.

'Did Penrose get his place at Wheal Vor?' Hamill asked, looking at Johanna.

'He's no longer with us,' she told him evenly. 'I believe he has lodgings somewhere out Godolphin way.'

'Handy enough for Wheal Vor,' Hamill commented. 'But that mine will have to close this year or next, you know. They're so sure the legal business will come to an end quite soon — and the judgement go against them — they've spent the last five years ripping out every pound of tin they can get, regardless of present dangers and future profit. And in all that time they've done no further exploration...'

It was the sort of anti-Grylls whine that had bored the three women through countless At Homes and dinners. By long habit they smiled and nodded — and let their fancy wander.

Johanna, secure in her love for Hal, assumed a mask of intelligent appreciation, nodding at Oliver's remarks, while she secretly considered his qualities as a suitor, in an entirely abstract sort of way. He was moderately handsome — well, pleasant-looking, anyway. Interesting sort of face. You wouldn't tire of seeing it about the house. And a good mind, too — well educated, but a trifle obsessive about things Cornish and Celtic. Still, it could be worse. Look at poor Mrs Nowlan, whose husband was building a one-hundredth scale model of Salisbury Cathedral out of fish bones. Haddock for breakfast, cod for lunch, whiting for dinner. Five lots of servants they'd had since last hiring fair. And Mrs Wearne, whose husband was only happy when he was photographing dirty, smelly little beggar girls.

No, on the whole, there was something to be said for an absorbing, scholarly sort of obsession like Hamill Oliver's.

'We are considering a pilgrimage to the Holy Land,' Nina told him.

'How very interesting,' he replied. 'Of course, you know that the Celts are, in fact, the Lost Tribe of Israel?'

Johanna revised her latest opinion: There was *something* to be said for his obsession, but not a great deal.

'Oh yes,' he insisted. 'When we Cornish return there — en masse, that is, not in dribs and drabs as pilgrims — the millennium will be complete and the apocalypse will be upon us. Will you be visiting Armageddon? That's where it will all happen, you know. Oh, I do envy you.'

For one dreadful moment Johanna thought that Nina was about to issue an open invitation for him to join their expedition. But then she told him: 'You must compile a list of things to do and see. And let us have it before we depart.'

Coming from any other person such a proposal would have sailed dangerously close to the wind but Nina managed to put that edge in her voice which made his exclusion absolutely clear. And in case his enthusiasm helped him to overlook the fact, she added, 'We'll report to you immediately on our return.'

The woodland around the Pallas demesne was now to their right. Oliver turned to them and said urgently, 'Don't look. Not just yet. In fact, may I ask you not to look up, or even about you, until I give the word? Shade your eyes, or bend your head, or something. Look only at the ground — follow my heels — until I give the word.'

'Is this some practical joke?' Nina asked.

'Far from it. You'll see. Follow me now.'

And he led them off the croft and into the woodland. Within a few paces it had grown so dark that they had difficulty in following his lead; but still they were too intrigued to look up and spoil whatever surprise he had prepared. Nina put an arm around each of the two cousins and gave them a reassuring squeeze. 'It'll be Cornish piskeys dancing in a ring,' she murmured.

Selina and Johanna had a struggle to suppress their laughter.

'I heard that,' Oliver told her with weary good nature.

'I shall be most dejected if it isn't,' Nina warned him. 'You have a reputation to maintain, Mr Oliver.'

'You won't be disappointed,' he promised. 'We're nearly there now.'

After a dozen more paces he stopped suddenly and cried, 'There!'

The women looked up and gasped in wonder.

He had brought them to an intersection of several rides in the heart of the woods, which were mostly of beech with a few elms and oaks in among them. All the trees that flanked the rides, though, were beeches. Their lower branches had been pruned away during their centuries-long climb toward the sky so that they soared up, up, up into the canopy, where a million twigs made a dense and intricate lacework of the afternoon light.

'It's. . .it's a living cathedral!' Selina murmured in awe.

'Exactly so, Miss Visick,' he replied, full of admiration for her. Had he said no more, their delight would have persisted; but he could not let it be. 'You see it at once,' he went on. 'A living cathedral. How men could know that this is possible and then go and build a great, dead monstrosity like Exeter or Lincoln is beyond me. The finest medieval church in the world is but a clumsy pastiche of this living temple.'

He skipped to the very centre of the intersection and beckoned them to join him. 'Tell me now,' he said as they approached. 'Standing here, looking about you, can you honestly believe in a God who is jealous? A God of vengeance? Could the God who created this space be the same God as the one who visits pestilence and war, famine and death upon mankind? No wonder our bishops and priests have fled to their tombs of dead stone! Nothing out here will support their old theology.'

'I'm sure you're right,' Nina told him. 'You know you've got saddle fungus in a couple of those beeches?'

Johanna saw the despair creep into his eyes and her heart went out to him. Poor young fellow! If there were any justice in the world — or even a little generosity — then faith and enthusiasm like his would carry some weight. Instead he was fated to play the gentle loon until he died. And there was nothing she could do about it, except, perhaps, ease the pain a little as she passed.

'It would be quite an idea,' she said to the other two, 'to hold an open-air service out here — in the summer, of course.'

'In a Cornish summer?' Nina asked. She pointed to some larger stretches of uncluttered sky. 'Mind you — an appeal for the roofing fund would not fall on the usual deaf ears.'

Hamill Oliver had sense enough to laugh and they turned downhill into the ride that led to the house. Johanna took his arm. 'You must forgive our levity,' she said. 'You know how confined a life I have led – and Miss Visick, too, to some extent. Thanks to Lady Nina's bounty we are much too happy with our freedom to be as solemn as you might have wished. But I promise you I'll never forget my first sight of your living cathedral.'

She could feel the tension in him. He was like a newly broken colt, his muscles still more than half-wild. She waited for him to say something but all that happened was that he grew even more tense. She released him then and walked easily at his side. 'How do you explain all those evils, then?' she asked.

'I believe the world was created by God but it was finished by a different Power. Satan, Beelzebub, the Prince of Darkness ... Belial ... men have called Him a thousand different names but they have all recognized the reality of His contribution – all except the Christians. Look at the contortions their theologians have to go through to explain it. Free will! God gave man free will. It is man who has abused the gift and thus brought evil into existence. But if God is so all-knowing, He must have realized what man would do. And all-loving? All-merciful? What loving, merciful father puts poisoned bait in the path of his children? And what about all-powerful? What father, seeing his children take up the poison, would not use every power at his command to undo the mischief?' He chuckled. 'They'll tell you there is no simple answer. And they devise the most convoluted theologies to prove it. But there *is* a simple answer, you see. The world, mankind – all that we inherit – is a battleground. A cosmic battleground between a cosmic Good and a cosmic Evil.'

'And free will?' Johanna asked, craning her neck to see what was holding back the other two. They appeared to be deep in conversation. 'Come on!' she called.

Nina waved to her without looking away from Selina, which gave the gesture a curiously dismissive quality. Johanna felt the first pangs of that jealousy against which Nina had cautioned her.

201

Hamill Oliver's voice impinged once more. She had missed whatever he said about free will; now he was telling her that Evil was not simply the absence of Good − the space left when Good departed − it was a Power in its own right. 'It is here,' he assured her, 'in this earth, these trees. In you. In me. It can exist alongside Good. That is the most frightening thing of all, yet the Christians hardly face it. The noblest man or woman who ever lived − the most Good − can also be the most Evil. Our finest actions can do untold harm.'

Johanna wished the others would hurry up and join them; she didn't feel equal to this sort of conversation at all. 'Is that what you were referring to last week?' she asked. 'On the witches' croft or whatever it's called?'

'Something of the sort. Are you interested at all?'

She smiled awkwardly. 'It would be a lie to say yes.'

'A white lie. There are white witches, you know.'

'I'm sure there are, Mr Oliver. And stamp collectors and people who build model cathedrals out of fishbones. What a dull world it would be otherwise.'

But, like most enthusiasts, he needed more than a gentle hint to stop him. 'Don't you believe that Evil and Good are quite separate things then, Miss Rosewarne?' he asked.

She shrugged. 'If a painting has highlights and shadows, I'm sure I'm not required to believe they were painted by separate hands. Tell me about your family's collection. Before my father died I was very interested in art. I wonder how much has survived in me?'

They were approaching a little gazebo. It guarded a rustic bridge over a small, artificial brook that was piped from the Pallas stream into the demesne and then ran through it to rejoin its parent lower down the valley. The other two women caught up just as they drew level with the door − whereupon they all nearly jumped out of their skins.

'Aha!' cried the unmistakable voice of Mrs Ramona Troy; it came from within the little building. The next moment she was standing in its doorway, giving each a look that would have wilted ripe mustard. 'The Visick girl. What is your name, child?'

'Selina, ma'am.' She dropped a curtsy.

'You are the first Visick to be seen at Pallas since. . . well, in more than half a century.'

'It is very gracious of you to have invited us, Mrs Troy,' Nina said.

The woman smiled acidly at Johanna and repeated the word: 'Gracious.'

'Indeed,' Johanna replied.

Mrs Troy turned to her grandson. 'You may take the others into the house, young man,' she said. 'I desire a word or two with Miss Rosewarne.'

She waited until they were out of earshot before she spoke again. Johanna, standing on the bridge, watched a waterlogged twig being rolled down the bed of the stream until it vanished beneath her. She waited for it to appear on the other side but it must have lodged somewhere.

'What is there between you and that young idiot?' Mrs Troy asked quietly.

'Mr Oliver?' Johanna asked.

'At least you know the collar for the dog.'

Johanna sighed. 'For my part, Mrs Troy, there is nothing "between" us, as you put it.'

'Well, there's a small mercy. You must realize, of course, that there could be no possibility of anything of that kind?'

'I don't think that is quite the question,' Johanna replied, surprised to find she could be so calm.

'Eh?' The other was jolted for a moment.

'I mean, it is not for *me* to realize.'

'Ah, I see.' The woman looked her up and down with renewed interest. 'You are not quite as I expected you to be, child. So nervous and tongue-tied the other afternoon — and now so collected. What has happened to you?'

Johanna gave her a brief smile.

Mrs Troy plainly decided on quite a different tack. 'Tell me, then,' she said, taking Johanna's arm and beginning to lead her toward the house. 'What d'you suppose we can do with the poor young fellow? He knows he has only the most miserable income of his own. He must marry a gel who can support him in the style to which I wish he would become accustomed. And what does he do? Goes calf-sick, mooning over you.' She gave a reassuring squeeze. 'I can see now you're in no way to blame, my dear, but I should be grateful for your help. The whole family would.'

'He knows nothing of me,' Johanna pointed out. 'Not as

I truly am. So it can't have any...'

Mrs Troy was shocked. 'But no man ever does! Not even of the gel he marries. If they did, the generations would end here and now. No, that is not our problem. Think again. Why did little Selina turn down so eligible a suitor as Doctor Moore? She seems rather too sensible for that. Tell me about her.'

Johanna hedged. 'I fear I know her almost too well, Mrs Troy. I don't mean I know her darkest secrets. Indeed, I'm sure she has none. But for everything I might say about her, I could immediately think of a dozen contrary things that were also true. I'm sure it's the same for all of us, isn't is? We are all so full of contradictions.'

She remembered in passing what Hamill had said of good and evil. Her spirit sank. Was his obsession going to claim her, too?

'Contradictions?' the other mused aloud. 'You are so fortunate these days, you young people. We were denied them utterly. If you were to encourage Miss Selina to start taking an interest in my grandson, how should you set about it?'

Cut off his tongue, Johanna thought of replying. 'Forbid her?' she offered. 'Or that might be too obvious. Point out to her the many disadvantages of taking such an interest at all.'

As she spoke, Johanna was aware of a quiet voice within her, whispering, *Judas!* She recalled her little pang of jealousy. Was that why she was saying all this?

Mrs Troy was smiling appreciatively. 'And young Hamill. How to' – she rejected *disabuse* and *cleanse* and settled for – 'how to *redirect* his thoughts in that more fruitful path?' Johanna almost treated it as a genuine question, but Mrs Troy answered herself. 'I'm sure some way will occur to you, my dear. You strike me as a most level-headed and astute young woman. Pity you've no inheritance – in all other ways, you'd be the ideal person to manage him. It will be a matter of a thousand tiny nudges, I think, don't you? Not some grand, blinding flash of revelation...' She sighed and a weary sort of disgust overcame her. 'Men,' she groaned. 'The labour of it! The sheer, unremitting drudgery of finding them and moulding them into the form we require

— and then *keeping* them there! Thank God it's over for me — except that, I don't know, having to do it by proxy is almost worse.' She patted Johanna's wrist sympathetically as she let go. 'And you, poor child, have the whole long war ahead of you, still. Well, if I can offer you any crumb of comfort, it is this: We can win, my dear. And with sufficient patience, we always do.'

'I'm sure I shall have occasion to think of it in years to come, Mrs Troy,' Johanna replied dutifully.

'I'm sure you will.' Her echo of the thought was infinitely sad.

They had reached the drive by now, a mere dozen yards from the front door. 'My other word of comfort for you,' Mrs Troy continued more briskly, 'is of immediate importance. It is this: If you play your full part in bringing about this consummation (which we both, presumably, desire), my entire family will be deeply appreciative — and will find some appropriate way to show it. You understand me, I'm sure.'

'Perfectly, Mrs Troy.'

Chapter Twenty-One

The granite exterior of the house did nothing to prepare the three women for the glory of its contents. Of course, they all knew the Pallas collection was famous; but that is not at all the same as seeing it for oneself. Nina had visited the house before, during an At Home in the summer. However, the entry to the drawing room on that occasion had been directly from the garden by way of the French windows, so she had seen nothing of the other rooms – not even the entrance hall. As with most houses, she had assumed that the pick of the family collection was displayed in the drawing room, but when Hamill closed the front door behind them, and her eyes grew accustomed to the dimmer indoor light, she knew it was not so at Pallas.

The hall was vast and was finished in a grand, classical style, rising to a domed lantern on the attic floor. Every available inch was filled with pictures, large and small, oval, round, and oblong. There was no pattern in it; portraits hung among landscapes and still lifes amid history pictures; there were frames of plain waxed wood beside elaborate creations in gilded plaster. From the dimmest recess glowed little jewels in water colours while there, in pride of place at the half-way landing, hung a vast canvas by Rubens, one of his several portrayals of 'The Rape of the Sabine Women'.

For a long moment they stood there, trying to take it all in. It was too much, of course, like being served all seven courses of a banquet on one large plate.

Johanna and Mrs Troy soon joined them. Johanna, too, felt a sense of wonder that bordered on bewilderment. Time and again she found her attention returning to one rather sombre picture, hanging beside the Rubens. It was a portrait of an unkempt old man standing in the gloom and looking out into space with eyes that had already seen too much, a man at once weary and tolerant of the world, sickened by it and yet resigned to its ways, a man so tempered by distress that he now seemed beyond all further harm.

'Is that a Rembrandt?' she asked, pointing it out.

'It is, indeed,' Hamill told her. 'One of the later series. You know them?'

'I remember my father telling me about him and what an awful life he led.'

Hamill smiled. 'I could show you some drawings of his darling Saskia that we have in a folio in the library. I don't think life was so awful for him, you know. Not all the time.'

'It never is,' Mrs Troy commented.

'But an artist's life in general,' Selina said, 'is fairly beastly, don't you think?'

'That's pure fasion!' Nina scoffed. 'If patronage decrees that artists shall be rumbustical Falstaffs, they'll carouse till the red rosettes run out. But when patronage wants its artists pale and consumptive and dying of the ineffable sadness of it all, why then they'll serve up the sickly spirituality with a malt-house shovel.'

They all laughed, even Mrs Troy.

'What did the old crow want?' Nina whispered to Johanna. 'Anything important?'

Johanna shook her head.

'Talking of the malt,' Hamill was saying as he led them into the dining room, 'would anyone care for a glass of beer?' He went over to an elaborate sideboard, inlaid with ivory and silver.

The women declined the offer. 'But don't let us deter you,' Nina told him.

'Never touch the stuff.'

'Is this *toile de Jouy?*' Nina asked, laying her gloved fingertips upon the wallpaper with careful reverence. It was green silk printed in the French manner with idyllic scenes of peasant life. 'We have the same at home, I remember, in a creamy colour.'

'And look – ever so many more paintings!' Johanna murmured, hardly knowing where to let her eyes rest next.

207

Proudly their host wandered around the room, blessing the air with a wagging finger as he called out the names: 'Poussin, Reynolds, Tintoretto, Rubens again, Gainsborough, yet another Rubens . . . Zoffany. The Opie portrait is old Sir William himself, my great-great-uncle on my mother's side. He's the founder of all this feast.'

'And he never married?' Nina asked.

'He finished her off very young,' Mrs Troy said grimly. 'After that he never even had a female servant. In the twenty years he occupied this house, no female ever crossed its threshold.'

'Not even you and his other female relatives?' Nina asked.

'Certainly not. My husband always dined here alone. That was much less common in those days than it has become since. Women were much more part of Society then.'

'Whereas now they *are* Society,' Hamill grumbled.

'Exactly so!' her agreement surprised him. In fact, it surprised them all — and she saw it. But she made no attempt to explain. Instead, she went on, with relish: 'But the minute the old tyrant was dead — Midsummer's Day, 1811, I'll never forget it — I was in here. I laid him out, old Martha Trevaskis and me.'

'Extraordinary fellow,' Nina commented.

'He agreed with the early Christians,' Hamill said, avoiding his grandmother's eye, 'that women have no souls and are to be considered part of the brute creation.'

The old woman stared at him fiercely but as she drew breath to speak Selina stepped between them with a teasing question: 'And is the affliction hereditary, sir?'

'Quite the contrary, Miss Visick,' he assured her solemnly. 'I seem to have acquired a double share of the opposite wisdom in that field — perhaps the extra had been intended for him, but it overshot by a generation and lighted upon me, instead?' Seeing her furrowed brow, he started to explain: 'I hold that any religion which believes it can safely ignore the Female Principle in the cosmos. . .'

'Hah!' Mrs Troy snapped. 'Little you know about it, you and your ancient druids! The Female Principle, forsooth! You said it yourself, young man. The Female Principle is taking over Society — and a more shrewish, censorious, carping, whining, vapid, mawkish assembly has never before been seen.' She looked around at the circle of astonished faces and smiled. 'It was not so in my young day.'

After a ruminating silence Johanna asked, 'Where's the Tintoretto, by the way?'

Hamill frowned in bewilderment and pointed to a 'Marriage at Cana' halfway up one of the walls. 'There. Did I pass over it?'

'I'm sorry. I meant the Veronese, of course. How the names come back to one! I'd forgotten I ever knew them, even. Tintoretto, eh!'

'What can you tell us about Veronese, Jo?' Selina asked, giving Nina a mischievous, sideways grin.

Johanna considered her answer. Pale, silvery, yellowy colours? Big, confident, sunny pictures? 'The Triumph of Venice' — his great masterpiece. 'Not much, really,' she said.

'He was an important influence on Tintoretto, so your confusion wasn't so out of place, Miss Rosewarne,' Hamill told her.

They wandered about the room awhile, looking at the pictures in silence, making only the occasional comment. Johanna, who had never before seen so many pictures brought together — so that one sweep of the eye could take them all in — was surprised to discover how differently the male and female subjects were portrayed. The men (depending on where your eye happened to alight) were emperors, soldiers, fishermen, masons, gods, fully robed saints or discreetly unrobed martyrs... and so on. By contrast, few of the women were modestly attired; those who were tended to be madonnas, or mothers, or mistresses of the household and their servants. The vast majority were naked as babes. Even worse — though perhaps it was the taste of the old misogynist who founded this particular collection — a disproportionate number of them seemed to be undergoing some form of humiliation or torture.

Here were three being thrust to the ground by grinning satyrs; a solitary bather was leered at by peeping elders; another half dozen were being carried off like sacks of swag by licentious soldiery (who wore full armour, of course).

Here was one pierced with arrows, another − in chains − menaced by dragons, a third broken on the wheel of martyrdom.

Her Uncle John, she thought, would give half his dividends to be allowed to wander here! The gentlest of these nudes simply stood in sylvan glades or sat by purling streams or lay in their quiet bedchambers and connived at the violation of their privacy going on outside the picture.

It shocked Johanna to realize that so much of what the world agreed was its greatest art bore this character. No doubt the pages of the *Art Journal* had told the same story, though she had been too young to follow it. Also, it made a difference to see many paintings hanging cheek by jowl like this, blinding you with colour by the acre. By contrast, those discreet little woodblock engravings, safely locked up in columns of gray text, were no preparation at all.

She glanced at Nina to see whether she was equally affected by it. But she and Selina were standing by a rare picture of the opposite kind; it showed a Hercules of a man and two beautiful youths on the verge of manhood, all naked as they wrestled a pair of sea serpents; the canvas flickered with rippling male muscle. 'These proportions,' she was telling Selina − and casually touching the bare thighs and torsos as she spoke, 'are absolutely classical, you know. I think they called it the Golden Mean. They measured I don't know how many dozen Greek statues and found they all used it.' As an afterthought she added, 'Michelangelo used it, too. It does make a difference, don't you think?'

Selina nodded vaguely. 'It must take an age to paint such a picture. And people stare at it for just a few minutes and then pass on to the next. I'm sure it's extremely disheartening.' She suited action to words, drifting away to leave Nina admiring the picture alone.

Mrs Troy came to stand at Johanna's side. 'A little overwhelming, is it not?' she commented.

Johanna smiled at Hamill who was hovering nearby. 'They are disturbing,' she agreed. 'Why so much... beastliness?'

'You didn't know the man.'

'Yes − but nor did the painters, either.'

The woman gazed at her shrewdly. 'How very true. That had never occurred to me. One just thinks of them as tradesmen who do as they're bid.' Outside in the hall a long-case clock struck a sonorous quarter-hour. 'I shall go and arrange for our tea,' she went on. 'Fifteen minutes, Hamill.'

He nodded.

She took Johanna's arm and led her part-way to the door. 'I hope we see more of you here, my dear,' she said. 'Remember what I told you — and don't imagine that your invitation comes only by courtesy of *that* young idler.' The words were loud enough for her grandson to hear. The woman patted her hand and cast her adrift with a movement that was almost balletic.

By chance it left her at Nina's side, in front of the naked men and the serpents.

'Well?' Nina asked.

'I honestly don't see the point of most of it,' Johanna replied.

'Oh dear!' Nina took her arm and called over her shoulder. 'There's work here for you, Mr Oliver. Young lady thinks art should have a purpose.'

'Heaven forbid!' he commented as he joined them.

'Oh, I can see purpose to some of it. Portraits. Nice landscapes — the sort of pictures we had at Lanfear. They brighten up a room. But why show the elders leering at Susannah while she bathes, just because it's in the Bible? Or St Catherine being broken on the wheel? Or this... wrestling match with snakes — whatever it is?'

'That's Laocoön and his sons in their death struggles with the sea serpents,' he told her. 'It was the turning point in the Trojan War.'

'Well, I can see how the Trojans might be interested. But to us it's just... well... look at it.'

'It's a universal story,' he insisted. 'Laocoön was a priest of Troy. He warned his fellow citizens not to bring the Wooden Horse inside the city walls. It was all a trick, he said. The horse was full of enemy soldiers. And he threw a spear at its flank to show it was hollow. But they didn't believe him. No one ever does. So he made a sacrifice to the god Poseidon. But the gods were angry that he'd married without their consent, so Poseidon sent a pair of sea serpents

211

to devour his two sons. He died trying to rescue them. And here they are, as you see, in their last moments of life. However, to Aeneas and his followers their deaths were an omen that the priest's warning was true, so they secretly departed from Troy. And as a result they were saved when the rest were massacred.'

'And that's honestly what you think of when you look at this painting?' Johanna asked.

He nodded vigorously. 'Don't you see — there's a universal message in it: Those who ignore true prophecy will perish.'

Johanna turned in disbelief to Nina, who was still half-lost in admiration of the painting itself. 'A universal message?' she asked. 'Can you see it?'

Nina smiled without actually looking at either Hamill or Johanna. 'Indeed I can,' she murmured. 'Everyone sees what they wish to see, my dear.' Then she turned to Johanna and said, almost as if it were an accusation, 'Even if it is something they cannot bring themselves to face.'

'Oh foldelol!' Johanna laughed uncomfortably. 'Let's go and look at this Tintoretto.'

'Veronese,' Hamill corrected her yet again. He led them back into the hall, where they were joined by Selina. 'It's on the top landing,' he explained. 'Immediately above us here.'

'In about twenty years from now,' Nina whispered to Johanna, 'I think Hal will look rather like the father in that painting with the serpents.'

'Oh. . .' Johanna gave a single tut, half-amused, half-vexed, and moved a little apart from her.

All the way up the stairs to the first landing her eyes were held by the great Rubens canvas — mountainous with tumbling females in insecure drapery. Though striking all the conventional attitudes of terror, they hardly troubled to make it convincing. She felt profoundly disturbed by the proximity of all that soft, vulnerable flesh to the hard, brightly polished armour. She longed to challenge Hamill to make some lofty universal moral out of it all, but managed to restrain herself. Knowing him even as little as she did, she feared he'd succeed.

When they stood on the half landing, immediately below the Rubens, he turned and flourished an arm toward the

212

opposite wall, above the stairhead. 'There!' he cried.

Both Nina and Selina cried, 'Oh!' simultaneously, for the resemblance between the young page in the painting and Johanna was uncanny. 'You could have been the actual model, darling,' Nina said, looking from one to the other as if no amount of familiarity would bring her to believe it.

In a daze Johanna threaded her way among them and walked alone to the upper landing. The years fell away and once again she heard her father's voice, almost as if he were beside her, telling her how devious and clever the artist was. But what had been only dimly apparent in the engraving shone here with a radiance that none could doubt: The merchant may have bought his nobility, but his page had been born with it.

Nina was standing beside her. 'It's an omen,' she whispered.

'Mmmm,' Johanna replied, thinking Nina was beginning to share her father's insight.

But Nina went on, 'It almost begs you never to let your hair grow again. Be yourself, as you are now.'

Johanna's disappointment at so shallow a conclusion must have shown for Nina asked, in slightly wounded tones, 'Don't you agree? What's wrong?'

Johanna stared at the two portrait faces, master and servant, and wondered how Nina could possibly have forgotten her explanation − or the more important half of it, anyway. 'Nothing,' she replied.

Nina was even more deeply hurt. She was not used to being excluded like that − not once but twice, and in short order.

Selina, standing a little way off and viewing the work more critically, asked, '*Is* it a boy? I suppose it is.'

Nina turned to her swiftly and smiled. 'Behind the obvious nobility,' she said, 'which the painter seems almost trying to force on us − as a conjuror forces cards upon the chooser...'

'Yes!' Selina laughed and clapped her hands, well aware what was really happening. 'Behind that façade there's a certain...what would you call it?'

'I was going to say − a certain nonchalant arrogance. Now that is decidedly masculine, wouldn't you say?'

Hamill, sensing that the words had barbs, but thinking they were intended for him, cut in with: 'On the other hand, there is also a demure sort of petulance. That light in the eyes — d'you see it? Something that says, 'Let others make the decisions — I'll amuse myself by criticizing them.' A feminine trait, most decidedly.'

And Johanna, who had endured her loneliness for so many long years, and who had been so overjoyed at the thought that it might at last be coming to an end, suddenly realized that nothing had changed. She was as lonely now as she ever had been. Here she stood, with three fellow humans — all enjoying themselves hugely — and yet her father, dead these many long years, was still more alive to her than any of them.

Her thoughts sped at once to Hal. No matter what Nina might say, she would go out to Goldsithney at the very next opportunity.

Chapter Twenty-Two

Charley Vose stood at the door of the Golden Ram, smiling at the world and wishing it could be twice as thirsty. Or twice as populous with the same thirst. Or with the same thirst as now, only more fairly distributed. That would be best. The difficulty with the present state of affairs was that the few drank too much while the many drank not at all. He had once worked it out that if everyone in the parish downed just a quart of ale a day, and children under six a mere pint, no one would ever be drunk and he'd be the richest man among them. But the preachers refused to see it that way.

'Make a law,' he told them when they came complaining of drunkenness. 'Everyone to drink a quart a day, and I'll affidavy you — no man shall ever pass drunk out of my doors again.'

They wouldn't even listen. The result was a downward spiral of despair: He was constrained to serve the drunkards or die a pauper; and the drunkards created endless sermon-fodder, which, in turn, kept away the very trade that would enable him to say no, and so take his pew among the righteous.

Meanwhile the gentry could drink itself under the table every night of the week and twice on Sundays and none would say a word against it. Discreet sin — that was the thing, now; any sin was permissible so long as it were discreetly done.

'Evening,' he cried out to John Barnicoat. 'How are 'ee, my handsome?' He winked. Charley Vose's wink was a most singular action; it never referred to any particular

215

mystery, or joke, or cementing of comradeship. Rather, when offered to a male companion, it suggested in a vague, generalized way that all men had secrets to guard; but when offered to a woman – which was more often the case – it hinted that all people had secrets to share.

'Proper,' came the reply, over the shoulder. No stopping.

Proper, right enough, Charley thought. There was one who'd never so much as call in for a sup – though he could put away enough at home. 'Hope your missis is better,' he cried after him.

Barnicoat stopped and half turned. 'How?' he asked.

'I seen she down Widow Jewell's this afternoon.'

That would give him something to think about! Widow Jewell sold home-made remedies to the poor, everything from love potions to cures that would prevent the fruits of love from ripening. Mostly honey and spices, laced with alcohol – as he should know, for he supplied her with the bulk of it. And she paid him in kind – the kindly act, as she called it. Either her or one of her twin daughters. 'Take your pick,' she'd say. 'And none is here to take no offence.'

Built up quite a trade in kindness, she had, this past year or so. But she was riding for a fall. She carried the profit on her back instead of into the bank. The respectable poor resented the finery; a ruin'd maid should look ruin'd – before sunset, anyway. And then again that little two-room cottage of hers wasn't enough. There'd been times last summer when the patrons had lined out to the lane and she'd had to send up to the village for temporary help from other kindly women. (Which accounted for the worry that Charley now hoped was gnawing at Joel Barnicoat's spirit.)

'Are you going to stand out there all evening?' Rose Davey, Charley's present mistress, called from within. 'I can't tend the bar and cook they pasties all to the one time.'

'In two shakes,' he called back. To Thomas Jellinek, who squeezed past him at that moment, he added, again with a wink, 'A creening woman'll live for ever.'

The man winked back. 'I'll tell she that. Her'll be glad to hear of it.'

Charley was about to follow him indoors when he saw a young lady in a pony trap, coming up the road; though the gathering dusk made recognition difficult, there was something vaguely familiar about her. He decided to wait until he could see her more plainly.

Yes, Widow Jewell and all her little jewels... they'd soon have the law down on them. Not discreet enough — there it was again. Discreet. If she were only firm with her callers — sent them up to the Ram to wait their turn out of sight — she could retire a rich woman without a stain. Charley decided he'd better have a word with her before the spring. Perhaps she could move some of her trade up to one of the empty cottages at the bottom of his garden, here at the Ram. Paradise Row, they called it, so what could be more fitting than that! He and she come to some amicable agreement. Where was the harm? He didn't invent the appetite, no more than he'd invented thirst.

He recognized the woman in the trap now. Whatsername, the orphan girl at Lanfear. Unlike him to forget a name. Thinking too much about kindly widows, that was his trouble.

Johanna Rosewarne — he had it. Where did she get they clothes, then? Not Widow Jewell's way, surely? My soul, a fine young cuzzle-an-taige she'd grown into! His heartbeat rose a notch or two when he realized she was going to stop at the Ram.

'Evening, my lover,' he called out. 'You'm some prinked up, then.'

Johanna stared back at him and realized she had almost forgotten what he looked like. His reputation had soured her mental portrait, so that the reality came as a refreshing improvement. Not that he was handsome — far from it — but he undeniably possessed a certain roguish charm. People said, 'He's a dreadful man, yet there's something about him you can't help liking.'

His face was flat and lopsided, almost babyish; it reminded her of a butter bean — and his nose was curiously bean-shaped, too. He had a baby cigar in the corner of his mouth, which he rescued from death with a brief puff every now and then. His eyes twinkled with jokes he would not share. And you knew — within a minute of meeting him, you knew — that never a thought passed through his mind unless it touched on his own eternal advantage and profit.

She glanced toward the upstairs windows. 'You have a Mr Penrose staying here, I believe, Mr Vose?'

'Beg leave to doubt that, Miss Rosewarne,' he replied evenly.

'Perhaps not at this particular instant, but he has a room here, I think.'

'There's no law against thinking. I'm not unbeknown to the gentleman, that's true. Now if I was to have some idea of the matter in hand...?'

'There's no "matter in hand," Mr Vose. I just happened to be driving to Lanfear House and I thought I'd come the extra mile and see if he were in.'

Charley raised an eyebrow. The distance to Lanfear was closer to three extra miles — six, counting both ways. 'Lucky, that,' he said, favouring her with a confidential wink.

'Lucky?' she asked warily.

'Yes, I got a delivery of ale for the servant's hall at Lanfear. You can put the boy and the barrel with 'ee, if you'd be so kind. He can walk back hisself.'

Johanna's heart fell. She had not actually intended going to Lanfear at all. She was just about to tell him she'd already paid her visit when he added, 'I know t'will be come over dark by then, but if you was to put the lad back here again, I daresay you might get a more decided answer to your question concerning Mr P., Miss Rosewarne.'

He knew she had no choice but to agree. The moment she'd spoken he had known it by the light in her eye, the tone in her voice. 'Very well,' she said. 'It looks as if there'll be a goodly moon.'

Five minutes later she was driving back the way she had come, with young Harold Blight and a firkin of ale as extra load, heading toward the last place on earth where she'd wish to be.

'A clever man, your master,' she told the lad.

'He in't so bad, miss.'

'And how long has Mr Penrose been with you?'

'Dunno, miss.'

'Two or three weeks?'

'I 'speck so, miss.'

Under further questioning he opened up a little. It

218

transpired that he was a lad of all work. He fetched water for the brewing, stoked the boiler, swept the yard, caught slugs and snails (or 'dewsnails and bulgrannicks,' as he called them), drove the mule with ale for delivery, cleaned the boots of any overnight guests...

'You clean Mr Penrose's, then,' she guessed. 'He doesn't have anyone else to do it for him?'

'No, miss.'

'No visitors at all?'

'I don't hardly think so, miss. He do just eat and sleep. Five o'clock next morning, he's out again, every day.'

'Even on Sundays?'

'Yes, miss. The railways do put passengers up Redruth, Sundays.'

'Poor man,' she said happily. 'It's all work, isn't it.'

''Tis for most on us, miss.'

Half an hour later they arrived at Lanfear House. The horizontal rays of the newly risen moon gave the place the appearance of a stage setting, as if a limelight were concealed somewhere in the shrubbery. In only two of the rooms were the lamps kindled, the drawing room and her Uncle John's study. She tried to imagine what they might all be doing but it was like struggling to recall a previous existence.

'You take the trap round to the back door,' she told young Harold. 'You may wait in the kitchen for me.'

Even by moonlight she could see that the brass bell-pull had not been polished of late. But the sound of its jangle did more to revive her memories than all her conscious recollection had done. It drew the house around her like a shroud, and she had to fight an almost overwhelming urge to turn and flee.

Mary, one of the under-maids, answered the bell. 'Why, Miss Johanna — you shouldn't never ought to ring. Come in, come in.'

Johanna drew a deep breath, expanding herself against all those ancient and subtle forces of the house; the moment she was over the threshold they seemed to press on her from every side, crushing her back into the old forms of meekness and subservience.

''Tis Miss Johanna,' Mary said, re-enacting her surprise

as she pushed open the drawing room door.

'Why, Johanna, my dear, so you decided to come...after all.' Theresa's voice faltered as she saw the beautiful clothes her niece was wearing.

Deirdre and Ethna came running to her. 'Oh, Jo, what a lovely dress! Where did you get it?'

'Lady Nina thought I ought to have it,' she said apologetically.

The grate had seen no blacklead this week.

'Oh, lucky you!' the girls chorused. And then, sourly, 'Is Selina having a new dress, too?'

'I should just think not,' their mother answered crossly. 'The very idea!'

'Well, if Lady Nina takes a notion into her head...' Johanna finished the sentence with a shrug. 'Still, I can't stop long, I'm afraid. I have to get Harold Blight back to Goldsithney. He came with a new...'

'Hah, let him walk!' her aunt exclaimed.

'I believe there's an empty cask to return.'

'They can send for it.'

'In any case, I promised Lady Nina. I don't wish her to worry.'

'I trust she hasn't let you out alone?' Theresa asked sternly.

'Aunt, dear — think of all the times I've been out alone from this house.'

'Yes, but...' The woman's voice tailed off. She could hardly point out that that was in the days when she had no value in the matrimony stakes. 'I shall have a word in her ear,' she finished lamely.

'I just thought I'd look through my old things and see if there were one or two bits worth keeping.'

There was a pile of fluff parked behind the writing desk.

Her aunt stared coolly at her. When she spoke it was with a weary, tentative sort of huffiness. 'I don't know why you should take that tone. They are all good, serviceable clothes.'

The girls mobbed her to the door. 'Can I have your embroidery, Jo? Can I have your seashells? Is it true Selina's going with you to the Holy Land?'

They followed her upstairs, where the racket brought

their father out onto the landing. Whatever he may have intended to say was choked at the sight of his niece. Beneath his surprise, habit slipped the challenge: 'Well, young miss!'

'Good evening, Uncle,' she called out as she swept on by. 'I trust you are keeping well?'

'Johanna?' He followed them up but she did not turn. 'Go below, you two,' he ordered.

'Oh, but Papa!' they whinged.

'Below, I say, or I'll fetch the rod to your backs.'

They retreated without a further word.

And without so much as a by-your-leave he followed her into her old room. It had not been dusted since she left. The mattress was folded and several of the wooden slats had been exchanged for ones that were even more splintered from the maidservants' beds above. She started to rummage through the drawers, uneasy at his presence. 'You ought to get a housekeeper, Uncle,' she told him awkwardly. 'They are good girls, but they are bound to take advantage.'

'That rebellious human spirit!' he sighed. 'If only there were some other way...'

'Aunt Theresa has many sterling qualities, I'm sure, but I doubt that the minute management of half a dozen maids is...'

'Oh, you're talking about them. I can't take a rod to maidservants, more's the pity. The law will have us wiping their noses for them next. No, when you said 'rebellious,' I thought you meant Deirdre and Ethna. Them at least I may chastise.'

'Much good may it do them.' She put aside her writing things.

'It never harmed you, did it?'

She glanced at the floorboard beneath which all her diaries lay hidden. If only her uncle would go!

'Did it?' he repeated.

'Did what?' She added a shawl to the pile, one she had crocheted herself.

'Your skin healed. It is as fair as ever it was.'

He reached out and stroked her arm, making her flinch.

'We miss you, little Jo,' he murmured. 'More than we thought possible.'

221

She opened another drawer a mere inch and then closed it again with her knee. 'I really don't think there's anything else I need take...'

'Jo?'

She faced him squarely at last. 'Uncle — when I think of what so nearly happened, and in this very room, on the night before I left! You surely can't expect that I might change my mind?'

'I believe your going was the shock we all needed, Jo.'

'And why are you calling me Jo all of a sudden? And being so pleasant? Not once in your lives did you...'

'I believe that if you came back to us now, it would be on such a different footing.'

'Please put all such thoughts from your mind, Uncle. Even if I were at death's door — and returning beneath this roof were my only salvation — even then I would not come back.' She gave him a wan, pitying smile. 'Now I really must fly.'

He spun on his heel and stalked angrily away. But he had taken only a few paces before he turned again, almost bumping into her. 'We'll see how long your little *affaire* with her ladyship lasts! You'll be back, young lady — and begging us to take you in again, mark my words.'

'If you say so, Uncle,' she muttered as she edged past him.

'D'you suppose all that woman wants is your companionship, eh? Your scintillating conversation? Pure and sweet? Well, you're in for some shock, that's all I can say.'

Johanna laughed. 'Well, she's hardly after my inheritance, is she.'

'You'll see,' he promised grimly. 'You'll learn what she's after soon enough, I think.'

All the way back to Goldsithney, as the trap wound its way among the black and silver hedges, Johanna played and replayed this absurd little scene in her mind. Her anger would not let go of it. How dare he! When she thought of the difference between him and Nina — his mean spirit, her generosity; his cruelty, her infinite kindness; his... But why go on? There was no point on which they were close enough to allow the slightest comparison.

She drove around into the yard behind the Ram, where Harold could more easily unload the empty barrels. There had, in fact, been two for collection − further evidence of the slackness now creeping in at Lanfear House. She asked the lad to give the pony his nosebag and went at once indoors.

Except for a bowl of what looked like pigswill and a large paper bag full of woodshavings, the dimly lighted passage was empty; but she could hear the racket from the four-ale beyond. The Ram was busy tonight. She had taken only a few paces, however, when a slatternly woman came out of the kitchen. 'Yeah?' she asked on catching sight of Johanna.

'I beg your pardon. I'm looking for Mr Vose.' Johanna thought she knew the woman slightly; she could not recall the name but somehow she felt sure she hailed from Penzance. She wasn't a bad looker, either − or wouldn't be if only she took more care. 'I'm Johanna Rosewarne,' she added.

The name meant something to the woman, too. But before she could respond, Charley himself came out of the taproom. He laughed. 'My soul, you was some quick then. What sped your wheels, I wonder?'

'I just came to tell you we're back with the barrels − so I'll be off.' She walked reluctantly back toward the yard.

He let her reach the edge of darkness before he called after her, 'He's home here now if you mind to see 'n.'

She made a brief play with her watch. 'Well, as I'm here...'

'If 'tis Hal Penrose, Miss Rosewarne,' the slattern cut in, 'he's in the room facing the stairhead.'

'Who asked you?' Charley snarled.

'I couldn't possibly go up to his room,' Johanna said, wondering if she mightn't, after all.

'See!' Charley told the woman, as if that had been his meaning, too. 'And look at this mess! Didn't I say clean it up?'

'Yes. And you also said do another ten pasties. And broach the new ale.'

Charley walked past her before he said, 'And now you may tell Mr Penrose he has very particular company in the garden.'

'Garden!' she sneered as she stumped away up the passage, wiping her hands, back and front, on her hips.

'Big mistake, that,' Charley murmured confidentially to Johanna as he edged her outside again. 'A housekeeper's a housekeeper and anything else is . . . whatever it may be.' He smiled at her as if she had already expressed sympathy for his unhappy state. 'You aren't housekeeping up Lanfear no more, then?' he went on.

'So it would seem, Mr Vose. Not that I was any such thing, mind.'

'You had the reputation without the pay, miss. That's the top and tail of it. All fame and no fortune. They're in some old pickle now, by all accounts.' Again he leaned close to her and chuckled, suggesting that the pair of them could, uniquely, share the humour of it.

Johanna said nothing.

He nodded toward the inn. 'Place like this doesn't run hisself.'

'I can imagine.'

He sighed. 'If my old woman had lived, now, we'd have made quite a go of it.'

She suppressed a gasp at the effrontery of this observation, for it was notorious that Charley Vose had used up the health and strength and purses of three wives. What had he been when he started? A slaughterhouse attendant!

'Yes.' He patted the wall affectionately. 'That's a little gold mine in there — or could be with the right touch.'

'Hah!' came Hal's voice from the passage. 'King Midas himself would resign the office!' His shadow preceded him into the yard.

'I'll leave 'ee in peace, then,' Charley said, actually squeezing past Hal in his sudden eagerness to be gone. By habit he turned and winked at them before he left.

'Well!' Hal said, smiling awkwardly toward her in the dark.

Johanna put a finger to her lips and nodded in the direction of the roadway. 'I'm sure he'll be trying to eavesdrop,' she whispered as she started leading him toward the yard entrance.

He looked at the pony and trap. 'Yours?' he asked.

'Yes. Or Nina's, really.'

'Then I have a better idea. You shouldn't be out so late – not alone.' He raised his voice. 'Harold – bring out that gray for me, will you? And his saddle – but don't put it up. Lay it in the back of the trap.'

The boy ran to obey. Hal added, 'It's Cunningham's horse really. I've just borrowed it.' He took her arm and led her toward the trap, which, to her surprise, he mounted first and then turned to pull her up.

'What's this?' she asked.

'I'm going to see you home.'

'Oh, you don't need to do that.'

He touched her cheek gently with his fingertips. 'I do, you know.' And then he turned to be sure that Harold tied the gray properly to the tailboard.

'You don't by any chance wish to go via Lanfear?' he joked as he drove them out into the highway.

'I've just come from there.'

'Oh.' His disappointment showed he had assumed her only purpose was to see him.

'You didn't write,' she chided.

The mines must be doing well at the moment; there were candles burning in almost every window as they passed. After a silence he replied, 'It's *what* I didn't write that matters.'

She waited for him to explain.

'D'you want to know?' he asked.

'I don't follow?'

'The words I didn't write...couldn't bring myself to write. D'you want to hear them?'

Of course she did – but she didn't wish it to seem like her imperative, so again she sat tight.

'I'll tell you, anyway,' he went on. 'I wanted to say that when we parted I was confident that, within two days, I'd have forgotten my infatuation for you, and that you'd become just another face with...well, rather fewer memories than usual attached to it. But just another face.'

She stared at the ribbon of road ahead; the moon was well up by now, and almost painfully bright. Why did he have to speak at all? Why didn't he just put his arms around her. She had felt his need the moment she saw him; could he not feel it pounding just as fierce in her?

'But it hasn't happened,' he went on. 'Instead I find you possess me with a force I have never before experienced.'

She stopped listening to the words. The sound of his voice, the nearness of him, sent shivers through and through her. At last he broke off whatever he was saying and stared at her. Obviously he had asked her a question. She strained to catch its dying echoes – on the air, in the outer layers of her mind. But there was nothing.

'Aren't you even listening to me?' he asked.

She reached up her fingers and touched his lips. 'Every word.'

He dropped the reins and took her head between his hands. 'Oh, Jo,' he murmured.

More words. She stopped them with her lips, which he accepted, tenderly at first and then with an increasing urgency, with a hunger that only fed on itself. One hand moved behind her head, to press her more firmly to him.

She raised her knee and slipped it over his, spreading her thighs; she edged a little nearer – closing the last few inches between them. His hand dropped to her waist and, with one powerful heave, he raised her on to his lap. She threw her arms about him and crushed herself against his huge body.

'Jo...Jo...' he whispered into the air above her head.

'Ssssh!' she commanded and raised her lips toward his face again. And again there was a long, hungry, ecstatic silence between them.

She undid several buttons of her coat. He slipped his hands inside and began to caress her back; she thought she would almost pass out at the pleasure of his touch. After a while she wanted him to touch her elsewhere. She pulled away from him, just a few inches, to allow him the chance.

'Jo?' he said.

'Ssssh!' she repeated and leaned against his arm, willing it to move.

'Talk to me?' he begged.

And is this not talking? she wondered. *Of a kind?*

'Tell me how you felt.'

'I thought I was.'

'I've been so miserable.'

'When you remembered me at all.'

He gave a dry chuckle. 'Aye — sometimes, to be honest, I must confess. . . sometimes I was able to put you out of my mind for a whole minute on end.'

'Oh, Hal!' It was half endearment, half frustration. 'You should have written.'

'I'm no great hand at it. But I will. I promise. From now on, I will. I'll write every single day.'

Greatly to her surprise, his words at last proved even dearer than the touch of him. The immediacy of her yearning dwindled — or, rather, the anxiety upon which it had fattened began to die away. She felt the first glow of confidence in the *fact* of his love. 'I've been so alone,' she was able to say.

He gave a single, surprised laugh. 'And I thought you wouldn't have a minute to yourself! Has her ladyship dropped you as fast as she took you up?'

'No. It's not that sort of loneliness.' She sighed. 'Hark at me! I must seem the most ungrateful creature who ever. . .'

'No, Jo, I know what you mean. One can be in the jolliest company and yet. . .'

'Oh, don't talk about me! Tell me about you. What are you going to write of in your letters to me? Can't you manage three a day — morning, afternoon, and evening?'

He laughed, and then, growing serious again, asked, 'Does Nina ever talk about me?'

'In what way?' Johanna was guarded.

'Does she. . . warn you or anything?'

She chuckled and snuggled tightly against him. 'She doesn't, as a matter of fact — but then she hardly needs to. It's a service I perform often enough for myself.'

He tensed. 'Eh?'

'I know you, Hal. I know your reputation.'

He said nothing.

'Tell me you came by it unfairly,' she challenged.

'I'll tell you one thing. God preserve in her innocent happiness the wife whose husband never outlived the curious schoolboy, the adventurous youth, the bachelor libertine.'

'It's the bachelor libertine who worries me. I could cope with the other two.'

He cleared his throat. 'D'you really wish to talk about all that?'

'It's the only thing that worries me.'

'Then you're wrong, Jo. You worry in vain. This love I feel for you is quite unlike any other, any previous...'

'And how often have you said that?'

'Never. Not once. Not to any other girl.'

'And there have been...many?'

'Too many. You talk of loneliness. I now believe that love itself is loneliness. To fall in love for the first time is also to know the beginning of true loneliness.'

'Why have there been so many, Hal?'

'Just let me finish. Perhaps it's also the answer to your question. Until now, until I met you again, I was happy enough – I mean, I could find myself happy enough with any one of, I don't know, a dozen or so girls. I thought I loved them all.'

'That's not possible.'

'But I thought it was, you see. I thought that all those poets who wax so lyrical over a single grand passion were just trying to mask their own inadequacy. I have known so many women, and all just peas in a pod to me. I took the same pleasure in each, and each found the same pleasure in me. And so every one of those easy loves progressed to that point of common pleasure – and there it lodged. I never knew a woman of whom something within me said, *This one and none other.*' He hugged her to him and added, 'Until now.'

She could think of nothing to say. She could not even decide whether there was anything that needed saying.

'D'you wonder that I fought it?' he asked. 'I resolved never to see you again. I even...' He gave a self-mocking laugh.

'What?'

'Never mind. It failed. The dreadful thing about it is – here are we, you and I, and our – whatever you might call it – our acquaintance with each other has not progressed one tenth as far (I do not mean as deep, mark you), but it has not progressed one tenth as far as my acquaintance with other women and yet, already, I know it will be utterly unlike anything that has gone before. With every other woman, I find I reach a point – a very shallow point, I confess – where it seems impossible to know her better. I stand, as it were, in her outer lobby already knowing that the rest of her is forever locked away from me. We might mistake it for love, might marry, might rear a family — yet *her* I should never know. I had almost begun to suppose that such was the natural order of things — that men and women are forever condemned to their mutual ignorance. And when you consider most of the marriages you know of. . .well, it's not an unreasonable conclusion, is it?'

'I suppose not. How is it different with me? D'you think we shall ever fully know each other?'

'Of course not — but the reason is exactly the opposite. We are not locked away from each other. Indeed, we are almost too open. The moment you are near me I feel an intimacy between us, between my spirit and yours. . .as if we're. . .not twins. . .more than twins — as if we were somehow extensions of each other. And yet I feel that that part of my spirit which is already united with you will, nonetheless, never know you fully. I feel I could spend the rest of my life learning about you and still die with an infinity left to discover.' His lips grazed her neck. 'Do you realize just how wonderful you are, my darling Jo?'

The sound of his voice, the touch of him, made her tingle all over. 'How is it lonely, though?' she asked — not really to hear the answer but to make him go on talking in those tones.

'Because our discovery of each other is not like the discoveries we learned about in school. When I learn something about you, the knowledge flows into me and *changes* me. Love is that infinite openness to change. . .an infinite willingness to break yourself up and be refashioned.' He checked himself and laughed. 'I daresay you can tell I've spent more than an hour or two alone these past weeks!'

'You mean you think you're rambling? I don't. But I still don't see how it's like a loneliness?'

'Because there is no longer any truly separate you and separate me. And yet from now on there can be no one else, either.' He sighed. 'I suppose you'd have had to be like me — you'd have had to endure one shallow love affair after another, or even at the same time, to really understand.'

He let the silence grow. Obviously, she realized, he now wanted her to tell him how she felt, what she wanted.

But what she wanted was *not* to tell him. She wanted him to know it all without any need for telling. Specifically, at this very moment, she wanted him to tie up the pony and trap and lead her to some sheltered spot and lie together and just be a man and a woman. She wanted it so much she almost burned.

'Penny for them?' he prompted.

Now it was she who sighed. 'Why can't we get married at once?' she asked. 'However poor we were, d'you suppose I couldn't manage for us?'

'Because I want to do the thing properly.'

'It's only your pride that keeps us apart. And it's going to cost us the happiest hours of our lives.'

Why couldn't they just go into one of these fields? There were horse blankets in the trap, and her coat. If she were any one of the other women in his life, he'd probably have been scheming toward that end all evening. All he'd need was one little sign of encouragement. Like, suppose, if she caressed him...*there!*

'Jo!' He was shocked. Then he hugged her tight, almost crushing the breath from her. 'Oh, my darling, please be...you are all the world to me. I love you so much I sometimes think I'll go mad with it. But please just...'

'What?'

'Be easy with me. Be patient. Don't encourage me to confuse you with...the other. Also you could tell me you love me, too.'

'You know I do. That's the only thing on earth would make me want you like that. Perhaps *that's* what makes me different from them? Can't you accept that and be done?'

'Soon,' he said. 'I promise. Soon. And now, since this might kindle...well...' He left the rest unsaid and lifted her back to the bench beside him, pulling her tight against him, side by side, almost as if it were a consolation. 'Let's talk of more practical things.'

'Very well,' she said at once. 'Why d'you have to go to America?'

And then he spoke the words that, in the long history of

human affairs, have done more to divide man from woman than all the cruelty, all the selfishness, all the hatred that ever was. He said: 'I'm doing it for *us!*'

Chapter Twenty-Three

Hal worked on through Christmas and into the new year. He finished the survey so quickly that he felt he had not earned his fee, or, rather, that Cunningham might be justified in such an opinion; so he filled out to a reasonable time — mid-January — by surveying the best minor variations of the line, with estimates of their time and cost.

Cunningham was overjoyed with the result. 'Well, Penrose,' he said, 'between us I think we may fairly boast we have done the company proud. I make no promise, mark 'ee, but there may yet be a bonus in it. We'll see.'

Though he had not actually been paid a penny as yet, it was all Hal could do not to spend this half-promised bonus at once in a grand celebration at the Angel. Instead, he accepted Lady Nina's invitation to a more intimate dinner at Liston Court. She had a triumph of her own to celebrate — the successful erection of Brookesy's menhir on the front lawn — so Hamill Oliver was there, too. Terence Visick evened up the numbers.

Before they went in to dine, Terence made a few hesitant plays for Nina's attention, keeping a weather eye on the other two men. To his astonishment they both seemed far more interested in his cousin Johanna, whose face was her entire fortune. That it had a certain beauty he could not deny; but for two almost penniless young men to be swayed by such a trivial consideration seemed to him the very height of irresponsibility. However, since it left him a clear field, he was not about to complain. All through the dinner his flirtations grew bolder.

The ladies left the men to their port, with the usual

injunction not to tarry. Terence, who was nearest the cigar case, opened the lid and offered it to the other two. But not one of them, as it turned out, wished to smoke.

'Our hostess commands us not to tarry,' Hamill observed, 'and for once I'm inclined to obey.'

'Yes,' Hal agreed. 'We'll just give them time to plant their sweet peas, and then...'

'A little longer, perhaps?' Terence put in. 'They must also have scope to shred our characters. It is my experience that a woman is never so charming to a man as when she has just torn him to fletters behind his back.'

They laughed. 'I can imagine our hostess at such work,' Hamill said. 'But surely neither of the other two.'

'Oh, Selina's up to it,' her brother assured them. 'And Jo, too, unless I mistake her. She has changed greatly from the maid who shared our roof.' He turned to Hal. 'You, too, Penrose, if I may say so — since you turned your back on Nineveh. Independence seems to suit you both.' His eye twinkled. 'Mind you, though it's no bad thing in a fellow, I cannot believe it good for a lady.'

'Why d'you say that?' Hamill asked.

The young man placed his hands together and clapped a silent applause in time with his words. 'We are too easily taken in by their gentleness and frailty, which is entirely assumed to flatter us and procure them their privileges. The reality is quite otherwise — and I speak with all the authority of one reared with three sisters and a female cousin. At sheer hod-carrying labour we may outpace them, I grant you — and the reasons for that would make an interesting subject for inquiry — but in all other ways they have us beat into a cocked hat. In constitution they are stronger, in purpose more robust. They are born with a picture of an ideal world already etched upon their brains — and with it comes an indomitable will to ... to ... oh, what is the word? Something between constrain and deceive...'

'Conceive?' Hal suggested.

Terence waved him away with a laugh. Hamill said he thought perhaps some other topic...

'Coerce!' Terence found his word. 'They coerce us. They have this indomitable urge to coerce us into remaking the world along the lines of that inborn ideal.'

233

'Ah!' Hamill caught his drift at last. 'Now there I agree, Visick. Yes, indeed. You speak, you see, of the Female Principle at work. Our barbaric forefathers understood it so much better than we.'

'Our hostess is a case in point,' Terence went on smoothly, as if he were actually developing Hamill's theme rather than his own. 'She has her own fortune now. She has acquired some considerable experience of the world. Her title guarantees her social position. And look what she is doing with it all! Why, I'm told she's in and out of the bank like a jack-in-a-box – a judy-in-a-box, perhaps – with orders to sell here and reinvest there.' He shook his head and pursed his lips. 'It is most ill done.'

'You think she'll lose it all?' Hal asked, beginning to worry for Johanna's sake.

'On the contrary, man. That would be too much to hope for. No, she's well on the way to doubling what was already a considerable fortune – and without so much as a word of manly advice! She manages it all by herself. What makes it worse, she has a cousin on the Dublin Exchange. I happen to know this because he's a close friend of John Walshe, who married the youngest Lemon girl a year or two back, you may remember. Anyway, it's dear Lady Nina who writes to Dublin – not *for* advice but *with* it!'

'You seem to know her affairs remarkably well,' Hamill commented gruffly.

'I hope I know the affairs of every eligible woman this side of Plymouth,' Terence responded. 'When one's fortune depends on the price of tin, as I hardly need tell either of you gentlemen, a wise man will elevate his vision to life's loftier elements –such as endowments, unentailed estates, and hard cash in the consolidated funds.' He smacked his lips. 'The port is with you, Penrose.'

Hal passed the decanter to Hamill with a smile. 'He's warning us off the widow, I think, Oliver old fellow. Wants the territory for himself.'

Hamill, who had drunk nothing but seltzer all evening, passed the port on immediately to Terence. 'Ill-bred as it may seem to pass comment on one's hostess, I feel bound to say that, for my part, he is welcome. The man who wins that lady's hand wins a great deal more than he bargained for.'

'That would be something for him to master,' Terence replied evenly. 'My purpose in speaking at all — and hang the breeding, I say, when one's living is at stake — is to draw our attention to the perils that now face two young and impressionable ladies.' He dropped his supercilious tone and spoke quite earnestly. 'You have heard of this scheme to spirit them away on some independent tour of Austria, Italy, and the Holy Land?'

'With your mother's blessing,' Hal reminded him.

'It was never more than mere assent,' he replied. 'Coolly given and now regretted.'

'But where's the harm in it?' Hamill asked. 'I myself have encouraged them with a list of antiquities of especial interest to people of Celtic...'

'Where's the harm!' Terence echoed. 'Why, they will come back to us thoroughly infected with this spirit of independence and rebellion.'

'I'd hardly call Lady Nina rebellious,' Hamill objected. 'If she is, even to the slightest degree, she is most discreet in it.'

'Indeed. She sits top of the class in that sort of cleverness. But her very refusal to consider remarrying is in itself a monstrous act of rebellion. It flies in the face of all the most civilizing trends in modern life. She is flaunting — to my sister and my cousin, mark you — she is flaunting the values of our grandparents, which were barbarous and tolerant to a degree that is surely no longer acceptable.'

'Then will your mother forbid this pilgrimage?' Hal asked.

'No,' he answered reluctantly. 'That would probably do more harm than good. The arrangements are too far advanced. It would be better now to use the time they are away to good effect.'

'Indeed?' Hamill remarked. 'May one ask how?'

'There is a circle of ladies in and around Helston, many of them still young and impressionable — in a word, not yet bent to their husbands' will — who are captivated by the example our hostess dangles before them. So, while her seductive influence is absent, it will be our pleasant duty to make them realize that civilization would come to an end if all women arrogated to themselves the subtly charming privileges that Lady Nina claims.'

Hal laughed scornfully. 'Good luck to ye! You won't change her, you know. And as for wanting our women submissive – "bent to our will," as you call it – well...'

'Oh, it is not our purpose to change *her,*' Terence cut in. 'In any case, we could hardly even attempt it in her absence. But what we can hope to achieve is a change in the climate where she presently basks. If we can reawaken her acolytes to a sense of their moral duty – of the obligations they owe to the society that protects them – then she will return as no more than an amusing eccentric. One of those charming, jiggety-minded females found in every circle, who set themselves up as exceptions but who, by their very failure at the game, only succeed in proving the general rule.'

'And the two acolytes closest to her?' Hal asked, unimpressed at Visick's scheme.

'When they see the harsh new light that shines on their idol,' he replied, smiling with a now unshakable conviction, 'well...women are the most wonderful conformists. It is the only weapon they hand to us.'

'I must say,' Hamill grumbled, 'these are damnably jaundiced sentiments from one who courted the lady so assiduously throughout our dinner.'

'What interests me,' Hal put in, 'is your views on our obligations – a gentleman's obligations – to womanhood in general. Since they are all, according to you, implacably opposed to us.'

Terence smiled at him pityingly. 'But there is no such thing as womanhood in general. There are women who see things as we do – and though they are principally ladies of our own sort, they are to be found in all classes, from highest to lowest. Our obligation to them is to protect the purity of their ideals and to make their duties toward us and our children as pleasant as God intended.'

'And the rest?' Hal asked.

He grinned and said, 'War! Win them whatever way you can. No weakness. No mercy.'

Hal chuckled and turned to Hamill Oliver, who was shocked at what he had just heard. 'Somehow I thought he was going to say that, didn't you?' He rubbed his hands and spoke to both. 'And now, shall we join the...battle?'

* * *

The moment Nina and her two young companions had settled in the drawing room she said, 'I hope they don't follow us *too* quickly, my lambs, for I want your opinions of them. Especially' — she turned to Selina — 'of your remarkable brother.'

'Remarkable?' she echoed in surprise.

'Yes. What does he imagine he's doing?'

Selina hesitated. 'Is it good breeding to discuss one's guests?'

'In his case, it's a matter of survival, I feel.' She laughed. 'And I never thought that breeding and survival might find themselves in opposite camps!'

Johanna answered, 'I imagine he's surprised to discover that neither Hal nor Mr Oliver is paying you court.' She turned to Selina. 'Did you know he keeps a notebook in which he lists every eligible widow or heiress between Land's End and Truro?'

'No!' Her cousin was both amused and aghast. 'How d'you know?'

'Because I've supervised the dusting of his room. That's how I discovered it.'

'But he keeps that bureau locked,' Selina objected.

'So!' Nina pounced. 'You've peeked and pried on your own account!'

Johanna smiled. 'He knows I know all about it.'

'Anyway,' Nina went on, 'tell us what's *in* it — what's it for?'

Johanna kept a cautious eye on Selina. 'There's a new name on each left-hand page — so, two pages for each female. And then it's like a miniature *Debrett* with a genealogy and so forth — but limited to the descent of title, if any, and wealth, or the expectation of it.'

'A pedigree of the beauty *and* the booty,' Nina suggested.

They laughed.

'Anyway,' Johanna went on, 'that can take the best part of the first page. The rest is . . .'

'You mean you've read through them?' Selina was incredulous.

'In his presence. I've even added the odd snippet from my own gleanings — things picked up through the servants' 'change.'

Selina shook her head sadly. 'Dear Jo! And to think how deeply I've wronged you all these years!'

Johanna looked askance. 'Do you say so?'

'Yes. I've hated you as an impossible ideal. Always so competent about the house...adored by the servants, who, even so, never took the slightest advantage of you...busy with your needle...cheerful, uncomplaining...you were such a monster of goody-goodiness. And now the truth comes out! Kissing the men at every sly opportunity ... spying on Terence *in flagrante* with the maids ... and this! Can you ever forgive me for misjudging you so?'

'I told you, I read with his consent.'

Nina grinned. 'You were about to describe the remaining page,' she said.

'You might call it a character testimonial. Cool but not unjust.'

'And how did he assess me?'

Johanna screwed up her eyes. 'I'm not sure that would be fair.'

'Listen, my lamb, you saw him at table just now. In this kind of war, all's fair. We are, you might say, our own Triple Alliance here. If we cannot hang together, they will dangle us separately.'

But Johanna could not entirely yield her own sense of honour. 'If you guess,' she promised, 'I shall nod or shake my head.'

Nina rubbed her hands, relishing the idea of such a game. 'Let me see – you join in, too, Selina, my precious – he supposes me to be vain, self-willed, headstrong, capricious...'

To each Johanna nodded.

'...beautiful, clever, generous,' Selina cut in.

Johanna shrugged, and then was surprised to observe that Nina was blushing. Selina saw it, too, and became embarrassed. 'I put the words into *his* mouth,' she explained.

'Oh...' Nina exaggerated her disappointment.

'No, *I* mean it, too...oh dear...'

Almost from the moment she had met Nina, Johanna had known how skilled the woman was at seizing on others' emotions and using them; she hadn't thought ill of her for it.

After all, though Nina's purposes might be 'selfish' in an absolutely literal sense, they were never spiteful or mean. But what had never struck her until now was that Nina performed the trick entirely unconsciously. She truly could not help it. As a mountain climber does not think twice about using whatever grips and holds his surroundings may offer — enlarging them or reshaping them if need be — so, too, did Nina with those far less tangible holds in *her* chosen environment, the feelings of everyone around her.

The deeper she thought about this comparison, the more apt it seemed. Nina was, indeed, a kind of mountaineer. She climbed among the peaks of the emotions, always seeking some as-yet-unscaled summit. The very air about her seemed to vibrate with wordless suggestions that she could lead you to... what? Nothing so crass as mere pleasure. It was more ethereal, more subtle than that. The plateau beyond that summit was a land where joy was the actual climate, the natural medium of life, as air was the natural medium down here in the humdrum world.

However, it was only a suggestion, not a promise. There was also something of the contrary about her — a sad, gray awareness that such a land might not even exist and that the whole of one's life, so short, so precious, might be wasted in a futile search for it.

Day by day, as she watched Selina fall under the spell of that suggestion, Johanna, who had been there before her, felt it losing its grip on her own emotion to a corresponding degree. How long before Nina became aware of it, too? And, more important, what would she then do about it? Whatever it might be, it would rise within her as instinctively as everything else.

Johanna rejoined the game. 'The thing you have to realize about Terence,' she said, 'is that he's exactly the opposite to you, Nina. Where you work by intuition he works by calculation.'

'Intuition!' Nina laughed.

'Yes. Look how you persuaded my aunt to let Selina and me go with you to the Holy Land. The actual arguments you used — if you'd written them down on paper — well, they wouldn't have convinced *me,* and I already wanted to come more than anything else in the world. But Terence... well'

− she turned to her cousin − 'you tell her how he'd have gone about it.'

'He'd have set forth twenty Grand Reasons and argued the hind leg off her.'

'There.' Johanna's hands delivered the verdict to Nina. 'Also − perhaps you, dear cousin, know this side of him less than I do − he'd make a list of your weaknesses, or what he supposes to be your weaknesses, and he'd try to work on them.'

'Ah! Now how d'you know that?' Nina asked, eyeing her shrewdly. 'It's not just this book of heiresses, is it. There's more.' She grinned. 'Do tell!'

Johanna felt a moment of panic. The impossibility of keeping anything from this woman for long! 'He thought he knew my weaknesses once,' she admitted. A glint of triumph flickered briefly in her eyes at the memory. 'What I'm saying is that whereas you have an instinct about people, he has absolutely none. That's all.'

But Nina scented a more exciting game and was not going to let this flattery deviate her. Her eyes flashed a promise at Selina before turning again to Johanna. 'It was after you spied him with the maid, wasn't it. Did he get tired of such easy game and turn his attention to you?'

Johanna bit her lip and blushed.

'Jo!' Selina was goggle-eyed. 'You didn't . . .'

'Didn't what?' Johanna challenged her to say it.

'Didn't tell me that,' her cousin complained lamely.

'Never mind that.' Nina leaned forward. 'What did he imagine were your weaknesses?'

Johanna, thinking she was being offered a way out − in mutual scorn of the poor, insensitive Terence − responded eagerly. 'He thought I'd want presents. Little trinkets. Quite large trinkets, in the end. He thought that was what my life must lack.'

Now Nina began to draw in the noose. 'How absurd! But I can easily imagine him thinking it. However, did you tell him where he was wrong? Did you let him know what might have worked?'

'Nina!' Selina was shocked at the suggestion that *anything* might have 'worked.'

'Yes,' Johanna replied evenly.

'Jo!' Her cousin's shock grew deeper. But then, seeing the amusement in the faces of the other two, she changed her tone and added, 'What? It must have been something enormous.'

Nina turned to her. 'That's right, my lamb. We all have that ultimate sticking point, to which we screw our courage. It pays us to know where it is.'

She turned back to Johanna, who replied, 'I told him my price would be the same as any woman's: a flash of gold...here.' She held out her wedding-ring finger.

'And?'

'He didn't imagine I could possibly be serious.' She chuckled. 'He said I disappointed him, because all women start out by saying that.'

'And isn't he right?' Selina stared from one to the other.

'He's right that all women start out by saying that,' Nina conceded.

Johanna glanced testily at the clock. 'They're taking their time,' she commented.

But Nina was relentless now. 'What would young Hal Penrose need to offer?' she asked.

'The same,' Johanna swore, but she knew her ears were giving her away.

Selina giggled and pointed a finger at her. 'Ha-al! Ha-al!' she mocked, keeping her voice down almost to a whisper.

Nina turned to her and patted a curl on her forehead, letting her knuckles brush the girl's cheek as her hand fell again. It was so exactly the sort of gesture a tolerant mother might make to an obstreperous child that Selina grasped its meaning at once and desisted.

Immediately Nina said to her, 'You're the real enigma here, my angel. How do *you* feel about this evening?'

'In what way?' Selina was genuinely puzzled by the question.

'Well, two of our guests are paying fairly assiduous attention to that shameless hussy over there while the third – in whom, admittedly, you can have no romantic interest – is lying doggo for me. And you do not seem to mind a jot. How can this be, we ask ourselves?'

'Oh that.' Selina was disappointed the mystery turned out to be so trivial. 'If I don't *seem* to mind a jot, it's because I don't, in fact, mind a jot. You're welcome to them all. The entire male kingdom for all I care.'

Nina patted her arm tenderly. 'I sometimes think you're the wisest among us,' she murmured admiringly.

And Johanna, watching them, seeing how Selina basked in this almost meaningless praise, realized she had been right: When Nina did such things her action was entirely spontaneous. She would be quite incapable of calculating her effect in advance. In fact, to ask her to try would be to paralyse her — like the joke about asking the centipede how on earth it manages to walk.

They were both of them creatures of instinct; their truest actions were all born of impulse. They calculated nothing and remained barely aware of what they were doing or where they were heading.

In an odd way it made her feel almost infinitely more mature than either of them; but it was a maturity she would gladly have exchanged for a single day of living like them.

Chapter Twenty-Four

Hal knew something had gone wrong when Cunningham failed to meet him, as arranged, at the Pendarves Arms; he knew something had gone badly wrong when the man was not to be raised at his latest haunt, the Liberal Club, either; and he knew it was disaster when, acting on the wildest surmise, he ran into the fellow as he was about to board the Truro-bound coach that connected with the mail coach for Plymouth – and as an outside passenger at that.

'Ah, Penrose!' the man called out with queasy bonhomie. 'You got my message then?'

Hal frowned at him.

'Left word for you with the landlord at the Pendarves Arms – and with the porter at my club, come to that.'

'My fee would have made a better leaving with either,' Hal told him.

'Ah, yes, well, it was about that, you see.' He consulted his watch, somewhat desperately.

'You've fifteen minutes. Come into the bar and tell me.'

'Oh dear – I don't wish to lose my place.'

'Safe enough, sir,' a helpful coachman told him. 'You're the only outside man this run.'

Reluctantly Cunningham descended and followed Hal into the private bar. 'The thing is, you see,' he said as soon as they were alone, 'there's been a dreadful run in railway shares. I don't suppose you follow such things but the market's been quite absurd. Scrip that only a month ago would have bought me a life's annuity at five hundred a year wouldn't now buy a week's groceries.'

'You're saying you have no money? You can't pay me —
is that it?'

'Not at all. Not at all. I have assets in Plymouth quite
independent of my railway dealings. It's just that I can't
realize them at arm's length. But the minute I'm there...in
fact, if you come back here two days from now and meet the
mail coach from Plymouth, the first thing into your hands
will be two hundred golden sovereigns. There now!'

'And there's no doubting you have this...'

'Not the faintest shadow of it, old fellow.' He grinned.
'Fact is, I have other reasons for needing to leave this district
in rather a hurry. Remember the two young beauties who
flirted with me so outrageously that first day?' He winked.
''Nuff said, eh? Four new feet for baby boots have made it
necessary to create a sudden dearth of Cunningham in these
parts.'

'And you can get it in cash?'

'Bags of the stuff.'

'Good!' Hal smiled.

'Capital!' Cunningham smiled back.

'You're fond of me, I trust?' Hal asked.

'Aye,' the man replied dubiously, staring at him slightly
askance.

'Always enjoyed my company?'

'Aye.' This time there was an embarrassed laugh.

'Excellent — for I can now tell you the coachman was
wrong. You're not the only outside passenger to Plymouth
on this trip.'

Cunningham swallowed heavily. 'But...but, I say, I
mean you're hardly dressed...'

'No more are you. I expect it's the thought of so much
cash just waiting there to be picked up — that's enough to
warm the cockles of any man's heart, eh?'

Cunningham smiled wanly and said, 'Good-oh.'

After a moment's silence Hal went on. 'There isn't any
cash there, is there.'

The other stirred uneasily.

'You're simply vamoosing — isn't that the truth of it?'

He slumped. 'There is some cash there — in Plymouth, I
mean.'

'But nothing like two hundred.'

'I'm afraid not, no.'

'What's happened to the survey? Didn't you get paid?'

He nodded glumly. 'I used it all up, I fear. I had to meet a call on some scrip. It was my only way to get my hands on it, fully paid – because I wanted to sell. Thought I'd sell out at a good profit. Dammit, the stuff was ten times over par when I paid up. It looked a dead cert.'

'And now?'

Cunningham thrust his hand deep into an inside pocket and pulled out a sheaf of grand-looking certificates, all bearing the legend SOUTH DEVON RAILWAY COMPANY. 'Have them if you wish. Six hundred pounds at par. Worth twenty if you find the right idiot.'

'It's a start,' Hal said evenly. 'Will you indorse them to me?'

Cunningham had plainly not intended his gesture to be taken up but he complied willingly enough – anything, it seemed, to keep Hal sweet and off his neck.

'And your surveying tools?' Hal asked. There was another fifty pounds there, even at knock-down values.

The man gave a dispirited nod. 'They're wherever you left them. I didn't have the heart to go back.' Then he remembered his charade and gave another wink. 'The two wenches, you remember.'

Hal, realizing that clever play would yield more from this fellow than any threat of the law or direct violence, forced himself to chuckle. He even gave the man's arm a playful punch. 'You're quite a card, aren't you,' he said.

Cunningham did not really know how to take it but he gave a lopsided grin and muttered something to the effect that it was good of Hal to be so reasonable.

'Cards on the table now,' Hal went on cheerily. 'How much cash is there for you in Plymouth? You say there's some.'

'About eighty guineas.'

There was more – Hal felt sure of it. Perhaps not money, but something. 'Where were you going to go next? You must have realized that the moment I blew the gaff on you, as the criminal fraternity say – and you're now among them, as I hope you understand? Anyway, the moment I raised the hue and cry, you were as good as in debtor's gaol already. Hence my question — what were you going to do next?'

Cunningham shrugged. 'Take a new name — try and begin something afresh.'

Hal shook his head. 'I'd love to believe that, Cunningham, but I can't. There's something more — I can feel it — something you're still not telling me.'

The post horn blew its final challenge.

'I must go,' Cunningham said with relief. 'Come to Plymouth if you like. You'll see I'm telling the truth.'

The coachman came apologetically into the bar. 'If you please, my lords?' he told them.

'We've postponed the journey,' Hal replied. 'Perhaps only for a day or two. I take it my colleague's ticket will still be valid?'

'Now see here!' Cunningham protested, rising to obey the summons.

Hal stretched out a hand the size and weight of a small steam hammer and pushed him back into his seat.

The coachman nodded and backed out hastily. 'Whenever he wishes, sir,' he said. 'No difficulty at all.'

'You've a damnable neck, Penrose,' Cunningham protested when they were alone once more.

'And you'll have a broken one in a minute,' Hal murmured. To the barmaid he called: 'Bring us a bottle or rum and a single glass, if you please, miss. And a half of mild ale for me.'

Cunningham frowned in bewilderment.

'One way or another,' Hal assured him, almost sadly, 'you're going to tell me all.'

The fellow was stubborn; he fought with all his resources not to say more. But Hal kept forcing the rum on him and, by the time he was several sheets to the wind, it all finally came out.

The fact was, he had an uncle, a ship's master, who traded between England and America. He would be calling at Plymouth in a week's time on his way to Boston. 'So you see, I'm going to America,' he explained in his drunken drawl. 'In this country, if you haven't got a coat of arms and enough quarterings to sink a man of war, you're nobody. But over there . . .'s different. Cousin Jonathan doesn't give a hang for all that. What he's looking for, you see' — and here he tapped Hal's chest portentously — 'is...is...what was I going to say?'

'Cousin Jonathan is looking for something.'

'Oh yes — genius! 'S very simple. Genius. I'll be a ...no time at all. I'll come back here. Buy out the lot of them. Genius.'

On which rosy thought he fell in a stupor. Hal patted him gently on the shoulder and said, 'God bless me, Cunningham, old fellow, but this may be a greater reward than any straight payment in gold. It all depends on your uncle — but it's my belief he'd rather carry and victual *two* to Boston than see you languish in gaol.' He tossed off the rest of the man's rum and smacked his lips at its fire.

Chapter Twenty-Five

Hal started twenty letters to Johanna and finished none. He knew it was futile, anyway; soon he'd put away his pen and go to see her, even if it meant walking all the way through the storm that now threatened. And yet he feared the encounter — the possibility that his resolve might weaken at the last minute. He feared she would tempt him with the thought that fortunes were as easily made here at home in Cornwall as anywhere else. For others that might well be true, even in times like these, when capital seemed to have vanished and trade was withering almost daily. But for him? No, not for him. Here he was branded as a ne'er-do-well orphan, fond of company, over-fond of women, handy in a fight — but trouble. And yet, even in that unsavoury reputation there was a certain seduction. He was widely known, and popular; folk would greet him with a smile and a clap on the back in dozens of places, from great houses to miners' hovels. He'd never starve here. He'd always get by. But he'd never be taken seriously, either. He'd never be a heavyweight — except in the ring.

So he had to get away, somewhere far beyond the reach of his reputation. Even in America that might not be easy — considering the number of Cornish folk who had gone out there of late. He was resolved, then, to go. The opportunity offered by Cunningham's misfortunes was sent by the Fates themselves. It was an omen he could not ignore. The only thing that might deviate him was Johanna. Those eyes...her lips...the slender delicacy of her neck...

There came a knock at the door.

'Eh?' he called out, startled from his reverie.

'Same as "come in," I hope?' Charley Vose stuck his head into the room.

Hal smiled and waved for the rest of him to follow; it included a couple of tankards of new ale, clear and lively. 'Compliments of mine host,' Charley said. Then he surveyed the wreckage of unfinished letters. 'Send it from Boston,' he advised curtly. 'You got the whole voyage to get 'n polished.'

He set down the tankards and pulled up a chair, craning his neck to glean what he might from the scraps. 'To that Miss Rosewarne, is it?'

'You know more than is good for you,' Hal told him.

'Ah,' the man answered lightly. 'Come to that, boy, you're some disappointment to me, too.'

'How?' Hal took a sup. It was good ale. You couldn't fault Charley there. If he'd been a different sort of a man, there'd be brewery drays travelling half the county with 'Vose's Ales' on their sides. But Charley was always too clever for his own good.

'Why, when you first come to stop here, I thought to myself, "Hello! Now we shall see a score o' pretty faces about the place." That's what I thought.' He winked his accidental-style wink, the one that could just as easily be a puckering of his eye against the fumes from his last-gasp cheroot. 'And there hasn't been no more than one − and she never come but the once!'

'Good heavens,' Hal responded. 'Is that my reputation? A lifter of skirts?'

Charley backed off about two miles. 'You and a dozen beside, boy. All names as was mentioned in' − he eyed Hal warily as he said the name − 'in that Joan Ninian business.'

Hal did not twitch a single muscle.

''Course,' Charley went on to fill the silence, 'I calculate there was more cock and bull about that than ever truth was told.'

'And you heard that *I* was mixed up in it?'

He grinned; his cheroot drooped with the corners of his mouth in placatory scepticism. 'Cock and bull, like I said.'

'Well then . . .' Hal stared out through the window. It was a cold, blustery afternoon; the storm looked even more threatening.

249

'I always thought,' Charley went on, 'she was very loyal not never to name no one, like she done.'

He's just probing, Hal thought. He *can't know a thing.*

Charley went on, in tones that suggested he was discussing the events of several generations ago, 'I believe most of it was a scandal got up against her. That Captain d'Acre, see, he was grown tired of her. That's where it's to. And don't forget — he'd fixed up some pretty old match with the Sutherland girl.' He rubbed his fingers around imaginary gold. 'And that, in my humble view, was how he wanted shot of Joan Ninian.'

Hal thought he might as well play along with this blatant fishing trip as sit and stare at the worsening weather. He shook his head in wonder. 'So none of those officers who stood up in court and swore they'd had carnal knowledge of her, not one of them...?'

Charley nodded with great confidence. 'All lies, boy.' He winked the definitive I-know, and you-know, and we-each-know-the-other-knows wink, 'Yet she did have that child.'

Hal screwed up his face, as at something almost impossible to recollect. 'Yes, I was going to say. Very shortly after the nuptials, wasn't it?'

'Three months. And the captain was right when he claimed the poor little bastard wasn't his — 'cos he was in India at that time.'

He'd actually been in Spain, but Hal saw the trap. 'Funny old world,' he said, wondering whether Charley could possibly know the child was his. One thing was certain — Joan would never have breathed a word. 'Still,' he added in tones that dismissed the subject entirely, 'the woman did well enough for herself in the end. Married that lawyer in Penzance, didn't she?'

'So I heard tell,' Charley replied. 'And now he's dying, they say. She'll be left a tidy sum I shouldn't wonder. Makes you think.'

'Aye,' Hal supped his ale.

'Here's you and me, Penrose, working the skin off our fingers — and the harlot goes about in silks!'

'I wouldn't know about that.'

''Tin't right, boy. 'Tis neither right nor fair. I do cater to an appetite as was sanctified by the Good Lord hisself at

Cana, when he turned the water into wine. Yet there's days I can't hardly move for customs and excise, and the magistrates, and the constabulary. And there's Widow Jewell, spreading the gentleman's relish at Sunny Corner, which is a sin of abomination in every book in the Bible. But...'

'Is that true?' Hal asked. 'All that scandal about her?'

'Surely you heard tell of it?'

'There was some talk — oh, a few weeks back. I overheard some talk when I dined at the Liberal Club, in happier days.' He grinned. 'In Mr Cunningham's happier days.'

'Talk!' Charley echoed sarcastically. 'That's all 'tis — just talk. But what about when the law do go a-knocking out there? 'Tin't with no truncheon nor yet no warrant — 'tis with a bloody half-crown held fast between the fingers. Yes, boy — a different kind of knocking! That's the law for you.'

Hal shook his head sadly. 'So that really is her trade, these days? I thought it was just the usual gossip that everyone fastens on a poor widow.' He shook his head, not wanting to think about it any more. 'There's one in every village, surely?' he asked dismissively. 'If not a couple.'

'Couple!' Charley snorted contemptuously. 'She've had half a dozen maids on their backs there some nights last summer — bal maidens from the village, all working *flat-out* as you might put it. And the lane full of idlers, fishporters, and I don't know what-all, just waiting their turn.'

'Ah!' Hal began to glimpse the point of this unexpected visit. 'That's what worries you, is it, Charley? All that coin jingling in all those pockets along all the highways and byways leading to Goldsithney — and none of it going on ale when it gets here! Poor old bugger!' He downed the last of his tankard with relish. 'You're in the wrong trade — that's all.'

''Tis an abomination in every book in the Bible,' Charley repeated.

'Live and let live, man. Pity Sunny Corner's just a furlong too far from here. Else you could make some arrangement whereby they wait their turn at your bar.' The thought led him to an inspired leap. 'But look here, man — you've still got those two cottages empty up the top end of your garden here, haven't you?'

Charley had missed his vocation; he should have been on the stage. You'd swear the idea had never struck him until that moment. 'Well,' he said as his eyes lit up with the discovery. 'That's a thought, now!'

'Only one drawback,' Hal warned.

'What's that?' Charley asked irritably. Now he could blame the inspiration on Hal, he resented being hindered in his further apparent exploration of it.

'You'll have to rewrite every book in the Bible.'

'Ah, well now . . .' He held up a cunning finger and gave his take-it-from-me-and-God wink. 'If you do study it a bit more careful like, you'll see that the abomination is in the public flaunting of the trade.'

'How d'you reckon that?'

'Stands to reason. All they bigwigs — kings and judges and high priests and prophets and that — they were only men, weren't they. Only flesh and blood. They must have had their houses of resort, too. They paid their half-crown, same as the rest.'

'Five guineas, Charley.'

'Eh?'

'For women up in that class it's five guineas just to cross the threshold.'

Charley's eyes almost popped out of his face. Petty calculations of profit and risk — calculations that must have kept him awake many a night — were hastily revised; the view from the top end of Goldsithney was transformed into the panorama from Mont Blanc.

'Anyway, you were saying?' Hal prompted. 'The superior classes must have had . . .'

'Ah yes — stands to reason. They were there — in Jerusalem and Babylon and Tyre and Sidon and that — cunny warrens for the high and mighty. But where are they called out, eh? Riddle me that. Where's the wrath of Providence poured down on them? Nowhere, boy! Not a word against them — not nowhere in the whole bloody Bible.'

'You verified that, did you? Cover to cover?'

Charley ignored him. 'Discreet, see. So that's all right, then. Are you certain-sure 'tis five guineas?'

Hal nodded confidently. 'Take it from me that's only the

ante. Mind you, we're not talking about any old carrion now.'

Charley winked and the man-of-the-world was back in charge. 'They young Jewell twins — there's a delicacy there as none could call carrion. Had a fair bit of eddycation, if I remember.' He laughed. 'A lot of good it did them! But yes, they could be made into something. I'd not say five guineas, mind . . .'

For Hal, the humour suddenly went out of the situation. Jenny Jewell had been a sweetheart of his for a brief season two summers ago. Not that there had been anything wrong with her to make him seek another. All his sweethearts until now had been 'for a brief season.' But the thought of what she had since descended to saddened him.

However, the last thing he wanted was for Charley Vose to get a whiff of it, so he returned to his former banter with the man. 'You were saying? About discretion and being too blatant in public?'

'Yes, 'zackly. 'Tis the public business God can't abide. "Thou hast a whore's forehead, not ashamed." Jeremiah. Blatant, see? He can't abide it.'

Hal pursed his lips dubiously. 'On the other hand, Charley — "Whoredom and wine take away the heart." Hosea, Four.'

'How about this, then, mister: "Publicans and harlots go into the kingdom of heaven before you." Matthew, Twenty-one. Swallow that while 'tis warm! You can't argue down that, not in the Good Book.'

'My! You *have* made a study of it — the whole business, eh, Charley? When do you and the generous widow open up shop?'

'Why,' Charley replied angrily, 'I only now thought of it. 'Twas you put the idea in my head.' He sniffed to signal a change of tack. 'Anyroad, 'tin't hardly for I to go talking to she. That do put the boot on the wrong foot altogether. No, her must come to I. Her must be the one to ask first. Trouble is — she don't understand what danger she's in.'

So there it was, then — the obscure point of this enormous roundabout of a little friendly chat. And in case Hal doubted it, here came the next question: 'You going Helston, are 'ee?'

Hal shrugged. 'Since Cunningham took back his horse...'

'Ah now, that's another thing I meant to tell 'ee — you can have the lend of my old grey if you mind to. Just till next week, see? Shame to keep that pretty Miss Rosewarne on tenterhooks!'

Hal didn't need to ask about the price.

Ten minutes later the abortive letters were reduced to glowing ashes in the fireplace and Hal, carrying fisherman's oilskins against the threatened storm, set out for Helston. Charley was out in the yard, staring up the garden at his two cottages as if he'd forgotten them until Hal spoke. 'I'll tell 'ee a funny thing, boy,' he said over his shoulder, not turning round.

'What's that?'

'Used to be five houses up there, all in a row. Know what the name of it was then?'

'I've no idea. What?'

'Paradise Row!'

Hal laughed. 'They saw you coming, Charley.'

'I reckon so, boy.'

Hal made a short detour at Sunny Corner. Widow Jewell came bustling joyfully up her garden path at the sound of an approaching horseman. 'Why, Mr Penrose,' she cried out in unfeigned pleasure. 'Now here's a nice surprise, indeed. Jenny!'

'No!' Hal began — but it was too late.

'Jenny — come-see who's a-calling on 'ee now.' To Hal she added. 'He's turned some bitter. So cold as a quilkin in a cundard. Never mind — you'll soon be where 'tis always nice and warm.' She turned and called again: 'Jenny!'

'That's not what I came for, Mrs Jewell,' he told her as he dismounted.

She laughed. 'You aren't the first to say that, my lover,' she assured him. 'Never fret. No matter what your errand, you comes-on in for a dish o'tay, now. You might change your mind yet.' She ushered him ahead of her up the garden path. 'They do usually tell me all they want is a wart cure, or a love potion. But I should hardly think you'm in need of either.'

As they neared the door it opened. Jenny, in no mood —

or dress — to get cold, had waited to the last polite moment before she answered her mother's summons.

The first sight of her, after almost two years, was a shock — or, rather, a series of shocks. He remembered the Jenny he had so briefly loved as a frail, slender girl with large, haunting eyes. Well, the eyes were still there, still large, still haunting; but there was something else in them besides — a confident, knowing sort of roguishness. And she was no longer either slender or frail, but robust, well-fleshed, and glowing with health.

'Hello...' she drawled, not immediately recognizing him. Her next word would have been 'Charley' or 'Jim' or one of those standard greetings in 'the gay trade.' But then the penny dropped and she saw through that anaesthetizing mist of man-business to the real person who stood there. 'Hal!' she cried and reached forward two soft, pink tentacles to clutch him indoors. 'My lucky day! Didn't I just say it, Ma?'

Behind her the widow laughed softly.

The repeated disclaimer rose into his throat — but would not be uttered. Not that it was any less true, but it would seem rude to begin again, to renew what had been the warmest of friendships, on such a note of rejection. To his consternation, though, she led him straight to the bedroom door.

'No,' he said earnestly. 'I wish to talk with your mother.'

'First?' she asked.

He hesitated. That decided her. Squeezing his arm urgently, two or three times, and signalling him desperately with her eyes to make no protest, she dragged him into the room and swiftly closed the door behind them.

'Listen...' he began at once.

But she hushed him to silence and stood with her ear against the door. What she heard was obviously to her satisfaction for she relaxed and smiled at him — a genuine smile, too. She walked past him, picked up a shawl, and wrapped it around her neck and breast, which until then had been exposed to within a hairsbreadth of decency.

'I should explain,' he tried again.

'No need, my lover. I know by now when a man has cat eyes — and when he hasn't. But listen...' She put her ear to the door again and then gave out a sigh of apparent ecstasy.

'What are you doing?' he asked.

She grinned and nodded toward the parlour. 'Keeping her at bay, I hope. Now listen. I've had as much of this way of life as I can stomach. The minute I saw it was you, I knew this was my lucky day. Didn't I say it? So can you get me away from here? Please?'

'Me? Lord, Jenny, how may I do that? You may not have heard but I've troubles enough of my own.'

'I could help.'

'You?'

She came closer to him and let the shawl slip a little. 'It's working for her I can't stomach. But' – she toyed with one of his shirt buttons – 'if you were my fancy man...now that'd be different. Why did you leave me? I thought we were sparking on fine.'

He nodded but said nothing.

'Frightened you, did I?' She grinned. 'You could hear the bells in my ears? Well, I'd be a fool to hope for that now. But we could still...spark along.'

He shook his head. 'You had education, Jenny. You shouldn't have to. ...'

'Hah!' she cried scornfully. 'What good was that to me? Except that I can surprise one or two gentlemen with "refayned" talk and so shame them into paying a little more.'

Hal drew away from her and went to stand at the window; two young boys went scampering off down the garden.

'So you won't help me at all?' she asked bitterly.

'I can't, love. I'm going to America.'

'They all say that – this year, next year, sometime, never.'

'Well, it's this week as far as I'm concerned. This Saturday from Plymouth, to be precise.'

'A precise lie is still a lie,' she said.

'As you wish.'

A silence fell between them.

'Where's Diana?' he asked, to fill it.

'Visiting the afflicted of the parish, bringing relief and good cheer.'

It was not long before the mother came in, bearing a bowl of hot water. She halted in consternation and stared from one to the other. 'What's this?' she asked. 'I thought . . .'

'I was trying to break it to her gently,' Hal explained, 'that I came to speak with you, not . . .' He waved his hand toward the bed.

'And I was telling him I wish more men of his kind came down our garden path.' As she spoke she crossed the room and took him by the arm, leading him back toward the parlour. 'The things I could tell you about some of your fellows, my dear.'

'If only there were time.'

She grinned. 'The man who made time made more than enough for me.'

He frowned uncertainly, but before he could ask what she meant her mother cut in with, 'You wished to speak with me?'

'To warn you, really, missis. I was dining with a friend the other night at the Liberal Club in Redruth . . .'

'Half of whose members are patrons here!' the woman interrupted proudly.

'Three-quarters,' Jenny corrected, in a tone more acid than proud.

'It may not help,' Hal added. 'Not even if they're all patrons here. One group of gentlemen were discussing this establishment of yours, Mrs Jewell — and in terms far from complimentary.'

'Oh? And why, may I ask? Did they get clapped here? Or got drunk and then robbed? Did they not find more value than they've any right to expect in return for . . .'

'Mother — it's no good talking like that. You know they've as many faces as a pack of cards.' She turned to Hal. 'What were they saying? Was it something particular?'

He now strayed beyond the bounds of literal truth. 'No, no particular complaint, you know. Not like rowdyism or drunkenness and such like, but . . .'

'I should think not, indeed!'

'Ma — do let him say.'

'The general feeling seemed to be that these cottages were too public — too open. In fact' — he brightened — 'not two minutes ago I put up a pair of lads trying to peep in at the bedroom window.'

'That's Harry Campion and Tommy Meagor, I'll be bound.'

'Whoever they were, Mrs Jewell, it's the sort of thing that starts complaints of public disorder and...well, you know the rest.'

The poor woman made a trapped, hopeless sort of gesture. 'But where else can I go? This is my cottage. 'Tisn't as if I did choose it deliberate like. I don't know what else I can do.'

'Try and find somewhere more discreet, if I were you. Somewhere well away from the road.'

'Oh yes − like the middle of Bodmin Moor, no doubt!'

'I'm sure there's somewhere nearer,' he said vaguely. 'Anyway, that's all I came to tell you. I thought I ought to pass on the warning, that's all.'

As he left by the front gate he turned about for one last look. Jenny was there, as he had expected, watching him all the way out of sight. But the expression on her face was not in the least bit wistful or sad − and that was something he had not expected to see. In fact, he felt slightly hurt to discover her so cheerful.

He remembered all he had heard about the fickleness of gay women. It saddened him to find her so far gone in it after so short a time. The next customer, or so he assumed, passed him at the head of the lane.

Jenny let Hal get out of earshot before she said, 'Ma, you'll have to oblige this next gentleman. I have to follow our last caller.'

'You'll do no such thing,' her mother replied stoutly, waving the man indoors without a second glance at him. 'The impudence of it!'

Jenny turned on her wearily. 'D'you really imagine that was just an innocent little visit? An act of kindness in passing? You still believe in acts of kindness, do you?'

'What are you talking about?'

Jenny was glad to hear the doubt and fear beginning to invade her mother's certainties. 'That was the opening round of some game,' she said. 'And I'm damned if I'll let him choose his own time and place for the next little skirmish.'

She didn't truly believe it herself; it was no more than a possibility that had flitted through her mind at some point during Hal's brief visit. But it was enough to scare her mother into compliance.

For the truth was, Jenny now had an exciting new game of her own to play.

Chapter Twenty-Six

The skies opened as Hal came down Sithney Common Hill. He had been aware of another rider behind him, a woman, ever since Godolphin. In fact, he had slowed his pace a couple of times, hoping she might catch up and so lighten both their journeys with some conversation; but, obviously not in the mood for company, she had slowed down, too. When the rain began in earnest he looked back toward the hilltop, expecting to see her dismount and take shelter until the worst of it had passed. Instead, to his disappointment, she spurred off the turnpike and took the old packhorse lane, which led directly down the hill to Trevose's mill. She must be in some hurry to go that way on a day like this. He spurred onward and continued his longer but gentler descent of the same slope. He would be turning off at the mill, where the two roads met again, so he might just get another glimpse of her, except that she would be ahead of him by then.

He wondered why the thought pleased him. And what about that earlier sense of disappointment, too? Here he was, battling through the elements to meet a woman who was dearer to him than life itself – a woman for whom, if she asked it, he would readily forsake the company of every other female on earth – and yet there lurked within him some demon that had wanted to meet this unknown woman, a person who had never been more than a speck in the landscape. Despite the threatened cloudburst he had tarried in the hope she'd catch up; and when she turned aside, his whole spirit had drooped. Experience told him she was probably all of three score and ten, toothless, haggard, and dim. But no matter. That eternal sexual optimist within him had fleshed her in pink, trimmed her age and waist below twenty, polished her eye and her cheek...in fact, come to think of it, had turned her into the very replica of young Jenny Jewell.

Not unwillingly, he turned his attention to that encounter. In his new conscience-searching mood, he had to admit that part of his readiness to undertake Charley Vose's unspoken embassy to the widow had been the thought of seeing Jenny again. He remembered walking her through the summer meadows around her home, to Chynoweth woods, or to the waste halvans at Halamanning...her bright talk, her large, hungry eyes. And how she had lain with him and whinnied with the pleasure of it, and begged him to stop and go on in the same breathless breath.

What had he hoped for now – or not him but that dreadful optimist, the old demiurge? Had it hoped to lie with her again?

Nothing so definite as that. It neither collected nor sought such precise experiences; rather, it sniffed the emotional breeze, seeking the merest whiff of a chance. *That* was what it collected – chances. It led you by the nose to the threshold of each and said, 'The rest is up to you, boy – make of it what you can.' And even while you obeyed, it had its snout in the air again, on that old, everlasting quest for the next and the next and the next occasions.

Would there ever be ease from its tireless demands? Would he survive his time in America without yielding to its offerings? Johanna would undoubtedly repeat her plea, 'Take me with you.' Would that not be the safest course? And if he still answered no, what would his true reasons be?

These thoughts so preoccupied him that he actually forgot to seek out the horsewoman when he turned off at Trevose's mill. He did not realize it until he reached the gate at Liston Court; then he laughed aloud. Perhaps there was hope for him yet. Anyway, he took it as an omen.

The rain had slackened to the merest spattering as the dark cloud of the storm moved inland, toward Carnmenellis and Redruth. Over Porthleven there were even fitful shafts of sunlight. Their brilliance was reflected off the sodden granite of Brookesy's menhir. It was the first time he had seen it by daylight. He knew of many such standing stones, for they were almost as common as mushrooms in the fields of West Penwith. But no degree of familiarity had ever quite dulled his sense of awe at their bulk and their antiquity; to stand near one, in the shadow of its Presence, always brought a tingle to his spine. He had feared that Nina, by taming one in her garden, might at last break their spell. He was pleased to find it was not so. Already its tenure seemed vastly more ancient than that of the house; its old, weather-beaten stone actually conferred a new dignity on the dwelling.

Selina threw up a window and called to him. 'Hello, Hal – isn't it magnificent? Nina wants to plant a bed of maiden-hair fern around the base of it. What d'you think?'

He laughed and went to join her. One of the grooms came out and took his horse. 'I think, how very like her,' he called back.

Beneath the grand portico, before he went indoors, he took off his oilskins and shook them. 'I never know whether these things are worth it,' he told Margaret Tyzack, the maid.

'I know,' she agreed. 'You get so damp inside from sweat as you might from the rain.' She bore them off to the kitchens to dry.

Selina took him by the arm and led him directly to the drawing room, where there was a grand fire roaring. 'Are the others not here?' he asked.

'They'll be back soon. They went to call on Miss Grylls. I didn't feel up to it.'

'You're not ill?'

She gave him a naughty-girl grin. 'The only thing I feel up to in weather like this is sitting by the fire, sipping chocolate, and reading novels. Oh, Hal – you should see some of the novels Nina's got!' She forced her eyes wide in pretended shock. 'They don't think much of marriage, do they – these novelists?'

'Is that why you're reading them – to reinforce your own conclusions on the blessed institution?'

'Not really. But when you think – most of the readers are married women, and they don't toss these books aside and say they've never read such ill-informed nonsense. They just sit there, glued to the page. It makes you wonder, doesn't it?'

'Does it? We've all read *Robinson Crusoe* without sharing his privations – or even wishing to. I never thought tilting at windmills was much of an occupation but I enjoyed *Don Quixote* all the same.'

She threw herself down on the sofa and stared moodily out of the window. 'I don't want to hear things like that.'

He stood in his own rising steam, staring down at her, and – inevitably – found himself wondering what she'd be like. Prickly, no doubt. And petulant. Easily pushed off the boil. But once she took to it...

He shook his head angrily at this train of thought. His meeting with Jenny must have unsettled him more than he realized. 'When will they be back?' he asked.

'Soon. I thought you were them, in fact. Do I make you uneasy, Hal? Nina says that women who are self-reliant by choice make men uneasy.'

He gave an awkward laugh.

'There you are, you see. She's right.'

'Has your brother spoken to you recently?' he asked.

Her eyes narrowed. 'Why?'

'I think he believes your opinions are pure folly and that Nina is a thoroughly bad influence for encouraging you to persist with them.'

She stared at him in alarm. 'Did he tell you that.'

He shook his head sadly, not in denial but at her naivety. 'The alternative would be that I'm just making it up.'

'Yes.' She ducked in a pantomime of apology. 'It wasn't a very grown-up question, was it. I am becoming much more grown up here, you know.'

'No doubt of it.'

She smiled again. 'And now you're not uneasy with me any more. It was the same with Tony Moore. There always has to be that point – and once you're past it, everything is marvellous. We walked the whole length of Praa Sands and had such an interesting talk. I can't remember a word of it now, mind. But there it is.' After a thoughtful silence she added, 'I do miss Tony now – much more than I would ever have thought possible while he was here.' She sighed dramatically and went on, 'The thing is, if I refuse to be a brood mare, what can I do with the years ahead?'

'Write one of these novels you enjoy reading so much,' he said with an impatient glance at the clock. Only then did he realize there was nothing in all the world for him to be impatient about. For the first time in his life he could look forward to three whole days, filled with hours that no one had bespoken. He relaxed and settled himself in one of the armchairs beside the sofa. Then he turned to Selina, only to find her staring at him open-mouthed.

'What now?' he asked.

'What you said. It's such a bright idea, Hal.'

'I see — I'm not supposed to have bright ideas, eh?'

'Well, not about me. I've never known you suggest anything about me. But you're absolutely...I mean, I've always enjoyed writing. Once I kept a diary for three whole months!' She grew reflective again. 'But what could I write about?'

'I'm surprised you need to ask. Write about the one topic on which you insist you know more than the whole of Society put together.'

She stared at him in withering scorn; but she could not sustain it, for a new idea had seized her. 'You really are going to America, aren't you?'

He nodded. 'This very Saturday. On the good ship *Starflight*. Why?'

'And you really are going to work and work and amass a fortune and come back and lay it all at Johanna's feet?'

He smiled. 'That would be one way of putting it.'

'It shall be my way. You must write to me, Hal — every single week. Promise? It needn't be true as long as it's authentic. I want Red Indians and buffaloes and fur trapping and wolves and river steamers and noble nigger slaves with cruel masters, and swamps if they have them — or is that Africa? Anway, keep your eyes peeled for every little novelty and put it all down and send it to me. And while you're living your rather humdrum life in the tin mines of Virginia or wherever it may be, I shall rearrange it into the stirring adventures you might have been having if...'

'If I weren't so busy writing it all down for you!'

She laughed, but immediately added, 'I'm not joking, Hal. The minute you said it I got that special ticklish feeling in my neck and I just *knew* it was what I really wanted to do. And it'll be fun for you, too, won't it?'

He nodded judiciously. 'It'll certainly keep me out of mischief, my dear.'

Her eyes went large with sympathy. 'It must be just awful to be a man.'

Her earnestness brought a smile to his lips, which she resented. To give her annoyance scope he pretended to mock: 'You, to be sure, soar loftily above all such temptations.'

'Yes!' Her eyes flashed. 'I truly do!'

Perhaps Nina was right about self-reliant women, he found himself thinking. The vehemence of her assertion both exasperated him and left him vaguely disquieted. Despite a strong impulse to leave her happy and secure in her delusion, he could not resist pitting himself against that ivory wall of smug assurance.

He said nothing. He left that faintly mocking smile on his lips and stared her out. She had not yet developed the resources that would enable her to withstand so skilled an assault. She blushed and lowered her eyes.

At once he hated himself for what he had done. Not that she hadn't asked for it, but who was he — of all people — to go about handing out lessons? How many bruised emotions had Selina left in her wake compared with him? To make amends he said the first thing that came into his head: 'If you've done with these games, Selina, I'll tell you what I really think about you. I think the day will come when Tony Moore will wish himself dead for having failed with you.'

'What d'you mean?' she asked in a quivering voice well above her usual range. He could see the fluttering of her pulse in a vein at her neck.

Committed now, he had to go on. 'I mean that the man who is privileged to fight his way through your thorn-thickets of indifference and plant on your brow the kiss that will awaken you . . . that man will find in you a gem beyond compare.'

She gulped. She blinked back a few incipient tears. And then, collecting herself with surprising speed, she said, 'Oh, Hal — if you only knew me as I know me! Ask Johanna, if you don't . . . I am not the nicest of people. I hope you make

265

your fortune quickly over there, and come back and take Jo away. I fear I . . .' She fell silent.

'You needn't tell me, if you'd rather not,' he prompted.

'Perhaps if I do tell you, it'll make it less likely.' She drew a breath, squared herself, smiled, and said, amost brightly, 'I sometimes feel the most dreadful urge to hurt her, to say things that will wound her, to pour poison against her in Nina's ear. I can't help it, you see, even though it makes me feel simply dreadful.'

He sucked a tooth and shook his head, suggesting he hardly knew where to begin against such a barrage of nonsense. 'And do you honestly suppose . . .'

But she, being as yet more interested in confession than in the consequent absolution, rattled on. 'I mean, she's my best friend. She's always been so good to me, while I . . . She's even better than Nina because she has so little to give, only herself. Well, I don't need to tell you how splendid she is. And I have this awful premonition that I'm going to spoil her life. I won't mean to − and yet, in a way, I will. Mean to, that is. And actually do it, too.'

Confession had run its course at last. She just sat there, staring at the fire. He watched her as she withdrew, in spirit, from the room, from him − perhaps most of all from the self she had just revealed. Was she mentally casting herself into those flames?

The daylight had almost gone by now. No servant had come in to light the lamps, so they sat there, bathed in the radiance from the hearth. It struck him that, had it not been for Johanna, he could very easily have fallen for Selina instead.

'Is it so amusing?' she asked.

He had not known he was smiling so obviously. 'Yes,' he told her. 'I've just ridden six miles through some of the foulest weather of this winter. But it was as nothing compared to the self-laceration that was going on up here.' He tapped his skull. 'You measure yourself against one person, and you judge your actions with regard to her. How many d'you think I might put in a similar balance against me? Fifty? A hundred? Easily a hundred. Fortunately the bruised heart mends, and I am not so arrogant as to suppose I have inflicted wounds that will never heal. But I have left

266

very little in the way of goodness behind me, Selina.' He frowned and shook his head, as if reviving after a blow. 'Here, enough of this or we shall talk ourselves into the very pit of melancholia! What's done is done. It's tomorrow that matters.'

But she had a last fling. 'You see, even when I suggested you write to me each week — that was part of it. I'd have flaunted those letters, oh so casually, in front of Jo. And even while I was asking you, I knew that was what I was going to do. You see how deep it runs!'

He stretched and yawned as he replied. 'All I see is that your villain — and you must have a villain, of course — is going to be a woman and that all the journals will say you have made an astonishing study of such a depraved creature. And you and I shall enjoy a good laugh together because we'll know the truth about her.'

A faraway look came into her eyes and she murmured an almost ecstatic, 'Yes!'

At that moment the door opened and Johanna came hurrying in. Her flustered expression gave way to a cry of delight when she saw Hal, springing to attention beside the fire. 'What a lovely surprise! But why are you sitting here in the dark? Oh! Selina?'

'We were just sitting here, putting the world to rights,' he told her. 'I say, Selina, just look at that huge eagle out there!'

She obeyed instinctively — and then with a laugh — while Hal and Johanna melted into each other's arms. But soon she grew tired of the game and turned back to watch. *It really is the most absurd thing for two grown-up people to be doing to each other,* she thought. And as for that other thing, *It,* the business Jo had seen Terence doing with one of the maids, the very thought of it made her want to hoot with laughter.

Hal started guiltily. 'Where's Nina?' he asked.

'Oh. . .' Johanna pulled reluctantly away from him and let go. 'She's found another little waif and stray at her gate. But somehow I don't think she'll be inviting this one in.' She bit her lip. 'Hark at me! I must sound the most terrible ingrate.'

'See?' Hal grinned at Selina. 'We are *all* doing it.'

Chapter Twenty-Seven

Nina gave Hal the strangest look when she came in. She was soaked to the skin, despite her supposedly storm-proof coat. She shrugged out of it and threw it at the maid, almost bowling the girl over. 'Oh,' she cried, 'winter never died in a ditch.' She held out her hands and advanced toward the fire as if it were the eighth wonder of the world. 'Throw on a log or two, Hal, there's a . . . brick.' Her voice tailed off. He saw that some novel idea or discovery had that moment seized her and he was about to inquire what it was when she gave him the look.

'What have I done now?' he asked instead.

She swiftly recovered her ebullience. 'Not you. It's Terence, but I feel sure you know of it. It seems that, having broken my bread, he's now trotting about the county, biting the hand that fed him.'

'I presume this . . . young person you met at your gate,' Hal began.

'Yes,' Johanna joined in. 'Do tell us about that. I thought she looked rather . . .'

Nina cut her short. 'In a moment,' she promised. 'Let's hear this man first.'

Hal glanced at Selina, who responded with a sphinx-like smile; he saw then that he had no choice but to repeat what he had already said. 'Master Visick believes you are wrong to encourage his sister in her unconventional beliefs about the state of holy wedlock.'

Nina waited for more.

Hal shifted uncomfortably. 'You've obviously been told everything. Why do you wish me to repeat it?'

'I wish I'd heard it from you, Hal. I wish I were hearing it *all* from you, now. I feel you have broken rather more than my bread.'

'You think I've let you down?' He stared at her angrily.

'Well? Have you?'

'Over young Terence Visick?' he asked scornfully. 'I do not consider him a serious person.' He apologized to Selina before continuing: 'Besides, Nina, you must already be well aware of the widespread scandal you're causing by not mourning Colonel Brookes with greater solemnity, to say nothing of the open and gleeful way you talk up your future independence every chance you get.'

She tossed her head impatiently.

He went on, 'I hope I needn't tell you I am not in that lobby myself. Indeed, I rather applaud you. But I never supposed you'd thank me for carrying every bit of tittle-tattle to the contrary.' He laughed. 'Good Lord — just imagine it! Imagine me coming to you and saying, "Oh dear, Nina, what d'you fancy I overheard Major Ives saying about you? And you'll never guess what Charley Vose tells me Rose Davey heard from Milly Jones who got it from"... and so on.'

Nina conceded his point with reluctant tetchiness — almost as if she wanted some cause to sustain her anger at him. 'Very well. But Terence Visick is different. You and he have sat at my table. That must make a difference. I suppose he mentioned it then? All right. You needn't tell me if you feel it might betray a confidence. But if he threatened to *do* something about it, that would be treachery — especially if he did it under my roof. And there can be no confidence in treachery. So I ask you: Did he?'

Hal smiled and made a hopeless gesture, preparing her to hear something so trivial she'd regret having raised the matter at all. 'He said someone ought to bend you to his will.'

'Hah!' Selina hooted with laughter. But when she saw how angry Nina was, she fell hastily back into silence.

'Meaning himself, I suppose! Bending me to his will, indeed!'

'Nina — he's one of a legion of gentlemen who would dearly love the honour of taking you up the aisle. When you throw down the gauntlet before them so provocatively, how else are they to express it and retain their sense of honour? All they truly seek is your fortune. Put that into their hands and they'd drop the rest of their ambition like a hot coal. You'd be as free as a bird again.'

Nina had not expected so neat an analysis of her situation. She clenched her fists and, turning to the window, shook them at the whole conniving world, giving out a strangled cry of frustration. Selina rose and took her arm, stroking it affectionately. 'It's hardly Hal's fault, my dear,' she said.

'Of course I'm not blaming him,' Nina replied. 'I'm just so angry to have to admit he's right.'

Johanna stared at Hal in surprise that Selina should have leaped in to defend him so swiftly. He tried to signal that he didn't understand it, either, while at the same time keeping half a nervous eye on Nina. She was up to something, he was sure of it.

Selina compounded matters by turning to him and asking, 'What should she do, Hal?'

The honest answer was that she should do the same as before – marry another rich man in his dotage and try, this time, not to give him a happy death. But he could hardly say that. 'Grow a third eye in the back of her head,' he advised. 'And a third ear in the sole of her foot.'

Nina turned to him, the thinnest of smiles upon her lips. 'Hal, dear – I don't know if you were expecting to dine here tonight, but, in the circumstances, I hardly feel. . . .'

He bowed stiffly. 'As your ladyship pleases.'

'Nina!' Johanna was mortified at this sudden turn of events.

'What?' she asked crossly.

'These are his last three days.'

For a moment Nina seemed at a loss. 'Oh, very well,' she said curtly. 'Go dine with him for all I care. Take my carriage. I'm not answerable to anyone for your reputation but I'll send Margaret with you.'

Johanna laughed and ran to her. 'Oh, you angel! You darling!' She tried to hug her but Nina pushed her away. 'Don't try me too far, child,' she warned gruffly.

However, the moment they had gone her demeanour changed entirely. She clapped her hands, gave a little laugh of triumph, and said to Selina, 'I never supposed I should manage it so easily! Was I too severe?'

Selina just stared at her in bewilderment.

'I planned he should dine here tomorrow night, you see. I presume by Friday he'll be Plymouth bound. If I send him a little *billet doux,* d'you think he'll forgive me and come tomorrow after all?'

'I don't understand. What is the...'

'No, no — of course you don't. How could you? But, my *dear,* I have just been told *the* the most extraordinary story. I didn't take it all in at once. I didn't think quickly enough. But the moment I came in here it all fell into place — then I knew I had to get those two out of this house for the evening. Come all hell and Connaught against me, I just had to do it. Was I terribly, terribly blatant?'

'No.' Selina was still at a loss.

'Come on then. You'll understand more as we go along.'

'Where to?'

'To the kitchens. The girl is waiting for us. Oh, why did I not see it at once? She is the answer to all my hopes.' And again there was that laugh of triumph.

The ostler took charge of the horse and carriage the moment they arrived at the Ram. Then Margaret discovered she'd left her shawl on its seat and ran after him to get it back. While they waited, Johanna asked, 'Can I hit you?'

'Eh?' Hal replied.

'Punch you in the stomach like Jim Rogers did — the mint-humbugs man at Harvest Fair, remember?'

He laughed and braced himself for her assault.

She drew back her fist and twirled it. 'Hard as I like?' she asked.

'Hard as you like.'

She struck him a piledriver that hurt her wrist. He didn't even grunt. 'Fleas are biting tonight,' he commented mildly.

She tried her other fist, with the same result. Then, thinking he couldn't keep himself braced for ever, she started a regular hail of blows, right and left in rapid succession. He might as well have been a side of beef for all the effect it had. Her heart began to race, she grew short of breath — and then it dawned on her that the excitement she

271

felt was something out of the ordinary. She wanted to provoke him to genuine anger, so that he would grab her arms, pinion her, tear off her clothes . . . and then he would see her, and suddenly all his anger would evaporate, and he'd fall to his knees, and put his arms around her nakedness, and beg her forgiveness, and they'd sink to the floor . . .

She saw it all happening in her mind's eye while she went on pummeling him. It made her stop in confusion; but the erotic pleasure it had given her was slower to die.

'Feeling better?' he asked, taking up her hands and kissing them tenderly. He knew very well what it had done to her. Their eyes met and all her uncertainties about the rest of the evening vanished.

They dined privately in Hal's room, three old school friends with lots of gossip to catch up on. When they had washed down the last of the spotted dick with what was by no means the last of the ale, Johanna turned to Margaret and said, 'One thing I meant to ask — when we came in — from the way you spoke to the woman in the kitchen . . .'

'Rose Davey?'

'Ah, you do know her then?'

'She's cousin to Bert Williams who married my half-sister Alice. Her people do live out Chynoweth.'

'Splendid.' Johanna smiled at her.

'Why,' Margaret asked.

'Oh . . . I just wondered — since you do know her — well, you probably have some news to share? Downstairs — with her?'

Margaret laughed at her boldness but glanced uncertainly at Hal.

'About half an hour's worth,' Johanna prompted.

The girl came to her own decision and winked. 'I dare say we might even find a bit more'n that.'

Hal remained impassive. When he had left Liston Court he had been too angry at Nina's unreasonableness to think properly; but now he remembered his earlier feeling that she had been up to some trick. It became plainer by the minute that her anger had all been assumed. She had come into that drawing room determined to get the pair of them out of the house for the evening. Why else had she been so complaisant about Johanna's coming to dine alone with him, when up until now she had guarded her reputation as fiercely as a Spanish duenna?

As soon as Margaret had gone, Johanna sat herself down in his lap, put her arms about him, and began to cover his face with kisses.

He responded for a while but then broke off to ask, 'Did *you* get the impression Nina wanted us out the house for some reason?'

She went on kissing him, now adding urgent little sighs to the gasps she was already having to make for her breath.

He began to take fire from her. She put her hand in at his collar, to caress his neck; she felt how his pulse was raging. 'Oh, Hal,' she murmured.

There was something wrong. It was not going the way she had imagined it. He was both yielding to her and holding himself back. At last she had to ask what was wrong.

'You know,' he said in a voice husky with longing.

His disorder made her tingle. 'Know what? All I know is I want you and want you and want you. Oh, my darling. . .'

'And I want you, too. Oh, I've never wanted anyone so much. But don't you see? It's because I love you, and truly love you. . .'

But she was no longer listening. Anything more than a murmured phrase, a cry of love, had already passed beyond her comprehension. She pulled his shirt free of its confining belt and thrust her hands up inside, taking up handfuls of muscle, raking his flesh with her nails.

'Johanna. . .' He was now drowning, too. Instincts too old for conscience brought his fingers to the buttons of her bodice.

They undressed so slowly, discovered each other with such loving care, that nakedness, when it came, seemed as natural as the night. She had to tell herself, in so many words, *This is a naked man and these are parts of me no man has seen before and this is naked manhood . . . wanting me . . . wanting him . . .*

And then it was as she had always known it would be — the sweetest and most passionate thrill, consuming every particle of her, rising, endlessly rising, from one impossible plateau of joy to another, still more impossible. Surely one would soon assail her with such force it would tear her apart?

When it happened for her it happened for him, too. Something within her − the wild, elemental female − felt the muscles of his thighs gathering for withdrawal. *No!* Quick as a cobra, it flung her legs about him, clasping him to her.

Of course, his strength prevailed. He collapsed upon her and she felt the most of him pumping to exhaustion between their bellies while he said oh and oh and oh in tones she hardly recognized. And she lay there, too, blinking at tears she did not remember shedding, wanting it to go on and on, with him back there inside and never stopping.

'Whoooo!' he breathed when he was calm again. 'That was touch and go.'

She pushed her hand into the sweat between them. The thing that always happened to horses had happened to him, too. 'How long...' she whispered, 'before...?'

'Oh, Jo!' He kissed her ear, sending a new paroxysm through her. She eased out from under him, feeling peeled and raw in the chill of the night. His hand went to her breast but she pushed it onward − lower...lower. He began to caress her there. She arched herself off the bed to meet him. His finger found the spot; she collapsed and began to spin herself around its rhythm. By the time she was back on that plateau he was hard again, too − and so, transfixed between the extremes of vigour and exhaustion, they passed a further hour before the world and its demands grew insistent enough to intrude.

He slept for a few minutes and then came wide awake. His eyes were troubled. She kissed him tenderly. 'It'll be all right,' she whispered.

'You're sure? You know, do you?'

She blew in his ear and giggled.

'What time of your month is it?'

'It'll be all right,' she repeated.

She tried to imagine herself carrying his child, and him five thousand miles away knowing nothing of it. Not a twinge of worry or conscience disturbed her. It *would* be all right. Something as wonderful as this could not be wrong.

With his immediate doubts resolved he turned to his

former worry. 'Why would Nina want us out of the house?' he asked. 'She picked that quarrel over absolutely nothing. She manufactured it.'

Johanna settled against his mighty chest and listened to the sound of his voice. The words just flowed over her. How could he talk of anything but the two of them at such a time as this? Men were the most extraordinary beings.

'It must be that person you said she met. Describe her — maybe I know her.'

Johanna made a half-hearted attempt to remember something distinctive about the girl. 'I don't know,' she replied. How raw her voice sounded. 'A beggar girl, I thought. Soaked to the skin and all bedraggled. Someone must have given her an old ball gown. But it didn't fit. Anyway, what does it matter?'

'How old? Dark or fair? Disfigured . . . starved . . . pretty. Tell me.'

'Oh, Hal, I don't want to think about her now. How can you?'

'It's important — or it could be. Try!'

'Talk about us. Tell me . . . what you feel. You know.'

There was a knock at the door.

Hal called out, 'We're coming.'

Margaret must have heard 'Come in!' for she opened the door, stuck in her head, cried out, 'Oh my gidge!' and vanished twice as fast.

Hal chuckled. 'You are one long surprise tonight,' he told her.

'In what way?'

'You didn't stir a muscle when she saw us.'

'I imagine she knew what we were doing. And another thing — I don't feel any shame at it. I know exactly how Adam and Eve must have felt before the serpent taught them shame.'

He wanted to get back to the subject of Nina, but he could not resist pointing out that Adam had not felt the shame of nakedness until God came looking for him. 'And we're not told whether Eve felt anything at all,' he added.

'Well, I'm quite sure she didn't — not shame, anyway. How could God make it such an exquisite pleasure and then fill us with shame at it? Anyway, why are we talking about them at all. Why are we talking about anything except us?'

After a pause he went on, 'It must have been someone who knows Terence. Perhaps a servant who overheard him talking... No, you'd have recognized her. Unless it's a new girl at Lanfear since you left?'

Johanna forced herself to think about the encounter. 'I don't believe she was a servant. I don't know how you tell someone's class when they look like a dying duck in a thunderstorm, but she spoke... well, I'd say more like a tradesman's daughter.'

'You said a beggar girl.'

'That was when I only *saw* her. But when she spoke there was just that bit of refinement. Anyway, why does it worry you? Nina isn't our enemy, you know.'

'Well...' he said dubiously.

'She isn't.'

'I've sometimes had the feeling she doesn't want us to be in love. Or not to marry each other, anyway.'

Johanna, still lying heavily on his chest, shook her head vehemently. 'She's never breathed a word to me about it.'

'I can well believe it. No, she's too clever for that. But just you be on your guard now while I'm gone. She'll find some chance to put the poison in your ear.' He smiled to himself at the second appearance of the phrase that day.

What a world!

Thank heavens there were people like Jo in it, too. 'Oh God,' he murmured, turning and gathering her to him for one last embrace, 'I do love you, my darling. So much. I didn't know such love was possible.'

She kissed him, over and over. 'That's the antidote to all the poison in the world,' she said.

Chapter Twenty-Eight

The Royal Mail ran via Truro. Normally the connecting coach from the Swan at Redruth left at some ungodly small hour, and Johanna had resigned herself to the knowledge that, even after their absolutely final and concluding and ultimate last farewells, Hal would still be in the county for several hundred more minutes, each of which would drag like a penance for her. But then Cunningham had got wind of an excursion to a fatstock show at Exeter; the coach was run by the same operator as had been going to carry him to Plymouth the week before — and it had two outside seats going begging. (Cunningham, however, gave Hal a different explanation. 'I've found this farmers' excursion,' he said. 'Much more convenient. What's more, one of the honest rustics practically owes me his life.')

This alternative coach left the Swan at the more reasonable hour of eleven in the morning, allowing for an overnight stay in Plymouth. When Johanna heard that, wild bears could not have kept her at Liston Court. She borrowed the fleetest of Nina's horses and flew the ten miles to the Swan. There was snow on the slopes of Carnmenellis and all the remainder of the way into Redruth, but it was the merest powdering and the wind had swept it clear of the highway.

She dismounted before the archway into the coachyard and gave the horse into the care of one of the ostlers. She herself, hoping to preserve her surprise until the last, slipped among a group of farmers and their wives who were entering the yard at that moment.

She need not have troubled. Hal leaned against a railing,

cast so deep in gloom that she was able to walk right up to him before he even noticed her. But the joy he showed when he realized who she was would have been worth a journey a hundred times more arduous. One of the farmers announced that their treasurer had had trouble with a farrowing sow that past night and would be delayed a further half hour. 'The gods are with us,' Hal told her. 'Shall we take a stroll?'

They followed the footpath to the Wesleyan chapel, a short way out of town. Here, on the weather side of Carn Marth, the snow lay thicker than it had up on the windswept tops, making the boundaries of the path uncertain; it was all the public excuse they needed to cling tight to each other, every step of the way.

'You couldn't have done a nicer thing,' he told her. 'I was...'

'You looked the picture of abject misery, poor darling.'

'That's what I was saying. When you saw me back there I had just arrived at the conclusion that I'm about to do the most foolish thing ever.'

She cleared her throat delicately. 'Are you talking about going to America at all – or going to America alone?'

He pulled her to him. 'I've told you about that. If it looks like I'll need more than two years, I promise I'll send for you.'

'Nina probably can't understand how I could wait two years – whereas Aunt Theresa, I'm sure, would think it shows monstrous impatience.'

'And should anything...I mean if you...well, if there's any need to come out earlier, you know what I mean – remember, Nina would always advance you the fare – and I'd repay her.'

And so it went on. They had said all these things before, of course, a score of times. But their separation from each other was now the only important fact in both their lives; they needed to confront it a hundred times a day; they had to look in the other's eyes and see how it haunted them – each ruefully drawing an odd kind of comfort from the other's pain; they tried to talk of different matters but soon found that all they wished to hear – yet again – were the promises, the resolutions, the brave words.

278

They passed the chapel and found themselves on the very fringes of the town. Before them stretched a mile or more of rising ground — a patchwork of tiny fields, isolated farmhouses, and open moorland. Mines and their wastes sprawled indiscriminately over all. From within the drab olive greens and the faded muddy browns of a Cornish winter the snow had discovered a new landscape, meshed in dry-stone hedges and littered with screes of rock and fine-grained debris; these features stood out, dark-etched upon the fields of white and gray. The pair of them stood awhile in silence. She gazed skyward, where a flock of gulls was protesting at the day and the threat of yet more snow.

He stared at her until he thought his heart would break. Some instinct told him he would need more than the image of her to carry through the months ahead. His eyes released their hold upon her and scanned the countryside, instead, seeking landmarks that were universal and yet somehow special to this hour and place. There was a lone pine in a distant garden, a dark and vivid scratch upon the snow. That would do for one. There was a fitful shaft of sunlight sweeping up the hillside to kindle a brief fire in the stones of the ancient fort atop Carn Brea. That was another. And close at hand a kestrel circled and fluttered, mewing with tremulous anger at finding no thermals to sustain him today. That was the third. Wherever he went in the New World now, he would never see a hovering bird of prey, or sunlight upon stone, or a lone pine against the sky without instantly remembering Johanna, too — precisely as she was, here and now.

He turned to burn that final image of her in his mind and found her eyes grown cool upon him. 'What's this?' he asked.

'You're already three thousand miles away,' she accused.

And he could not deny it. 'Ah,' he said, tapping his forehead. 'But when I am there, I shall also be back here.'

'And I shall always be here,' she promised.

They clung to each other so long they had to run all the way back. They only just made the coach in time.

She was still breathless when the party pulled out of the yard. The clatter of iron tyres and iron-shod hooves on the

279

cobblestones was almost deafening, even without the yapping of stray dogs and the blast of the coachman's horn. She ran after it into the roadway and waved and waved until it passed out of sight. Every second was so precious.

Back on her own mount she had to fight the urge to turn his head toward Truro. She could ride alongside, she told herself. The way from Truro back to Helston was surely only a mile or two longer. Where would be the harm?

But now she felt a curious emptiness within her; all her feelings seemed to have taken wing, flying in search of him, as the siren voices were urging her to do in person. She squared her shoulders, clenched the saddlepost firmly in her knee, and headed the creature for home.

All the way back she found herself thinking, *Only an hour . . . only ninety minutes. . . only two hours ago, I was here, going the other way, and the joy of being with him was still before me. And now it is over, and I may never see him again!* At Wendron she had to dismount and lean against a tree and cry till the salt ran out.

In her misery, she would have given all her tomorrows to change places with that happy, Redruth-bound Johanna whose shade taunted her at every new mark along the way. But by the time she arrived back at Liston Court, the old narcotic of grief had dulled the pain and enabled her to face the world and her own future once more.

Nina was waiting. She came running out across the snow-dappled lawn and lifted her arms to help Johanna down; the groom led the horse away. 'Oh, child – I'd almost begun to think you'd deserted us. I felt sure you were halfway to Plymouth by now! Will they get through with all this snow?'

'The coachman seemed to think there'd be no difficulty. I had to fight myself not to ride with him.'

Nina hugged her tight. 'Your eyes look red as fire. Poor angel! We must think up something special for this afternoon to take your mind off everything. Shall we go out to Pallas and tease little Hamill Oliver? You decide. Anything you want.'

'I just want to go to bed and pull the covers over me and never get up again.'

'Exactly!' Nina gave her one more squeeze and let her go. 'That's why we must get out somewhere. I know! We'll go down to Bullion Cliffs and watch the waves breaking over the rocks. It'll be quite spectacular after these gales. I always think there's nothing like the sea — the power of the sea — to make our own turbulence of spirit seem utterly trivial.'

Johanna shook her head. 'Not the sea, if you don't mind, Nina dear. I don't think I want to see the sea for quite a long time.'

'Good!' Nina was brisk and businesslike again. 'That settles it, then. Poor Hamill!'

Plymouth is really three towns in one. The city proper lies to the east, flanked on that side by Sutton Pool and the Catwater. Amost two miles away to the west, at the mouth of the Tamar, the river that divides Devon from Cornwall, stands Devonport, nine-tenths of which is an Ordnance dockyard of recent creation. And in the middle, both in years and in geography, is Stonehouse, on a tongue of land between Stonehouse Pool and Mill Bay. The coach put down its passengers at the Duke of Cornwall Hotel in Buckland Terrace, on the boundary between Stonehouse and the old city. There Cunningham was told that the *Starflight* lay at anchor in Sutton Pool. 'Good,' he explained to Hal. 'We shall pass my bankers on our way.' Hal wondered how long he would sustain that particular fiction. Anyway, Sutton Pool seemed a fitting enough point of embarkation, being the very harbour where the *Mayflower* had rested before setting out on an almost identical voyage of hope, one summer's day over two and a quarter centuries ago.

They left their baggage at the hotel, with the intention of sending a porter to collect it once they had located their ship; then they set off, free of its burden and glad to be stretching their boneshaken frames once more. Even had they not been able to see the masts of vessels over the rooftops, there could have been no doubting that this was a seaport town. The houses resembled nothing so much as a fleet of landlocked ships. Many had walls entirely of wood (bits of which had, indeed, sailed to the south seas and back) and they sloped outward in tiers, which, at the attic level, almost met across the street, blotting out the already fading light of day. The heavy carving, some of it gilded, the brass furniture on the doors and windows, the thick glazing, all tightly puttied in, the swinging lanterns...everywhere the eye came to rest in that cheek-by-jowl confusion it found the hand of the nautical architect rather than of his landlubber colleague.

Hal was astonished when, as they crossed High Street, Cunningham said, 'There it is,' and vanished into a none-too-imposing house with a brass plate outside, bearing the legend, DEVON COUNTY BANK. 'Shan't be a tick,' he called back over his shoulder. And, in surprisingly short order, he was back with a leathern pouch holding, he said, eighty guineas. As he handed it to Hal he added ambiguously, 'You'd best look after that. I shouldn't think even the most desperate ruffian would dare tackle you.' So Hal could not determine whether this were part payment or whether he was merely appointed its custodian. He tugged at the thongs and glanced inside; it was, indeed, full of gold coin and banknotes. Wonders would never cease. What was one to make of this enigmatic fellow? He loosened his belt and threaded it through the loop of the thongs, hanging the whole where it dangled uncomfortably but oh-so-reassuringly inside his trousers and against his rump.

'You're a bundle of surprises, Cunningham,' he commented.

'Man of my word,' came the laconic reply.

At Sutton Pool there were a dozen ships of ocean-going class, half of them flying the Blue Peter; but among them was no sign of the *Starflight*. They inquired in several waterside inns until at last someone told them she was, in fact, at Mill Bay, not a furlong from where the coach had set them down. Cunningham seemed not the least put out. Indeed, he was if anything rather relieved. 'Listen, Penrose, old chap,' he said as they set out to retrace their steps. 'We'll be afloat soon enough, and out of the company of complaisant women for a good few weeks, I venture. What say we brush off the loose chaff before we embark, eh? Union Street's the place, I'm told.'

Hal laughed and patted him on the arm. 'You go ahead,

dear fellow, if that's your bent. I'll stroll back over the
Hoe. It's not much out of the way...see the lighthouse...'
He was about to add something about the view of
Plymouth Sound in the twilight, and Drake's bowling
green, and so on, when he realized why he was padding out
in such detail this quite ordinary preference − so as to
disguise the fact that what he really desired was to see the
house of Dr Anthony Moore, who had come to Cornwall
to ask for Selina's hand and had ended up in love with
Johanna. He had noted the man's address on a card
marked PPC among the dozens that littered Nina's
mantelpiece.

As he mounted the hill towards Windsor Terrace, it
struck him, rather belatedly, that he was not alone in
dissembling his true purpose. Cunningham, if he ran true
to form, was almost certainly not the apple of his uncle's
eye that he pretended to be. The poor chap had been
uncharacteristically subdued all the way between the Duke
of Cornwall and Sutton Pool − even what should have
been his moment of boastful triumph, actually producing
the promised cash, had been oddly low-key. Now why? Hal
wondered.

Maybe he was pondering how to keep Hal at a distance
while he soothed his relative's prickles. In that case he had
made his suggestion for a frolic in Union Street knowing
full well that Hal would refuse. And if Hal had not
volunteered to stroll slowly back by a longer route,
Cunningham would then have had good cause to ask for an
hour or so before they joined up again and went to see his
uncle − during which time he'd race ahead and beard the
lion without losing face. What a quaintly twisted world it
was, Hal thought. A moment later he arrived at Windsor
Terrace, which turned out to be a row of august dwellings
almost half a mile in length.

Dr Moore's portion of it, somwhere near the middle, was
not a terrace at all but a row of new villas in the Gothic
style. Only the inland side of the street was built upon, so
their windows looked out over the Promenade and the
eastern end of the Hoe to the magnificent sweep of the
Sound and the English Channel beyond. It was a humbling
experience for Hal to stand there and see what a superb

home Johanna had refused on account of her love toward him; for a second or two he even felt guilty, almost as if *he* were denying her the chance of a life among all this grandeur.

He crossed the road and stood with his back to the Promenade. There he glanced in turn at each of the villas opposite, trying not to reveal his interest in that particular one. He had intended no more than a brief survey before moving on to the Hoe, but now he realized he wanted above all to see this man whose comeliness had all the girls a-flutter yet who could never, poor chap, consolidate his advantage. It occurred to him that the man didn't actually know him; so he could easily pretend to have a vague sort of pain somewhere... 'Just wanted to be sure it was nothing serious, you see, doctor – because of this long voyage.'

Yes, that's what he'd do. He could get a good close look at the chap while he prodded and listened for murmurs and so on.

He had just started across the road when he saw something that stopped him dead. True, the light was now fading fast, but by what remained of it he could swear that the young female who was at that very moment emerging from the tradesmen's entrance to the house was none other than Jenny Jewell.

She saw him, too – though that was strange, for he had the remaining daylight behind him and she could not possibly make out his features. But she recognized him all right. Was she then expecting to see him here? Or, at least, in Plymouth? Oh yes – he had told her of it, hadn't he. Still – why was she at Dr Moore's?

She turned and scurried away down the street as if the hunt were baying at her heels. He let her go, knowing he could easily outrun her if he wished.

But she was quicker with her brain than with her heels; the scurrying carried her no more than twenty yards before she slowed to a halt, turned, and stared at him uncertainly. 'Hal?' she asked, with just the right amount of doubt in her voice.

'You know full well it is,' he said evenly, not moving a step in her direction.

She came toward him, crossing the street to his side. He stepped back onto the footpath and waited, his mind racing. By the time she joined him, a few wild conclusions had already formed. 'You don't seem too surprised,' she remarked. She herself was shivering like a willow; her voice was up and down, all over the place.

He risked a guess. 'Ever since I realized it was you following me into Helston, during that storm the other day, I've been expecting something to happen. Not this, I admit — but something.'

She took his arm, making the gesture seem coquettish, though, to judge by the way she leaned upon him, she truly needed his support. 'Did you come up here to...I mean, did you know I...?'

'I was on my way to the Hoe.' He turned and, still supporting her, resumed his stroll in that direction.

'He's probably watching us.' She kept her voice down as if she feared being overheard.

'Dr Moore?'

'Yes. Don't turn round. He's probably standing at one of his windows, watching us.'

'It's all right. He doesn't know me from Adam.' He laughed. 'In fact, I was about to call...here, you're cold. Put up my coat.'

'No, I'm just shivering with the shock. It'll pass.'

'Put it up nonetheless.' He draped the garment over her shoulders and went on to explain how he had been about to visit the doctor when she had suddenly appeared.

'I suppose you know everything?' she asked. 'Or can guess.'

He risked a further surmise. 'Just one thing — was it Lady Nina's idea or yours?'

'Hers, of course! Lord, Hal, if you can ask that, then you know nothing. This is Lady Nina's scheme from start to finish. She may call me a traitor but my intention was always to tell you as soon as...well, no matter, we'll come to that. But when I followed you into Helston that day, it was simply to learn...I mean, you didn't visit Sunny Corner off your own bat, as they say. Someone put you up to it. I calculated you'd go straight back to that same person. But then Lady Nina learned who I was and...

everything else followed. Anyway, I had no choice.'

He saw then that, though he might have been right in certain details (it *had* been Jenny who followed him to Helston, and Nina *was* somehow involved in this 'scheme,' as Jenny called it), he was hopelessly adrift when it came to her motives. 'You're right,' he admitted. 'It seems that I know nothing — or only the superficial circumstances. I have painted you blacker than the devil in my mind, but now I begin to think I've wronged you. Why don't you tell me your side of the affair?'

They had gained the Hoe at last, but the view was rapidly being swallowed up in darkness. Except for the last dim resonance of land, sky, and water, the world was now largely defined in pinpoint bursts of artificial light, whose brilliance only served to deepen the circumambient black. Down in the harbours and out on the Sound, masthead lanterns were being kindled and carried aloft; once set, they trailed shimmering fingers upon the water, all pointing at the Hoe. On headlands and islands, from Mount Batten in the east to Cremyll in the west, burned the gentler, steadier illumination of candles and oil lamps. And far out to sea, fourteen miles from where they stood, they could just discern the glimmer of the Eddystone light. Hal remembered an old sailor telling him of the storm that had swept away the first such structure on those shoals and sunk a whole fleet of merchantmen. 'You could walk from shore to shore over Sutton Pool,' he had said. ''Twas wreckage floating all the way.' Hal tried to forget how soon it would be before he himself was to embark on that same uncaring ocean.

Jenny gave a sigh. 'I meant to tell you any road,' she said. 'You'll just have to believe that. I meant it to be the first thing I . . .'

'If that's true, you were leaving it pretty late!' he commented. 'Why are you in Plymouth at all? And what business have you with Dr Moore?'

She did not immediately take up either question. 'When Lady Nina came across me, waiting outside her house like that in the rain . . . she's a good-hearted lady, you know. I don't want to say a word against her in all this. I mean, she thinks she's acting for your own good. I still thought she was your fancy woman, remember. So I tried putting her off you. I tried sort of hinting that you were, well, as good as promised to me.'

'If she had been my "fancy piece," that would certainly have endeared you to me!'

'You'd do the same,' she assured him darkly.

'Listen, Jenny — you may have all the time in the world, but I have a boat to catch.'

She stiffened for a moment and then relaxed. 'You'll see soon enough,' was all she replied to that.

'Anyway?' he prompted.

'Yes. Anyway — like I said, she has a heart of gold, that Lady Nina. She asked me if I wished to come in and dry myself by the kitchen fire and have a cup of hot broth or suchlike. So I thanked her, pretty-like, thinking I'd hear from the servants something of your business in that house.'

'And did you?'

'I learned that Selina Visick was there, too — hah, I could tell you a thing or two about her brother!'

'Not much that would surprise me,' he began to say — and then he remembered how Nina had behaved immediately after this waterlogged encounter. 'But you told *her*, didn't you!' he added. 'You told Lady Nina about Terence Visick.'

He felt her stiffen with surprise. 'You're too swift for me, Hal. How d'you work that out?'

'Swift! This is getting us nowhere. You're explaining nothing. Never mind about Terence Visick. Just tell me what you're doing here in Plymouth?'

She appeared to think the matter over but when she spoke it was only to change the subject yet again. 'You tell me one thing first,' she said. 'Why did you come out to Sunny Corner like that, the day before yesterday?'

'I didn't come *out* there. I called on my way to Helston. I've been living at Charley Vose's, or didn't you know?'

'No. So you didn't make a special visit of it?'

They had reached the eastern edge of the Hoe by now and were starting the brief descent through narrow, cobbled streets to the quays at Mill Bay.

'I'm afraid not. So — to return to the point — exactly

when did you come here to Plymouth? It must have been yesterday. And *she* must have sent you – Lady Nina. Amn't I right? And *she's* the one who gave you Dr Moore's address. But why?' He squeezed her arm, not meaning to hurt. 'What message did you carry between them? And what is she hoping for now I'm gone away?'

She protested at his strength and jerked her arm from his grip. Rubbing it tenderly she said, 'Oh Hal, my dear, haven't you worked it out for yourself yet?'

'I know that for some strange reason she's opposed to my...to Johanna and my...to our love for each other. Not that she'd say a word directly. Oh no, she's all honey and...'

At that moment there came a cry from the bottom of the street: 'Penrose! Penrose!'

It was Cunningham, sounding extremely agitated. 'I'm here!' Hal called back, already breaking into a trot. Then he remembered his coat. He was about to stop when he realized Jenny was keeping up at his side. 'Cunningham!' he called out. 'Here – I'm coming.'

'Thank God,' the fellow cried when Hal had caught up with him. He did not wait but set off at once along the waterfront. 'Come on – they've already weighed one anchor. I'd almost given you up.'

'Our baggage,' Hal reminded him.

'All aboard. If you don't hurry, she'll sail without us. In ten minutes they'll have lost the tide.'

They were all three running toward the ship by now. 'Ahoy!' Cunningham shouted as soon as they came within earshot. '*Starflight* avast! Hold the gangway!'

'You...needn't...run,' Hal told Jenny, a word at a time between his gasps for breath. He galloped lopsided, hitching up the bag of coins which would otherwise impede him painfully.

'Must...say...proper...farewell,' she replied in the same breathless fashion, but with a laugh in her voice as well. She had to sweep up her skirts so as to keep pace over the granite setts of the quays.

'You're idiotic,' he panted back.

'I know.'

Hal and Cunningham tumbled aboard at the last possible

moment, in a confusion of curses from the crew and cheers from those idlers who had no stake in the business.

'Oh hell − my coat!' Hal cried the moment he was safely on deck. He rushed to the railing and stared out into the pools of fitful light upon the quay. 'Jenny?' he cried. 'Where are you? My coat!' He had learned nothing from her and had lost his coat into the bargain.

A moment later the garment was slipped over his shoulders from behind and her voice, husky with exhaustion, murmured in his ear, *'Now* do you understand?'

PART THREE

STRANGERS IN PARADISE

Chapter Twenty-Nine

The Arab tribesman took careful aim and fired again. Between the towering walls of the narrow Siq the explosion cracked sharp as a whip and its reverberations were long in dying. The three Englishwomen just stood their ground and stared at him in astonishment. Nina turned to Usn, their dragoman, to see how he was responding. There was a sneer on his lips — but that was nothing new; Usn was a second-generation city-dweller and the ways of his desert fore-fathers always made him sneer. He had the most superbly chiselled lips, Nina thought, like the Egyptian carvings in London; upon them even a sneer was worth a lingering glance.

'What *does* he imagine he's doing?' Selina asked.

'*Dhahab!*' Usn said in disgust. 'Buried treasure. For the sake of it his goats are straying and his family wants. Everything must go on powder and shot. Later, he'll come begging. Leave him to me.'

The man took another shot. This time, lacking the element of surprise, they had a chance to discover his target.

'Good heavens!' Nina laughed, still not quite believing her eyes.

'Doesn't he realize it's solid stone?' Selina asked. 'Like everything else here.'

'For him there is knowledge-through-the-senses, which is worthless, and knowledge-from-legends, which is beyond truth. His legends tell him that the whole of Sela — which is their name for Petra — is the work of a Pharaoh who was a black magician of supreme power. And the Pharaoh hid his gold and rubies in the heart of the rock — most especially in that urn on top of the temple. So this zany and his gun will go on shooting at it until it splits open and yields its *dhahab.*' He gave his stupid-Arab laugh, the one that always concluded his explanations of local customs.

Nina turned to Johanna. 'You're very quiet,' she said.

Johanna took a deep, luxurious breath. 'Mmmm.'

'What are you thinking about?'

'What else?' Selina asked with jovial mockery.

'I was just marvelling — here's this temple, as big as Liston Court, all carved out of living rock, and somehow it manages to dwarf the very cliff into which it's carved.'

They resumed their stroll toward the upper end of the Siq. The tribesman paid them no attention as they passed. *What unknowable people they are,* Nina thought. *If we were camels, rather than strange, foreign women, he'd watch us out of sight — and recognize us again a year from now.*

At the head of the narrow gorge, just beyond an ancient and by now dangerously derelict archway, Usn showed them where they could peep into the Tunnel, a triumph of Roman engineering that even now, after twenty centuries of neglect, still carried the annual floodwaters through the heart of the mountain to watertight cisterns in the city below. He explained how, 'many untold years ago,' those waters had carved out the gorge of the Siq and, indeed, the entire basin in which the ruined city now lay, 'half as old as time.'

He pointed northward, out into the desert beyond the gorge. 'And there stretches the ancient trail through Philadelphia to Byzantium and Trebizond, to Babylon and Damascus.'

Selina gave a little shiver. 'You never think of them as real places, do you. It's eerie to actually see it. What did they bring down the trail, Usn?'

'Carpets, ginger, hashish...a thousand miles!' He opened his mouth and touched his tongue. 'What people will endure for the sake of a new flavour here!' He did a mime of intoxication. 'Or a new way to forget.'

'But how did the citizens of Petra pay for it all?'

He grinned and stroked the palm of his hand. 'Like market folk everywhere. Other traders came up from Gaza and Egypt, with brass and jade and slaves and all new wonders from Rome. Also from Zanzibar, from China, with silk and medicine — from the Araby Gulf, with gold and rare spices and camels and fine leather and frankincense . . .' As he spoke his hands carved out the four quarters of the compass and beckoned to the ghost caravans of camels and donkeys. His presence was so imposing, his voice so hypnotic, that, for the three women, the empty vistas of the desert and the forsaken solitude of the Siq bustled once again with the life that had made this the hub of the ancient orient.

They re-entered the gorge not so much as tourists but as living echoes of those earlier hordes who had passed this way — stragglers too late for the actual feast but determined, nonetheless, to enjoy its fantasies.

Selina pictured herself as a Greek scribe or scribess or whatever they were called, recording her impressions for the all-powerful emperor in Rome. Everyone flattered her, for everyone wanted a good report. Her restless eye missed nothing. Lord, how they all went in fear of her!

Nina was a slave-girl, but different from all the rest. Her fame had spread throughout the orient so that the king of Petra, the richest man in the richest city in the world, had sent his Grand Vizier to Damascus to buy her from the Sultan there. She was to become the flower of all his thousand concubines. And there was no taint of sin because things were different in those days and anyway she had no choice in the matter.

And Johanna was something more timeless than either of her companions. The handmaiden of a great lady on her travels, secure in the love of a husband half a world away — then as now, her pleasure was all focussed on the new little life within. A woman who has just felt the first queasy wriggling of that miraculous gift no longer dreams about herself, her past, and all that might have been. Her fancy has a more rewarding focus altogether.

'There!' Usn proclaimed as they rounded the bend in the gorge where the Khasneh had been carved — the building with the fabulous (and now shot-riddled) urn on its pediment.

Suddenly they understood why he had insisted on breaking off their tour of the ruined city and coming up the Siq instead. In the half hour since they last stood there, the sun had risen to the point where it now shone directly down into the gorge. It fell upon the russet stone, making it burn with an incandescent light that struck fiery resonances into the shadows all around — a display of silent majesty that would last ten minutes at most. They stood entranced, lifted out of themselves, beyond all fantasy — in a way, beyond time itself. It touched them with a paradox, a sensation of passing immortality. Since their arrival in the Holy Land they had seen many wonders of which they had said, 'For that alone our journey was worthwhile.' But of nowhere was it more true than here. For this moment of sheer magic their entire lives seemed vindicated.

Later, back in the ruins below, the palimpsest of former selves returned. They stood among the fallen colonnades, upon what had once been fair boulevards of marble, and rekindled their sense of wonder at the sight of so many palaces and temples, all carved from the cliffs of rose-red stone. And Usn once again brought it back to life. He guided their feet through bazaars thronged with people from the caravans. He boxed the ears of importunate urchins. He pulled them aside, out of harm's reach, when arrogant slaves walked twenty abreast through the streets, clearing with their whips a path for the king. He flung out an arm to protect them when a centurion and his men passed by, fed up at trying to keep the wild Beduw tribes at bay, and now seeking oblivion from their failure in wine and women.

His eyes glowed with pleasure as he brought it all back for them — the teeming markets, the taverns...the theatres, fountains, gardens...the grand houses, the mean alleys, the crowded tenements. Watching him in fascination, Nina realized what an utter romantic he was, this would-be city swell. His grandfather might have tended goats amid these ruins, which would have seemed no more wonderful to him than they did to that hopeful musketeer up in the Siq. But now, one generation away from the tents, from the vast, empty deserts, from the sky with a myriad eyes, and his soul was starved of a romance the bazaars could not sell nor the city nurture. And he found it here, by flirting decorously and oh-so-correctly with foreign ladies among ruins that his ancestors had ignored for fifty generations...by telling them tales he had learned from books written not by *his* kinsmen but by theirs — books by doctor this and professor that, with imprints in Paris, London, Rome. What a topsy-turvy world it was becoming, to be sure.

Then she looked at Johanna, whose eyes were fixed dutifully on their guide, who smiled and laughed at all the right places, yet whose thoughts were plainly a million miles away. She had changed so much since coming out here. Selina was bright as always, writing everything down, sketching, making notes of it all; she would go back with enough details to rebuild the orient from scratch if some Old Testament catastrophe were suddenly to wipe it out. And yet Johanna would probably take back more — except that it had all soaked deep inside her, become part of her very fibre. She carried the whole desert in her eye; its peace was now at one with her blood.

The person who had gained the least, she reflected dourly, was herself. She felt, if only by proxy, Selina's busy excitement; she knew, if only from its outward marks, the serenity Jo had found. But she herself had discovered nothing beyond what she had known these ten years and more — that she was desperate for the loving touch of a man and would burst a vessel if something did not happen soon.

That evening the Beduw musketeer came to them with the offer of a sheep. He was annoyed they would spare no cartridges; his nearest supplier, a Turkish trader, lived half way to Philadelphia. Still, to carry a few small coin there was better than driving a sheep. He slaughtered it ritually for them before he left; of the four who watched, Usn was the most disgusted — but he roasted the chops on the fire and ate them with as much relish as any. He roasted a joint, too, and set it aside for the morrow before giving the rest to their Arab bearers, who finished the carcase in what sounded like one long, gleeful squabble.

They dined out beneath the stars, eating off a slab of marble that had left the mason's hands almost two millennia ago. The sweetness of the meat, the purity of the desert air, the serenity of the night — and above all, the certainty that they would never again repeat this experience — filled them with a nostalgia close to tears.

Later, Nina had troubled dreams. She was on a railway train but the line had been removed in places and the engine

had to find its own way as best it could. She walked ahead
with Usn to find where the track began again. They
discovered it running gently downhill beside a bridge, then
curving round to pass beneath its arch. But it was a false
hope; it, too, gave out as it emerged on the other side. Usn
became Hal. The bridge was the one he had sketched for
crossing the valley at Chacewater. She and Hal turned back
to warn the driver but it was too late. The gentle slope had
become very steep. She woke up shivering as the engine and
all its carriages tumbled into the abyss.

Unable to return to sleep, she pulled her thickest coat
about her and crept from her tent. The moon was so bright it
hurt her eyes for a moment. But then, as she grew more
accustomed to its brilliance, she began to make out the now
familiar details of the ruins – the Tomb of the Pharaoh, the
Unfinished Tomb, the Nymphaeum, the Roman walls and
towers – their brilliant hues reduced to a sort of pearly pink
in the moonlight.

With no particular aim in mind she strolled toward the
Nymphaeum, near the mouth of the Siq. The way led along
the foot of a low wall, which had once been far higher to
judge by the size of the gate near its western end. There she
was startled by one of their Arab sentinels, who gabbled
incomprehensibly at her, pointing several times toward the
Nymphaeum. She assured him that all was well and that she
intended going there anyway and he seemed satisfied
enough; at all events, he returned to his vigil. They certainly
took the threat of the *bakhsheesh*-seeking hordes of Abu
Zeitun very seriously. 'Pay them and run,' had been the
advice of the consul at Aleppo – who had nonetheless
assured them that women would be far safer than men
among the Beduwiyn.

At the Nymphaeum she was surprised to see Johanna,
sitting as though carved in anthracite, silvered by the moon.
'Well,' she said.

'Ah,' Johanna replied. When Nina sat beside her on the
ruined wall, she added, 'That sentry back there sent his
companion here to watch over me. See if you can make him
out.'

After the most minute inspection of the landscape, Nina
had to admit defeat.

'Look at that row of little tombs carved in that cliff above the entrace to the Siq.'

Nina saw the man then. 'They're not taking our safety for granted, are they. I suppose Usn's right — we should return to the Dead Sea tomorrow, before word of our arrival here can spread.'

'We shan't be harmed,' Jo assured her.

Nina gave a single, dry laugh. 'I envy you that calm, Jo. I must confess this land unsettles me. The heat...'

'I'm sorry.'

'Oh, I know it has the opposite effect on you.'

'I'll never be able to thank you enough, Nina, for giving me this chance.'

'All too soon over, I fear.' She patted the cool marble and ran her hand along its wind-honed surface. 'What does Nymphaeum mean, I wonder?' she asked.'D'you think it's what it sounds like?'

'I think it means 'fountain'. At least, it does in Leptis Magna. *Murray* says there's a huge one there.'

'Just being coy,' Nina said confidently. 'I'm sure those places had fountains, too. But the nymphs were what gave them their name. That's what Usn meant this afternoon when he pictured the Roman soldiers for us. Did you see how he stared at this place?'

'No.'

'Well, I did.' She rose to her feet and strode about, restless once again. 'Imagine it — being one of those young nymphs — standing here among the fig trees... I don't suppose they were here then, but still. Imagine standing here, listening to that squad marching up the road, knowing they were coming here, knowing that one of them was going to point to you and say, "I'll take her!" And you'd have no choice in it. You'd have to hold him by the hand and lead him' — she wandered uncertainly toward the back of the ruin, seeking the remnants of ancient cubicles but finding none — 'somewhere here. Or there. Or there or there — the whole squad.'

After a silence she added, 'Men are so lucky.'

'D'you think so?' Johanna was surprised. 'I think it must be terrible for them — to be so ridden by their demon that almost *anyone* will do.' When Nina said nothing further she asked, 'Or isn't that what you meant?'

'No, I mean everything's arranged for them. They know where to go, what to do. And then it's done. No obligations...nothing. 'Til next time. Marvellous!'

Johanna gave a small chuckle of disbelief. 'I can't imagine anything less attractive than a special house where we could go and pay to get ourselves in child – even by the stranger of our choice.'

'But if you were already married, and had given your husband a couple of undoubted heirs...well, he couldn't really crib about the tail-enders, could he?'

Johanna cleared her throat diplomatically. 'I imagine you'd have to ask him that question. I know what Hal would say.'

'Hal!' Nina cried out in vexation. 'Oh, Jo, can't you see how your world has shrunk since you've known him? What is the fascination of that man? I should have thought you, of all people...' Her voice tailed off as she saw Johanna stir herself at last and come walking toward her.

Her first thought was that she had said something to anger the girl; then she saw the smile on her face – like the smile of someone half asleep, or half in a waking dream.

'Give me your hand,' Johanna said. 'You shall be the first.' She took it and raised it to her lips, kissing the open palm in benediction before she slipped it inside her bodice and pressed it tight against her belly. After a moment she added, 'You probably won't feel anything yet.'

Nina's throat went dry. 'Jo...' she whispered in horror. 'Can you?'

'Jo – you don't mean...?'

'I felt it move today – that's the first time.'

Nina leaped away and hid her face in her hands. She pinched her forehead and cheeks, hoping this was some even more nightmarish sequel to the train disaster.

'Don't take it so,' Johanna pleaded, giving a brave little laugh to recruit Nina's mood to hers. 'I've never been so happy.'

Nina slumped; she seemed to shrivel from the touch of her own clothes. Her hands fell to her sides and she looked vaguely about for somewhere to sit down. 'What are we going to do?' she asked.

'Send a letter to Hal, of course — as soon as we're back within reach of the mails. Tell him I'm coming over to join him. You have the fare — he told me. Else I wouldn't have...' Whatever she had intended saying, she thought better of it.

'You wouldn't have what?'

Johanna shook her head. 'Nothing, really. Anyway, you do have the fare, don't you?'

Nina felt a surprising reluctance to tell a direct lie — surprising to herself, for she had previously decided she would do anything to protect her darling friend. Hal was wrong for Johanna. No question of that. Wrong, wrong, wrong. Soon, for the poor girl's own sake, she would have to inflict a wound that would seem to tear the heart out of her, but not yet. 'What month is this?' she asked.

'May.'

'No — I mean *your* month.'

'Oh, I don't know. Hal said something about months, too. I didn't understand it. I just told him everything was all right.'

'Oh, Jo!' Nina came forward and grasped her hands tight between her own. 'Such wisdom and such ignorance, crammed into that beautiful head! Haven't you noticed — the cardinal's not been paying his regular visit lately?' Her eyes lit up in a wild hope. 'Or has he? Is this all some false...'

'No, he hasn't.' Johanna announced it like a discovery — something she'd been too busy or excited to notice before.

'And has no one ever told you of the connection between that and your present "interesting condition"?'

Johanna remembered one of the maids once being overwhelmed with relief when she could 'fly the flag again,' as she expressed it. So that was what she meant! It all seemed so logical now she was amazed she had never made the connection before. 'No,' she admitted.

'So how long has it been? Actually I know — you needn't tell me. It was two nights before he left, wasn't it. There was that big storm. And you and Margaret went over to Goldsithney — that was it.'

Jo gave her a conspiratorial grin. 'And the next night, too, when he dined with us. After he left he came back and

301

shinned up a drainpipe to my bedroom window.'

'And I thought he was a gentleman!' Nina exploded.

'To come back like that? But why shouldn't . . .'

'No! I mean to leave his quickening inside you. A gentleman should know how and when to withdraw.'

'Oh, but that was me. I stopped him. I almost stopped him the first night but he was too strong for me. But that last night was different. I was ready for him then.'

Nina stared at her, mouth open. She looked in one eye, then the other, as if she hoped one of them might give this confession the lie. 'You *wanted* it to happen!' she said at last.

'Of course I did. I knew it would be all right — I mean, *will* be all right. You can lend me the fare. There are boats going to America every week in the summer. Even if we're not actually together, we can marry by proxy once I'm there.' She laughed. 'Another baby born six months premature at full weight! He'll join a goodly flock in Cornwall.'

'Listen.' Nina appeared to come to some decision. 'No matter what may happen, I shall stand by you. I want you to know that, my lamb. I shall never, never cast you out.'

Johanna was nonplussed. 'Well, that's very kind of you, Nina, I'm sure. I mean, it's exactly the sort of generosity I'd expect. But it won't be necessary. As I was saying . . .'

'No — don't say it again. The truth is, Jo, my pet . . . oh dear! The truth is — I don't think you will be going to join Hal. There!'

'But of course I will.' Johanna was just beginning to realize this was not a teasing game of the sort Nina sometimes liked to play.

Nina shook her head; her eyes were two great pools of sympathy.

'I will!' Johanna insisted, fighting a growing desperation inside her. 'You must give me that . . .'

'I've been dreading having to tell you, darling. In fact, I decided not to. I just hoped that once Hal had gone, you'd see it was no more than infatuation and . . . well, there'd be no need. I never for one moment suspected . . .'

'What d'you mean — infatuation!' Johanna shouted.

'Ssssh! You'll wake Selina.'

'I don't care if I awaken the dead.' She faltered at the

302

word. 'Hal! He's not...you're not saying he's ...dead?'

Nina sighed and shook her head. 'That would have been the kindest...oh, even now I can't bring myself to tell you.' She turned toward their tents. 'The best thing I can do is show you.'

'Show me what?'

'Come.' She held out her hand, which Johanna took reluctantly.

'I don't care what it is,' she warned. 'I shan't believe it.'

'I think you'll believe this. It's a letter from Dr Moore.'

'Hah!' Johanna cried scornfully − and with reviving hope. 'If that's all it's going to be, a plea from a desperate man...'

'It's nothing like that.'

'I'm sorry for him, of course. But he didn't give a fig for Selina's feelings − and he wasn't to know then how cool they were. And I feel the same about him.'

Nina let a silence grow before she went on. 'You do know, don't you, that Hal has a keen eye for a pretty face?'

'Yes,' Johanna laughed wearily. 'Such an unusual fellow!'

'And more than a pretty face.' Nina was relentless. 'He'll go all the way with any woman who takes his fancy and gives him the chance in return.'

'Why, that must make him almost unique!'

'All right.' Nina chuckled. 'You're not as green as my cabbages, then. Very well − let's go in by the other gate. You tell me what *you* know about him in that way.'

'I know he's cut a fair swathe among the maidens of West Penwith. But I don't imagine there's many who grudge him what they yielded. I certainly don't.'

'Ah! But you know he loves you. You know he's going to marry you. But just suppose that were not the case! Suppose you were one of his many cast-offs − what then?'

Johanna was silent.

'You still wouldn't grudge him? No, perhaps you wouldn't. Your inability to harbour a grudge is quite extraordinary. Selina's told me a thing or two about...but never mind that. However, even if you held no grudge, surely you'd at least *hope*? And if he went off after some other woman, and then you saw a chance to get him back with you again... are you trying to tell me you wouldn't take it?'

'Of course I would.'

'Very well.' Nina fanned her face in a parody of relief. 'Finding common ground with you is like trying to discover Atlantis. So — next question: Do you know a certain Mrs Jewell? Lives in Goldsithney.'

'I know her by sight. She lives at Sunny Corner. She used to wash for us.'

'D'you know anything more recent about her?'

'I've heard nasty gossip.' She remembered that young Harold Blight, the lad who had made the delivery with her to Lanfear that evening, had passed on some unpleasantness about the poor woman and her semi-orphan family.

'You know she has twin daughters, Jenny and Diana? And that the three of them are very obliging to the wandering man? They gaily take all in their stride, as the saying goes?'

'So do half the women in Cornwall, if you believe a quarter of what idle tongues can...'

'And do you also know that Jenny and Hal were sparking together a couple of years ago?'

Johanna sighed with exasperation. 'Listen, Nina, if all this is a preamble to the revelation that Hal paid the occasional visit to Widow Jewell, all I say is tell me more — it'll help put me to sleep.'

She smiled to hear herself speaking like that. If it were Hal beside her, making such a confession, she doubted she'd be quite so tolerant; but she was damned if she'd give Nina the satisfaction of putting her nose out of joint.

All Nina said, however, was, 'Wait out here. I'll bring a lantern.'

In fact she brought more. When she had placed the lantern on the block of marble that had served as their dinner table, she handed Johanna a folded piece of paper. 'This,' she said, 'is what I hoped you would never see — or even get to hear of. Read it yourself.'

It was, as she had promised, a letter from Tony Moore, dated from Plymouth on the very day Hal had sailed:

My dear Lady Nina,

I write to tell you of a most puzzling and disturbing occurrence, and to ask your advice upon the matter. Yesterday I received a visit from a young woman by the name of Jennifer Jewell. She told me she had visited you the previous day in Helston, having been brought to Liston Court by Mr Hal Penrose. (Now you see at once *my* interest in the matter, for my feelings toward Miss Rosewarne have not diminished in the smallest degree since we spoke together in Helston last year.) The tale she span was fantastical to a degree. I did not believe a word of it and shall not dignify it with ink. In a nutshell, she claimed that *you* had sent her to me! When she saw what effect this vile slander had upon me, she quickly changed her tune and said she got the entire tale − of Miss Rosewarne's connection with Hannibal Penrose and of my interest in the matter − from your servants. I cannot even believe that is likely, but I imagine she has picked up a certain amount of gossip from *somewhere*.

She also informed me that she and Mr Penrose had been lovers in the summer of 1846 − in every sense of that word. But he, as is apparently his way with women who yield to him, quickly tired of her and moved on to pastures new. She has never got over her loss of him, she said, and would do anything to get him back. Mr Penrose, she informed me, was sailing to America the following day − which is this very day, as I write. Her proposal was this: If I would pay her fare to go with him, she would guarantee that he would never trouble Miss Rosewarne again, nor even think of her.

I sent the girl away, telling her to return today for an answer. To be sure, I was sorely tempted. What man as hopelessly lost in love as I would not respond to such an offer? I had no sleep at all last night, being buffeted between conscience and that lack of scruple which only those in love may understand. I remember once I said to you in jest that if Mr Penrose ever wished to emigrate, you were to give him the fare to Timbuktu or the moon and I should happily reimburse you. However, if push had come to shove, I do not think I would have carried out that promise, for, when the girl came back today, conscience had won and I told her I would not give her the passage money. (I gave her ten shillings, though, for her lodging tonight and her coach fare home, which I swiftly regretted, for she at once abused me in a shameless and ungrateful way.)

I had seen her out by the tradesmen's entrance, not wishing her to have contact of my own servants here. When she was a safe pace or two from me she turned and dropped the money where even a doctor could not delve for it and said, 'What sort of milksop are you, then? Anyone with the bowels of a true man would have paid double the fare to get his rival out of the way.'

She is right, of course, but I know my chance of finding the happiness I crave with Miss Rosewarne is near hopeless, so it is my conscience I must live with, not her.

The Jewell creature had one more pearl to cast. 'Anyway,' she said, 'I have meanwhile acquired the fare in my own way. As soon as I came here yesterday I knew I could not rely upon the likes of you.' (Not quite her exact words but *they* were unrepeatable.)

The truth, I suppose, was that she already had the fare when she came to Plymouth, otherwise it was a long journey to be risking. She merely hoped to coax a little extra out of me. However, imagine my surprise when, only moments later, I went to my window and saw her linking arms with none other than the great Mr Hannibal Penrose himself! – whom, you recall, I saw dining with you and Miss Rosewarne one night while I was staying at the Angel in Helston. There he stood as bold as brass! He hadn't even the common sense, or sensibility, to wait around the corner. They linked arms and went off laughing up to the Hoe. I watched them out of sight and they were very tender with each other. So now I believe it is pretty clear how and from whom she 'acquired the fare in her own way'!

My dilemma, dear Lady Nina, is this. I now know that the woman I hold dearest in all the world has entrusted her heart to one who will break it. Suppose I were merely her good friend, would I not find some way to tell her this? Of course I should! I could not shave myself if I failed in such a duty. But I am – or would dearly like to be — so much more than a mere good friend to Miss Rosewarne, and that must inevitably colour the picture. Clearly I must tell her what I have seen, even at the cost of losing her esteem for ever. But that is a step I tremble to take.

In any case, I write within an hour of the unfolding of these events — much too soon to come to any sound conclusion. I am resolved, therefore, to set the whole matter aside until I have heard from you. I know you love Miss Rosewarne as tenderly as I; yet you will be able to view the business from a calm perspective that will always be beyond me. I therefore commend into your care the troubled heart and conscience of,

Yr. devoted servant,
Anthony Moore.

Johanna folded the letter calmly and passed it back to Nina — who stared at her in astonishment. 'Have you nothing to say?' she asked at last.

'No.'

'You don't even wish to know what I replied?'

Johanna shook her head and smiled. 'It is poison,' she said. 'Hal told me to expect it. I don't for one moment blame you for being deceived by it, Nina dear. And I'm grateful you've shown it to me at last. I wish you'd done so earlier, for I could have saved you much heartache. . .'

'But how can you say that?' Nina shook the letter open again and held it before her.

Johanna ignored it, and the interruption, both. 'You see,' she said, 'There is one great difference between us. For this particular poison' — she placed her hand on her midriff — 'I carry the antidote always about me.'

Chapter Thirty

They had not intended revisiting Italy on their return voyage to England, but now Nina said she 'thought it best'. After all, they had 'no particular reason to hasten home'. Johanna knew this was said in provocation of her but she held her peace; the less fuss she made, the sooner Nina would drop it.

They arrived one evening, hot and tired, at a little inn a dozen miles southeast of Florence, just outside San Gimignano on the fringes of the Monti del Chianti. 'It will be cooler here than down on the plains,' Nina said. 'And the wine is out of this world.'

The house and its extensive garden occupied a long terrace cut in the northern side of a steep valley, running more or less east-west at that point. Immediately in front of the house this terrace was almost certainly natural, for the lemon grove between it and the valley was bounded by a low wall built on the very edge of a bluff that fell sheer, more than a hundred feet. In the heart of the lemon grove, just inches from that wall, was fixed a vast oak table of considerable antiquity. Around it, massively carved in the same enduring wood, were armchairs fit for a medieval Florentine prince.

'Oh, do ask if we may have our dinner out here,' Selina said.

'Ask?' Nina echoed with amusement. She went indoors and told the man, 'We shall eat out there.' He looked at her in tolerant surprise, as if he expected she might go on to explain that they would wash in water and sleep in beds.

'It seems that this is the dining room anyway,' she remarked as she returned, chastened, to the others.

They were already seated, staring out over the valley beyond. After a long silence Selina murmured, 'I imagine paradise will be like this.'

Immediately below them, over the wall, they could peer down into the dark-upon-dark of a citrus grove, almost lost in a deep pool of shade. From that rich floor the valley rose through levels of increasing poverty — through an abandoned olive grove where the drab-coloured trees had grown wild and rangy, on up through a labyrinth of tamarisk scrub and goat maquis, until it arrived at a bare scree of sun-bleached rock where no green showed at all. The evening sun fell aslant this wilderness, making a kaleidoscope of jagged shadows and shouting highlights; somewhere in that confusion a shepherd was playing his pipes — a nonstop dirge on five notes whose every combination was purest melancholy.

The same rays crept beneath the lemon trees and warmed the three of them where they sat.

'I hope so.' Nina answered Selina at last.

The table was pallid from the sun and scored with the years of rain and frost. The lady of the house came out and spread an ample white cloth upon it; she chatted with them easily for a while. Nina, who had the best Italian, did most of the answering. When she had gone Selina said, 'That's something we don't really have in England — a peasantry. Something between a yeoman and a labourer. That woman may call you milady, yet she yields nothing in equality. I like it.'

Nina smiled at Johanna. 'Incipient revolutionary here!' She nodded her head in Selina's direction. 'I don't think her mama's going to agree that our Grand Tour has done her lamb much good, do you?'

Johanna shook her head fondly. 'Doesn't it all seem a lifetime away — Cornwall and...everything.'

'We'll be back there soon enough, precious.' She left the disturbing notion to swell during the meal. On several other occasions she found an opportunity to mention the imminence of their return to Helston and a society in which they would once again have to remember whose eyes were upon them.

They had pasta and saltimbocca, washed down with the

local white Vernaccia — which was Nina's real reason for choosing this spot. 'You know what Michelangelo said of this wine?' she asked. 'He said it kisses, licks, bites, thrusts, and stings.'

'And all in one bottle!' Selina laughed.

'Not bad value for less than one scudo.' She grinned conspiratorially at the other two. 'I say, shall we stay an extra day and go and see those sculptures again?'

Selina agreed with enthusiasm.

'Also,' Nina added, 'more seriously — there is one other thing we must do.' She stared at Johanna who gazed back and asked, 'What?'

'Well, you won't be able to stay in Cornwall for more than another month or two, my dear. A certain degree of enlargement could be put down to the pleasures of my table. But more than that and the locus of the presumed pleasure will certainly change.'

'Pleasure?' Selina murmured sadly.

Johanna ignored the provocation and waited for Nina to speak more plainly.

'I mean' — Nina was annoyed at being forced to spell it out for her — 'you will have to come back . . . *we* will have to come back here to Italy this summer and rent a discreetly shaded villa.'

Johanna was shaking her head wearily. They had been through all this a score of times already.

'*And* arrange for some good, reliable people to rear the child for you,' Nina added.

That was something new. Johanna sat sharply upright and blurted out, 'No!'

'It's the only way, Jo,' Selina told her gently.

Had they been talking about it together? Well, of course they had. But was it all neatly stitched tight between them? Johanna stifled the panic that was beginning to rise within her. 'You mean *that's* why we've stopped in Italy? The only reason?'

'I know it'll be hard, darling. But if you can start getting used to the idea now . . .'

Johanna shut her eyes, bowed her head, and shook it vehemently in time with her words. 'Not now. Not tomorrow. Not next month. Not in the summer. Never!'

Hearing only silence she looked up at them; they stared back at her with the eyes of unwilling attendants at a beheading. 'I've told you,' she insisted. 'As soon as we get back home I shall take passage to America and...'

'And what shall you use for payment?' Nina asked in as kindly a voice as she could manage.

'I shall go to Tony Moore for it if you won't honour what I assume was your promise to Hal. I'll beg in the streets. I'll hang a placard round my neck. I'll steal your silver... I don't care! I *am* going to America and I *shall* marry Hal Penrose.'

'You wouldn't!' Selina's eyes were bright with admiration at this outburst. 'Would you actually go to Tony and ask?'

Nina merely stared at her, saying nothing, revealing no emotion.

'And why not?' Johanna asked truculently. 'I'd say, after writing that cowardly letter, it's the very least he can do to make amends. If Hal were here, he'd kill him. And when Hal returns, Tony is going to need something to set against the harm he has done, or tried to do.'

'You just cannot face the truth, can you,' Nina remarked bitterly.

Johanna thought it best not to respond.

Nina went on, 'Any dispassionate person reading his letter would know at once that it was written by a man of the highest principles who found himself in an impossible dilemma.'

Johanna turned to Selina. 'If I asked you to compose a letter such as might be written by a simpleton, could you do it?'

Selina looked uncomfortably at Nina. 'Tony's no simpleton,' she said.

'That's not the point. Could you do it?'

'I suppose so.'

'If you were writing a novel and one of the characters was a simpleton, you could compose a letter as it were from him?'

Selina made a trapped, expansive gesture — as good as an admission.

'Or the letter of a snake in the grass?'

311

'Why not?' She repeated the gesture.

'Or of a man of the utmost nobility?' She turned to Nina without waiting for Selina's reply. 'You see the point without my labouring it, I'm sure?'

Nina shook her head sadly. 'You forget one thing – I have also met Dr Moore. I know the man, too. He would be quite incapable of...'

'You met him for ten minutes,' Johanna said. 'He stayed at Lanfear almost three weeks. I remember how, while he was there – under my uncle's roof and supposedly paying court to Selina – I remember how he followed me out to Godolphin Hill and took me in his arms and kissed me. I don't call that very honourable, do you?'

Selina let out a breath, as if she had been hit in the stomach. 'How utterly unfair!' she cried. 'He did nothing of that sort until *after* we took our walk along Ptaa Sands – when I freed him from any obligation he might have felt towards me.'

Nina tried to pour out more of the chianti but Johanna pulled her glass away. 'I'm not *drinking* for two, you know.' She intended it as a mild joke but somehow it didn't come out that way.

Nina poured herself and Selina a full glass each. 'Here!' Selina protested with a nervous laugh.

'Oh, I think you may safely let yourself go a bit tonight, darling,' Nina told her. She seemed quite suddenly restored in humour. 'Every woman should know her own limit and what it feels like when she's close to it. Anyway, if you're going to be a writer, you should stop saying no to new experiences. You should say yes to everything. Landlord – another bottle here!'

Selina, who had been kept on the tightest rein until now – no doubt for fear of what she might blurt out in her innocence once she was back home again – drank eagerly and waited with the dutiful curiosity of a budding writer to see what tipsiness was like.

Johanna grew even more alarmed. For some time now she had been aware of a great tension in Nina, the sense of an impending explosion. She would do something, or say something, that hinted at wildness or abandon – and then immediately quash it with a joke or a gesture that would smooth it away, suggesting she had been talking for talking's sake, trying out an idea as one might hold up even the most obviously unsuitable dress material, because there was just the remotest chance it might prove seemly. Then she would laugh and flash those wonderful, wild Irish eyes and it would all be forgotten.

Except... not quite. Something would linger each time, the remnants of her abandoned abandons, gathering as flotsam gathers in the unswept corners of a busy port, eventually threatening to impede the normal traffic there. Tonight there was a sense that the normal traffic between the three of them — the traffic of words, of mutual contentment, of all those fleeting but important emotions — was about to choke.

Nina held up her glass to the setting sun and turned it delicately between her fingers. Her fair skin was suffused with pink and her blue eyes sparkled. 'Intoxication,' she murmured. 'There are some who will never risk it and some who seek it night and day. Perhaps if we had a bacchanalia once a month — a proper institution of society — and abstinence in between, things would go better for all of us.'

Selina giggled and took another draught.

'What about someone like Isaac Wills?' Johanna asked. 'Drunk almost every night of his life then he goes to just one prayer meeting — gets converted — falls down in a swoon — and hasn't touched a drop in the last three years. Now he's the most popular preacher in Cornwall, some say.'

'Sure don't you see? The man's still intoxicated night and day. The brew may be different but the mania hasn't changed at all. There is this urge in all of us.'

'That's an easy argument.' Selina set down her glass with elaborate care so that it touched precisely two folds at right angles in the linen. The precision of the action, especially when she felt the rest of the world was turning very imprecise, was enormously satisfying. 'You could just say that anything anybody wants to do very much is a mania. Then you can prove anything.'

'But isn't it?' Nina asked quietly. 'Isn't there a mania lurking in each of us? Often all unsuspected, just waiting for the right combination of circumstances to spring the lock?'

313

'Not here!' Selina chuckled brightly. 'Nothing lurking in here.' She tapped her forehead confidently.

'Solid ivory.' Johanna smiled sweetly at her.

'I'm serious,' Nina told them. 'I believe there is in everyone − absolutely everyone − a potential . . . what can I call it? If you don't like *mania,* let's call it *addiction.* There is a potential addiction in each and every one of us. All it needs is the right circumstances and there it is, with its . . .'

'Cacaoëthes!' Selina exlaimed proudly.

'I beg your pardon?'

'That's the word. Not *mania,* not *addiction,* but *cacaoëthes.* A wicked and insatiable longing.'

'Where do you get such words?'

'From *your* library, Nina dear. You should try putting your nose into it sometime.'

Johanna smiled to herself. She had no idea what Nina's purpose might be in raising this subject − nor in permitting Selina too much of the grape − but it was not going the way it had been planned.

'Anyway,' Nina said brusquely. 'I prefer *addiction.* And what I was saying is that it's in everyone − the possibility, the potential . . .'

'The propensity,' Selina said.

'Thank you, darling. Always there with the right word. Now, I daresay . . .'

'D'you know,' Selina said to her cousin, 'I think the sun has bleached your hair a bit. It's quite red in places. You're a secret redhead.' She turned to Nina with a laugh. 'A secret ginger-nut! That's what's lurking in her − a red-hair caca . . . whatsit. You'd better be careful how you try her temper.'

Nina forced a smile and chewed her lip for a moment or two. 'Actually, Jo's a case in point,' she went on. 'When she left Lanfear that night, I doubt if anyone could imagine a less likely candidate to support my argument. Think of the way your parents brought her up, Selina. She always knew she'd be the last of you girls to get married − if, indeed, she ever did. If she wanted a quiet life, she had to buckle down and suppress her own . . .'

'Not to start with,' Selina interrupted mournfully. 'Poor thing! She had a terrible time of it. She had a wicked, unruly spirit, Papa said. He used to bind her limbs to the frame of the bed and whip her bare botty until Mama had to intercede.' She leaned forward and stroked her cousin's arm.

Nina turned to Johanna in surprise. 'You never mentioned this.'

'It was a long, long time ago.'

'He was going to whip her again the night she left,' Selina added. 'That's why I helped her get away. He used to whip us, too, you know — but not so often as poor Jo. And Terence was always left to keep his trousers on when he was whipped. I always thought that was so unfair.'

Nina wanted to touch Johanna, too, in sympathy, but the mild, unspoken estrangement between them prevented it. 'You poor mite,' she said. 'Don't you sometimes wonder what harm it may have done?'

Johanna shrugged uncomfortably. 'Skin heals quite fast, you know.'

'I wasn't thinking of your skin.' She shivered. 'I can't even bear the thought of it.'

'Were you never whipped?' Selina asked in surprise.

'Never!'

'How did they punish you, then?'

'They reasoned with us. And if that didn't work, they bound us by the ankles and hung us upside down from the rafters. Thirty feet up — very effective, I can tell you! They never had to do it to me beyond the once.'

'You always *pretended* to see reason?' Johanna asked.

Nina laughed. 'You may very well be right, my precious.'

Johanna knew the woman would never rest content until she had said her say in full; she decided to confront the matter head-on. 'So in what way — according to you — do I now support your argument, Nina?' she asked. 'What is this secret addiction within me?'

'But you have already told us, darling. For what would you go through fire and storm, beg money from a man you claim to loathe, brand yourself thief?'

Selina emptied her glass and communed with the tablecloth. 'There is nothing like that in me,' she told it.

'I'm coming to you in a minute,' Nina said, without taking her eyes off Johanna.

315

Johanna shrugged. 'You call it addiction. Everyone else would call it love. Anyway, I don't see where it brings us.'

'I know where it'll bring *you*.'

Johanna gave a vaguely concessionary nod. 'One can't deny that most marriages do not bring all the happiness the couple hoped for. But some do.'

'And nowadays, when more and more are marrying for love, as they think, it's getting worse, not better.'

'But I have no choice − just as I had no choice when I forced Hal to start this baby with me. I know it doesn't seem like it. I mean, a judge in a court of law might say I was perfectly free to do whatever I wished. But he wasn't there. He could have no idea how overwhelming...'

'But Jo − dear Jo − every petty drunkard could say precisely the same about the bottle. It's overwhelming. The need for it − the drive, the urge − is overwhelming.'

Selina poured herself another glass and then, belatedly, filled Nina's, too.

'So?' Johanna shrugged. 'What then? All this must be leading up to some plan of yours.'

Nina put her hands to her face and rubbed her forehead briskly for a moment. 'It's not a simple matter of my drawing up a plan and then persuading you to follow it, my love. It's much harder than that. It goes much deeper. What I have to do is to persuade you to an altogether different way of seeing things. We've made some progress already. I mean you can admit that love is just a kind of addiction. Now I don't care what addiction we're talking about − for the bottle or religion or the man of one's dreams − all kinds of addictions, they are all ruinous.'

'To the ruin'd maid!' Selina toasted them both.

'I know what I'm talking about,' Nina went on. 'Believe me − the way Brookesy and I managed it was by far the best. I didn't love him − at least, not in the mindless, self-destructive way that you call love. But even so we had the most wonderful...' She vanished amid her own thoughts for a moment. 'Well, never mind that. He was old enough and wise enough to know that love and marriage simply cannot mix. And if he hadn't died, we'd have come back to Helston and I could have had my little love affairs with other men − younger men − if I'd wished. He knew it, too. And it wouldn't have upset our...'

'Did he say as much?'

'He didn't need to. But that's what I mean about the occasional bacchanalia, you see? Neither *total* abstinence nor *total* addiction — something in between. That's always the best.'

Johanna considered the argument. She could see not the slightest merit in it from start to finish. 'Little love affairs.' There was the phrase that gave Nina away. *Little,* indeed!

However, to allow it all out of the woman's system, she commented, 'Perhaps I could see it more clearly if we started at the other end. I mean, suppose I saw it your way, what course of action would I then choose — and what advantages would it bring me? Perhaps if I could see the advantages, I might be persuaded to the argument itself.' She finished with an encouraging smile.

'Well,' Nina answered eagerly. 'I should have thought that was obvious. When you first came to live at Liston Court you told me that Tony Moore had kissed you and that it wasn't in the least unpleasant and that you'd half-agreed to a plan of his to go and live in Plymouth...'

'Yes but that was...'

'I know what you're going to say: That was before Hal. Never mind that. My only purpose in mentioning it is to remind you that you didn't always feel the same towards Tony Moore as you now claim. You *were* able to enjoy his company and even contemplate a course that might eventually lead to marriage. Your head obviously ruled your heart in those dim, distant days. And my advice — if there is any spark of that Johanna still alive in you — my advice is to harken unto her. She knew clearly what was best for you. And as long as you didn't deceive Tony — and, of course, you'd have to give him the heirs he's entitled to expect — but as long as you kept that part of the bargain, he'd be a monster of ingratitude to deny you the occasional moment with Hal. Or whoever else had stormed your heart by then.'

Johanna turned to see how Selina was taking it. Her cousin pulled a face. 'I could never do that,' she said. Her cheeks had gone very white all of a sudden.

'Of course not, my pet.' Nina patted her hand. 'Your case is entirely different. Johanna wants a home and family of

her own. She doesn't know it, of course. She fondly
imagines all she wants is Hal — Hal, Hal, and only Hal. But
if the man himself came home tomorrow and told her to put
the child out for fostering because they were going to travel
for the rest of their lives and live in hotels, no home and no
family — well, believe you me — she'd be looking for a new
man before the next shower of rain!'

Selina closed her eyes in ecstasy. 'Oh, I'd love that.
Travelling forever and hotels and no household!'

'You see! Your case *is* quite different. You want to be
someone, make something of yourself, without having to be
grateful to any husband.'

'I shouldn't mind being grateful, as long as he didn't
want...' She shivered.

Nina laughed. 'At least we have *one* thing in common,
you and I, my precious: We both need husbands in order to
mask our true desires and make them seem respectable.' She
turned back to Johanna. 'Anyway, my lamb — have I even
dented the armour of your self-delusion?'

Johanna pursed her lips and let a long silence grow. 'My
happiest moment with Hal,' she said at last, 'was not, as you
might think, when we lay with our limbs intertwined — in his
room or mine. It was just before he took the coach from
Redruth. We went for a short stroll out toward the hills.
Everything was covered in snow. And when we reached the
end of the path we just stood there, our arms about each
other, gazing around, not saying a word. And then I looked
into his eyes and I saw he was already thousands of miles
away. And at first I was furious. I thought how could he!
With only minutes to go before we parted, perhaps for ever.
So I made some grumbling comment. But he just smiled and
said, "Ah, but when I'm over there I shall be back here."
And I suddenly realized he had been trying to...to
photograph it all in his mind — carrying a complete picture
of Cornwall, and me in it, wherever he went. So I told him
I'd always be there. That was all! Just a few seconds out of
our lives. But that moment of understanding in me was
...so intensely happy I couldn't begin to describe it. Now
you explain to me, Nina dear — how do I arrange for such
moments to happen during that brief monthly bacchanalia
that you and Tony Moore will so generously permit me to

enjoy? Because without moments like that, let me tell you, all those rather obvious pleasures (which are all you seem to have in mind) are just trivial.'

Selina's eyes were full of tears. 'I think that's beautiful,' she murmured. 'I think it's the most beautiful...' She turned to the low stone wall and parted company with her supper.

Her two companions rushed to help. But she was giggling. She gazed down into the valley — at what might have been no more than a few scraps thrown for the birds and foxes. 'Now I know my limit,' she said.

Chapter Thirty-One

When it dawned on Hal that Jenny was, indeed, to be a fellow passenger for the next few weeks, and that Nina had arranged it so, his anger overcame even his instinct for self-preservation. He went at once to the bridge, where he demanded to see Captain Cunningham, his companion's uncle. Unfortunately he chose the most delicate moment in the business of leaving port in an adverse wind: Anchors were weighed, the after-yards braced on one tack, head-yards on another, and her head was paying off nicely. At any moment it would be time to square the after-yards and fill all sail. At such a moment a distraught passenger demanding to be returned to the quayside is somewhat less welcome than a platoon of excise men. What followed was a pyrotechnic display of fury that made Hal's own seem like the tantrums of a four-year-old; he was lucky to escape back to the main deck without legirons. Jenny, to the salvation of her own skin, had gone to the female dormitory below.

Hal and Cunningham found an out-of-the-way spot beneath the open companionway that led up to the foredeck. There they stood, leaning on the rail, watching the lights of Plymouth pass before them as in review. They made good headway for the first mile, with a fair sou'-sou'-westerly on the starboard beam.

'You must be growing weary of life, old man,' Cunningham chided.

Hal clenched his fists but said nothing. They would be passing Drake's Island soon. He could leap and swim for it, perhaps?

'If it truly is urgent,' his companion went on, 'I might talk my uncle into flagging down a passing coaster and transferring you by daylight tomorrow. Only you'll have to make amends first. We're invited to his table tonight, by the way.'

In his frustration Hal grasped the rail and tried to shake it out of its fixings. 'Being stuck here and not knowing,' he said vehemently. 'That's the worst.'

'Not knowing what?'

'Oh . . . Lady Nina is up to some divilment, as she calls it. She's never wanted this attachment between Miss Rosewarne and me. You saw that girl who came aboard with us just now? Her ladyship sent her. It's part of some plot to discredit me. I have to go back and stop it.'

After a pause Cunningham said, 'You can't expect a whole ship to put about for something like that. You'd do better to search for typhoid aboard.'

'I know, dammit! But it doesn't make it any easier to bear with.'

'You've questioned the girl very closely, I take it?'

'She's told me enough. I'd get no truth from her anyway.'

'Well, so you say. But with your permission, I'll have a crack at her myself. I have a certain way with them, you know.'

Hal gave a reluctant laugh and clapped him on the back. 'You're a grand fellow to travel with,' he said. 'By all means "have a crack." And I promise to make amends with your uncle this evening.'

There was a great deal of hauling at sheets on the deck and tacking and untacking of sails up aloft. They had reached the island and were now having to come about so as to beat their way into Plymouth Sound. Although the harbour roads were a good thousand yards wide, the wind, still strong, was now scant on the starboard beam; even worse, it was made wayward by the islands and hills on that quarter, so that they were taken aback two or three times and had to fall off to the lee to regain their momentum.

In the depths of a mine, choked with dust and near killed by the heat and damp, Hal had often envied the matelot his life aloft in the cool, pure air, letting the wind do all the hard work for him. But watching them now, cold and wet, perched several dozen feet above the heaving deck, dark shapes against the paler dark of the sky, with only her navigation lights and the newly-risen moon to guide them...he swiftly revised his opinion.

'We must dress for dinner,' Cunningham reminded him.

Hal was as good as his word that evening; within half an hour he had charmed the captain into putting the whole incident behind them. He did not canvass the possibility of being transferred to a coaster but he felt sure that, when the time arose, the man would be receptive enough to the idea.

Later, when he and Cunningham were standing once more by the rail, enjoying a cigar before turning in, his friend said, 'Care to tell me a little more, old boy? Two heads better than one, after all. I'd love a farthing for every man I've been able to help out of a scrape like this over the years. I tell you – there'd be no necessity for such a voyage as this.'

More for the sake of thinking aloud than in hope of actual assistance, Hal told him as much as he knew – and was now able to surmise – about the immediate affair of Jenny, Lady Nina, and Dr Moore. When he had finished, Cunningham was silent for a while.

'It's sinister enough, don't you agree?' Hal asked. 'The girl told me it was Lady Nina's idea from start to finish.'

'But your only informant is the girl herself,' the man replied.

'Naturally.'

'And you don't feel there's a whiff of self-service about it somewhere? I can't see Lady Nina behaving in quite that way – and I'm a pretty fair judge of the distaff tribe, you know. Ask anyone.'

Hal cleared his throat. 'Perhaps there's something in that.'

'Take my word for it, man, she's not told you the half of it. But *nil desperandum* – if there's more to be told, I'll squeeze every last word of it out of the little dovey after breakfast tomorrow. Are you a good sailor?'

'I don't know.'

'Well I am. So...as long as one of us is compos mentis. Plenty of time. Could be a couple of days before we see blue water. Anyway, a free passage to America is a lot to give up for what might be an out-and-out lie.'

Hal forbore to observe that the passage was hardly free,

and that, even taking the fare and the eighty guineas and the set of surveyor's instruments into account, he was still out of pocket when measured against Cunningham's original promise.

'Coming below?' the man asked.

'I'll just finish this cigar. Damn thing's gone out. I'll be down soon enough – leave us the matches, there's a good chap.'

Alone again, Hal stood at the rail and stared out over the waves. The sky had cleared and the moon was almost full; there was a medium swell running beneath a breeze strong enough to peel white horses off the tallest waves. Unfortunately their course lay into the teeth of it, so they had to wear ship every few miles to bring the wind onto the other beam. This involved turning full circle and running downwind, actually back toward Plymouth, for a good mile before turning her on the other leg. To Hal it seemed a period of dangerous confusion – the taking in of sails, which were then almost immediately set again, the cries of 'Luff!' and 'Brace up!', the swivelling of the yards, the shivering of loose canvas as the breeze got across it, the turning of the wheel, first this way, then that . . . how anyone made sense of it was beyond his comprehension. But at last the sails filled with a satisfying *thwack!* and she leaped forward once again, now safely on the new leg and with the breeze soughing evenly through her rigging. Even then, though, the seamen had no rest. They stood along the rails and on the yards up aloft, feeling the tension in the sheets and adjusting them to keep her in perfect trim.

The captain's cook came out during one such manoeuvre and Hal took the chance to compliment him on a fine dinner. He accepted it nonchalantly and stood there awhile, until the vessel had come right about. When it was done he smacked his lips in appreciation and commented to Hal: 'Now if you've any compliments to spread around, young sir, our master's your man! Many a captain these days'll leave the mizzen-top square till after the head-yards are squared. Put all the work on the rudder, see? But not Cap'n Cunningham. He'll save us a mile every time we tack about.'

'Imagine!' Hal replied. He hoped that sometime during

the next few weeks these words would acquire meaning for him.

The cook spat for luck and went back to his galley. Hal, remembering his dead cigar, took the matchbox from his pocket. He was just about to open it when there was a rustle at his side and a delicate hand stole it from him. He knew it was Jenny's even before the match flared and the light fell upon her. 'D'you still want to cast me overboard?' she asked as he puffed his cigar back to life. 'The way my stomach's feeling at this particular moment — it doesn't seem such a dreadful idea.'

'I don't know what's to be done,' he replied as he moved aside to make room for her. They stood in silence awhile, watching the swell as it ran beneath them, shimmering dark green and black beneath the moon.

'I'm sorry,' she said at length.

'Was it the truth, Jenny? I have to know.'

'Why? What does it matter now?'

'So it wasn't true — what you told me?'

After a long pause she said, 'Some of it.'

'And the rest?'

'You'll be even more furious, I warn you.'

When she volunteered nothing further he said, 'Go on.'

'Lady Nina is not the. . . I mean, it was my idea, not hers. Isn't that enough? Isn't that all you really need to know?'

'I want to hear it all.'

'Give us a puff.' She took several before she passed the cigar back. 'Very well. It began, of course, when you turned up like that, out of the blue, back home. I suddenly remembered. . . I mean, I realized I'd forgotten. . .' She buried her face in one hand. 'Oh, Hal — I wanted you. I'd forgotten what it was like to want you. Or to *want* any man. But I could see straight away there was someone else. I could read it in your eyes.' She looked up at him and smiled wanly. 'I don't know if you can understand, but I just had to find out who she was. Funny to think I'd gain any comfort from that, but there you are. I had to know. So I gave my mother some line and set out after you. Never went back.'

'Yes, that's a puzzle — where did you get that horse? That's why I didn't recognize it was you.'

'You said you did.'

'Well, if we're now putting all our cards on the table. . . I didn't actually guess it until today, up on the Hoe.'

'I met Isaac Watts in Godolphin, and he. . .'

'The temperance preacher. Who used to be such a drunkard?'

'Yes, well, he has other cravings now, which I would be in a position to know more about than most. So it wasn't hard to persuade him to "lend" me his nag.' She bit her lip. 'I hope he got it back!'

'Where did you leave it?'

'At Lady Nina's.'

'So − we come to her. Tell me exactly what happened when you met.'

'I tied Watts's horse to a bush farther along Cross Street, where the lawyer lives, and walked up to Liston Court. And I was stood there by the gate, thinking Lady Nina must be your new lover, when she came on in her carriage, and that Miss Rosewarne with her.'

'You know Miss Rosewarne?'

'By sight. When father died, the old woman used to go up Lanfear, washing days. I saw her then a time or two. Anyway, Lady Nina leans out of her carriage and asks me if there's something I want. So I asked her if that was Hal Penrose just went inside − I wanted to see her face, you understand.'

Hal chuckled. 'That gave you a bit of a startle, eh? I'll lay she wasn't at all pleased.'

'Well, funny thing, that − the first she did was to turn round to see if Miss Rosewarne had heard me. But she hadn't − the rain on the roof and that, I suppose. So she unrolls that great umbrella of hers and steps out. 'Go on indoors, my dear,' she says to Miss Rosewarne. 'I fancy there's a nice little surprise for you inside.' And then she walks with me round the back and. . .'

'There must have been more than that. Miss Rosewarne told me she heard you speak.'

'Nothing to any purpose. Anyway, after a lot of beating about the bush Lady Nina gets it out of me that you and me once were sparking.'

'Anything else? I mean, did you tell her what you've been doing since?'

Jenny gave a cold laugh. 'Very likely! Mind you — as you yourself came to warn us — 'tin't exactly the best-kept secret, not locally. Why *did* you come to see us, by the way?'

He was about to say he'd explain it later when it struck him that a spot of mutual confession might help loosen her tongue still further; so he told her what Charley Vose had, obliquely, asked him to do.

She laughed. 'You should have said it out straight. The old woman would leap at the chance. She's got pretty girls off the bal applying for work there every day, almost. And the trade in the summer is . . .'

'Yes, so I heard. Tell me what happened then at Liston Court.'

'Charley Vose may call them "cottages", up Paradise Row. To us they'd be mansions. He'd die rich then, if that's what he wants.'

'You'd got to Liston Court.'

She sighed. Was it, he wondered, at the thought of all that had just slipped through her grasp? 'Very well,' she said. 'She asked me if I still had a yearning for you. Which I answered her.'

She waited for him to press her to be more specific but he simply went on staring at the waves. Was he really so totally indifferent to her? she wondered. Had he come to Sunny Corner merely because Charley Vose had asked him to?

She continued: 'So she told me that *if* I still entertained hopes of you, I was to abandon them. You were lost to another. I said I didn't believe it — wanting for her to tell me everything, you see. She said it was, in fact, the young lady who had shared her carriage. I asked her name — pretending I didn't know — but she wouldn't tell me. But then, just when I was ready to give up and go, she came out with something else. Oh, that's right! I asked her. I said was this "other person" just as sweet on you? And she said yes. And I asked how she knew and she told me the young lady had turned down an offer from one of the most eligible men in the whole of the West Country. So I asked who *he* was and again she wouldn't tell me. All she said was that this young man was still heartbroken for her.'

Hal thought that an odd piece of information for Nina to throw in, but he made no comment.

'Anyway,' Jenny went on, 'she said I could go in by the kitchen fire and dry out.'

'Aha – now we have it – the vixen! Of course, you immediately set to gossiping with the servants and so got the name of Dr Moore in ten seconds flat. Oh, she's no fool, is our Lady Nina!'

'True – but I can't say she even so much as hinted at me for to do that. Not a hint, not a wink.'

'Ah, she'd summed you up, though. She's quick enough at that.'

'She's a bit odd, if you want my opinion. She asked me if I knew the Parable of the Talents, so I said I did. I said it was Matthew, Twenty-five, so she'd know I wasn't just pretending. This was when she came back, about a half-hour after she left me to go in by the fire.'

'In other words, after Miss Rosewarne and I had gone?'

'Yes. She took me to the backyard door and gave me a guinea. 'You are to do with this,' says she, 'as the servant with the five talents did in the Bible. And you shall let me know whenever you can, how you make it multiply.' And no receipt asked for it, nor nothing!'

'In fact, she was giving you your fare to Plymouth.'

'She never said that. In any case, the fare was no more than five bob. Sixteen shilling to spare!'

'And you went to Plymouth the following day – yesterday, in fact? Didn't I ask you that up on the Hoe? Was it yesterday?'

She shook her head. 'The day before. I travelled that very same night on the Royal Mail. Sat inside!' She laughed at the memory. 'Made two gentlemen there – travelling with their wives – made them very uncomfortable all night, I can tell 'ee! And then went directly to Dr Moore, which I mentioned.'

'And he, of course, gave you the passage money like a shot.'

She shook her head. 'Not him! He hemmed and hawed and said to come back next day – today, that is. But I could see straight off he wasn't going to.'

'So how did you. . .' His voice tailed off.

'Yes,' she said. '*Passage* money, right enough!'

'So why did you go back to see him at all?'

'To force him to say no. To have the pleasure of telling him what a feeble little milksop he was and how someone like him, with water for blood, didn't deserve even to know the likes of Miss Rosewarne...'

'I say!' Hal protested. 'You'll give him a rival's backbone yet!'

'Not him!' she said with a mixture of scorn and mortification.

Hal had meant the comment sarcastically, but as soon as the words were out he saw it was, indeed, the truth. That was what she intended. However, he preferred to let the implications of it remain unspoken between them.

Another thought occurred to him. 'If you never went back home, your mother and Diana can still have no idea where you are?'

'They will soon enough. I wrote this morning.' She closed her mind to the thought of what she had said in that letter.

'Also,' he continued, looking her up and down, 'you must only have the clothes you stand up in. D'you know how long a voyage it'll be?'

She smiled, more to herself than him. When a man looks you up and down in that way, and wonders about your clothing, all is not lost. 'You don't think I'm a mite more plump than when you saw me at Sunny Corner?' she asked.

He frowned in bewilderment.

'I bought another set, man. Mind you — if I can have the lend of your greatcoat again — or your next-best one — I wouldn't say no. I'd only need put up one outfit to a time then.'

'Consider it yours, Jenny.'

'You got a cabin, have 'ee?' she asked.

'Me, Cunningham, and two other gentlemen. Why?'

'I'll leave some of my things with you, then, if you will. I don't like the look of some in that female dormitory. And it's so crowded. Like pilchards in a barrel.'

'It will be worse after we call at Queenstown. The Irish famine's so bad again that every ship is sailing scuppers-down with emigrants.' He threw the butt of his cigar out to sea; it painted a dim red trace on the air before it died. 'What'll you do over there?' he asked.

'Well, there's one trade I'll not follow again,' she replied stoutly. 'I'm not jumping from the griddle onto the bakestone. That's news for nothing.'

'You had a good education. You speak well.'

'You think I'd make a nanny?' she asked. 'Or even a governess? I wonder do they have such things over there?' Almost at once, though, she answered herself: 'It wouldn't work. There's so many going over from Cornwall every month, some kind, good-natured friend would be bound to see me and peach to my mistress.'

'It's a big country, Jenny. Perhaps if you stayed in Boston someone would spot you. But if you went out to one of those communities on the edge of civilization, I'll bet you could go a lifetime without meeting another Cousin Jack at all, much less one who knew you.'

'We shall just have to see. It's a long voyage ahead of us yet.'

After a pause he said, 'Anyway, I'm glad you're not going to...you know.'

She leaned her head briefly against his arm. 'I'm glad, too. I mean...it's nice to know you care one way or another. I'll tell you — the number of people I thought were my friends! You soon find out.'

'I didn't exactly come running to help, Jenny.'

'What help could you have offered? Weren't you as poor as us? At least you didn't come running for...the other thing.' She shivered. 'Some men I can't understand. I mean, the *difference* between when you're just sparking, man and woman, like, and when they're paying for it — master and slave. 'Tin't the same fellow at all. You wonder what they enjoyed about it before.' She shivered again. 'D'you mind me talking about it, even?'

'Not if it helps. You want for me to get you that coat now?'

'No. It wasn't that. No, I'm fine with these two heavy dresses up. You surely never thought I was so fat as this?'

He gave a single, self-mocking laugh. 'I never thought at all.'

'No. Your thoughts were *elsewhere.*'

'Won't it seem strange? Going from I don't know how many men a day to absolutely none? So suddenly, I mean?'

She was about to tell him it would be utter heaven when it

occurred to her that he — perhaps quite unaware of it himself — was skirting a delicate opening toward her. She decided to put up the flimsiest of barriers and see what he did with it. 'Just at this moment,' she replied, 'it's the last thing on my mind. The way I feel now, I don't want to part my thighs for another man — not ever again.' She clutched his arm impulsively. 'That's why I'm glad to be making this voyage with *you,* Hal, dear. I think I'd feel safer with you — that way, I mean — than with any other man on earth.'

'Indeed?'

She was pleased to note that he did not sound altogether delighted at the testimonial. 'Yes. In the first place, we both know everything's over between us. Second, you know what I am — or was until this morning. And third, you belong, mind, body, and soul, to another woman. We can be as easy as you like together. Brother and sister. Tell me what she's like? She's a lot older than me, isn't she. I always looked up to her, I know that.'

He chuckled. 'Somewhere, Jenny,' he said, putting an easy arm about her shoulder and facing her toward the bow, 'somewhere ahead of us there, in America, there's an unattached young man, dreaming of you — whom he's never met. But when he does, he'll know it at once — that you're what he's been waiting for all this time. Just as I knew it about Johanna Rosewarne the moment I clapped eyes on her. And when it happens — in your case, I mean — I just hope he'll be everything to you that she is to me. And I couldn't wish better on you than that, not even if you were truly my own sister. So there!' He gave her an affectionate squeeze and said, 'And now I must go below or Cunningham will think I've made a swim for it.'

'Why should he think that?'

'Oh, we were going to hail down a coaster and get me back ashore tomorrow. But now I've heard the truth, I think a letter from Queenstown will suffice.' He stared at her quizzically. 'It *was* the truth, wasn't it?'

'The truth and nothing but the truth.'

He did not notice the omission of the third possibility. They shook hands and he turned to go. 'What about you?' he asked over his shoulder.

'Yes, I'll follow you down.'

She stood at the rail, feeling with her hands for the warmth he had left in them, gazing out over the vast, restless water. In a while the tears began to flow. She wept for so many small things — principally that when Hal had stopped calling at Sunny Corner, she had not followed her instincts and camped on his back. She wept, too, at the heedless, lighthearted spirit in which she had undertaken this voyage, despite Lady Nina's warning that her hopes of Hal were forlorn. And most of all she wept at the emptiness — the space she now occupied, which, only moments earlier, had caged the magic of his person — all that warmth, all that strength, all that marvellous ... bearlike ... embraceable ... Hal.

But when the weeping had run its course she perked up again. It was, after all, a long voyage with little or nothing to do. He was a man alone. And if life had given her nothing else, it had taught her more than any woman ought to know about the care and feeding of the lonely male.

Chapter Thirty-Two

Liston Court, newly painted and decorated during Nina's absence, sparkled in the June sun, giving her and her two companions a bright welcome on their return. Brookesy's menhir reared its venerable bulk from a new bed of maidenhair fern; ornamental doves fluttered up in brief, ungainly alarm before they resettled to their strutting and foraging; two lawn-mowing ewes ran to the ends of their tethers before deciding there was no panic after all — then they stood, grinding their mouths with those astonishing rotatory jaws, and staring balefully at the intruders.

'Home at last!' Nina said. 'I'll bet there's enough mail for a month of reading.'

And, indeed, there was; she had it all carried up to her room in two large bread panniers. Johanna had to go and knock on her door to see if there might not be one or two — but especially *one* — for her as well.

'Who is it?' Nina called.

'Me.'

'You don't need to knock, darling.'

'I do when it's locked.'

Nina opened her door. 'Silly me! We've spent too much time travelling. Do come in. What is it?'

'You know perfectly well, Nina. Don't tease.'

Nina did not smile. 'Are you quite sure...'

'There is one, isn't there.'

She nodded. Johanna made to go past her but Nina held out her arm. 'I'm not going to prevent you, my lamb — not if you insist — but just hear me out. Please? What you do in the next few minutes could set the course for the rest of your life. But just consider this: I know Hal is everything a girl might dream of . . .'

'And more,' Johanna interrupted.

'Right, pet. But it's that *more* which makes him so wrong for you. Oh, why can we always see things so clearly when our feelings are disengaged? Why do our emotions make us so blind?'

'But I think that's what's wrong with *you,* Nina. You're the one whose feelings are all tangled up here, not me. Tell me honestly — on the first night he slept in this house — you remember I awoke early and came into your bedroom. This room, in fact.' She looked around at its new decor as if it had deceived her. 'And he was sitting here . . .' She pointed to the spot where Hal's chair had been. But then she lost her nerve and could not pose the question.

Nina did it for her. 'And you thought he had just sprung there fresh from between my sheets!'

'I did not!'

'You did! I let you into the warm half of my bed and you straight-way felt the other half to see if it, too, was warm.'

Johanna could not suppress a smile at the memory. 'All right. It was a natural thought, wasn't it?'

'Very natural!'

Johanna swallowed hard. 'And had he — in fact . . . you know?'

'But you felt the sheets yourself . . . ah, I see. You mean we might both have been in the same half. Yes, well, it wasn't for want of trying on his part, let me tell you.' A sudden realization filled her eyes. 'And there you are! He was supposed to be newly in love with you, bowled over and all that. You were only two rooms away down the corridor. And yet he saw, or thought he saw, a chance with me. *And he could not help but take it!* There you have him. Fickle as a hare when it's trying to run straight. He cannot help himself. Now can you imagine the *hell* of being married to such a man as that? The day-long, night-long, year-in, year-out hell of it?'

Tears started to Johanna's eyes. Nina put her arms about her. 'Oh, my love — it is so hard, so hard. I know.'

But Johanna was shaking her head.

'What?' Nina asked.

She pulled away and spoke as from the depths of fatigue. 'Even if all you say is true, Nina, I, too, cannot help myself. If there is a letter from him, I would rather read it and die than leave it and live.' She shrugged her shoulders in a gesture of petty despair.

'I tried!' Nina said as she went to one of the baskets. 'Here. Not just a letter, but sealed in an envelope, too.' She returned, rubbing it between fingers and thumb. 'And something inside it. God send it's not a ticket.'

Johanna waited only long enough to kiss her on the neck before racing away to her room — where *she* locked her door and, with fingers that trembled almost too much to obey, slit the cover open.

There was, indeed, an enclosure — not a ticket but a second envelope, folded double and marked *General*. The letter itself read:

My darling Johanna,

No stranger to love (among whom I now count our friend Lady Nina) can possibly know the exquisite torments of such a separation as this. The greatest pleasure is that it compels my mind, my heart — my all-of-me — into an endless reverie of that which I most lack: the sweet, adorable nearness of you. Another compensation is that, in one sense I do not lack you at all, for you are all about me, always. When I turn in my bunk you are there beside me; when I gaze on the vast face of the ocean, I see only you before me. . . I look at my hands and say, 'She was here! These have briefly held that most magical of persons!' Every minute of my waking day, my dreaming night, is passed in adoration of you.

And yet I should gladly sacrifice a century of these imaginary joys for one moment of your actual presence again. So I know full well they are but the trumpery with which the grieving spirit consoles itself, and that I shall find no true happiness until we are united again. Now, in the depth of that sweet grief, I must write to you of certain practical things.

I make no doubt but that my *dear* friend Lady Nina has found many occasions to attack your love for me — no, to attack *our* love — with 'unwilling' but oh-so-honeyed words concerning a certain Miss Jenny Jewell. Let me now tell you what truly happened.

Some few days before we embarked — it was the day of the downpour, when you dined with me at Goldsithney, a day we shall, I believe, forever remember and treasure — upon that same afternoon, along my way into Helston, I called at Widow Jewell of Sunny Corner with an errand from Charley Vose. He supplies her with the alcohol she uses in her receipts and potions, and with certain other spices. Her daughter Jenny, the elder of twins, was once a 'couranting companion' of mine, two years ago, for a brief season. We had parted on good terms so there was no uneasiness in our conversation on that day. And that was that — or so I thought.

But this same Jenny took it into her head to follow me into Helston, notwithstanding the weather. She it was whom you first took for a beggar girl and then a wet and bedraggled tradesman's daughter. She must have said something to awaken Lady Nina's interest — and that was why our hostess, your protector, contrived to expel us from the house and set aside her duty toward you. Which, you recall, perplexed me at the time.

What followed next is not clear. It is a different tale each day. But this much at least is certain: Lady Nina invited Jenny into Liston Court and quizzed her most particularly — as a result of which she saw a chance to put the girl in my path in circumstances that could be made to seem woefully suspicious to you; she gave her Dr Moore's address in Plymouth (presumably with the thought, or perhaps the certainty, for who's to say what plots he and she hatched between them that morning after Harvest Fair? — that he would furnish her the passage money to sail to America with me on the *Starflight*); and, most damning of all, she gave her a guinea for her five-shilling fare to Plymouth.

Jenny took the coach that same night and saw Moore the following day. She says he would not give her the money. Well, be that as it may, she nonetheless acquired it *somehow* and was here, on board, awaiting me — and not as a stowaway, either.

Now why trouble you with these base contrivings? For

this reason alone: If Lady Nina has mentioned nothing of it to you, then I have wronged her and she is innocent. The same goes for friend Moore. If, on the other hand...the conclusion I leave to your native wit.

And to set your mind at rest as to what has happened *since* we sailed, I have so well convinced Miss Jewell she had best pin her hopes elsewhere, she has done precisely that. There is on board a certain widower called Jeremiah Timson of Chard in Somerset, who has a 'dry goods store' (a species of grocery or hardware, I believe) in a community called Fortunata in the new state of Wisconsin. To be precise, the store is his brother's, but that unfortunate man is not expected to see another winter, so Jeremiah is to take it over. On our first full day at sea he approached Jenny, as an unattached female, and asked her if she would kindly nurse his younger son Thomas, four years old and suffering abominably with the seasickness. In fact, it proved to be the smallpox — which, you may be sure, is a secret known to but half a dozen souls aboard this ship. Jenny has milked cows enough to be immune to it, so she has volunteered to nurse the little fellow all the way over if need be, as it probably will. The cabin is in strict but secret quarantine, of course. If the poor little lad survives (and perhaps even if he doesn't), I believe there will be a second Mrs Timson by the time we land in Boston. And I am sure the passage money for her family will be dispatched on the proximal boat for England.

I tell you all this because Jenny, despite all my urging, will not write to her mother and sister until the cat is in the bag. But I know Charley Vose! I believe he will be too eager to contract certain business with the two who remain at Sunny Corner, which it were best you did not know of. So I ask you earnestly, without involving yourself in any detail, to find some way of getting word to Widow Jewell soon. Do not visit her yourself, mind, but alert her to what I say anent Mr Timson and urge her to put off any decision touching Charley Vose, at least until she has heard from her daughter. Mrs Jewell has never done me aught but kindness. Like Lear, she is more sinned against than sinning; unlike him, her daughters bear the yoke of it, too.

336

Oh, my darling, as I write these words I imagine you setting forth upon your social round. I see you in your pony and trap on a beautiful Cornish morning in summer (as it will be by the time you return and read this), with the sun dappling through the leaves on all the hedgerows, and I am almost there with you. In spirit I *am,* of course, and that is where you must imagine me, too. Do you wish to know what an utterly foolish fellow you have engaged yourself to? I sometimes stand on deck and think, *This is the wind that will soon kiss her!* And so I lay a thousand kisses of my own upon its invisible fingers. Thus, if there be storms ahead, do not mind them for they bear my love to you all the more swiftly!

Enough of this folly. I shall write again, both soon and often. In the meanwhile, I enclose a general letter that you may read it aloud and give it Selina to copy for her penny dreadful.

Your ever-loving Hal

P.S: I have had the vaccination against pox, so do not worry on that account. I also consider myself vaccinated against Jenny Jewell, Lady Nina, and all that might come between us. I trust this will fortify your resistance to that plague, as well.

The general letter was full of particulars about the ship, its passengers and crew, its rigging, what a landlubber could make of the complexities of sailing her, the messing arrangements, the conditions of the emigrants, their reasons for going, their hopes for the New World . . . in short, all the minutiae an observant man with time on his hands could set down — and certainly all that Selina could wish for. As Hal explained, in an aside to her: 'You shall find no excuse in me if your critics accuse you of feeble observation or unconvincing detail!'

He added some more personal remarks on Cunningham's astounding knowledge of seamanship, the Atlantic currents, the American Indian, cures for seasickness ('on which we *must* defer to him since he has tried them *all!*'), and the romantic inclinations of every female aboard.

There was then a sombre postscript, written after they had docked in Ireland, concerning the pitiful conditions there as revealed in the wretched state of the emigrants they took on board. 'No time or space for particulars now. It will have to wait for my next — which, I fear, will be some months after this unless we have a fortuitous exchange of mails in mid-Atlantic. However, your long absence in the orient will telescope that interval for you.'

There had obviously been no 'fortuitous exchange,' for this was his only letter to await their return.

Selina, guilty at the length of time she had been away, felt she ought to go home that very afternoon — if only to tell them that Nina had extended her invitation to stay for an indefinite period. Johanna arranged to go with her — to which Nina, having so much correspondence to catch up with, made no objection.

However, when the pony and trap drew near to Lanfear, Johanna said, 'I can't go in, Selina. Don't ask me why — I just...' She gave a theatrical shiver. 'D'you mind?'

'Not for myself, Jo, but I could be *hours*. I'd feel awful to think of you waiting out here all that time.'

'Well,' Johanna replied dubiously — as if the thought had only just struck her — 'Hal did mention some papers he forgot at the Ram in Goldsithney. I could go and see if they're still there. And get a barrel of Charley Vose's beer, perhaps?' She smiled. 'I never thought I'd miss good old English beer so much. I'll call back for you at teatime. I'll come in then, tell them.'

'Well...' Selina looked toward the house, which was now in view. 'You shouldn't be alone.'

'Go on. I'll be all right.'

And so, rather reluctantly on Selina's part, it was agreed.

Johanna found Charley in one of the fermentation houses, adding water to his latest brew of ale. He tilted his shiny, pink, bean of a head to one side and said with mock solemnity, 'Now! You shall *have* to marry I, Miss Rosewarne. I belong to let none see this but family.' He held forth the remains of a slice of toast on which was spread something like grey butter. 'What's that, then?' he challenged.

She sniffed at it and, somewhat bewildered, replied,

'Yeast?' He winked his confirmation. 'Yeast in *brewing?*' she asked.

He nodded. ''Course, the yeast do play no part in the brewing itself, but he do give 'n a proper flavour, see. That's the secret of Charley Vose's ale — a good bit o' yeast for the flavour.'

'Does it affect the specific gravity?'

His eyebrows shot up. 'My dear soul!'

'We used to brew our own at Lanfear for years, so I do know a little about it. In fact, we only stopped when Terence persuaded you to supply us.'

'Ah.' He turned and drew off a tall glass beaker of the diluted brew. He bore it into the light, where she stood, and she saw that a hydrometer was afloat within it. 'How 'bout that then?' he asked. 'The black line is where he started out.'

'Proper job,' she replied.

The head tilted the other way. The little cheroot crackled to life and died again. 'Come for that old dressing gown, did 'ee, maid?' he asked.

'Dressing gown?'

''Es, that there Hal Penrose, he left 'n behind in his room. They was going to throw 'n out but I said no. That little maid, says I, she'll be back to fetch 'n afore long. Didn't 'ee know?'

Johanna blushed and shook her head.,

'You shall have 'n afore you go. Well now, if 'twasn't for that old gown, what was it? You want that housekeeper job, do 'ee? He's still open.' He winked to flag the joke for her.

'Yes please.' She spoke so swiftly and so firmly that for a moment he believed her.

Then he laughed. 'That's a good 'un, that is.' The head came up straight. Man-to-man question coming. 'To what do we truly owe the honour of your visit, eh?'

'It's only half a joke,' she replied. 'The fact is, I cannot sponge on Lady Nina Brookes for ever. I will soon have to look for a position somewhere. I remembered what you said that time and . . . well, I wondered if you, too, were only half joking?'

He turned on his heel and mounted the ladder that led up to the open lid of the fermentation vessel. There he trapped the neck of the hydrometer between two fingers and let the liquid pour out again. Then, with equal deliberation he descended and came all the way back to her. 'Mebbe not,' he said. 'What 'zackly had you in mind, now?'

Surely that cheroot would burn him soon? She glanced toward the inn, then at the brewhouses. 'I should supervise the labour,' she told him, 'but perform none of it myself.'

''Es.' It was not an acceptance, just an encouragement to continue.

'Such a task would not occupy all of my time. I'd want my afternoons to myself, between the hours of two and seven.'

He frowned suspiciously. The cheroot burned his lips at last; he spat it out like a cat with a lodged fishbone. 'That's a long time.'

'Unpaid.'

'Paid or unpaid, he's still a long time.'

'You can always say no, Mr Vose. But that's the only condition on which I'd undertake the work.'

He was going to refuse; she could feel it. As he opened his mouth to speak, she said, 'I can, however, assure you of one thing. What I do in those hours will be very much to your advantage.'

He shook his head, still dubious − but he stepped back from the brink. 'I should have to know.'

'Oh, have no fear − you'll be the very first.'

He fished out another cheroot and puffed it to life, dipping his head in an ambiguous gesture that might be either acceptance or rejection. At least it was not outright rejection. She knew better than to try enlarging such a bridgehead all at once. She also saw no point in mentioning that the very idea of working for him at all was well down on her list of possible occupations, only to be considered if she could not raise the fare to America.

'Was you thinking of starting on *now,* or what?' he asked.

What he meant was, in that case, he'd say no at once. She smiled as if letting him off the decision. 'No, I'll return this day week and you can tell me what you reckon I'd be worth. As I say, it's just half an idea at the moment, so there's no rush.'

He looked her up and down and a cheeky glint entered his eye; the cheroot wagged like a hound's tail at a death. She knew he was toying with some salacious reply but she was just a little too 'high quarter' for him. She stared him out.

As she turned to go she said, as if it were the merest after-thought: 'Your proposed business with the Widow Jewell, by the way...' and let the sentence hang.

From Hal's careful instructions and Nina's earlier direct-ness on the widow's character and trade, she had surmised enough of the truth not to be fishing in the absolute dark.

''Es,' he said with a nervous wink. The fact that his eyes could not quite meet hers gave his smile a sort of shifty bravado.

'Nothing irrevocable has been decided, I hope.'

'How?'

'That sort of trade could not be permitted under the roof of the Ram if I were housekeeper here. I hope that's perfectly understood.'

He chuckled and relaxed again. 'Perfectly understood, Miss Rosewarne. Nothing of that sort at all. Not under the roof of the Ram, as you say.'

He looked her calmly up and down − and in that one gesture their whole relationship was changed. When Charley Vose talked to a woman − any woman from the freshly nubile maid to the crone in her dotage − he some-how conveyed the suggestion that a small impropriety was on its way. He invoiced it in his smile, the tilt of his head, the confidential lowering of his voice, the quick-look-around-whew!-safe! as he spoke...the sparkle in his eye. He invoiced it but he never delivered. It was a game he played with them all. But in that moment of inspection he ceased to play it with Johanna. She had somehow penetrated his jocular armour and convinced him there might be a genuine, man-to-man conspiracy between them − with the sug-gestion of advantage in it for him. She obviously had a notion or scheme of some kind; but he was skilled enough at the game to know that profit lies not in grand ideas, nor wondrous manufactures, nor in effectual arrangements to sell − it lies in people, in those who have the presence and determination to go out and make it happen.

341

And he had just glimpsed such a person in her.

When he finished his scrutiny, he said, 'I can't make 'ee out at all, maid.'

'In what way?'

He went indoors, speaking over his shoulder as he walked. 'All lawdydaw and 'corum one minute...next minute – this! Widow Jewell and that.'

He returned shortly with Hal's dressing gown, as promised. She longed to hug it to her, to bury her face in it and revive memories no other sense could stir; but she waited until Goldsithney was well behind her. Then, as if the garment were a kind of armour, she decided to return by way of Sunny Corner. Hal's caution had been to protect her from learning what Nina and local gossip had already made crystal clear; so where was the harm?

As she went she was surprised to note that her heart was starting to beat a little faster than usual. She had expected such a reaction earlier in the afternoon, on her way to see Charley Vose – but, oddly enough, it had then remained quite normal. So why should the prospect of meeting the much less formidable...well, not that Charley was exactly what you'd call formidable – the much-less-to-be-reckoned-with Mrs Jewell...why should that seem more daunting?

Of course, it wasn't the woman herself, but what she did, the unimaginable things that went on in her house. Johanna recalled her conversation with Nina by the Nymphaeum at Petra. The look in her eyes as she had started to become, in her imagination, one of the supposed 'nymphs' of that place. At the time, Johanna had simply pooh-poohed the idea. But what was her real feeling? Easy enough to call forth all the reach-me-down responses you could make without thinking. Without the *danger* of thinking.

Did she fear to discover within herself an echo of Nina's response? If Charley Vose turned down her proposal, or made a derisory offer she could not afford to accept...if she fell out with Nina over her determination to have and keep Hal's baby...if, when her condition (and brazenness) became the public scandal it undoubtedly would, and all other doors were shut in her face...would she take Widow Jewell's path to survival?

No, she would lose Hal for ever, then.

Oh! Was that her only reason? Nothing in herself would draw that line?

How could one tell? What did one ever know about oneself until, as Tony Moore put it, 'push came to shove'? When she left Lanfear House (almost nine months ago now, she realized with a shock) she would have laughed at anyone who suggested that, a year to the day, she might be working for Charley Vose! So who could tell, indeed?

Those penny dreadfuls the servants used to devour were full of clergymen's daughters and other highly respectable young ladies reduced by cruel squires and ill fortune to the 'gay' life. She had assumed — in the case of the few she herself had read — that the writers invented such detail merely to make the stories more piteous and amazing; but perhaps it did sometimes happen just as they depicted it. However, the moment she allowed them that degree of realism, she was forced to suspect their honesty on a different front. The 'unfortunates' of popular fiction were haggard, consumptive, starving wretches, with 'the fruits of their debauchery etched in the myriad lines that disfigured their sunken countenances'... such, at least, were the morally satisfying exteriors they exhibited to the righteous world. But the two 'unfortunates' whom she now met, sunning themselves before their aptly named cottage, seemed healthy to the point of bursting.

'Afternoon, my lover,' Mrs Jewell called out. Her smile was knowing and none-too-friendly.

The daughter, Diana, surveyed her with guarded hostility. She was quite pretty, after her sultry fasion — as Johanna realized with a pang, for, being a twin, the girl bore a striking likeness to her sister.

All at once she regretted the impulse that had carried her here, born in the euphoria of her successful encounter with Charley Vose. Mistrust and dislike congealed the very air between them. She smiled broadly, to show she did not judge them. 'Good afternoon, Mrs Jewell. What ages it seems since we last met! I have word for you from Hal Penrose.'

That surprised them. Mrs Jewell could think of nothing to say beyond, 'Oh my gidge!'

Johanna dismounted from the trap, to dispel any suggestion that she was passing gentry stopping to impart a few kind words to the lesser breeds. 'I don't know if you heard from Jenny at all? You know she took the same ship to America as Mr Penrose, I suppose?'

Some of the woman's truculence returned. 'That's one way of putting it, I dare say.' She laughed harshly and Diana joined in.

Johanna ignored her tone. 'Well, Mr Penrose, writing from Queenstown in Ireland, about two weeks after they sailed from Plymouth, says that Jenny has been engaged by a Mr Timson, from Somerset, to nurse one of his children who is sick.'

The sneer on the widow's lips was now so marked Johanna was forced to respond. 'I'm sorry – perhaps this is no news to you at all? Has she written you? They must surely have reached Boston weeks ago.'

The woman gave an all-knowing nod. 'And I bet you haven't heard nothing since from Master Hal. And I bet you don't, neither.'

'That is surely my affair.' She smiled again, to soften the rebuke. 'But I'll be on my way. You clearly know all the news. Jenny has probably explained why you should have no truck with Charley Vose?'

'Oh, we heard from she true enough, Miss Rosewarne. But her advice is directly to the contrary purpose.' She turned to her daughter and jerked her head toward the cottage. 'Go get that letter.'

Johanna put her hand to the seat of the gig, ready to remount. 'Pray do not trouble yourself. There's no need for that. You clearly know your own business. I merely came to pass on what Mr Penrose asked me. He said you never did him aught but kindness and he thought you should be...' Her voice tailed off.

Diana was coming down the path, carrying the letter with such an air of triumph that Johanna knew she would lose more by going than by seeing this business through. The girl came right up to her, almost crowding her against the mudguard of the gig; she thrust the letter into Johanna's hand with the words, 'See for yourself, if you mind. Black and white.'

The hand was well formed and the lines neatly spaced. It read:

From Queenstown, Ireland.
My dear mother and sister,

When I wrote from Plymouth I said as Hal Penrose was to meet me there and put me to America with him. I only said it to explain my haste. Truer to say as Hal knew nought of it, as it was arranged by Lady Nina Brookes in her clever Way, which was to say nothing direct but to allow me to discover, that a certain Doctor Moore would likely give me Passage Money on the *Starflight,* so as to be rid of Hal and have his darling Miss Rosewarne to himself. But he, being such a Timdoodle, he would not do it, which I knew the Minute I set eyes on him. A Shab-Rag if ever I saw one. Give me Hal Penrose any day. Selfish he may be, a Rogue and a Cheate, too, but there's a warming Honesty in him as *honourable* Men all lack (as who should know better than we who have carried so many of that Breed!). So I must open up the Apple-Dumpling Shop one more Night to get my fare. I never traded so brisk, I can assure ye!

All was well then and I got aboard with Hal. We almost missed her sailing, I having been told she was to leave on the Tide next morning. Being ignorant of Emigration Ships and having done all in such Haste, I had made no Provision for my Vittles, the Master being obliged to provide nothing but potable Water, which I knew nothing of. But Dame Fortune smiles on this Adventure! That first day out a merchant called Timson with a sick Child, a darling little Lad of five (the very best age for a Man, as I believe!), asked me, to nurse him to Health. The which I am now engaged upon in return for a Mattress in their Cabbin and my vittles to Boston.

Poor little Timson is much taken with me, and I could if I wished hook him into the marriage Bed. If Hal were not on this Boat, if I did not see him Morning, Noon and Night, I believe such would be my End. Proprietress of a large 'Dry-Goods Store' in Wisconsin — who would

credit it? And all for running away in the Rain! Hal
urges me strongly to this Formula. So strongly, I
declare, that I suspect he wishes the Temptation of me
to be gone!! But while the Temptation of *him* is here I
cannot even think of it. I know it is the worst of Folly.
I know Hal will be the Ruin of any Woman who lets
herself be snared by him, unless she can school herself to
be as fickle and careless as he. And I, of all Women,
should know the Worth of Men in general, since they
have often enough measured it out for me in their Coin
and their intemperate Flesh and their choaking Breath.
Yet I cannot help myself. I am as much his Slave as I
would be knowing none of this.

He, to be sure, will have nothing to do with me in that
way. He is as warm to me as he is to all the World. We
might be Brother and Sister for all that I can do to make
him hotter. He stands by the Rail, sighing his Heart
toward our wake and whispering the name of Saint
Johanna Rosewarne to every little Breeze. So I must be
a little cleverer than my slavery makes me seem. His
Companion, Mr Roger Cunningham, an amiable but
empty know-it-all from 'Yaaksheer,' is determined to
travel with Hal wherever he may go, so I am, to a like
Degree, determined to let our Roger adore me — which
he is already more than apt to attempt. But this little
Cockalorum, who no doubt hopes to find himself a
Jolly Roger in the open Sea (or C!), will find the Tide
gone out instead. I think I may dangle him at least a
Year — long enough for Hal to become himself once
more. Whereupon I shall undertake his Cure for good
— and with a better Remedy than the learned Dr Moore
would dream of applying, too.

Such, at least, is my Design. I tell it you mainly so
that, you shall know you have no immediate Hope of
my sending you Money from America for some long
Time yet. Also because Hal is so earnest I should marry
Timson he may write it home as Accomplished Fact and
you may, by some roundabout way, come to hear of
it.

Time is up! I think of you often, with Affection. Oh —
I almost forgot. The Reason Hal called at Sunny Corner

346

was to fire the first Broadside in a Skirmish by Charley Vose to get us (now you and Diana and as many other flash Girls as may be needful) to leave Sunny Corner and take up the Trade in the two empty Houses up Paradise Row, whose Gardens touch the Garden at the Ram, along the back lane to Trevabyn, where you will be less of a public Temptation to the Pigs in Blue. An excellent Notion, I believe. We tempted the law too much at Sunny Corner. Only that we were so careful to please so many Magistrates, we had been taken long before. I know Charley will want his share. But what's *your* share if you're both in Helston Lock-up? So if Vose has not fired the second Shot yet, go meet him broadside on!

Love, Jenny.

Johanna folded the letter and handed it calmly back to Diana. 'Poor Jenny,' she murmured. 'To make such a rod for her own back! But I thank you for showing it to me. It has cleared up so many things in my mind.'

The other two said nothing — they just continued to smile in that knowing, triumphant way.

Selina was waiting in some impatience by the time Johanna returned to Lanfear House.

'I said I'd come in,' she reminded her cousin.

'No — don't,' Selina said. 'Not ... well, not this time.'

'Is something wrong?'

'No, not wrong, but ... well, it's just not convenient. I'm going to stay the night — I promised them that, at least.'

'Is it something I might help with, Selina?'

'No. Really no. You go home and make my apologies to Nina. I'll come back tomorrow. Perhaps everything will seem quite different then.'

Johanna put down the reins. 'I simply can't leave you like this. Obviously something has happened.'

'Please!' Selina insisted.

Johanna stared into her cousin's eyes and saw how determined she was. 'You won't even tell me?'

Her cousin forced a smile. 'Tomorrow. It's not much, really. You're compelling me to make a mountain out of it. Now go!' And she gave the pony a smart crack on his flank.

Johanna waved her farewells over her shoulder as she

fought to rein back the startled creature. She puzzled over this exchange all the way back to Helston, but at last took comfort from Selina's final assurance and the reflection that if her cousin had ever been in a serious pickle, her first response had always been to come running for help.

When Johanna entered the door of Liston Court, she found Margaret Tyzack grinning broadly and holding out a letter. *Another* letter. The telescoping of time, as Hal described it, had worked its magic: Again the envelope held two letters, one for her alone and a general missive for them all. She read it even more avidly than his first. But, between his forwarding address in Boston and the long row of *X*s that adorned the foot of the final page, there was not even a mention of Jenny Jewell. Plenty about Cunningham . . . about the voyage, which had been slow, against a foul wind most of the way . . . about his endless longing to be with her again . . .

There was even a brief reference to the splendid recovery made by the little boy. But of his erstwhile nurse (and step-mother?) not a whisper.

Hal must know enough of a lover's fears, she thought, to realize that his first letter, being all hopes and few certainties, would in no way calm her misgivings. Why had he not followed it up with the assurance he must know she craved?

Jenny's letter had, of course, provided an all-too-obvious answer. For the first time since their parting she began to feel that the antidote she carried within might not, after all, be enough.

Chapter Thirty-Three

That same night, while Selina was at Lanfear, there came a gentle knock at Johanna's bedroom door, just as she was on the point of going off to sleep.

'Who is it?' she asked. In her drowsy state she half expected it to be one of the servants, unwilling to disturb their mistress; the sight of her former home must have revived the expectation, for no such thing had ever happened at Liston Court.

'Me, dear.' It was Nina. 'May I come in?'

'Of course.' She sat up, preparing to rekindle the lamp, but saw that Nina had brought her own. 'Is anything the matter?'

The other smiled wanly as she set down her lamp. 'Not really.' Though the night was warm she clutched the seams of her dressing gown together as if there were an autumnal chill on the air. 'I just couldn't sleep, so I thought I'd come here and torment you instead.'

'Are you cold?' Johanna moved across to the cool half of the bed — deliciously cool in this weather.

Nina lay down and, for a moment, seemed to fall asleep.

'Worried about Selina?' Johanna suggested.

'Oh, about everything. Travelling is so unsettling. Having started, one should never stop. Don't you feel a dreadful...dull...dead...*eeeurgh!*' She shuddered in resentful frustration — and then opened her eyes and laughed at herself. 'Oh, Jo — thank God you're here. I don't know what I'd have done without you.'

Johanna, not knowing quite what to make of this, felt her brow. 'You've no fever, anyway,' she reassured her.

Nina lifted the hand away, as if even that gentle pressure were too heavy; but she gave the fingers a glancing kiss before she let it go. 'The touch of...' she began, and then changed it to, 'The human touch.' More crisply she added, 'Did *you* notice anything amiss at Lanfear today?'

'Well, I have to confess I didn't actually go in. When we got there I simply couldn't face it. So I went on to the Ram at Goldsithney to buy that beer and have a general sort of chat with Charley Vose. If ever you need to know what's going on in the district...'

'Oh, don't worry on that score, my dear. I have a thousand friends only too eager to tell me!'

For a guilty moment Johanna supposed she was hinting she had somehow learned of the visit to Mrs Jewell. But who could have reached Liston Court so swiftly? And no one had called since her return. Then Nina went on: 'Quite a deputation. Mrs Knox and her ghastly offspring, Wilhelmina and Grace. Mesdames Wellbeck and Ivey, all in ostentatious black — and people I hardly ever see, like Mrs Treloar, Mrs Rogers, Lady Wentworth.'

'Good heavens! All at once?'

'Not quite. Not in concert, anyway. But all moved by the same kindly intention — to be the first to warn me (oh, ever so obliquely, mind) that *things have been happening* while we've been away.'

'What sort of things?'

'I couldn't make head nor tail of it, they were all tripping over each other to remain discreet. If only one of them had called, she'd have blurted out the lot. But with all of them there it was looks and sighs and would-be significant lollings of the head that signified absolutely nothing to me.'

'So you still don't know?'

Nina smiled. 'Fortunately, Miss Grylls called after they'd all gone. She can see our carriage sweep from her upstairs drawing room. And I got it from her. Not to beat about the bush, it seems that your *cher cousin* Terence has become the most assiduous preacher of morality while we were in the Holy Land.'

'Never!' Johanna laughed at the impossibility of such a change.

'Oh, I don't mean all wild-eyed and foaming at the

mouth. Much more cunning than that. It's all hints and suggestions with him, full of 'I may be wrong, but...' and 'I wonder if, just possibly...' A most artful dog, your Terence.'

'He's nothing of mine,' Johanna protested.

'Of course, he knows he's working in fertile ground. Don't you feel it?' She reached across and patted Johanna's tummy. 'If you don't, you soon will, I fear. There's an insidious, creeping sort of...what can one call it? An aversion to the easier ways of our grandparents. I mean, up until now there's been a sort of general understanding that as long as we kept ourselves reasonably private – didn't alarm the *hoi polloi,* so to speak – we could more or less do as we pleased. You remember all that fuss about Joan Ninian? Everyone already knew what an Athanasian wench she was. It only became a scandal when her husband brought it all out in public. That was her crime.'

'*Her* crime!'

'The way of the world, my dear. Still she married that solicitor and redeemed herself. So fairy stories do sometimes happen. However – what I was saying is that there's a new mood of moralistic fervour that's seeking to change it all.'

'Well I can believe that – but not that Terence has any part in it.'

'He's not leading it. That would be too much to swallow. Or if he is – in our circle, anyway – he's leading from behind. I think the serpent in Eden must have been very like him. Eve had already made up her mind, of course – and the serpent knew it. All he needed to say was, 'I may be wrong, but...' and 'I wonder if, just possibly...' and she did the rest. What is it in women nowadays? I don't know. Life used to be so pleasant. We observed the outward proprieties *and* we enjoyed ourselves. But now there's such a mean, canting, pettifogging, *nasty* spirit going about. Women are such sheep. I could see them today, vying to outdo each other but only by a tiny little bit. Like children at a dance. Shuffling forward. I hate women sometimes, don't you?' She sighed. 'Except...'

Whatever the exception was, she did not speak it. Johanna said, 'I can see I'll have to leave here soon.'

'No!' Nina turned to her in surprise. 'Damn them, I say!

I'm an earl's daughter. I will not let this spawn of tradesmen dictate to me. They can stew in their own self-righteousness for all I care.'

'It would be easiest of all if you gave me the fare, Nina. I'll go to America, marry Hal, come back a respectable matron.'

'And we'll all live happily ever after!'

'You said yourself — fairy stories do sometimes happen.'

Nina turned and clutched her arm. 'I couldn't do that to you, darling. Listen, I've been trying to think of something that would convince you. You remember how — in those days after Harvest Fair — when Hal came to dinner once and he wouldn't look at you or talk to you or anything?'

'But I understand that.'

'Do you? All right, you tell me.'

'He saw his freedom vanishing over the horizon. He told me himself — he'd never been in love like that. He felt imprisoned by it.'

Nina let go and stared at the ceiling. 'Then you baffle me entirely. Or is it that you think he's now reconciled to it?'

'I know he his.'

'Hmmmph!'

'He *is.*'

Nina shook her head sadly. 'Not him. Believe me. He'd walk you in circles. The sort of woman he needs is one as passionate as himself and yet with as cool an eye, too — one who can match his roguery, wound for wound.' She gave a single laugh. 'That's me, of course! I should have stolen him from you that very first night. I could have, too. If only I'd known what effect he was having on you.'

'There's nothing I can say will make you change your mind?'

'At least admit I'm right.'

Johanna stared at the ceiling and nodded. 'It doesn't seem to make any difference.'

'Well! Here's a change at last.'

When Johanna said nothing, Nina went on, 'You have been doing *some* thinking, then?'

Slowly, deliberately, Johanna replied: 'I haven't yet told you everything I did this afternoon. In addition to calling on Charley Vose, you see, I also stopped by Sunny Corner.'

The name clearly meant nothing to Nina.

'The Widow Jewell?' Johanna prompted.

Nina closed her eyes. 'Hal's letter,' she murmured.

'Yes. He told me the other side of what Tony Moore wrote about. Hal had nothing to do with all that, did he. And you know it.'

'Except that he did call at that place – Sunny Corner? He did go there.'

'And d'you know why?'

Nina laughed, as if the question were naive.

'Wrong,' Johanna told her. 'He went with a message from Charley Vose. I can see exactly what's going on in that mercenary little mind of his. Last summer every man in West Penwith with the Irish toothache was...'

'Johanna!'

'Isn't that what they call it? How would you put it?'

'Go on. You never cease to amaze me.'

'The trade must have been brisk or Charley wouldn't be so interested. But the distance between Sunny Corner and the Ram is just too far for him to feel the benefit of all those extra mouths and bellies in the parish. Not to mention purses. So he wants to set up the obliging widow and her girls in those two empty cottages in Paradise Row, at the back end of the Ram, where it'll all be very discreet and orderly – and under his control.'

'Paradise Row!'

'Yes, I know, but they were called that long before.'

'You seem to know *all* their business.'

'Mrs Jewell showed me a letter from Jenny, you see.'

'Oh. Did she...' Nina fell silent.

Johanna smiled. 'Between the lines, Nina dear, she reveals how you allowed her to discover Tony Moore's existence and his interest in me – without saying a single direct word on the subject.' She reached forward and touched her arm, hesitantly. 'I don't blame you, love. I know you think it's all for the best. You're doing it for my own good, and nothing in it for you.'

'Don't you be so sure!'

Johanna gave a bewildered laugh. 'But how can you possibly benefit?'

Nina raised herself on one elbow and turned to her.

'Don't you know?'

Johanna shook her head.

'I can't imagine this household without you, darling. I'd be desolate if you left us.'

Johanna made an embarrassed little noise in her throat. 'There'd still be Selina.'

Nina stared at her, showing no emotion at all, for a long, unnerving moment before she said, 'You've already decided to go.'

'It was decided for me. The night I came here.'

'Why? What did I do? Was it something I...Oh! You mean Hal.' She flung herself back on her pillow. 'Oh, damn all men! What good have they ever been to us?'

'Damn the women. Damn the men,' Johanna commented.

Nina did not take up the remark. In a voice that was curiously flat and distant she inquired, 'Will you go and ask Tony Moore for your passage money?'

Johanna shook her head. 'I don't think Hal would like that. I only said it to try and shock you.'

'It's only what Hal thinks that matters, is it? Nothing in you would feel dishonoured if you went and grovelled for the money?'

She chuckled. 'I was pondering something of the sort earlier today, after I'd spoken with Mrs Jewell. You know that Tony didn't give Jenny the money?'

'Well, he told us that.'

'Yes, but I didn't believe him. However it seems he was telling the truth. But she got it nonetheless. In her letter she said she 'opened up the old apple-dumpling shop' for one more night and got it. In one *night,* Nina − over twelve pounds!'

Nina was staring at her, aghast. 'You weren't thinking of...'

Johanna gave a rueful smile. 'I think it'd be the best way of losing Hal for ever.'

'And that's your only reason?'

'How do I know? I've often thought myself the most miserable creature alive, but I've never even been close to that sort of desperation. So how can anyone know?'

Nina just lay there, eyes closed, hardly breathing. Her jaw

was open but her lips were together, causing her cheeks to fall inward, giving her a haggard, defeated look. Johanna felt a sudden upwelling of pity. 'D'you want to spike Terence's guns?' she asked.

'Mmmmm?'

'I suspect the Jewells know quite a bit about that lad. And I don't for one moment suppose his new-found love of righteousness among the teacups has led him to discontine his visits to Sunny Corner − knowing him as I do. D'you want me to find out?'

'I don't want you going back there.'

Johanna tried to think of some other way to break the rest of her news − which she now realized it would be cruel to keep to herself.

'You're not going to, are you?' Nina pressed.

Johanna, feeling too warm for comfort, threw off the bedclothes and sat up, hugging her knees to her chin. 'There was something else in Jenny Jewell's letter. She's passing the voyage as nurse to a sick child belonging to a widower from Somerset. Called Timson. He's keen on her, apparently, and Hal keeps urging her to marry him. He's quite well set up. But she told her mother she won't do it. Instead, she's going to pretend to be sweet on poor Roger Cunningham, who had decided to throw in his lot with Hal over there.'

'Poor Hal.'

'It's Cunningham I pity. Hal can look after himself.'

'I never doubted that!' Nina gave a sarcastic laugh. 'You think Jenny's scheming to stay close to Hal and win him from you?'

'I don't need to think it. She makes no bones about it.'

'And you're afraid she'll. . .'

'She hasn't the ghost of a chance, Nina. But even she knows it. That's what I was really going to tell you. She said something to the effect that she knows full well Hal is a rogue and a cheat and will be the ruin of any woman who's foolish enough to fall for him. But. . .'

'There you are!' Nina, too, threw off the clothes and sat up, her eyes filled with joy., Even she says so! Isn't it exactly what I've been telling you?

'More or less word for word. But − as I was going on to say − she added that she couldn't help herself. She's as much his slave as if she knew nothing of all that.'

'So there are two of you.'

'And one of us is on this side of the ocean.'

There was a long silence after that, during which Nina tried not to make the obvious offer. Then Johanna took her breath away by saying: 'I'm beginning to wonder if I haven't made the most colossal mistake.'

Nina was completely at a loss to know how to take this confession; then she saw Johanna's eyes were brimming with tears. Awkwardly, waddling on her knees, she crossed the few feet that separated them and threw her arms about her. 'Oh, Jo, don't cry, my love. Please don't cry. I'll give you the fare. I should have given it to you weeks ago. Please don't make yourself miserable.'

Her entreaties faded. Johanna was not responding in any way — and certainly not with the outburst of joy one might have expected.

'No?' Nina asked.

Johanna shook her head. Sobbing openly now — yet trying to speak as if she were nonetheless in full control of her voice — she replied, 'When I read those words of Jenny's — knowing she loves him as deeply as me, even...she does love him — but when I read those words, and then when you said the same sort of thing...I don't know. I just don't know what to do any more.'

Chapter Thirty-Four

Selina did not return to Liston Court until after lunch. Her mood was sombre, even downcast. 'I don't know what's to be done,' she said. 'I never saw my mother so unhappy. And poor Deirdre and Ethna. It's a changed household, Jo.'

Johanna, thinking she knew what had gone wrong at Lanfear, replied, 'I did wonder if it was altogether wise for Aunt Theresa to try and manage the entire establishment on her own.'

'Oh , but that's not it,' Selina told her. 'She did, in fact, employ a housekeeper — shortly after we left for Paris. The poor woman lasted about a week. It's my father, you see.' She paused a moment, lost for words. 'He takes it into his head...' This time the silence was complete.

'D'you think I should...I mean, is there anything I might do?' Johanna asked with sinking heart.

'No!' Selina was horrified at the thought. 'Certainly not in your present condition.' The animation deserted her and she added, 'My mother wonders if he hasn't perhaps become a little unhinged.'

'About what?' Nina asked. 'Are the mines doing badly? Tin has taken a tumble, I see.'

'Well, that hasn't helped, of course. But it's more serious than that.'

'What does Terence say?' Johanna asked.

'He's gone. He and father actually came to blows. He's taken a set of chambers here in Helston. In Coinagehall Street. I must go up and see him. Find out what he thinks.'

'You started to say,' Johanna reminded her, 'my uncle

takes it into his head...to what?'

Her cousin stared mournfully at her. 'I don't want you to suppose it's your fault, Jo.'

'What isn't?' She closed her eyes, almost guessing what was coming next and dreading to hear it.

'Well, it seems he was very upset by your leaving. For a while he ranted on about ingratitude. And now he seems to have taken against all females — young or old, no matter. Whether he knows them or not, even if they've done him nothing but kindness all their lives, it's all the same to him. Peggy Machin, you remember, who's cooked for him since he was in pantaloons? He abused her so dreadfully she had to give in her notice.'

'No!' Johanna was aghast. Lanfear without old Peg was almost unthinkable.

'And he terrorizes my poor sisters.'

'And Aunt Theresa?'

'No, that would go too far against his own self-interest. He's ill-tempered with her, but otherwise cautious. She broke down and told me she has considered means of restraining him.'

Nina and Johanna exchanged glances. It struck them both that Selina had not herself broken down, nor come even close to it, at any time during her account; she might have been discussing the household of some distant relative.

'And you're sure Terence has nothing to do with this?' Nina asked.

Selina frowned. 'Why should he? As the cause of it, you mean?'

'I'm told he's become quite the moral evangelist while we've been away — stirring up the already considerable fervour of a certain set of local ladies.'

'Terence?' Selina echoed in disbelief.

'That's what I said,' Johanna told her. 'But it seems to be true.'

'But why?'

'To clip my wings, of course,' Nina answered scornfully. 'My flagrantly enjoyable widowhood is to be so exposed to public censure that I shall fly to the altar for protection. With him, or so he hopes.'

Selina pulled a face. 'Perhaps I shouldn't see him, after all – about the goings-on at Lanfear, I mean.'

'Do, by all means.' Nina laughed. 'He's no more threat than a flea to a dog.'

Selina stared out of the window, shaking her head at the incomprehensible turn things had taken.

Nina, filled with sudden misgiving, went to her. 'There's more, isn't there, my lamb? You haven't told us everything.'

She nodded and said, morosely, 'He only let me come back here on condition I gathered up my belongings and returned to Lanfear.'

'But you're over twenty-one.'

Selina gave a hopeless shrug.

'You're free to do as you please,' Nina urged.

'Legally yes, but that's not how people will see it – the fervent ladies of Helston, all our friends. As far as Society's concerned, I'm a poor, weak, frail, young spinster. I'm still under his protection until some gallant husband relieves him of the dreadful burden.'

Johanna watched Nina's knuckles turn white; that bitter frustration, never far from the surface with her, was about to erupt once more. She leaped in and said, 'I have an answer.'

They turned to her with eyes so wide and eager that she quailed; she had not been brought up to suppose her ideas might be taken so earnestly. 'I'm not entirely serious,' she warned, 'but we could throw their whole stupid notion into their faces. Selina and I could go up to the workhouse, find two male paupers on their deathbeds, marry them – I'm sure they'd agree in return for a decent funeral and a known resting place. And then we'd be three widows under one roof. Perfectly acceptable in Society's eyes. . .my baby would have a name. . .all our problems solved at one stroke! And wouldn't they be furious!'

'Oh yes!' Selina turned to Nina. 'Let's! Why can't we do it?'

Johanna had achieved her purpose. Nina laughed good-humouredly and said, 'But, to be serious, we now have two reasons for asking Terence to call – or, rather, each of us has one.'

'What is he living on?' Johanna asked.

Selina shrugged. Nina raised her eyebrows, as much as to say the thought had not struck her.

'Then all three of us have questions,' Johanna said. 'But, alas, mine will have to wait. I have inquiries of my own to make – elsewhere.'

Just as she was about to set out, however, the postman came with the third delivery – a single letter, addressed to her, and posted that same morning in Goldsithney. 'The Widow Jewell,' she exclaimed in surprise the moment she opened it. The message was brief. The woman apologized for her incivility of the day before and would be obliged if Miss Rosewarne would call at her soonest convenience. Johanna passed it to Nina with a significant lift of her eyebrows. 'I wish you wouldn't go,' Nina told her, but her tone already conceded the action.

The pony almost made his own way to Goldsithney by now. It was another balmy day, not so hot as yesterday but still fine. As they passed the mines between Pednavounder and Carleen – Wheal Metal, Pallas Consols, Wheal Vor, Greatwork – she counted more than half the chimneys idle; and there were men and women lying drunk in the hedges at almost every bend, an uncommon sight for a Wednesday afternoon. When tin took a tumble, people weren't slow to follow, she reflected.

Mrs Jewell was in her garden, seated to one side of her front door, shelling peas. Diana lay at full length beneath a parasol on a travelling rug that almost completely obscured their tiny patch of lawn. She opened one eye, saw who it was, and went back to her dozing. Once again Johanna felt the pain of her likeness to her sister – and the thought that her mirror image was there with Hal, day and night, flaunting her availability.

'You were some quick, Miss Rosewarne,' the widow said as she set down her bowl and advanced up the path, nervously wiping her hands into her pinny. 'I didn't hardly expect 'ee afore tomorrow.'

'I had other calls to make in the district,' Johanna explained. 'What was it you wished to see me about?'

The woman glanced at her daughter and then, with a deferential touch, turned her visitor back toward the gate.

When they were in the lane once more she said, 'I was up to Charley Vose last evening, thinking all was settled and just hoping to get the key...well, I mean to say, all *is* settled, decorations done and everything. Anyway, he says to me as you must have the final say in the matter, seeing as you're to be the new mistress up there.'

'Is that what he said?' Johanna was surprised she was able to sound so calm; her pulse was racing, partly from anger at Charley and partly from excitement at the glimpse of power that was being offered – which suited her perfectly at this particular moment.

'Isn't it true?' Mrs Jewell asked. 'It fair took me aback, I can tell 'ee. I'm the one who paid for all the decorations, see.'

'"Mistress" needs clarifying – and he and I shall have words about that. He's offered me the position of house-keeper – which I've told him I'll consider taking if I may also have the opportunity to...well, another opportunity connected with his trade at the Ram.'

'Ah,' the Widow said bitterly. 'Now we come to it – *this* trade, you mean.' And she jerked her head back toward her cottage.

'Not at all. Quite the contrary. Indeed, I told him there could be no question of that. What exactly did he say to you?'

'Aaa. He told me as you said that but he also said mebbe you were a touch hasty. Mebbe if all the facts were beknown to 'ee, you'd see your way different?' Her voice rose hopefully.

'What are these facts, then? I wouldn't want you to think I'd said no out of hand.'

It had also struck Johanna since the previous evening that in a couple of months now, whenever the baby started to show beyond all doubt, she'd make herself a laughing stock for having taken such an uncompromising moral stand against the trade. Whereas the people engaged in it could hardly object to her – on the same grounds.

'Well...' Mrs Jewell had obviously not prepared any case – not having expected this encounter before tomorrow. A last-minute woman, then, Johanna decided. 'I s'pose the first fact is that the day I took to this business

I hadn't eaten in forty-eight hours, the girls were bailing and squailing with the hunger, and you couldn't pinch a rasher of fat off of my ribs. And now there's a handful on every one of 'em.'

'And what about your daughters?'

'Plump enough, too, I tell 'ee. Well, you've seen Diana for yourself.'

'No − I mean why did you have to involve them, too?'

A man, a stranger to Johanna, entered the lane; when he saw her he hesitated, but Mrs Jewell beckoned him on. He was an old farmer with two unopposed teeth left to show; his weatherbeaten hide was as brown as his gaiters and every bit as tough. Johanna knew him vaguely by sight; he farmed over beyond Nancegollan, she fancied − about six miles to the west. When he raised his hat, it was almost as if he removed a skin, for his domed head was pink, hairless, and shiny. As he advanced he kept looking at Johanna but Mrs Jewell disabused him of any notions he might be forming behind those porcine little eyes. 'My Diana's a-waiting for 'ee, my lover,' she said.

He did not give up so easily, though. He tilted his head almost imperceptibly toward Johanna and hesitated. 'Diana,' the mother repeated even more firmly.

He turned slightly from them and spat in the hedge. 'You, then,' he told her, making a grab for her arm.

'Not just now. You wait ten minutes if you mind to − else, like I say, 'tis the girl.'

He gave Johanna another once-over, the implications of which made her flesh creep, and went scowling toward the cottage.

'The *gay* life!' Mrs Jewell commented.

Johanna waited for more but the other just stood there, biting her lip. 'He'll only go and take it out on she, poor thing,' she muttered. 'I don't s'pose you could wait just five minutes?'

She was so full of concern that Johanna ushered her homeward. 'Please,' she said.

'Maid!' her mother called as they reached the gate.

Diana turned, pulling her arm out of the man's clutch.

''Tis all right. I'll look after he. You see to our visitor here.'

Showing no relief — indeed, no emotion whatever — the girl changed places with her mother.

'A deliverance for you,' Johanna commented when they were alone.

Diana looked briefly toward the house and then shrugged. ''Tis all one to me, now,' she commented.

'Truly?'

The girl sniffed.

'You mean if the most handsomest fellow you ever saw came down the lane now, you wouldn't prefer to go with him than with that awful man?'

Diana shook her head. 'If the money's good.'

'And was it like that from the very beginning?'

The girl said nothing — just stared at her with those great, incurious eyes. 'Will you leave us go up Paradise Row?' she asked at length.

'How old are you, Diana?'

'Twenty, miss. Nigh on one and twenty. Will you?'

'I'm trying to understand it, my dear. I don't want to say no just out of ... but also I don't want to say yes out of ignorance, either. I want to understand.' A thought occurred to her. 'Your mother was explaining to me how it all began — for her at least — all of you starving and so on. But she didn't tell me how you two girls got into it. I mean, presumably she was earning enough to keep all three of you by then?'

Diana gave a single dry laugh and shook her head.

'It's not just idle curiosity, I assure you. If I'm left to make this decision, I want to be fair.'

That jolted the girl out of her sullenness at last. 'How did I start? That was over twelvemonth back. The old woman was doing fifteen...twenty a day and near killing herself. But you can't turn people away, see? So, anyway, there was these four fellows, waiting like, and one of them says he couldn't hold on no more, so he grabs Jenny and puts she on her back, out the hayfield. And then one of the others took me the same way. And I'll tell no lie now — 'twas the easiest ten shilling we ever earned between us. So then that was it. Didn't seem much point in holding back.'

'I see. Tell me another thing then. When that man came down the lane just now, he wanted your mother but she told him to go to you. Then she changed her mind. She said he'd only take it out on you. What did she mean?'

'He'd slap me about a bit, I s'pose.'

'Instead of...what he paid for?'

The girl laughed.

'You see, I don't understand. You mean he'd slap you about and then...what d'you call it?'

Diana chuckled. 'You'd need paper so big as Cornwall to take down all the names for it.'

'Just one word.'

'Strum? Put a leg over me? Play three to one? Take a turn among the parsley? Do it...'

'Do it!' Johanna settled for the most neutral term on offer. 'You mean he'd slap you around a bit and *then* do it?'

She nodded.

'It's beyond my comprehension.'

'There's a lot of men like that. Some *only* want to slap you. Some want you to slap them.'

'And you do? You let them?'

'They pay, of course. If it's only slapping with hands, we can take that for the extra coin, but if they do want to use whips or canes, we do send out for Angie Viggers. 'Course, if they want us to ply the cane on them...'

'Is that the Angela Viggers who used to live over to Lanuthnoe, over St Erth?'

''Es. She still do.'

'Why d'you send for her?'

'Because she do claim to like it, but if you ask me, she got no feeling in her bum — nor yet nowhere in her back at all. And she do like the money, too. A hand-slap is only sixpence playful and a shilling hard, see? But with the cane 'tis a half-crown for each cut. And a extra half-crown for every one that draws blood.'

Johanna had to reach out and steady herself against the hedge. Partly it was a straight reaction to this matter-of-fact recital of depravity, but behind it, hovering just at the rim of her consciousness, was an awareness of what might really have been taking place during those sessions at Lanfear House — when she supposed she was being chastised, justly or not, for her transgressions.

Diana, seeing the effect of her revelations, now began a retreat. 'Of course, I wouldn't say it do happen every week. Nor yet every month. And I daresay we only send for Angie five or six times since we started, like. We don't really look for that class o'trade, see. I mean, there's proper houses down Penzance and up Falmouth where they're equipped for all that caper. That's where Angie do work regular, see – down Penzance. Behind the Duke of Wellington in Wherrytown.'

'Good heavens, Diana, from the way you talk. . . I mean, how many houses are there?' The surprise of this new revelation did much to revive her from the shock of the previous one.

'This side of Truro? Well, there's a dozen I could name, so I should think there'd be at least twice that many. There's two in Helston.'

'I don't believe it!'

'Suit yourself. There's one down the bottom of Lady Street and the other's out 'long Meneage Street, almost opposite the workhouse.'

'Well! Each has an appropriate address, in its way. I had no idea.'

'You've no cause to. But I tell 'ee – any man walking that way, he'd know it straight off. No second glance. He'd know it.'

Johanna laughed at her own naivety. 'And *I* thought Charley Vose was proposing to start something new and foreign down here!'

'My dear life!' Diana laughed, too.

'But if there are so many houses, why don't you go and work in one of them?'

'Because they do take half of all you earn. Some do want more. The girls are never free of debt there.'

'And what's Charley Vose going to want?'

'We're still higgling over that, but we do think he'll accept eight shilling in the pound. The suppers and the beer is his real profit, see?'

'These men. . .the ones who hit you.' Johanna returned to the topic only because the germ of an idea was taking shape in her mind. 'Is it as if they *have* to do it? It's not just the sort of high-spirited prank that young bloods might egg

365

each other on to try just once – the way they'll try anything?'

'Oh no, miss. Different breed altogether. I had a young fellow here once –' She paused. Johanna felt sure she was about to mention his name, but she obviously thought better of it and went on: 'He tried it like that, just for a prank, see. He slapped me once and then he giggled so much he couldn't go on. And then I got a fit of the giggles, too. We had a good old time after that. You've got to see the funny side sometimes.'

'I'm sure. But about those others...'

'Oh, yes, they need it right enough. And they want you to beg them for mercy. You've got to tell them you've been a naughty girl and deserve whipping to an inch off your life – and all that. Angie can do it, proper job.'

'And afterwards – are they apologetic? Ashamed? Or what?'

'Quiet as lambs. All the fever gone. And that's another good thing why we're here. I often think of the respectable women who walk safe on account of we, and with their skin unblemished, too. I believe they'd think more kindly on us if only they knew.' She carefully avoided Johanna's eye as she spoke what sounded like a prepared text.

Her mother and the farmer returned to the lane at that moment. He was now as jovial as Punch; all his brusque nerviness had gone. When he drew level with Diana he put an arm around her and said cheerily, 'I shall have a little wetting to give 'ee next time, maid.'

He glanced at Johanna but only long enough to see the frost in her eye. Diana kissed him warmly on the cheek and said she'd count the hours; but the moment he had his back to her she pulled a face for Johanna.

'I thought you said it was all one to you,' Johanna accused her after he had gone.

'When they pay,' she replied. 'He never paid a penny for that hug he gave me.'

'One more respectable maid walks safe tonight,' Mrs Jewell said portentously, staring up the road after the farmer.

'I did that, Ma,' Diana warned.

The mother turned to Johanna. 'So, what do 'ee say, Miss

366

Rosewarne? Is it yes or no?'

'I have one more question,' Johanna told them. 'Then you shall have my answer.'

She paused and looked sternly at one, and then the other.

'Yes?' they encouraged her eagerly.

'Tell me everything you know about my cousin Terence.'

Chapter Thirty-Five

There was a storm brewing in the north. About ten minutes
before it struck, the door was flung open and a portly old
gentleman cried, 'Helloa there! Where under heaven *is* the
folks. Git a-joggin', can't ye?'

The silken bolster he carried over his shoulder slipped to
the ground, grew two dainty slippers and a head of hair,
dusted herself down, and, with a fearful glance at the
sulphureous skies, said, 'Oh, Paw!'

Hal and Cunningham sprang to their feet and asked how
they might help; but the old trapper pulled Cunningham
back into his seat and motioned to Hal to sit down, too.
'Damn Yankees!' he muttered.

Micajah Owen, the builder and proprietor of this two-
room log-cabin and a plain Quaker man of mild and
primitive habits, came in with a basket of logs for the
kitchen stove. 'Thee are welcome,' he told the newcomers.

'Ah, you sir,' replied the Damn Yankee, 'we require three
rooms for the night. Pray be so good . . .'

His wife, some fifteen if not twenty years his junior,
interposed herself. 'If you have a small space, sir, where we
may shelter out this storm? We'll be mighty obliged to you.'
While she spoke she caught her husband by the collar and
hauled his ear down to her level. Into it she muttered
something that made him cough, and then mumble, 'Your
pardon, sir. Didn't understand. Thought this was one of
your regular stages. Harvey Butts, your humble errmerr.
Mrs Butts. My daughter Clarry. My servant is seeing to the
team.'

Micajah nodded to each, introduced himself, and added,

368

'Thee are welcome to shelter here. All thee see is all we have.'
Then he continued his interrupted journey to the kitchen.

A well-made, ruddy-complexioned young man squeezed through the door and closed it against the wind. 'Frank Ashburn,' he said with a bluff nod to the party around the fireplace before he turned to Butts. 'Well, that's the team settled,' he told him.

'The luggage must be brought in.'

'I should jes' think it had oughter.' He began to peel off his gloves. 'An' ef'n 'twas mine, that's jes' what I should do, too.' His eyes found Jenny. He winked at her — or rather, at a point somewhere between her and Cunningham.

'Now see here, sir,' Harvey Butts began.

'No, *you* see here,' Frank told him. 'I'll set to and help any man upon a pinch. But I didn't engage to wait upon ye. I ain't nobody's nigger. I came on for your teamster. And you should know the difference between a help and a servant. And *now* I'll fetch in the luggage.'

Hal stood up and joined him. 'And I'll give a hand.' He pointed to his seat and nodded towards little Clarry.

She was really too young for such courtesies, but only by a year or so. She accepted in a bewilderment of daring and coquetry.

'You made a conquest there, feller,' Frank told him as they bent themselves into the van of the storm.

'Hal Penrose,' Hal told him. They shook hands awkwardly, being all triced up against the blast. Between grunts and cries of 'To me . . . your end first,' they continued their conversation.

'You headed west?' Frank asked.

'Northwest. We're making for Galena, Wisconsin.'

'Mining, eh?'

'Yessir.'

'From North Carliny? Or Luzaany — by the sound of you?'

'No, we're from Cornwall in England — or next-door to England as some of us would say.'

'I was born back there, in Liverpool, but I can't remember it. Who is 'we'?'

'The man who was sitting by me and the young lady next to him. Name of Roger Cunningham and Jennifer Jewell.'

369

'Yeah, I noticed her!' He gave a guarded chuckle. 'An' him – squirmish kinda feller. Are they going together?'

'She's kind-of with me, Mr Ashford.'

'Plain Ashford'll do. *Kinda* with you, huh?'

They went indoors with the first of the trunks and returned to haul the second. Frank gave Jenny a lingering scrutiny as he closed the door. 'Jes' my luck,' he commented. 'We was in Wellington last night, and I'll tell ya – that is something less than a one-horse town. So' – his voice changed pace suddenly – 'you're a miner, Penrose. And looking for a bonanza, I'll be bound?'

'If that means what it sounds like – yes, we are.'

'I hear the Cornish in you now. I ran across a passel o' you Cousin Jacks, you call yoursel's. But you're kinda different, somehow.' He put down the trunk, which he had only just begun to lift, and stared shrewdly at Hal. 'I take you for some powerful, high-larnt man, Penrose.'

Hal gave the trunk a shake. 'I've had my share of schooling.'

'Geology's in there somewheres, I opinion?'

Hal conceded with a nod.

'An' mineralemonology an' augurs an' figgerations an' all them hiramglyptix, too, eh? Take my Bible on it.'

'I have a smattering of it, yes. Come on – it's going to pour.'

Frank toted his end and laughed. 'A smattering! Now how did I ever take you for an American?'

'What's in these trunks anyway?' Hal grumbled.

'Would you believe it? Two thousand dollars – all in bits an' picayunes. Not a figger less. Listen – we must have a jaw, you and I, afore we part.' After a pause he added significantly, 'Ef'n we do part, that is.'

The meal was served almost at once – or, rather, the food was placed upon the table and then, after grace, it was 'set by an' reach to.' Cunningham was the last to join, having been sent out to the spring house for the buttermilk. The storm broke as he sat, almost as if it had been waiting for the signal.

It was quite a spread. When Micajah Owen had prayed, 'Oh Lord, for these thy bounties...' it had been no mere convention. The centrepiece was a loaf of wheat and Indian meal, large as a grindstone; there was half a cheese, almost as great, with cold pork, peach pie, apple pie, and — because it had been baking day — a huge rice pudding in an earthen pan.

And it was quite a party that shared it, too. The Owens had a son, Israel, who never spoke, and two daughters, Beulah and Amy, strong, homely girls, full of laughter. There was Johnny, the trapper, named Jonathan Bonny in full — 'Though folks usually call me Bonathan Johnny for short.' There were the three Buttses and Frank; and lastly, the three immigrants from Cornwall — thirteen in all. When they noticed that, Johnny wanted an extra place laid but Micajah would have no truck with such superstition.

Honours for the entertainment were divided evenly at first between Johnny and Frank. Johnny told of stampedes and Injun hunts and rough justice 'on the frontier,' which set Hal and his companions to wondering, for the land they had travelled these last few days had seemed already quite frontier-like enough for their taste. Frank, who made himself out to be something of a rolling stone ('Cain't stop nowheres longer nor manure on the slope of a red sand hill,' was how he expressed it), matched him tale for tale, with a swamp fire in Florida, a fight in Illinois over a bee tree, which ended up in the state supreme court as an all-time precedent on pre-emption rights, and two judges who schemed so mightily against each other that neither got elected. In the end, though, it was the girls who won.

Johnny was impervious to their charms; no man ever radiated a purer beam of misogynistical self-sufficiency. But Frank was quite the opposite; for a fleeting smile or a soprano giggle he'd lay on his back and stretch all four legs toward the skies. So, what with Mrs Owen and her daughters, and Jenny and Clarry, all hanging on each new revelation from him, it turned into no contest at all — except among themselves as to which flutter of which eyelash could provoke the most outrageous revelation.

The following morning Frank rose early to tend his team of horses, which were loose in the corral along with Hal's. He found Hal already there, grooming his pair. The storm had passed and the day promised sunny and warm, though with less dust along the trail.

Hal was worried enough about his horses' shoes to ask Frank's opinion.

The man took his time answering. 'Shoes is no light matter, Penrose,' he advised. 'Not like hitchin' to a gal or settlin' down and sich foolery.' He studied all eight feet with care; he gauged the weight of the horses; he consulted his mental map of the trail ahead. 'Good for another hundred,' he said. ''Course, ef I knew how you tool these animals...?' He rose and fixed Hal with his eye. 'Like ef I knew you done tol' the truth 'bout Galena...'

Hal laughed. 'Why should I not?'

''Cos I think you're headed same way as me, boy – Fort Laramie, South Pass, Fort Bridger, Salt Lake City, the Hastings cutoff, Donner Pass...and glory-be! Now, does that jump a whole card of efs an' ands an' mebbes? We're all headed for Cally-for-nigh-ay, right?'

'Is it true, then?'

'Is it true? Man, where you been hibernatin'?'

'One hears so many rumours.'

'Rumours? Ain't no rumours. True's preachin', is all.'

'We intended going as far as St Louis and then either upriver to Galena or head west if it proved true.'

'Head west, huh?' Frank chuckled and tapped his cranium. 'These ol' cogs was a-whirrin' all night – done tellin' me, "Boy, this Penrose an' Cunning-ham an' that purty li'l Jenny sure hit lucky the day they met young Frank Ashburn." Was you ever on the prairie? Ever meet a Injun?'

'Several.'

'No, I mean a *Injun* Injun, a kill-or-get-killed Injun out to raise hair. Now I have carnal knowledge of them fellas. Tell you 'nother thing – you'll hit the Humboldt the worst time o' year. You know how to locate water in the Sierra?'

'Is that where you're headed, then? With the Buttses?'

'No siree. He's aimin' to build hisself a hotel in St Louis. That's where my contract ends. So, seein' as we're both headed for ole Mizurah, we can chew the fat along the trail.'

Cunningham joined them at that moment. He and Hal split a whole cord of wood for the Owenses while Jenny banked up a couple of rows of potatoes and 'joshed' with Frank. Every now and then she checked to see how Hal was taking it.

And just as frequently, Hal did the same service for Cunningham. After a while the man became aware of it. He gave a lopsided grin and asked, 'D'you suppose there's a chance he might take her off our hands, old man?'

Hal raised his eyebrows. 'That's an odd way of putting it. But I thought you were quite keen?'

'You know me. I've too much for any one woman. I should have been born an oriental potentate.'

'Ah. Yes, of course.'

'Besides, I'm none too sure of her sincerity. I used to think she was playing with me to rouse your jealousy, but now I believe she senses what sort of man I'll be one day. She's just waiting to clutch at my coat-tails.'

'Lucky you spotted that,' Hal told him. 'I must say, I had my suspicions.'

'Well, of course, so did I. You don't suppose our teamster friend would try to take advantage of her, do you? She's obviously completely innocent in that regard. I'd hate to have to teach him his manners.'

'I think the surprise would be on his side — if he tried it,' Hal assured him.

'Jove yes!' Cunningham laughed at the prospect. 'She certainly knows how to say no.'

After breakfast, when they were all setting out once more, Mr Butts made the mistake of slapping a five-dollar bill down on the table. Later, when they stopped for a noontide bite and to rest and water the teams, Frank took Hal aside for a stroll and showed him that same bill. 'Owen done give it me,' he explained. 'He said, "You give this back to that fine gentleman o' yourn. Tell him I heared they got emporiums in them big cities where a man can walk right in and buy some manners. So you tell Mr Butts to git hisself five dollars' worth on *me!*" That's what he done said. An' that's the pleasurablest commission this particular feather of the American Eagle ever got given. Can't hardly wait for St Louis.'

'Nor can we, as a matter of fact, Ashburn. I talked it over with the others along the way, and it looks as if we'll head straight for California with you.'

'The gal, too?'

'The "gal" too.'

'Yahoo! Why she makes a man feel like a June bug is crawlin' up his trousers, and the waist band too tight for him to git out.' He grinned craftily at Hal. 'She's kinda sweet on you, I suspicion. The way she was tryin' to rile you, joshin' with me this mornin'.'

'I wouldn't draw too many conclusions from that.'

'You didn't seem too all-fired steamed up?'

He laughed. 'Well, Ashburn, you may draw any conclusion you like from that!'

Chapter Thirty-Six

The night of her visit to Sunny Corner, Johanna composed a letter to her uncle. It cost some effort, when the only letter she really wanted to write was to Hal. What tipped the balance in favour of the other was the knowledge that, whatever she might send to America, even if every word were true, would be an hypocrisy. The things she left out would ultimately rebound to her shame. So while she said nothing at all, she postponed that unpleasant choice.

The following morning, while Nina was busy with her correspondence (including, though Johanna did not know it, one of her regular reports to Tony Moore) and Selina got on with her journal — or whatever it was called today — she took the letter with her and paid a surprise visit to her cousin Terence at his chambers in a narrow, winding alley off Coinagehall Street.

'Good God,' he said as he answered her knock — in person, she noticed. He looked as if he had only just risen. 'You!'

'Welcome, *ma chère cousine*,' she said brightly, speaking for him. 'How nice to see you after your long sojourn in foreign climes. You must have so much to talk about. Do come in!'

He stood aside. 'Come in, anyway. But after seventeen hours of Judea and Damascus and Paris and Florence and Petra yesterday afternoon, I'm not so sure about the rest. Anyway, how are *you?*'

There was a special solicitude in the question that made her uneasy — particularly when he guided her toward a chair and added, 'After what Selina told me yesterday, you're just about the last person I expected to see going about town.' He put a hand to her waist. 'But you're right. Nothing's showing yet.'

She felt the blood draining from her face. 'She told you?'

'I suppose she thought family ought to know.'

Johanna felt sick with apprehension. 'D'you suppose she told my aunt as well?'

He pulled a dubious face. 'She didn't say she did. Ask her.' He thrust a chair behind her knees and put a token hand to her shoulders until she was settled. 'Cheer up, Jo. Bags of time yet. We'll find a good husband for you in due season. All's not lost.'

He pulled up a chair of his own and sat facing her with an encouraging smile.

'Is that what Selina told you I wanted? Was Lady Nina there, by the way?'

'No, she'd gone out to her carriage already. Show of tact, I thought.'

'Well, don't mention it to her. She'd have an apoplexy if she knew Selina had told anyone, even you.'

He frowned. 'Dammit, Jo, you've got to let the family know. We must rally round. I know you're only a cousin, but we can't have you dragging the family name down like that. I'll marry you myself if it comes to it.'

She searched his face for irony but he was being quite serious — and, she realized, noble and self-sacrificing in his own estimation.

'The only help I really want is the fare to America.' As she spoke she took stock of his quarters. Apart from his clothes, some of which she could see lying on the bedroom floor, he appeared to have brought nothing of his own from Lanfear. His model galleon, which should be on the mantelshelf, his prints of 'Great English Generals,' his cricket bat, his framed William and Mary shilling — all his former enthusiasms — none had followed him here.

'Well, it's no good coming to me,' he said. 'I don't know how I shall live as it is.'

'Yes. How *are* you managing?'

'Bread and cheese and precious few kisses.'

'Who's looking after you?'

'Situation vacant.' He raised his eyebrows hopefully.

'Unpaid, of course, but you're used to that.'

'Be serious, Terence.'

He tilted his head awkwardly. 'I'll get by for a while. Rogers suggests the Indian army. An officer can actually live off his pay out there.' He sighed. 'If I'd been more studious at engineering, like your darling Penrose, I could enlist with the sappers here.'

She shook her head crossly. 'Why talk such nonsense to me. We both know very well what you'll do. You'll marry page three or page four or page five of your Book of Heiresses. I hope you've given up all idea of Lady Nina?'

He grinned lazily. 'Not at all. I detected a keen interest there when she called yesterday.'

'Don't deceive yourself, my dear. It was no more than the curiosity of a bug hunter at finding an unusually repellent specimen.'

He was taken aback. 'What's happened to you, then? You were never like this.'

'How might you know?' she smiled, but there was little warmth in it for him. 'I wonder how *you'll* take to it, Terence? Having to become a meek little nonentity because you daren't be your true self. Perhaps playing the Great White God in India is all that's left.'

He stirred uncomfortably, never having seen this Johanna before and having no means of coping with her. She kept her cool gaze fastened upon him. 'I could set you free from it all, you know. But I wonder if I should.'

'You?' he sneered — and was then forced to moderate himself. 'How?' he asked; but there was the glimmering of a genuine interest.

'It'll be harder for you,' she mused.

'Hot air,' he snapped.

'Very well.' She squared herself to the decision. 'You might not even be able to grasp what I'm talking about, but at least I'll know I tried. I was driving out Godolphin way yesterday. There seems to be a lot laid off from the mines around Carleen.'

'Oh, thank you! That's all the reminder I needed!'

She ignored his interruption. 'People lying drunk in the lanes ... the *stench* of poverty. And thinking about it afterwards — last night — it occured to me that although

377

I've been reared poor — I mean, when I walked out of Lanfear I literally hadn't more than a few pounds to my name. I still haven't, come to that — I've never known a moment's poverty, not actual poverty. You know what I mean? We've been brought up — you and I and all "our sort" of people — we've been brought up, so to speak, on a raft afloat in a vast, shapeless sea of poverty. We don't look at that sea, we don't examine it, we're just desperate to keep clinging on to our raft. Oh, occasionally we approach the more deserving elements out there with soup and uplifting tracts, but we don't ... tsk! I had the word for it last night. Yes! We don't *confront* it. All we do is fear it. We say, "That must never happen to me." We don't confront it.'

Give him his due, Terence was trying. He asked, with no hint of the sarcasm she had expected from him: 'And that's what I must do, is it? Confront the spectre of poverty?'

'It isn't a spectre. That's the first thing to realize. It's the country where our common grandfather lived — and look what he made of it! Poverty is truly as varied and intricate as the life we think we enjoy on our raft. Society, I'm talking about. That's what our raft is. Society.' She relaxed and eyed him speculatively, preparing him for a change of tack. 'Actually — Nina will be horrified to hear it, but she was the one who first set me to thinking like this. When we returned from the Holy Land and learned what good work you had been doing among the more fervently righteous ladies of Helston ...'

'I?' he echoed with a mixture of truculence and bravado.

'You still have a lot to learn about the women, my dear. They couldn't wait to tell Lady Nina how the tumbrils were already rattling up Cross Street to Liston Court.'

'And they mentioned me?' He was aghast.

'Of course not.' She shook her head sadly. 'As I say — a *lot* to learn. Anyway, Lady Nina's immediate response, after they had gone, was to cock a snook at them all. "I am an earl's daughter," she said. "They are the spawn of tradesmen." Isn't she magnificent?'

He didn't think so. 'Just wait till her name stops appearing on people's guest lists!'

She stared at him in pity. 'How little you know her. She'll

manage it. She'll confound you all. But so shall I — in my own much smaller way.'

She spoke quietly but in her eyes he glimpsed a steeliness of purpose he had never supposed she could muster. 'You were saying?' he reminded her. 'The sea of poverty?'

'Oh yes. When you look into that sea . . .'

'Confront it?' he suggested with a cheeky smile.

She grinned. 'Just so. When you confront it, you soon realize it's not all one uniform gray.' She painted the air with a sweep of her hand. 'There are people "down" there making fortunes that would take your breath away.'

His eyes gleamed, as she had hoped they would, but she went on to disabuse him of that simple thought. 'I'm not just talking about money — though, of course, we know how important it is. There are ways of living "down" there, and friendships, and . . . it's so hard to describe to those who've never seen it. There are *rewards* "down" there that are richer and more' — she tapped her breastbone — 'than anything we ever dreamed about. But we can't see them — not even see them — until we leave Society, until we get out of its all-embracing shadow.'

'Get *out?*' he asked in bewilderment.

She lowered her hand to her midriff. 'This little fellow is going to get me out, whether I would go or not. So you can just brush all these fine words aside, if you wish. Tell yourself I can't afford to think anything else. But I hope you won't, Terence. I think you and I, together, could . . .' She smiled, leaving all possibilities open.

He gave her a dubious look. 'Are you proposing to me, Jo?'

'Not marriage. But I think we both have a pretty cool appreciation of each other. I probably know your faults better than any other person on earth, man or woman, and — dammit — I'm still quite fond of you. Now that must count for something.'

He smiled, but his eyes were narrowed in mistrust. 'What sort of proposal is it, then?'

'I'll tell you soon. I'm not absolutely sure myself.' She gave him a rueful smile. 'Everything starts out seeming so easy. You plan it in your mind and it's . . . pffft!' She swept aside a set of imaginary obstacles. 'The reason I was out

Godolphin way yesterday was to visit Sunny Corner.'

He tried to brazen it out but he could see she was not merely fishing. 'I can't imagine why,' he said at length.

'Nor can I, now. I wanted to help Nina. I thought I might collect enough about you.'

He rose with a cry and lifted both hands towards the ceiling, almost touching it. 'Little Jo!' He spoke as if inviting witnesses. He turned and stared at her. 'You! Who spent all your life rooting in the linen cupboard and writing lists of groceries and looking as if butter wouldn't melt in your mouth!' A further thought struck him. 'I hope Selina knows nothing of this?' He seemed to take in his own words then and his eyes flashed with anger.

'Of course she doesn't. But what an interesting response, my dear cousin. I notice you feel no equal solicitude on *my* behalf.'

'What could you have been thinking about? Not your reputation, that's certain. Nor ours. In most people's eyes you're still part of the Visick household, you know.'

'Terence,' she said wearily.

'Well . . .'

'You've said the right things, now just drop it. I *know*, you see.'

'Know what?'

'The hypocrisy of it all.'

He smiled, not quite meeting her gaze. His tone became soft, reproachful. 'What did you hope for, eh? What did you suppose you'd learn out there?'

'Something that would help me drive a wedge between you and the good burgesses of Helston.'

'And what *did* you find?'

'That you're no worse than nine men out of ten hereabouts.'

'Or the world over.'

'Aye.' She nodded. 'I'd be baling out Loe Pool with a cockleshell.'

He grinned. 'What did they say about me? Did you talk to Diana?'

So he didn't know Jenny had gone to America — or, rather, that she'd gone with Hal and Cunningham. Otherwise he'd surely tease her with it.

'Did you?' he repeated.

'I did.'

'She's very sweet on me. What did she say?'

'Oh, I think she'd tell you that for nothing, Terence. Especially for *nothing!* Just try going there without your half-crown.'

'Five shillings is more like it,' he said ruefully.

'Really? Hmmm.'

'My God!' the implications of her interest in the exact fee began to dawn on him.

'Don't be absurd,' she told him angrily. 'You men make me sick.'

'Well, what am I to think, Jo? You come in here, you talk in riddles, you confess to these ... these unspeakable ... things ...'

She laughed bleakly, ignoring him. 'Those bluestockings in London who're making such a fuss about wanting to be taught all the masculine subjects — mathematics, natural philosophy, engineering ... Even if they get their way, they won't know the half of it, will they!'

'Half of what? What are you talking about?'

'The world, Terence. The way the world actually works.'

'And you think you've learned that at Sunny Corner?'

'No. I need conversations like *this* to bring it home.' A new thought struck her, the implications of which made her forget her anger. 'In fact, Sunny Corner is the last place. In a curious way, the Jewells are as ignorant as any other women. They don't know the *other* half of it!' She smiled at him again. 'But why are we falling out? It's not as if you're to blame for it all — just as it's no fault of mine that I now have to start learning rather fast. Well' — the smile broadened — 'a very tiny fault, perhaps. But we shouldn't fall out, my dear. You're the one man in Cornwall to whom I may talk without hypocrisy. Don't you feel the same?'

He was willing to be won over, but not all at once. 'I hardly feel I know you at all,' he grumbled.

'Well, there's a goal to aim at. But if you try kicking for it while you're up there on your high horse, you'll only fall off and look ridiculous.'

He laughed, still reluctantly. 'I wish I knew what you expect of me.'

'I'll tell you soon enough – I've already promised.'

'Anyway, I thought you were hell-bent on getting to America.'

She sighed and half slumped in her chair. 'I brought this upon myself.' She looked down at her stomach. 'This little creature wasn't Hal's carelessness. I did what I did knowingly, deliberately.'

'Jo!'

'Yes, I willed it. I thought it would be something so awful, so unthinkable, so monstrous, that practically everyone I knew would press the money into my hands and pack me off to Hal as soon as they could.'

He pulled a sympathetic face but did not risk a comment on her folly.

'Well – ha ha! Nina offers a discreet *accouchement* in Italy followed by a tidy adoption. Can you imagine a child of Hal's and mine tending goats and plucking olives? And you offer a marriage of convenience to someone – even your gallant self in the last resort. So! Never mind. I have learned something of the world. If you put the fare into my hand at this moment, I'd take it and go. But in my heart of hearts I know that I must not carry this burden to Hal and encumber him with it over there. I will be a better wife to him – though unwed – by staying here and doing what I must to preserve us, our child and me. And he will be a better husband to me on his return, too.'

'He'll be furious. I know I should.'

'We'll weather that storm. I shall tell him as soon as it starts to show. If I don't, others will. So he'll know what he's coming back to.'

'He may not come back.'

'I'm learning to face that prospect, too, my dear.'

His gaze was almost admiring. 'I'd never have thought it of you.'

'And d'you think *I* would have?'

'But what'll you do, Jo? Fine words butter no parsnips.'

'I'll tell you next time. I promise. Meanwhile, may I ask you the most enormous favour? Would you ever go into Penzance . . .'

'You caught that from Lady Nina. She says "would you ever".'

382

'Would you go there with this letter to your father and give it a postmark he'll not associate with me?'

He took the envelope from her and looked at the writing. 'Who is it from?'

'Me. I disguised my hand.'

His suspicion deepened. 'What have you said to him?' he asked.

'Words that I hope will spare your poor sisters any further bruising.'

Chapter Thirty-Seven

The bursting of the railway bubble, the resulting commercial crisis, and especially the collapse of tin, had all played havoc with Nina's finances. She put a brave face on it, saying: 'I'm almost back to the state of poverty in which Brookesy left me.' She added that she would have to spend the afternoon over at Grylls's bank. 'So why don't you two darlings go over and torment dear little Hamill Oliver? Tell him about those Celtic treasures we found simply *littering* the Holy Land.'

Johanna, who now had her own reason for wanting to get Selina alone, accepted before her cousin could say she'd rather stay at home and write her 'novel,' which was today's word for the pile of used paper she was assembling. They left soon after luncheon, which was a decidedly hair-shirt collation. 'Our days in the Land of Cockaigne are numbered, I fear,' Selina commented as they set out.

'Mine certainly are. Why on earth did you blurt it out to Terence about me and the baby?'

Selina did not reply.

'Did you also tell your mother?'

Still no response.

'Selina, I have to know. Because if you did, all the servants will know by now — and then you might as well have put it in the *Cornishman* straight away.'

Selina sighed heavily.

'Why?' Johanna pressed.

The girl burst into tears and flung away the reins. 'I don't know! I don't know!'

Johanna caught up the reins and, almost in the same

movement, took out her own handkerchief, which she poked between her cousin's hands and face. Selina spoke between sobs: 'As soon as I said it, I knew . . . Oh, Jo, why did I do it? Now you'll never talk to me again.'

Johanna overcame her own anger sufficiently to lay her hand on the other's arm. 'It's too important for that, dear. That's just childish. "Never talk to you again!"'

The sobbing abated rather swiftly, even for Selina, whose moods were ever mercurial. 'I've ruined your life,' she said lugubriously.

'Don't be so dramatic. What you have done is left me with rather less time than I'd hoped for.'

'Time?' The eyes came out of their cradle of tear-moistened gloves.

'To do what I have to do. That's all. No one's ruined my life – not even me.'

Selina gave a fleeting smile. 'Oh, Jo – you have a *plan!* How like you. I wish I could be so competent. I'll never have a plan.'

'Did you tell my aunt?'

The face fell. The lips trembled once more. The head nodded a fear-filled confirmation.

'So be it.' Johanna sighed.

Selina's relief was just as swift. 'How did you know Terence knew?'

'Because I called on him this morning.'

'Was he up?'

Johanna laughed despite herself. 'Only you could ask such a question. Just about, is the answer.'

'And he told you I'd told him?'

'After he'd offered to marry me himself – if the worst came to the worst.'

Selina laughed, not believing a word of it. 'And what is this plan of yours? You know Nina will stand by you whatever may happen.'

'Yes, but I couldn't harm her like that. No, that's going to be the hardest part – persuading her to tell people she turned me out the moment she learned of it.'

'She'll never do that.'

They turned the corner by the church, where they had to wait for a farm cart that had already entered the narrow section of the lane, coming downhill toward them. 'Shh, there's the curate,' Johanna murmured.

'Good afternoon, young ladies,' the man called cheerily. 'You've picked a splendid day for a little jaunt. And how was the Holy Land? We must have a good chinwag about that. I'm longing to hear it all.'

'Yes, we must, Mr Pelham,' Selina told him. Then, because the cart was still blocking their way forward, she added, 'I hear you preached a rousing sermon last Sunday. We're only sorry we weren't back from our travels in time.'

'I fear it might have been over your heads,' he replied mournfully. 'The vicar has told me to be more simple.'

The way before them was now clear. 'We look forward to the fruit of that advice,' Johanna told him as they set off once more.

'Ninny!' Selina muttered. 'I'm sure I shouldn't have heard it anyway. All I can do when he preaches is watch his adam's apple going up and down. It's like a dumb-waiter delivering words. Over our heads, indeed!'

'You can just imagine what he's thinking about us. Two charming young maidens out for a "jaunt", looking for wildflowers to press − and no doubt to take inspiration from in our embroideries during the long dark evenings to come. Poor creatures!'

'Curates? Or us?'

'All men. And all of us, too, perhaps.'

'We might as well live on different continents,' Selina concluded with a sigh. Then remembering who were, at that moment, actually doing precisely that, she added, 'Sorry − not the most appropriate . . . whatsit? Metaphor is it? Or a simile? Figure of speech, anyway.' After a pause, she said, hesitantly, 'Talking of figures . . .'

'No don't!' Johanna said firmly. 'You've already done quite enough talking on that subject as it is.'

'I was only going to ask what your plan is. You still haven't told me.'

They reached the brow of the hill, where the view gave out across several miles of rolling countryside to Tregathennan and Trigonning. 'I never saw so many bare mine chimneys,' Selina added.

'Wheal Vor's going, and Greatwork, and Wheal Fortune,

and Wheal Pallas. And that's it. The destitution in the villages will be terrible soon.'

Selina shuddered. 'And you expect Nina to pretend she threw you out into that world! *Have* you a plan?'

Johanna sighed. 'It was to have been my last resort. But now . . .' She gave an unwilling heave to her shoulders.

'I'm sorry. I'm sorry. I'm sorry . . .' Selina repeated the words with needless vehemence.

'Never mind. I'm sure everything else was just a pipedream.'

'I thought your suggestion that we marry a pair of dying paupers was . . .'

'I'll tell you what I shall do — since it'll be common knowledge soon enough. Before Hal left . . .' She laughed at what she had been going to say. 'Yes, well, of course you know I went up to see him at the Ram! Anyway, the first time I called, he hadn't returned home. And I had a sort-of conversation with Charley Vose.'

'He makes my flesh crawl.' Selina made her flesh crawl to prove it.

'Yes, but you say that about most men. To get back to Vose, he made one of his usual jocular suggestions — that since I was no longer unpaid housekeeper at Lanfear, I might . . .'

'Oh did he! The impudence of the fellow!'

' . . . I might like to consider a paid position in that category at the Ram.'

'As if you would!' Selina sneered. She turned to share her scorn, only to find her cousin smiling broadly. 'Jo!' Disdain turned to horror. 'You *wouldn't!*'

'That's not even half of it. Oh, I know it would suit the world very nicely to see me vanish among the *hoi polloi*, as Nina calls them — the great unwashed. I'd be fodder for a couple of simplified sermons from that simpleton back there, and then my name would never be mentioned again except in whispers from mother to daughter when complaints about tight chaperoning grew too shrill.'

'And that's just what will happen,' Selina warned. 'I think, if you do that, Nina will just about have to disown you.'

'Good. Well that's one less hurdle.'

387

'But you *can't!*' Selina insisted. 'Think of us! In everyone's eyes you're almost a Visick, you know.'

Johanna smiled. 'Yes – including the Visicks themselves. Tell me then – what do you say I should do?'

'Well, I've put in a lot of thinking about that. And Nina. We're sure there's a retired clergyman somewhere, a widower who needs a housekeeper-companion. No one would think the worse of him for showing you a little charity. I mean, they've practically *got* to show it when they preach it so much. But you may be sure no one else will. I'm sure the Reverend Grylls could arrange it.'

'Which Reverend Grylls!'

'Any of them. You could get a place up in Yorkshire somewhere.'

'Or Mr Cunningham. He was the sort of man who could arrange anything.'

'Yes!' Selina spoke before she caught the sarcasm. 'Well, even his kind of anything would be better that what you're suggesting.'

'Ah, but you don't know what I'm suggesting. That's only the beginning.'

Selina covered her ears with her hands. 'I don't wish to hear it.'

'Can I have my handkerchief back, then?' Johanna asked quietly.

Selina gave it her. When Johanna began humming a formless little tune she went on, 'Oh, well, I suppose I'd better know the worst.'

'Good. Hal told me a couple of times – and Terence has often said the same – that Charley Vose is always scheming his little plots to make money by some shady, lazy means . . . and yet all the while he has a potential fortune within his grasp. But lazy's the word. He's too idle and contented with himself to get up and do it.'

'Do what?'

'His idea in taking me on a housekeeper is that I shall be able to give the Ram that little touch of *bon ton* which he never could.'

'Well, of course you would.'

'Make it truly the Golden Ram. I admit he's a little off the beaten track, but, on the other hand, there isn't a good inn anywhere between Penzance and Helston. The only tolerable one is in Marazion.'

'Oh, you've sampled them all, of course!'

'No, but on my way back from seeing Terence I stopped for a word with the coachmen outside the Angel, and if anyone should know, it's them. So, Charley's no fool.'

'Jo,' Selina interrupted, 'you're actually relishing this, aren't you.' It was an accusation, not a question. 'You're even looking forward to it.'

'It's a challenge,' she admitted. 'But then, as I said to Charley Vose himself . . .'

'You've accepted the offer, you mean?'

She smiled. 'He doesn't know it yet.'

'Thank God for that!'

'You won't talk me out of it.' She smiled, sweetly acid. 'For one thing, you've run me out of time for argument. But do let me get to the point! As I said to Vose when I promised to *consider* his offer — all right? — I told him I'd do no domestic labour myself, not of any kind. He's to employ servants for all that and I shall oversee them down to the smallest task.'

Selina gave a dramatic shiver. 'Poor things!'

'Not if they do their work well. In fact, they could grow quite rich — in tips. Anyway, I also told him that I'd take every afternoon free.'

'For the baby.'

Johanna closed her eyes. 'Don't! I haven't dared face that yet. No. The potential goldmine Vose is just sitting on — the thing Hal and Terence were saying — is his beer. Don't you agree it's some of the best you've ever tasted?'

'For those who like beer, I suppose.'

'Which, fortunately, is nine out of ten — quite enough to support a very lively trade.'

Selina laughed. 'And so you're going to take up brewing in the afternoons!'

'No. I already have the services of a very good brewer. Shall we get out and walk? I don't think this poor beast can manage this hill with us up.'

She dropped the sprag, tied the reins loosely, and went up to the creature's head. 'Come's on then boy!' She clucked him into renewed effort. The sprag, trailing on the road, made a drone to their conversation. Selina walked beside her, slashing at the hedgegrow with the long driving crop. 'I'm lost,' she said. 'Vose is brewing away like a demon and you've got every afternoon off. It doesn't make sense.'

'Why is most of the ale sold in the public houses around here so atrocious, eh? Because the landlords can't be bothered. How can Vose prosper at all, with an inn on the way from nowhere to nowhere? Because he *can* be bothered. Didn't you notice, when we were travelling in England, how many brewery drays there were? The inns up there have practically given up brewing their own. That'll start happening down here, too, once they improve the roads. In fact, it's already happening in the towns. Now I don't see why the name on those drays shouldn't be Vose. That's all.'

'Yes, but I still can't ...' Selina's voice tailed off. She stared at Johanna, not daring to give shape to the monstrous, impossible thought that was just beginning to form itself in her mind. 'Not ... you don't mean ... *you?*' She shook her head, forgetting to breathe. 'But you can't.'

'Just watch me – first thing tomorrow. Why waste another day? I think we could get back into the gig now.'

Selina, still in a daze, accepted a pull from her cousin.

'You should join me,' Johanna said. 'You'd gather a lot of scenes and characters for your novel – things that other writers wouldn't even know about. Not even men writers.'

Selina just stared at her. Johanna could not tell whether she were angry, shocked, dazed, or in a wide-eyed coma. Then, though trying hard not to, the girl smiled. 'You!' she accused.

'What?'

'You manipulator!'

'There is another name – a *synonym*, as you would say.'

'For manipulator? What? Lawyer? Serpent? What?'

'Saleswoman.'

Selina thought it over. 'I think you must be mad,' she said at length. 'Isn't this our turning to Oliver's cottage?'

'Time will tell. No, it's the next.'

'People could forgive you for being housekeeper to Charley Vose, but ...'

'You mean they could wash their hands, and souls, in the sight of my disgrace.'

'Exactly. Mixed metaphor, by the way. But one thing they'll never forget is for you to do something outrageous like that and make a howling success of it. Or a success of any kind. The Visicks will never forgive you at all, of course.'

'What, not even one of them?'

Selina laughed. 'I hope you don't even need to ask that.' She became serious again. 'Indeed, it's I who should ask forgiveness of you still. Don't tell Nina I blurted it all out, will you? I must warn Terence.'

'I've already done so. No, I'll say it was me.'

Selina clutched her arm and laid her head briefly against her shoulder. 'Oh, Jo, will it ever change? All our lives you've taken the brunt of my rashness. "How 'scaped I killing when I crossed you so," eh?'

Johanna gently shrugged her off. 'Don't exaggerate. I say, isn't that Hamill Oliver — out in the road?'

Selina looked at her in surprise. 'It's some young stonemason, surely.'

'I'll swear it's him.'

Moments later the man himself resolved their doubt when he raised his hat, a dirty old stovepipe that had seen a better century, and called out, 'Good afternoon, ladies!'

When they drew closer he said, 'There's more of an art to building the Cornish hedge than you might suppose.'

'Trying to see how little stone you can get away with?' Johanna asked, eyeing the huge earth-filled gaps between his courses.

'No. I shall have to tear it down and start again. Well, I'll do it tomorrow, now you're here. You'll stay to tea, I hope? We've just had some fresh clotted cream sent up from the Home Farm, and the strawberries this year are the size of beetroot.'

Selina clapped her hands. 'You knew we were coming, you darling man! You knew we'd make you almost our first port of call after our return from the Holy Land.'

His face fell. 'Alas, I cannot claim that degree of clairvoyance, Miss Visick. No — the strawberries were not picked in that certainty. But guess who *is* coming?'

On an inspiration Johanna replied, 'Your grandmother — Mrs Ramona Troy.'

He looked at her in astonishment and she felt sure he was about to say something about *cendl an wrea,* her supposed powers of witchcraft, so she added, 'Why else would you be out here masquerading as a labourer — if it wasn't particularly to annoy her?'

He tried not to laugh, which would have been like admitting the charge at once, but in the end he succumbed. 'Would you mind if we wait until she comes into view? She won't be long. And it's a pleasant enough day. Go and take a turn in the garden, if you wish.'

'No, we'll stay here and torment you,' Selina told him.

And for the next quarter of an hour they told him all the things they had made up and agreed between themselves about Celtic associations with the Holy Land. He grew more and more excited — so much so that they began to regret what they had started. At last he decided to abandon his plan to annoy his grandmother so that he could go indoors and write it all down. Selina assured him it was already written down and it was only her empty-headedness and stupidity that had caused her to forget it at Liston Court.

And then Mrs Ramona Troy herself hove into view, being driven in a gleaming open landau from Pallas House — driver, two footmen, and all. It made the quaintest contrast with her grandson, in his moleskin trousers and battered hat, up to his elbows in puddled soil, and his face all muddy where he had wiped off the sweat.

She took one look at him and said, 'You're making a pizzle of that wall, whoever you are. Clear all these stones out of the road at once.' Then, smiling sweetly at the two women, 'My dears — what a happy chance has brought you here! My grandson is no doubt waiting for me indoors. Do join us for a dish of tay. He has promised some strawberries of quite exceptional character.'

'Good afternoon, Grandmama,' Hamill said cheerily. 'I was showing Miss Visick and Miss Rosewarne how ...'

'Drive on, Harker,' she told her coachman, though the gate was but a ho! and a whoa! away.

By long practice the fellow made the awkward turn into the yard at Wheal Leander seem child's play. The moment she passed out of sight, ramrod-straight, looking neither right nor left, Hamill grinned at his other two visitors and said, 'Now we can go in.'

'Aren't you going to change?' Johanna asked.

'We'll eat in the garden,' he replied, as if it fully answered her question.

The tea — that is, the physical servings of buttered scones and strawberries and cream, and the brew to help it down — was superb. But the other tea — the social occasion — was a frosty affair indeed, with Hamill, looking as if he had been dragged through a hedge backwards, and several other directions, too, chatting away, as cheerful as a linnet, while his grandmother played the arctic queen, ignoring everything he said and behaving as if the real Hamill would join them at any moment.

At last she said, 'I'm so glad you decided to call today, young ladies. It's always a pleasure to see either of you — let alone both together. I should, however, welcome a private word with you, Miss Rosewarne — that is, if Miss Visick will not think that somewhat rude?'

'Not at all, Mrs Troy,' Selina assured her. 'I shall take a turn around the garden and collect flowers for pressing. We shall have such fun working them into our embroideries during the winter. Not the flowers themselves, of course, but their inspiration.'

Mrs Troy smiled indulgently. 'How delightful it is to observe that some of your generation, at least, know the difference between those occupations that are fit for gentlefolk and those that are not. My grandson will be down soon. I cannot think what's keeping him. He will tell you the names of any you cannot identify.'

'In Cornish, if you like,' Hamill added.

But his grandmother was already wafting Johanna toward the little gate that led to the croft.

The moment they were alone, Mrs Troy became a different person. 'I'm not sure about leaving those two alone for long,' she said. 'I've had second thoughts on that subject.'

Had the word of the deteriorating situation at Lanfear House reached Pallas, then, Johanna wondered? 'I'm afraid,' she replied, 'that I didn't develop much in the way of *first* thoughts, myself. And it wasn't for lack of trying, I assure you.'

'Well your instincts are sound.' She gave an angry sigh and looked around for something to blame for her displeasure – a tuft of gorse, a bird, a cloud ... anything. 'What am I to do with that fellow?' she asked. 'That lout. That clown. A spell in prison would jolt him out of it, I sometimes think.'

'Rather drastic?' Johanna offered timidly.

'Do you have any answer, my dear? You're such a level-headed gel.'

Johanna decided to take the bull by the horns. If Selina had told her mother about the baby, it would not take long to spread. She said, 'I'm glad I have the opportunity to tell you my news before it is a matter of common gossip, Mrs Troy.'

'Oh?' The woman smiled encouragingly.

To Johanna it seemed absurd that so august a person should show the slightest pleasure at being made party to her news ahead of the crowd – she being of no social importance at all. She began to suspect that behind her patrician ways, she felt rather lonelier and more isolated than she would ever admit. 'It's not good news, I fear,' she warned. 'At least most would not call it so. You see – I'm going to have a baby.'

'Ah!' Mrs Troy was clearly taken aback. But then, after the briefest pause for thought, she said, 'Well, these things happen. From the way you talk, I am to presume the father isn't ... that is, won't or can't ... '

'He would if he were here. He's in America, though.'

'Penrose!'

Johanna was surprised at the speed of this deduction. 'Have you heard our names linked?' she asked.

The other smiled ruefully, as if Johanna had caught her out. 'I've pursued a rather closer interest in you, my dear, than you might guess. I was very taken with your replies to my questions, last time we met. Well, well, well – this does change matters. I suppose you intend to wait for Penrose to return from America? You know that a subsequent marriage, even to one who acknowledges paternity, will not legitimize the child?'

'Forgive my asking this, Mrs Troy, but are you not shocked?'

She smiled. 'I shall be, of course, when I hear it in the usual way. Shocked to the marrow. But as for now . . .' She shrugged. 'I wonder if, being such a sensible and level-headed gel as I know you to be − I wonder whether you'd consider an alternative to whatever you're planning?'

'I'd welcome any suggestion − especially from you.'

'You face so many uncertainties, you see, if you are thinking of having the child. When is it to be, by the way? I see nothing of it yet.'

'November.'

'Hmmm. Time enough, then. Good. As I was saying − if you intend brazening it out down here, I'm afraid you can have no notion of the cruelties that will be heaped upon you. This is a canting, unforgiving age. You will be treated worse than a leper. Will you stay at Liston Court?'

'Certainly not. In fact, I shall leave tomorrow. I was just explaining to Selina on the way.'

'That is characteristically generous of you, dear, but even more foolhardy. Every door will be closed to you, you know.'

'Well, I was never destined to be anything but an unpaid housekeeper to my aunt and uncle. So a housekeeper I shall become once more − except that now I shall be paid.'

'You do surprise me.' Mrs Troy stared at her, suspecting a joke or some other meaning. 'Does your mistress-to-be know of your condition?'

Johanna smiled reassuringly. 'Have no fear, Mrs Troy. This establishment would never appear on your visiting list. It is a commercial place. An inn.'

The other woman was too surprised to comment.

'As it happens,' Johanna went on, 'my new employer does not know yet, but by the time he does, I trust I shall have proved too valuable for him to send me away.'

Mrs Troy shook her head in bewildered admiration. 'And on that slender trust . . . ? Well, perhaps it will make you even more suggestible to my proposal. The reason I brought you out here was to ask you if you would consider marrying that idiot grandson of mine?'

'Me?' Johanna gasped.

'Having thought about nothing else since you went away, I had come to the conclusion that it was the answer to the entire problem. He won't make much of a husband in bed, I fear. But now, in any case, that isn't likely to disturb you for a year or so. Plenty of time to cultivate the other side of it all – which, you may take it from me, is the only important side, anyway. Making the beast with two backs is a highly overrated game for a woman, let me assure you.'

She waited for some comment. When Johanna said nothing, she grunted, 'I see. Well, you're young yet. It will pall, believe me. But we were talking about uncertainties. It isn't only your social position, you realize. You appear to be discarding that quite recklessly. But there is also the uncertainty that Penrose will ever return from America. I suppose he's caught up in this gold fever in California?'

'I don't know. The latest letter was just after he landed in Boston.'

'Well, anything could happen to him. And even if he does come back ... people change. He hasn't the grandest reputation in the world for constancy.' She touched Johanna's arm to soften what she was saying. 'I only tell you the things you have to consider – and not for yourself alone, now. The child can never be legitimized, as I say – once born a bastard, a bastard it will remain as long as it lives. Bastard – try repeating the word to yourself as you fall asleep tonight! As I was saying – no, hear me out – Penrose might change. If he comes back with a fortune, that in itself might change him. He had the rearing of a gentleman; if he comes back with the wherewithal to support the claim, is he likely to want to marry an inn-housekeeper with a bastard in tow? Now you may be sure in your own mind that the answer to all these doubts is a certainty. Only you can weigh it. But let me tell you what's in the other pan.'

She had led the way across the croft to a small rise, the last foothill of Little Tregathennan. At the crest of it she halted and turned Johanna to face back the way they had come. And there, in the centre, stood Wheal Leander. A 'cottage' they affected to call it, but that was just their inverted snobbery. It was, in fact, a villa – a perfectly sited little jewel of a Cornish villa.

Indeed, it was so perfect that Johanna had a sudden intimation of what was coming next. 'If you'll marry young Hamill and manage him for me,' said Mrs Ramona Troy, 'that house is yours — outright. Moreover, I shall settle upon you two thousand pounds a year.'

Johanna gasped.

'Oh, you'll deserve it, have no fear. You will also get a husband who adores you to distraction — as I'm sure you already know. A man with an interesting and original mind that lacks nothing but the right sort of guidance — and I can think of no one better equipped to provide it than you. And finally, if, when Penrose returns, he proves still to be true to you, then you shall have my assistance — which is considerable — to meet him as often as you wish and for whatever purpose.'

After a long pause, Johanna drew breath to speak.

But Mrs Troy gripped her arm, almost painfully. 'Don't,' she said. 'Just think it over. Thank heavens you told me in such good time! There is no immediate urgency for your answer.'

Chapter Thirty-Eight

They sat in the shade of a chestnut tree that had been planted at Liston Court on the day of Brooksey's birth.

'What's keeping Selina, I wonder?' Johanna asked.

'I asked her to give us a few moments,' Nina replied, 'I want to talk about what Mrs Ramona Troy said to you yesterday.'

'But Selina knows all about it. We spoke of nothing else all . . .'

'It isn't that.'

'I know your opinion anyway, Nina. You think a marriage of convenience is always best.'

'Do I?'

'You've said so often enough.'

'Yes . . . well.' Smiling to herself Nina opened her pocket book and began rummaging inside. 'Circumstances alter cases,' she said vaguely. 'Ah, here it is.'

The search was a bluff, for the chamois-leather purse she now produced must have filled more than half the bag. Nonchalantly she tossed it into Johanna's lap, where it fell with a reassuring weight and jingle.

'What's this?' she asked, feeling it but not daring to look inside.

'A hundred guineas. Your fare to America — and across the continent, if need be. Money for your lying in . . . money to spend. Yours, anyway.'

Johanna pulled tight the drawstrings. 'I can't!'

'I thought you'd say that,' Nina told her lazily. 'Consider it a loan, if you wish. There's a clipper called *Moonraker* sailing from Falmouth for New York next Tuesday. It should arrive early in September. Six weeks will allow for an exchange of letters with Hal, wherever he might be, and that will give you time to go up the lakes to Chicago, which will be the best way to travel in your condition. Perhaps there's a railway all the way? No one here seems sure of it. Anyway, Hal can be there in time to meet you and give the child a name. You see — I have made fulsome inquiries.'

Johanna tipped the purse out into her lap. There were only twenty guineas in coin; the rest was Bank of England notes, which remained inside the purse. She stared at it and swallowed hard. 'Why?' she whispered, unwilling to trust her voice to anything longer.

Nina did not immediately reply. At length, and still somewhat reluctantly, she said, 'I could give you all sorts of practical reasons. On my way back from the bank I met master Terence, who told me you are considering some madcap . . .'

'But he knows nothing.'

'You must blurt out more than you suppose, darling. Why did you tell Mrs Troy, of all people? No, you needn't explain it to me, because I think I already know.'

'Do you?' Johanna started returning the money to its purse.

'You're burning your bridges, cutting off your own escape — in case you're tempted to go back on your decision. I don't know precisely what that decision may be, but you want to make it inevitable.'

'Hence this?' Johanna asked, replacing the last of the coins.

'It seems to involve your accepting a degrading position of some kind, or undertaking degrading labour.' She raised her hands to ward off explanations Johanna had not been going to offer. 'I don't wish to know. And I also don't wish you to do it.'

'Hence this,' Johanna repeated, no longer making it a question.

'No. As I say — I could give you all those practical reasons, and they wouldn't be a lie. But they'd only skirt the truth.'

'Ah.' Johanna waited to hear what that might be.

'Watching you and Hal,' Nina went on, 'and thinking of

what you've risked to have his child, and all the sensible advice you've turned aside — and now this magnificent offer from Mrs Troy, which takes my breath away, and which you also say you're going to reject . . . I've begun to realize I have no idea what love *is.*' She gave an awkward laugh. 'You remember once, it must have been the first week you came to Liston Court, you said on an impulse that you wished you could be a passionate sort of woman — like me? Remember that?'

Johanna smiled at the memory.

'Well, I think there's more true passion in the lobe of your ear than there is in the whole of me. Or ever will be. I'll give you another memory: the opera in Rome. You said wasn't it absurd for people to destroy themselves for the sake of such fervours and raptures, remember? Of course, it *is* absurd when it's simplified into the plot of a grand opera — and yet it is exactly what you're going to do with your own life now.' She looked at her and added, with a mournful kind of admiration, 'I envy you, Jo — the way you once, quite wrongly, envied me. I hope that someday, perhaps just for an hour, I hope I'll feel for someone that sort of all-consuming love you obviously feel for Hal. My loves are incandescent. They flare and are gone. But yours smoulders on. The other day I thought you'd finally begun to go cool about him. But no — it's burning away again, isn't it?'

Johanna nodded. 'It goes up and down.'

'But never out.' She smoothed her dress and looked toward the house. 'So accept that purse. Call it a gift, a loan, a bribe, a tribute of envy, an act of love — call it what you will. But take it and go to him.'

The following Monday, after an infinity of tearful-cheerful farewells and promises to write and assurances that she'd come back to Cornwall, with Hal, at the first opportunity, Johanna sat alone in her cabin aboard *Moonraker* and contemplated the adventure that now lay ahead. Tomorrow they'd slip anchor and head out into Falmouth Bay — and onward, past the darling landscapes she knew so well. They'd round the Lizard and sail into the great open hand of Mount's Bay, and she'd be able to make out Loe Bar, where she'd started her pebble and shell collection . . . and Porthleven, in whose sheltered cove she'd learned to swim — or discovered she already had the knack of it without knowing ... and Breage and Trigonning, from whose lofty vantage she'd taught her spirit to resist so many adversities ... and Lanfear House and all its continuing unhappiness. Then she'd run the gauntlet of all that coast, right down to Penzance — all those coves and villages where she had hoped to ...

Hoped to what?

She pictured herself as she had often done of late, in her daydreams, sitting in her gig and taking round her samples of Charley Vose's ales — to the Lion and Lamb at Ashton, to the Queen's Arms at Breage, the Coach and Horses, the Falmouth Packet ... and to the houses of the gentry, too — to Godolphin Hall, St Michael's Mount, Clowance and even, yes, why not? to Pallas House itself! Later, with the custom engaged, there would have been the deliveries, which the lad would make, of course ... the money pouring in ... a dozen drays with VOSE'S ALES on their sides.

It mocked her now, that once-bright vision. 'How did you suppose you might ever do such a thing?' It sneered. 'Did you think you'd have it in you? Why, miss, the only thing in you is Hal's baby.'

She took out Hal's dressing gown, the one he had left at the Golden Ram, and clasped it to her — something she had done so often by now that no trace of him lingered within its folds. 'What shall I do?' she asked aloud, as if it were him. Her only answer was the voice of that self-mocking imp: 'Go — run to him, as fast as sail and steam will carry you. Throw all your problems onto his broad shoulders.'

She went up on deck to escape its taunts. They were moored at the mouth of the inner harbour, off Trefusis Point, sheltered from the open sea by the arm of Castle Peninsula. On the opposite shore she could just make out the end of Flushing Quay, where the river ran westward, up to Penryn; and then, to the east, across Carrick Roads, lay the beautiful rolling landscape of the Roseland peninsula, running seaward to St Mawes, where stood the twin castle, guarding the harbour and denying the whole of West Cornwall to any invader.

What a beautiful country it was! And so much of it she had never seen ...

She thought it would be safe to torment herself with this kind of ready-made nostalgia, which is the tribute every emigrant pays the motherland as a kind of tax on leaving. But other memories soon intruded. This was the River Fal whose banks Hal had claimed he was following in Cunningham's survey – never for one moment imagining that mere women would be so practical as to check his lie against a map.

Oddly enough, that rankled with her now more than it had at the time. He might think her the most divine creature that ever left heaven, but it didn't change his opinion of her in more down-to-earth ways, where 'angel' was translated into 'mere woman.' Odd how two such contrary beliefs could cohabit in the same mind. One set of values for those special moments of loving and quite a different set for the day-to-day business of living. That was it: Living was a thing apart from loving for him. For all men, perhaps. Which meant there'd always be a part of his life she could never share.

For the first time she pictured herself as she might appear to him at the moment of their meeting – in Chicago, or wherever it might be. There she'd stand, eight months gone, looking like a balloon, unsure of her welcome ... the mere woman who had made a mess of it and bolted across half the world to burden him with the result. The bad penny in skirts.

He'd smile with delight, of course, and hug her as hard as he dared. And he'd marry her in all sincerity, meaning every vow. And he'd say how deliriously happy he was – and he'd mean that, too. But there would always be a part of her that would despise her own weakness – the fact that she could think of nothing better than to go running to him.

Would it not find its echo in Hal?

Her flesh crawled at a sudden new thought. It would be even worse if he *didn't* despise her – if he assumed that such weakness was natural in a woman. Then he'd consider it part of a man's honour to accept her feebleness. That would be the worst of all, for it would put a gulf between them that nothing could ever bridge.

The dream of the might-have-been returned once more – not in mockery but with a more subtle form of goad. Would she now live out the rest of her life with one small regret gnawing away at her? With one half of her saying, 'You might have done it,' and the other half sneering at her pretensions, and the third half (as Nina would say) telling her she'd never know.

'Did you survive all those years of pain and humiliation at Lanfear House,' it asked, 'only to collapse at the first challenge out there in the big wide world?'

She did not underestimate the size of that challenge, but once she had put it to herself in those terms, she could not turn her back on it, either.

Captain Spring, the ship's master, was very understanding; he was even good enough to return one fifth of her fare, with a promise of the rest if he sold her cabin at Queenstown. She gave him her direction at the Ram in Goldsithney. It was seven o'clock that evening before she found herself once again at Liston Court. The scrunch of iron tyres on the gravel brought Nina to the drawing room window at once. She came running to the front door and answered it in person. 'My darling! Is something wrong? What's the matter? You're not . . . ?' She let her eyes stray to Johanna's stomach, completing the question.

'No. I just couldn't go. When it came to it, I just couldn't.'

Nina closed her eyes. Her whole body seemed to fold in upon itself. 'You'd better come in, anyway,' she said tonelessly. 'Oh, Jo, what are we going to do with you.'

'Say good riddance, I should think.'

'Well – I thought we had!' Nina laughed with little humour.

'I'll be gone tomorrow.'

'Have you eaten? You must be famished.'

'I'm past hunger, I think.'

'Well, eat something anyway.' She did not even need to nod at the footman, who went off at once to arrange a meal. She took Johanna into the dining room and almost pushed her into her seat.

Selina came from the library across the corridor. 'Good heavens!' she said.

Her cousin gave her a weak smile. 'Did you tell Nina about my plan?' she asked.

'Yes!' Nina gave an indulgent laugh, to show that she

could see a joke as well as the next.

'That's what I'm going to do,' Johanna told her, handing back the purse in the same moment. 'I owe you sixteen pounds, which I shall repay as soon as . . .'

'You will not!' Nina told her vehemently.

'It may take a few months, but . . .'

'I mean you will not engage in this travelling tapster business. I never heard anything so preposterous in all my life.'

The footman came in with a plate of cold roast pigeon and salad. Nina signified that he could leave them alone. As Johanna ate, dutifully rather than hungrily, she tried to think of some way of making Nina understand — but as she had passed the entire return journey in the same pre-occupation, she felt little hope of success.

Nina gave an encouraging smile as she reached across and touched her. 'Never mind. There'll be another ship next week. There's still time.'

'You needn't talk to me like an invalid, you know,' Johanna told her. 'It wasn't easy — changing my mind and coming back here.'

Nina bridled. 'I'm sure you've no call to take that tone with me, either.'

'Let me try to explain. I'm sorry. I'm all on edge.'

Nina, not truly mollified, waited impatiently for whatever she might have to say — and ready, Johanna realized, to pounce on it and shred it at once.

'Can you put yourself in Hal's shoes?' she asked. 'Imagine him having heard these tales we've been hearing about gold finds in California. Only he'd have confirmation of it. So there he is, somewhere in the middle of the continent, just ready to set out and make his fortune — our fortune — when he gets a letter from me saying . . .'

'But he won't just be getting ready to set out,' Nina interrupted. 'He's missed this season. The *Cornishman* is already advertising sailings to Mexico and overland as the swiftest way to California. So he'll be working somewhere on this side of the continent, and saving up for next spring.'

'Oh . . . never mind all that.' Johanna felt her will caving away inside her. 'Wherever he is, whatever he's doing, I just pictured myself turning up like that, looking like a whale . . .

I mean, I might as well write across my forehead, *Now you've got to marry me!* What a way to start a life together!'

'Well, you won't be the first girl to say that. Anyway, what's the alternative?'

'For him to come back in his own time, and still with the choice – so that if he says, "Will you marry me?" it'll be because he wants it. Not because I've practically put a gun to his head, which would be the case now if I followed your plan.'

It was obvious that Nina could not grasp the point she was making. 'And I thought you loved him!' she said.

Johanna pushed away her plate and buried her face in her hands, more in weariness than sorrow. 'I don't know any more,' she said. 'If I truly loved him, how could I deceive him so?'

'*Deceive* him?' The word astonished Nina.

'I'm going to have to write letters pretending all's well – telling him everything, all the news, except the single most important event in my life. Isn't that deceit? Yet I'm doing it out of love. Because I cannot burden him.'

'Burden him – I like that! He's the one who's burdened you, my girl. Oh Jo, you are so confused!' She smiled encouragingly, as parents do to children who have hurt themselves slightly. 'You can't make proper decisions in this frame of mind. Why don't you have a good long sleep – round the clock, if you wish, eh? Then, when you're quite refreshed, we'll talk about it as long as you like. And we'll arrive at the best possible decision.' She smiled with joking accusation as she added, 'Again.'

Feeling more cowardly than tired, Johanna followed her advice. She had just undressed and slipped between her beautifully cool sheets when Selina came like a ghost to her bedside. 'Remember,' she said, 'if you do decide to go to the Golden Ram, remember you promised to take me out on your rides. My Adventure is going swimmingly but I need good lower-class characters and colour and all that.'

A thought struck Johanna. 'Forgive me, darling, but in all this confusion I forgot to ask. How are things at Lanfear? Didn't your father insist on your returning there?'

'Oh . . . no. I went to plead with him but I didn't need to.

He's quite different — much more like he used to be when you were there.'

Just before dawn, came another tapping at her door. Nina had lain awake for hours recalling that glint of stubbornness she had seen in Johanna's eye, even at the height of her misery and confusion. The girl was not going to America, and that was that. Nina knew she herself would have to capitulate; she had lain in bed, her mind churning over the possibilities and dreading the moment of confession. Now she tiptoed up the corridor, word-perfect in her mind: 'You may have your baby, Jo. And you may stay here at Liston Court — and damn Society! I would rather have your solo friendship than that of the local Upper Thousand. Jo, my darling Jo — please just stay here with me!'

There was no reply to her knock.

She pushed open the door and crossed swiftly to the bed. No adorable young head with its dark, glossy hair dented the pillow; a single sheet of notepaper was pinned in its place. 'Dearest Nina,' it read, in letters broken by grief. 'Forgive me. I do what I must but I shall always love you and be in your debt. Your tormenting, tormented, Johanna.'

Nina dropped the letter and stood there, for a moment on the verge of tears. But she mastered it, squared herself as if to some unpleasant task, picked up the letter again, and tore it to confetti.

At that particular moment Johanna, on foot and with daylight advancing behind her, was drawing near to Goldsithney — actually, at the head of the lane to Sunny Corner. On an impulse she turned aside. When she reached the cottage a few minutes later, the light was strong enough to enable her to make out the notice nailed to the gatepost. It read: INTERESTED PARTIES TO THE GOLDEN RAM. In the narrow space above this bold declaration a more hesitant hand had squeezed the words: COTTIJ FER SALE WITH HALF AN ACER.

Fait accompli! Johanna thought.

And her every bridge was now well and truly burned.

Chapter Thirty-Nine

From Hal Penrose to Johanna Rosewarne:
Dudley, Iowa
Friday, 28th July, 1848

My dearest darling Johanna,
Thank you a million times, from the bottom of my heart,
and more than I can ever express, for your beautiful
letter, telling me of all your doings in the Holy Land,
Italy, France – and your return. Yes, yes indeed, we
must, we shall one day, visit all those places together. The
very moment I have fulfilled this trivial task of making
our fortune, it shall be done!

I have read every word you wrote, twice a day, and
every day since it arrived, and have slept upon it so
heavily it is flatter than ship's biscuit. You need not fear
that the mails go astray here. Considering the size of the
country and the temporary nature of so many
settlements, the system is amazingly competent. I met
John Thomas from Pengiggan last week, passing
through, and he told me he wrote home to Cornwall on
the 1st March from Independence, Missouri, and had his
reply on 5th May in Iowa City – a degree of despatch that
is quite commonly achieved if the trade winds are fair. So,
take heart my precious, we are not as far apart in time and
space as we once feared.

Well, from my last you will have expected to see
'Galena' at the head of this; yet here we are in 'Dudley,'
two weeks short of Kanesville on the Missouri, which is
the present vanguard of civilization. Don't go searching

for Dudley in your atlas, though. I'm sure Nina has the very best but you still will not find it, for it is no more than a gleam in the eye of its founder, an extraordinary man called Jeremiah Church, who describes himself as a 'Peripatetic Builder.' However, if you can discover the confluence of two rivers, the Des Moines and the North, then that is where the gleaming eye has alighted, and we (Cunningham, Frank Ashburn, and I) are, for this winter at least, his temporarily non-peripatetic builders. He has already erected an hotel, though nothing that name may arouse in your mind will in any degree match the reality, for it is but a many-roomed log cabin. We are to build a log-cabin saloon, a log-cabin store and post office, and as many one-room log cabins as we can − all for our keep and a handsome 'bonus' in the spring. Then, in April, hardened by our labours and well set-up in pocket, we shall sally forth to Kanesville, and thence, by way of the Mormon Trail, to Sutters Creek, California − which name, I make no doubt, will sufficiently explain our change of plan. This entire territory − nay, continent − is in the grip of gold fever; and we, by leaving as early as possible in April, are 'fixing' (as they say) to be ahead of the main rush. I am sending you separately from this a new-printed *Latter Day Saints' Emigrants Guide*, by a man who went with Brigham Young last year. From it you will share every twist and turn of our way, for I never read a more thorough work. If you will picture me this coming winter, then see me committing every dot and comma to memory.

Frank Ashburn is an astonishing man, too. The extraordinary thing is, he was born in Liverpool and yet has become so thoroughly American in the space of one lifetime. You should understand that there are not many Americans out here in the west. They are all settled, as is only natural, I suppose, in the established states. Here the accents are almost all English, Scots, Welsh, Irish, French, and some other European tongues. Yet I make no doubt but that in time − in one lifetime − Frank and his kind will grind them all to his extraordinary diction and way of thought, just as 'twas with him.

And it *is* a different way of thought from ours. When

you have seen the American frontiersman, and woman, too, assert their equality, and equal merit in the eyes of the Lord, with any crowned head in the Old World, you can understand why our aristocracy fought so hard to quell them. However, I am not blind to their faults, either. Our aristocracy, having lost that war, can content itself with the knowledge that the free American is now too busy establishing his equality *over* the aboriginal Indian and the nigger slave to disturb Europe and her old ways for yet a while.

I did not mean to say any of this. Take it as a sample of our serious talk while we hew our logs and shape them into cabin walls. A regular hedgerow school we make of it! Cunningham is the greatest surprise of all. Under the influence of heavy manual toil, and lacking the support of a Society that will always turn the blind eye if the proper pedigree be there, he is becoming a useful and, at times, even shrewd 'hoss,' as Frank himself admits. And in Frank's vocabulary there's nothing higher, unless it's an 'all-kill-fired smart hoss.'

What I meant to say was that, whether or not we make our lucky strike, and whether or not I bring back to Cornwall no more than an adequate competence, this first-hand knowledge of what it is to be a free man and the equal of any other on Earth, will still stand to me as the greatest profit on my days invested over here. Perhaps these are hardly the sentiments to send to you, living as you do with dear *Lady* Nina, surrounded by servants who *are* servants, and not needing to lift a finger to get you through the day; but then, I reflect, that quality of humble pride is innate in you; none of the indignities heaped upon you by your kinsfolk has dimmed it in the least degree. I accept all you say about Nina, by the way. I am almost convinced it was an accident or misunderstanding, and yet if you could have spoken to Jenny, as I did, you would be less sure. However, let us leave all sleeping dogs (like all ambassadors abroad) to lie.

I mentioned the women. The easiest brief chronicle of them is to say they are bal maidens in new clothing, rough in their ways, yet not coarse, as ready to be heard in our village councils as any man, and as willing to shoot in defence of what is theirs, too. They do not, however, grow on trees out here. Cunningham, who feels the loss of their company more keenly than I, has counted twenty males to every one female. Were I still the slave of my former wantonness, I should no doubt be able to tell it you to a dozen places of decimals; but thanks to you, I am now indifferent to all that. On the subject of clothing, there are but two colours, for men and women alike — oatmeal homespun and pale blue Kentucky jean. Excepting Jeremiah Church, who wears black worsted and an old stovepipe hat and is very singular to remark as he goes about *his* town.

Well, it is all most novel and interesting, and there are enough excitements to sweeten the bitterness of this long separation from you. Yet I never forget you, my darling, not for a moment. Even when you are out of my conscious memory and thoughts (can there be *un*conscious thoughts? — a topic for our hedgerow school, I believe) but even then, my awareness of you persists. You are the most compelling force in *my* world, New or Old. Everything I do, all I strive for, what little I achieve, takes its value from you, from the mere fact that you are there and that I am bound to you by ties that men have struggled, and failed, to understand since the dawn of time. I cannot ponder this mystery without trembling at its power.

Now that we have this temporary base, I shall strive to correspond with greater frequency than was possible along the way. I write to you every hour, of course, in my mind. So, in the loving hope that I am never long absent from yours, either, commend me to my friends and know me to . be yours alone and always, Hal.

Johanna did not receive the letter until the first week in August; by then her life had changed out of all recognition. (Her figure, however, had not yet begun to swell — at least, not to an extent that might cause comment. Also, much to her relief, word of her condition had not spread from Lanfear House, either.) She hardly needed that telltale crossing out to know that Jenny was still of the party. Diana had already taunted her with a letter from her sister, also written from Dudley, Iowa. It had, however, failed to upset Johanna because, although the girl still claimed to be baiting her traps for Hal, it was fairly plain, reading between the lines, that she was falling rather heavily for this Frank Ashburn fellow instead.

Besides, Johanna was finding enough to worry her in her daily life at the Ram, without needing to invent phantasms to haunt her from six thousand miles away. Charley Vose was well nigh impossible to understand. Though scrupulously clean and orderly out in the brewery (which was why his ale excelled), he was as slovenly as they come in the rest of his establishment, and his lax ways had infected his servants, new and old. They had learned that a superficial appearance of order and cleanliness was all he required of them.

For Johanna, by contrast, nothing less than the reality itself would do. She began with a thorough spring cleaning of the inn, from the attics to the cellars. For the first day or two all had gone well. The servants had expected something of the sort and had worked with a will, thinking that once they had shown willing and done their token stint of hard labour, they could all smile, clap each other on the shoulder, and drift back to the old routines; when it became clear that these extraordinary efforts were no more and no less than the everyday standards henceforth, the rebellion began — or rebellions, rather, for they were incapable of doing anything in concert for long.

Charley, preoccupied with his new line of trade in Paradise Row, wanted no part of their squabbles. 'Tis your affair now, maid,' he would say. 'You must put all to rights your own way.'

'It's all very well for you to say that, Vose,' she replied. 'I just wish you'd tell *them* when they come whining to you. Instead you go all sympathetic and promise you'll have a word with me and they come back smirking all over their faces because they think they've won you over. For heaven's sake show them a bit of spine.'

After several skirmishes of that kind it dawned on her that her only hope of succeeding was to make Charley more afraid of her than he was of upsetting his servants, especially those who had idled away so amiably at his side down the

411

years. Her one ally was Rose Davey, Charley's fancy woman and cook, who had been trying to bring about some order ever since she had started to work there more than a year ago. 'But I did give up,' she told Johanna. 'They do know, see. They do know 'ow 'tis with me. That Charley, all he needs do is touch me and I'm all giddy. And he won't stand out agin they. All he do want is a quiet life — and bugger off up Widow Jewell's.'

'I don't understand him at all. What did he want me here for if he's not going to ... ?'

'So he could forget the inn and put the blame on you.'

'You know Willy Rodda? He told me Vose was in the Star in Marazion last week, boasting to John Durro about getting me to work here. Why does he do that and yet refuse to support me? Trying to make him stand up for himself is like trying to make a feather bolster stand on its end,' Johanna said bitterly. 'The slightest push from them and he falls over. How can we stiffen his resolve?'

'There's not much about Charley Vose as I can seem to stiffen these days, somehow,' she replied.

They both stared up the garden. 'There lies the trouble,' Johanna said.

''Es, that's where 'e's to. You been down there, ave 'ee, Miss Rosewarne?'

'Never!'

'Nor yet me.'

But the answer lay there, too. A month or so after Johanna had begun her uphill task at the Ram, The Penzance Philosophical Association arranged to hold a dinner there. They spent the afternoon visiting the old smuggler haunts of Jack Carter, the 'King of Prussia,' and took tea at Pengersick Castle, beside Praa Sands; but as soon as their dinner was served, and the ale began to flow, it became clear that their main goal in devising this outing lay up there in Paradise Row. Charley's notion that the attractions of each enterprise would enhance the profits of the other was starting to bear fruit.

The meal, however, was poor — and the philosophers were the very opposite of philosophical about it. Their president, Mr Jethro Humphries, sent for the housekeeper to be brought before him.

Johanna half-delighted, half-fearful, answered the summons. He told her of the cold soup, the fitful service, the greasy plates, the blackened silver, and the cheerful, casual familiarity of the serving maids — 'Which is what we expect to find at the *other* end of your garden,' he concluded with a smirk.

Johanna froze him out; she wanted it as widely known as possible that what went on up there was no concern of hers.

His eyes fell and the stoop of his shoulders came as close to an apology as he could make without sacrifice of dignity. She relaxed and told him she hoped it wouldn't happen again. 'But it's not an easy thing to promise, sir, when the proprietor himself considers it of only the airiest significance. A threat in his ear, now, would strengthen my hand. Especially coming from such an eminent personage as yourself.'

When the Association had finally been led up the garden path, Charley erupted in fury. He came storming into the pantry, where Johanna was putting a flea in the ears of the two most sluttish of the maids, Verity Jones and Abigail Thomas. 'How am I to satisfy them buggers up there if you set out to poison 'em down 'ere?' he shouted.

Johanna wafted his words on toward the two girls, as if she thought Charley were talking to them; she nodded in grimly satisfied agreement and said, 'There now.'

''Tis you I'm talking to, maid,' he spluttered.

'No you are not, Vose,' she flared back at him. 'You are talking to these two wretches — and the rest of them. And what you're saying — at last — is what I've been trying to drive into your thick skull for the last . . .'

He made a hissing noise like a steam boiler about to break its bands. ''Ow dare you?' he almost screamed.

Johanna turned to the two girls. 'Be off,' she said sharply. They needed no second bidding. As Johanna shut the pantry door behind them he resumed his attack. 'Don't 'ee never dare talk to me like that again,' he warned.

'I most certainly shall,' she told him. 'Every single time you come down here and start bawling at me in front of my staff.'

'Oh *staff* is it now? My my!'

'No it isn't — thanks to you. It's a rabble. An ill-disciplined motley of lazy good-for-nothings whose only qualification for working here is that they know how to put up with you.'

'Well! 'E's some different tune o' you now you think you'm safe and snug in 'ere.' He eyed her speculatively; she knew he was turning over the idea of dismissing her.

'I think no such thing. Indeed, quite the contrary. You have proved the greatest disappointment to me, Vose. You are not one half the man I took you for.'

'Oh, I s'pose you think you can fare better!'

'Indeed, I do. John Durro at the Star in Marazion has already asked after me, if you want to know. Now *there's* a place that might truly become a . . .'

He laughed, but the wind had vanished from his sails. 'You never would,' he asserted.

'And why not?'

'Well . . . because. That's why. There's one thing we got that they haven't.'

'A nine-day's wonder – yes! How many gentlemen are going to return here, d'you think, for the novelty of being served by maids with dirty fingernails, on plates garnished with last week's grease?'

'Fuss fuss fuss,' he said crossly.

'All I'm saying, Vose, is that you need me more than you need your servants.'

'That's all you are – bloody servant.'

'Very well.' She lifted her shawl and resettled it. 'I'll go and pack.' At the door, to give him his chance, she turned and said, 'You won't last a month.'

He let her get all the way to her room before he followed her. She made him knock twice before she bade him enter. 'I don't rightly know what you expect,' he mumbled.

'Are you asking me to stay?'

'I thought you was going to take afternoons off.'

'Don't change the subject. Are you? Asking me to stay?'

He shrugged.

'Because in that case,' she went on relentlessly, 'I'll tell you what I expect. I expect you to go downstairs, this minute, and muster your rag, tag and bobtail, and inform them that from this moment forth I, not you, enjoy the last word on their continuation in employment here. If I decide they go, they go — and any appeal to you will fall on deaf ears.'

He shook his head and sucked at a tooth that was no longer there. 'Don't hardly seem fitty like,' he said.

She just stood her ground and stared at him.

'Rag, tag *and* bobtail, eh?' he echoed.

She could tell from his smirk that some indelicate observation was about to emerge. 'You may keep that sort of humour for the other end of the garden,' she told him frostily. 'I've made it quite clear that I neither know nor wish to know anything about it.'

''Es, there's another thing now — that there Mr Humphries, he said as you was proper scratchy about it.'

'That's entirely in your hands, Vose. If you wish to avoid that sort of unpleasantness with those of our guests who come for something more than the food and ale, then it's up to you to inform them I have no part in what goes on up there, and I want none of their winks or digs in the ribs or their feeble, tasteless witticisms.'

'All right, all right,' he responded grumpily.

'I am no part of those arrangements.'

'Yes!'

'And whether or not you tell them, I most certainly shall.'

'I said yes. What more do 'ee want, maid?'

'All right, Vose, I just wanted to be quite sure we understood...'

'And you should call I Mister Vose. Not just Vose. 'Tisn't fitty.'

She dipped her head to flag a concession she felt she could easily allow. 'I agree — on condition you'll call me ...' She thought quickly. *Miss* Rosewarne was going to ring a little strangely in a month or two. 'Mistress Rosewarne.'

His eyes went wide in surprise.

'Not just plain "mistress," now. "Mistress Rosewarne" — always the two together.'

That had been the first important test of her authority at the Ram. Charley was furious all over again when he learned that John Durro had not been making overtures to her, but she passed if off as hearsay from a third party for which she was not responsible. 'Probably he overheard *you* boasting to the man about securing my services,' she suggested — knowing he could not deny having done such a thing.

A few days later he remembered the question with which he had tried to divert her anger — the business of her afternoons off. Until then she had worked almost round the clock, bringing everything at the Ram into line with her idea of a well-managed hostelry. 'Perhaps it's about time,' she conceded. 'I shall take this afternoon off, then — with your kind permission Mr Vose?'

He almost told her they'd all subscribed a round robin begging her to do it, but thought better of it even as the taunt rose to his lips.

Her outing, however, was not to be.

She had changed into her afternoon dress when Rose came running upstairs to say that a young lady was desirous of seeing her.

'Does she look like an applicant for the Other Business?' Johanna asked. There had been a regular rain of them, what with trade continuing so bad everywhere.

'Not this one,' Rose replied.

'Did she give a name?'

'Sara Vavasor or some such.'

Johanna shrugged. 'It means nothing to me. But, if she looks as respectable as you imply, you'd better show her up.'

'Selina!' she cried the moment 'Sara Vavasor' was announced.

'Sssh! Don't let anyone know I came here.' She crossed the room and gave her cousin a rather desperate hug.

'Darling — what is the matter?' Johanna asked, holding her at arm's length and searching her face for an answer.

'Everything! It's all so beastly . . .'

'At Lanfear?'

She nodded. 'There, too. Poor Mama is worried about the mine shutting down for good. Did you know it had closed?'

'I heard, yes. I'm so sorry. But I'm sure it's not permanent. This slackness cannot last forever. Things will pick up again soon, I'm sure.'

'Well, you know Mama. The only bright side to it is that

Papa is much gentler with them at home now. It must have been the worry.'

'I'm glad about that. Tell me, is he often in Penzance?'

'I don't know.'

'And how are things at Liston Court? All well, I trust?'

Selina shook her head. 'Nina has become impossible, all because of your leaving.'

'But I left her a note.'

'She tore it to shreds.'

After a moment's stunned silence, Johanna said, 'I don't believe it.'

Selina nodded. 'She's grieved more at your going than ever she did for Brookesy, or so Margaret Tyzack says.'

'Oh ...' Johanna bit her lip. 'I don't want anything of that sort. I know, I'll write to her now. Can you wait? Will you carry it back?'

Selina shook her head sadly.

'Why not?'

'She's got over her grief, all right, but it's dissolved into a most terrible bitterness.' She eyed Johanna nervously. 'How are you? Is ... ?' She half-pointed at her cousin's waist and then touched her own.

'Fine! Kicking lustily now. No one here knows yet, by the way. And your mother, for once, seems to have minded her tongue. Why? Did Nina ask you to find out?'

'No! I was just wondering whether or not to tell you – except that I have to tell you anyway. Promise you'll never let Nina know I was here?'

'Of course – but why?'

'Promise.'

'But I did. Very well – I promise. Now what is it?'

Selina swallowed hard. 'She says you took some money with you.'

'My fare to America! The bit that wasn't refunded immediately. But she knows about that. I told her.'

'I know, dear. And so have I. So now she's got the servants counting everything – all the silver, all her jewelry, and even things you'd have needed a horse and cart ... I mean, I'm only surprised she hasn't checked to see whether or not you stole Brookesy's menhir!'

'Stole?' Johanna echoed the word in alarm. 'But I stole nothing.'

'Of course, darling. We all realize that. It's just Nina. Talk about hell having no fury like a woman scorned! That's what it is, you realize.'

'Scorn her! But I did it all for her sake.'

Selina shook her head. 'You don't understand. She *loves* you. Or did.'

'Me too! I still do. I did this for love of her.'

Selina shrugged and gave up.

Johanna, to change the subject, said, 'When you walked through that door just now, I thought you wanted to accompany me. I thought you must be a mind-reader, because today is, in fact ... '

'Oh that! No, that's out of the question now. Jo − if she finds something missing, she'll go straight to the police.'

'Well, they can search this place all they ...' Her voice tailed away. The very last thing they could do was search the Ram − at least, with her as the cause of it. 'Oh God!' She closed her eyes and sank upon the end of her bed. 'I shall just have to go to her.'

'She won't let you in.'

'At least I'll have tried.'

Selina started up guiltily. 'I must go back. I told her I was going to Lanfear, of course − which I did. But I must get back there. I wouldn't put it past her to come out and check on me.'

'Well! She must have changed, that's all I can say.'

At the door Selina paused and turned. 'Jo?'

'Mmmm?' Johanna was preparing to write a letter to leave at Liston Court in case Nina refused to allow her in.

'About Nina ...'

'Yes?'

'Did she use to ... with you, I mean ... did she use to ... sort of creep into your bedroom in the small hours?'

'Yes. Well, early morning, anyway.'

'And get into your bed?'

'Yes. Once or twice, anyway.'

'Oh.'

418

'She's very lonely, darling. And haven't you noticed how she hates being on her own? Why, d'you mind it?'

Selina shrugged again. 'It's a bit strange to me, that's all.'

Chapter Forty

The letter to Nina cost Johanna all her remaining free time that afternoon, and even then it finished in the waste-paper basket. She tried again after midnight, when her evening's work in the Ram was done. The air of respectful dread toward her, now exhibited by all the servants, was just the tonic she needed and she fell asleep in moderate satisfaction with what she had written. But, on reading it over in the chill light of dawn, she was assailed by fresh doubts. However, there was no time to make yet another fist at it; and in any case it was now more important to see Nina and talk to her than to write her a hundred letters, no matter how brilliant. So, shortly after lunch, she took Charley's gig – the use of which was one of her perquisites – and set off for Helston.

Being so unsure of her reception, she thought it wisest to leave her pony and equipage at Miss Grylls's – who might also have news of Nina's latest intentions. She found her friend in a state of some excitement. 'You'll never guess!' she kept saying as she ushered Johanna indoors. 'Come and see. I hope we can make it out from the attic.'

When they arrived at the very top floor she stood on an empty fruit box and peered out through one of the roof lights. 'Dear me,' she sighed. 'They've taken it in. Oh, botheration! But I don't see why. It's surely not going to rain? I'm sure you'd have recognized it.'

'Recognized what? Do tell me, dear Miss Grylls. You'll have to now.'

The woman led her back downstairs. 'I've heard all about it, of course. This contretemps between you and ... yes – it's so absurd, but ...'

'Goodness! Is it all over the town then?'

'Oh no — fortunately. No. Selina Visick was here earlier. She came to return a little cerulean blue she'd borrowed from me — at least, that was her excuse. Truly, though, I believe it was simply to unburden herself. Poor child!'

'She came out to see me yesterday.'

'I know. She told me. But just as she was going she let slip that Dr Moore — from Plymouth, you know? She said he'd suddenly turned up on their doorstep and that Lady Nina had at once spirited him away to her boudoir.'

'When was this?' Johanna asked at once. 'D'you mean he's there now?'

'Oh — I wonder? Perhaps *that's* why his trap has gone. Still, he can only be up at the Angel. Surely he wouldn't try returning to Plymouth immediately?'

Johanna thought quickly. Would it not be better to confront Nina while some third party was there. It would force her to curb her wilder flights of fancy ... and there could hardly be a better third party than Tony Moore. 'You wouldn't recognize him, of course,' she mused aloud.

'No, dear. I was away, you remember?'

'Only too well!'

'Oh yes — that's how it all began!'

'I wonder if I might ... do you have such a thing as a pair of opera glasses?'

A maid duly fetched them and Johanna went to the window, where she trained them on Nina's boudoir; she did not need to return to the attic, which had been necessary only to see over the wall into the stable yard. There was no mistaking the figure of Dr Moore, who was striding around the room, now approaching the window, now receding into the shaded interior, talking and gesticulating in a most lively way — quite unlike the shy, taciturn fellow she had known.

She laid the glasses on the mantelpiece and said. 'He's there, all right. Miss Grylls, will you think me most dreadfully rude if I ...'

'Fly, my dear!' her friend laughed. 'Such excitements! Only do let me know everything that passes as soon as you can. Oh, I'm not sure my brain can stand it!'

It cost every ounce of Johanna's will not to dash across the road to Liston Court — which would have drawn all eyes to her and set the tongues of the town wagging for a week. She walked sedately, as if out for a stroll and wondering whether or not to revisit this or that old friend, for all the world as free of care as the early bird itself.

She chose the gate that was least visible from Nina's room and kept in the shade of the chestnut tree until she arrived at the laurels that bordered the portico on each side; they gave her cover all the way to the front door.

She did not bother to ring but pushed it open and went straight in. Margaret Tyzack, half-dozing in the porter's cubicle, ready to answer double knocks, started up in alarm. 'Here!' she exclaimed. 'My orders are not to let 'ee in. Miss Rosewarne. Not on any account.'

'It's all right,' Johanna called back over her shoulder. 'Shout after me if you wish. I'll make it plain I forced my way.'

Margaret's idea of a shout was too feeble to carry up to the boudoir, or at least to penetrate what was probably a most animated conversation. Once again, Johanna pushed open the door without knocking.

There was no conversation of any kind in progress. Tony Moore, in contrast to his earlier animation, was now standing at the window, hands behind his back, head sunk in the very picture of angry gloom. Nina sat at her dressing table attempting to conceal the evidence of what had plainly been a copious flow of tears. Johanna, with a dozen opening remarks on the tip of her tongue, forgot them all at the sight of this tableau. The other two turned and stared at her like one returned from the dead.

But she had eyes only for Nina. She had never seen her friend looking so ill and haggard. She ran at once to her side and fell to her knees, throwing her arms around her and hugging her for dear life. For a moment Nina was too astonished to react in any way. Then she gave out a cry, an animal howl of 'No-o-o!' and her fingernails sank themselves into Johanna's flesh, in her neck, her ears, her cheek ... And all the while she cried, 'Hoor! Thief! Slut! Traitress!'

Johanna offered no resistance. It was Tony who leaped forward and tore her away. 'Oh, my God!' he cried, pulling out a clean kerchief and staunching the blood where it

flowed most freely. 'What has she done?' Over his shoulder
he shouted, 'Look what you've done!'

Johanna did not take her eyes off Nina; by now they, too,
were full of tears. Nina could not withstand that mute
accusation for long. She rose and flung herself from the room.
Johanna collapsed to her knees upon the carpet, forcing Tony
to follow, going down on one knee beside her and still holding
the handkerchief to her wounds. She paid him no attention.
'What have I done?' she asked the air rather than him.

'Nothing that may be laid at your door,' he assured her.
'It is my opinion that woman is certifiable. And I mean
professional opinion.'

She turned to him then appeared to see him for the first
time. 'You should go,' she murmured gently.

'What can you mean?' he asked in astonishment.

'I mean . . .' She relapsed into silence.

'We should get some iodine upon these wounds,' he said.
'Could you bear it?'

'Hamill Oliver was right,' she answered – or said as if in
answer.

'Whoever he may be.' He lifted the cloth experimentally
and watched the rate of flow. 'That's better.'

'There are forces that we simply cannot . . .' She rose and
went to the window.

He followed anxiously, kerchief at the ready.

Her eyes rested on Brookesy's menhir. 'I wonder?' she
mused.

'What *has* been going on?' he asked.

She turned to him again and said flatly, 'I'm going to have
a baby.'

His eyes narrowed and she suddenly realized how often a
doctor must face such a blurted-out confession, either from
the *enceinte* herself or from her agonized parents. She
smiled coldly. 'By "going to" I mean "intend to",' she
added.

He blushed, not having realized what his face had
revealed.

'I'm surprised Lady Nina hasn't already told you,' she
went on.

'So am I. She's accused you of almost every other sin in
the calendar.'

'This was no sin, Dr Moore. It is my careful and deliberate choice.'

'Tony,' he said.

'I knew what the consequences would be — for me, I mean. And I realized I could not force Lady Nina to share them.'

'Did you give her the choice?' he asked, not with any hint of accusation. But nor did he speak idly, like one who wishes to keep the appearances of a conversation alive and who will therefore ask whatever comes into his head. He truly wanted to know. It was an important moment in that it went some way toward re-establishing their former friendship. At least it made her realize he was something more than a mere passive bystander in the present situation, which was all she had assumed or conceded until then.

'D'you think I should have?' she asked. 'Yes. Perhaps you're right.'

He nodded. 'I fear it's too late now. Much too late.' He sighed. 'I have my bag downstairs. D'you think you could . . . ?' He raised his eyebrows. 'It'll sting,' he warned.

'Sharper than a serpent's tooth,' she said tonelessly. 'I was like a child to her, you know.'

'Something rather more than that, I believe,' he said as he guided her to the door, where he peeped out almost as if he expected Nina to be waiting with a gun.

But she was nowhere to be seen — nor even heard. Margaret Tyzack, standing bewildered at the half-landing, told them that her mistress had gone rushing out of doors without even putting on her hat.

He pinched the lint as tight as he could, so as to leave the narrowest stain upon her skin, and dabbed at her cuts; it certainly did sting, but she held back her cries, taking a savage relish in it as a kind of punishment for what she had done, or as he had pointed out, what she had *not* done.

'Brave little soldier,' he murmured, parodying the sort of thing one says to children.

He really was a nice man, she realized, touched by his gentleness. She raised her hand to his cheek and smiled — for the first time with some warmth. 'Get up and go now,' she advised. 'Leave us. You should not become involved in all this.'

'And what *is* all this?' he asked.

'How can I say? I don't even understand it myself. How, therefore, could you?'

'Ah!' he said, with a smile that suggested her question had an obvious answer and that, one day, he might let her in on the secret. As he put away the iodine he asked casually, 'Has anyone examined you? D'you mind my asking?'

'No one.'

'Well – making certain obvious assumptions – you ought now to be . . .' He hesitated and then went over to shut the door. On his way back he said quietly, 'One never knows.'

'I don't think I care who knows now.'

He let it pass. 'I was about to say – you should now be . . . what? Almost six months into your term. I have to say you don't give any appearance of it.'

'Yes, appearances matter, don't they!' she smiled tolerantly. 'On the other hand – d'you know anything else that feels like a live fish in here?' She patted her stomach. 'D'you mind if we go out onto the lawn? This house oppresses me now.'

'Of course.' He opened the french windows and let her pass ahead of him. She felt his scrutiny upon her as she passed.

'I must allow you have all the other signs,' he said, following her out. 'Your skin always was fine, of course. Oh well, let's take it you're one of those who don't actually get very large. It does happen. What shall you do?'

She stopped and looked at him. 'I don't wish to seem rude, Dr . . . Tony.' She gave a small cry of frustration. 'How can I call you Tony in one breath and tell you to mind your own business in the next!'

He smiled encouragingly and waited.

She turned and saw Selina at the french window. 'Here,' she called, holding out an arm in welcome.

Selina took a pace backward.

'Come on!' Johanna held out both arms, feeling it was absurd to have to encourage her like this, as if she were a shy child.

Reluctantly she obeyed. 'Hello, Tony,' she said as she joined them.

'Selina.' He nodded.

Then she noticed the scratches on Johanna's face and neck. 'What happened?' she asked, already shaking her head at the anticipated answer.

'I tried,' Johanna told her.

'Oh lord! Where is she now?'

'Who knows?'

Selina, unable to look at the wounds any longer, turned to Tony Moore. 'What a happy time you have chosen!'

'Indeed.'

'I've told him,' Johanna said. 'Everything.'

Her cousin, wide-eyed at the news, stared at him.

'And I,' he said, 'am waiting to know what she intends doing next.'

The wide eyes traversed toward Johanna. 'Next? Have you left the Golden Ram?'

'No. He doesn't know yet. I was about to tell him.' Her hands offered the office to Selina instead.

Johanna expected the recital to be in tones that said, 'Isn't she stupid? What a goose! Can you believe it?' Instead, she found herself listening to a justification that she could not have bettered herself – indeed, she doubted she could have managed anything so lucid and fluent. It had a practised ring to it, as well, and Johanna was suddenly struck with the thought that Selina had spoken these very words to Nina, last night, perhaps, during some argument over her 'desertion.'

When her cousin had finished, and before Tony could respond, she said, 'You mustn't take my side, you know. The last thing I ever wanted was to stir up bitterness in this house, where I never knew a single unhappy moment. Even if she says things you can't agree with, you should just stay silent.'

Selina shook her head. 'You don't understand. The night you "took leg bail," as she puts it, she came to your room all ready to tell you you could stay on any terms.'

'Terms!' Johanna repeated angrily. 'I sought no terms.'

'I know. I'm just trying to explain to you what happened. She was going to tell you you could stay here and have your baby and . . . just let the rest of Society go hang.'

Johanna appealed silently to Tony. 'She told me that,

too,' he said. 'Also about putting you on the ship to America and your getting off again . . .'

'Did she tell you why? No — she doesn't understand it herself. Nobody does.'

'I hope I do,' he said calmly.

They both looked at him in surprise; then at each other. 'You?' Selina asked.

He nodded. 'This . . .' He sought for a word and then, smiling at Johanna, said, ' . . . little fish is a kind of tyrant. I have seen men in a boxing ring standing up to a battering that ought to have laid them out cold at the start. Yet they go on and on, taking it all, and — sometimes — they even come through it and win. But I tell you, that is nothing — a few moments of bravado — nothing — compared with what I have seen women endure and survive, for the sake of that new little life within.'

'It's not that,' Johanna said. The last thing she desired was to be turned into some kind of martyred heroine.

But he held up a finger, begging a few moments more. 'Not directly, perhaps. The question it raises is, does that doggedness, that durability . . . is it always there, waiting for times like that to call it up? Or is woman a frail, vulnerable thing, prey to every passing vapour, and only whipped to those superhuman endeavours at certain special times? That would undoubtedly be the popular view.'

'But not yours?' Selina asked.

'My admittedly limited experience, in my practice, leads me inescapably to the opposite view.' He turned to Johanna. 'I believe you had no choice but to do precisely what you have done — though you did not realize it until you found yourself alone and about to sail for America.'

'And you don't condemn me?' she asked.

He shrugged. 'As the farmer condemns the otter for undermining the river banks. Your action is undermining Society . . .'

'This aloofness,' Selina interrupted, 'this Olympian detachment from the ordinary woes and cares of women, does it lie there within all doctors waiting certain special circumstances to call it up? Or are doctors really warm, sympathetic people who are whipped to a godlike severance from the rest of mortals by the mere sight of a woman in need?'

'Selina!' Johanna laughed. 'That's clever but very unkind.'

Tony took it on the chin, though. 'No, no – she's right. A degree of aloofness is a necessary protection; but it should not become an ingrained habit.'

His submission to Selina was more apparent than felt, though. Their eyes locked for a moment, gleaming with the relish of combat, and Johanna – like Nina before her – could not help thinking what a splendid couple they would have made. He turned to her at length and said, 'However, both from a detached and from a sympathetic point of view, I am bound to say that I think your plans are brave to the point of foolhardiness. Your path would be stony enough even if you wore sackcloth and ashes and made yourself a satisfying moral example of penitential meekness to others. But . . .'

He seemed to realize that the argument was already falling on deaf ears.

'I'm sorry,' Johanna told him, thinking it a most inadequate response.

'Just remember this,' he concluded. 'Those friends I mentioned to you once, Charles and Eleanor Dugdale, they are *good* people. And while they would condemn what you have done, they would not condemn *you*. The very fact that I can speak for them like this . . .'

At that moment there was a commotion at the gate. Nina, still hatless, came striding in, looking like some latter-day portrait of Diana the Huntress, with a large, sweating constable in tow. 'There she is,' she said, changing direction to join them on the lawn. 'Just about to run away again, no doubt. Search her. I demand that you search her.'

'Lady Nina . . .' Tony began.

'You hold your tongue, sir,' she snapped. 'You were not invited to be part of this. There she is – Johanna Rosewarne.'

'I know the young lady very well,' the constable said.

The moment he eased off his helmet Johanna recognized him. 'Joseph Clements,' she said. 'How's your father now?'

'A little better in this weather, thank you, Miss Rosewarne.'

'Never mind all that,' Nina shouted. 'Do your duty, man. She has stolen . . . things.'

The constable raised an eyebrow and looked at Johanna.

'If she says so, it must be true,' Johanna replied.

He looked at them all in turn. Tony, out of Nina's line of vision, shook his head.

'You heard her,' Nina said. 'She admitted it.'

He patted his pockets, one after another, slowly. 'I done a stupid thing, my lady,' he said at length. 'I left my handcuffs up the station, I shall have to go and get they now.'

'But you may take her without all that. You do it every day — I've seen you.'

'Ah.' He shook his head sagaciously. 'Misdemeanours, yes. Drunk and disorderly. Brawling. Yes. But theft's a felony, see? And if we're going to apply the full rigour of the law, we must do 'n fitty-like. Proper job.' He turned on his heels and left them. 'I shall be 'bout a half hour,' he said heavily as he reached the gate.

Nina stared at the others, saw no support among them (but failed to notice their concern for her), and ran after the man. She pleaded with him, but he was not to be deflected. She wandered back in a daze. With only half the ground covered, her emotions overwhelmed her and she turned to Brookesy's menhir — almost fell upon it, indeed — and clung to it as a drowning woman to a rock. They saw that she was racked by sobbing, but not a sound came out of her.

Johanna went hesitantly to her side, touched her on the shoulder. 'Darling,' she murmured. 'I'm sorry. Tell me what to do. I'll do anything — anything you want. Just tell me.'

Not raising her head, Nina turned and fell against her exactly as she had against the stone — swinging from one support to another. She allowed herself to be folded into Johanna's embrace, caressed, comforted. Her hair irritated one of Johanna's wounds, making her inch away from the contact. Nina lifted her head just enough to see the cause of this apparent withdrawal; her eyes, swimming in tears, alighted on the scratches, which were made to seem twice as fierce as they were by the iodine. 'Oh!' she cried, and then broke down into open, uncontrollable sobbing.

Johanna queried Tony with her eyes. He gave her an encouraging nod. Nina tried to kiss the wounds. Johanna winced and let her. 'Do you want me back?' she asked.

But the question had the very opposite effect of anything she might have intended. Nina froze, and then pulled herself away. 'No!' Her voice was strangely unlike anything Johanna had heard from her before.

Nina took a pace backward, bringing herself hard against the menhir once more, but now facing Johanna. 'You're starting it all over again!' she accused. 'You'll worm your way back into my house . . . into my affections . . . and then you'll take control of me again.' Her hands gripped the stone and then patted it, almost as if she wondered what on earth it might be, lurking behind her there. She turned and inspected it, then back to stare at Jo, with the light of discovery dawning in her eye. 'It's this, isn't it! Hamill Oliver was right — and we just laughed at him. You are a witch!' She turned to Tony and shouted, 'She is a witch! Don't you see what she's done to you? Look at you, man!' When he did not respond she turned to Selina and repeated the accusation for the third time.

Tony went to her. 'Come,' he said gently, 'let me take you indoors and give you something.'

'No!' She backed away from him and looked wildly around the garden. Her eye fell on one of the temporary gardeners. Harry Dyer, an out of work miner. 'You!' she called out. 'Come over here!'

He began to amble. 'Run!' she shouted. He ran. 'You're a miner, aren't you?' she asked. 'You know all about breaking up granite? Blasting powder . . . all that?'

'Yes, m'lady.' He shifted uncomfortably and glanced at the others.

'Go and get some then, and others to help you — whatever you need — go and get them. And you are to see to it that this . . . this . . . monstrosity is broken into tiny pieces. I don't care how you do it. That is your business.'

'Nina!' Johanna said gently.

But Nina spun on her heel and, with movements more like those of a mechanical doll than a human being, stumped away indoors.

Harry Dyer turned to the others. 'What am I to do? We can't go blastin' away in the middle of Helston.'

'Just find some way of breaking it up,' Tony told him.

The man left them, still scratching his head.

Johanna went right up to the stone and touched it. There was no electric spark, no thrill, no surge of power. It was just a lump of granite. 'What a shame,' she said. 'After all that. Hamill Oliver will be heartbroken.'

Tony turned to Selina. 'I keep hearing that name. Who is he? The Pied Piper of Helston?'

She laughed. 'A painful case,' she replied. 'A sad case, anyway. He's a bit touched when it comes to Celtic mysteries — anything Celtic.'

'Ah. An eccentric old gentleman. I see.'

'Not at all! He's no older than you — if that.' She gave him a conspiratorial smile. 'And what's more, he's head over heels in love with Johanna — even though he admitted she's a witch.'

'He did no such thing,' Johanna said wearily. 'This isn't getting the work of the world done.' She stared briefly at the house and said, 'I tried.'

'Are you leaving?' Tony asked.

She nodded. 'I left my trap at Miss Grylls's.' She turned to Selina. 'Shall I see you soon? Will you let me know about . . .' She inclined her head toward the house. 'If you can talk her round to some sort of reconciliation.'

Selina rolled her eyes heavenward. 'I'll do what I can. I'll call on you anyway. Are you going to start . . . you know?'

'Two o'clock each day.' She turned to Tony and held out her hand. 'Thank you for trying, too,' she said.

However, when she took her leave of Miss Grylls, some fifteen minutes later, he was waiting for her at the gate. 'May I hitch my nag to the tailboard?' he asked. 'There is still much to talk about, I fear.'

Chapter Forty-One

Johanna demurred at first but when Tony added that he intended calling at Lanfear anyway — indeed, that was the original purpose of his visit to Cornwall — curiosity won and she allowed him to make at least the first part of the journey with her.

'It's a strange thing,' he said as they went down into St John's, 'but, even though I've told you how foolhardy I think your decision is, I feel more unease at leaving poor Selina alone in that house than in seeing you return to Goldsithney.'

'Is that why you're going to Lanfear?'

'Indirectly,' he replied. His tone revealed it as less than a half-truth. 'Do you often hear from America?'

After a silence she said, 'I've had a number of letters. One of them warned me of what you and Nina might try to make of . . . certain events in Plymouth.'

'Quite right,' he told her.

'Oh? Here's a new tune!'

'I wrote under the stress of . . . I wrote too hastily, I admit it now. There are entirely honourable and fortuitous explanations of what I saw. I should not have . . .'

'Oh, Tony!' she shouted.

'What?' He stared at her in surprise.

'You're so *fair* and . . . impossible!'

'I'm sorry.'

'I know you are.' After a pause she added, 'And it's your own fault. Talk about something else.'

He remained silent.

'Tell me what you and Nina were discussing with such

high fever.' She smiled at him. 'One can see into her boudoir from Miss Grylls's drawing room, you know.'

'Ah.'

'Well?' she had to prompt. 'Here — you drive. I can see you're itching to.' She passed him the reins.

They were at the junction of the main road at the foot of Sithney Common Hill. He had to wait to let a cartload of dressed granite go by.

'Rough ashlars,' he commented. 'A fine new face for someone.'

'I think they're refacing Bolitho's Bank. It's a fine time to be doing it, I must say.' She watched him, sidelong, so that he would not be immediately aware of her scrutiny. He was much less jumpy now he had something to occupy his hands. She began to recollect her original feelings toward him — an affection that fell a long way short of love, but an affection nonetheless. At least it had once been strong enough to induce her to accept his offer of a place with the Dugdales.

What a chancy thing love is, she reflected. *Why this man and not that?*

'Well?' she prompted yet again as they started up the hill.

He spoke reluctantly. 'It is not normally a topic on which I . . . not with a lady.'

Johanna let the gathering silence press him for her.

'Lady Nina mentioned . . . well, I'm not reverting back to the subject of Plymouth, you understand, but she mentioned Miss Jenny Jewell. When I refused to give her the fare to America, and she came back the following day and told me she had it anyway . . .' Johanna heard him swallow audibly, even above the grinding of the tyres on the gravel; his hands were unsteady.

She rescued him. 'Lady Nina explained to you how she probably earned it.'

'Yes.' After silence he added, 'But that was not all.'

'Do you want me to go on guessing? I'm sure I could.'

He sighed. 'I would rather not talk about it at all — except that you have to know the sort of thing Lady Nina is . . . oh dear, I do wish she had not shown you all of my letter. Now you will imagine I have ulterior motives in everything I say and do.'

433

'Dispose of them first, then,' she advised.

He gave her a wry smile. 'So practical always! I'm not mocking. I mean it. In everything you do you are to me a paragon. My feelings toward you have not wavered, not once, never for a moment. But I have changed around them. When I left here last year, I was in hell. I could not eat. I could hardly sleep. I had no means of coping with those feelings, you see.'

Johanna just sat there, wondering how to stop him. She had not expected — and assuredly had not wished for — anything so revelatory as this.

He sensed it and said, 'Soon be done,' as if he were still dabbing her with iodine. 'Now I *can* cope. I have learned to accept it and live with it — or live around it. Just as I teach my patients to live with far more disabling conditions. I have simply learned that I cannot help having these feelings toward you — just as you cannot help not reciprocating them. And there it is. Ordinary life must go on. And, hey presto, it does . . . somehow!'

She reached out and gave his arm a reassuring squeeze.

'Even if my heart occasionally stops!' he said urgently, as if it were a warning to her. And then he laughed again.

'And what does this have to do with what Lady Nina told you?' she asked.

'I was hoping you'd forgotten that.' He clicked the pony to greater effort and then said, 'I think I must get down and ride my own nag to the top.'

It seemed to be understood between them that the topic could not be aired until he was at her side once more. At the brow of the hill, she asked him if he wished to go to Lanfear first.

'How do you feel about it?' he asked as he retied his horse to the tailboard.

'I ought to pay them a visit, it's true. And it's something I'd rather not do alone. Would you mind?'

'Lanfear it is, then,' he said as he climbed back beside her.

She waited to see if he would take the reins from her, as if it were now his right; but he did not. Strangely pleased, she handed them to him.

He needed no third prompting but took up the postponed conversation at once; she guessed he had been working out

434

what to say as they toiled up the hill. 'Lady Nina told me of Miss Jewell's family background. Sunny Corner, is it called?'

'Yes. I'm afraid we shan't pass it on this road.'

He did not respond.

'I mean . . .' she stammered. 'I didn't mean to imply . . . oh, never mind.'

He laughed. Then she joined in. After that it became easier. 'Well,' he said, 'at least we know we're talking about the same thing.'

'Which is the topic you would not normally discuss with . . . et cetera.'

'Quite.'

'And Lady Nina suggested that I am now somehow involved in what goes on at Sunny Corner — or rather, what used to go on there?'

'Oh.' His tone was troubled.

'So she told you that the Jewells have moved their trade to the Golden Ram?'

'Is it true?' He sat stiff as a carving, waiting for her denial.

'I don't know by what means she's learned that. I'm sure Selina had no inkling of it — though she did visit . . .'

'Johanna!' he cried.

'Well, it's true to the extent that Charley Vose, the landlord of the Ram, is also the owner of a couple of cottages, and they, too, are in Goldsithney — in fact, they're situated just over a furlong from the back door of the inn. And he has let them, or come to some arrangement — I don't know anything about it, nor do I want to. Anyway, Widow Jewell has moved her trade to those cottages.'

He remained silent.

'And now,' she told him, 'you may get back on your snow-white charger and ride off into the sunset. Except,' she put in as an afterthought, 'your home is in the opposite direction.'

When he still said nothing, she added, to herself, 'Still, you could always sneak back by way of Hayle. The gesture is the only thing that matters these days, after all.'

Reluctantly he said, 'One cannot touch pitch and not be defiled.'

'True,' she said lightly. 'Which of us does not? Every day. All of us.'

'But this!'

'When I used to go into Penzance and see those girls standing down on the quays . . .'

'You mean — you knew?'

'Tony! Everyone knows. I should think even Deirdre and Ethna know that. They may be a little vague as to the exact . . . well, never mind. When I used to see them there, I did what everyone else does. I simply walked past as if they didn't exist. And that's exactly what I do now in Goldsithney. I'm sure you do the same, especially living in Plymouth!'

'Yes, but Lady Nina says they dine first at the Ram and then . . .'

'Not the girls. The first girl who dares cross my threshold gets thrown out with a pail of water for company.'

'But the men.'

'Oh yes — and they also arrive by hackney coach, some of them. Must I never travel by hackney now because Widow Jewell's customers also use them? Where does one draw the line, Tony?'

He cleared his throat. 'Well, it's not for me to say.'

They drove on in silence, but hardly easeful.

'I say, is that Trigonning Hill?' he asked.

'Yes.'

The silence returned.

'You must have some opinion on the subject,' he said at length.

'Indeed, I do. I would wish to live in a world where such places and people were not necessary.'

'You suppose they *are* necessary?'

'They would hardly flourish else.' Her tone softened, as if pardoning him. 'Perhaps you should come and meet the good Widow, early one afternoon, when she can spare the time to enlighten you.'

'I can't imagine what she might say that would induce me to . . .'

'Tell me, Tony, do you believe it's only a particular *sort* of girl who takes to that trade? D'you think they're *born* brutish and corrupt? D'you suppose that Nature somehow obliges the male half of mankind with a steady stream of predestined . . . ' She sought a polite word for it. Her eyes lit up and she said, 'Hoors! So that's what Nina meant!' She turned to him. 'And that's what all this is about, isn't it?'

He stared morosely at the road ahead.

'Or do you think it might happen to any woman — given the right degree of ill-fortune and the world's usual indifference to it?'

After a pause he said, 'I don't like the implications of this conversation.'

Their eyes met. She smiled. 'Beginning to wonder whether the Johanna you love so much has any existence outside your own imagination?' she asked.

He weighed her up before he replied. 'Perhaps you jumped ship for something of the same reason?'

She was immediately seized with rage. How dare he offer such a thought? She snatched the reins from him and clucked the pony into a trot. For a long time she waited for him to apologize; but he said nothing. By this silence she realized he had meant it not as a provocation — something her taunt had stung him into saying — but as a possibility she should consider quite seriously. She was not willing to do that, however.

Then it struck her that *her* silence might mislead him into believing she was thinking it over, so she swallowed her anger and prepared to exchange smalltalk with him. They were going through Breage at the time; she remarked that the place seemed dead. He agreed. She told him the tin trade was very depressed. He said, 'Ah.'

Some twenty desultory minutes later they arrived at Lanfear House. From the road all seemed well; the garden was a little neglected, perhaps, but nothing out of the way.

'That curtain in my aunt's bedroom,' Johanna said. 'Is it torn?'

'The middle window? Yes.'

She sighed.

No one answered their knock. After allowing a decent pause, Johanna opened the door and pushed in — and it was a push, too, against a box full of old newspapers that had been deliberately placed against it.

'The spring's gone,' he said, twisting the useless handle round and round.

There was a vague noise from the direction of the kitchen and a moment later a slatternly young girl came out into the passage and stared at them.

'Who are you?' Johanna asked.

'Betty, m'm,' she replied, making an attempt at a curtsy.

'Betty what?'

'Ferns, m'm.'

'And where is your mistress?'

'In the garden, m'm.'

'And Miss Deirdre and Miss Ethna?'

The girl just nodded.

They walked toward her – or, rather, towards the kitchen door, which led into the garden. She backed away as if she feared they might strike her.

'Easy!' Tony told her. 'We mean no harm.'

'Are you the only servant here?' Johanna asked.

'Not for long,' was the immediate reply.

'Well, I've never seen a place so altered,' Johanna murmured.

'Nor I,' Tony agreed.

'Selina said things weren't good but she didn't even hint at this.'

Out in the garden her aunt and cousins were nowhere to be seen. The grass on the side lawn had not been cut for weeks. 'Aunt Theresa?' Johanna called once more.

'Who is it? Johanna?' The cry came from the kitchen garden and a moment later, Aunt Theresa herself stood at its gateway. Her face fell a mile when she saw Tony Moore there, too. As they approached she made a futile attempt to block their view – but there it was, plain as daylight: the two young girls were lifting potatoes and their mother – it could have been none other – was carting off the tops in a wheel-barrow, which now accused her from just within the gate.

'Good groundsmen are impossible to come by down here, Dr Moore,' she said grandly. 'We are between gardeners at the moment, I'm afraid.'

'And cooks, and housekeepers, and upper maids?' Johanna added.

Her aunt smiled vaguely in her direction. Down the

garden the two girls had just caught sight of their visitors. Johanna waved at them. Less inhibited than their mother, they came running to greet their cousin. Their skin was as bronzed as that of any field hand; they looked awful — though they seemed healthy enough, and cheerful, too. Underneath that unsightly tan, on their upper arms at least, Johanna noticed some bruising. She looked to see if Tony had noticed it, too, but he was still trying to accommodate the change in Aunt Theresa.

Thinking the woman might unburden herself to him more if they were alone for a while, Johanna said, 'Come on, you two. Let's go and make some tea. You all look as if you could do with a break, I must say.'

As they went indoors she saw him leading her round to a seat at the edge of what, last year, had been the front lawn.

As soon as they were in the kitchen, Johanna, ignoring the presence of Betty Ferns, turned on her young cousins and said, 'All right. You'd better tell me.'

But they were already doing so, both talking at once, finishing each other's sentences, tripping over their tongues to get it all out.

'Papa says we've gone smash,' was the burden of it.

Then it was Johanna who could not contain herself. 'When?' she asked. 'How long back? Does Selina know? Why hasn't she said anything — why didn't one of *you* come and tell me?'

'She said not to bother you.'

'She said you had troubles enough of your own.' Deirdre, greatly daring, put out a hand and touched her waist.

Johanna closed her eyes and tolerated the inspection. 'The little idiot!' She tried to think clearly but the ideas and possibilities crowded her mind. 'Where is my uncle now?'

They looked at each other and shrugged.

'He's gone Penzance,' Betty chimed in; she was struggling to scrape a burned roasting pan back to metal.

Johanna nodded at her and turned back to the other two. 'Is he still whipping you at every slight excuse? What are those bruises?'

'Ancient,' Ethna said — a touch proudly.

'No, that's stopped,' Deirdre confirmed.

'And what are you living on?'

'The garden, mostly. And every now and then we sell something.'

Ethna burst into tears. 'Oh, Jo, it's horrid here. Take us away, do – find work for us. Anything.'

Deirdre joined in.

Johanna held out her arms and hugged them both into her embrace. She stood there, staring out of the window over their heaving shoulders, feeling more useless than she had ever felt in her life. Deirdre was almost as big as her now.

And the window was filthy.

'You could start by cleaning up this house,' she suggested. 'There must be some value in it. You could sell it and move.'

'Sell Lanfear?' They started howling again.

'All right, then, clean it because you love it so much. But, one way or the other – clean it.'

Deirdre pulled away from her. 'Does that mean you're not going to take us with you?' she asked.

'I can't, darling. I'm just Charley Vose's housekeeper now. But I'll think of something, I promise. Talking of promises – they'll be wondering what's happened to the tea.'

While the two girls put the finishing touches to the tray, proving that the household could still rise to the occasion when necessary, she went up to her old room, intending to retrieve the diaries she had left beneath the floorboards, almost a year ago, now.

But when she reached the room, she found that someone had moved a heavy chest of drawers so that one of its feet stood four-square upon the loose board – and she dared not risk attracting attention by trying to move it. If she failed, someone else might twig and then come back and do the job for her – or, rather, for themselves.

She wandered back downstairs before they could come looking for her. None of the furniture had been sold, anyway – or not yet.

Later, when she and Tony had resumed their drive to the Ram, it was she who broke the silence. 'I simply can't believe it,' she told him.

He remained at a loss for words.

'Even though I saw it. Why didn't Selina say anything yesterday?'

'What will they do?' he asked at length. 'It can't be just the recent decline in trade. They must have been going downhill for quite some time.'

'Well, I wouldn't have known about that. The money for the household was always there. That's all I knew. I must go and have a word with Terence.'

'What'll they do?' he repeated.

'Exactly. They've had no training for anything. I don't think the girls can even sew.'

'Could they teach? What were they like at lessons?'

'Average. Not very good.'

After another silence he said, 'There must be *something*.'

Their earlier conversation was uncomfortably recent.

She still held the reins. She had decided to take the slightly longer way round, past the gates of Godolphin Hall, because the woodland drive was prettier than the direct way through Millpool. At the top of Tregembo Hill, where the road winds down into the valley of the River Hayle, they heard a strange noise, which sounded at first like a great gathering of rooks. As they drew nearer they realized it was a crowd of people, but they could still see nothing.

'A wrestling match?' Johanna mused. 'But I'm sure I'd have heard of it — especially this close to Goldsithney.'

They had already passed a number of drunken people, lying in the ditches and propped up against the gates, but nothing unusual for the time of day, particularly with most of the mines idle. At the next bend, with the roaring of the crowd increasing all the time, they came upon two more drunkards — as they at first supposed; but then they saw that blood was pouring down the face of one, a woman, and that the other, a miner by the look of him, had several open wounds on his hands and arms. 'Good Lord,' Johanna said. 'That's Jack and Kitty Lanyon from Breage.'

Tony was already leaping down. 'The first time in my life, I think, that I left my bag behind! Wouldn't it happen? Where's the nearest running water?'

She pointed toward the bottom of the valley. 'Lanyon,' she cried out. 'What is happening, man? What have they done to you?'

He laughed and, with Tony's assistance, rose to his feet. He was drunk but not incapable. 'I done worse to they,' he crowded. 'Me and my missus. Didn't us, old girl?'

She cackled and rolled over on her back.

Tony shifted him to where he could support his own weight upon the mudguard. 'We must dress those wounds,' he said, dropping to his knees beside Kitty.

'There's a thousand more down there, master,' he said, rolling his eyes as he tried to fix them on Johanna. 'Miss . . . miss . . .' He hunted for her name, too.

'Rosewarne,' she told him.

'That's it. That's the very person.'

'What is happening, Lanyon?' A dreadful suspicion was forming. 'Have the Breage folk come over here looking for a fight? I thought the place seemed deserted.'

''Twas a challenge,' he confirmed. 'St Hilary folk against Breage folk. St Hilary against Breage. St Hilary . . .'

'How many?' she asked, though the roaring from up ahead was answer enough.

'Thousands!' He repeated the word several times as his hand described a great arc in the sky.

Tony came back to the gig. 'I can't move her on my own without risking those wounds opening up again. She seems to have clotted fairly well.'

'You've no call to worry about she, master,' Lanyon assured him genially. 'But there's a woman down there whose throat she cut. Now if you want to see blood!' Laughing at the memory he fell beside his wife.

Tony stared down at them in disgust. 'I suppose they'll live,' he commented. 'It sounds as if we could be more needed down there.' He leaped up into the seat beside her – then immediately down again. He went over to the woman, put his hands under the hem of her skirt, caught hold of a petticoat, and pulled it off in one swift jerk. Then he returned to the seat beside her.

'Filthy,' he said. 'But better than nothing at all. Tell me, is there, by any chance, a pair of scissors in that handbag of yours?'

'And needle and thread,' she said, opening the bag and taking out her 'housewife,' as soldiers call it.

'Yes – we'll need them too. No, you drive. Just the

scissors for now. I'll make bandages of this.'

He cut off the waistband, which he set aside for a tourniquet. Then he ripped it along its seams, giving himself a couple of yard-square sheets to work with. He made a series of rapid cuts about an inch apart all along the hems.

'It's not the first time you've done that,' she commented admiringly.

'Only last month, funnily enough. A runaway horse in Cobourg Street went slap-bang into a crowd. Can you tie a bandage?'

'I expect so. Oh, my God, look at that!'

The pony stopped, too, and started backing crabwise across the road. She urged him to a stand with difficulty.

The entire hillside was covered with a seething mass of drunken combatants. But what had caused her outcry was the tableau immediately before them. Six men were struggling to hold down a seventh — a Goliath of a fellow, roaring and thrashing beneath their combined weight. And above them reeled a strapping great woman holding aloft a hedging stone that must have weighed all of half a hundred-weight. Her purpose, clearly, was to dash it upon the giant's head the moment her companions could hold him still enough.

'Stop!' Tony cried, casting scissors and bandages into the gig behind him. 'Give me the whip,' he said to Johanna.

They paid no attention; it was doubtful they even heard him. He leaped down and struck out at the woman, she being the most immediate threat to the man on the ground — indeed, to all men on the ground. She staggered at the blow, turned half a circle, and then fell against Tony, allowing the stone to drop upon her own leg. Even Johanna heard the bone as it broke.

The woman's shriek tore the afternoon in two. Several of her companions left the giant and came to what they supposed was her rescue, kicking any part of Tony that showed, and stamping on his arms and legs. Johanna leaped down and, taking up the whip from where Tony had dropped it, drove them off before too much harm was done. The giant rose to his feet and staggered off downhill with the rest of his attackers still clinging to him, like so many mastiffs on a bear.

'Is it bad?' she asked, helping him back to his feet and dusting him down as gently as would do.

'You cannot possibly stay here,' he told her, flexing his limbs gingerly. He examined the woman, who had passed out by now. 'Splints,' he murmured, more to himself than her.

'Nor can you. It'd be suicidal.' She had to leave him to catch the pony, who was once more backing across the road. His horse, too, was becoming restive.

A miner's hammer, the kind they call a bucking iron, fell near them from nowhere — from out of the sky.

'No,' he agreed, taking charge of his horse. 'How far is Goldsithney?'

'A mile and a bit. Are you all right?'

'As rain.'

'You're thinking of a place to treat these people?' she asked.

'The ones who need to go to hospital, yes. What about the Ram?'

She nodded. 'The yards and stables? I'm sure they'd do.'

There was a sudden chorus of whistles. The quality of sound down on the field of battle changed — from roars of anger and drunken delight to shouts of alarm. 'That must be the police, at last,' Johanna said. 'Mount up — see what you can see.'

He did as she suggested and stood in the stirrups. 'Yes,' he cried. 'Looks like a whole platoon of them. Thank heavens for that.'

The ragged armies made for the road and started fleeing up the hill toward them. Johanna sought a gateway where he and she might shelter. But a moment or so later, this new impetus petered out and they began scattering in all directions, over the hedges and through the surrounding fields. Tony and Johanna turned around and saw that a second contingent of the constabulary was advancing toward them down the hill.

'After them, boys!' shouted the officer. 'Give them a pasting they won't forget this side of Christmas.'

Whooping and yelling, the men broke ranks and started a chase across the pasture and ploughland that would leave many a sore head in St Hilary and Breage over the next week or two. Tony dismounted again.

'A lucky escape, sir,' the officer commented jovially as he approached them. He looked at Johanna and his smile broadened. 'Miss Rosewarne, isn't it?'

She recognized him then — William Kemp, the excise officer who had once kissed her during a search for contraband at Lanfear House. 'I had no idea you'd joined the constabulary, Mr Kemp,' she replied.

'Inspector,' he said, smiling to show that his insistence on the title was jocular.

'Congratulations. This, by the way, is Dr Anthony Moore, of Plymouth. We were about to see to some of the wounded.'

'Or join them, more likely!'

'Yes, so we discovered.'

Tony cut in: 'Where is the nearest hospital, Inspector?'

'Penzance, Doctor,' he replied. 'And I should think there'll be a good few dozen who'll require it.'

Tony turned to Johanna. 'Can you go on and prepare things at the Ram? I'll do what battlefield repairs I may and pass them on to you. Send out what you can in the way of bandages. Also a strong packing needle and button thread. Make it a couple of needles.' He hitched his horse once more to the tailboard as he spoke.

She tossed him the bandages he'd already made and the housewife, whose needle and thread would do to be going on with. As she drove off he was already organizing a supply of splints and tourniquets with Willie Kemp.

On her way to the bridge at the foot of the hill she passed two undoubted corpses and up to a dozen who had bled so copiously they were probably on their way to join them. There was a half-naked woman lying face down in the river. If she hadn't died before she fell, she was assuredly dead now. On the farther side of the valley she overtook a stream of the wounded, escaping toward Goldsithney; she had never seen so much blood in her life. The arrival of the police had not restored sobriety but it had changed their drunkenness from the rowdy to the morose variety. People lay against the hedges where they had collapsed, holding their heads, moaning, weeping, vomiting . . . There was one man, limping along, trouserless, and attempting to hold together the two halves of a great seeping gash in his thigh; she called out to tell him there was a doctor back where he had just come from, but the fellow paid her not the slightest heed.

She drove on, having no time to stop and argue. Several of his fellow sufferers started to urge him to go back for treatment but he merely lunged at them with his free hand. As she neared the top of the rise she looked back and saw that a fresh fight had broken out among them.

What could one do with such people? She did not think Willy Kemp's answer was much help — break a lot more skulls to deter them next time. But against that she had nothing of her own to offer.

Charley Vose came down the path from Widow Jewell's cottages while Johanna was still organizing the clearance of the livery and coach-houses. He nearly threw a fit when she explained. 'What, maid,' he roared. 'Would 'ee bring bluebottles swarming all over my place? What sort of caper is that?'

She went on with what she was doing. 'You'll never learn, will you, Mr Vose. If something the like of this happened in Helston, where would they take the wounded?'

'I don't know. Anyway, this isn't Helston.'

'They'd take them up the Angel, and you *do* know it. And if you want this place to have as good a reputation ...'

'Yes, yes,' he said impatiently. 'I do know all that. But they still can't come here.' His eyes strayed to the two cottages at the top of the garden.

'Here!' Johanna thrust the besom into his hand and told him to finish sweeping out the coach-house. 'I'll see to that,' she said.

She strode up the path she had promised herself never to take. Fortunately it was one of the slack times of day in Paradise Row.

If she surprised herself, she astonished Widow Jewell. However, her amazement swiftly turned to alarm when Johanna explained that the premises below might soon be swarming with police. The girls, who had come from their rooms on hearing the doorbell jangle, started to panic.

'Don't just vanish,' Johanna shouted above their twittering. 'Put up something respectable and come down to the Ram. You can help make bandages, and tie them, and bathe wounds, and comfort the dying.'

'Can that be right, Miss Rosewarne?' asked one of the bolder women. 'The likes of *us* soiling your beautiful back yard down there?'

'Treasure in heaven, dear.' Johanna smiled sweetly and left them. She had just noticed the first of Tony's patients being brought in.

For the next four hours she worked without a pause, as did they all, even Charley Vose. During that time something like eighty badly wounded people, about a quarter of them women, passed through their tireless hands on the way to the infirmary in Penzance. At last the flow fell to a trickle, and, at the very end of it all, Tony himself came in, covered in blood and ready to drop. Behind him was a wagon piled with ten corpses, five of them women, including the one who had drowned and the one with her throat cut. The wagon was backed directly into the first empty coach-house and left there under guard to await the arrival of the coroner.

Johanna gave Tony Hal's dressing gown and got one of the maids to wash out his suit in a great kieve of rainwater.

'I shouldn't bother,' he said. 'It's ruined anyway.'

'You'd be surprised,' she assured him. 'Abbie'll get that looking as good as new by morning — won't you, dear?'

If the girl had had no intention of getting it even half so clean before, she certainly had it now. 'You'll see, mistress,' she promised.

'I can't stay till morning,' Tony protested.

'Well, you're certainly not going all the way back to Helston,' she told him. 'I'm sure the Inspector or one of his men will carry a message in there for you?'

Willie Kemp nodded. 'I'd be obliged if you'd stay, sir — to assist the coroner, you see? He'll be out here first light, I dare say.'

'Landlord!' Johanna turned jovially to Charley Vose. 'I think this calls for a hearty dinner for the brave doctor and all our gallant men in uniform. What say you?' And as his jaw fell she added, 'Not forgetting all our ministering angels from the village, too.'

Not even the greenest constable there had the slightest

doubt as to who these 'ministering angels' really were. The various parties, from Mrs Jewell and Charley Vose to Dr Moore and Inspector Kemp, stared incredulously at each other and then, being all on the edge of exhaustion, burst into laughter — which went on and on while, with mock gallantry, the gentlemen took the ladies by the arm and led them in to dinner as if they were all at some grand municipal occasion. And though it was but the scraping of the stockpot and a cut off every cold joint in the larder, they all declared it the grandest dinner they'd enjoyed in many a year. What private confidences and invitations passed between the various parties may only be guessed at, but when they took their farewells, which was close to midnight, it was with many a smile, many a nudge, many a wink.

Tony and Johanna went out into the yard for one final check on things. The Widow was just a few paces ahead of them. While Tony lingered for a word with the guard upon the temporary charnel house, Johanna looked up toward the cottages and said, 'You left a good few lamps alight.'

Mrs Jewell grinned. 'And three girls to trim the wicks,' she said. 'Well — us couldn't have desperate men coming down the Ram saying where's Rosanne, could us!'

'You mean . . . all the while we've been sitting down here, with more police than I've ever seen in my life before, they've been . . . whew!' She fanned her face at the boldness of it.

Tony joined them at that moment and the Widow bade them both good night.

'I'll bet you're exhausted,' he said as soon as they were alone.

'No!' She spoke the word with surprise, as if his question had forced the discovery upon her. 'I feel strangely restless. But you must be.'

'I don't think I'd sleep a wink, even if I took a draught. To be honest, I feel like a walk. Not far. Shall we just go to the end of the village and back? D'you mind me in this dressing gown?'

'Not at all. Who'll see you, anyway? And when we get back we'll have a glass of Vose's best contraband rum — and then perhaps I could sleep. What a day! D'you know, I'd completely forgotten my own injuries.' She took his arm and pushed him off toward the road.

'Are they hurting?'

'They feel a bit hot, but that iodine numbs them.'

'Good. I'll have another little peep at them when we get back.'

He was very tense. She took his arm. 'Relax yourself,' she said.

'Sorry. We have supped full of horrors. What's the quotation? Actually, supper was the one good part of it. But as for the rest! What induces people to behave like that?'

'It's quite an ancient tradition here — though I must say, this was worse than any I've seen, or heard of. I don't know what the answer is.' After a pause she added, 'I don't know what the answer to *anything* is.'

'We used to think the workhouses would cure it all. But obviously not.'

They passed a couple kissing in a doorway.

'G'night!' Johanna teased.

They paid no attention, but Tony chuckled. 'You've a decidedly mean streak,' he accused.

'It had to come out sooner or later,' she allowed.

After an easy silence he added, 'That moon! It's almost painfully bright.'

'A harvest moon. Or this time next month it will be. You'll be home in Plymouth by then.' There was no response. 'Will you come back for the inquest? I suppose you'll have to.'

He cleared his throat. 'Whatever about that . . . I'd like to be here for your lying in, Jo. I couldn't bear it if . . . Will you let me be your doctor for that time at least.'

'Oh, Tony.' She leaned her head against his arm.

'What? Will you?'

'I wish you could be . . . I wish we were just friends.'

'Surely we are? At the very least.'

Delayed exhaustion suddenly claimed her. 'Let's go back,' she suggested. 'This is the end of the village anyway. I'll bet you didn't think it was as short as that!'

They turned about and looked down the street toward the Ram. 'Lord,' she sighed. 'If there had been just one more casualty this evening, I think I'd have screamed.'

'You organized it marvellously, I must say.'

They walked most of the way back in silence.

If they had been talking, they would have missed it on their homeward walk as well. It came from a little way up the lane to Trevabyn, the lane that led past Paradise Row. It was the sound of someone – a woman by the timbre of the voice – retching.

Had that been all they would probably have shrugged their shoulders and passed on; it was not so uncommon a midnight sound in the back lanes around most of the public houses in the land. But this woman was also weeping – a forlorn, moaning sound as piteous as any they had heard that whole long, piteous day.

'Oh no!' Johanna said.

They looked at each other and, without a further word, turned off into the lane.

Chapter Forty-Two

She was a thin, frail young girl — not drunk, or at least with no smell of liquor about her. She was stooped against the hedge, clasping a gnarled ash stem, weeping bitterly and, every now and then, retching on an empty stomach. Johanna looked at Tony, thinking it a case for him; but he nodded encouragement at her, instead. She gripped the girl at the elbow. 'There, there, little one. Tell me what's the matter? Were you in the fighting this afternoon?'

The girl made an obvious effort to contain her tears; she straightened herself a little, but still without turning around. Somehow, in that slightly more upright posture, she seemed even wearier than before.

'This gentleman is a doctor,' Johanna went on. 'Can he help you? Are you hurt anywhere? What is it? Do tell us.' The poor thing's arm was nothing but skin and bone.

The girl took a deep breath and held it. Then she turned round and, wiping her tearstained face into her sleeve, said 'Thank you, miss, but I shall be all right. It's just . . . I shall be all right.' She stared down toward the highway like one seeking escape.

'Have you eaten?' Johanna asked.

She gave a single, dry laugh and nodded her head toward what she had left in the hedgerow.

'Perhaps the doctor should look at you?'

'I shall be all right, like I said.' She began to edge past them, feeling among the tussocks of the ditch with her feet. Johanna noticed she was barefoot; but her dress, though a little tawdry, seemed almost new.

'Is it to do with the fighting?' Johanna asked again.

The girl shook her head. 'I know you do mean kindly,' she said, edging still further past them.

Johanna turned to Tony. 'One can't help someone who simply refuses it.'

'I can,' he replied and reached out a hand to detain the girl, grasping her lightly by the arm.

'No!' His touch electrified her. Johanna had never seen such panic over so trivial a cause.

'I thought as much,' he said, letting go of her again. 'It's something to do with those houses, isn't it?' He nodded toward Paradise Row.

The girl broke down completely at that, and would have fallen if Johanna had not caught her. Now there was no holding back her tears. She buried herself in Johanna's embrace and sobbed her heart out. While she was still racked by this sorrow, Tony got behind her, lifted her in his arms, and started at once for the Ram. There was a momentary return of her panic but Johanna caught up her hand and held it tight, and that seemed to be all the comfort she now needed. 'Light as a little bird,' he commented.

Rose Davey had started a new stockpot that evening; its thin gruel, mashed with a morsel of oatmeal, was all the girl thought she could manage − though she ate ravenously enough for three. She was shivering, despite the warmth of the night.

Johanna mixed it for her. She took a sip, wrinkled her nose, and − for the first time − smiled. It was a shy little effort but it transformed her face.

Now she was in the light they could see she was much younger than her dress had led them to suppose − hardly fifteen, Johanna thought. She had auburn hair, let down loose over her back, straggling at the moment but not generally uncared for. Her face was a pixie shape, with high, freckled cheekbones and deep-set eyes. The freckles ran on in a band over her nose, which was slightly turned up.

'Have you a name?' Johanna asked.

'Hilary, ma'am. Hilary Cardew.'

'And where do you live?'

She shrugged. 'Nowhere. Not really.'

'Well, where did you sleep last night?'

'Old Ma Jewell, she said we could sleep out along Sunny

Corner for a time, until he's sold like.'

'We? Who is we?'

'Our mother, and my sister Iris, and the two boys, Peter and James.'

'And your father?'

'He died down Wheal Vor last year.'

'Does your mother work, Hilary?'

'She went up Godolphin Hall, looking for ... well, scrubbing floors and that − this afternoon. I don't know if she found it.'

'And did she make this arrangement with Mrs Jewell?' Tony asked.

Hilary had lost her fear of him by this time. She gave a wan little smile and nodded. Then, more to herself than to them, she murmured, 'But I can't.'

'How old are you, my dear?' Johanna asked.

'Fourteen last Michaelmas, ma'am. Ma Jewell said if I do catch on, like, then Iris could start up there, too. But I ...' She broke off and stared at them, almost as if she were apologizing. 'I can't go back there. I don't know what we shall do now.'

'And how old is Iris?'

'Twelve, ma'am. Twelve this week.'

Johanna herself felt sick by this time. She could not even look at Tony, who now assumed her role of gentle inquisitor. 'Your mother will be waiting for you, then,' he commented. 'Back at Sunny Corner?'

Hilary slipped her hand inside the waistband of her dress and pulled out a leather purse from which she tipped a handful of coppers and silver. The purse also contained a small bottle, which she must have forgotten, for she now tried to conceal it. 'That's what she's waiting for, sir,' she replied, stirring the coins unnecessarily, to distract their attention. 'Five shillings and sevenpence three-farthings. What am I going to do now?'

'Well, we must talk about that.' Johanna had not the first idea what she might propose. 'The main thing is to see you safely home. Are you sure you've had enough to eat?'

She nodded, put her hand to her stomach, and smiled.

'D'you think my suit will be dry?' Tony asked.

'I hope not! It would shrink beyond recognition.'

453

'Well, I shall just have to come in this dressing gown.'

Johanna laughed — which encouraged Hilary to a daring chuckle. But he insisted. It was a warm night. The world was asleep. And their business was too important for such petty considerations as dress to weigh against his coming.

Johanna did up a parcel of scraps and they set off under a bright moon in an almost cloudless sky. The whole village was silvered and asleep. A cat stared incuriously at them from the sill of a larder window, just above their heads, and then returned its stare to another cat, on the garden wall beside the house; it gave them more wary attention as they passed.

'Have you applied to the poorlaw guardians?' Johanna asked as they reached the edge of the village.

''Es ma'am. They said as they'd take Peter and James in the orphanage, put Iris and me on a field gang, and the old woman could work in the laundry.'

'It wouldn't have been for ever.'

'It would for James, ma'am. He've got a fliction in his chest. She said he wouldn't last three weeks, not in there, not even in summer. That's how we went up Ma Jewell's, see? For the physic. And then she said how I could pay for it.'

'The bottle in your purse,' Tony said.

'I do earn the physic for James.'

'And the money you showed us?' Johanna asked.

'Tips,' she explained. 'I'm sorry to put both of 'ee to all this trouble.'

'Might I examine the — physic, please, Hilary?' Tony asked.

'It's very good,' she assured him, making no effort to get it out.

'I'd still like to see it.'

'How d'you know it's good?' Johanna asked.

'Well, he slept right through last night.'

'So tonight was not your first up there.'

'No, ma'am. 'Tis the third.'

'And have you been made ill by it every night, or was it something particularly bad that happened tonight?'

'I been sick every night, ma'am. I thought I should get 'customed to it, like. But now . . .' Her voice trailed off into a wan silence. ''Tis only worse, not better.'

'Please let me see this physic, Hilary,' Tony repeated.

'He may be able to give you something a lot more effective,' Johanna explained.

Still reluctantly the girl passed over her precious, hard-won bottle. Tony pulled out the stopper, sniffed at the contents, put a drop on his tongue, and then recapped it before handing it back to her. 'I should just think he did sleep! Did you give him the lot?'

''Es, sir. He did seem to want'n like.'

'What's in it?' Johanna asked.

'Mostly alcohol. Laudanum, too, almost certainly. And something slightly bitter − juniper berries, at a guess. You could get any apothcary to make it up for fourpence.'

'Ooooh!' Hilary's eyes went dark with anger. 'That old shimshanking scadger! She told I ten shillings! I done four gentlemen for that. And 'twas only for a penny each!' She almost burst into tears again but another thought intervened. 'The old woman needn't have gone out scrubbing, neither,' she added bitterly.

'But it did work on the boy,' Johanna pointed out to Tony.

'He probably has asthma. Anything that relaxes or makes the sufferer drowsy would help. Certain kinds of asthma, anyway.'

They turned off down the lane that led to the cottage. At the sound of their approach another young girl − it could only be Iris − came running up to meet them. 'Oh, Hilly, Hilly − what shall us do?' she cried. 'Ma went out this afternoon and now she haven't come back.' At that she broke down and cried.

It was Hilary's turn to play the rock of the family. 'She must have crossed path with someone,' she said confidently. 'And they got in liquor. She's sleeping it out somewhere, you'll see.'

'Yes, but there was a fight back along the road today. A big one.'

'I know, I know. But that was Breage folk and locals. She wouldn't have tooken no part in that.' The masquerade was wearing thin; it would not be long before both sisters were in tears again.

'Describe her to me,' Johanna said. A dreadful numbness was invading her stomach.

'Dunno, I'm sure,' Hilary responded.

'Tall? Short? Fair haired?'

'About your size, ma'am,' Iris said. 'And her hair is the same colour as Hilly's.'

'And worn long like hers, too?'

''Es.'

'And her dress, was it a sort of faded blue cotton — patched in several places round the hem at the back?'

She was describing the drowned woman — as Tony soon realized. When the girls assented to Johanna's question he, who had examined the unfortunate woman closely, asked, 'And had she these three teeth missing?'

''Es, sir.' The agreement was little more than a whisper.

Johanna and Tony looked briefly at each other, wondering how to break the news. Johanna took a pace forward and put her arm around Hilary. 'Have you eaten?' she asked the younger sister.

In a daze, Iris shook her head.

'Well, here are some scraps to be going on with. Eat them all, if you like. Your sister and I will go back to the village and return very soon with some more for you.' She gave Hilary a squeeze to stifle the questions that were no doubt clamouring to be asked.

None of them spoke until they were back on the highway. ''Tis the old woman, isn't it?' Hilary said flatly.

'It may not be,' Johanna answered lamely. 'We saw several women dressed like that today, some of them hardly even injured at all. She may just be in the infirmary in Penzance.'

'What about they teeth?' the girl objected. 'See many like that, did 'ee?'

When they reached the Ram, Johanna went indoors for a lantern. Charley came down in his nightshirt, still half asleep. 'How are you still up, maid?' he asked.

She explained the immediate circumstances, but glossed over Widow Jewell's involvement in the business.

'No rest for the wicked,' he commented as he yawned his way back to bed.

Short of the rest eternal, she thought as she returned outdoors — where Hilary ran to join her. 'Where's Dr Moore?' Johanna asked.

456

'He said to wait on you, ma'am.'

Remembering how the corpses had been left, Johanna realized he had gone inside the barn to lay out Mrs Cardew with some respect.

It was her mother, of course. Hilary remained absolutely impassive when the lamplight fell across the lifeless features; she reached out, touched the stone-cold cheek with her knuckles, and withdrew her hand rather more hastily. 'That's all about it, then,' she said tonelessly.

All three of them could see her life stretching before her now; there was no question but that she would have to swallow her disgust and go back to Widow Jewell's — night after night after night.

'Had she anything put by for a funeral?' Johanna asked, thinking it best to direct her mind toward the immediate, practical things.

The girl just shook her head. She gave her mother a pat or two on the arm, as if it were she who needed the reassurance, and turned toward the door. 'You been very kindly, ma'am,' she said, in that same monotone. 'Now 'tis me got to shift for all on us.'

'Go back and get some sleep, my dear. Don't wait for the food. If you bring your brothers and sister up here tomorrow morning, I'll see you get a good, hearty breakfast.'

The girl walked away from them, across the yard, without a further word; nor did she glance back when she turned the corner.

Tony shut the barn door and leaned against it as if an infinity of weariness had suddenly fallen upon him. He closed his eyes and turned his face toward the sinking moon.

All at once she realized he was crying — silently, evenly, with no effect on his breathing; but a stream of tears ran down either cheek. She went to him, feeling more lost for words — indeed, for feelings, too — than at any time in her life. 'Oh, my dear,' she whispered.

'Did I say horrors?' he asked the sky. 'Horrors? They had not even started. Four-teen-years-old!' He gave each syllable precisely equal weight. 'Four *gentlemen*, she called them.' He raised his voice and cried out, from the pit of hell, 'Oh God, where are you?'

He opened his eyes then and searched the heavens with a wild, accusing sweep. 'There is no God.' His despair hammered every word.

And she could do nothing but clutch at his arm, and wait.

'There is no God.' He repeated the words in a more conversational tone. 'And therefore' — he even managed a smile — 'the work must fall to us.'

He smacked his lips and made small, brisk movements, encouraging himself to abandon his despair. 'Up to us,' he repeated.

'Us?' she asked.

'All of us. You, me, everyone.'

She smiled and faced him toward the back door of the inn. 'Your bed's turned down,' she said. 'Let's sleep on it — I mean on the problem — poor little Hilary's problem. We'll find some answer in the morning.'

'No,' he laughed. 'You don't understand. How could you? I didn't tell you — or, rather, you never asked.'

'Never asked what?'

'What business I had with your aunt.'

'Oh. No — other things . . . somehow intervened.'

'In point of fact, I went to see her about buying Lanfear house. I shall sell up in Plymouth, you see, and move down here.'

'But what for? I mean — will you get a practice down here?' She thought it extraordinary of him to start telling her his own plans at such an hour — and after such a day and night as this.

'Perhaps there is a God after all,' he conceded, making a vague gesture toward the road where Hilary must now be walking. 'And that is a sign from Him.'

She closed her eyes and shook her head. 'My brain is just numb.'

'Ever since I started my practice in Plymouth, I've known that something was wrong. Charming people, lovely area, splendid air . . . good income . . . wonderful friends. And yet, something was missing.' He smiled at her. 'And now it isn't.'

'Good!' She turned toward the door. 'I'm glad for you — the bits of me that are still awake.'

'No, no — you still don't understand. Look — I have an

458

income such that, if I never did another hand's turn in my life, I'd still be very comfortable. I don't *need* my lucrative practice. I can come here and start afresh with the very opposite sort of people. The poor. The Hilarys and Jameses of this world. Now d'you see?'

She couldn't see. Her exhausted brain could only grasp at small points, one at a time and there wasn't any time left. 'Free?' she asked.

'Of course.'

She shook her head. 'It won't work. Poor people are proud. You'll have to charge something. A few pence a visit, something like that.' As she spoke she felt herself drifting out of her body, floating away, and listening to herself in astonishment. Part of her knew that Tony had just presented her with a grand notion – the most earth-shaking decision of his life. And there was she, that strange, third person, stranded down there in the yard, marooned on her own fatigue, nattering on about how much to charge! Why couldn't she just shut up and marvel at his dream?

She came down to earth with a bump, though, at his next utterance. 'Oh, Jo,' he said, taking her arm. 'So practical always! Thank heavens you're there.'

PART FOUR

HAPPY FAMILIES

Chapter Forty-Three

When Johanna next wrote to Hal she told him she had left Nina because she could not sponge on her for ever. She described the transformation she had made at the Golden Ram and how well her work there was now progressing. Both the volume of the trade and − more importantly − its quality, were improving all the time. 'Last week we had the assize judge, several guests of the Duke of Leeds, the Chairman of Penzance Board of Guardians, and other gentlemen of almost equal eminence. We are assisted in this,' she added, 'by the new fashion, which has long held sway in England and has now begun to cross the Tamar, too, namely for gentlemen to dine out alone, or with only each other for company, and without their ladies. You are not to think of following it, my darling, when you come back.' She said nothing of Paradise Row, though he would hear about it from letters to Jenny. He would have to assume that her reason for silence was the same as his − to avoid embarrassment between them. And he would have to make the same assumptions about her honour as he expected her to make about his.

She told him of the Great Randy, as the fight on Tregembo Hill was now being called. It had become a local scandal, of course, as soon as the number of deaths − a dozen in all − was reported. The police response − to thrash everyone in sight and then allow the matter to drop − was not then satisfactory to public opinion. Thirty-six exemplary arrests had been made. 'And since they all carry the evidence into court upon their skins, they will all be transported,' she remarked. 'Which will leave thirty-six half-orphaned families thrown upon the mercies of the parish and to be a charge on the purses of those who bayed most loudly for this retribution.' She thought it best not to mention Tony's part in the proceedings. If Hal was keeping quiet about Jenny to save his beloved from anxiety, she could do him the same service in the matter of Tony. She and the doctor *were* just friends, and no more than friends ... rather better friends each day, to be sure, but still *only* friends. And never would be anything dearer than that, no matter what Tony might hope for. She had the matter quite firmly settled in her own mind. Indeed, she never even considered the possibility of something stronger.

Or only very, very rarely – the way anyone might speculate idly about anything under the sun.

She wrote of her intention to encourage Charley Vose to do more in the brewing line, adding that it was really Hal himself who had first put the notion into her head. She was less forthcoming on the part she intended to play in the process, even though, on the day following the Great Randy, she took the afternoon off, the gig, a firkin of ale, and the liberty of leaving free samples at several houses in the neighbourhood, both public and private. But then, she hadn't even informed Charley Vose himself as yet.

She said nothing about the baby, of course, which was at last starting to show. So much so, indeed, that she was compelled to say things like, 'Goodness, I shall have to sample less and serve more of our dinners here!' and 'Isn't that the way of things! I eat to plump out my cheeks and it all settles to my waist!' She estimated it might give her another month before a scandal became inevitable. Her greatest ally was her own reputation. No one would believe that the prim young martinet who ruled the staff at the Golden Ram like a military academy and who would never permit so much as the name of the Widow to be mentioned, much less her actual business ... no one would believe that she herself could stoop to such folly.

Charley, who had almost dismissed her because of her refusal to allow that the Widow's business was any part of the trade at the Ram, now received many a congratulation on his shrewdness from his (and Mrs Jewell's) clientèle. There is a species of English gentleman that loves nothing so much as a night out 'slumming'. He will consider himself 'no end of a dog' if he can boast of some friendship with a genuine member of the Great Unwashed. Not with any old hedge-trimmer, mind you; the 'pal' in question must be something of a 'dog' in his own right — a card, a scoundrel, one who is rumoured to have a finger in every gamey pie but who is never caught with the gravy on it.

The prospectus fitted Charley to a *T*. Respectable gentry who could endure a month of Sabbaths without a smile, would dig him in the ribs and say that his choice of La Rosewarne was the stroke of a master. At first he had thought they referred to the aura of respectability she conferred upon the place — implying it would deceive the gentlewomen left at home. 'Not at all!' one of the franker dogs enlightened him. 'They know full well what goes on up your garden path, old man. Dammit, most of them are only too happy to be relieved of our attentions and the consequent nine-month sentence. No, but don't you see — Miss Rosewarne keeps up such an *appearance* of propriety it covers our reputation, and, naturally, theirs along with it.' He laughed. 'But don't for one moment suppose they don't *know!*'

In a letter to Hal this reported exchange became, 'Vose says our guests inform him that I have raised the *bon ton* of the Ram beyond all measure.'

She told him, too — as he did in every letter to her — how much she loved him; how, the thoughts of him filled her day; how, in those moments of despairing loneliness, when it seemed they would be parted for ever, she loved to steal into his former room upstairs and hug his old dressing gown to her, and so refresh her inward springs of hope and confidence; and she stressed how much she needed her present exhausting occupation to preserve her from despond. Stretching the truth a little, she told him it was the same despond which had driven her to leave Liston Court, where 'the days were just too perfect and only mocked the melancholy it furnished me with enough time to indulge.'

She told him about the terrible depression in trade, which had hit the Trahearne-Visick partnership badly. She hinted that the Visicks, in particular, might be 'smashed', but left the revelation of it for a future letter, because it would involve some mention of Tony's part in their rescue.

All in all, she reflected sadly, each letter she wrote was an unfortunate tally of omissions and partial truths. She did not feel she was actually deceiving Hal, but nor were they enjoying the sort of bare-all entanglement of two souls she had always thought to be the very essence of true love. 'Never mind,' she would comfort herself. 'My reasons for omitting certain facts are all eminently practical and are rooted in my desire not to trouble him or give him pain upon my behalf. And I do think of him constantly, every day. And this baby is our love incarnate, which no one and nothing can ever take away from me. And when Hal sees him, or her, he will surely understand and forgive what must seem like my distrust of him now.'

And his letters, too, were filled with equal assurances of his love for her — and never a mention of young Jenny, who, as Diana made quite sure of informing her, still wrote regularly from that same 'Dudley, Iowa'.

Frank Ashburn had moved into his own log cabin, which, he avowed, would astonish any other log cabin in Iowa. 'He said he was right smart tired of too many Gals,' Jenny wrote. 'And that I am a miserable fine Woman who can take the Lint off all for *pretty* any day in his Estimation and that I could take his Hat but he was of the Opinion we should annexe up to each other until we come across some handy Circuit Rider and make it right with the Good Lord above. In short, Mother and Sister dear, he and I now live in happy Concubinage.' She added — as if to spare their blushes on her behalf — that 'such an Arrangement is far more usual here than ever at Home'.

Hal, of course, said only that Frank had moved into a log cabin of his own. 'We are raising these buildings,' he wrote, 'according to a Swedish system, which is quicker, neater, and in every way superior to the American style, and we complete just over four every week. Our mentor is an immigrant called Carl Rehnqvist, which no one can get their tongues around. Frank calls him Charlie Renko, and that name has stuck, poor chap. A log cabin built to his system is as impermeable to the elements as a wall of our Cornish granite . . .' There followed an entire page on the

Swedish system, which made Johanna smile — but it also made her realize what it was she loved so much in Hal: his ability to enter heart-and-soul into everything he undertook.

There were no half measures with him. He couldn't just build log cabins for a wage and be done. He had to go into the whole science and art of the business and be sure he was making the best possible job of it. He even seemed surprised when Jeremiah Church, the great Peripatetic Builder himself, congratulated them on the result and offered them a partnership in his new town. But Frank had scotched that one. He said that 'Dudley' was just an expensive way of clearing farmland. 'The very next overflow will carry every rentable morsel clear down to Luzanny,' was his opinion. And it was at his insistence that they were paid at least their basic wage by the month. Johanna liked the sound of Frank Ashburn — and not only because he had removed the threat of young Jenny Jewell.

It amused her to think that, if Hal had been open about Jenny's presence from the start, he could now write of her with a clear conscience — especially about her 'concubinage' with Frank. It amused her somewhat less to realize that a similar situation was developing in her letters to him. Since Dudley was slap-bang on the main trail to Kanesville and onward, across the continental divide, to California, Hal would likely meet with dozens if not hundreds of Cousin Jacks, most of whom would know of the closing of Wheal Venton and the Visicks' smash. They might not know Tony's name but they would all tell of a 'young doctor from Plymouth' who was buying up Lanfear house; Hal would supply the name at once.

She was surprised he hadn't already twigged that Jenny's news must filter through to her. But perhaps he did? Perhaps his silence on the subject was no longer prompted by the embarrassment he must initially have felt when Jenny decided to throw in her lot with him and Cunningham; he might have worked out that, thanks to Jenny's letters home, she, Johanna, already knew the entire story. She would then wonder at his silence and — in her turn — work it out that he was doing it out of tenderness for her. His silence would thus become yet another way of saying, 'I love you.'

What a web! she thought.

Tony was meanwhile pressing forward with his plan to buy Lanfear. Much to her relief he had said nothing further about enlisting her help in any of his projects – and she certainly wasn't about to raise the matter. The very morning after they had found Hilary in such distress he moved all four young orphans to the gardener's cottage at Lanfear.

Johanna, meanwhile, went to pay a call on the Widow, intending to demand that Hilary be given her full due. Mrs Jewell had somehow got it into her head that Johanna had swallowed her principles last night and come up the garden path to warn her of an intended police raid. She therefore yielded at the first mild skirmish, and was only too happy to oblige. Over the previous three nights Hilary had, in fact, earned fifty shillings, of which she would normally have kept twenty. Mrs Jewell, unsure of Dr Moore's status and possibly sensing trouble from him as well, coughed up the lot – and said she'd throw in the physic as a bonus.

Seeing what mood the woman was in, Johanna pushed her luck a little further. 'I think we'll have no more truck with girls under the age of fifteen, Mrs Jewell,' she suggested.

The Widow pulled a dubious face. 'Twelve is the law's age of consent, mistress. And I'll tell 'ee another thing – a lot of the gentry do like 'em "with no parsley," as they say ... smack smooth. They reckon as there's less risk of waking up in *Clapham*, if you take my meaning. That assize judge, he's very keen. Wants me to find he a brace in single figures, he does.'

Johanna knew by now how to win a concession by seeming to make one of her own. 'I would not dream of telling you how to manage your affairs, Mrs Jewell. But I would entreat you to consider this – we tread a narrow path between lawbreaking and tolerance here. Never mind what our fine gentlemen may say, we shall be tolerated only as long as we do not offend their wives. Those women will not blink an eyelid at your employing a girl of fifteen. Fourteen would make them uneasy. At thirteen it would turn to disquiet. At twelve to alarm – even if the law may permit it. Single figures would be an outrage which I doubt we could survive. However, as I say, the choice is entirely yours. You know my opinion of your business. I detest it. I do not say one thing to your face and another behind your back. And I really want nothing more to do with it than my own position at the Ram makes unavoidable.'

Thereafter, no girl under fifteen found work with Mrs Jewell. Johanna wished she could have made it twenty, but then her entire argument would have been laughed out of court.

When she handed over the money to Hilary the girl's ears turned scarlet. At first she wouldn't even touch it.

'The money itself bears no taint,' Johanna told her. 'It's as good as anything that goes in the collection plate of a Sunday. D'you want the doctor to look after it for you?'

But she didn't even want him to know about it. She took up the money then, gingerly, as if she feared it might burn. And then she did a most singular thing: She clasped it to her, almost cuddling it between her tiny breasts, and closed her eyes, and gave out a long, deep sigh. Johanna watched in fascination.

Everything was in that simple gesture. It was an interment of all those horrors by means of which she had come by so large a sum — to earn which she would have needed half a year as scullery maid. It was also a subdued cry of triumph, which almost justified her ordeal, at least insofar as she had survived it and gone on to reach this new pinnacle of achievement — this milestone in her young life; for it was far and away the largest sum of money she had ever held between her own two hands. And it was all hers. And she had earned it.

The moment was ... *ecstatic*. One could not describe it any other way. Watching her, so spontaneous in her pleasure, Johanna began to understand how some of the girls up there could tolerate it. That moment when money changed hands ... until now she had thought of it as the time when the woman forfeited her humanity, her self, her free will, and became instead a thing, a play-thing, a chattel of the giver. She had not seen this side of the transaction at all. By some extraordinary paradox the taking of the fee reunited the woman with her own sense of respectability as the provider of an obviously valued service. Without it she was just another wanton.

The girl must have realized it, too. Even as she shared that briefest of ecstasies with herself, part of her must have been alarmed at its strength. For when she opened her eyes again Johanna saw them fill with panic. She knew exactly what was going through her mind. From this hour forth, and for as long as she kept her youth and beauty, she would never arrive at a moment of financial crisis without remembering this. She would remind herself of the horrors, too – of how she was found vomiting into a hedge at the soul-destroying awfulness of it all – but she would also remember herself surprised like this.

She thrust the money from her, back into Johanna's hands. 'You look after 'n for I, ma'am, if you mind. And never tell Doctor, please. Please?'

'He's bound to ask. The way you were cheated shocked him even more than it did me. I'm a pessimist. I expect people to behave like that. I'll just tell him she made it up to you and leave it at that, eh?'

She nodded. 'Only if he do ask, mind.'

When they were safely installed at Lanfear, the two girls set about cleaning the house from top to bottom; the young lads, Peter and James, gathered snails at a penny a bucket and cut the grass and mucked out the stables and did as much as two young sprigs could do, given such little supervision. James's asthma improved greatly. The Visicks, somewhat grudgingly, accepted an equally grudging invitation to stay with their erstwhile partners, the Trahearnes of Nineveh, pending the successful completion of the sale. There was talk of their buying a villa along the seafront at Wherrytown, just outside Penzance, and running it as a boarding house.

Tony himself divided his time between Plymouth and Lanfear – equally at first but gradually the stays in Cornwall grew longer until they coalesced into a permanency. He was by then master of Lanfear. All the world wondered that he had no cook, neither of the Cardew girls being any good in that line. They wondered even more that he bundled them all into a gig each evening and drove them over to the Ram at Goldsithney for a slap-up meal all round. Even Charley Vose, who benefited most from the arrangement, drew him aside to tell him what a great mistake it was to feed one's servants too much red meat.

Johanna, meanwhile, had continued her visits to likely customers for Charley's ale and, in addition to leaving free samples, was now soliciting orders, too. The man himself did not catch on to what was happening until it struck him that the brew he was about to commence was, in fact, the third one that week – when he had never before done but two. Of course, there was a considerable increase in trade in the dining room – and up beyond, in Paradise Row. But then, on the other hand, he had been discouraging the patronage of the heaviest beer swillers, the labourers and miners – except for a few token 'characters' whose bucolic custom created the authentic 'pub' aura that some of his gentry customers admired. Taking one thing with another, then, the consumption of ale ought actually to have declined a little. That was when he turned his attention to the list of orders Johanna had given him.

She was watching him through the scullery window.

He skimmed it. He read it. He went down it a line at a time, using his finger as a stop for his eye. He stared at the inn, but she knew he could not see her for the scullery was too dark. He shook his head and started to read it once more. Then she knew it was time to go to him.

'Can't you make out my writing?' she asked as she crossed the yard.

''Tin't that,' he answered with a sigh.

'What then?' She was beside him now.

He tilted the list toward her. 'Jack Tremeer – who's he when he's home?'

'He farms down Higher Keneggy. Chapel folk, they are.'

Charley stared at her in bewilderment. 'Well, what's he want buying beer off of we? He's got Coach and Horses ... Falmouth Packet ...' He began listing all the public houses that were nearer than the Ram.

'He said he'd rather drink ditchwater than some of their muck.'

Mollified but still puzzled he returned to the list. ''Tin't just he, though. I don't know half these folk. Ebenezer Scadden ... Mrs Ellacot ...'

471

'Penhale ... Rosudgeon ...' She supplied the locations as fast as he reeled off the names.

'Are you telling me they do come up to 'ee in the street and say, "Put I down for a dozen of ale," or what?'

'Something like that,' she admitted. 'You should never have started obliging just a few regulars, Mr Vose. You should never have let my cousin Terence talk you into it. Once people get a taste of Vose's ale, you see, they can't get enough of it. Word is spreading.'

His eyes narrowed and they began to shine with the light of a dawning understanding. 'Word is spreading, eh?' he echoed tartly. 'Now that wouldn't have nothing to do with your afternoon drives in the gig, I suppose? Out the kindness of your heart you do deliver this order and that order, perish the thought you'd take another half dozen orders beside!'

'What am I to do?' she asked in wounded tones. 'Am I to turn away? Do I tell them Charley Vose has lost all interest in money now? Incidentally, you mentioned the Falmouth Packet just a moment ago. There's a new landlord there.'

'John Moyle, I do know he.'

'Yes, so he told me. Anyway, he's not impressed with the brewing equipment he's inherited from ... who used to own that place – Stanley Morcom?'

'You do know a damn sight too much for my comfort, mistress.'

She laughed. 'Moyle has been talking with Joel Saunders, brewer in Penzance, about supplying all his ale in future. So I left him a sample of ... *ours*.'

It was the first time she made that leap from *your* to *our*. He did not seem to notice. 'You what?' he asked, as much astonished as angry.

'I also left him looking mighty thoughtful,' she added. 'They do a fair trade on the main highway there. Wouldn't it be a grand feather in our cap if most of the beer he sold was ours? I'm sure he'll contract with Saunders, as well, but their beers can't hold a candle to ...'

'Just ... just ... just a minute.' He finally slowed her to a halt. 'Are you seriously suggesting I should work double tides here – and most of that time for a competitor?'

'Funny sort of competitor who sells *our* beer,' she told him scornfully. 'If you work double tides ... well, that's up to you, Mr Vose. It's hardly my place to tell you how you manage that part of our new trade. If it were me, I'd train up the lad.'

'There you do go again!' he complained, having noticed her usage at last. '*Our new trade!* What sort of animal is that? When did I say us had any sort of trade – new or old?'

She gave him an apologetic smile. 'You're quite right, Mr Vose. I'm too soft-hearted. That's always been my trouble. Ever too ready to oblige. Well, you just go down that list and cross off those names you're not willing to furnish with ale. I'll go round and let them know they may apply elsewhere. I didn't actually promise them – not in so many words. So – no harm done, eh?'

Greatly relieved he pulled out an atrocious little stub of a pencil and struck through a good two-thirds of the names she had compiled. Mentally she totted up the cost of the cancellations as he made them.

On his final flourish she said, 'Twenty-five pounds, eight shillings and sixpence. Just like that! You're a bold brave man, Mr Vose!'

'What are 'ee talking about?' he asked testily.

'That's our lost trade. A year's wages for three dining-room-maids – and you strike it out, just like that, as I say.'

He stared again at the list but could not see it. 'What price did you give they?' he asked at length – just when she was beginning to think the question would never occur to him.

'Five shillings and sixpence a dozen. Quart bottles, of course. Plus a halfpenny deposit on each bottle.'

He gaped in disbelief.

To rub in the salt she added, 'And fourpence if they keep the crate – returnable. Six shillings and fourpence a dozen.'

'No!' He laughed, quite convinced she was pulling his leg.

'Yes,' she insisted.

He surveyed the list once more, rubbing his baby-smooth

473

chin the while. Absent-mindedly he took out a new cheroot, even though the usual half-dead gasper already smouldered in the corner of his smile. 'I reckon we'd just so well give it a go,' he said.

No hint of triumph showed in her manner. If anything, she expressed a concern that he might be taking on too much altogether. 'Whatever you feel is for the best, Mr Vose. I'd hate you to think that I had in any way brought this decision upon you.'

He just stood there and roared with laughter. 'Perish the thought!' he said between fits.

Chapter Forty-Four

Charley Vose had decided to open a new passageway to the
yard, to save his guests the indignity of having to pass the
kitchen and scullery on their way to Paradise Row. This, in
conjunction with a new path through the garden, leading
round the back of the stables, would also ensure that a guest
was at no time exposed to view from the highway. A pergola,
suitably draped with mile-a-minute and traveller's joy,
would complete his protection from the worst of the
elements as well. The profitable congruence of facilities at
the Golden Ram was beginning to assume an air of
permanency.

In the last week of the old arrangement, the bubble of
silence that surrounded Johanna's condition was finally
pricked. The suspicion was already abroad, of course; she
could see it in people's eyes. Several times Charley himself
had cleared his throat and pushed his cheroot from one
corner of his mouth to the other; but that was as far as it had
got. He needed only to look into her eyes to think better of it.

It was not exactly a trick she had – and certainly not
something she had sat down and worked out in that cool,
methodical manner of hers. Indeed, she had discovered the
way of it almost by accident. When she first approached
John Moyle, the new landlord at the Falmouth packet, she
had simply knocked on his door, put her proposal to him in
a straightforward manner, and left him to think it over.
Later, when he knew her better, he confessed she could have
struck him down with a feather that day. 'Pretty young maid
like you, ladylike and all ... I don't mean lawdydaw, now
– but ladylike, and no mistake. And there you was, talking

quantities and discounts and credit like any regular traveller. It took me on the ground hop, I can tell 'ee. Agape, I was.'

'It didn't show,' she told him, thinking he was seeking that sort of reassurance.

''Course it never!' he replied. 'I dursn't let it. I mean, you was so calm and direct about it all, I thought to myself I shall look a right edjack if I go and pass some remark on it. So I just carried myself on, normal-like.'

'Well!' She gave an awkward laugh. 'I'm the one who's taken aback now.'

'Old Jack Tremeer, he said the same. He said first time you come down Higher Keneggy there, you mismazed he into buying. He wouldn't never have done it else. 'Es – proper bewaddled, he says he was. But you carried on like you had more right to sell than what he had to buy, so he held his tongue. 'Course, now he got the taste for your beer, you couldn't get he to drink nothing else, not if 'twas free.'

'Not my beer,' she corrected him. 'Vose's.'

From this encounter she concluded that if you did a thing with enough conviction – even something that others might think outrageous – then so long as you behaved as if it were the most ordinary thing imaginable and not even worth a comment, most of the world would let it pass.

Whether it would work with something so scandalous as having a baby out of wedlock was another matter; but still, it was the only line of defence now open to her. And, considering it had come spontaneously from within her – she hadn't, after all, *planned* to 'mismaze' any of their customers into buying – she felt she might just be lucky enough to carry it off.

So when the bubble finally burst – when one of their regular customers, Squire Pellew, a local justice, mumbled something jocular about 'a woman in your condition –' she was ready for him. They were in the passageway outside the kitchen – she coming inward from the scullery, he going the other way to Paradise Row. He stepped aside and, imagining he knew her fairly well by now, uttered his fateful remark – the first that publicly aired her situation.

She had backed against the wall to let him pass; she simply froze there and stared at him. There was no anger in her eyes, nor humiliation; nor was there challenge, nor outrage. He found himself staring into a nothingness – a vast, glacial coldness: the mask of the basilisk.

He averted his gaze at once and hurried on. She followed him with her eyes, all the way across the yard, where he blew upon the tips of his fingers and waved them in the air. And she smiled in satisfaction. It had worked. There were storms ahead, but she now had one small shield against them.

Later, when the place was all locked up for the night and she and Rose Davey were sitting alone at the great kitchen table, relaxing, as they did at the end of almost every day, over a cup of hot chocolate, Rose lowered her voice and said, 'I seen what you done to poor Squire Pellew. Proper job! That'll spread the word to leave 'ee be.'

Against an approach so cleverly oblique she had no defence – for what was there to react to? Instinctively she gave back her cold stare – but the woman wasn't even looking at her. She was gazing into her steaming mug, with a smile of admiration on her lips, and she was saying, 'Poor old Charley – he's dancing seven jigs about it. Every morning he do wake up and say to me, "I shall talk to that maid today. I shall go down and have it out with her." And every night he do lie there and say he never had no time, or the proper occasion never showed itself.' Only then did she look up at Johanna, a merry twinkle in her eye. 'He won't be sleeping now. I'll lay any odds he's up there, tossing and turning, fretting how to tell 'ee.'

During this speech Johanna had realized that Rose would actually make the very best kind of ally. She heard everything that happened at the inn – on both sides of the service door; the kitchen was the high 'change of all gossip among the staff. Moreover, she was privy to Charley Vose's thoughts and fears. And above all – as her little speech had signalled in the plainest manner – she had no moral judgements of her own to offer.

'Tell me what, Rose?' she asked.

'Well, 'tis his opinion you got to put yourself away till you shed a bit o' weight again.'

'And what is your opinion, as to that?'

'I do say that's entirely your affair, mistress. 'Course, you do belong among they high-quarter folk who hold 'tis a nine-month infirmity, and needs six month of convalescence after. But my mother, now she had me in a field in harvest time — out Sethnoe Farm in Breage, 'twas — I could take 'ee to the very place. And she swaddled me up and put me fast the hedge and went back to binding her sheaves. And you know what my father told her? He said, "Don't 'ee fret, missus," he said. "I finished your row for 'ee."' She laughed. "Es, that's what he told she: "I finished your row for 'ee".'

Johanna joined her laughter. 'I don't think I'm quite in the same class of heroine as your mother, Rose. But, if I had to choose which path to take, it would be somewhere closer to hers, I trust. In short, I intend to continue working here for as long as I feel able — without, of course, hazarding the . . .' Her hand made a vague movement near the belly.

Rose smiled at her unwillingness to actually come out with a name for it.

'. . . the little mite,' Johanna said.

The other swilled the dregs of her chocolate around. 'I can't see no face in here,' she remarked, peering at the bottom of her cup. 'You finished yourn, have 'ee?'

She half held out her hand but Johanna hugged her cup to her as if it held a secret.

In that way the father's name was fished for and refused.

Rose tried another tack. 'That Jenny Jewell, her mother showed I a letter from she, the other day.'

Johanna yawned. 'I sometimes see them, too. And, of course, I hear quite regularly from Hannibal Penrose, who's in the same town until spring.'

'Ah.'

'Which reminds me — my cousin Selina hasn't seen the last couple of letters. I've neglected her shamefully.' She sighed. 'But there are only so many hours in a day. Really, Mr Penrose writes to both of us, you see. She's gathering material for a great Cornish-American romance she's writing.'

The woman stared at her evenly, waiting for this stream of persiflage to reduce to a trickle. 'That Diana, she's some little letter writer, too. She give a whole catechism to Henry Collet in the village. You know he's off looking for gold in Californey? Him and three others.'

Johanna stood and went to rinse her mug at the tap. 'With the state of the mines here, who can blame them?'

''Es, there's dozens at it. I should think if you wanted to hear all the news and cooze in Cornwall, your best place would be to stand on the Californey road.'

'It's amazing,' Johanna agreed airily, stretching and yawning once again. 'The last letter I had took less than a month to get here.'

Rose, pretending to an equal nonchalance, stood up and rinsed her cup, too. 'I've forgotten rightly where they are,' she said. 'Mr Penrose and his party.'

Johanna gave her an affectionate pat on the shoulder. 'See you in the morning, Rose. You'd need a hammer and tacks to keep my eyelids up.'

But she did not go immediately to her bed. Rose was right. Even if no one else carried the news of her pregnancy to Iowa, dear little Diana would revel in it. Why had she not faced this reality before? It alarmed her that she could hide so much from herself. She sat and wrote a second catechism for Henry Collet to carry with him along the Californey road:

My own darling Hal,

And never were you more dear to me than now. By the time you read this you will be a father. If you did not know it already, I make no doubt but that Henry Collet carries a letter for Jenny Jewell in which no detail is spared. And the first thing you will ask is why, why, why did I not tell you? Why did I perjure my soul to assure you all was well?

My purpose is shrouded and confused, even to me. At the time, I told myself it was to force Nina into parting with my fare and sending me after you. I did not understand that I would, by those means, extort my wedding ring out of you, no matter how willing you might feel. And even now, my love, I can still only see it as a very abstract sort of truth. My heart is so much united with you that all questions of extortion − of any ill usage − are, as it were, in another country.

However that may be, I have to ask myself why I tarried so long in telling her. If such were my plan, I was

479

disgracefully slow to carry it out. Perhaps a part of me, in secret from my thinking self, already knew what she would say. When finally I confessed it to her, she told me at once that you and I are as wrong for each other as any two mortals could be. She showed me a letter from Dr Moore, who saw you embrace the Jewell girl outside his house the day you sailed from Plymouth. (He has since retracted the implications he read into the event in a most honourable way. He wrote in the heat of anger, he confesses.)

When, despite this revelation of your 'perfidy', I nonetheless insisted on joining you, Nina changed her ground. She, Selina, and I should spend the summer and autumn in Italy; I should lie in there; and our baby would be reared as an olive farmer and goatherd. I did not even consider it, not for one second.

There were a dozen other projects for me, all of equal absurdity. Mrs Ramona Troy offered me two thousand a year and the freehold of a house if I would marry her grandson Hamill Oliver and keep him in check. Absurd, as I say. On your returning to Cornwall, she would facilitate our liaison to any degree we might desire! The morality of the upper classes is only amazing.

Now I am called stubborn and perverse and unbending and I don't know what else. But I disagree. I know (there is something within me that knows) what is right – and I do it. That is all. I have more patience than most other people. That is all. I know it is right to bear this child, to keep its father's name to myself until he owns it of his own free choice, and to look the world in the eye. I shall never feel nor own a moment's shame, so do not grieve for me on that score, either. But to come back to Nina.

Eventually she yielded. She did not simply give me the fare, she arranged everything – vessel, cabin, and the onward journey to Chicago, where we should meet and give our baby a name. It was all I had ever desired of her. And this brings me to the most difficult part – to explain to you why, sitting in that cabin, and with all that wonderful vision before me, I went back on it all. Yes, I jumped ship and returned here to certain disgrace, to a Nina who now hates me, and to lay a stigma upon our child that nothing can ever lift, not even your owning of it and marrying me.

But disgrace (in the eyes of the world, not mine) was no new prospect to me. I had faced it daily over the five months while Nina persisted in her refusal. It held its Terrors, to be sure, but they were no longer unknown. I formed a plan. Put baldly, it will sound absurd. In fact, this is the first time I have committed it to words, even in my own mind. I planned it in pictures, not paragraphs.

Here she wrote several more sentences and then scratched them through.

See! I still cannot. Let me tell you instead that it works. Morning, noon, and night, I am housekeeper at the Ram. (What goes on at the Jewells' place has nothing to do with the inn. I do not permit so much as their names to be mentioned here, nor may anyone make any reference to that business in any way. Even Charley Vose himself concurs in these rules. I don't know why these people obey me. I have no sanction over them – in Vose's case, quite the reverse. But I have commanded it so, and so it remains.) And then in the afternoons I climb into Vose's gig and go about the neighbourhood soliciting orders for our beer. We now brew for six local public houses, four of them on the Penzance highway. We are also brewers by appointment to the Duke of Leeds, the Lord St Aubyn, General Thomas, Squire Pellew of Skewjack hall, and a dozen notable families beside – and some fifty genteel households on top of all that.

I have done all this. I am paid commission only, and yet I earn more than Mrs Jewell and all her creatures put together – which I wish they were and sent to Van Diemen's Land. Vose does not like it, you may be sure, but I set it all forth in the form of a letter which he has signed so he cannot slip me now.

And it was because I knew all this was possible, and that I, and perhaps only I, could make it come about, that I jumped ship and came back here. I should have held myself in contempt for the rest of my life had I turned my back on that certainty and instead come running to you, saying, 'My problem is thy problem. Whithersoever thou goest, there also shall I hang about thy neck . . .' *et cetera*. In honesty, I should have had to sign myself your loving leech.

Now you know all the truth, my darling, and you will think me the most forward, shameless hussy ever — except that I hope you remember me better than to let my pride and boasting stand for *all* of me. Were you here now, I should melt in your arms and you should find me as soft and as yielding as in your fondest dreams. If other men say I am hard or perverse, it is because all the power to move me has been gathered up and bestowed upon one single man — yourself, compared with whom they are less than dust.

Your next thought, then, will be to abandon your dreams of California and come home to me at all speed. Again, that secret part of me which thinks without thought has made such action futile. It breaks my heart to say you must stay, but what sort of life would we face if you came back now? So go onward, my darling. Enlarge your dream for the two of us. The deceit between you and me is over. I have often written with a heavy hand, knowing how much I have left unsaid. My sole excuse must be that I did it to spare you the worry, just as you kept silent about the Jewell girl on my account, to spare me a like anxiety. But now I shall write with a will! You may build a house in California out of paper sent from Goldsithney. A house, did I say? A mansion!

I ache for you always, my love, my marvellous man. You are the light that brightens my day, the dark that shrouds me in slumber, the savour of all I eat and drink, the zest in every word I say, the sweetness of my breathing, the *chaleur* of my smallest thought. What more can I say?

The following afternoon, having sealed her letter and given it to the Collet lad, she called, as she often did, at Lanfear; she was on her way to collect orders from the Queen's Arms in Breage and from some of the larger houses in that neighbourhood. At the final bend in the road, just as the house came in sight, she took a battered old post horn from under her seat, put it to her lips, and blew. What emerged from the other end was closer to a rasp than a musical tone. The only living creature to pay her any heed was the pony; he bolted half a furlong before she reined him back to a gallop — and only the sight of the entrance to Lanfear, where the Cardew children would be sure to spoil him dreadfully, induced him to halt.

Tony came out and stood on the front step — Selina at his side, Johanna saw.

'What was that?' he cried. 'We thought someone was torturing a donkey to death out there — was it you?'

Hilary came skipping out to take the pony in charge; her brothers were close behind. She gave Johanna a shy, impish grin. Her hair had not been combed and her clothes were dirty.

Johanna climbed carefully down. Selina went to help her, giving Tony an accusing glance as she passed; but he put out a hand to stop her, and shook his head — all behind Johanna's back.

Selina raised her eyebrows. He nodded confirmation: When that young woman wanted any help, she let you know.

'Hello, darling,' Selina said as she kissed her cousin's cheek. She looked down at her waist and added, 'There's no concealing it now!'

'Aye, it's going to be a bit of a nuisance,' Johanna agreed. She turned to Hilary. 'You could smarten yourself up a bit, young miss.'

The girl stared at her feet and said nothing.

'D'you hear me?'

'Yes, ma'am.'

'What on earth is *that?*' Selina asked, holding up the post horn.

Johanna grinned. 'My new wheeze. Often I have to wait five minutes at each place, while they find the right person, look out a list, assemble the empties . . . It soon adds up. So, when I found that old horn stuck up in the rafters at the Ram, I thought, proper job. Just the thing.'

Tony laughed. 'Just the little matter of learning to play it.'

'Well, at least you heard it.'

'No doubting that! From this moment forth I shall never

hear a dying donkey without immediately thinking of Vose's Ales.'

'Pay him no attention,' Selina advised. 'He's full of himself today because he's just ... well, he'll tell you.'

'Yes,' Tony agreed. 'Come indoors and take a small glass of ginger cordial with us — to celebrate.'

'Is it medicinal?'

'No, but our celebration's medical, and that's almost as good.'

He led the way inside. Johanna put her arm about Selina's waist and gave her a squeeze. 'It's so long since we've *seen* you, darling. I've got a couple of letters from Hal for you.'

'I know. The days have been rather ...' A wan smile supplied the missing adjective.

'How's Nina?'

'Very low.'

'Oh dear.'

'That's why I came to see Tony. I think she's making herself ill.'

Johanna, who had just entered the front door at that moment, could not help exclaiming, 'Goodness! Here's a difference, even since last week!'

'It's amazing what servants can do when you feed them red meat,' Tony commented. 'You may thank Mr Vose for the tip.'

'You could tell Hilary to take some soap and water to herself as well. I know what it is — your furniture's come ... beautiful furniture, too.' She peeped into the drawing room. 'Did you have all this in Plymouth? I see some of our old things among it, too.'

He nodded. 'We'll go in the morning room.'

Johanna turned back to Selina. 'I'm sorry — you were saying about poor Nina? How does she make herself ill?'

Selina sat down and placed her fingertips together. Why was her solemnity always so comical? Johanna wondered. Selina said, 'I was just trying to describe it for Tony. Nina always does everything to extremes. She finally gave up in despair about breaking up Brookesy's menhir last week — after all this time! Of course, being Cornish workmen, they only turned up one day a month. You'd pass them in the town every day, hanging a gate here, patching an old launder there. "I'm coming up your place tomorrow, milady," they'd cry – and you'd never see the scut of them, as Nina said. Anyway, she got fed up and commanded them to use gunpowder to finish it off quickly. Which they refused. So she found two drunken wretches from Praze-an-Beeble and they offered to do it for her.' Selina broke off and fanned her face. 'My dear – you never saw such a mess! I should think every house in Cross Street either has windows blown in or roof slates smashed. I'm surprised you didn't hear it out at Goldsithney. Now, of course, the air is full of writs for damages and she's taken to her bed.' Selina shook her head and then, before either of them could comment, went on, 'She knows, you see. Part of her is well aware how ... overdone it all is. She stood out on the lawn while it went up. The two oafs were cowering behind the gatepost. I was shivering behind the pillars in the portico. But she just stood there. How she wasn't killed I'll never know. And then there was this *almighty* bang. It ... I mean, people the other end of town ... well, if you've never been near a great explosion like that you've simply no idea! Anyway, while the smoke was clearing, and the sky was full of panic-striken birds – not to mention lumps of falling granite, slates, bits of lawn and maidenhair fern – everything – while all that's going on, she just turns round and laughs. "Isn't that just like me!" she says. So she *knows,* you see. She knows how she overdoes everything.'

Johanna nodded. 'And then, when people find they can't respond – or have different ideas from her – she feels utterly let down and deserted. She didn't really think Hal was wrong for me, you know.' She avoided Tony's eye as she spoke, even though he was actually putting the cordial into her hand at that moment. She murmured her thanks and pretended to be concentrating on not spilling a drop. 'I was writing to him only last night – telling him everything ... the whole truth out at last ...'

'Good!' Tony cut in, handing Selina her glass. 'I'm so glad.'

Johanna still did not look at him. 'And it struck me then. Did you know she once told Hal I was like a cuckoo – the way a baby cuckoo can force parent birds to neglect their own offspring and kill themselves to feed it, instead? I was very hurt, but only for a brief while. I realized it was her way of explaining that almost desperate need *she* feels to grab at people's lives and melt them completely into her own, which is what she tried and failed to do with mine ...'

'... which is what she's done with mine,' Selina echoed dourly. 'And succeeded.'

'It probably suits you,' Johanna told her. 'Otherwise you'd have got out, like me. Anyway, I think you have a marvellous restraining influence on her.'

'Hah! Tell that to the rest of Cross Street!'

'Otherwise why didn't the whole of West Penwith know about this baby the very day after I left Liston Court? I mean, you don't almost claw someone's eyes out one moment and then guard their most shameful secret as if it were your own life the next, do you?'

'You do if you're Nina.' Selina closed her eyes and strained at the effort of trying to explain this paradox. 'You simply cannot apply ordinary ... Try and think of it as if you were a man and she was your lover. Surely you can imagine a woman wanting to tear her lover to shreds but still not giving away his secrets. One is passion, the other would be just petty meanness. Nina can be passionate at the drop of a hat — or even if you just sat there *thinking* about dropping a hat. But you'd wait a century to catch her at something mean.'

Johanna saw the point — except that she wasn't a man and so Nina could not have been her lover; but it seemed pedantic to say as much. Tony thought so, too — she could tell it by the smile on his face when she at last looked at him.

'Cheers,' he toasted them both.

'Oh yes! Your news, poor man! What a selfish pair of cousins we are. Do tell us.'

He turned to Selina. 'Finish your tale first.'

She frowned. 'But I did.'

'Did the blasting powder finally break up ...'

'Oh no!' Selina laughed. 'No, it didn't. I forgot to say that. But it dug a hole so big that Nina just said, "Very well — push it down there and bury it!" We had to laugh.'

'And *that* was when she said wasn't it just like her?'

Selina had to think a moment before she agreed that it was.

Tony turned brightly to Johanna and said, 'Makes a difference, eh?'

'Tell us your news,' she said.

He pulled a face. 'Very dull after all that. The trouble with Cornish miners – from our point of view – is that none of them is employed by the mine owner, as you probably know. They each bid for a section of the lode and then work it on their own account ... you know all about that, do you?'

They both nodded, much as they would if he had tried to tell them how to ruche a collar.

'Sorry! It just seemed so amazing to me.'

'It's the way they've always done it down here. They used to have their own courts, their own laws, their own parliament ... money ... everything. Why is it bad from our point of view?'

'Because there's no association, no miners' lodge, no friendly society ... no banding together of any kind. Each man thinks of himself as a little, independent capitalist. So today's triumph – which is only a very small first step, mind you – is to have persuaded the miners of Breage, the ones who aren't facing transportation, that is, to band together at least to form a medical union. Each man pays in twopence a week, for himself – and wife, if any – plus a halfpenny a head for each child. And for that he gets free doctoring and medicine.'

'But the wonderful thing is,' Selina added, all eager to see Johanna's excitement at the news, 'Tony doesn't have to do any of the organizing – the administration. The miners are managing all that themselves.'

'Are they indeed?' Johanna asked grimly.

Tony merely smiled at her, a maddeningly knowing smile. 'They'll have a jolly good try, anyway,' he said, with exactly the sort of complacency he might have guessed would infuriate her.

'Like they had a jolly good try with the vegetable competition, I suppose? And the bellringers' fund. And the Troon Row pump repair fund. Aaargh!' She clenched her fists and shook them in frustration. 'If only I weren't so busy myself.'

'Yes,' he agreed mildly, topping up her ginger cordial. 'That is a bit of a shame, I must say.'

Chapter Forty-Five

Mrs Pellew of Skewjack Hall looked up from her writing desk, or, rather, her *escritoire,* distracted by the most amazing noise. It sounded like a drunken bugler. Then she saw it was the Rosewarne girl, coming down the hill to take the order for her splendid ale. She smiled. What would that young woman think of next? Still, all power to her. She had a good head on those young shoulders. She must have known about Visick's impending crash and got out in time. And she'd seen through that awful, decadent Irishwoman pretty smartly, too. 'Lady' Nina Brookes, indeed! It was only an Irish peerage. The earldom itself was hardly better than a courtesy title − her father had no seat in the Lords. And what's more, they had no knowledge of true descent. Why, when she had told 'Lady' Nina how the Pellews could trace themselves all the way back to Charlemagne, the impudent woman had just smirked in the most offensive manner. But Miss Rosewarne had not been deceived − so all power to her.

Mrs Pellew of Skewjack Hall was a Modern − in her own quiet, West Country way. She had read Godwin and the Bluestockings and Mary Wollstonecraft − though, being unsure how to pronounce the name, she usually spoke of her as Mary Shelley. She believed in female suffrage for females with more than £1,000 a year (she herself enjoying £1,900), for she considered it monstrous that farmers who doffed hats as her carriage passed by could vote into public office solicitors who bowed and scraped their way out of her home − and then went into the council chamber and decided matters on which she was ten times more competent than they. Apart from anything else, it was a public licence for impertinence. She knew exactly what those farmers and tradespeople were thinking as they fawned in outward respect.

Miss Rosewarne had lately become her ideal type. When one heard of a woman making her own way in the world, one's usual picture was either of some browbeaten governess, who truly did no more than point up woman's subjection, or a vulgar adventuress, trading on her charms. Betwen these two extremes was the sober, workaday world – almost entirely appropriated by men. Yet here came Miss Rosewarne, modest in dress, well spoken, calmly practical, straight as a die, making no strident claims – just simply getting on with it. One needed to look no further than what she had done in a few short months at the Golden Ram to see why she was so worthy of admiration.

Mrs Pellew had not actually visited the place but, judging by what the squire told her, Miss Rosewarne had taken an unremarkable village inn and turned it into a gentleman's eating house of the highest reputation. It had become a virtual dining club for men of quality and distinction throughout West Penwith. Of course, there was gossip; but that was the way of the world. Mrs Pellew refused to credit it. Miss Rosewarne would have nothing to do with *that sort of thing*. She ruled the place like an empress, Pellew said. One dubious gesture, one improper word, and her displeasure was on you like a ton of bricks – his own words for it. She was a modern young lady whose example was well worth encouraging ... in her own quiet, West Country fashion.

Mrs Pellew rose and went downstairs to greet her young heroine in person; she had chanced to be away for each of the last few visits and had missed her demure and straight-forward conversation. She found her folding her order book and tucking the pencil back into its spine; even that was so ladylike – bound in leather and gilded with the name *Vose's Ales* in a most respectable style of lettering. The same legend, she now noticed, was also painted on the side of the gig. Mrs Pellew could not suppress a slight touch of envy. Miss Rosewarne's life must be so full of interest and incident, whereas her own was one long round of duty, obligation, and support, and all for the sake of a man who did not truly appreciate her value to him.

'Good morning, my dear Miss Rosewarne,' she called out gaily. 'You're looking very . . .'

She paused, for she had just noticed that *enceinte* was the only possible word if the sentence was to maintain her reputation for forthright honesty.

'. . . bonny,' she concluded limply. Now she understood why Mrs Jackson, her housekeeper, and all the nearby servants, had been staring at her ever since she entered the yard. They were looking to her for a lead.

Well, she was never one to shirk that responsibility, however painful it might be.

'Why, thank you, Mrs Pellew.' Johanna beamed back at her. 'I'm sorry to have missed you these last few times. But I see the absence has done you nothing but good. These cold autumnal mornings are so invigorating, I find.' She smiled again and, with the observation that there was no rest for the wicked, turned her pony round and prepared to ascend into the driving seat.

'One moment, young . . . lady,' Mrs Pellew called out.

Johanna turned and looked at her — pleasantly enough but with that unblinking gaze that people found so unnerving. The woman's heart fell. She who had once dispersed several dozen riotous miners with no larger sanction than her tongue, found herself unable to ask a simple question like, 'What, pray, is the meaning of appearing at my house in your present condition?'

'I will walk a little way with you, if I may,' she said, cursing her cowardice.

'How pleasant that will be,' Johanna replied.

'Bring my hat and coat,' the woman called over her shoulder. 'And a muff.'

Johanna led the pony; Mrs Pellew walked at her side. 'I cannot help noticing . . .' she began, turning to Johanna with a kindly smile. Those eyes! '. . . er, how partial the squire is to your ale.'

'Vose's Ale.'

'Quite. I was thinking we might increase our order. Slightly, you know. Er — what is it now, may I ask?'

'Two dozen a week.'

'I say, is it really?'

'Shall we make it two and a half then?' Johanna suggested.

'Just over these cold winter months ahead. The squire likes it mulled, with a little cinnamon, you know.'

'And raisins steeped in it the day before.'

'I never tried that for him.' Mrs Pellew wondered how on earth she could break the thread of this absurd conversation.

The maid came up with her outdoor apparel. While the two of them helped her into it, Johanna decided to try something new.

The basilisk stare, she had realized, was a defence of limited duration. It was as a moat to a castle; the first brave person to establish a bridgehead across it would make a highway where a hundred non-swimmers might follow. This short walk, quite alone, with one of the social arbiters of the neighbourhood, seemed as good a time as any to try out her new notion. 'I'm constantly surprised,' she said when the maid had gone, 'at the variety of different ways our customers use our ales, in cooking, you know, and making up their own refreshments. I think I might compile a list of receipts and have them printed up − after the baby's born, of course. I could present them gratis to our most favoured customers − of which you shall be the very first, Mrs Pellew, having half-suggested it to me.'

'Did you say . . . er . . . that is, you would not mention our name in connection with it?' the woman asked, being too flustered by Johanna's calm mention of the baby to take it up at once.

'No, no, of course not. Discretion is our other name.'

Mrs Pellew saw a further chance and, once again, turned away from it. 'I don't know why it is. People have such strange attitudes, don't they. We all enjoy it. It's as old as civilization itself. And yet − to see it in public − I mean, one's name over a receipt using beer, in a public print . . . I don't know . . .'

Johanna thanked her for showing such tactful understanding.

Only later, on her walk back to the Hall, did Mrs Pellew realize why the girl had responded with that slightly odd phrase. They had parted company soon after, and she had

still found herself unable to say a word about her being
apron-up.

'It's an outrage,' she told the squire that night. 'You must
do something about it, Pellew.'

'I agree, my dear.' He smoothed the air about her as if
warming his hands at her anger − all the fury she had been
unable to show at the proper moment. 'But what can I do −
she has broken no law.'

'The brat will be illegitimate, so she must have broken
some law. Ask your court clerk, he'll tell you.'

'Indeed, I shall, my love. And I shall bear his reply back to
you as swift as thought. As always, you know precisely what
to do in all circumstances.'

She knew full well he'd do nothing of the kind; he was
simply burying the subject in a heaping of sugar. 'And at
least you could get Vose to dismiss her. I'm astonished he
hasn't done so.'

'Oh yes! He's very likely to do that! What − kill the goose
that's laying all his golden eggs?'

'But that's only because . . .'

'Permit me to conclude my sentences, my dove? Vose
never made more than the most precarious living out of
those premises − until she came along.'

'Yes, well one hears − I'm sorry − have you quite
finished that sentence?'

'For the moment.'

'You don't wish to interupt me with another − yet again?'

'Not for the moment.'

They were united in a fit of acid smiling.

'I was about to add that one hears *other* explanations for
Vose's sudden launch into opulence. I did not believe a word
of them − until now.'

Their eyes locked.

'All success,' he opined, 'gathers to it a scum of
detractors. Decent people show their contempt by refusing
to credit the scandal of knaves and rascals, who, lacking the
virtue to improve themselves, impute vice to those who have
it abundantly.'

She shooed the words away like a swarm of troublesome
gnats. 'Twist it how you will, the girl is a whore.'

'She is a mother, or mother-to-be, who has the misfortune

not to blessed with a husband to love, honour, *and obey*. That does not make her a whore. Why your own sister . . .'

'That's quite enough of that, Pellew. I'll thank you not to mention Laetitia in the same breath, indeed the same *day,* as the Rosewarne creature. Laetitia stooped to folly, that is true. But she had a wedding ring on her finger before the child was born.'

'By three hours. And Cedric was not the father.'

Mrs Pellew sensed that her husband could devote the rest of the conversation to equally unprofitable genealogies, in both their families, if she persisted in this line. She therefore changed tack. 'And who is the father in this case, I wonder? Does anyone know — including the woman herself?'

'Oh, you may be sure she knows. The candidates are her cousin Terence, and his father, John Visick — on grounds of opportunity. Hannibal Penrose, now in America — on the grounds that they still correspond. That fellow Cunningham — cousin to the Knoxes — for the speed with which he departed these shores. That doctor scoundrel who's bought the old Visick place — because he's a free-thinker and they've been seen together. William Kemp, now in my constabulary, because someone once saw him kiss her. A footman at Liston Court. And sundry persons unknown, in Paris, Vienna, Italy and the Holy Land.'

His wife could not wait to burst in with: 'See! Is that not the very chronicle of a whore? What a catalogue of depravity!'

'The depravity, Mrs Pellew, is in the minds of those who gazette so many candidates as if they had all confessed to it. You, I know, would never stoop to such contemptuous vilification without copper-fastened, triple-proof, aqua regia certainty. And even then, knowing you as I do, I suspect charity might seal your lips.'

'Then who do *you* suppose it to be?' she inquired frostily.

'I am sure it is none of those. And the business — well, that is none of mine.'

'Oh, you are great in Christian charity, Pellew, when your belly is well served! But let us, indeed, talk of the business. Rosewarne is certain to be preached at from the pulpit. Ask yourself this — how can the fine gentlemen — the exemplars of Society to whom the lowliest ragamuffin is taught to look for moral example — how can they escape the preacher's contumely if they persist in gracing her table?'

Pellew shifted uncomfortably. 'It is not her table, it is Vose's.'

'We shall see.' Her smile was filled with righteous satisfaction, for the way forward had just been revealed to her.

'Anyway,' he returned to an earlier thought. 'This is an about-face for you, is it not? I thought Miss Rosewarne was your Ideal Modern Woman — refusing to accept an inferior position while preserving all the attributes of a Lady.'

The smile grew a shade more savage. 'It is quite clear to me that, far from refusing it, she shows every sign of having *enjoyed* an inferior positon while *displaying* all the attributes of a whore!'

The following Sunday, Johanna called at Lanfear House as usual, to collect the Cardew youngsters and bring them to matins; she still worshipped in Breage, preferring to be among people she knew. True, half of them pretended not to know her, and some of the rest were uneasy at giving her a distant nod; but there still remained a goodly sprinkling of friendly faces. On this particular morning, Tony surprised her by expressing a willingness to join them.

'Is this a sign of faith returning?' she asked.

'On the contrary.' He shook his head. 'The bile is in need of a little stirring.'

She laughed. 'You won't find much bile — or much you could call stirring, either — from dear old Canon Pryce.'

But, he insisted on coming nevertheless. Along the way he said, 'If ever you leave the Ram, Jo, you know how welcome you'd be at Lanfear. To say nothing of how sorely needed you are there.'

She darted him a glance of surprise. He had not referred to his feelings — not even as obliquely as that — since . . . she could not remember the last time. The day of the Great Randy, perhaps.

'In connection with the Medical Union,' he added.

'Ah.' She felt an odd sense of let-down — which she at once repented, for if she did not return his feelings, how dared she expect him to go on exposing them, just to please her vanity?

'Your doubts about their ability to organize are proving well founded.'

'I'll see what I can do,' she promised vaguely.

'No, I don't mean that, I mean if you *have* to leave the Ram.'

She laughed. 'It's very kind of you, Tony, but that fear has receded. I had a brief but highly interesting conversation with Mrs Pellew this week. I took a risk and it paid a handsome return. She is very sympathetic to me. I think I shall, after all, weather the storms ahead.' She reached out and gave his hand a grateful touch; but he held on to it briefly, as if it were she who needed the reassurance.

Theirs was the front pew in the south aisle, facing the lady chapel and the perpetual light. It helped to keep the young boys quiet, Johanna had learned; the notion of a light that burned for ever seemed to fascinate them. Then came the usual rituals − which also helped to keep them quiet. First, she made sure that all of them had pennies for the collection plate. Then she gave them spills to mark the hymn pages. And finally she showed them where they'd find the psalms and lessons and collects for the day.

There was a slight rustle of surprise when the processional began and it became clear that Canon Pryce was not officiating today; his place was taken by the Reverend Claude Greep, vicar of St Hilary. It was not the first time Greep had preached here; in fact, in the weeks following the Great Randy, the two vicars had taken turn and turn about in each other's pulpits, as part of the work of reconciliation − even though, as many pointed out, rather self-righteously, at the time, most of the rioters had been chapel folk (or nothing at all), and the gesture was lost on them.

'You'll enjoy this,' she murmured to Peter. 'He's a very powerful preacher. That's why there's such a huge congregation − look, people must have come from miles around.'

Then she noticed that Hilary was staring at the vicar in a peculiarly intense fashion. 'What is it?' she asked her.

But the girl just smiled back, shook her head, and paid him no further heed. Only then did Johanna notice how filthy her ears were; but the service had started by then.

The first intimation that this was not quite the normal

matins came in the second lesson, which should have been taken from Luke 15. Instead, Squire Pellew, who gave the reading (and that was odd, too, because the Pellews always worshipped at Marazion), announced that it was taken from the Second Epistle of Peter (which is appointed to be read just before Christmas).

'They knew you were coming,' Johanna whispered to Peter.

'The Lord knoweth how to deliver the ungodly out of temptations,' Pellew read in his ringing baritone, 'and to reserve the unjust unto the day of judgement to be punished. But chiefly them that walk after the flesh in the lust of uncleanness, and despise government. Presumptuous are they, selfwilled, they are not afraid to speak evil of dignities. But these, as natural brute beasts, made to be taken and destroyed, shall utterly perish in their own corruption. Spots they are, and blemishes, sporting themselves while they feast with you; having eyes full of adultery, and that cannot cease from sin; beguiling unstable souls, an heart they have exercised with covetous practices. Cursed children!' He looked up and stared about the church — at every part of it except the pews in front of the lady chapel. 'Here endeth the lesson,' he snapped.

Tony, the only one who had followed the text in his Bible, whispered, 'The bits he left out are quite interesting.'

'Sssh,' she replied, indicating with her eyes that he shouldn't say that sort of thing in front of the children.

The service then proceeded in its tranquil, age-old majesty until it was time for the sermon. 'My text,' said the Reverend Greep, 'is taken from St Paul's Epistle to the Galatians, Chapter Five, at the Twenty-fourth Verse: *And they that are Christ's have crucified the flesh with passions and lusts.*' He stared around at his temporary flock. It was an old church with stained walls and small windows; in that dim, fitful lighting the guttering pulpit candle struck an almost hypnotic fire into his eyes. 'You may be surprised to see me back here so soon,' he went on. 'But I have had no choice in the matter. I am called here by one in my parish, a notorious and flagrant sinner, who — for reasons that have lately become plain for all to see — will not worship with my flock, but rather comes crawling here to fasten on those in whom ancient friendship and once-deserved sympathy may induce a tolerance.'

For Johanna the world suddenly lost its everyday solidity. Everything around her — the children, Tony, the pews, the pillars, the vaults above — all turned to one seething, shifting sea of fragments. They began to whirl. There was a roaring in her ears. One small focus remained, still and deadly — the pulpit, the candle, and the man. The fragments circled him, rising, rising, falling, falling — yet somehow never moving. If Tony had not linked his arm in hers at that moment, she might easily have passed out. Later, he thought that would have been a mercy.

'Believe me,' Greep continued, 'this is the most distasteful duty a minister may perform. For are we not all sinners? *I come to call the sinner to repentance.* Is it not that call to which we make our Sabbath answer every week? And even if our sin be only in our minds, yet still it is sin. *Whosoever looketh on a woman to lust after her hath committed adultery with her already in his heart.* We are none of us free of that taint. As St Paul also says — and I must echo his words, *I keep my body under and bring it into subjection: lest that by any means, when I have preached to others, I myself should be a castaway.*'

'D'you want to go?' Tony whispered. 'There's no reason why you should stay and put up with this.'

But she was watching Hilary. From where the girl was placed, the pulpit was masked by a pillar. She sat there every Sunday and, normally, did not, by leaning forward or craning her neck, attempt to see the preacher. But now she was doing both. 'It *is,*' she said to herself, but loud enough for several people round to overhear. She turned to Johanna and repeated the words: 'It is.'

A man in the pew behind leaned forward and tapped her angrily on the shoulder with his ear trumpet.

'Sssh,' Johanna told her; she even managed a little smile. The need to shield the children, by not going to pieces in front of them, put some iron into her backbone.

'Let's go,' Tony suggested.

'Not on any account,' she told him. Her heart was fluttering like a minnow and her whole body was shivering, but nothing would now make her leave that place.

He gave her arm an almost desperate squeeze — and then held on to it for the rest of the sermon.

The ear trumpet descended on her shoulder now. She turned and stared the man out. A hundred other eyes were upon her — all hastily averted as she gazed around. At the back she was surprised to see Hamill Oliver, who gave a cheerful wave. Craning her neck she saw Mrs Ramona Troy beside him, determinedly *not* looking her way.

How far and wide the word had spread, she thought. And why had she heard nothing of it? Even Tony had known, else nothing could have dragged him here.

'. . . yet if the sinner repenteth not of her sin,' Greep was saying, 'if the sin be flagrant, and fragrantly flouted . . . that is, flagrantly f-f-f . . . blazoned forth, then it is another matter entirely. The sins we repent, the sins that make us cringe with shame — these we offer up each Sunday in the sure and certain faith that — if our repentance be sincere — then we are washed clean in the Blood of the Lamb. But what of the sinner who revels in her sin, who *flaunts* it' — he found the word at last — 'before the world? What of her? In Biblical times the answer was plain enough. *If this thing be true, and virginity be not found, the men of the city shall stone her with stones that she die. So shalt thou put evil away from among you.* But we who live in more clement times have to seek God's will in more merciful ways. For, since those early days when God gave us His Word in Deuteronomy, He has sent us His Son with a later message of hope. "Come unto me," He tells us. "Say with Job, *I abhor myself and repent in dust and ashes,* and I will wash away your sin." He offers us a new chance. But for those who do not take that chance, the ancient wrath is ever near. *I gave her space to repent of her fornication and she repented not. Behold, I will cast them that commit adultery with her into great tribulation. And I will kill her children with death.*' He paused to let the awful message sink in.

Hilary turned to Johanna; she had not looked so troubled since the night they found her. She raised her eyebrows in some obscure query but Johanna shook her head and smiled.

'But we cannot leave it all to God.' The sermon ground remorselessly on. 'He requires it of us to stand up and be numbered, too. And no matter where you seek among His Words, you will find the message writ plain. *Hate the whore and make her desolate and naked.* So that perdition may *eat her flesh and burn her with fire.* Lo, see here where she sits in all her vanity and pride!'

He was the only one who did not turn his face toward her. 'But let her know that *pride goeth before destruction and an haughty spirit before a fall.* And let her remember that *those that walk in pride He is able to abase. For a bastard shall not enter into the congregation of the Lord – even unto the tenth generation he shall not enter.* Such, dear brethren, is the detestation of the Lord for harlots like her. For *when lust hath conceived, it bringeth forth sin; and sin, when it is finished, it bringeth forth death!'* He nodded with vigour, assuring them that all this was indeed so. The candlelight danced in his eyes and no one could now turn from him.

'For these harlots,' – his voice fell almost to a whisper – 'for the fragrant . . . the flagrant ones who know not how to repent – there can be no mercy. There must be no mercy – not among us. Mercy is the prerogative of the Lord; it is not ours to usurp. There is nothing godly which men cannot corrupt. We usurp His mercy and we corrupt it to mere tolerance. We tolerate the harlot and we lay the foundations of a new Babylon. But *Babylon is fallen, is fallen, that great city, because she made all nations drink the wine of her fornication.'*

Hilary leaned across Tony and tapped Johanna on the knee. 'Lend I five shillings?' she whispered.

'What for?'

The girl's eyes begged her mutely to comply, to ask no questions.

Johanna shook her head and returned her steady gaze to the pulpit. Her panic was now yielding to an odd kind of exhilaration. She knew that the entire congregation was willing her to break down, to wail out her penitence, confess her shame, abase herself before them. But the more she felt the press of so many wills, the stronger she grew in resistance to it.

Unseen by her, Tony slipped a pair of half-crowns into Hilary's gloved hand.

'The choice is stark indeed,' Greep told them, 'but we may

not shirk it. *Shall I then take the members of Christ and make them members of an harlot? God forbid!* He gave a triumphant smile as he echoed the words: 'God' — his finger stabbed at the air before him until every member of that congregation felt its point — 'forbid! God forbid! St Paul's words, not mine. God's Words, my brethren. You may choose to be of the party of Christ, or you may choose the party of the harlot — but between the two is fixed a gulf that all humanity cannot bridge.'

Hilary rose to her feet.

'No!' Johanna said and clutched at her skirt — but she had already passed out of reach. 'Hilary — don't,' she called after her, though she had no inkling of what she was trying to forbid.

The girl did not even turn round.

Greep must have supposed he had at last provoked his victim to some action. He fixed a grim smile to his lips and pointedly refused to turn his head toward the source of this commotion. *'Hate the whore!'* He repeated his earlier quotation. *'Make her desolate and naked!* Let perdition ...' His voice tailed off as he saw it was not the abstract whore of his sermon now approaching him but one of that sisterhood whom he had far less scriptural cause to recognize. 'Let perdition ...' he murmured. But he had lost his thread just as surely as he had lost his audience, for now all eyes were fastened on this least expected sight of all — a young stranger, walking calmly toward the pulpit.

Johanna rose to go to her assistance, but Tony barred her way. 'Have faith,' he advised her urgently. With great reluctance she complied — not that she had much choice, for the other end of the pew was plastered into the wall.

Hilary was known by sight to many in that congregation. Some knew her as an orphan of the Great Randy. But one alone knew what three days in Paradise Row had made her — the one who now stared in horror from the pulpit, as a murderer might stare at the ghost of his victim if it rose to haunt him in court.

She arrived at the foot of the pulpit.

He leaned over and whispered, 'I did not mean *you.*'

But oratory was in his blood. That whisper died among the farthest rafters of the belfry.

Hilary stared at him a moment and then, as deliberately as if it were part of the morning's ritual, dropped one half-crown at the foot of the stairs. Then a second.

And then, with the same slow dignity, she turned and glided back to her pew.

Greep shuffled his notes. 'We conclude then ...' The ringing tone had deserted him. 'That is, I conclude, as I began, with the words of our beloved Paul. *Lest when I come again my God* — *"come among you again*," he means. He writes to the Corinthians but here I apply it to you. To us.' His conclusion was one long gabble: '*Lest when I come among you again my God will humble me and that I shall yet again be called upon to bewail one which has sinned already and has not repented of her uncleanness and fornication and lasciviousness* which she has committed and now we shall sing hymn number five hundred and twenty-nine ...'

Somewhere out of sight, over in the south chancel, the bellows lad leaped to his feet and began cranking his pole as if salvation depended on it. The organist tried a note but it subsided; he had to wait for more wind.

Half the congregation rose; the rest waited for the blessing — then, seeing the half that rose, joined them ... only to find that they, seeing their fellows still seated, resumed their places, too.

Greep was also playing jack-in-a-box. Half way down the pulpit steps he saw the silver coins, lying where Hilary had dropped them. He shrank back, and then remembered that he had not given the blessing. He returned to the top and went through the motion: 'And now unto God the Father ...'

It gave him the necessary time to gather himself and collect his shaken forces, so that when he next descended the steps he was able to ignore the coins that lay there.

During the hymn the collection was taken. The sidesman, Gerald Loy, broke with his usual practice and walked along the aisle in front of the foremost pew, presenting the plate to each worshipper in person. It soon became clear why. Tony refused to contribute so much as a penny. Johanna put in her usual sixpence. Mr Loy, whom she had counted as her friend these ten years and more, pointedly removed it from the plate and handed it back to her; he saw the pain in her

502

eyes and he flinched from it. But he moved on inexorably, until the plate was handed into the row behind. Only then did he return to the aisle. 'Why?' she murmured at him as he passed, but she might as well have saved her breath.

She turned to let Tony know she wanted to leave, only to find him already bustling the youngsters from the pew. As he helped her out he noticed she still held the sixpence in her hand. He took it from her and flung it at the pulpit steps, where it briefly sang like an angel before it curled up beside Hilary's weightier accusations.

On their way out all eyes were upon her — except those particular eyes she happened to fix with her own; they deliberately turned away.

As she drew near the porch she saw that Hamill Oliver was having a tussle with his grandmother, who would not let him past her into the aisle. When he saw Johanna, he leaped up on the pews and strode across their tops, creating a sensation among the worshippers in front.

'Can't bear the stench here a minute longer,' he called out cheerily as he leaped down into the aisle. 'One dead lily reeks worse than a whole field of dead weeds, what?'

When he saw his humour did not work, for Johanna remained as ashen and shivery as ever, he turned and bellowed at the congregation at large: 'Whited sepulchres! God is not mocked!'

The verger collected the burliest sidesmen and advanced upon him, but by the time they slammed the door he was outside, following the little group of outcasts down the path. 'Miss Rosewarne!' he called.

She turned round. 'Go back in, Mr Oliver. Make your peace as best you can with your grandmother. The last thing I want is to bring division among families. You, too, Tony, my dear. I'll never forget your support, but take the children back inside. You must have no quarrel with those people — nor must the children.'

The two men ignored her pleas; the children, taking cue from them, held their ground, too.

Hamill walked straight up to Hilary and clapped her on both shoulders. 'Young lady,' he said, 'I do not have the privilege of knowing you but I salute you from the bottom of my heart. What you did there was magnificent. No, no!

503

Pray do not explain it. The entire action was so complete in itself — like good wine it needs no bush.' He pointed his face at the sky, from which a gentle rain had now begun to fall. 'Oh,' he cried. 'At last I feel the presence of God. He must be wondering how to wash that vile mass of . . .'

'Mr Oliver!' Johanna called sharply. 'Stop it this minute! They are good people in there. Good friends to me. They are misguided and bewildered at the moment. Most of them don't know *what* to think. And I *have* done wrong — at least in their eyes. I knew that when I took the risk. I did not ever imagine it would come to this — and I still don't understand why it has. But I must now live with it. And, as I told you, I shall be mortified if you let it make a rift between you and your family. Or' — she turned to Tony — 'between you and this village.'

He smiled placidly. 'How many people . . . here, let's get out of this rain.'

They all crowded under the canopy of the gig. The hymn slowly wound its way through the final verse.

'How many people were there actually from this village?' Tony took up his deferred question. 'I didn't count more than twenty. Not a single member of my Medical Union, either.'

'I invite you all back to luncheon at Wheal Leander,' Hamill said grandly. 'If you, in turn, will invite me to share your gig. I doubt if my grandmother's carriage any longer holds a place for me.'

'I shall lunch at the Ram, as usual,' Johanna said firmly. 'Hilary, is there the makings of a meal in the pantry at home?'

'Yes, ma'am.'

'Then — after you've given your ears a wash — you children and the doctor will eat there.' She heard Tony drawing breath to protest. 'Yes!' she insisted. 'This has changed everything.' She nodded her head toward the church, where the concluding organ voluntary had just begun.

'Not here.' He touched his breast. 'It has changed nothing here.'

Hamill looked at him sharply, then at her.

'I have to see Charley Vose before news of this reaches him.'

504

Tony was wavering.

She persisted. 'I'm fighting for something very important to me. You know that.'

'You have allies, too.' His glance took in Hamill Oliver.

'I can't forget it.' She sighed. 'But this will be between me and Charley Vose. And there you cannot help me.'

Indeed, who can? she wondered as the congregation began to emerge and she clucked the pony into motion.

Chapter Forty-Six

The small pile of luggage, all her wordly possessions lying heaped against the passage wall, confirmed her worst fears. It had been stacked between the kitchen door and the yard, as close to the outside as possible without actually exposing it to the rain. Johanna walked in, straight past it.

Rose Davey came to the kitchen door, wiping her hands nervously into her apron. 'He don't want to see 'ee,' she warned.

'I'm sure he doesn't!' She strode on without a pause. 'Is he in his room?'

Rose wouldn't reply out loud. Johanna turned and saw her pointing to the cellar door; the tittle-tattle finger then rose to her lips in a mime of *hush*. Johanna nodded.

She gently pushed open the door and saw a dim light flickering against the wall at the foot of the steps; Charley must be working at the farther end of the cellar. She gathered up her skirts and, holding them close to her, clear of the wall, and keeping as near the edge as possible to reduce the risk of a creak from one of the treads, she reached the bottom without alerting him. The cloying reek of his saliva-soused cheroot was everywhere.

He was pretending to check the stock – a task he had completed in earnest only the week before. Her spirit rose in nauseated contempt. Slowly she wound her way among the cobwebby wine racks and casks of ale, feeling ahead for debris whose shifting might give her away. At last she stood not four paces from him, in full view if he cared to glance her way; but all his attention was on the floor overhead. He would begin a count of the bottles in one rack, then, hearing a footfall in the passageway above, he would freeze, staring at the beams and ceiling boards as if they might turn transparent and reveal her.

'Did you suppose I'd walk off with a dozen of your finest claret, Vose?' she inquired calmly, making him jump out of his boots. The cheroot fell from his mouth but clung like a dark brown slug to his chin.

'Why damn 'ee, maid,' he complained as he stuffed it back. 'You'll put I up the infirmary.'

'What is the meaning of throwing out my things like that?' she snapped. 'You try that just once again and I'm warning you now — I'll leave you.'

The effrontery of the threat took him aback for a moment, long enough for her to follow up with, 'And if you suppose you can manage this place without me, then you're even more witless than this little game with my luggage makes you appear.'

He made several vaguely pugilistic gestures — shakes of the head and so on — like a wary sparring partner. 'I shall just have to find someone, shan't I.'

'Someone who'll tolerate you! And d'you imagine we grow on trees?'

He poured himself a whisky, or, to judge from the level in the bottle, another whisky. ''Tin't you made this place what he is,' he grumbled. ''Tis Widow Jewell, if you want to know. You think all they high-quarter folk do come here for the sake of your *consommy dew jewer* and your *tureen der vernaison,* do 'ee?' He laughed, shaking himself with a number of single-shoulder shrugs, now the left, now the right — again like a boxer wasting time.

'They come because what I have done here at the Ram provides them with a cloak of respectability for a subsequent visit across the garden.'

'Respectability, is it! Well, where's that to now, then? *That* cloak is shot full o' holes.'

'By a parson who is himself, and quite obviously, no stranger to Paradise Row. Is that the sort of man Charley Vose allows to run his affairs for him nowadays? Weekdays for wenching and Sundays for sermons.'

''Tin't just he, maid.'

'Who stole your backbone, Vose, or did you never get one? Doesn't it sicken you, man?'

''Tis all our customers, see?'

'The one thing I've always admired about you — just about the only thing, in fact — is your contempt for hypocrisy. You never made any secret of what you're ...'

'Even Squire Pellew, now — and he's a champion to you, or was — but even he said he'd have to stop his visiting here.'

She stared at him in astonishment. 'I don't believe it.'

''Tis true. He come here.'

'I simply don't believe it. I even spoke with Mrs Pellew on the matter. She seemed to me most understanding.'

Charley was shaking his head. ''Tis on account of his wife, see. He says for his self he wouldn't worry overmuch, but for he to frequent the house of a notorious woman — that's what he called 'ee, a notorious woman — would be rubbing the dirt off on Mrs Pellew. And he couldn't allow that.'

'He can't have meant me,' she said. 'Notorious woman? That can't be meant for me.' But she could hear her voice fighting to maintain its conviction, for she had just remembered the relish with which he had read the lesson. 'He can only have meant Mrs Jewell.'

Charley leaped in upon the ground her hesitation had yielded. 'Mrs Jewell, is it? I never yet heard no sermon preached against *she*. And if one of her young pretties do get theirselves belly-up, they don't go flaunting the fact round ten parishes — blowing bugles and saying there's no rest for the wicked.' He sized her up with his beady little eyes before he risked adding, 'And doing men's work.'

She knew then that she had lost. Something he had said ... she couldn't put her finger on it yet, but something he had said was the death knell of her ambitions. She fought on, but only because yielding was not in her blood.

'Yes! There we have it,' she cried. 'Mrs Jewell and all her "little pretties" *are*, of course, doing woman's work, aren't they! Yet I'm the one who's preached at as a whore. I who have lain with but one man in my life — and would not for the life of me lie with another while he lives — I am the whore. But that's just a cloak. That's a gift from me to them. My real sin is that I'm out there every afternoon, doing what would normally be done by a man. Isn't that the top and bottom of it?'

'You're as well able to fathom it as me, Miss Rosewarne. I got no choice in the matter. You stay on here and I might just as well turn off all the new staff we took on — and tell the Widow to cut back to just herself and two pretties. Now you do know I can't do that.'

'Why not? You'd still have the brewing business. That'll make you far more money.'

'I don't want 'n, maid. That's my whole point now. I never wanted 'n. You astonished me with 'n, and I went along, but I never wanted 'n, and that's a fact.'

'I don't need to go out and about any more, if that's what's worrying you. I was going to suggest this anyway. Put a couple of good men out on the road each day.'

'I don't want 'n.'

'Your trade could expand tenfold this year. I'll stay here — never even show my face, if that'll suit you — and manage ...'

'I don't want 'n, I tell 'ee.'

'Will you stop saying that. How can you not want it? You could have an income of several thousand a year.'

'There's better things than ...'

'You have the knack of brewing the best ale that's ever been known in these parts. Or in living memory, anyway. And the time was never better.'

'I aren't interested, maid. You got me rising at six of a morning and I got yeast rising, eleven at night. I never wanted no ...'

'Then train someone up to it. Train the lad.'

'I don't want none of it. And that's all about it. I'm happy with the Ram and I'm happy with Paradise Row. I never wanted more. Brewery! That's your idea, not mine. Well you're welcome to 'n, and good riddance.' His words stirred some of his old instinctive cunning, for he was always the soul of generosity with anything he did not himself require. 'Take the trade,' he urged. 'I shan't grumble. You talk of knack. There's no knack to brewing. Good hops, good malt, good yeast for the flavour, and good water – and keep 'n all good and clean. That's all the knack there is to it.'

A sudden weariness overwhelmed her. She covered the few paces that separated them, picked up the whisky bottle, and refilled his glass. 'Go on then,' she said, handing it to him. 'Stick where you are – which is nowhere. You think that all you need do is get rid of me, and then everything here will just go on running like clockwork. You can spend your days down here at the Ram, drinking and gossiping, and your nights up there in Paradise Row.'

''Es! And a bloody good life, too. So there – put that in your pipe and smoke it.'

She stood her ground and stared at him.

'Well, I don't see nothing wrong with it,' he muttered.

'No, of course you don't – that's the sort of man you are. You can't see beyond the end of your nose – even when you cut it off to spite your face. But let me tell you – because I'm the only person hereabouts who can see beyond the middle of next week – a year from now, d'you know where you'll be living?'

'Here.' He asserted.

She snatched up the whisky bottle and pointed her finger half an inch from its bottom. 'Here,' she said.

She turned and took two paces back into the dark. 'This is your last chance, Vose,' she said, not turning round as yet. 'If I go up those stairs, and no word to the contrary from you, then I go on walking – out the door, out of the Ram – out of your life.'

He stopped breathing; that gurgling wheeze was stilled while one kind of self-interest wrestled with another. She turned and faced him. Even as she did so, she felt it might have been a mistake. From what slender threads of chance are our lives suspended! If she had not turned, he might have relented, she would have stayed at the Ram, working out of public gaze until the next nine-day (or nine-month) wonder caused memories to fade ... some compromise would have been worked out and her life would have gone on more or less as she had planned it.

But she turned and faced him. By that she offered him one grain of challenge more than he could swallow, and he choked on it. He told her she could walk off the edge of the world for all he cared. And from that moment on nothing could ever again be as she had planned it.

As she passed the kitchen door Rose came out, eyebrows arched, the very picture of worry and suspense. Johanna threw her arms about her and hugged her. 'Goodbye, Rose dear,' she murmured. 'I'm bound away.'

'Why' — the cook was almost in tears — 'see how you'm shivering, poor mite! Tell 'ee what — work up a tear or two and go down on your bended knees. He can't never say no to that. Soft as a brush, he is.'

'But this trembling is not sorrow!' Johanna pulled away from her. 'It's anger, Rose. I have never been so indignant and resentful and enraged in all my days. If that ... that ... toad down there was to go down on *his* bended knees and weep an *ocean* of tears, I would not come back. Tell him I'll send for my things.' She turned to go but then hesitated. 'I am sorry to leave you, though. If you'll harken to me, you'll get out while this place still has reputation enough to carry you to a good position elsewhere.'

The woman just gave her a sad smile, admitting both the wisdom of the advice and the impossibility of accepting it.

Johanna walked out into the yard and round the back of the inn, past the stables and brewhouses, to the exit gate. There she gazed right and left, up and down the village street. Which way to go? All the roads in the world were now equally open to her — and equally empty, too. The baby made a couple of painful readjustments — painful, that is, to her. The alarms and excursions of this day were not to its liking.

'Take the gig, woman,' Charley Vose shouted at her from the middle of the yard behind.

'I wouldn't take your gig if ...' She sought for an image but gave up. No condition was extreme enough to mention in the same breath as her refusal.

Only then did she notice how heavy the rain had become. In a few minutes she'd be soaked to the skin.

'At least take they.'

She turned and was almost bowled over by a great heavy

511

mackintosh and an oilskin hat such as fishermen wear.
'You want boots, do 'ee?' Charley added, hefting them to
toss after the clothing.

'No thank you,' she called back as she struggled into the
coat. 'I've got a good pair up.'

It was not the heroic sort of exchange on which life-
hinging partings are usually made; but the clerk of the
weather wanted the last laugh that day.

Once again she faced the choice − right or left. To the
right lay Penzance, with branches off to the Falmouth
Packet or the Coach and Horses. She could put up at either
inn, at least until this rain passed over. She had money
enough not to worry for a bit, anyway.

To the left lay Helston, with branches off right to
Lanfear and Breage, and, left again and much father on, to
Wheal Leander.

She ought to go to Tony at Lanfear; that was the obvious
thing. Her time was near − another month at the most −
and, as she had said, she owed it to the child if not to
herself to accept the best medical care she could get. Yes,
she decided; she'd go back to Lanfear.

A closed Stanhope came over the brow of the hill from
her right. Well, here was a stroke of luck, indeed, for it
belonged to Squire Pellew. Of course! It was Sunday, she
realized. How could she have forgotten that! On Sundays,
after a heavy morning in church, he almost always
dropped down for a rum toddy and an hour or two with
the nymphs of Paradise Row; he'd surely let his coachman
take her on to Lanfear, especially on such a day as this.
She went and stood beneath the front porch, where he
would soon alight.

As the coach drew up, she stepped forward and opened
his carriage door. 'Good day to you, Squire.' she called out
merrily. 'What inclement weather it is, to be sure.'

He climbed down ... and stared right through her.
'Must get this door seen to, Jenkins.' he said conversation-
ally. 'The fucking thing opens itself.'

'Indeed, sir,' Jenkins said imperturbably.

'Squire!' The shocking word hit her like a steam hammer.
She drew off the oilskin hat. 'Do you not recognize me?
Johanna Rosewarne.'

'Throw something over the horse and then you may have your usual quart of Vose's stingo.'

'Oh,' Johanna cut in. 'I was rather hoping he'd take me on to Lanfear ...'

Her voice petered out as the squire turned on his heel and went indoors. She turned in amazement to the coachman, Jenkins, whom she had known for years — long before his present employment. He checked nervously to see that the door to the Ram had been well and truly slammed before he muttered, 'That's the way of it now, my lover. I'm sorry and all, but that's the way of it.'

He pulled out a ragged piece of tarpaulin and threw it over the horse.

She went forward and caught his arm. 'But you know what he's gone in there for. How dare he!'

She stared around at the sky, the houses, the muddy pools underfoot — as if, somewhere in all that mire, she would surely find words strong enough, foul enough, to express her outrage.

'That word he used,' she went on. 'How dare he use that — as if I weren't there?'

'That's what he was a telling of 'ee, Miss.'

'Dear God! I shall just go in there and put all ten commandments on him — then let him tell me I'm not there!'

'I shouldn't do that, miss. He is chairman of the bench.'

'Aaaargh!' In her rage she grasped the upright of the porch and shook it mightily. An extra shower of rain-drops was all her reward. 'Well I won't stoop to his vile level, but if I did, I'd say *that-word* all of them. The hypocrisy of it! The vile, stinking hypocrisy. You tell him that!'

And before her fury could reduce her to tears, which he would surely misinterpret, she stumped off into the rain. She had barely reached the edge of the village, though, before she realized that, whatever she might or might not owe the child, she certainly owed it to Tony to stay as far from him as possible, at least for the immediate future. This absurd fuss would die down. It always did. Look at Joan Ninian — after nine officers of the Duke of Cornwall's had sworn on oath that they'd all enjoyed her carnally before she married that captain. That had been a far greater scandal than this could ever be. Yet now she was back in good society again. So of course it would blow over, in time. But meanwhile the work Tony was doing was far too valuable to be muddied up with a scandal like this.

She decided to go to Helston, to see Terence.

She could not put Squire Pellew out of her mind. This canting morality that allowed such gentlemen to take their pleasures in Paradise Row, and yet conspire to have her dismissed, was beyond all enduring. Even the man who had slandered her from the pulpit was part of it. She indulged herself in fantasies of impossible revenge. She would collect duly sworn affidavits from Widow Jewell's girls, or from those who had tried the work there and found they couldn't tolerate it (for Hilary had been by no means the only one); she would compile a list of all those fine, upstanding gentlemen and take it to the police.

No, the fine upstanding gentlemen had broken no law — naturally, since it was other fine upstanding gentlemen who had framed the law with such care in the first place.

Take it to the newspapers.

They wouldn't print it. Who, after all were their shareholders, their patrons, their advertisers — the fine upstanding gentlemen.

But surely if their womenfolk knew ...?

Reluctantly she had to admit that the womenfolk did know. Looking at most of those men, what sensible wife would wish for any one of them even to come near her, pawing over her body, risking her life yet again in a fifth ... sixth ... seventh child. They did not simply tolerate the system; they caused it. Behind their public prayers for morality they must offer up secret thanks that such houses and women existed.

She could stand up and read out her list in church. No, she'd be pounced on by vergers, sexton, sidesmen — indeed, by every fine upstanding gentleman in the place. And she'd be brought up in court for disturbing the peace.

At least she'd have her day in the dock. Evidence from the dock was privileged. Her heart leaped up as she pictured it. Name after scandalous name placed in the public record. The dumbfounded magistrates – Pellew among them. The embarrassed lawyers. The sensation among the public. People running out into the streets, shouting 'Amazing revelations! Come and hear this!'

But it wouldn't be like that. 'The accused female then attempted to recite an adumbration of eminent personages whom, she alleged, had at some time essayed the patronage of the demimonde. It would ill become this reputable organ to compound her calumny by even the most partial or selective repetition of her attempted defamation.' Thus would they boil it down – hardly a report to set West Penwith alight!

Was a sermon privileged, though, she wondered? Had she civil cause to pursue the Reverend Greep through the courts? Now that would be worth looking into.

It was then that she recalled what Charley Vose had said: 'Widow Jewell's pretties – when they get belly-up, they don't go blowing a bugle around ten parishes and saying no rest for the wicked.' Something like that. It suddenly struck her that the only place she had said 'No rest for the wicked' was in the back yard at Skewjack Hall. She had meant it in the conventional way; only after the words had escaped her lips did she realize how inappropriate – or too appropriate – they were to her condition. After that she had been careful not to repeat the blunder.

So who had heard her say it? The housekeeper, the stable lad, one of the maids – and Mrs Pellew herself. And which of them was most likely to have passed it on in such a form that Charley Vose would trot it out like that? The betting was a thousand to one bar one: Mrs Pellew – who never had a word for her that wasn't kindness itself. Mrs Pellew, the champion of the Modern Woman. Ought she not to know what her husband was doing, probably at this very minute?

It was one of those rare questions that combined duty and pleasure in a single answer. Skewjack Hall was only a mile or so off the road. She thought it worth the detour, even in such foul weather as this, just to see the woman's face. The turning was, in fact, within sight.

But when she had covered about half the distance a

carriage came round the bend behind her and slowed down to offer her a lift. She realized that Mrs Pellew would have to wait. When the vehicle drew level, the window went down and a voice Johanna recognized as that of Mrs Wellbeck, a friend of Nina's, called out, 'I say, do you require ...' And then she saw the object of her intended charity. 'Oh,' she said.

'I quite understand, Mrs Wellbeck,' Johanna assured her. 'Do close your window or you'll catch something dreadful, I'm sure.'

The poor woman was racked with doubt. She poked her head out and glanced fearfully up and down the highway. Another carriage was coming, from the direction of Godolphin. Johanna spared her further embarrassment by turning on her heel and resuming her long trudge through the mud and carriage ruts to Helston. 'Pass by on the other side,' she called over her shoulder.

The window went up with a bang and she heard the furious rap-rap of the signal hammer beneath the driver's seat. Mrs Wellbeck sailed by without a sideways glance. What had all her sweetness and smiles and apparent friendship ever amounted to? Johanna now wondered. It was the same as with Mrs Pellew. Well, if she desired a world without hypocrisy, she had certainly achieved some part of that dream today!

The carriage from Godolphin went by; it was no one she recognized, but the driver called out a cheery greeting and added the uplifting news that, in his opinion, worse weather was on the way.

When she reached the turn to Skewjack, she felt herself overcome by a powerful reluctance to turn aside. It was stupid to stay out in this weather a minute longer than necessary. Already she was sticky-damp all over – more from perspiration trapped inside the coat than from any rain that might have penetrated it, but still, wet was wet.

There was another mild protest from the baby, and that decided her. She would stay on the Helston road – and hope for someone who hadn't heard of her disgrace to come by. As she set off once more it suddenly struck her that she had walked past Sunny Corner without so much as a glance in its direction – nor had it raised even one of the many thoughts it might have invoked. What had blotted it out? Dreams of revenge. The impression of them now came back to warm her. There had been one in particular ...

Ah, yes – could she sue the parson for what he had said?

She was so deep in the pleasurable contemplation of this peculiarly apt form of retribution that she walked up Tregembo Hill without a single thought for the Great Randy, either. She was just passing the gate to Sunrise Farm, still lost in her reverie, when a voice behind her made her jump with fright. It said, 'What a werry inconsiderate day it is to be sure, young lady.' In the same moment, as if his voice had conjured them out of the air, she also heard a great rumbling of cartwheels and the steady plod of horse hooves in the mud.

She turned, and for a moment she felt sure she had somehow slipped into a world of total fantasy. For there, instead of the expected wagon and the clodhopping shires to pull it, was what looked like a giant snail shell on wheels being pulled by two pure white chargers, straight out of some fairy tale.

She peered at it and saw it was, indeed, a giant snail shell on wheels – glistening blue and green and gold in the rain. The opening of the shell flared out toward the front, creating a platform on which was bolted a temporary driver's seat. And there sat a grinning fellow – young, or middle-aged, or old, it was hard to tell – saying, 'Well, d'you want a lift or don't you?'

'Oh yes please sir,' she told him and turned to mount as swiftly as she could.

When he realized what condition she was in he became all apologetic and leaped down to help her. 'Go within, do,' he told her, with a nod toward the snail shell. 'My wife will settle you comfortably. Lord, who'd send you out on such a day as this!'

She saw iridescent white puddles forming beneath the wagon and realized that it was some kind of paint being washed off the horses' coats. He saw she had spotted it and laughed as he opened the door for her. 'Yeah,' he commented in disgust. 'I need hardly have bothered, need I!'

A buxom young woman stared up in surprise as daylight flooded the windowless interior. 'Mrs Snell, my love,' he called to her. 'Here's a poor young gel in an awkward way.' He turned to Johanna. 'Going to Helston are you, my dear?'

'I am, sir, and I'd thank you for ...'

'Say no more.' He bundled her inside almost brusquely. 'Say no more. You have met with the right *ekiparge*.' There was a strange odour inside the place. It reminded Johanna of something but she could not remember what.

'Sit down, my dear. Oh, my poor dove, you must be perished.' Mrs Snell led her to what seemed to be the only chair. The moment she was safely ensconced, the door slammed and they were plunged into absolute darkness.

'I'll soon get us some light, don't fret.' The woman was just a foot or so to her left.

She opened the latch on a little stove; its dull embers threw a narrow red glow upon the floor. But the paper spill she eventually persuaded to take fire revealed an Aladdin's cave of delights. Its flame, transferred to the wick of the lamp, kindled a sense of warmth that the stove had failed to impart.

'I usually travels in the dark,' she explained, as if apologizing. 'To save the oil, you see.'

'Oh, but I'll gladly pay you for your trouble,' Johanna assured her. 'Believe me, I am by no means penniless.'

The woman laughed and patted her on the shoulders. 'Snell would never hear of it — and no more would I. Say no more. My word, but you must be soused. Why don't you get out of that coat and I'll stoke up the fire ...'

'Oh please no, not on my account.'

'What?' The word was almost a challenge. 'I'm glad of the chance, I tell you. And as for saving oil — that's only what I say. To gain the merit of being thrifty, see, when the truth is I've seen more of the inside of this thing than I ever want to remember.'

All the while she spoke she was poking fresh twigs into the stove, making it flare up; all it did, though, was belch smoke into the room itself. 'Ooops!' she cried and pulled out the damper. 'I allus forgets that.' From then on it burned brightly and soon began to throw out a welcome heat.

'Are you from London?' Johanna asked. 'My name, by the way, is Johanna Rosewarne.'

'Pleased to meetcha I'm sure. We're Snell, like you heard. John Snell and Jemima Snell. Which side was you walking?'

Johanna nodded her head towards the wall behind her.

'Ah. If you'd been on the other side, you'd have seen we calls ourselves "Snail." 'Tis but a short hop from Snell to Snail, Snell allus says. And since a snail can't hop, the Snells must. Yes – *Snail's Happy Families*. That's us. Would you like to see all our little ones?'

Johanna stared about them, wondering where in so confined a space they could hide one child, let alone a family.

Laughing, Mrs Snell rose to her feet and, carrying the lamp, squeezed behind her to what Johanna had taken to be a table covered with a large cloth of green baize. But when this was pulled aside she saw a cage filled with a number of startled animals – a cat, a small dog, a monkey, several mice, a guinea pig, a pair of rabbits, three canaries, and a jackdaw. ''Ello darling,' cried the jackdaw. 'My what a face!'

The creatures soon overcame their astonishment and settled back to sleep out the journey in one big heap. That was the strange smell, of course; and then she remembered where she had sensed it before – in the menagerie on the night of the Harvest Fair when she had fallen in love with Hal. Now it brought everything back to her in that immediate, visceral way that only the sense of smell can achieve. She almost broke down at the power and the suddenness of it.

'Snell's got 'em trained up to all sorts,' his wife was explaining. 'The cat marries the dog and the parson's the monkey, with the guinea pig for bridesmaid and the rabbit for best man. And the budgies fight a duel and one of them dies and the monkey puts it in a coffin and buries it. And it don't move. You can't hardly see it breathe, poor mite. It's marvellous – first hundred times you see it, anyway,' she added with a heavy sniff.

'Amazing,' Johanna agreed. 'Have you ever thought of doing the same miracle with a cage full of people?'

Mrs Snell laughed as if it were the funniest thing she'd heard in years. Then, as she wiped her eyes, she said, 'Still — I know what happy family I'd choose — if the choice was ever offered, that is.' And her hand stole out and gently touched the swelling of Johanna's abdomen. 'Not long now, is it?' she asked wistfully.

Chapter Forty-Seven

Terence was a long time answering Johanna's knock at his door. When he finally opened up, he just stood there – in clothes that had obviously been thrown on in some haste – staring at her through one bleary eye; then he said, 'Oh, you!' and slumped against the wall. 'I suppose you wish to come in.'

'Not if it's inconvenient. I mean if you have . . . a caller?'

He opened both eyes and then grinned at her. 'Well I do now.' He made an exaggeratedly heroic effort to collect himself. 'Come in. Don't mind the mess.' He relieved her of her raincoat as she passed.

'Well, only for a cup of tea or something. I haven't had a bite since breakfast but I'm past all hunger now. Did you hear what happened this morning?'

She found an old rag – part of his once-best shirt, she realized when she examined it more closely – and wiped a chair seat clean enough to allow her to sit down.

'Oh good,' he commented. 'I've been searching everywhere for a duster like that. Aren't you clever. Tell me what happened this morning. I've been conscious of nothing since the small hours. When you say 'tea or something' would gin count?'

'No. Never mind. A glass of water will do.'

'No no no. I can make tea. It's just so boring, that's all.' He went out into the passage and filled his kettle at the tap. 'Poke a bit of life into that fire, will you?'

She was surprised to find the embers still glowing brightly, so someone had tended the stove quite recently – within the past three hours, anyway. 'I was named from the pulpit this

521

morning,' she told him. 'Or rather, the man made it so clear who he meant, he didn't actually need to say my name.'

'What?' Terence returned with the kettle. 'Old Canon Pryce?' he asked in amazement.

'No. The Greep from St Hilary. May I ask who stoked up your fire? That hasn't been going since last night.'

He laughed as he echoed her words: 'Stoked up my fire, eh?' But he would not elaborate further. 'So what shall we do?' he went on, rubbing his hands to mark the return to weightier matters. 'Go out and put a torch to his tithe barn?'

'No. Anyway, I didn't come to talk about all that. Except – I wonder? You don't know a good lawyer, do you?'

He grinned and tapped his breast.

'Be serious,' she said crossly.

'But haven't you heard? Hasn't Selina told you?'

'What?'

'We screwed that idiot Moore to such a good price for Lanfear House, there was enough over to apprentice me to the law.' He gave a jocular bow. 'Terence Visick, Indentured Clerk-atte-Law – and atte your service, ma'am.'

'Well!' Her laugh was mostly surprise. 'It's better than the Indian army, I suppose. What happened to the Book of Heiresses?'

He dipped his head gravely. 'Some things take much longer than one realizes. What happened to the great career you were keeping up your sleeve for me?'

She mimicked his gesture. 'Some things take much longer than one realizes. So – you're to be a lawyer, eh? Yes, you'll be good at it when you . . .' She left the rest of the sentence to a withering glance around the room.

'You may look at anything except the kettle,' he warned her. 'A watched pot never boils, you know.'

'That I may swear too!' She rubbed her stomach significantly.

'Oh – yes. I wasn't going to raise the topic, but . . .'

'Why ever not?'

'Women are funny about it. How is it all going?'

'Won't be long now. This side of Christmas anyway. Terence, since you do know a good lawyer, I wonder if you could find out whether a woman who is libelled from the pulpit can . . .'

'It's slander if he spoke it. Libel is written. Slander's spoken. See how much I know already! Anyway, you want to know would she have grounds for action? Interesting question.'

'And the answer?'

'I couldn't say. If he didn't actually name you . . .'

'I thought about that. A writ would force him either to deny he referred to me, in which case everyone would scorn him, or to acknowledge it. And then there would be grounds.'

Terence laughed in delight. 'I think perhaps the wrong member of the family has taken out the indenture! Exactly what did the fellow say?'

She gave him the gist of it and added, 'I'm not really interested in restoring my own name — I mean, it would be more than a little futile even to try. What I want to do is to show him up for the hypocrite he is. I could call witnesses . . .'

'But that's no grounds for claiming defamation — at least, I can't imagine it would be. If a thief calls an honest woman a thief, she can't prove defamation by showing up the thief for what he is.'

'You see, I can call witnesses — real harlots — who can prove he used their services.'

'No doubt. That still wouldn't prove he slandered you. Only that he has a neck made of brass.'

'Damn!' she said.

He looked at her in astonishment.

The kettle began to sing.

'There must be a way,' she insisted.

'What you've got to do . . .' He broke off and stared at her. 'No, by harry, I shan't tell you. You'd only go and do it!'

'What?'

'I didn't say a word. Goodness — I have to keep reminding myself that this is dear little Jo. Meek as a lamb! Wouldn't harm a fly! I still can't believe it.'

She shook her head, refusing to join his orgy of *just fancy!* 'The only thing that changed, Terence, is that opportunity came into my life. I was always like this — underneath.'

'Lucky Pater and Mater — think what they've escaped. But no, Jo, that's just not true. Sorry and all that — but the opportunity to go selling Vose's beer around the district, that didn't just "come into" your life. You made it happen. Tell me about Charley Vose, by the way? How's he taken all this? Or doesn't he know of it yet?'

'He knew even before it happened. I think everyone did. Even Tony Moore.'

'And he didn't tell you? The cad!'

'I'm not so sure. He's a strange man — for all that you think him so nondescript.'

'Limp, I'd say.'

'You're wrong. Today, during the sermon, young Hilary stood up and . . .'

'Just a mo — who's young Hilary?'

Johanna explained a little of the background. 'And obviously Greep was one of the men who . . . used her. He must have paid her five shillings, because that's the sum she asked me to lend her, during the sermon. I said no, of course, but Tony must have given it her because she stood up, holding it — two half-crowns — in her hand. And it was quite clear to me she was going to return it to him in the most . . .'

'What! During the sermon? In front of everyone, you mean?'

She nodded. 'Naturally I tried to pluck her back. But — this is the point, now — Tony stopped me. He knocked my arm down and murmured, "No — let her do it."'

'And was he right? Was it the right thing to do?'

The kettle began a series of small explosions.

'I think it was. It taught Hilary something about herself — how much courage she has . . . what she's capable of. She's been a cheerful young soul since she went to Lanfear — slovenly but cheerful — but there was often that strange sort of withdrawn look in her eyes . . . a wistfulness . . . a sense of something lost . . .'

He chuckled. 'You're being romantic, Jo.'

'I think not. When a woman sells herself like that, she loses something intangible, some — I don't know — some way of measuring herself. Something precious that is so hard to get back. I think Hilary got it back this morning.'

'And darling Tony knew it would happen just like that?'

The kettle boiled. She took it and heated the teapot – surprised to see how clean it was. Her cousin's nameless visitor must also be partial to tea, she decided. 'Tony knew that unless she tried, it would always elude her. And I think he did the same with me. He let me walk into the lion's den of that church this morning in exactly the same spirit. Oh, I nearly died a thousand times, Terence. But I'd have truly died – of apoplexy – if I hadn't been there.'

She went to empty the pot out of the window. Tony followed her with the tea caddy. 'Sounds pretty callous to me,' he commented.

'Only if you think we're made of porcelain and will crack at the first bit of a stress. Actually, Tony paid us the highest compliment – Hilary and me – the highest *true* compliment he possibly could.'

He laughed. 'Steady the buffs, *chère cousine!* You'll be marrying the fellow next.'

'Oh no!' She joined his laughter. 'There's too much friendship between us for that. Anyway, this is getting silly. None of this is why I came to see you, you know.'

'Yes, I've been wondering about that. Sugar?'

'Twice, please. This little creature seems to have given me a sweet tooth. Ouch – stop it!' She pretended to smack the baby through the dress.

Her cousin eyed her nervously. 'Not going to drop out all over my carpet, is it?'

'No. One must expect these twinges over the next few weeks – or so the other women tell me.' She took her cup and stirred it, watching the bubbles rise from the dissolving lumps of sugarloaf. 'The reason I came here was to offer you the chance to carry on what I started with Charley Vose – the brewing business. That was to have been your great career! But if you're happy learning to solicit – or whatever solicitors do. I suppose it *is* better than the Indian army?'

'Yes and no. A lawyer's a queer sort of cove – like a doctor or a parson. They're not considered to be gentlemen and yet, if they rise to the top, they do get asked out to dine occasionally. They *pass* as gentlemen.'

'And what about a wholesale brewer?'

525

He shook his head. 'He'd have to be very big — and buy a fair bit of land. The land would qualify him then.' He chuckled. 'Why — don't tell me Charley Vose will ever be so big?'

'Not him,' she said calmly. 'But you could be.'

His smile was deeply sceptical.

'These last three weeks,' she said, 'I made . . . by way of commission . . .' She paused and sipped her tea.

'Yes?' he urged.

'Twenty pounds a week.'

He almost fell out of his chair. 'I can't believe it!' His eyes vanished briefly inside his skull. When they returned to her he said, 'A thousand a year!'

'Terence.' She put down her cup and stared at him earnestly. 'That is nothing. I tell you, that is nothing — compared with what it could be, or could have been, I suppose I must learn to say.'

'Why?'

'Oh, of course, I didn't actually tell you. I've been thrown out. Charley Vose has turned me off!'

'The devil he has!' Terence rose as if he would fly to Goldsithney that instant and run the man through.

'Calme toi, mon cher,' she urged. 'I was naturally beside myself with fury. But, thinking about it on my way here . . .'

'You haven't walked all the way?' he asked in horror.

'No. Mind you, it was no thanks to Squire Pellew and Mrs Wellbeck, who behaved as if I had ceased to exist. No, I got a ride with some wonderful . . . I'll tell you about that later. Anyway, thinking about it, I've begun to believe that leaving Charley Vose is the best thing I could possibly do. The brewing business I started to build up with him will fall to bits now. He's simply not interested. But it would have happened anyway. The man has no vision — and he's as idle as a pig. So all I need, you see, is some premises to start brewing in . . . a good supply of water . . .'

For the second time that afternoon, someone laughed as if she had just made the funniest statement in years — only this time she wasn't joking.

'And you thought of me?' He was still choking. 'Is that really what you had in mind for me — back in the summer?'

She nodded.

His laughter redoubled. 'I thought you'd gone a bit soft in the head *then*. But now I'm sure of it.'

'Why?'

'Because, *ma chère cousine,* can you honestly see me as a brewer!'

'Yes.'

'Then your case is even worse than I feared. Anyway, the obvious location for your million-barrel, gas-powered brewery is Lanfear House. And the obvious man to partner you in something so fanciful is its present owner.'

'No ... no ...' she started to object.

'Yes, yes! For one thing he won't miss the money, which you will certainly lose. For another thing, he won't miss his reputation, since he has none *to* lose. And for a third, the poor chump is still calf-sick in love with you.'

She stared into her cup before she drained it. 'Well,' she said wearily. 'That was just so much wasted time.'

Chapter Forty-Eight

Johanna lingered at Terence's rooms only long enough to write a short note for Nina, in case her former friend still refused to admit her.

'I suppose,' her cousin mused as he led her to the door, 'having more or less grown up with you, one doesn't see you in quite the same light as others.'

'No, I suppose not,' Johanna agreed, not wishing to pursue a conversation that now seemed fruitless.

But he was not to be stopped by anything so artless as that. 'People have asked me if you're quite all there.'

'Really?' She was not offended; she merely took it for some new line in banter.

But he was quite serious. 'Yes, really. And I've been as surprised by the question as I see you are. I know a lot of women, but there's only a handful among 'em I'd want to spend much time with — and you're the very top of that class, Jo.'

'Aha!' She spoke knowingly. 'I ought to warn you — I have no cash to spare.'

He laughed. 'There you are, you see. To me you're as natural and as easy to talk with as my own twin. And you always make the day a little brighter. And yet I can see what they mean — the people who ask that question. Here's a woman who quite deliberately chooses to keep her hair cropped like a convict . . .'

'Only because Hal likes it that way.'

'. . . and to have a baby out of wedlock, and who goes about blowing a bugle and selling beer . . . you sound like some wild, free-thinking revolutionary virago. And yet when one talks to you, you're so normal and reasonable and . . . well, persuasive about it. Dash it, you have me saying to myself, "Yes, what is so unusual, after all, in what she's doing?" D'you see what I mean?'

She shook her head. 'You speak as if I live by making big, bold decisions. Bang, bang — just like that. But it isn't just like that. I have to admit I sometimes look about myself and ask, "How on earth did I get *here?*" And the answer is I shuffled into it, one teeny-tiny step at a time. In fact, it was so slow, the snails just whizzed past!' She laughed.

'Why is that so funny?'

'The couple who gave me a ride into Helston were called Snail — or Snell. No . . . I haven't time to explain all that now. I'll tell you next time.'

'You always leave something to tell me next time.' He opened the door for her.

'Often you know, it isn't a decision at all. It's like sleep walking. It's something I just know I have to do.'

'Yes. Of course, there are special places where they put people who think like that.' He settled her mackintosh around her shoulders, as if it were a cape.

'Do you think I'm unhinged, Terence?'

His smile was that of an indulgent parent letting a child off the worst of some punishment. 'I'd settle out of court for "eccentric",' he told her.

'You'll make a good lawyer, *mon cher cousin.* You're interested in almost everything but you never let any single thing assume an overwhelming importance.'

'Except sloth,' he replied, falling asleep against the doorjamb.

She pecked him hastily on the cheek and walked off down the passage. When she reached the end she looked back. He was still leaning against the door, and trying not to smile.

Outside she found the rain had abated, but dark clouds that were massing over toward Porthleven announced that the respite was temporary. What an odd fellow her cousin was, she thought. Talk about eccentric! If they hadn't grown up in the same household — and if she hadn't met someone as overwhelming as Hal — she and he could easily have fallen for each other and enjoyed a warm, happy marriage down there in the foothills of love. They had always been easy and contented together.

But then that was equally true of other men. Even Tony, for instance; they got on wonderfully now, since he had learned to accept the limitations of her feelings for him.

Who else? Hamill Oliver, once you allowed he was slightly dotty — imagining that a people who had become extinct hundreds of years ago were still somehow lurking in the blood hereabouts — he was as easy to be with as anyone.

Come to think of it, she couldn't name a single man of her acquaintance with whom she felt awkward and uneasy. She remembered many conversations she had had at the Ram with that ever-widening circle of gentlemen who formed the unofficial dining club there; how swiftly they had passed from mock gallantry and nervous heartiness to normal, unfeverish, interesting conversation with her. Often, she now remembered, she had noticed a sort of alarmed surprise in their eyes, as if they could not quite believe what was happening, or as if they distrusted her. Coupled with Terence's judgement — eccentric — it set her thinking.

She passed in front of the memorial to Humphrey Grylls. The saviour of Wheal Vor, they had called him. And now it had shut down — for ever, they said. Nothing lasts. The first drops of the next downpour began. She put her coat on properly and buttoned it right up to the neck. The baby gave her another twinge. Lord, but she'd be glad when the weight and bulk of it was gone.

Do I seem eccentric to everyone? she wondered. It was a bit of a shock when you'd grown up thinking of yourself — and knowing that everyone else thought of you — as modest, retiring, hard-working, demure ... all the things a young lady ought to be; and then, without any big change in your own opinion of yourself, you were suddenly slapped in the face with 'eccentric ... not quite all there ...' and hints of worse.

How did other women behave?

Most of the married ones — 'safely married,' as they would put it — supported their husbands loyally in public; smiled at their speeches or nodded gravely as the occasion required, echoed their opinions, et cetera — and then cut them to fletters when speaking *entre nous* with other wives.

But what about their behaviour with other men?

It seemed to Johanna that they carried on very much the same as unmarried women, except, perhaps, with a larger foundation of confidence, as the sovereigns of their own secure little empires. Some flirted, mildly or outrageously — like Nina. But, as Nina herself had once said, flirting was a splendid way of keeping them at a proper distance without entirely shutting off all intercourse with them. A man could leave your house after a whole evening of delicious flirtation and be not one whit the wiser as to your true opinion on anything or your true character in any particular circumstance. And when Johanna had remarked that she saw no point in it all, Nina just laughed, leaving her to feel naive and ingenuous.

Selina wanted nothing to do with men, or so she still claimed. She was hearty, bluff, direct with them ... but her eyes gave out none of those secret signals that keep a man and a woman smiling and wishing to persevere with even the most humdrum conversation. Selina, therefore, didn't count.

Deirdre ... no. Unfair. Too young to judge. And yet Johanna felt sure she was going to grow up and join the other category — that large pool of blushers and flutterers who knotted the tongues of young men and left them grumbling to each other that no one could ever understand women anyway. So off they went in search of a jolly little flirt. Poor Wilhelmina Knox was the perfect example of the type.

Did that explain Terence's comments? When his cronies found she was not a flutterer, did they assume she was a flirt? And when they found she was not that, either, but just a ... a what? Just an ordinary person. Did they then have no word left but *eccentric?*

At the bottom of Lady Street, all along St John's, people were driving wooden boards between their front-door jambs and piling sandbags against them. One of them told her that the Cober had already broken its banks in a couple of places above the town.

As she ascended the hill again, into Cross Street, she recalled coming up this very road, on a day as cold as this, though hardly so wet — was it just fourteen months ago? —

and finding Miss Grylls's house all shuttered and dark. And then Nina . . . taking her in without a second thought. What true generosity that had been! Really, it was charity, and yet Nina had never once made her feel it. A cynic might object that it was very easy for someone so rich to be generous at such little cost; but Johanna knew better. She had seen rich men − and women − being 'generous' at the Ram, and didn't they just make sure you appreciated the fact! But with Nina, if you tried to mention it, she became embarrassed and laughed it off and made it quite plain she wished the whole notion of gratitude would just go away and never come between you again.

Images of Nina tumbled through her mind: Nina laughing at a joke she or one of her two young protégées had just made; Nina, moved by some powerful feeling, searching your eyes and begging you to share her intensity of emotion; Nina, discovering some new wonder in Paris or Florence or the Holy Land, and wanting to sweep you up in her response to it; Nina, wasting a whole morning on their way into Rome, stopping to sniff at every patch of wayside flowers, always hoping for one new fragrance . . . Nina, tireless in her search for the new, the exotic, the strange, the unknown pleasure that would exceed all others. Nina, always desperate for more.

And what united them all, this patchwork of Ninas who had seized her humdrum little life and filled it with laughter and hope and passionate feelings about the obscurest trifles? The golden thread that drew them all together was one of terror and desolation. For, by insisting that every experience was potentially the ultimate experience, that every patch of weeds might yield the impossible fragrance, that every waif and stray might become her profoundest soul-mate . . . Nina laid herself open to hurt from all directions. If the process had been more conscious, you would have said she invited it.

That vulnerability one sees in young children, which compels one to shield them at whatever cost − in a curious way Nina had carried it with her, naked, into her adult life. Johanna now saw all this for the first time − a bitter pill with a coating more bitter still. For, by failing to see how vulnerable Nina was, she had wounded her far deeper than she had ever supposed.

Her 'desertion' of Nina had been the shallowest part of

her 'crime.' The real wrong lay in her very inability to respond to Nina as Nina wished. And yet if she had asked, 'What is it you want of me?' Nina could not have told her. 'Something surprising,' she might have said, or 'The ultimate,' or simply, 'More!' And there was nothing in Johanna that could yield those nameless superlatives.

Now, by those strange internal laws wherewith the soul judges itself guilty or free, Johanna found herself unable to plead. It was of no consequence to say that she could not help the way she was made ... to tell herself that she had even discussed it with Nina at the time: 'I wish I could be passionate like you,' she had said; and if she herself had failed to recognize what warnings lay behind the desire, then so had Nina, despite her vastly greater experience of such things...

None of this was mitigation in the slightest degree. She knew, as surely as each step brought her nearer Liston Court, that what she had done to Nina was beyond forgiveness, beyond penance, beyond expiation. She felt the emotional tentacles of that house reaching out, seeking her, touching her, enfolding her, drawing her inward − a curious combination of violence and enticement that was uniquely *Nina*. A dreadful premonition filled her − that if she were now to enter that house once more, she would never again leave it while Nina breathed. It was absurd, of course; it was exactly the sort of exaggerated alarm in which Nina would revel. But, even as she acknowledged its absurdity, she knew there are some fears so irrational their power becomes infinite.

Liston Court had become the centre of some wild, ungovernable vortex of Nina's making, and which only Nina could control. Johanna could feel it whirling in front of her now, as if the very pavements and walls were moving. One step more and she would be into it, starting on that inexorable spinning, drifting, inward fall ...

She shook herself as one waking from a nightmare. What was happening to her? She stared about her. The rain was falling in stair-rods; its drumming on the ground was like the distant roar of an army on the move. The skies had grown so dark that the light seemed to come by magic from out of the earth itself − powerful, muted colours, shimmering in the rain. Yet this was Helston as she had always known it. This was Cross Street. That was Miss Grylls's house, with Lawyer Grylls's office above the entrance...

Once again she tried to walk on, but now no rational power on earth could move her forward half a step.

She yielded at last and turned about, and went once more into the valley at the foot of the town. This time no directing impulse moved her. One foot followed another, each taking her where it would. She was half way to Lowertown before she realized that Helston was lost in the black deluge behind her. And Lowertown had vanished, too, before it struck her that she must be heading for Hamill Oliver's cottage out near Tregathennan.

The rain continued to pour but, after a while, its steady thrumming ceased to register. Then a curious silence settled over the deserted fields and lanes -- almost, she thought, like a deafness. The water poured along the rutted byways, overflowing the upper ditches to flood those on the downward side – eventually uniting to form brief canals at every dip in the way. New rivers overspilled the hedges or gushed forth in a dozen spouts between the stones, dashed in spate across the road, and plunged headlong down the hill below.

At Truthal one knocked her off her feet. She sat in the mud, with the water seething round her, and all she could think of was that it no longer felt wet at all. She was past wondering at it; all she could do was note it as a fact.

Not until then did it occur to her that the baby was about to be born. That, too, was just a fact. So was the pain. Quite a lot of pain – which was why the water didn't feel wet and why the rain was so silent. Her conscious mind had no room for trivia like that; it was too full of the pain.

Soon, the pulsating, throbbing torment of it became the only fact in the universe. Through it she stared out upon a strange, deserted, alien world, where cold and wet and hunger and fatigue had ceased to be. And hills as old as time, and immemorial fields, and dwellings that had outlived a dozen generations – all were reduced to mere landmarks in the epic struggle of one more generation to be born. Time itself had lost its usual measure. The murk of the rain-shrouded sky combined with the natural dusk to give a premature night — which had imperceptibly become the genuine thing by the time she crawled past the Pallas gates.

Was she actually down on her hands and knees by then? Who can say? When at last they found her, the mackintosh was in shreds and the skin it had briefly shielded was so torn and bleeding she might have crawled a mile — or but a hundred yards. She had struggled past shelter, and the chance of a safer delivery, at a score of cottages along the way, not to mention the gatelodge of Pallas House itself; but something kept her to that goal of Wheal Leander; nowhere else, it seemed, would do.

She did not know it, but it was not Hamill who found her, lying unconscious at his gate. It was Tony.

Chapter Forty-Nine

She weighed, so far as they could tell on the rather primitive scales that Sara, the maid, brought up from the kitchen, just under seven pounds. Johanna recovered her senses before the actual birth began but, being somewhat fevered, passed in and out of consciousness until midnight, when at last it was over. In one lucid moment she chose the name Hilda; but by noon the following day, when the high point of her fever had passed, she claimed she had never intended anything but Hannah — Hannah Nina Penrose.

'She'll be Rosewarne for the moment, of course,' she added. 'But we'll change her name by deed poll to agree with ours after the marriage. Oh I must write to Hal.'

'You must get some rest,' Tony told her. 'And those knees must be poulticed again in two hours. That's enough "musts" to be going on with. Do they hurt?'

'Everything hurts. Oh, Tony, it was good of you to come. Did Hamill send for you?'

'Never mind that now.'

'But I want to know. I can't rest. If I even close my eyes everything whirs around and I feel shivery again. Just talk to me. Talk about anything. I shan't listen, I promise.'

'Shall I read to you?' He went over to Hamill's bookshelves, for, though this was the guest room at Wheal Leander, his books spilled into every corner of the house. 'How's this — *Holy Warriors: Lives of Cornish and Breton Saints Compared*. That should send you off to the Land of Nod in three paragraphs flat.'

She smiled at the thought. 'How long have I been here? And don't you agree she is the most adorable little bundle that ever was? Look at her! Shall I wake her up and feed her?'

'You did – just over an hour ago.'

'Did I?'

He sat at her bedside and stroked her brow. 'Jo,' he said after a while, 'why did you struggle all the way out here? That's what we can't fathom.'

'I don't know. I can't remember. No, don't stop.' She reached up her lips and kissed his hand; the comfort of his touch was great.

'I began to worry about you shortly after we parted. I couldn't get away at once because some of the miners wanted to see me, but then I went over to Goldsithney and I met Pellew's coachman, Jenkins. He said you'd gone down the Godolphin Road, on foot! And in that weather! I couldn't believe it. Then Rose Davey came out and told me what had happened.'

'Which you could believe.'

He nodded glumly. 'I'm afraid so. Anyway, I set off after you as fast as my horse could go.'

'Did you see a large snail-shell on a wagon?'

'Yes, I discovered about that later. I must have ridden straight past you. Why did I not stop and ask? I wasn't thinking very clearly by then, I fear. Just panicking.'

'Tony!' She patted his hand.

'I didn't think of Terence, either, or not at once. I went directly to the Angel – to see if you'd taken a seat on the night mail coach. Of course, you hadn't. So then I went down to Nina's.'

'D'you think she'll agree to be godmother? If she just saw the child!'

He hesitated and then said, 'I'm sure she will. It'll just take a little time. So – as I was leaving, Selina advised me to try Terence. And then it took me some time to find him.'

'And even longer to wake him!'

He chuckled. 'And he said you'd gone an hour before – by which I knew you must have taken a ride with someone. And the only vehicle I'd passed was that snail-shell thing. And Terence seemed to recall you'd said something about snails. Anyway, *they* were easy enough to find! And they confirmed it. But by then it was getting dark – properly dark — and I realised you could have gone anywhere. And that's when I remembered Hamill's invitation to us all after church.'

'Oh Tony, Tony — why did you bother? I deliberately didn't go to Lanfear. The last thing I wanted was . . .'

'But why? That's what I just can't fathom. Miss Davey said Vose offered you the gig. Why didn't you just take it and come straight back to us?'

She shook her head. 'Now I've hurt you — and that is the very last thing I wanted.' She closed her eyes. 'The reason I stayed away is that I've obviously become a pariah now. They should give me a bell and let me go about shouting "unclean!"'

'Jo!'

'But it's true, Tony. Your work is going to be difficult enough without my adding another burden.'

'Burden? I will not listen to another word of this. Those miners who came to see me today — yesterday — d'you know the last thing they said?'

She opened her eyes and waited.

'Now I hadn't so much as mentioned you — so this was straight off their own bat. They all said what a disgraceful thing it was for Greep to preach your name like that.'

'Was it only yesterday?' she murmured.

'They've had no love for him ever since he blamed Methodism and Nonconformism in general for the Great Randy, in those smug sermons he preached on his earlier visits to Breage.'

'Thank you, my dear. I know you're trying hard, but where the Church of England and the Nonconformists are concerned, it's any stick to beat a dog. I doubt I have a genuine champion in either of those camps.'

He clenched his fists and fought with himself. 'I wasn't going to tell you this — in fact, I still don't think I should — but, as you say, any stick to beat a dog. Do you know Trevanion Body? Lives along Baker's Row.'

'Short fellow? Thick set, very powerful-looking?'

'Yes. A cut above most of them. A good man, in fact. Well, just as they were leaving (I think he at least guessed the cause of my agitation) he turned back and buttonholed me. They'd just been saying how disgusted they were, and so on.

And he said, "When you do look at what she done up the Golden Ram . . ."'

Johanna broke into laughter. 'Why me 'ansum,' she said in heavy dialect, 'I never heard 'ee talk fitty-like afore. Proper job!'

'Listen!' he commanded — pleased nonetheless. 'He said, "When you do look at what she done up the Golden Ram, why, if old Charley Vose do turn she off, wouldn't she just make this-here Medical Union buzz!" That's what he said.'

'Go on.'

'That's all. That's what he said.'

'When a Cornishman tells a story, he always repeats the last bit of it.'

'Don't evade the issue.'

She sighed. 'I shall have to think about it.'

'Very well. You're still half-evading the issue but — as your medical adviser — I think I have to permit you that.'

After a silence he went on, 'D'you suppose you might sleep now?'

'In a bit. Talk to me a little more.'

'Why did you call on Terence?'

'Did he tell you all his friends think I'm sixpence short of a shilling?'

He rose and went over to the fireplace where he poked up the embers and threw on another log. 'This was poor Hamill's best applewood. He was keeping it for *Yuletide,* as he calls it. For some ceremony in his one-man Celtic Church.'

'Is he here? I should see him and thank him and so on. It's all a bit embarrassing. I can't even remember why I chose to come here. I tried to go to Nina, really, but it was like a . . . like a wall of glass.'

'He's gone out to walk around some circle. Three times, he said — but he'll be back in time for tea and toasted pikelets. The liturgical rituals of the Celtic Church are obviously very well adapted to the gastronomic rituals of the landed class. Oh dear, one shouldn't mock. He's the soul of kindness. Heart of gold. Well!' He rubbed his hands briskly as he returned to her bedside. 'You didn't say why you went to see Terence.'

'Nor I did. I don't know . . . I can't believe it was only yesterday.' She changed her position slightly and winced. 'Could you bear to poultice these knees now, Tony? I know it hurts to begin with but the heat does seem to do something.'

It took ten minutes, with the help of Sara, to prepare everything. She stayed and pinned down Johanna's feet. But after that first violent stinging was over, she was able to go and take the old poultice with her. The doctor told her to throw it all in the stove but as it was good bread, and most of it unbloodied, she reserved the best bits into a bag for her father's fowl at home.

'Terence is a very odd fellow,' Tony went on, as if no time at all had intervened. 'D'you know what he told me? I asked him why you'd called on him, you see — thinking it might give me some clue as to where you'd gone. And he said "Try all the local breweries."'

Johanna laughed, despite the pain from her knees.

'I'm afraid my response was a little more severe than that. But he swore that your only purpose in calling on him seemed to be to offer him the chance of becoming a brewer himself.'

She sniffed. She shrugged her shoulders. She made several awkward movements, preparatory to speech. And then she fell back into silence. But from the look in his eye she knew he was not going to let it drop. 'What else did he say?' she asked.

'Oh, it was only a flying visit.'

And that seemed to be the end of it — until just before he left her, saying she really must try to sleep a little; almost his last words were, 'I have been wondering how best to use all those stables and outbuildings at Lanfear House.'

Johanna turned on her side and settled to sleep. Little Hannah lay all tightly swaddled on the bed beside her. That's what your real, actual living baby looked like! Had the two old cribs been cleared out when the family left Lanfear? Such a placid little thing! Would it last? She hadn't heard her cry or even make a sound yet — or if she had, she'd forgotten.

Ugly, really. She could admit it to herself though she would never have spoken again to anyone else who said as much. Long black hair and blonde, all mixed — longer than her mother's! — wrinkled face, lips peeling, her head squashed like a hatchet . . . but what did it matter? Nothing could take away from the fact that she was the dearest, darlingest, little bundle that ever breathed . . .

She awoke again at four when, like some engine being put

in steam for the first time, Hannah began a soon-to-be-familiar chant. It started from a barely voiced 'Eheh ...' and progressed through a crescendo of increasingly confident repeats, pausing only for a triple sneeze, to its climax in a single, sustained wail of astonishing power and volume.

'A second Jenny Lind,' Hamill said from the door, or from the four-inch gap he had opened. 'May I come in?'

'Hamill!' She rose on one elbow − knees not too painful, she was relieved to note − and held out her other arm toward him.

'The Cornish nightingale,' he added as he strode toward her. Tony was hard on his heels. 'How are your knees?' he asked.

'Well enough.' She retrieved her hand from Hamill, who, having brushed it with his lips, seemed at a loss to know what more to do with it. 'Hamill,' she said. 'What must you think of me? Turning up like that ...'

'But where else could you possibly have gone?' he asked. Her question seemed to shock him. 'You came to *crows-an-wrea.*'

She avoided Tony's eye. 'You're such a good man.'

He shook his head. 'Aren't you going to feed her? I'm sure that's what she wants.'

Johanna looked askance at him. Tony came to her rescue. 'Let her cry a bit. It's the only exercise she gets.' He dropped a face towel on the chair beside the bed and nudged Hamill toward the door.

Hamill looked as if he would argue the point but Johanna said, 'I'll call you back the moment I'm done,' leaving him no choice.

'Come along then, little cooze!' She began to unpeel the swaddling that bound the child. 'This imprisonment can't be good for you, I won't believe it.'

The crying faltered at the sound of her voice.

'Look at your little hands, all white and bloodless. Yes yes yes ...' She tried to kiss some warmth back into them. Such teeny little fingers! How could anything so small and delicate be alive? 'I don't care if he is a doctor. Doctors don't know everything.' The crying stopped the moment both arms were free − which they celebrated in a flurry of independent windmilling.

'Yes, I know what you're groping for. It's coming. It's coming.'

She raised her chemise and put Hannah to her breast. At first her nipple lay against the baby's cheek. She readjusted her seat, intending to improve the alignment, but the speed with which the little thing managed the job unaided was only amazing. 'Oh, such greed, such hunger,' Johanna cooed.

Tony said she'd already been fed but Johanna had no memory of it; as far as she was concerned, this was the first time. The pleasure of it! She closed her eyes and breathed deeply and told herself that no matter what dreary future lay ahead – between now and Hal's return – there would be moments like this nothing and no one could take from her.

'Hannah,' she murmured, gazing down at the guzzling little bundle in her arms. 'You don't even know your name, do you, Hannah? Listen to it: Han-nah. It's the same both ways, you see. There's a name for that, too, only I've forgotten. Hippodrome or something. Selina will tell you. You'll love Selina, though I'm not so sure how she's going to feel about you. She's your cousin once removed – and you're the same to her. I'm sure she's going to make a joke about that. And then there's Nina, your godmother – I wonder how long it'll be before you see her? I know what she'll say. She'll say she'd give her right arm to have skin like yours. She'll say why is beauty wasted on babies? And isn't she right? *You* don't appreciate it. All you want is ... my goodness, have you drunk that one dry already? All right, all right! Patience!'

She watched with astonishment as the contented little face screwed itself up in a sudden fury – even during those two or three seconds it took to get her to the other breast. The corresponding change, back to contentment, was equally sudden.

'You've no consideration for others at all,' she told her mournfully. 'It's all: "I want, I need, I must have." How are we ever going to turn you into a civilized young miss whom one can safely put to a County Ball?' Her arms gripped a little tighter and some of the playfulness left her voice as she added, 'I can promise you one thing, anyway: No one is ever going to strap you to a bed and birch you till you bleed. You have your mother's word on that.' Then she laughed. 'Listen to me! You don't even want to think about things like that, do you? All you want to know is will there be more milk in a few hours' time? Well, I think I may promise you that, too. As to the rest ... we've just got to take each other as we find us. And I'm afraid, darling Hannah, dear little thing, I'm afraid you've picked a bad 'un. Oh yes! This great milky lump you're attacking with such gusto is what they call sixpence short of a shilling. And what may that mean, I hear you ask? It means she's got a sharp little brain when it comes to the next hour or two, but as for thinking about tomorrow ...! Don't even ask her. Another thing is she gets bees in her bonnet, too. D'you want to hear the latest?'

Hannah paused and let fall a great windy curd of milk, most of which Johanna caught in the towel that Tony had left. 'It's not that bad,' she assured her. 'The latest bee is that she can't stop thinking about brewing and selling beer. Beer is to grown-ups what this ... yeurk ... is to you. Yes, they sometimes do the same thing with it, too. But there's your poor demented mama for you – can't stop thinking about it. Morning, noon, and night. Well ... that is ... she thinks about Hal, too. He's your papa. She thinks about him a lot, too. Oh – all the time. Often and often.'

Hannah fell away, her lips parted in a smile of milky exhaustion.

'And now you have to pay the price of all that gluttony,' Johanna warned as she raised the child over her shoulder. 'Come on. Up with it!' And she began a rhythmic patting and stroking, whose only effect was to send the little thing into the deepest slumber.

'Well, at least I know how to put you to sleep.' Johanna pressed a warm, firm kiss on the baby's neck. 'Yes – you're the same as all the rest. All I need to do is start telling you everything about brewing and what an amazing future it offers us!'

Chapter Fifty

In the Year of our Lord 1849, everyone left for California too early. Monday, 2 April, found the Cornish party, augmented by Frank Ashburn, in a long line of wagons and a great mass of cattle, waiting at Kanesville for the Mormon ferry to take them across that turbulent, fast-flowing highway of dilute mud known as the Missouri, which at that time formed the last bastion of the new civilization. Ahead lay more than a thousand miles of trail through the wilderness, through the lands of the Pawnee, the Sioux, the Cherokee, and others; and although the present mood of the tribes was described as friendly, the smallest lapse, the least trespass, could bring them down in terrible wrath.

As soon as Frank had realized how many other hopefuls were also bent on crossing the great divide, he abandoned his idea of riding light and rough, living off dried buffalo and hard tack; then he thought it safer to join a larger party, anything between one and two dozen wagons, which could be drawn up for mutual defence. Besides, thanks to their winter work, they could now afford to travel in greater comfort and safety. Between them they had a one-horse buggy with two spare horses, a covered wagon and three yoke of oxen, two ponies, and four milch cows.

The ferry was a flat boat, manned by six oarsmen. It could take no more than two wagons at a time, and at a dollar each – so the morning was well advanced before their turn came. They cut out their own cattle and herded them down to the water's edge, driving them in with blows and shouts, leaving them to swim across as best they could.

'We should orter a' put our brand on their horns,' Frank

said, surveying the motley herd that had already made the crossing. 'Keep one good eye on them critters now.'

They crossed at a diagonal, to counter the stream, landing at a stage precisely opposite their departure point. From their vantage on the wagon the prospect ahead could not have been more daunting – or so it seemed to Hal. The view gave out over one vast, unrelieved grassy plain, seemingly infinite, and strangely empty; thus, before they had even set foot upon it, the mighty wilderness that lay ahead already taunted them with its vistas of unattainable horizons. He had expected this to be a moment of high excitement; the sense of foreboding was a surprise.

Jenny's scrutiny was more practical. 'Look, honey, see that small wagon with the quilt cover?' she asked.

He searched and found it soon enough. 'Yes?'

'Do the three men just this side of it seem sort of familiar to you?'

He took out his surveying telescope and trained it upon them. 'Can't say as they do,' he told her, handing the instrument over.

'It is!' she cried the moment she located them through it. 'That's Henry Collet and Arthur Kenny and Pig-eye Gee from Goldsithney. Ahoy! Henry Collet!' She began shouting and waving though they were still too far away to be heard over the general hubbub along that farther bank.

'What was that last name?' Hal asked.

She laughed. 'Pig-eye Gee. His real name is Percy Collet – he's first cousin to Henry. But the teacher asked him to spell *pig,* and he said, "Why that's easy – Pig-eye Gee!" And that's been his name ever since, poor feller.'

They managed to attract the attention of the three just as they made landfall; with gleeful yells the lads rode over and immediately set to, helping them to round up their cattle. 'We thought you was already in California,' Pig-eye said. 'A man we met in Iowa City swore it. Henry's got letters for 'ee. Scores on 'em.'

'Who? Which of us?' asked the three compatriots eagerly.

'All on 'ee.'

'Scores' was a bit of an exaggeration. There were four for Cunningham; three ending in, 'Your prompt attention would oblige,' and one from Wilhelmina Knox. 'Kindling,' he said as he dropped them into the dunny bag.

Jenny had two. Hal had four, but he would have traded the other three, and a hundred others beside, to have had the fourth a few months sooner. He read those three lesser ones swiftly, avidly, before he even took up the fourth. It was, he saw, dated last October — since when he had heard nothing from Johanna at all. True, the winter storms had been bad and several vessels had been lost at sea, all carrying mail from England; but her long silence, whether intended or accidental, had weighed on him. If Jenny had not been there, the worry would have ruined him.

Now — with Jenny there — he hesitated to open it.

'Anything interesting in yours?' he asked her, knowing that Diana always included the latest gossip about Johanna, especially if it were disparaging.

'Nothing much,' she replied, but in such a heavy tone that his sense of foreboding deepened. 'Aren't you going to read yours?'

He pointed to the three opened letters, and she said, 'Ah.' But they both knew that was not what she had meant.

'Later,' he told her.

'We can all go together, if you're agreeable?' Henry Collet suggested to no one in particular, though his eyes happened to fall on Frank.

'Whatcha toolin'?' he asked. 'And did you brung much plunder?'

'The quilty.' Henry nodded toward the wagon Jenny had noticed. 'The only plunder is mining gear. They told us that's scarcer 'n gold now in California.'

'Yeah. Us too. Oxen or horses?'

'Oxen. Two yoke.'

Frank gave a dubious shake of his head. 'Should a' brung three. Mebbes you can pick up one more at Fort Laramie.'

'Two were all Arthur's uncle could spare. He staked us back in Wisconsin.'

'We'll manage,' Frank assured him. 'We ain't fixin' for no speed, I suspicion. Too many folk here seem to believe in hosses. How's about gettin' clear a' this landin' and find us somewheres we can brand our cattle?'

The system they had devised on their journey from Dudley was for Jenny to milk the cows at dawn. She would then strain the milk into a wooden churn tied to the back of the wagon, where the lurching and jolting would turn out a decent little pat of butter and leave some sweet buttermilk to wash down the evening meal, their main meal of the day. On this particular morning, however, when they had realized what a rush there would be for the ferry, they had set off before first light, and even then found several dozen ahead of them.

So she now took the chance of their early 'nooning' to catch up on her routine. The three men set about branding the cows and oxen in their horns. The lads from Goldsithney went off to do the same for their cattle. The first party, of some three dozen wagons, would set off just after one o'clock.

As soon as it became clear that two men could handle the work with ease, Hal excused himself and wandered off to open the letter from Johanna: *By the time you read this you will be a father* ... it began. His eyes scanned the words again and again, feeling their shock, undiminished even at the tenth reading.

His hand fell to his side as he turned and stared back across the Missouri. This changed everything. Obviously, he must return to Cornwall; he must get to Johanna as soon as possible. Or perhaps he could send her the money to come out here.

But Nina could have lent her the money. How could she have allowed this to happen? She must have known months ago.

He saw Jenny had paused in her work and was staring at him — a gaze so desolate, so forlorn, it made him flinch. She knew, too, then. Diana must have told her.

He returned to the letter. Now, knowing that Jenny could not take her eyes off him, he tried to master his expression and seem as unconcerned as possible. With each new revelation — the extent of her quarrel with Nina, her work at the Golden Ram, her knowledge that Jenny had not gone her own ways at Boston, and, above all, the fact that she, Johanna, had actually been put on a clipper to New York and had herself jumped ship — his nonchalance became more difficult to maintain. At last, when he read her closing endearments with their command to go on to California and make a fortune big enough for the three of them, he had to turn away to hide his face from Jenny.

A moment later she was at his side. ''Twasn't your fault,' she assured him. 'You never even knew.'

'Leave me alone,' he snapped. Then he turned and said, more gently, 'No, I'm sorry. What does your letter say?'

'Same as yours, I reckon, from the look on your face. You're a father by now.' She gave a single, derisory laugh. 'And not for the first time, I'll be bound.'

He ignored the comment. 'Have you ever mentioned, in any of your letters home, did you ever say you and I were together?'

'Well — I said in the same party.'

'You know what I mean.'

''Course not. We agreed that. I told them I was with Cunningham. Then, 'cos I knew they'd never believe it that long, I said I'd gone over to Frank. I told you all that. Why — didn't she believe it? You said she'd work it out for herself that you were keeping silent to protect her?'

He nodded miserably, unable to disagree.

'Didn't it work?' she asked.

'That's what's so awful. This letter ... she's just so ... oh God!'

'Well if she doesn't suspect, I can't see what you're worried about?'

He closed his eyes. 'Why didn't we part company at Boston? Why? I feel so ... unworthy.' He looked at her. 'She must never learn of it!'

'Oh, of course, nothing must be allowed to disturb the saintly Miss Rosewarne's peace of mind! You can do anything you like — break my heart — be as heedless as you wish — and as long as word of it doesn't get back to *her,* the world's all right!'

He gripped her arm and squeezed until she would have cried out but for her determination not to give him the satisfaction. 'If you so much as breathe one word about us ...' he threatened.

Her lips curled in contempt. 'You know nothing about women, do you,' she taunted. 'If you did, you'd realize that hot coals wouldn't tear it from me. I know full well I'm no more than a bedwarmer to you. When you make your fortune in California, with me aiding you every inch of the way, you'll buy me off with the least your conscience will allow, and . . .'

'I'll go back to Cornwall and marry Johanna. I've never made any secret of that, Jenny. I told you so as we sailed from Plymouth. Or from Queenstown, anyway. It was your choice. And I said it again in Boston, when you had the choice of going on with . . .'

'And you think that frees your conscience, I suppose! The fact that I . . . oh, never mind!'

'No – go on, say it.'

'It doesn't matter. What I was going to say was: When you do leave me for good, the sweetness for me will be knowing that it's *her* turn next. And the double sweetness will be that in her case it's for *ever*. I can't think of any two people who deserve each other more.'

'Well, if you feel like that, why don't you up sticks and leave now? You could take your pick. Look about you. The one thing there's a powerful shortage of, this side of the river, is women.'

Misunderstanding between them was now complete. He meant no more than that she could have her pick of husbands; she felt sure he was about to tell her she could make a fortune at her old trade without even going to California. She struck him a stinging slap across his face and ran back to finish her milking.

Hal, knowing that both Cunningham and Frank were watching him in amused interest, deflected the hand that was on its way to rub his cheek and made it, instead, compress each nostril while he blew the other clean upon the sod. Then, grinning like a whipped boy who hasn't blubbed, he joined them. 'She'll pay for that tonight,' he murmured. 'In thumps of a different kind.'

Jenny saw the three of them throw back their heads and laugh. What unrewarding creatures they were, really, she thought. Then Frank gave her a cheerful nod and a friendly wink. Frank wasn't so bad, actually.

Her words had sown a seed in Hal's mind. That afternoon, when they set off across the vast, featureless plain, it had plenty of opportunity to germinate and grow.

In his heart of hearts, or souls of souls, or wherever it is that people judge themselves, he had no great opinion of Hal Penrose. It was all very well to say that Jenny had thrown herself at him – which was, indeed, the truth – but it was a long step from there to concluding that he therefore had the right to use her as a common-law wife while it pleased him, fully intending to leave her one day and go back to marry Johanna. Even though he had told her as much, and reminded her of it – and often – it still did not absolve him from judgement, least of all his own.

The trouble was, he knew himself too well by now. Place him within range of an attractive woman, young or old, and all his resolutions fled. When that certain light danced in her eyes, when her eyelashes fluttered and seemed to brush her cheeks, when her cheeks burned red, when she smiled, when she walked and all her petticoats sighed like silk, when he caught her fragrance, heard her voice, touched her hand . . . then the compulsion within him would not be restrained.

And she could sense it, too, whoever she was – untried maid or experienced dame – she could feel that raw urgency of his longing, which she must then answer. And if the answer were yes, then there were two whom nothing could restrain. And so it had been with Jenny. But if it had not, if she had somehow found the strength to bid him farewell at Boston, then there would have been Clarissa or Evelyn or Pam or – what point in naming them now – the ships that had passed in the nights of this last twelvemonth, few of them even suspected by Jenny.

Her taunt that Johanna deserved him now made him wonder. Could he honourably go back and ask her to marry him, even with a million in gold? Did he have the right to inflict himself upon her like that? At least with Jenny he had been honest: 'Here and here are the limits of our love.' She had known that from the start. She might imagine she had seen a different promise in his eyes but that was her affair. He had spoken the honest truth. But to Johanna he had never promised anything but an absolute, endless, and unconditional love. And yet look how, on the very night he realized he had fallen for her, he tried to slip between Nina's thighs.

Even with the complication of the baby, had he the right to make her life a misery with his broken promises?

But then, no sooner had the obvious conclusion begun to take shape in his mind than another voice told him that Johanna represented his only chance ever to rise above his deceit and lust. Did he not truly love her? She was the only woman, in all his wide experience, to haunt him day and night. Every new marvel he had seen since his arrival here — his first thought had been to wish Johanna were there to share it. Even at his most perfidious moments, when he lay with Jenny, he always imagined she was Johanna. That was partly, he knew, to salve his conscience, at least at its most primitive levels; but also it increased his pleasure. If that didn't prove he loved Johanna beyond all others, nothing did.

Which, then, would be the nobler action: to go back on all his promises to Johanna because he was unworthy of her — to spare her the misery and pain of his falsity; or to accept the offer of her love, match it with his own, and from that fastness, pinch out all his shortcomings?

Fortunately he had a year or so to find the answer.

They made no more than five miles that day before they came to a spring where they decided to camp for the night. They saw no Indians, no buffalo, no deer — but plentiful signs of all three. When the first of what was to be many a westering sun set before them in a great red ball, they could still look back and see it strike with a borrowed fire off the Council Bluffs in Kanesville. Through the telescope they could even make out the caves where the Mormons had spent their first winter there, three years ago.

The only timber they had passed that afternoon was a stand of cottonwood fringing a stream that, like them only not so directly, was making for the Elkhorn River. Others in the party had cut them down but Frank had brought along enough firewood to keep them supplied for at least ten days. To conserve it, the Cornish party doubled up on the one fire. They ate hard tack and eggs and some of the buttermilk. The rest Jenny kneaded into her dough while Hal dug a pit beside the fire for the baking kettle. When the dough was inside, they raked the fire onto its lid and left it to cook overnight.

There was some jollification that evening, a little singing, a recitation or two; but no dancing and – in marked contrast to life east of the Missouri – no hard drinking. Out here one slip could spell disaster – under a wagon wheel, in a quicksand, before panicking cattle . . . there were a dozen ways or more before one even mentioned 'Injun'. Sudden death was already too close for comfort. A head clouded by liquor brought it closer still.

By eight o'clock only the lookouts, and the cattle turned loose to graze, were awake. For the next hundred days or so, dawn would never be far enough off for aching muscles and weary bones. Cunningham and Frank usually slept in the wagon, though tonight Cunningham and Pig-eye had decided to try the experiment of sleeping out, spreading their blankets under the wagon. Hal and Jenny slept in the buggy. They had managed to be civil enough to each other while the rest were about but as soon as they were alone a frost settled between them and they undressed – at least their outermost garments – and went to sleep in silence.

In the small hours, though, Hal came wide awake and found himself shivering with longing for her. He just lay there, willing himself with all his might not to move, not to touch her, not to give in. But something – perhaps his very stillness – woke her up, too. And his yearning must have communicated itself for, moments later, she was filled with that same overwhelming desire. Her petticoats had already ridden up around her waist so all she did was slide herself back until she just came into contact with him.

He still hated her – for loving him, for the power of her sex to subdue him, for showing him his weaknesses. And she still hated him – for not loving her, for imprisoning her in this endless carnal duel with him, for showing up her frailty. And in the extreme of their hatred they almost wrote off the springs of the buggy.

Chapter Fifty-One

On the outside of the envelope, Hal had written: 'This left my hand, where and by what means you shall discover within, 500 miles from the nearest post office, on Friday, 1 June, 1849.' The letter itself, which reached Lanfear House toward the end of July, read as follows:

4 April, 1849
My dearest darling Johanna,

You may imagine with what consternation I read your letter, sent via Henry Collet & Co last October, which did not reach me until two days ago. Any letter sent since by the regular mails has also not yet arrived. We had just begun our Great Trek across the untamed half of this continent. I literally saw the Collets (who now are travelling with us) as we crossed the Missouri. They had heard we were already in California and so had ceased to look for us in the East. Naturally, the moment I had read your first paragraph, I was for quitting the party and returning forthwith to Cornwall. But as I read on, your wisdom sobered me and by your conclusion I was persuaded to continue and carry out our ideas as we planned them from the outset. I begin this letter two days out into the trackless plain, looking for the Elkhorn River, and not knowing when or where my words will be sent back to you. Perhaps from Fort Laramie, which we hope to reach in the middle of May.

But oh with what pride I now strike out into each day's unknown (to me) territory! I a father! And of a fine, healthy son, I trust? Yet if she be a daughter and she have one tenth the charm and character of her mother, my pride, I think, shall still be boundless. I am sure even the 'easiest' birth is not truly easy, albeit I hope you had the easiest time possible of it. By my calculating it should have been in the early half of December last. I curse myself that while you were suffering to bring our child into this world, I was a quarter of that world apart from you, carefree and heedless in the yet-unborn town of Dudley.

If it would be possible to be married by proxy across our two continents and the ocean between them, and if witnessed affidavit of mine be sufficient to the purpose, then to whom it may concern I, Hannibal Penrose, late of Nineveh House in the parish of St Erth, do hereby affirm my solemn, unwavering, and absolute desire to take in matrimony Johanna Rosewarne, late of Lanfear House in the parish of Breage and to acknowledge my paternity of her child, born on or about December last, 1848, and to recognize said child in every way if he or she were my sole legitimate heir and successor. Also I wish that the utmost powers of the law may be applied in order to encompass these ends.

His signature was witnessed by Frank Ashburn, Teamster, and Roger Cunningham, Gent. The letter continued:

I shall not write on the back of that section of this paper so that you may scissor it asunder and use it as best fits the case. And if it be not possible, then you are to insert it as a paid advertisement in the *Cornishman,* prefacing it with: 'Mr H. Penrose has communicated the following affidavit to Miss Johanna Rosewarne'.

6 April: 2 more days have passed in which I have thought of you constantly yet written not a line. Nothing has prepared us for this fatigue. If it does not rain, we perish in dust; if it does, we squelch in a prairie of glue. Forgive this shaking hand of mine; my very blood feels exhausted.

Frank, ever practical, has assigned each wagon (we are

now 24 in all) a number. Each new day the eponymous wagon (e.g., wagon number 4 on the 4th day) will lead, the others moving up in line and enjoying (if that is the word) progressively less dust. We are 15, 16, 17, and have some way to go still. I am too exhausted to write a continuous narrative — much less make a separate notation for Selina. And since neither she nor Nina has sent me one line except messages by you, may I prevail upon you to excerpt which bits will spice her narrative best?

9 April: We have already lost one of our milch cows to Pawnee Indians. The first party, whom we met before the Elkhorn, demanded only money, which they got readily enough. No one truly objects to a toll on passing through what is after all their land. But the next lot demanded a cow, which, to our horror, they slaughtered and ate on the spot, before our eyes. A cow yielding near a gallon a day! They also took some flour.

They came back today and stood in a most insolent manner between where we had settled for the night and the spring of water we hoped to use. Something in their attitude reminded me of a gang of Wheal Anchor bullies who once sought to prevent our Wheal Venton men from going down. I recalled how we had faced them out, simply walking through their line as if they were not there. So I took up a pail and did the same with this bunch of painted louts. On my way back I thought they would strike me down but they laughed and clapped me on the back as if I were one of them and we had shown up the Paleface. And so they went their ways. A most singular people! Cunningham said he had been on the very point of doing the same when I stepped out and so pre-empted him.

I meant to add at the foot of the previous page that from the moment I digested your news properly I have considered myself married to you, and you may take it that I already feel myself bound by every vow I shall one day make with you in person, as set forth in the Book of Common Prayer.

16 April: Progress woefully slow, little over 7 miles each day. We are camped by the Loup River, which seems to be disputed between the Pawnee and our next marauders, the Sioux. Even as I write, and notwithstanding a violent storm raging outside, they are engaged in a rowdy battle not half a mile away. Our train is too large for them to attack, but the Mormons who man the ferry were mighty glad to see us. They say this storm will not last. The worst ones are in May and the wagons often have to lie up a day or two before the trail is passable again. We awoke this morning to blistering heat, gnats, and mosquitoes. Now we have hail, rain, and sleet.

19 April: Having picked up half a dozen wagons along our way, we are now reduced to 17. The other 13, with the reek of gold in their nostrils, have pulled on ahead. Frank says they will only exhaust their oxen and horses. Lakes and ruts everywhere; grazing poor; very unrewarding country for us.

24 April: The Platte at last. But why have we anticipated it so keenly? Flat, monotonous, dismal, everything wet and no firing to dry it. Frank told Cunningham the miasma off the river will give one 'rheumatiz'. Cunningham asked, 'Inflammatory or chronic?' Frank: 'Well, I ain't much given to bottle names, but I reckon it's the worst kind. And jes' 'bout th'only way to claim pre-emption on it is to sleep in wet clothes.'

Well, there he picked the one commodity not hard to come by. Cunningham tossed and turned all night in wet buckskins and now has the Adam and Eve of all colds in the head. Frank enjoyed the company of his usual bedwarmer and seems to have escaped cold, rheumatiz, and miasma — as indeed did I, with only our love to keep me from harm.

29 April: The Sabbath is no day of rest here. Our service is a brief reading, then it is a day of toil — or of toiling forward — like all others. We seem to have been rolling

for ever. In places the Platte is two miles wide, and when the sun gets up and starts to shimmer, and a haze sets in, the farther shore is invisible. Then I can easily imagine I am wandering among the dunes at Hayle Towans, where the sands stretch to Godrevy light. I try not to think too often of Cornwall for fear that even now I should turn and run to you. Yet I think of *you* constantly and that only spurs me forward to secure our future, all three.

Occasionally we see a cottonwood or a willow or poplar, but usually it is a featureless, empty world, with plains to our right, water to our left, and sky above. The water is undrinkable. Though only a few inches deep, it flows so swift it is always full of sand, and too foul even for washing. Several have tried drinking it, including poor Cunningham, and have proved it more effective than cascara, Epsom salts, bad pork, or any other traditional aperient. But the buffalo drink it without harm. They are a constant hazard to us. A herd of them can fill the plains to the horizon and when it comes thundering down to drink, nothing can stand in its way. The pounding of their hooves enrages our cattle. Our oxen, particularly, go frantic to break their harness. And even though we can usually avoid them en masse, we have to stumble over their tracks, which puts a fearful strain on axles and spokes.

However, their meat is most acceptable and their droppings, called buffalo *chips,* when dried after several years on the plain, burn as good as charcoal. We walk a little apart on either side of our wagons now, picking them up as we go. We are now 300 miles from Kanesville, and every one hard won.

3 May: Near caught in a quicksand today at Cave Creek. Had to throw all our plunder out on a sandbar and by the grace of God got the wheels turning again. Then lost our best ox, frightened in a buffalo stampede, which it took us all morning to search for, and with no success. Our flour is all damp and we are trying to dry it without losing too much to the breezes. Fortunately the weather is fine though strangely elastic. More

desertions today by the impatient. Even the Collets wish to press on faster. We are now reduced to 12 wagons, only just enough to ward off attack. Fortunately the tribes between here and Ft. Laramie seem pacific enough. Our way is littered with buffalo skulls on which earlier migrants have left messages. Some tell of old massacres, so we remain in high vigilance.

5 May: A band of Sioux came by today. V. friendly and gave us quantities of fresh buffalo meat. Frank says they were gauging our strength, which is probably just too great for them. This evening, far off on the western horizon, we got our first glimpse of Chimney Rock; when we reach it we shall be one day's hard ride from Laramie. Already we can spy Laramie Peak, which lies well beyond the Fort. How pathetically we long for each new landmark; and how, in this flat wilderness, they taunt us for days before we reach them! And then they are like yesterday's bright news and we bend our eyes westward, ever westward, for the next. One image is always before me, sustaining me, and that is you, my love.

6 May: 20 more groaning, panting, dust-choked, treeless miles, with the one lone finger of Chimney Rock to beckon us every inch of the way. And then, just as we break off to camp, we find a beautiful spring of clear running water in a marsh, a furlong south of our trail. It must be the one Parkman described in the other book I have sent you. He says it appears just in time to breathe new life into battered humans and animals. When I read it in the dirt-floor luxury of my Dudley log cabin, I smiled at his poetic licence. Now I marvel at his sober restraint of language.

Scott's Bluff, where the poor clerk was left to die, is majestic in the evening sun, all in delicate shades of pink, like the cliffs of elvanstone at Trequean Zawn.

7 May: All our spirits are lifted, for tomorrow we shall be in Laramie. Today was 21 miles of unrelieved sun

through ... the American has an exact word for everything, and his exact word for this terrain is *badlands*. Yet here we are camped at Spring Creek, where I caught us some fine trout for supper, and there are wild sunflowers shooting up and lavender and daisies blowing, and all our aches and pains are forgotten. I doubt not that when we look back on this dreadful journey, we shall remember only such moments as these and think it the prime idyll of our lives. How I wish you were here to share it. And the child.

8 May: A 25-mile forced march (no other term will do) through the Robidoux Pass and more and yet more badlands and here we are at (I shout it) LARAMIE! We are camped outside the fort in the heart of an Indian village, a motley of Sioux and Cheyenne, who have made a treaty with the government and are to get tens of thousands of dollars a year for it. The govt. is also buying the fort from the fur company. These Indians are the finest we have seen anywhere in America. Tall, manly, full of vigour — and very keen traders, too. 'Me good Indian,' they say. They live in fine tents of tanned buffalo hide, which we, with our bleached, patched covers, envy them. They expect many thousand Palefaces to pass this way before the next snows, so they have every incentive to trade and none at all to 'raise hair,' as Frank puts it. And yet those very numbers, I fear, will eventually put an end to their fine, free way of life.

10 May: Though it would content me to send this letter now, I feel, on reading it, it would dampen your spirit with our hardships and *ennui*. And also, when you look at the map, you will see we have so far still to go. A captain at the fort says we are bound to meet a letter carrier along the way, so I shall wait until we reach the Great Divide. Then you will be assured that our worst, or at least the uphill portion of it, is behind us, and you will be able to imagine us already in California and

bringing up great nuggets of gold with the toecaps of our boots wherever we kick the sand.

The same man told me that they were fools who pressed on so hastily. They burdened themselves down with all kinds of needless provender and will find their way blocked by snows between Devil's Gate and South Pass for several weeks yet. The Collets, though disinclined to believe Frank, seem to have taken this fresh warning to heart. We have bought another yoke of oxen for their wagon.

A good omen as we were about to draw out: Our best ox, which we lost at Cave Creek, was brought into camp by an incoming train. They were sad to part with him but could not argue with the brand. We gave them our spare cooking pot since they had to stop theirs with rye meal every day and that cheered them up.

The country here is a Paradise compared with the Purgatory down on the Platte. In reality, of course, we are still following the Platte, or the North Fork of it, but here the land is beautiful rolling pasture, high meadows laced with gushing streams, full of wild roses, larkspur, mountain cherry, and blueflax. I write this in the evening, when the breeze is charged with the fragrance of pine and cedar and sage, with which we make our fire; and we awaken to an air so pure and fine we feel like gods, and equal to whatever challenge lies ahead.

15 May: Fate must have been peeping over my shoulder as I wrote the above. Paradise, indeed! Down on the prairie she bludgeoned us; here she employs subtlety instead. The way continues beautiful to behold, the weather settled and fine, but these are badlands *in excelsis*. The hills are savage. Frost and rain and wind have combined down the centuries to litter our way with razor-sharp fragments of rock, which damage the hooves of our cattle and cut even our stoutest boot leather. And the sucking mud of the river bottoms seems alive in its malevolence. In one creek today the Ferrises' wagon was smashed in pieces; and had we not found a wheel, abandoned nearby when some previous

traveller met with a like fate, they would have been forced to go back.

Perhaps they would have joined the Indians. I forgot to say that two couples who came with us to Laramie decided to stay and live as Indians — making more than a dozen who had chosen that life in that one camp alone.

Thanks to these diversions, we made but five miles today. The altitude, near 5,000 ft, makes everything doubly strenuous; and always our way goes up. Even when we descend into a river bottom, our way out is 'twice as up as it was down' (Frank).

No sign of any letter carrier yet.

20 May: Another working Sabbath. Our preacher, an old circuit rider named Jackson, took as his text, 'Come unto me all ye that are heavy laden.' Which some thought appropriate but others too near the bone. The meadowlands are behind us and we are back in a treeless waste of grey and brown, where sagebrush seems to have sole pre-emption. Frank shot an antelope today, which gave us good meat, but for that we should be as low as at any time since leaving Kanesville.

The land, both hills and plains, is scored with deep, volcanic fissures. We drop stones into them, as young lads do into abandoned mine-shafts back home, to estimate their depth. Some are cloven several hundred feet. Talking of cloven feet, the trail is now of deep sand, which is the hardest going of all for our poor oxen. All of them now wear half shoes, which at least prevents lameness though it does nothing to ease the burden of draught.

The wayside is littered with the shards of wagons which we collect for firing, since the sage is so poor at retaining its heat. It breaks one's heart to use it, when one thinks of the poor people who came so many hundreds of miles — through what strains and privations we know all too well — only to see it all end here, in this waste of boulders and hills and nothingness.

We also come across stoves, cooking pots, bread

kettles, coffee cans — all that extra plunder bought up
by the feckless at Ft Laramie and now shed as so much
hindrance. Those poor people who were so glad of our
spare pot in return for finding our oxen will kick
themselves for their gratitude when they pass this way!
Even sadder are the graves. *Tom Vernon,* said one, *B.
1818, Spitalfields, London. Head crushed by wagon
wheel.* Another commemorated *Baby Simpson, died of
colic, Aged 4 days.* Their clothing is usually left with
them. Tom Vernon had a fine coat, which I would not
have left behind. The Indians are too superstitious to
rob these graves, but one winter will undo them utterly.

Still not one single letter carrier going east. I think I
was deceived.

23 May: Today Frank ordered a day of rest since
tomorrow is alkali country and we shall need every
ounce of strength and all our reserves of it. I thought I
would catch up on this letter but we spent all our time
cutting up fat pork and laying it down in meal, also
filling every container to the brim with water. And so
early to bed. No letter carrier again. I shall give this to
the first who comes, whether we have reached the
Divide or no.

24 May: Now indeed I have endured Hell. As we set off
I saw a flock of magpie, an omen of luck at home. I
greeted them respectfully, as any normal superstitious
Christian should, and perhaps our luck was to have
survived this day at all. They are different to ours, with
long, green-hued tails — the longest tails I yet saw on
any bird here.

The alkali desert itself is one vast, trackless waste of
sand, scorched by the sun and baked to granite
hardness. It is mottled with stagnant pools filled not
with water but with a scum of soda, sulphur, and
copper. The stench is as if all the cess pits in a large city
had been thrown open at once — and all the bad eggs
in the world thrown into them and smashed. Frank's
stratagem of eating no meal before we set off worked no
better than ours, Cunningham's and mine, which was to

eat little — nor, indeed than the Collets', which was to eat a lot. We all retched miserably — the entire train, the evidence of which upon the sand only added to our nausea.

Wind devils descended out of nowhere and whipped up the alkali dust to sting our eyes and coat our ears and nostrils, and anywhere our sweat had gathered — just in time for a hellish red sun to bake it hard. Our cheeks are peeled and our lips are split open so that, as Frank said, fingering his gun, 'The first to make a joke, man, woman, or child, I'll search his carcase for a heart.'

But our chief problem was the cattle. Through all these torments, no matter how red or itching our eyes, we must keep them *peeled* (and in that desert the word has an exquisite meaning all its own) for the cattle, that they did not drink from the poisoned pools; for one swallow will bring a swift and horrible death — the only remedy for which is a forced feeding of pork fat. And hence our labours of yesterday. Fortunately none was needed. Indeed, as I write these words I am bathed in the most delicious aroma of frying lard and eggs and baking bread.

The Lord is indeed merciful. At the very height of our torment we all smelt it simultaneously, even the cattle. I mean, by then desperation had honed our sense of smell as keen as theirs. And soon we saw it, too — the darling white ribbon of the Sweetwater River, the most beautiful mountain stream in the world. And it will be our companion for the next 100 miles, though it still flows east it will bring us to the Divide. It is in spate at the moment, which suggests an early thaw ahead.

26 May: Another landmark, this time a huge, badly baked loaf of bread called Independence Rock, a single monolith of granite, a third of a mile long, a furlong wide, and thrusting up out of the desert to tower almost 200 ft above our head. We felt puny, indeed, which is perhaps what induced us to do what hundreds who had passed this way before us have done — paint our names in tar upon its flank.

There we nooned before passing on to Devil's Gate,

a gorge of 65 fathoms depth carved through the rock by the Sweetwater. The name must have been given by a party travelling east. In our view it should be called Heaven's Gate, for the land beyond it made us rub our weary eyes. As far as the horizon it is one endless water-meadow carpet of wild flowers and prairie grasses, all blowing in the gentlest of zephyrs, nodding and swaying to the very tops of all the hills. It looks as if those impatient ones who went on ahead have been lucky with the thaw.

28 May: I have long suspected Frank of having a better education that he 'lets on'. Today he said the Sweetwater is, 'The cantankarest durn sample of hydrographic sinuosity I ever seed.' I put him top of the class for observation, too. Half a fathom deep and two chains wide, I doubt if its longest stretch in any one direction exceeds ten paces. We walked in it for a while, including the oxen, to cool our feet, which it did excellently. But the twists and turns so detained us that in the end we returned to the trail, which is over a very hard granite, smoother and less fractured than our Cornish stone but cruel on the feet. Five miles was all we managed since nooning. The cattle prefer the dry buffalo grass along the water margin to the succulent looking meadows all around. We must assume they know what is most nutritious for them. The sagebrush here grows to ten feet and its pale, dusty green is very restful to our eyes. Evidence abounds of a lengthy encampment here, so perhaps those who forestalled us were not so lucky after all.

Today we saw signal smoke in the hills to our north. Later a half-breed wandered among us, going east, and he said they were war signals and that the Crow were fighting the Blackfoot to control this part of the country. He said to corral the cattle at night for when they are at war they cannot hunt and so risk the white man's guns to steal his meat. He also spoke of another party just a day and a half ahead of us; so that is all they gained!

31 May: Today we have parted with the Sweetwater, just a mile or two from the summit level of South Pass. Remnants of snow on the peaks all about, but nothing along the trail.

The air is cold and crisp and somehow one can feel its thinness. I could not help stopping and saying to my companions, 'This water we see before us will by this time next year, be mingled into the Gulf of Mexico, and from there, by way of the Gulf Stream, it may, a decade or a century hence, be dashing itself against Bullion Cliffs or upon Praa Sands in our own, beloved Cornwall. The next water we meet will never make that journey.'

It was a truly awe-inspiring moment and yet we need these childish reminders before we can grasp the majesty behind such a dry geographical term as Great Divide.

The road through South Pass was hard granite gravel and easy going, fringed with beautiful scented flowers including daisies. Though we were some way short of the actual Divide, I could not resist a practice with my (formerly Cunningham's) sextant. Thanks to which I can categorically record that we have reached an altitude of 7,085 ft at Latitude 42° 18′ 48″ north and Longitude 108° 40′ west. We then floundered through another alkali swamp, though nothing like so bad as the first before going down on our stomachs and drinking from Pacific Springs. We marvelled at the sight of water flowing west and wished it a hundred times greater in volume, that we might have built a raft (out of what, though?) and float all the rest of the way.

Still no letter carrier.

1 June: A letter carrier at last! An intrepid man on one pony and leading a second has just ridden in among us. He has come all the way from California, picking up mail as he goes, which he will carry back to civilization for fifty cents apiece, plus whatever their onward postage will then be. His reports of the gold finds in California are extremely favourable and have put fresh heart into all of us – even those who intend going to Oregon, such is the infection of hope. Our hasty friends

now only a day ahead of us, which we can tell from the warmth of their hearths as we find them.

I must seal this and send it at once. Did Providence hear me when I wished to wait until now before releasing these pages? I love you, my darling — or my darlings I must now write. And now you are two, and both so dear to me, I have twice my former reason to make a swift success of the business ahead and return to you with God speed, and never ever be parted from you again. I could match each *word* of the foregoing with a whole page of endearments but this fellow is in a hurry.

Your ever-loving and ever-faithful, Hal

Chapter Fifty-Two

'Your ever loving and ever faithful Hal,' Johanna repeated as she folded away the letter. 'That's your daddy. Dada? Dada? Say it — you said it beautifully yesterday. Dada.'

Hannah just grinned and gurgled and kicked the thin cotton coverlets away.

'Oh, who d'you get that stubbornness from?' Johanna asked with playful weariness. 'Listen — you're going to meet your godmother today. Yes, you're going to be baptized at last, just to torment your Uncle Tony. But she's not at all well, so I want you to be very, very good. Promise?'

'Does she understand all that?' Hilary asked shyly from the doorway.

'Come in, come in,' Johanna told her. 'Of course she does. Every single word. I'll just change her napkin and then you may ...'

'Oh let me?' the girl begged.

Johanna, who had got no farther than lifting the baby's skirts, blew a raspberry on her naked tummy, pulled a face at the reek of the present napkin, and gladly resigned the office. Since the baby was born, Hilary had turned over a new leaf and become quite fanatical about cleanliness.

Hannah, seeing only that her mother was leaving her, began at once to howl.

'Louder!' Johanna encouraged her. 'Come on, I can't hear you. That wouldn't make a fly turn around. Louder!'

Hannah stopped.

'See?' Johanna said. 'Every single word.' At the door she added, 'Put her out in the garden when you've done. In the shade but...'

567

'. . . in the shade but out of the breeze.' Hilary said it like a litany. Then, more respectfully, she added, 'The boys are waiting on you, ma'am.'

'Oh, such impatience!' Johanna called over her shoulder as she left. To Tony's maternal grandmother, whose portrait hung at the head of the stair, she added, 'I'm not going to bottle it if it's not ready.' And to the old lady's husband, who hung at the half-landing: 'They'll just have to wait.'

She had been brewing table beer for some time now, and had found quite a good sale for it. Table beer was easy. You sent it out in cask, still fermenting, and people used their own isinglass or fish skin to fine it. But everyone had told her how much they missed Charley Vose's beautiful pale ale. So at last she had taken the plunge, even though she had never tried to brew anything more forbidding than porter, which was generally agreed to be about half-way in difficulty between beer and ale.

Her maltster, Thomas Tregear of Hayle, had tried to palm her off with the same high-dried malt she'd taken for the beer; but one thing she had remembered from her brief time at the Ram was Charley Vose's insistence that the malt for his ale – indeed, the malt for any stock liquor – should be dried slowly and carefully. Any mark of singeing and he'd reject it. That was where she had gone wrong with her porter, though that had been back in her time with the Visicks, when she hadn't known any better. So she had battled with Tregear a whole afternoon, and in the end she had cajoled him into supplying the quality she desired.

This first ale brew had been like another baby to her. She had practically slept on top of the fermenting tun when they first led the mash into it. Tony had played his part, too. 'I believe Charley Vose may have been even more clever than he supposed,' he said. 'Look at the enormous increase in the yeast by the time fermentation is complete.'

'That's where the flavour comes from,' she told him. 'That was always Charley's secret.'

He shook his head dubiously. 'It must be more than that. I believe the yeast must play some part in the actual fermentation, too.' He had to agree that none of the standard treatises on brewing mentioned yeast, except as an accidental by-product. However, acting on his suspicions, he had 'bred' a portion of baker's yeast through several accelerated fermentations until it could survive comfortably in alcohol above ten percent.

And despite his crackpot theories Johanna had to allow that his 'special breed' of yeast proved very steady, giving a long, slow, cool fermentation from which the liquor could be raked off as clear as glass and with no need for finings — at least, such was her hope for today; yesterday there had still been a slight cloudiness. She wanted to use no finings, if possible. That was another thing Charley had once told her: 'Finings in, flavour out.'

Peter and James were larking around in the brewhouse doorway, leaning on one jamb and walking up the other; James, though younger, was a perfect length for this trick and so proved the equal of his brother, who got more and more angry to find himself matched at each attempt.

'You could at least have swept out the brew-house,' she chided them as she came across the yard.

'We did, ma'am,' they said in sheepish chorus as they straightened up.

'And washed the bottles? We may need them today.'

'Iris is doing it now, ma'am.'

'And you couldn't help her, of course.' She strode between them, tousling their heads. Such knobbly, bony things, boys.

'Help I?' Iris queried sarcastically from the dark interior.

'How's it coming?' Johanna raised one of the bottles and held it to the light. 'We'll make a brewer of you yet, young woman.'

Iris basked in the implied approval. Johanna rounded on the boys. 'Clean, clean, clean,' she intoned, 'Dirty fingernails turn good ale to bad vinegar. Let me see them.'

They held out their hands and waited intently, mouths agape, for her reaction. Amazingly, they were clean. 'You're learning,' she said severely. 'Come on — let's see if we've made some ale at last.'

She reached one of Tony's apothecary cylinders off the shelf and passed it to Iris, who swilled it and gave it back. She squatted before the first of the racking barrels and eased out the top bung, letting the gas escape slowly before she lifted it right out and then rested it loosely back in again. 'Why do I put it half back in again?' she asked. 'Iris?'

'To stop wild yeasts from getting in, ma'am.'

'And where are all these wild yeasts?'

'Everywhere.'

'Even on *skin.*' James said, as if skin were not the most disgusting thing imaginable.

She held the cylinder under the spigot. 'And why am I letting it run so slowly down the side of the glass? Peter?'

'To stop it so it won't de-gas, ma'am.'

'Good. Why shouldn't it de-gas, Jimmy?'

He tripped up his own tongue in his eagerness to show her he knew the answer. ''Cos it's . . . 'cos people wouldn't . . . 'cos they wouldn't . . . 'cos it's flat . . . 'cos . . .'

'Just try and say one thing at a time, lad.'

''Cos people wouldn't buy it,' Peter cut in.

'I said that,' his brother told him vehemently.

'Didn't.'

'Did. So there!' And he belted him with his fist as high as he could reach.

'Nyeh-eh!' Peter paraded his lack of hurt.

Iris lifted the flat of her hand menacingly. Johanna, still carefully racking off the liquor, said quietly, 'If you two don't behave yourselves, I'll twist your arms off and you won't get them back until Christmas.'

It was not the first time they had heard the threat, but the enormity of the image it conjured up for them was so thrilling they both laughed with delight and settled down to try and behave properly.

She rose and carried the glass to the door, where she raised it against the bright July sun. It sparkled like burnished amber, a clean, golden fluid that looked as good as anything Charley Vose ever made. 'Beginner's luck,' she murmured, to guard against being carried away.

Peter whispered something in Jimmy's ear that made him snigger. Johanna, guessing what it might have been, held her peace, but Iris cuffed him hard. Seeing him about to cry, Johanna said, 'If you ever say a thing like that again, I'll stand over you until you drink it. And I'm talking about drinking what you said, not this ale. D'you follow me?'

570

Poised precisely between disgust, giggling, and wanting to cry, he rubbed his stinging ear and nodded.

'Well!' Johanna passed the cylinder to Iris. 'Tell me if you think that's clear.'

All three youngsters crowded their heads together, staring intently at the glass, searching for the least sign of cloudiness.

Looking at their young faces, so alert and eager, Johanna could not help remembering their mother. Though she had never seen the woman alive, one glance at her corpse had been enough to show her as a coarse, drunken, befuddled creature – exactly the sort of woman who'd go to Widow Jewell for a linctus and leave her fourteen-year-old daughter behind to earn the price of it.

Tony was right. Only yesterday he had remarked on how much brighter and more alive the Cardew children were nowadays. 'It's because you talk to them all the time,' he told her. 'You're forever challenging them – never letting their minds rest.'

'But that's the trouble,' she grumbled. 'Their minds *don't* rest. Leave them alone and they're always up to some divilment, as Nina says. I don't call it "challenging" them – more like distracting.'

'Ah, but they were never like that before. One could see in them all the signs of that terrible, brutish lethargy of the intelligence. I often notice it, going round their wretched little cabins. I see youngsters of five or six, bright as buttons, full of zest and curiosity. But by ten they're starting to go dull. And at fourteen it's all gone. That's a terrible thing we do to them. Every new generation – they're born with that divine spark and we turn them into brutes.'

'Hardly *we*,' she objected.

'You think not?'

That lightly spoken question had caused her much thought.

Iris handed her back the cylinder. 'I don't think we'd hardly get 'ee much clearer 'n that, ma'am.'

She smiled at them. 'Then the three of you have several hours' employment in there.'

The two lads skipped gleefully indoors. Iris asked if she wasn't going to test the specific gravity again but Johanna shook her head. 'That won't have changed since yesterday. But it's good that you think of things like that.'

She showed them how to rack the ale off slowly into the bottles; how to use the corking machine; and how to paste the labels on, making sure each one was straight with the bottom edge and a quarter-inch above it. 'And when I come back from the christening, we'll have a tea party on the lawn — but you won't be invited unless you've finished up here *and* done the job properly.'

The label, all in dark brown and red and gold, was her special pride. She had designed it herself and Tony had got it printed secretly in Plymouth by a friend he knew they could trust. It took the form of a heraldic shield with her own initials, *JR,* at the top where the crest would be; and, like some crests, they were slanted over to one side. 'They look a bit drunk to me,' Tony had commented — not realizing that was the point until he heard himself making it. The shield itself was ornamented with hops and barley, and the only bits of text read: 'Fine old pale bitter ale,' and, at the bottom, 'Brewed in Cornwall'. The point of choosing her initials, she said, was that the local gentry had a fad for talking about a 'jar' of beer; every time they did so, they'd already be half-way to choosing her brew above someone else's.

She admired it all over again before she reluctantly picked up the cylinder and left the youngsters to argue it out as to whether they should specialize in one of the processes or whether each was to cork and label the bottle they filled. She gained the yard just as Hilary was wheeling the bassinet across to the orchard. Tony was with her. 'How can you just walk away from a racket like that?' he asked admiringly.

'Hannah?' she asked.

'No. The brew house.'

'Oh, they'll work better if they pick their own tasks.' She passed him the cylinder. 'We seem to have made a brew to equal anything Charley Vose ever managed. What d'you think?'

He took a sip and swirled it round his mouth before swallowing it. 'Not half bad,' he murmured, smacking his lips.

He offered Hilary a sip; she swallowed it, smacked her lips, and gave an approving nod.

'That blend of bitter and sweet,' Johanna added, 'is very delicate. It's so easy to overdo one or other of them.'

'No, I think you've got that just right.' He grinned. 'Can you repeat it, though?'

She shrugged. 'That remains to be seen.' Together they sauntered back toward the house. 'I'll make a fresh lot of mash tomorrow and start the next brew.'

'Is that wise?' he asked. 'Shouldn't we wait for orders to start coming in?'

'I'm going to leave those bottles stand a while – see how they keep. This weather will be a good test of that. Really, I don't want to sell anything until it's been at least three months in bottle.'

His eyebrows shot up.

'I told you – it's a completely different business from brewing beer.'

He nodded ruefully. 'Yes, it is a *business*. I see that.'

She smiled to herself but he turned and caught it. 'D'you want it in pounds, shillings, and pence?' she asked, giving a provocative arch to one eyebrow.

He nodded.

'There are six barrels in there whose contents amount to twenty-three shillings each. Malt fifteen shillings; hops eight. If they keep that quality' – she tapped the cylinder, which he was still holding – 'those same contents will sell in bottle for sixty-five shillings wholesale and ninety-odd retail.'

His eyes popped out of his head. 'Whew!' he whistled. 'No wonder the big brewers are so generous at election time.'

'Don't mock the big brewers, my dear. You could be one yourself, someday.'

'God forbid!' He turned to more immediate topics. 'What are you going to do between now and the christening?'

'Make excerpts from Hal's letter for Selina. Actually, there's a bit of it I'd like to show you now – d'you have time?'

They went indoors by way of the kitchen, where Peggy

Machin, the cook throughout Johanna's earlier years at Lanfear, was once again installed. She delayed Johanna to taste one or two of the sweetmeats for the party that afternoon.

She found Tony waiting for her in the morning room, nervously drumming his fingers on the window sill.

'Sorry,' she said, 'Would you rather not?'

'Eh? Oh, no, it's not that. It's Nina this afternoon.'

'If you really think she isn't up to it . . .'

He sighed. 'Even if she's not, you can imagine what it would do to her to call it off.' He gave a sudden, reassuring smile. 'Oh, she'll be all right. What was it you wanted to show me?'

She took out Hal's letter and let him read the bit about his marrying her by proxy. His face remained impassive, even when he folded it and handed it back to her. 'And what will you do?' he asked.

'I just don't see any point in it,' she replied. 'Do you?'

It was hardly the answer he had been expecting. He just stared at her in surprise.

'Well – what's done is done. This wouldn't make a scrap of difference to Hannah.'

'But it would to you. It would change a lot of people's attitudes – especially if you want to start selling your ale about the place this autumn.'

She couldn't deny that. All she said was, 'It would be like admitting that I accept their way of looking at it – which I don't. D'you think I'm just a stubborn, cantankerous old maid?'

'I'd jib at "old",' he allowed.

She stared again at the letter, as if a different reading might release her from the need to decide. And he, for his part, stared at her in amused surprise. 'Are you really asking me to supply you with reasons for *not* marrying Hal Penrose?' he asked at length.

'It just seems a pointless way of going about it,' she repeated.

'Then don't do it.' He gave an exasperated laugh.

'No,' she said as if he had hit upon an answer that would always have eluded her. 'You're right. I won't. Thank you, Tony. Now you're not emotionally involved yourself, you

574

can see these things so much clearer than me.'

'Call on me at any time.' He managed to keep a straight face. As she went out by the door he asked, 'What about his other suggestion – an advertisement in the *Cornishman*? Will you do that?'

She frowned, having already put the whole thing from her mind. 'Oh no,' she said. 'There'd be even less point in doing that. Besides, it would make me look so abject – just begging to be accepted again. I'd never beg like that – would you?'

'No, Jo, that's something I'd never do either. Not beg.'

Chapter Fifty-Three

Because of Nina's illness the baptism was to be held in private at Liston Court. They set off just before three – Johanna, Tony, and Hilary with the baby, all wrapped up in a beautiful christening shawl that had belonged to Tony's grandmother. A couple of hours earlier the sky had clouded over, thinly, allowing the sun to break through in hazy patches from time to time. Despite the breeze the air was sultry. Movement was an effort and Johanna found herself yawning every half mile or so on the journey into Helston. And yet she could not rest. She fidgeted so much that Tony eventually passed her the reins, saying, 'Get some employment into those hands, woman. You're driving me mad.'

She checked that Hannah was safely in Hilary's arms and then took up the reins gratefully. 'I can't settle to anything,' she said.

'It's only a christening. I'm sure Reverend Pelham could recite the entire ritual in his sleep. Indeed, I believe he often does so.'

'It's nothing to do with all that, Tony, as I'm sure you know very well. It's the thought of seeing Nina again after – what is it, almost a year? – and in such awful circumstances.'

He nodded. 'But how do you suppose *she* feels?'

'Well . . . forgiving, obviously, but . . .'

'She's precisely the opposite, my dear. She's convinced that she's the one who harmed you. And if anyone has any forgiving to do . . .'

'No, no – she's wrong. She must be. Oh, I understood it all so clearly that time, the day Hannah was born. I wish I'd just had the courage to go and see her, that's all.'

'Whatever you lacked that day, I don't think it was courage. What did you understand so clearly?'

'Oh, I couldn't even begin to explain it. Just the way she is. Always searching for . . . more. Always hoping for more. Not in a petulant, childish sort of way, but just because she wants to get the most out of life. I recalled one morning when we were driving into Rome and she kept stopping every time we passed another patch of wildflowers. And she'd leap down and sniff them, because she was always looking for a new fragrance.'

'And did she find it?'

'No, that's the point. I realized that was exactly what happened between her and me. I was a weed she passed on the wayside, and whatever it was she sought in me, I just couldn't provide it. I let her down.' She shook her head in vexation. 'I haven't explained it at all properly.'

'But, Jo, she accused you of being a thief.'

'And wasn't it a kind of theft? To accept everything she gave me and not to give back whatever she wanted?'

His only response was to rake the heavens with an exasperated eye. She turned to him and caught the tail end of it. 'What's that mean?' she asked.

He pondered his answer carefully before he spoke. 'You know how sometimes, when you hear a new word, or new to you . . . like last Easter I heard the word "rubric" for the first time. I can't imagine why I'd never heard it before, but I hadn't. And suddenly I heard it on three separate occasions, in very different circumstances, all within a week. And it makes you think, "Have I been both blind and deaf all these years or what?" Does that ever happen you?'

'Quite often, but I don't see what . . .'

'Well, I get the same feeling now over this guilt of yours, which isn't like a real guilt at all − because one can't . . .'

'Oh, isn't it just! What d'you call a real guilt, then?'

'I was on the point of saying: one can't get at it with logic and show how groundless it is. It seems to run too deep for that. But the strange thing about it − and this is what I've noticed several times these last few weeks, though I'd never remarked it before in all my life − is that all the sufferers of this particular kind of guilt are women. Coincidence? Or a Genuine Phenomenon?'

Johanna, slightly annoyed to hear her own moral balance sheet lumped in as just one more 'case' among several, said, 'Well, as I know nothing about these other unfortunate females . . .' and let the sarcasm hang.

'One is Mrs Williams, whose baby was stillborn, with a defective heart, you remember. She blames herself for it and nothing I can say will shake her. Another is the daughter of someone in our union who was indecently assaulted just outside Breage, on the old road to Helston. I'm having the devil's own job persuading her she need feel no guilt about it at all.'

'Who was that?' Johanna asked.

'I'd better not say the name.' He turned and smiled apologetically at Hilary, as much as to say he wasn't singling her out as being particularly untrustworthy.

But she took it as an invitation to contribute — which she had wanted to do ever since he had begun on this theme. 'Yes,' she said eagerly. ''Twere the same with I, after all that old caper up Paradise Row. You remember, ma'am, how you kept telling I, "Put a comb through that hair, maid . . . put up a clean pinny, that one's a disgrace . . ."'

'And wash your face,' Johanna chimed in, recalling how the girl had gone through a slatternly phase in her first weeks at Lanfear House.

Hilary laughed at the memory now. 'And I kept saying to meself, "Can't her see it? Don't her understand that showing a pretty face and wearing nice clothes and that was what got me in trouble." I reckoned it was my own fault, see? I obeyed you, like, in the end, but I never really got over it until that day in church, when I give he back that five bob. That's when I saw 'twas no fault of mine.'

Tony reached back and patted her on the shoulder. 'You've answered my original question,' he told her. 'I *am* blind. And deaf. I should have realized.'

'You're not the only one,' Johanna added. 'Oh, Hilary — why didn't you *say?* We'd have understood. Did we seem such ogres to you that you couldn't speak out?'

''Course not.' The girl laughed awkwardly. 'It wouldn't have made no different how you was to I.' She touched her breast. ''Twas in here, see? I could tell myself I was just being dawbrained. I could see that. But it never made no different.'

Johanna saw a bolt hole for herself. 'Ah, now there is a difference between your cases and mine,' she told Tony. 'I don't tell myself I'm just being dawbrained.'

They were negotiating the sharp corner at the bottom of Sithney Common Hill. Taking advantage of Johanna's distraction he winked at Hilary and said, 'All right. Here's a case in point. I took young Hilary here under our roof very much as Lady Nina took in you — both in some distress, in the dark, at the side of the road.'

'Yes, all right — for argument's sake.'

'My reasons were — I mean, apart from the fact that Hilary was in need and so on — my own selfish reasons were that I wanted the help and support of one of the most honest, hard-working, cheerful, and kind-natured young servants in the whole of Cornwall. But just suppose I had wanted her in order to — oh, I don't know — to train her up to sing in grand opera, say.'

Hilary laughed at the notion.

'Well, pretty and all as her voice is,' he went on, 'my ambition to turn her into a second Jenny Lind would be a trifle absurd. So when, inevitably, she fails, and I get furious, and claw her face to shreds, and go about calling her a thief and all that, and then she starts feeling guilty at having let me down — is she being dawbrained, in your view, or would her guilt be well founded and proper?'

Johanna shook her head stubbornly. 'The cases are different.'

'I'd like to know how.'

'Because I'm me and nobody else is.'

Hilary nodded and gave him a sympathetic little smile, as if to say, 'You may not understand it, mister, but I know just what she means.'

They were going up the hill into Cross Street. At the very point where Johanna had felt that invisible wall of glass preventing her from going forward, the horse stopped dead. Tony was thrown forward and caught the nearest thing to hand, which was the lever that let down the sprag.

'That was quick thinking,' Johanna said admiringly. 'Come on, boy — gee up!'

The horse went on again. The moment he was past that point he behaved perfectly normally. 'What got into him?'

Tony asked, pulling back on the lever and raising the sprag once more.

'Just a dawbrained old horse,' she commented.

The air seemed to grow even more oppressive as they drew into the carriageway at Liston Court. Johanna turned her eyes at once to the spot where Brookesy's menhir had stood. Its place was now taken by a large pond, with red and yellow fish swimming lazily in its dense green water. Selina came out to meet them as they drew up before the portico. It was some weeks now since Johanna had last seen her; though she smiled a warm enough welcome, she was wan and pale.

'What an unbearably sultry day,' Johanna said as she kissed her. 'You look worn out, poor thing.'

Her cousin seemed to take it as a rebuke, for she straightened up and made a pointed effort to be lively.

'How is she today?' Tony asked.

Selina's shrug spoke volumes; her voice merely interpreted: 'Much as before. She took a little nourishment today but couldn't retain it.'

Johanna suddenly became aware that Nina was dying. In all their references to her long illness neither Tony nor Selina had so much as hinted at the possibility; they had not even referred to it as a decline. But now, in their mutual glances, in their tone of voice, in the very way they did *not* speak of it, Nina's impending death was the only thing that occupied them.

'Terence is already here,' Selina told them. 'You could take his godchild in to be spoiled for a few minutes, Hilary. Reverend Pelham sent to say he'd been unavoidably detained.'

'Which, in translation, means he overslept his lunch,' Tony commented.

'Nina wants a word with you alone, first,' her cousin went on. As Johanna was about to mount the stairs, she added, 'You will find her greatly changed, Jo. You know she hasn't been able to manage any food for some time.'

Johanna turned to Tony. 'D'you really think this is such a good idea?' she asked him.

'She absolutely insists,' he answered.

'I think it's now the only thing that's . . .' Selina could not finish the sentence. She smiled feebly at them both.

Full of foreboding now, Johanna went up the stairs to Nina's boudoir. As she went in, Margaret Tyzack rose and left the room, passing Johanna with the briefest of nods – a mere token of recognition. Even then, despite all her premonitions, and despite the air of death that was so thick in the house, she would never have recognized the wizened old lady in Nina's bed as that bright, fair, effervescent young woman who had brought her into this house almost two years ago now. She seemed more like a skeleton, lightly draped in onion skins, than a living human being. Only her eyes gave her away – pale blue, bright as ever, full of challenge and laughter and outrageous opinion . . . and the unspeakable sadness of things, all in one.

'Hello, Jo, me darlin' one,' she called out in a husky tone that was half whisper, half speech. 'Aren't I a sight!'

'Nina!' Johanna fell to her knees at the bedside. 'Oh, Nina.' She kissed her tenderly on her dark, shrivelled cheek.

'Don't go to pieces, my swan,' Nina warned. 'It happens to all of us sooner or later.'

Johanna buried her face in that hair which had once been so luxuriant. 'Don't talk so,' she pleaded. 'You're not going to die. Oh, please?'

'Shh, shh, child. Didn't you know? Didn't they tell you?'

Johanna shook her head.

'That was me, I'm afraid. Don't blame them. Sit where I may see you. So! That's it. God, but you're as bonny as ever. Motherhood must suit you. As bonny as a fightin' rabbit, as my old nurse used to say. Would you ever reach under the covers here and find my hand and fetch it out for me?'

Johanna did as she was asked, marvelling pitifully that so thin a limb still had room for blood vessels and sinews – it seemed to be all bone. Yet Nina's grip was strong, even though there seemed to be no muscle to provide it.

'I was a fool,' she said. 'The time I wasted, blaming you, cursing you – and not feeling how my own arrogance was eating me up from inside. Look at me – I'm nearly all gone.'

Johanna drew breath to speak but Nina gripped hard and shook her head imperceptibly. 'I have the power of my right hand and my jaw,' she said. 'Leave me use them while I may.'

581

'And your mind, darling. That's as sharp as ever. Can't you ... isn't it possible ...' She couldn't quite frame the words.

'Fight back? That was three months ago. Or was it three weeks? I've gone down so quick.'

'Are you in any pain?'

Nina smiled. 'Tony is very good. No, listen — there are things I must tell you. Stupid, eejit things about money and that but I have to tell you. Selina ...'

Her voice, such as it was, tailed away. Johanna thought she had lost consciousness, for her eyes were closed and her face was impassive, but then she saw a small tear roll down her cheek. She reached out, caught it on her fingers before it fell to the sheets, and carried it by instinct to her own lips. There was no salt in it. 'You were my sister,' Nina went on, still not opening her eyes, 'but little Selina was my child. She is a child, Jo. There's something in her will never grow up. D'you follow me now?'

'Yes.'

She opened her eyes then. 'All my inheritance from Brookesy was entailed to a cousin of his. The man was older than Brookesy, so how long he'll live to enjoy it, the dear alone knows. Had he died first, 'twould have been mine in ... what's the rigmarole? Fee something. Mine entirely, anyway. And then you ...' Her eyes sought and found Johanna and she smiled and gripped her hand as if she thought she had finished the sentence. 'I was so sure I'd outlive him. Man proposes, God laughs — who said that?'

'You shouldn't be taxing yourself with these things now, my love,' Johanna told her.

'No, no — listen, I didn't finish. Did I tell you what I want for Selina?'

'Not yet.'

'The increase on Brookesy's estate *is* mine. The money I multiplied out of it. That's mine and it's quite a tidy sum by now. It wasn't everyone went down in the big smash. Did I tell you what I want for Selina?'

'You were just about to, darling. You said you'd done with Brookesy's legacy what the good servant did in the parable of the talents.'

'Parable of the talents?' Nina frowned, trying to recollect

582

something. 'She never did let me know. Jenny Diamond, was it?'

'Jenny Jewell?'

'Yes! Whatever happened to her? She was supposed to write to me.'

'She married a friend of Hal's. You were telling me about Selina.'

'Married a friend of Hal's!' Nina chuckled. 'I'll bet they brewed that little tale up between them, to keep you happy.'

'I expect so. What about Selina?'

'But she'll find some way of letting you know, Jenny Diamond. Very nimble brain, that one. Are you sure she hasn't told you?'

'Not yet.' Johanna wondered how a body so frail could continue to support a mind so nimble — to use her own word for it — and, conversely, why a brain that was so obviously alive and in touch with the world couldn't force that enfeebled frame to repair itself and recover from whatever ailed it. What could it be, she wondered?

'Or perhaps she's got the measure of that braggart Hal. Perhaps she thinks you deserve every particle of him. Then, of course, she'd go to her grave swearing she married that friend. Be careful of that, won't you.'

'Yes,' Johanna whispered. She closed her eyelids tight, squeezing a tear out between them.

'About Selina. I've left you a small bequest — your half of the profit on the railway shares for working out what the Great Liar in your life was really up to.'

'Nina! There was no need for that.'

'I know. It doubled the pleasure. And don't tell me you can't make good use of it.'

'I hate this. I'd give all I own — and all you own, too, and all the treasures in Pallas House and all the tin in Cornwall — just to hear you say you're going to get well again.'

'Oh, I will. But not this side of the grave. I know the first soul I'll meet beyond is me darlin' oul' man again. And I know the first thing he'll want to do! You remember I always said he died *on* me in Venice?'

'Yes.'

'Did you know what I meant?' She chuckled.

'Not the first time you said it. But later I twigged.'

'The way time runs in Eternity, he's going to think he never stopped. He always said I'd led him into Paradise, and now he'll be able to say I told you so. Except I've no handles for his grip any more. He'll notice that all right.'

Johanna joined her laughter, though her heart was fit to break. 'Well,' Nina said, 'that's all there is to it. I told you about Selina, didn't I?'

'You did. You've told me everything you wanted to. And I think that's the curate at the front door now. They'll bring the baby up soon. Do you . . . are you sure you feel up to it, darling? You wouldn't like to rest a while?'

'It's all in my will, anyway,' Nina said. 'It's all in my will.' There was a long pause and then she repeated it again. 'It's all in my will.' Like her body, her voice had faded to almost nothing.

The clock struck the half hour — half past four, Johanna realized.

She bent over and kissed her friend on the lips; there was no sign of breathing. She knew then Nina was dead. She did not weep, though, for something within her refused to acknowledge it. The hand that had so lately gripped her she left loosely on the coverlet, as if she merely slept.

Selina led the way in. She went at once to Nina's side. Johanna tried to warn her with a glance as she went to welcome the curate and Terence. After a few conventional pleasantries she took the baby from Hilary.

When she turned about she saw Nina's death confirmed in Selina's expression. What to do now? She had no idea — nor the slightest feeling that anything ought to be done.

'I think the curtains had better be closed,' Selina said quietly. 'The light is beginning to oppress Lady Nina.' She turned to the curate. 'Could it be managed by candlelight?'

'It often is, Miss Visick.'

Margaret came in, carrying the bowl for the holy water. She nodded at Selina and went to draw the curtains and light the lamps. 'Only two of them,' Selina warned.

'I'll be as quick as is decently possible,' Pelham told Tony. He read the appointed text from St Mark, followed by the brief exhortation upon it; then came the Lord's Prayer and the Thanksgiving. Then he asked, 'What is the name of this child?'

584

'Hannah Nina,' said Terence.

Pelham turned toward the bed. Selina put her ear to Nina's mouth. 'What, dear?' she asked. 'Speak up.' A moment later she looked up and said, 'Hannah Nina.'

Pelham turned to face the bed. Selina held her hand over Nina's eyes, as if to shield her from the little remaining light.

'Dost thou, in the name of this child, renounce the devil and all his works, the vain pomp and glory of this world, with all covetous desires of the same, and the carnal desires of the flesh, so that thou wilt not follow, nor be led by them?'

Selina again lowered her ear to Nina's mouth. 'I renounce them all,' she whispered, as if confirming an even quieter promise from those dead lips.

And so the brief service drew rapidly to an end. The curate proved quite adept at handling the baby, though Hannah was robust enough by now to need no especial care in that way. She laughed at his long, upside-down face; she laughed when the water wet her brow; and she cried when she was returned to her mother's arms.

When it was over Pelham turned to Lady Nina, but Johanna forestalled him, saying very firmly, 'We'll join you gentlemen below in a moment.'

Tony took the hint and led the others away; at the door he looked back over his shoulder. Johanna shook her head and he went on.

'Was I right to do that?' Selina asked at once. 'Oh God, what have I done?'

'Possibly the one act in your life that will get you past St Peter and no questions asked,' Johanna assured her.

'D'you think so? Oh Jo, d'you truly think so? What are you doing?'

Johanna laid the still bawling Hannah down at Nina's side and put her dead arm about the child, who immediately stopped crying. 'There,' she said. 'Perhaps she hasn't quite left us. How can we tell? She was so alive only five . . .' Her voice began to break. 'Oh Selina she was so *alive!*' She fussed with Nina's hand, pressing it against Hannah's shawl; she hoped for some last flicker of life, some final spasm from the dying sinews, to transmit a touch of that vital continuity from godmother to godchild. But there was nothing.

She broke down then and buried her face in the pillow at Nina's side. There were no words to her grief, not even her dead friend's name. It was one long agonized howl of pain and bereavement. Something had been wrenched from inside her and would never grow there again; it would leave a permanent emptiness, which even now she could feel as a wound, a hurt that no physic could ever heal.

In that abject misery she was in danger of smothering the child. Selina picked her up and carried her to the window. She started to cry again, but only feebly now.

'One light gone,' Selina said as she quenched the first lamp.

'All light gone.' She quenched the second.

Then she paced the room with the tears running down her face, her whole body heaving in silent grief. She did not even notice when Hilary took the baby from her and went below, leaving the two cousins alone at last.

A short while later Tony tiptoed into the room, saw them kneeling one each side of the bed, their prayers and tears mingling in one joint cry for a comfort no earthly power could grant. He went quietly back downstairs without their knowing he had been there.

'She is sinking fast,' he said. 'I doubt she will last the night.'

Pelham nodded gravely. 'I thought as much yesterday. I was surprised to find her still with us today.'

'Yesterday?' Tony asked.

'Yes, she sent for me, for her final communion, you know? I'm sure she realized she was sinking. Should I go to her now, I wonder.'

'I think it might not be ... I'll send to let you know.' As Tony saw him to the door, and out into the drive, the oppression of the house lifted and he felt able to ask, 'If she does go today, will there be need for another baptism, with another godmother?'

'Not as far as the church is concerned, Dr Moore.'

'It seems rather strange – to survive such promises by only an hour or two.'

Pelham chuckled drily. 'I hear the tone of a confirmed sceptic, sir. But I tell you, if she survived her vows by only one second, or one infinitesimal fraction of a second, God may do more in that brief flash of time — *our* time — than all the most powerful men have done or will do between Creation and the Day of Judgement. It is not ours to question.'

'Not at this particular moment, perhaps,' Tony conceded.

'But my dear doctor — all of life is made up from particular moments. Good day.'

Chapter Fifty-Four

Nina, Lady Brookes, was buried beside the colonel in the southwestern corner of Helston churchyard, in the last plot near the gate; from there a path leads down between the houses to emerge in Cross Street almost directly opposite Liston Court. One panel in the memorial window, which had graced the church for a mere nine months, was removed temporarily to allow her name to be added. A few days after the funeral Liston Court was shuttered and shrouded and left with Margaret Tyzack as its sole caretaker, all the other servants being paid their notice and sent home. Even Margaret divided her time between there and Lanfear, where she was also housekeeper.

The responsibility for all these arrangements fell to Johanna, for Selina was almost inconsolable at the death of her friend and patroness. Even on the night of Nina's death she could not stay in the house but returned with the others to Lanfear, where she reoccupied her old room and took to her bed for several days, rising only for the funeral. The whole town turned out for the occasion and all the great families of West Penwith sent their representatives – people who had sneered at her in life and cavilled at her attitudes, all now in deepest mourning. Looking around at them – the pompous, the pampered, the pathetic, with their carefully composed mien of grief, their watchful eyes (all of them still avoiding her direct gaze), and their skins as thick and sleek as a wolverine's – Johanna kept her sorrow to herself, lest, by association with theirs, it should be defiled.

Not one of them spoke to her when it was over, though

Mrs Ramona Troy gave her a brief, conspiratorial smile, as if to say that she shared Johanna's view of all these people even if this was not the time or place to express the fact. Johanna's opinion of her, always equivocal, sank a notch or two. Hamill was unaccountably absent — though perhaps what Nina had done to his beloved menhir was cause enough for him to stay away. He at least was honest.

The cold-shouldering continued at the funeral tea, which — the day being fine and warm — was held on the lawn at Liston Court. Johanna made a game of it, wandering among them casually joining this group or that, saying not a word, but listening as respectfully as she would if she were an unmarried maid in good social standing. Some ignored her; some actually closed ranks and excluded her from their circle. As she went up to a group that included the Pellews, she felt an almost overwhelming temptation to ask him what was that word he had used when she had last met him — and then repeat it, loud and innocent. But Tony, perhaps alerted by some glint in her eye — though she had never told him what Pellew had said — came swiftly to her side and remarked, clearly enough for the others to overhear, 'They simply aren't worth it, Miss Rosewarne. They combine the airs and graces of the nobility with the morals of the gutter.'

She left them in a stunned silence before she could succumb to a fit of giggles, which would have owed more to grief than humour. 'Did somebody speak?' Pellew asked lamely when they were well clear.

The squire and his wife then went around, quietly talking to the other "mourners," and within five minutes they had all gone.

'Thank God for that,' Tony declared.

Johanna told Margaret to arrange for all the leftover food to be carried up to the workhouse. 'Say it was Lady Nina's express wish that the paupers were to have it,' she said. 'Will the overseers keep it for themselves? D'you think you should stay and see it fairly distributed?'

Margaret did not think so; Harold Blight, the present master, was a pretty fair man.

Ten minutes later there was but one lobster sandwich left,

and that was in Terence's hand. 'There's the reading of the will,' he reminded her.

'Is Coad coming then?' Johanna inquired.

'He asked me to do it, seeing the circumstances.'

'Oh, and what did he mean by that?'

'Well' – Terence shrugged awkwardly – 'seeing that Selina is my sister and you my cousin, I suppose.'

'You suppose!' Johanna echoed scornfully. 'When you sup with the devil, use a long spoon. I'm the devil. You're the long spoon. That's what he meant.' She stared at the house and sighed. 'I don't want to go back in there, somehow. Can we do it out here?'

There was a table and some chairs under the big chestnut tree. Terence led them there, taking a large and impressive parchment from somewhere under his jacket as he went.

'Which of us d'you want?' Tony asked.

'It might as well be all three of you. There are some small bequests for the servants but we can inform them later.'

When they were all seated he began what was plainly going to be a full reading, including all the legal rigmaroles and folderols. After the first paragraph Johanna stopped him, 'It doesn't mean a thing to us, *mon cher cousin*. Can't you just summarize it?'

He looked dubious. 'Coad said read it out.'

'We're all exhausted. It just goes straight in one ear and out of the other. You can sit here by yourself afterwards and read it all out – so you won't be telling him a lie – but just summarize it for us, eh, there's a good chap.'

Reluctantly he agreed. 'It's actually very simple. Did Nina ever talk about it with any of you?' He directed his question at Selina, who shook her head.

'She said something to me,' Johanna admitted. 'Just before Hannah was baptized. She'd left me a small legacy to look after Selina with – something like that.'

He raised his eyebrows. 'Her idea of small is not mine. She's left you five hundred guineas.'

'How much?' Johanna was aghast. 'That must surely be wrong.'

He found the page in the will. 'No. "To my dearest friend Johanna Rosewarne, who was a sister to me, I hereby bequeath the sum of five hundred guineas, being her portion of the profit we jointly made on the shares of the Hayle Railway Co." There it is.' He made a token offer of the page in her direction.

'Ah, I understand.' Johanna had meanwhile worked it out for herself. 'She said to look after Selina. So it's really only in trust to me, for Selina's needs to be found out of it.'

Terence was shaking his head, enjoying every moment of it now. 'The five hundred guineas is yours. Selina has the rest — all the capital that Lady Nina accrued on her own account, which amounts to something over twenty thousand pounds.'

Selina and Johanna stared at each other, quite unable to believe what they were hearing. Terence continued: '*That* is the sum which is now put into trust for Selina until she reaches the age of thirty, or marries — in which case there are some lengthy instructions here as to the deed of settlement.'

'What's the income to the trust?' Tony asked.

'You're also a trustee,' Terence told him.

'I know. She asked me a few weeks ago. She didn't say it was anything like as large as this, though. The income must be what — about eight hundred?'

Terence nodded. 'A shade under. Once she'd made the money she invested it very safely.' He turned to his sister. 'You have half of it, little face — lucky thing. Three-hundred and seventy-odd a year.' Selina could not take it in even now. 'The rest is at their discretion,' he added, with a nod at the other two. 'So be nice to them, eh?'

'Did she leave you nothing, then?' was all Selina could think of to ask.

He blushed.

Johanna laughed. 'Come on — tell us!'

'I'm to get all the *Peerages* and *Landed Gentrys* and every *Handbook to the Titled, Landed, and Official Classes* in her library.'

They could not help laughing. 'Come now!' he said sharply. 'This is not seemly. Remember the occasion.'

'Go on!' Johanna dabbed at her eyes. 'She put it in for that very purpose. She'd have hated our solemnity today.'

'Well,' he responded, 'I don't know what you've got to

laugh about anyway. What d'you think has happened to
the house and to the colonel's original bequest to her?'

'Oh, she told me that. It all goes to his cousin. Or
nephew? No, cousin. Some cousins are lucky, you see.'

'But if she'd survived him? Did she tell you that?'

Johanna had to struggle to remember. 'Oh yes – it
would have been hers entirely.'

'Outright and in fee simple. Yes. And who would have
got it then?'

Johanna shrugged. 'Someone on her side of the ...'

'You!' Terence said.

She almost laughed but he turned and pointed at the
house. '*Voilà!* All that – house, furniture, pictures,
library, a couple of farms, and something over twenty
thou' in the funds ... it would all have been yours. And
now it's all gone!'

'Thank God for that!' Johanna murmured, closing her
eyes and breathing out, as people do after a narrow
escape.

'Easy enough to say it now, *chère cousine.*'

'No. I mean it. Heavens, I felt guilty enough before –
I still do, over this five hundred guineas. Can I refuse it?'

'You may do what you please with it. Buy me a house,
for instance.'

She laughed. 'I'll stand you a bookshelf, my dear.' She
turned to Tony. 'Would it build us a clinic in Redruth?
And pay for a doctor and nurse?'

He patted her arm. 'Time enough to think of that.'
There was a familiar noise from the house. 'D'you hear
what I hear?' he added.

She nodded glumly and went reluctantly indoors to feed
Hannah.

Three weeks later, just when they were beginning to sort
through Nina's clothing and personal jewelry, which she
had left for the two cousins to divide between them, a
rather flustered Mr Coad came in person to Liston Court.

'There's been a mistake,' Selina said as she watched him
puffing up the drive. 'They've found a later will in which
she left it all to her cats.'

'But she didn't have any cats,' Johanna objected.

'That's her final irony.'

'But she wasn't like that.'

'I know. I'm just being pessimistic and silly. It's what would happen if I was making a story out of all this. We'd have borrowed from a moneylender on the strength of our windfall − and then suddenly there wouldn't be a windfall. And we'd have to do I don't know what to get back in funds again.'

'We'd better go down and let him in. I don't think Margaret can have heard him ring.'

He was even more flustered when he saw who answered the door. 'Oh, pray do forgive me, dear ladies, dear ladies,' he said several times, as if he had somehow compelled them to the menial office. He was even more reluctant to surrender them his hat, which Selina almost had to wrest from his hand.

'There's very little in the house, Mr Coad,' Johanna told him. 'We can offer you a lemon cordial and seltzer, I think. Or some excellent ale?'

'Your own ale, Miss Rosewarne?' he asked. There was an ingratiating edge to his voice.

'You've heard about that, have you?' she asked.

'Your young cousin told me. I think, yes, I might like to try a glass of it, if it isn't too much ... er ...'

'Do come into the morning room,' Selina invited. They went ahead of him and swept aside enough dust covers to reveal three chairs and an occasional table. 'There's something wrong with the will, isn't there?' she added.

Margaret came at last and Johanna asked her to bring the ale.

'Why no,' he was saying. 'At least, that is ... I don't know. It all depends. Tell me − I'm more sorry than I can say to have to bring up what must be a most distressing ... er ... but can you say what was the exact time of her ladyship's death?'

'The afternoon,' Johanna replied.

'Yes, but the hour. The exact hour.

'Have you not got the death certificate? I'm sure Dr Moore put it on that.'

Both women now had a dreadful premonition that their innocent deception was about to catch up with them.

593

'Not at this moment. It is with the registrar. I could go and look there, of course, but I thought I'd save us a day's delay. Can you really not remember?'

'Well,' Johanna said, carefully skirting an outright assertion, 'I remember hearing the clock strike half past four, and that was immediately before the baptism — at which Lady Nina became my baby's godmother.'

'Ah! And how is the dear little mite?' he asked jovially. 'I trust I may be vouchsafed a view of him before I go.'

'Her. She's a girl — Hannah Nina Rosewarne.' She laid no stress on the surname but he didn't bat an eyelid.

'Very pretty,' he replied. 'And in the circumstances perhaps, very appropriate, too — to have named her after Lady Nina.'

'Why so?'

'Could her ladyship still have been alive at five o'clock?' he asked.

Both women had wanted to avoid a direct statement that would link any one of them to the lie, but Selina, remembering that Tony had already committed himself to it in the death certificate, now said, 'Dr Moore certified the death as having occurred at six o'clock that evening.'

'Six o'clock!' Coad repeated it as if the words were a reprieve from hanging. 'You are sure? Quite, quite sure?'

'Six o'clock is what he wrote,' Johanna echoed. 'May we ask why it's so important?'

He smiled at her. 'Because, my dear young lady, unless there is some quite unforeseen circumstance, I believe you are now the proprietress of this entire establishment. You are Lady Nina's sole heir and assign.'

Johanna frowned. 'But the cousin ... the colonel's cousin?'

'Died at a quarter to five on that very same afternoon. Lady Nina's last will and testament therefore rules.'

The two women exchanged the unhappiest of glances. Selina, realizing that Johanna was about to blurt out the truth, said quickly, 'May we ask, Mr Coad — supposing it had been the other way about, supposing the cousin's will had ruled — who would be the beneficiary?'

'The crown, dear lady,' he told her, with a certain savage glee. 'Those licensed highwaymen known as the Lords

Commissioner of Revenue. The cousin, one Thomas Brookes of Crediton in Devon, died intestate. However, by predeceasing her ladyship, he has left both you young ladies as heiresses of considerable fortune.'

PART FIVE

PALE GOLD

Chapter Fifty-Five

Tony found Johanna in what, when he came to think of it, was the most obvious place – the brew house. 'You're not still going on with that, are you? he asked.

Her only response was to give the wort an extra vigorous stir.

'I looked everywhere else for you. Selina was sure you'd be up Trigonning Hill.'

'Hah! What would she know about it?'

'I didn't mind. I enjoyed the walk and the view and so on.' He watched her closely, waiting his moment to say what was really uppermost in his thoughts.

'I'm going to try an even hotter mash and an even cooler fermentation this time,' she said, more to herself than to him.

'What's happened,' he said, 'with Nina's will and so on, is probably the very last possibility she had in mind when she drew it up.'

'You mean it never even occurred to her that her doctor and her two closest friends – and sole beneficiaries – would connive at a lie to secure her estate? Oh, she was so innocent of the world!'

He held his peace.

'Well?' she prompted angrily.

'There are two quite separate issues here. Which do you want to discuss first?'

'I don't wish to discuss anything – first, last, or ever.'

'Ah.' He turned on his heel. 'Then I think I shall sit in the garden and catch up on that pile of *Lancets.*'

Twenty minutes later she came out and sat beside him. She

had discarded her apron and was carrying her pocket book; work was over for the day. Selina, staring out from her bedroom window, waved down at them and returned to her writing. Johanna waved back.

'I'm so glad she has that occupation,' Tony said.

After a pause she asked, 'What are these two quite separate issues?'

He laid down his journal with a smile. 'Would you care for a walk, Miss Rosewarne?'

'Where?' she asked guardedly.

'Let's see where our feet take us. D'you want to put on your boots?'

'I have them up already.'

'Black silk crinoline and boots,' he commented. 'That's you all over.'

'Selina?' she called up to her cousin. 'We're just off for a stroll. Care to come too?'

'No thanks. My hero is in dire trouble west of Laramie. Is that where Chimney Rock was? Or is?'

'No. It's Independence Rock after Laramie. A long way after. Why don't you go down to my cottage and get the Mormon guide. It's all there.'

'No thanks.'

'Go on. I'll bring it up to you.'

'No. I don't want to be chained down by mere facts. I'm after a deeper and more sublime truth than that. I'll just assume a rock, like Chimney Rock. Enjoy your stroll.'

'*West of Laramie* would be a good title,' Tony called back as they left.

She held up an approving finger and began to scrabble for the sheet of paper on which she was assembling 'good titles.'

This slightly absurd exchange had the effect of lightening Johanna's mood by several degrees.

'It looks as if she really is serious about finishing it at last,' Tony said. 'Has she let you read any of it?'

'Good heavens, no! It's more private and secret than . . .' She thought of her own diaries, which, when she had at last found the chance to move the chest of drawers, untack the carpet and roll it back, and lift the loose floorboard, proved to have been stolen.

'... than your own thoughts,' he suggested when she failed to finish her sentence.

'What are these two quite different issues?'

'One is the degree of our joint guilt at having quite innocently deprived the revenue commissioners of a handsome estate — when all we really sought to do was legitimize Nina's position as Hannah's godmother. The second is Nina's frame of mind when she made that bequest.'

They reached the lane that skirted the western foot of Trigonning; a right turn would take them to its summit, or on to Ashton; the other direction offered many choices, including Godolphin warrens, where they had first kissed and she had tentatively agreed to come to Plymouth.

'Well, you've been up Trigonning already this evening,' she said and turned left.

They covered the next hundred yards in silence, easeful to him but increasingly tense to her. 'You're never going to change, are you,' she blurted out at last.

'From what?'

'From this saintly patience. Any other man, having said there were two issues and then having described them, would go on and give his opinion.'

'But I know *my* opinion,' he said, laying delicate stress on the word.

She clenched her fist and struck out at him, quite hard but with imperfect aim, so that it caught him only a glancing blow on the shoulder. She was so surprised at herself, and so mortified, that she just stood there with both fists clenched against her jaw, and her mouth agape.

'Go on,' he urged, making no effort to defend himself. 'If you don't let it out, you'll burst with it.'

'Oh, Tony — I'm so sorry. I don't know what made me do that.'

'Exactly,' he said, resuming their stroll when he saw she was not going to take his advice.

'I presume you want my opinion then,' she said, falling in beside him once more.

'There are two kinds of patience,' he replied.

'Everything seems to be in couples today.'

'Very nearly. One is the lazy kind: Do nothing and matters

will sort themselves out. The other is your kind — the kind that goes with a cast-iron determination.'

'Me? I've got no patience at all.'

He shrugged. 'I may be wrong. Tell me if I'm also wrong in this: I believe the rage that's in you is due to the fact that you had an absolute determination — indeed, you still have it — to make a success with this brewing business. You can tell yourself you only started because Penrose pointed out the opportunity, and you're only doing it now to rub Charley Vose's face in your success, and, in a vaguer sort of way, to show all the world that however much they may cut you and try to exclude you, you'll still battle on and triumph.'

She drew breath to speak but his hand begged a few moments more. 'However, I believe you could take all those reasons away ... Charley Vose could give you his secret recipe book and say, ''The best of luck to you.'' The Mrs Pellews and the Mrs Ramona Troys of this world could beg you to open the next autumn produce show ...' He laughed as a new thought occurred to him. 'Or baby show! That would be a turn-up. And Penrose could write from America to say he absolutely forbade you to soil your hands with commerce. And none of it would make you hesitate for a single moment. You'd simply find a different set of reasons — and carry on trying to build up your trade. Or am I wrong?'

For reply she opened her pocket book, took out a handful of visiting cards, and passed them to him.

'What's this?' he asked.

'Read them.'

He flipped through them and whistled. They were from several leading ladies of the district — including Mrs Pellew and Mrs Ramona Troy. He passed them back to her.

'They were left this morning,' she said, 'Just as if I were a brand new arrival in the district.'

'You were even more honoured than that,' he pointed out. 'No unmarried lady, newly arrived or not, would get cards from such *grandes dames.*'

'Oh, she would if she'd just inherited a fine town house and all its chattels plus a few acres and twenty thousand-odd in the funds. I just hope you're not too clairvoyant, my dear.

It so happens that when I left the Ram, Charley Vose did indeed tell me to take over all his off sales, and he wished me luck with it, too. Not sarcastically, either. So if I now get a letter from America forbidding me to continue, I shall . . .' The conclusion escaped her for a moment.

'. . . trust me a little more in future?' he suggested.

'No, I shall report you to Hamill Oliver and ask him to investigate your credentials.' But that hadn't been what she was going to say, either. The fact was she was thinking about what Hal might command, now that she had no financial need to continue with her small business.

Tony knew it, too. Else why did he say, 'Suppose Penrose did command you to give up this trade — would you?'

She clenched her fists.

'Go on,' he urged. 'You'll feel better for it.'

She thought she saw a way to stop him from behaving like that — by shocking him, just as she had wanted to shock Squire Pellew at the funeral tea. This time she did not hold back. 'If you enjoy being beaten by young women,' she said. 'There are places you can go, you know.'

He turned bright scarlet. 'I . . . I . . . just don't know what to say,' he stammered.

'Good!' She laughed.

Her complete lack of discomfiture helped him surmount his own embarrassment rather smartly. 'I see,' he murmured, taking out his handkerchief and wiping his nose unnecessarily. 'Very well — if that's the way you want it. Let's talk about that very subject.' He refolded the handkerchief and put it away. 'But before that — you haven't yet answered my question.'

They reached the place where he had first set eyes on her. Of course, they had driven through it many times over the intervening couple of years; often enough, they would have said, to divest it of any special significance. But this was the first time they had approached it on foot; and at that slower pace, and with this odd emotional charge between them — which Johanna could not explain at all — some of its original quality began to seep back. She turned to him with a shy smile. 'D'you remember?' she asked.

He nodded, 'As if it were only a century ago.'

She chuckled. 'Yes. Rather a lot has happened in

between.' She saw he was weighing up his response carefully. Whatever it was, she didn't want to hear it, so she said, 'The answer to your question is, yes. Even if Hal commanded me to stop, I should go on.'

'And when he came back?'

'Well . . . he'd look at it and see how wrong he was.'

'Of course — I was forgetting.'

'What?'

'That well-known humility of his. Which way do we go now?'

Left would lead them eventually to Lanfear; right would take them past the end of Greatwork — or to Godolphin warrens.

'You choose,' she said. 'I don't mind.'

He turned right. 'I have absolutely no qualms about putting what I did on that death certificate,' he said. 'Professor Sahl, who taught us pathology, used to say, ''The only sure and certain sign of death is *rigor mortis.*'' And there's many would agree with him. Which brings us to the question of what was in Nina's mind when she made that bequest.'

'Oh, why do we have to talk about all that now?' she asked crossly.

'No reason at all,' he replied mildly. 'Let's talk about Mrs Pellew *et al,* instead. D'you think it's just money has fetched them up out of the sewers? You don't suppose there could be a little twinge of conscience there, too?'

'Conscience?' she sneered.

'Of a very self-serving, practical kind, I agree. But conscience nonetheless. I mean, now that the truth has come out about Greep and Paradise Row and so on, their big blunderbuss has exploded mainly in their own faces. So if there was the slightest spark of remorse there, about what they did to you, the occasion of your bereavement would be ideal for offering the olive branch.'

The word *olive* made her think of Italy, and of Nina's plans for Hannah's adoption . . . and of that evening when Selina drank too much wine . . . and of Petra — anything to avoid the implications of what he was saying.

'All right,' she challenged him at last. 'What do you suppose was Nina's state of mind when she made that bequest?'

'I thought you didn't wish to ...'

'Well, you obviously do and I'll get no peace until I let you.'

'Not at all,' he assured her genially. 'If you'd rather not, then, please believe me ...'

'Tony!' she shrieked, and for the third time during this brief stroll she clenched her fists to strike him.

Once again he braced himself for her assault, but made no preparations to ward it off. Her anger subsided. Airily she kissed her fingertips and patted his cheek with them. 'So clever,' she sneered. 'I know exactly what you're trying to do.'

'What?'

'That thing Selina was jawing about at supper last night. Catarrh, or whatever it was.'

'Catharsis. The lightning-rod theory of emotional discharge.'

'It sounds even worse than catarrh. Well, you won't provoke me, sir! Tell me about Nina's state of mind.'

He fell in beside her. 'I didn't mean "state of mind" in the sense of how sound she was. I only meant the likelihood of this or that possibility as it must have seemed to her when she called in Coad to draw up the will.'

'Did she know she was dying? Look — they're forking out Greatwork on this side of the hill.'

'Is that good?'

'Well, this is the deeper sump, so it means they want to reopen more of the workings, the lowest levels.'

'Thank God for that. We shan't feel so useless now — telling them their children really need more meat and milk and things.' He sighed. 'Did Nina know she was dying. There are several shades to that sort of knowledge. She certainly knew she had a malignancy. Whether she knew how short a ... well, no, she can't have. Even I was surprised.'

'And why didn't you tell me?'

'She didn't wish it, and it would only have fretted you to no purpose. You recall how haggard she was that day — the day of the — when we met again? Well, she remained like that, no worse, no better, until very recently. Her decline all happened in the last seven to eight weeks. I never saw anything so rapid. The flesh just fell off her.'

'Even so, Tony.'

'Well, to start with, all the time she just looked slightly ill, she kept saying she wanted to see you again − kiss and make up and so on − but not while she looked like that. The first thing she used to ask Selina every morning was, "Does Johanna know?" She always asked me, too − if I'd told you. And she always made me swear I wouldn't.'

'Oh, Tony, don't. It's awful.'

'And only when she said − finally she came out with it − she said, "I'm not going to get over this, am I?" then . . .'

Johanna burst into tears. He put an arm around her shoulder and squeezed with a strength that surprised her. She wanted to turn to him, to be folded within that strength and let him soothe her grief, but he resisted it. The power of his grip and the pace of his marching kept her going forward.

He went on with his tale. 'Only then did she ask to see you − and even so she made us swear not to tell you. It was hard for us, too, you know. But when people are dying one somehow respects the most awkward . . . I don't know now. I believe we were wrong not to tell you.'

'No, if those were her wishes, I'd only feel even more guilty than I do.'

'I expect she knew that. She seems to have known you rather better than any of us do.'

'She understood everyone like that. It was uncanny.' She almost went on to give the example of Jenny Jewell and why she would pretend to be married to that American when surely she'd want to crow over her 'capture' of Hal − but in the nick of time she remembered that it was Nina's invention . . . pure fantasy.

He took her remarks as a general comment. 'What she didn't know,' he said, 'at the time she drew up her will, was that it would happen so swiftly. She felt immortal, the way we all do at our sort of age. In her mind she was arranging for some remote possibility, forty or fifty years from now.'

Johanna nodded and sniffed back the tears from her nostrils. He passed her a clean pocket handkerchief, this one of silk. She buried her face in it, relishing its softness against her skin.

They were near the brow of the hill, where the path leads off into the warrens. He paused, 'Which way do we go now?' he asked, assuming a great innocence.

She gave him back his handkerchief and pushed him roughly along the path ahead of her. He had to stumble to save himself. 'Can't keep you down for long,' he said when he had recovered his balance.

'Nor you,' she replied, catching him up and passing him by. '"Which way do we go now!" You intended coming up here from the moment you first suggested this walk.'

He fell in beside her again. The way led down over springy turf and then up to a low stone wall. Hundreds of rabbits thumped the ground and scuttered off in a panic of flashing white tails. 'Have you been back here since that day?' he asked.

'No. Have you?'

'No.'

The answer surprised her — and was, she felt, to his credit.

'Even now I wonder if I should.' He was talking quite seriously again.

'Why?'

'You showed me a Cornwall that day which I've never been able to find since. I've driven through all those lanes — well, we both have, often together — the actual countryside you see from the hilltop ahead. But it isn't down there. It's a magic sort of Cornwall that you can only see from up here. Or perhaps you can only see it on special days.'

She slipped her arm through his and felt him shiver. 'That was a special day,' he added.

'I wish . . .' she began.

He did not press her to say what she wished. At the low stone wall he pointed to a space beneath an overhang of ling. 'There was a skull there, remember? You showed it to me and said a crocus grew out of its eye socket.'

She laughed with delight, 'I'd forgotten that. The things you remember.'

A short while later they arrived at the top of Godolphin Hill. He ran ahead of her, as if he was afraid the whole landscape might have altered or even vanished. She drew level with him in time to hear him give out a great sigh of relief. 'Still there,' she said.

'Still there!' he echoed.

She stared down into the nooks and crannies, the folded hills and secret places her eyes knew so well. But the day she remembered best — perhaps because it had been an August evening just like this — was after an especially savage flogging by her uncle, when every square inch of this view had cost a step deeper into pain, and yet she had struggled here to find that balm which nowhere else on earth could yield.

'It is magic,' she whispered, easing her position so that the skin of her back touched her dress as little as possible — favouring flesh that had long since healed.

The gesture, the unchanging landscape, the time of year . . . all conspired to bring it back to her with a sharpness that took her breath away. She remembered now something she had buried — not forgotten, like the rabbit skull, but buried, all these years. She remembered making a resolution to be a better girl in future, and not to plague her uncle with her wickedness, so that he made himself ill with remorse at having to flog her like that.

She glanced at Tony to check her irrational fear that he knew exactly what was going through her mind; he was still scanning the landscape, trying to capture every leaf and twig in his nets of memory.

Her mind made the first hesitant connection between those guilts of her childhood and her feelings now about Nina's death and the morality of accepting her bequest. But no, no, it was too fanciful; she shied away from a closer examination.

He turned to her with (as Nina once said) 'a smile that would deafen you were it a purr,' and pointed vaguely back the way they had come. 'Thank you,' he said. 'Now I'll be able to come here again. But I couldn't have done it alone.'

'Nor me,' she replied, stepping slightly off the path to let him walk at her side.

'Even though our reasons are different.'

'Yes. In my case . . .' She paused. Somewhere in what she had been going to say was the word *guilt*.

She couldn't say it now.

'Too many unhappy associations, I expect,' he said.

'I used to come up here after I'd been punished. I suppose all children have places like that.'

He took her arm and it suddenly struck her that she'd been wanting him to do that ever since they had set out; her feeling now was not of gratitude or pleasure, but anger that he had let so much time go by.

'And you accuse me of patience!' she blurted out, as if that bit of their conversation had only just taken place.

'Patient determination,' he said, like a fussy sort of revision.

The fact that he saw at once the connection she was making, though it was still partly obscure even to her, only annoyed her the more. 'You think you've only got to wait,' she said bitterly, 'and everything else will burn itself out, and you'll still be there. You think you're fireproof.'

'If there is some other course open to me, more likely of success,' he responded evenly, and in a tone that had already infuriated her several times that evening, 'do tell me. I would not dream of ignoring advice that came from such . . .'

At last it worked. They were in a hollow in the heart of the warren, overlooked by no one. She leaped in front of him, barring his way, and began to pummel his chest with her fists.

And he stood there and took it, raising one hand loosely to protect his face, no more.

His body was amazingly wiry and strong; she could feel that her blows, though they were the hardest she could deliver, had next to no effect on him. And yet it was wonderfully satisfying to be able to let go like that. Far better than kissing. That deep, hollow thump as each blow landed, the slight sense of give as his ribs absorbed the blow, the gasps as he alternately breathed and braced himself — these were thrilling in a way that she was now worldly-wise enough to recognize as erotic.

And that made her afraid. She changed her stance and began to hit him lower down, in the stomach, no longer flailing but using her fists and arms as piledrivers. Again he made no effort at defence, but braced his muscles to absorb her blows. Suddenly she remembered the last time she had played with a man in that way, and then the erotic feeling became overwhelming.

In panic she drew her fist for one knock-out blow. He watched her eyes. 'Above the belt,' he warned urgently, but it was too late.

He ducked to protect himself from an agony she would never have believed and her fist caught him smack on the lip. He leaped back, laughing, trying not to roar out his pain; and his chin was streaked with red.

'Oh, Tony!' All her aggression — and the desires it had roused within her — fled. 'I didn't mean it. I'm so sorry.' She ran toward him, fishing up her sleeve for her own handkerchief.

He could feel all the guilt in the world rushing back to fill that little hollow, drowning her and him.

'First blood to you, me proud beauty,' he cried. 'Now it's my turn!'

'No!' With a scream that turned to a laugh and back into a scream she fled, making a game out of something that had threatened to overwhelm her. But in her crinoline she managed no more than half a dozen paces before he brought her down. He fell on top of her. Still she screamed and laughed. Their faces were only inches apart. She saw his bleeding lip and went silent. He was stemming the flow by licking at the cut.

She rolled over until she was on top of him, mainly so that it would not drip on her. 'Poor lip,' she said mournfully.

'You'll have to kiss it better,' he told her.

Their eyes dwelled in each other's for a moment and then their lips were joined. In an instant she was transported beyond all questions of right and wrong. No inner voice told her she was faithless to her love. This was a debt she owed her body, her flesh, her blood — a debt long due.

She was so overwhelmed by her own feelings that, at first, she did not notice the change in him. Only slowly did it dawn on her that he was at some kind of war with himself — he who had tried so often this evening to provoke her into letting go was now having to struggle to hold himself in check. He was shivering with the effort. She would never have suspected that his calm, infinitely patient character might conceal such passion. Every muscle was locked rigid; he could hardly breathe, and there were beads of sweat upon his brow.

He broke the contact at last and moved away from her, but only enough to see her face more clearly. Again their eyes dwelled in each other's and she saw a more familiar Tony. Yet there was something new about him, too — something more. Those eyes were shrouded with an odd mixture of astonishment and fear — astonishment at the strength of that other self, hiding within him, and fear that he had come so close to losing.

'You know I would,' she told him.

He nodded, almost imperceptibly, as if too much movement would chance his frail stability. 'Just as you know I won't.'

'Why?'

'Not with things as they are.' He spoke more easily; with each word he regained the mastery of himself.

'Hal, you mean,' she said flatly.

Now he found the strength to roll away from her. He sat up, staring eastward to Tregathennan and the downs between Helston and Falmouth. She kept her gaze on him. They were in a shallow pool of shade from the evening sun, which flooded the landscape before them, saturating its colours and making the whole world seem languorous and easy. 'How do things stand there?' he asked at length.

'Why can't you ask that tomorrow? Why d'you need to know it now? Can't you just accept things when they're offered?'

After a pause he said, 'Because tomorrow, he's coming back.' He turned and challenged her to deny it.

She frowned in bewilderment.

'Or tomorrow, or tomorrow. What matters it *which* tomorrow? He will be back.' His eyes narrowed. 'Have you ever felt the pangs of jealousy, Jo?'

She shook her head.

He shrugged. 'Then there's little point in asking you.' He returned his gaze to the landscape.

She half rose and went to him, kneeling behind him and putting her arms around his neck. 'I'm sorry,' she whispered, kissing his ear.

He nodded.

'I do love you in a way, you know. But not the way I love Hal.'

611

'And what way is that?'

'Oh, it's just so impossible to describe. All the sensible parts of me disagree. They never stop singing your praises. I know you'd be a better husband ... a good friend ... faithful ... a more interesting companion. I know Hal is moody, a bit full of himself ... won't see me for weeks and then practically billets himself on me.'

'Can't keep his hands off anything in skirts.'

'Yes, I know all that.'

'So what can outbalance it?'

'Don't make me tell you, Tony. It's all feelings and no reasons — but, oh, if you only knew how strong they are.'

'And they haven't varied at all? Not once since the day he left?'

'Yes, of course they have. But they always come flooding back.'

'What made them weakest? Was it something he did, or something you did, or' — he cleared his throat hopefully — 'something I did?'

She laughed and eased herself away from him to stand up; her foot was going to sleep. 'You're an old fox and I'm not going to tell you.'

'Very wise.' He stood up and helped her brush the grass off her dress. 'To appear like this on the highway would certainly expose us to comment,' he said tendentiously.

'And all for nothing,' she added.

'Not quite,' he replied with great assurance.

'Oh, you think you've learned something useful, do you? Stand still while I ... ' She brushed the grass off the back of his trousers.

As they resumed their homeward walk she said, 'I don't suppose you'd accept something between the office of lover and that of good friend, Tony?'

He shook his head. 'I'll play the hand as dealt, I think.'

She had a fleeting intimation of an enormous strength in him, a moral strength, and a courage, too — greater even than Hal had shown on the night he went into the ring against those little ogres. It frightened her. She was not great at analysing her own feelings, nor at giving herself reasons for doing whatever she decided to do. As she had told Terence once, she just knew what felt right and did it. But now this fright, this brush with something of unexpected power within him, made her ask what she had wanted in kissing him like that.

A safe little flirtation, was the answer. Good old Tony — a safe man if ever there was one. Loved her in his mild-mannered way ... knew he had no real chance ... but stayed close all the same. Took what crumbs of friendship he could. The sort of man who'd never set any woman alight. Born to be a substitute for a real lover — why, he'd practically invited her to use him in that way.

And then, suddenly, there was this explosion inside him — which, by some superhuman effort he had managed to contain.

He cleared his throat and said, 'I think we will try and set up a new clinic in Redruth.'

'Yes,' she said, 'There's nothing holding us back now.'

'Will you — er, you know — help with the administration side?'

'Of course — why d'you need to ask?'

'I just wondered.'

After a pause she said, 'That was a mistake, what happened back there.'

'Yes.' The word was as flat and as neutral as any he had ever spoken.

'We must avoid ... that sort of situation.'

'Yes.'

'But we needn't throw away all the good things we share — our work, the things we talk about. Laugh about.'

'Bicker about.'

'Yes, those things, too.'

'Splendid.'

There was in his tone just the faintest hint of the provocation he had offered earlier — enough to make her say, 'It was your fault. You shouldn't have made me hit you like that.'

'It's stopped bleeding,' he said. '*Rigor vivandis* will set in shortly.'

Her next question came from nowhere — bubbling up from deep inside her before she could stop it: 'Did you actually enjoy being hit like that?'

'Ah.' He grinned at her — the Tony she had always

613

known. 'I wondered if you'd forgotten.' He sighed heavily. 'The truth is I have a confession to make. And an apology.'

'Over what?'

He chewed his lip awhile − the uncut half of it − before he replied. 'Several months ago young Hilary came to me in a state of high excitement. Her view of the world must be bizarre to say the least. She thought she'd found some long-lost documents belonging to one of the wives of Henry VIII.'

'Under a floorboard in her room?' Johanna asked, her heart in her mouth all of a sudden.

'Exactly. Well, of course, I've since realized whose they were − when Selina mentioned something once about the way your uncle used to flog you. But at the time . . .'

'You read them?' she asked. Her eyes begged him to say no, or just a few pages.

'Your handwriting then was so different. And there was no name in them, not anywhere.'

'I should have burned them. I should never have written them.'

They reached the road. He put his arm about her waist and asked if she minded.

'No, you weren't to know.'

'I don't mean that. I mean . . .' He gave her a squeeze.

'Oh!' she laughed. 'No − people can think what they like. Why did she suppose it had anything to do with Henry VIII?'

'Yes, we smile in our superior way at her ignorance of schoolbook history, but we give her no credit for seeing the essential connection. All she knows about Good King Hal . . .' He laughed at the reappearance of that name. 'I didn't mean that. All she knows about him is that he was a monster of injustice and cruelty toward a number of women. The details are obscure, but she leaped right to the heart of it.'

'I should never have written them,' she repeated.

'I believe it's what saved you, my dear. And I also think you should read them again. Destroy them then, by all means, but do read them.'

She nodded unhappily. 'What did you think when you read them?'

'Oh Jo! When I discovered it was you ... your words ... your experiences.' He shook his head at the impossibility of conveying it. 'I wept. I know that. But even before I knew. I mean, it was clearly the hand of a young girl. And the things she was writing — that she obviously felt a compulsion to write!'

'You found it revolting.'

'No! Not in the least. Well, the subject matter was repellent, of course. But that you — or this unknown young girl — was compelled to write it ... that was pitiable.'

'It seemed to help,' she said simply.

He hugged her tight again. 'He was mentally unbalanced, of course — but you discovered that for yourself, didn't you.'

She stiffened.

'You found a way to stop him from ruining Deirdre and Ethna's lives as he had almost ruined yours — and probably would have had it not been for your ability to write it all down like that.'

'And go out alone to Godolphin Hill. Did Terence tell you, then?'

'Indirectly. He doesn't know exactly what it was you got him to post in Penzance. He thought it was a straightforward threatening letter. He just told me you're a dark horse and everybody makes the mistake of underestimating you.'

'How did you know, then?'

'I know something of the pathology of these cases. Your uncle is by no means the only one, I'm afraid. And our modern theories of child-rearing are hardly calculated to discourage them.'

'If any man ever raises a hand to Hannah,' she said, 'I will kill him.'

The bareboned simplicity of her words and the monotone in which she uttered them made him shudder.

Chapter Fifty-Six

Mr John Liggat of Liggat and Mowbray, Publishers, of Paternoster Row, London, was so excited by the manuscript of *West of Laramie* that he undertook the awkward journey to Helston for the sole purpose of meeting its authoress. In some places, especially during November, it was a dangerous journey, too. Indeed, in the last few miles, while crossing Manhay Moor, the fury of the winds blew the coach into the ditch and all its passengers took a tumble. He arrived at the Angel somewhat shaken and required a number of brandies to fit himself up again. The first three of them restored his blood to its usual consistency; two more overcame the shock; the rest were for luck.

Selina was excited, too, and had to be restrained by Johanna from descending upon the hotel, bursting into the man's room, throwing her arms about his neck, and covering him with kisses of gratitude. Instead, having made sure that her impresario, her prince among publishers, was in the Earl's Chambers (as the astute hotel manager had lately decided to call the principal suite), overlooking Coinagehall Street, she prevailed upon the wife of the pharmacist opposite to allow her the use of her bedroom for half an hour. Into it Selina brought, not the ardent gentleman the good wife had expected, but Nina's (now Johanna's) binoculars, with the help of which she had once been able to lie in her bed at Liston Court and follow a game of whist in a house on the far side of Cross Street.

'Well?' Johanna asked when she returned home to Lanfear.

'He is chubby, genial looking, rather deliberate in all his movements — though that may be explained by the quantities of brandy he sank.'

'Ah.' Johanna's interest sharpened. 'Did he strike you as an organized sort of a man — everything in its place?'

'N-n-n-o.' Selina did not seem too sure. 'Mostly it was his manservant, of course. But several things he arranged, Liggat fiddled with and then the fellow had to rearrange them all again. There was a lot of that. And his own papers seemed to be — well, in the sort of mess mine usually are.'

'How does he dress?'

'Not fashionably.'

'Yes, but the quality. Has he a good tailor?'

'The suit he had up when he arrived was of excellent quality, but the one he changed into seemed fairly poor. Threadbare, almost.' She giggled and lowered her voice as she added, 'He also wears two sets of heavy underwear. Someone must have told him Cornwall is cold!'

Johanna rubbed her hands in gleeful anticipation. She had decided not to entertain the man out at Lanfear but to put on a bit of a show at Liston Court, which Margaret Tyzack and a number of temporary servants had been working at for the past few days. The following morning, before the man was properly awake, they drove into town and took up their apparent residence. Tony was too busy at the new clinic in Redruth to be able to join them before dinner that evening.

'Why are you going to such lengths?' Terence asked.

Johanna had told Coad she needed her cousin's exclusive service as long as Liggat was in Cornwall, a request the man had been only too happy to grant. At first he had been obliging to her because he thought the Rosewarne account would be good for some hefty litigation. But then the Lords Commissioner of Revenue had yielded to an unarguable death certificate. More recently his disappointment on that score had yielded to gratification at her growing skill in the line of trade. He was now happy once again to grant almost any request she might make, especially if it bound their common interests more tightly together. And he would not have asked why Johanna was going to such lengths to impress Mr Liggat.

'So the fellow will understand that any offer of a few guineas will be unlikely to interest your sister,' she explained to Terence. 'You are not a solicitor's clerk, by the way. I don't want Liggat to know anything about that. Today you are a gentleman, pure and simple — though, come to think of it, I never met a gentleman to whom either adverb would apply.'

'Perhaps it takes a lady to recognize it,' he responded haughtily.

'Epithet,' Selina corrected her.

It was all the more surprising then, that when Liggat came he was only charmed at the opulence in which his budding authoress dwelt and each new sign of her wealth merely made him the happier. He was in the suit that Selina had described — not unfairly — as 'almost thread-bare.'

'I hope our arrangements will be to your liking, Mr Liggat,' Johanna said after a brief tour of the pictures and a glance at the garden through the windows. 'We thought we would take a light luncheon now, followed by a drive out in the carriage to Loe Bar.'

'Ah yes, Miss Rosewarne,' he enthused. 'I am more than keen to see something of this wild and beauteous landscape.' He turned to Selina. 'The little I glimpsed yesterday has given me several ideas for your next *chef d'oeuvre,* Miss Visick.'

'If the wind has moderated still further,' Johanna went on, 'the sun may come out, and the waves in the bay will be magnificent. You could perhaps stroll along the Bar and discuss these future plans of yours.'

'Indeed, indeed — and the few very minor changes that are required in the present manuscript, too.' Again he smiled at Selina.

'Changes?' She bridled.

'Nothing out of the way, I do assure you, my dear young lady. But no novel ever written was fit to publish as it left its creator's hand. Why, as Mr Dickens was telling me, only the other day ...' And there followed a lengthy anecdote during which it emerged that *David Copperfield,* half of which was now before the public, owed its 'sublime convergence of imagery and plot' almost entirely to Mr

Liggat's happy intervention – 'Which was made entirely without pecuniary interest on my part,' he concluded virtuously.

But Selina was still not entirely happy at the idea of 'changes'. She began to view Mr Liggat in an altogether more guarded fashion, which pleased Johanna to see.

'And then,' she concluded, 'I thought we might dine at five – if that is not too late for you?'

Indeed it was not. In town he frequently dined as late as six. He spoke as if it were one of several minor martyrdoms he endured in the service of literature.

'And then we can discuss terms,' Johanna concluded.

Liggat smiled and nodded at Terence, assuming that would be his function.

During the luncheon the number of living writers who owed at least part of their eminence to the obliging Mr Liggat rose by the minute – Thackeray, Harriet Martineau, Southey, Joseph Ingraham . . . There was no topic of conversation that did not call at least one such luminary to mind – Liggat's mind – where they prompted memories that revealed how profound was their debt to him and (occasionally) to his partner, the saturnine Rupert Mowbray.

Mowbray, it turned out, had taken a violent disliking to *West of Laramie*; had it not been for Liggat's passionate belief in the book, and the power of his advocacy, Miss Visick would have received nothing but her manuscript back and a polite note of regret.

Selina was gratified to hear it, of course, but still uneasy about these 'changes'.

At the end of the meal Johanna offered him brandy. He looked at the day outside, where the wind had moderated to the merest zephyr. 'Something to fortify us against the withering blast, eh?' he said. 'I don't usually, you understand, but I suppose it might be a wise precaution in this weather.'

The first balloon was hardly wet before he set it down dry again. The second he took at greater leisure and discovered it to be excellent – and declared the fact aloud, too.

Johanna leaned toward him, as if about to divulge a

secret. 'It is the oldest, the palest, the most superior Hennessy,' she confided. 'May I ask how much you would expect to pay for it in London, Mr Liggat?'

He certainly knew his brandies. 'Sixty-four shillings a dozen,' he replied without a pause for recollection.

'Ah. Five shillings and fourpence a bottle. We get it by the half-hogshead here. Twenty-seven gallons at thirteen guineas – a fraction over ten shillings a gallon, which works out at around sixteen pence a bottle. A saving of exactly four shillings on every bottle.'

He stared at the glass in his hand. 'Contraband?' he asked, as if he thought it should be a different colour, or parade its illegality in some equally obvious way. 'Why then I was robbed at the Angel last night, for they charged me threepence-halfpenny a measure.'

Johanna smiled indulgently. 'It is an ancient Cornish custom, Mr Liggat. You should use the fortune your astuteness has no doubt earned you in the field of publishing to retire and buy a small estate down here. You could then enjoy the "Cornish privilege", as we call it, until you are called to that Other Land, where, let us hope, it runs free.'

He laughed, but she could see the thought taking root. However, he immediately pooh-poohed the idea that anyone who called himself a publisher could afford anything that called itself an estate. A tiny villa on some small chalk stream was the most to which he had ever aspired – and even that, he feared, was now but a vanishing dream. 'A few publishers,' he admitted, 'do as well as a few authors. But most of us live in the same state of abject penury as most scribblers, and for the same reason: the depraved taste of a public that values trash above quality – and even then is unwilling to shell out the price of a modest meal for something that has cost the writer his health and the publisher his fortune to produce.'

He laid his arms casually upon the table where all might see how worn was his suit at the cuffs, and how inexpertly darned at the elbows.

Later, when they were all in the carriage and on their way to Porthleven, he bucked up considerably. At the summit of the hill south of Helston, Johanna made the carriage

stop so that he could appreciate the wild beauty of the
Lizard peninsula, from windswept Goonhilly to the cliffs
of pure serpentine near Kynance. It was a perfect day for
such a view, with the last of the autumn colours on the
downs and the sea whipped to a frenzy of surf by
yesterday's gales. And then, when they set off once more
and were instantly plunged into the wooded dell around the
gates to the old Penrose estate, where a little brook —
today in spate — zigzagged and broke into a whole choir of
rushing streamlets, he could contain himself no longer.
'Oh, *this* is the land,' he said. 'Such possibilities!'

'For what, pray,' Selina asked.

'Why, for passion, for romance, dear young lady. And
you can do it, for you have the inestimable fortune to be
born here. It is in your very blood. I feel it in your
American romance, of course; yet I confess myself
astonished you did not set your tale here instead. In fact
...' A remote and speculative light shone in his eyes.
'Could we not do that? Transfer it all here! Have you no
mountains and wilderness of your own down here? Why
need we import an inferior American product into our
home-grown stories? I'm sure it would all move splendidly
— and with far less effort than you imagine.'

'Call it *West of Lostwithiel?*' Johanna suggested
solemnly.

He waved the suggestion away like a bothersome insect.
'The title will have to be changed anyway.'

'Changed?' Selina protested.

'Yes. Who, what, or where is Laramie? Ask any ten
people at hazard and they'd just stare at you. One might as
well call it *West of Witherspoon* or *North of Nowhere*.
No — our title shall be something grand and heart-stirring
and resonant with passion. No matter — t'will come to me
anon.' He smiled reassuringly at the company in general
and then continued, 'Has any of you read a little tale that
came out recently — *Wuthering Heights?*'

They all shook their heads. 'By whom?' Selina asked.

'Newby was the publisher. I forget the writer's name.
Bull or Bell or something. It was a pen name, anyway, for
I'm sure the writer was, in fact, a lady.' He turned to
Selina. 'That is another point we must settle — your *nom*

de plume. "Sara Vavasor" is not right for this tale. But to get back to *Wuthering Heights.* It is a tale of passion and intrigue with a dark, brooding hero and a wild, romantic heroine set amid the lofty braes and rock-embosomed tarns of the storm-tossed Yorkshire mountains. It's the sort of thing you could do wonderfully down here, for the scenery is almost identical — and you have the sea, as well!'

'I'm surprised we've not heard of it,' Johanna commented. 'Is it quite recent?'

'Last year, anyway. Newby didn't handle it at all well.' He nodded sagely, as if letting them into trade secrets. 'It shows the importance of choosing the right publisher. I thought it deserved much better success than it had. The public, I feel sure, is ready for morbid tales of that kind.'

'You would have proceeded quite differently?' Johanna asked.

He nodded with huge confidence but did not elaborate. 'However,' he added sorrowfully, 'as the advance paid was only fifty pounds, I don't suppose poor Newby felt justified in doing more than he did.'

Selina was considerably bucked at hearing this. A fifty-pound advance seemed more than generous; to hear it described as 'only fifty pounds' augured well.

Liggat, meanwhile, was licking his lips and eyeing the two ladies cautiously as he added, 'Much of that would have been swallowed up by the cost of printing alone, you see.'

There was something not quite right with that sentence, thought Johanna — though she had to repeat it mentally several times before she could put her finger on the knot. 'You mean — the author pays the printer out of the advance?' she asked.

'No.' His smile pardoned her naivety. 'The publisher does. Author and printer — *qua* printer — need never meet. Of course, most publishers are their own printers, too, as in our case, so the distinction is blurred.'

'Quite. But the publisher pays the printer — even if it goes out of the right pocket into the left?'

'Admirably put, Miss Rosewarne. And the payment is part of the author's advance.'

There it was again; they seemed to be back where they

started. 'So it *is,* in effect, the author who pays the printer?' Johanna insisted.

'In a roundabout way,' he admitted reluctantly. 'The author pays a general advance to the publisher. But how the publisher may employ that money is entirely at his discretion.' He made a conspiratorial grimace in Terence's direction. How did one explain the fearful intricacies of finance to women?

But Terence seemed equally puzzled. 'We have always assumed,' he said slowly, 'that the advance was paid *by* the publisher *to* the author.'

Liggat threw back his head and laughed. 'Dear me! Dear me! How your hopes must have soared!' He scratched his head as if he hardly knew where to start. 'If your name were Charles Dickens or William Makepeace Thackeray or – more to the point in this case, perhaps – Mrs Gaskell or Harriet Martineau, then, indeed, a publisher would gladly make a substantial advance on his expected sales. But with ordinary mortals' – he gave an apologetic shrug and invited them all to smile – 'how else is one to live?'

When no one took up his invitation, he added, 'I'm extremely sorry to have to disabuse you of any fantastical notions you may have formed in your ignorance of our trade. But that is, indeed, the way things stand. If you wish to see this book published, you will have to pay.'

The carriage had not actually gone down into Porthleven but had cut across the edge of the Penrose estate to Tyrock, a cove between the village and the Bar.

'The sea!' Terence exclaimed in an attempt to lighten their gloom.

They turned onto the coastal track, half a mile short of the Bar itself. Liggat judged it time to say, 'Naturally, if your book achieves any sales at all, the advance will be covered in a few weeks and the income will then be substantial. However, I presume that you, as a lady of quality, will not actually be taking any income from this book, so the question is surely rather academic?'

'Is that usual?' Terence asked.

'Bless my soul, yes. I make no claim to be a gentleman myself, you understand, and yet I trust I have the instincts of the same. But if I hadn't been blessed in that way, well!

I could name you half a dozen ladies of quality, all writing under the *noms de plume* of men and all of whom would be appalled at the thought of pecuniary gain from a labour that, to them, is the flowering of a free and ardent soul. They give their work to the public as the wayside blossom lays its fragrance on the air — and are happy and proud so to do.'

It was a subdued and chastened party that descended from the carriage at the end of Loe Bar — and a meek and receptive Selina who set off for a stroll with her publisher along its crest.

Johanna and Terence went directly down to the beach, where she gave vent to her frustration by hurling several large stones into the raging sea. The sand shelved so steeply on this part of the coast that even a twelve-foot wave would rear, break, roar, and expire almost on the same spot before it fell back with a vicious pluck at the shingle and tripped up its successor.

'No fortune for Selina!' Terence commented glumly. 'I thought his letter was too good to be true. Mind you, I wouldn't trust him as far as you're lobbing those stones even. He must think we're green as cabbages down here — wearing his tax-collector suit to show us how poor he is!'

'Why "tax-collector suit"?'

'We've all got one, surely — when they call us in to examine our accounts.'

'Ah — how clever!'

He looked at her askance and shook his head. 'You're the most baffling mixture of ignorance and astuteness I ever met.'

Her immediate worry resurfaced. 'Still — fifty pounds!' she said bitterly.

'He's going to ask for more than that. Remember he said it was "only" fifty.'

'Good heavens, Terence, for that much money I'm sure we could get a thousand or so copies printed ourselves.'

He shook his head dubiously. 'If it were so straightforward, why isn't it done more often?'

'Because everyone wants easy money. We'd have to work at it, like billy-oh.'

He patted her on the shoulder. 'And I'm sure you would,

chère cousine. But you have quite enough on your plate already. Talking of which, how are your plans coming on? Are you really going to build this new brewery in Penzance?'

'I'm going to sell Liston Court, anyway.'

'Is that an answer?'

'It means yes. It'll provide me with the capital I need.'

He gave a reluctant tilt to his head. 'I used to laugh, didn't I. You offered me the chance once, and I just laughed. Coad says you'll be richer than all the Gryllses put together one day. People just won't be able to go on ignoring you. Is that why you're doing it?'

'No, I've burned my boats there – properly, this time. They all descended on me with cards and olive branches when news of the legacy first began to spread. Mrs Pellew ... old Mrs Troy ...'

'Really? What did you do?'

'Nothing. Now they're furious, of course.' She hurled another large pebble into a breaking wave and was astonished to see it emerge on the far side and shoot up at a steep trajectory. So was a passing seagull. 'But I'm angry at this Liggat man,' she went on, 'and the disappointment for Selina.'

'You could pay it out of her trust.'

'That isn't the point.'

Her next stone also went through its wave; but it emerged flat and made a few ducks and drakes before ploughing into the face of the wave behind.

'Talking of easy money,' Terence went on, 'you heard what happened to Charley Vose?'

'No!' She dropped the stone she was about to throw and turned to him, all attention suddenly.

'Arrested last night.'

'What for?'

He laughed. 'What d'you think? He'll be bailed tomorrow, I expect, but it's the end of the road for him. He'll be sent to Australia.'

'Poor old Charley! Much as I disliked the man, I couldn't help a sort of sneaking ... what? Admiration is too strong. You know what I mean, anyway.'

'Yes. Everyone feels the same, I'm sure. But he has been

asking for it. Spending all his time up in Paradise Row —
plundering the stock, as Coad said. The place went down
and down after you left.'

'I didn't *leave,* Terence. I was thrown out. Literally. Into
the rain.'

'And heavy with child!' He made a dramatic parody of it.
'Never darken me doors again! Like one of Selina's tales,
isn't it.'

'It didn't feel like a tale to me, I can tell you.'

'I was there, my dear,' he reminded her. 'You came
directly to me.'

She touched his arm and laughed. 'So I did! I forgot — I'm
sorry. Yes, that's when I offered you the chance of coming
into the brewing trade. The offer's still open if you want.'

He shook his head. 'Thanks all the same. I find I quite
like the law. In fact, I like working. And I begin to pity all
those idle young gentlemen whose company I once aspired
to join.'

'And your Book of Heiresses?'

'Yes, wasn't that a shallow ambition, too. Let's go back
up to the carriage.' He threw a last stone at the foot of a
wave, which caught it up and dashed it down upon the sand
— where it bounced several times, coming to rest again
within six inches of his feet and almost exactly where he had
found it. 'There's magic abroad today,' he commented.

Which reminded her: 'I invited Hamill Oliver to join us at
dinner tonight,' she told him. 'And his grandmother, if
she'll come. If you'd like to suggest a young lady I might
invite for you to squire — one who won't snub me — we
should be evenly balanced.'

'I'll see. The notice is a bit short. Coad's daughter,
perhaps? He wouldn't refuse you, I know that!'

They returned to the carriage.

'Did you bring those binoculars?' he asked.

She lifted the seat and took them out of their case. 'D'you
want to see if your sister's casting herself into Loe Pool yet
— our local equivalent of a rock-embosomed tarn, I
suppose. What on earth *is* a rock-embosomed tarn?'

He chuckled as he trained them on the bay, about a mile
off Gunwalloe cove. 'I thought as much,' he said with a note
of triumph. 'That's no lobster fisherman. Cheeky devils —

626

and in broad daylight, too! I'll bet a Frenchman slipped in last night and filled his pots with bottles.'

'They must have a lookout,' she said, and, since the Bar to their left was obviously uninhabited – except for Liggat and Selina – she scanned the cliffs to their right.

It took her some time to see the man, standing by a clump of furze just below the abandoned working at Wheal Unity, half-way back to Tyrock.

'Ho ho ho!' Terence chortled behind her.

'What?'

He handed her the glasses. 'Look in the towans above Gunwalloe – just this side of them. Someone there you might recognize.'

She had to refocus the lens slightly; and then she saw him. 'Willy Kemp!'

'A combined police and excise party,' he commented. 'They must be hoping for something big.'

She turned next to locate the 'lobster fisherman' and his boat but in searching for him saw something even more exciting – an excise cutter running downwind from Newlyn, making directly for Gunwalloe, and thus for the lobsterman, too. She was already well out across the bay, with her own spray flying before her.

She handed her cousin back the glasses and pointed to this new element in the drama. 'In half an hour they'll have them boxed,' she said.

'How d'you know she's an excise cutter?' he asked when he found the vessel. 'She's flying no flag.'

'They'll break it out when they challenge. I've seen that boat scores of times from my old window at Lanfear. There's no mistaking her.' She turned to see whether the lookout had noticed her, too, and then realized that from Wheal Unity the cutter might just be hidden behind Rinsey Head. 'I'm going to warn him,' she said.

They trotted back along the coastal road as fast as her dress would allow. The lookout at first stepped back into the concealment of the furze, but when they started calling to him, he came running. Johanna handed him the glasses and told him where to find both the cutter and the shore party among the sand dunes.

Like her, he recognized the boat at once. His eyes raked

the nearby coast for a safe haven. Mullion? Poldhu? Porthleven? Or round the far side of Lizard Head? She saw him sizing them up in rapid succession.

'Porthleven would be best,' she told him. 'Even if they rounded the Lizard, the shore party could cut across the land and be ready to meet them.'

'Jo!' Terence laughed awkwardly. 'I'm sure the fellow knows his own business.'

'No, the maid's right,' the man said. 'Porthleven it is.' He handed her back the glasses and ran to the top of the hill behind them. There, silhouetted against the sky like a pilchard huer, he made several broad gestures with his arms, repeating the sequence until – as Johanna saw through the binoculars – his companions in the bay understood and signalled back.

'Do I know you?' she asked him when he came down again.

'No,' he said with a grin – and without pausing on his way. Over his shoulder he called back to her: 'But I do know you, Miss Rosewarne. So don't 'ee fret.'

'Now that warms the cockles of my heart,' she said as they began to stroll back toward the carriage.

'Spitting in the face of the revenue commissioners,' he chimed in with relish.

'The oldest sport in the world.'

'Second oldest.'

She laughed. 'Which reminds me – I didn't ask what's going to happen to the Widow Jewell. Was she caught too?'

'Same warrant – the Hard Labour Act of 1822.'

'Why d'you say it like that? Is it particularly harsh?'

'It means they're charged under statute law and won't be able to snake out of it with the old and well-tried common-law defences. Someone is determined to get them – that's what it means. But, as I said, they brought it on themselves. They started what they called gala nights – strict governesses on Mondays, whips on Thursdays ... that sort of thing. One night a month was "charvey night" – no girl over twelve.'

'That was it!' Johanna pounced. 'I warned her. She wanted to start that caper when I was there, but I put my foot down. Well, I don't feel so sorry for her now.'

'Diana's gone to a house in Penzance.'

She turned and faced him. 'You seem to know a lot about it.'

'She was the only one left at liberty. Came to see me — wanted us to represent them.'

'Are you going to?'

He shook his head. 'Sent her to Curnock and Carminow in Penzance.'

'Ah.'

They walked on in silence for a while. The lobsterman was now well on his way to Porthleven; and at the far end of the Bar, she was amused to notice, a squad of men in blue was running toward them, and making heavy going of it in the sand and shingle.

Terence broke the silence. 'Actually, I did use to go out to Paradise Row from time to time — not to take any of the girls upstairs, or not often, but just to talk to them.'

'Ha! I'm sure their conversation was fascinating!'

'Well — it's natural and easy, anyway. You've no idea how hard it is these days, just trying to meet a girl of one's own class and hold an ordinary conversation about ordinary topics. You're one of the few, Jo. But then you're my cousin, so it hardly counts.'

'Oh look,' she said, 'Liggat and Selina have turned about. Listen — I want to give that man a bit of a run for his money tonight. So stay close and keep your ears skinned, eh? I'll tell Tony the same. We may need witnesses.'

About five minutes after they regained the carriage, and shortly before the other two joined them, they were passed by a scarlet-faced motley of constables and revenue men, panting and sweating like pigs.

'What a life, eh!' Kemp shouted to her as he passed.

'You'll have to get a new cutter,' she called after him. 'Even I can recognize that old one by now.'

Selina looked as miserable as Johanna had ever seen her. 'Pretty bad, is it?' she asked sympathetically.

'Oh, no! Hardly anything at all! I've only got to move the entire story from America to Cornwall, kill off my present hero in chapter six, and make a brand-new hero out of one of the others. And three of my heroine's sisters must die because five girls is too many for the reader to hold in the mind. And she can't love two men at the same time because she'll lose the reader's sympathy.'

To each of these statements Liggat nodded his happy assent, as if Selina were now his star pupil, repeating her lessons word-perfect. 'And it's all there!' he asserted genially. 'It's all in her present text. It just needs bringing out properly. That's all.'

Chapter Fifty-Seven

The fourth delivery, which came to Lanfear while they were out at Loe Bar, had included a letter from California. Hilary brought it to Liston Court, where Johanna opened it eagerly:

Poste Restante, San Joaquin.
Saturday 22nd September, 1849

My dearest wife,

How to give you this news? Shall I say we have dwelt among clouds for the past week? Or that no dream is now beyond us? Or that ... but no! Let me put it at its most practical, for I know that is the realm where your mind ever dwells. In simple terms, then, my own darling: You may abandon forthwith your fond and foolish notions of becoming a brewer! I cannot even write it without laughing – just as I cannot imagine my quiet, biddable, modest little treasure ever getting such a quaint notion into her head in the first place.

(I may confess it now: I was annoyed when I heard you had gone to the Ram. Indeed, for an hour or two I was perplexed and alarmed beside – knowing what Vose had schemed with the Widow Jewell – until my native good sense assured me that no wife of mine would have any part in such a caper and that you would oppose it to the last. And I was heartily glad that you severed company with the man so soon, though I deplored the manner of it on his part and he shall account to me for it when I return.

631

What you have done since then and how you have lived is not clear. Your letters have hinted in passing that you are back at Liston Court, but Percy Collet (Pig-eye Gee) has a letter from home in which his mother says you are living in the old gardener's cottage at Lanfear, which is now the property of little Dr Moore. I know you have mentioned him, once, as having moved into the district, and that your paths occasionally cross, etc. But if Mrs C is to be believed, the occasions must be daily. Understand me, I write in no sense of suspicion or mistrust; I remember well how I kept silent over Jenny Jewell for fear of alarming you, and, though you knew she was of our party, you also knew I should never betray your faith (and my honour) with her. And I repose the same absolute trust in you. And yet I should have liked to hear this news from you instead of from a grinning Pig-eye Gee.

You may say the same of me, however, and with justice. So let me out with it now: Jenny was of our party from Plymouth to California, and she is here still. She tried all her wiles to woo me from you, but without the meanest success. Hardly a day passed in those first few months when I did not have to tell her that you were my first, my last, my only love. And when she finally realized I meant it and that nothing would sway me — well, then, of course, she took against me, and you, with all the venom she could muster. Now our intercourse is arctic indeed. Her best opinion of us — you and me — is that we 'deserve each other'. To which I say (inwardly) that I hope it is true. I never thought to deserve one so fine and loving and beautiful as you; and if you are so generous as to find the slightest merit in me, then you deserve it a hundred times stronger — and it shall be my undying endeavour to supply that increase when I return.)

There! This eternal parenthesis is done. I meant it to be a paragraph, not a page, but now I have made a clean breast of all my feelings and errors. And — as I began to say — I at last feel free to do so because our long separation will shortly end. It was a dream when we built Dudley; it was a scheme as we crossed the Great Divide;

632

and now, if I may borrow Selina's literary mantle, dream and scheme are a solid gleam – of GOLD!

We had almost given up. The worst was to see how ignorant, drunken vagabonds and wastrels (of which there are now tens of thousands in California) could sink a pick into the loose drift of some ravine and find a glory hole, a sump of gold that even a fool could assay with his eyes. True, these nonce finds are never the token of a large lode. They are erratics that support nothing but hope for years after their profit has been squandered. We have made a few small finds in that way ourselves, which has kept our heads above water. Nonetheless, it was galling that our careful survey, our educated choice of strata and dip, and our seemingly endless drift into rock, rock, and more rock, should for so long have yielded nothing but talcose slate, quartz, hornblende slate, porphyry, quartz, argillite slate, serpentine, yet more quartz ... and absolutely nothing that glisters.

I have written little to you of these mortifications. Our stray feelings, when committed to paper, assume a permanence that was never intended. But many a night we have gone to our beds weary with despair. Frank Ashburn made an equation of it: 'An ounce of toil over a ton of rock is equivalent to a ton of toil over an ounce of gold,' in its power to age a man. The proof of it was long in coming, but last week, as we were working down through a quartz gozan as pretty and kindly as you could wish, we saw the first veins begin to open up. Within an hour we knew we had gold at an ounce to the yard.

We worked the clock round, for we should never have slept anyway. By the following day we had the drift in so dangerous a condition that, had poor little Enion Hosking been here, he would have died of apoplexy and a blistered tongue. But we now had gold at three ounces to the yard! Since then, having shored up and made safe (if you are friends again with Nina, tell her it was 'horse-play' – she thought it a very comical word, I remember), we have gone a few yards deeper and find it settling to three and one half oz.

The signs are even better. The talcose slate on either

side of our quartz is largely unfragmented; the quartz forms a broad, intrusive dike of even thickness and quality; and best of all, the dip is steep. Everything tells us this is a deep, unbroken vein, a large intrusion that will not pinch out for ... who knows how many hundreds or thousands of feet? Guess a figure and add it to your prayers.

This discovery has changed everything, including our own expectations. All the reports that reached us spoke of the gold lying in broken veins at the foot of deep river gorges — and indeed, such has proved to be the case. Some of the gorges are a thousand feet deep, or more, and the quality of broken quartz in their bottoms is keeping tens of thousands busy; but they are scavengers, not miners as anyone in Cornwall would use the term. Except for their age they are like those broken down old tributers who pick over the old halvans around our mines at home. We are the first (or maybe the second, for I have this day heard of another good vein found in the Maripoosa Valley) to mine the living lode in an orderly, and at last, thank God, productive, manner.

We all sat down in solemn council this afternoon (which is why I write this now) and decided that our mine, which they kindly call the Penrose Mine, will be our 'banker,' as the term is. We shall use it for our staple income, a portion of which will buy proper Cornish stamps and buddles and vanning tables to handle the loose, river-bed ores in a sensible fashion. For there is no doubt that the scavengers leave behind more invisible gold than they remove in their eye-popping, glory-hole nuggets. And there is equally no doubt that those loose ores, when worked by men who know their craft, will yield even better than our proper mine (i.e. the Penrose Mine — I am still diffident of the appellation). Indeed, that is hardly surprising, since the barren slates and shales weather away quickly, leaving relatively more of the gold-bearing quartz behind than there is in our living rock.

Thus our notion of kicking up a quick fortune with our boots and rushing home to Cornwall with all speed must perforce give way to a plan whereby we spend at least the next five years out here. But by then — and I have seen enough of this gold-bearing country to speak with certainty — we shall all be able to retire and live out the rest of our lives without ever having to worry where the next penny, or even the next thousand pounds, is coming from.

Therefore I ask you: will you bring our dear little Hannah and your own darling self here to share our adventure? I have business in Sacramento next week and from there (having first deposited some ten thousand dollars' worth of gold!) I shall send you a draft that will bring you to Kanesville in style and comfort. I could meet you there in the second week in July next year (1850) and bring you back here to San Joachin — by a trail that will, I'm sure, seem oddly familiar!

Oh, my darling, my hand trembles now as I write the very thought! To see you again, and so soon! To hold you in my arms! To feel your head resting upon me once more, where I have imagined it so fervently all these centuries of days. And to put out the light, and to pull the blankets over us, and to discover and rediscover, as long as we live, those joys we knew so briefly in the nights before we said goodbye — man and wife at last!

Respond as soon as you receive the draft. If there is any trouble over cashing it, discount it at whatever rate you will, for I shall make it double what you really need. Go to Nina, even if you are at daggers drawn. Go to little Moore. Go to Charley Vose. Go to my uncle . . . go to anyone you can as long as you catch your ship and come at last to, Yr ever-loving, Hal.

PS: You omitted to send the copy of the paper in which you placed my announcement re paternity, etc.

Johanna hummed joyfully to herself as she took her bath before dinner. She had decided that, if she was going to act like a lady for little Liggat's benefit, she might as well enjoy some of the privileges of the station while the pretence lasted. She had moved back into her old room, where, during the drive to Loe Bar, the maids had built up the fire and set the bath to warm by it. Peggy Machin, who had come over from Lanfear to see to the cooking, had boiled the water. The two footmen had carried it up in pails just hot enough to bear, and now Margaret was tipping it onto the big white wingback of the bath, where it spilled deliciously, like a thousand glowing fingers, around her back and limbs; soon it was deep enough for her to poke her knees out into the air and sink to the tip of her nose in its steaming embrace.

'Oh, Margaret,' she said in ecstasy. 'When I'm living in Californa, I'll do this every day.'

'California?' the maid echoed in surprise.

'That letter was from Hal Penrose — well, I don't suppose you need telling. But they've found gold at last, not just chance little finds but in quantity in a proper bal. And he's sending me the money to go over and join him.'

'Oh!' Margaret said approvingly. 'You won't need to touch none of your own, then.'

Johanna laughed. 'No — he doesn't know about that yet. Last time I wrote to him I wasn't sure what to do with it, so I didn't say. In fact, I didn't say anything about ... Lady Nina or ... anything. But no, of course I won't wait for his money to come. I'll go straight away ...' She paused.

'Is it getting cold?' the maid asked.

'No, no — it just struck me — there'd be no point in going at once. I'd only be stuck for months in the East, waiting for the thaw.'

Oddly enough, there was no great sense of disappointment within her.

'That's a shame,' Margaret replied. 'Shall I scrub your back?'

'Yes, please.' She sat up, all eager. 'It's probably a good thing,' she mused. 'It'll mean I can finish the brewery and sell it as a going concern. Don't say a word to Terence about it, by the way — I mean, don't tell him the roof's almost up. I sort of allowed him to believe I hadn't even started building yet.'

'Why?' Margaret moved the sponge in great, lazy circles. 'I mean, of course I won't say a word, but why are you keeping it secret from them?'

'I just don't want them dropping over to Penzance every

636

other day, picking holes in this and that and plaguing me with their superior ideas when they know *nothing* about it. There's the topping-out celebration next week, and that's time enough for them to find out.'

'And does mister know?'

'Mister' was Tony. 'I couldn't say. He hasn't asked and I haven't told him.'

Margaret chuckled. Johanna asked her why.

'I was only thinking the other day,' she replied. 'You two are so cool with each other as man and wife.'

Johanna gave a derisive laugh. 'We're a million miles from being that.'

'If you say so.'

'Why? Are tongues wagging?'

'No, I didn't mean that. I meant you may be a million miles off of that, but what about mister?'

'What about him?'

'A millionth part of a mile, I should think.'

'Well then — perhaps it's better that we stay cool and correct. That's enough with the sponge.'

Margaret started rinsing off the soap. 'Some have all the luck,' she said to the furniture.

'D'you mean you find him attractive?' She looked up to see the girl smiling at her — and the smile said, 'You know I do, and don't tell me you don't.' Her lips only confirmed it: 'I didn't at first, mind. There's some men do sweep a maid off her feet — like one we both could name. Trouble is, they do sweep a lot of maids that way — off of their feet and flat on their backs. Like one we could both name.'

Johanna bristled with anger. 'Have a care, Margaret!'

'I speak as I find, and always have done. Turn I off, if you mind to. Hide yourself among a gaggle of yes-ma'am-no-ma'am women who'll go down the kitchen and giggle at 'ee. But there's scores of maids here can tell 'ee the same about Hal Penrose.'

'They don't read his letters. They don't know how much he's changed.'

'Anyroad, mister's the other kind. Slow and sure. I know which one I'd pick.'

'Ah yes, but what about when Hal Penrose came back? What when he looked at you with those eyes of his? And

637

if you went to a ball and he asked you for a dance ... when he took you in his arms — what then? Don't tell me you'd be able to ignore it all. I remember the way you spoke of him, in this very room, on my first night at Liston Court.'

Margaret grinned. 'If the cake was well and truly cut by then — why, who'd miss a slice or two?' The smile faded and she went on in a more serious tone. 'And that's all any maid who hitches herself to Hal Penrose will get of *him* — a slice or two. Men like that can't help theirselves.'

Johanna sighed. 'Oh, Margaret! I appreciate your frankness — don't mind me flaring up now and then. But if that's the world's opinion of Hal Penrose, then — as in so many other things — the world will just have to learn how wrong it is.'

The girl squeezed out the sponge and dropped it in her lap. 'You do the rest and I'll go lay out your dress,' she said. 'It's nice to work in a proper house again, I must say.'

'Margaret! Are you unhappy at Lanfear?'

'No, 'course not. But 'tis nice to work in a proper house again, that's all.'

As she finished soaping herself, Johanna looked about her. A proper house? She could see what Margaret meant; there was something *very* proper about Liston Court. Perhaps she wouldn't sell the place after all. It would make a nice town house for Hal to come back to — no, for Mr and Mrs Hannibal Penrose to come back to. And there was no need to sell it now, after all. They'd get a good rent on it while they were away.

In which case, this dinner for little Liggat was now somewhat pointless.

While Margaret dressed her she tried out her decision not to sell. The maid was all in favour. 'You make it a condition that whoever rents it must take me as housekeeper. I'll keep an eye on them for 'ee. And when you come back — oh my! The garden parties we'll have. And the balls. And the grand dinners. And you shall be At Home each week, just like Lady Nina was. And little Hannah and all your other children will all grow up proper little ladies and gentlemen and marry lords and ladies, I shouldn't wonder! And just let anyone try and cut you then! You could blight them with a single glance!' She giggled in delight at the thought. 'You'll be the next Mrs Ramona Troy of Helston — think o' that!'

'Yes,' Johanna replied rather bleakly. She went across the corridor to the nursery, where she read a bedtime tale and did Miss Muffet and Patacake and This Little Piggy and Round and Round the Garden. Then she sang 'Don't wander away, love,' and tucked Hannah up tight and kissed her and said very firmly that she was to go to sleep without any fuss.

'What's next week?' she asked the child.

'Birfday.'

'And what's a birthday?'

She replied in one great gushing giggle: 'Cake!'

'And?'

'Jelly. Whoss jelly?'

'You'll see — but only if you're good. What else?'

'Pwezunks.'

'Yes! Secret presents! Now is that enough reasons for being a good little girl tonight?'

Hannah, unwilling to admit it in so many words, turned on her side, stuck her thumb in her mouth, and began the slow, sensuous stroking of her nose that almost always sent her off to sleep.

Johanna kissed her tenderly once more and told Margaret to leave the lamp until she'd dropped off. The maid said not to worry about the child this evening; she herself would pop up and look at her every now and then.

On the way downstairs Johanna passed Nina's old bedroom. She thought of opening that door with Hal, going inside, putting out the light, drawing the blanket over them, and ... No, it was impossible. Not in that room. And yet, where else could the master and his lady sleep if not in the principal room? Hal would certainly insist on taking it.

She opened the drawing room door and went in to meet her guests.

Mrs Ramona Troy had come after all — though Johanna did not realize what a significant moment it was in her life until much later in the evening. 'My dear Miss Rosewarne,' she said, 'you are looking the very picture of health. It must be all that fresh air.'

What she meant, Johanna realized, was 'All that driving around in your governess cart, soliciting orders for beer!' Oh dear, was it going to be that sort of evening?

Terence arrived, with apologies for his lateness. 'I think you know Miss Coad,' he said.

Miss Coad was a tall, angular young woman who seemed to suffer from a permanent off-odour which she carried around just inside her nostrils. She held her head very high, as if to escape it. Then Johanna remembered that Selina had read out a passage from *The Drawing Room Companion* saying that heads were being carried very high this season. She studied the effect and found it not to her liking.

They went directly in to dinner: Mrs Troy with Liggat, who had been flushed out into his well-tailored suit and looked as if he had found a fortune since lunch-time; Hamill with Selina, who had recovered something of her composure over the 'death by a thousand cuts' of her romance; Terence with Miss Coad, who seemed to have lost touch with that unpleasant smell the moment she saw Mrs Troy was of the party; and Tony with their hostess, who heartily wished the evening over and done with now that she had decided not to try to induce Liggat to buy Liston Court.

The first course was mulligatawny soup, fried codfish slices in oyster sauce, or eel *en matelote*. The entrées were broiled pork cutlets and tomato sauce or *tendrons de veau à la jardinière*. The second course was boiled leg of mutton or roast goose or cold game pie. The third course was a choice of roast snipe or teal with apple soufflé, iced charlotte, champagne jelly, coffee cream, tartlets, or mince pies. And the meal was rounded off with the usual ices and desserts. No wine was served, but the ales, stout, porter, and (for those with delicate constitutions) table beer had all been specially brewed at Lanfear – not, it must be admitted, for this occasion but as samples of what the new Penzance brewery would be able to supply.

For a small, family dinner in November it was perhaps a trifle on the grand side; though, on any given evening, half a dozen other tables in Helston would have offered a fair comparison with it – and hundreds in the county as a whole. Liggat, at least, was most impressed and declared he had no idea provincial society did itself so proud. He seemed to think that every dish in every course had to be sampled; but as he ate twice as fast as anyone else, he did not delay the planned progress.

Not that the progress, for all its planning, was so very swift; no one expected to rise from the table until past nine. Meanwhile, the conversation flowed like Rosewarne ale. It turned out that Mrs Ramona Troy had read *Wuthering Heights,* the morbid romance of which Liggat had spoken so warmly. Unlike Liggat she did not pretend to have forgotten the author (which is a common trick among publishers to show the tyro writer how swift the scribbler's name can slip the midwife's mind).

'Ellis Bell!' he echoed happily when she let it out. 'I recall it now. She is — for I am convinced he is a she — she is a sister to that "Currer Bell" who wrote *Jane Eyre.* Now that was a successful book. Smith and Elder knew how to treat it, you see.' He smiled to underline the message for Selina.

'Piffle, sir!' said Mrs Troy. 'Currer Bell is Thackeray, and all the world knows it. He dedicated the book to himself to throw us off the scent. But the circumstance of the lunatic wife is too improbable to be coincidence. It gives him the lie.'

'You may well be right, ma'am,' Liggat conceded diplomatically.

'Are the two books at all similar?' Selina asked. 'I have read *Jane Eyre,* naturally.'

Mrs Troy drew breath to reply but Liggat leaped in: 'They could not be more different, in my view. *Jane Eyre* is about right and wrong — and indeed, rights and wrongs.' He smiled at the neatness of it, as if he had never made that conjunction before. 'The right of a woman, be she never so poor, to love whom she pleases. That question has never previously been placed before the reader of fiction. The Pamelas and Clarissas, the Molls and Roxanas of the past all knew their proper stations in life. But not our Jane. Though penniless and alone, she presumes to love her master, a gentleman both rich and powerful — and a man of the world, beside. But, alas,

.

married. There follows that most terrible struggle between her virtue and an easy collapse into vice. She champions a woman's rights to preserve her virtue against the most intolerable pressures from the tormented depths of her own heart.'

He smiled around at the entire table. Did he linger briefly when his gaze arrived at his hostess? Johanna thought he did and she shifted uncomfortably. They were some great gossips up at the Angel Hotel.

'And has this *Wuthering Heights* a theme of similar grandeur, sir?' Tony asked.

'In my view it is infinitely more profound, Doctor. *Jane Eyre* tells of a woman's struggle between right and wrong in the words of the woman herself. She speaks to us as if she were plaintiff and we the jury. But *Wuthering Heights* is a wild, fierce, grim tale of two doomed lovers, Heathcliff and Catherine — in which elemental Evil battles elemental Good to the death. Aye, and into the world beyond the grave, too. And it is told in the words of two of the lesser characters, who are themselves caught up in that struggle, so that the focus of it is constantly shifting and there is no firm ground anywhere. And thus we feel ourselves drawn in until we stand at the very rim of its vortex, staring down in pity and in terror at those poor, tormented souls ...' Again he stared around at them; his hearers hardly dared breathe now.

And then he laughed and went on in a most conversational tone: 'Of course, it is grossly overdone, as is the way of all fiction. In real life, Absolute Evil comes to the feast in a dainty mask. "Not such a bad fellow," we say of him. "Has his faults, of course, but then which of us is perfect?" Nonetheless, he can destroy a life as easily as Heathcliff destroyed Catherine's.'

Thoughts of Hal came to Johanna's mind. She dismissed them angrily. At that moment Margaret came in and told her in a low voice that a certain Edward Penaluna had called with a 'benefaction' for her.

'For me? What does he mean?' she asked. 'Is he religious?'

Margaret laughed. 'No one never accused him of that before. He's the best smuggler in Cury parish, they say.'

Johanna relaxed. 'I think I know what this is. Ask him to come in.'

'Here?' The maid looked askance.

'Yes, it'll amuse us.' She raised her voice. 'Mr Liggat — you recall the smuggling operation this afternoon? Here is its sequel.' The door opened behind her. Without turning round she called out, 'Mr Penaluna, you're very welcome. Go and warm yourself at the fire there, where we may see you, and tell us what happened.'

'Well, thank 'ee kindly, mistress.' As he passed he casually laid two bottles of Martell's finest on the table beside her.

'My, what can this be?' she asked, giving Liggat a wink. 'Well, did they get their hands on anything? The shore party passed us, red as lobsters and making all of three knots through the sand.'

'They got the boat,' he said, lifting the tails of his coat and warming his hands at the fire. His salt-cured face glowed at the memory. 'Which they must release tomorrow as there's no law yet against going lobster fishing and coming back with no catch.'

'No catch!' Johanna laughed and stroked the bottles.

'Did the excise cutter put in at Porthleven?' Terence asked.

He shook his head. 'Willy Kemp turned she back agin. I dare swear they was some wet by the time they got back Newlyn. And poor old Willy — he must have turned Porthleven upside-down and inside-out and forth and back.'

'And never found one of you?' Tony asked.

'Nary a one, sir.'

Johanna nodded to one of the footmen. 'Some ale for our friend,' she said, turning to check with Penaluna. 'Not too humble for your taste, I hope?'

He smacked his lips. 'I'd sooner have a drop of good ale — for myself, like — than a hogshead of that there brandy.' He supped it. 'That's very good stuff, that is. No need to ask where that do come from. Excise all paid, I hope?'

Mrs Troy took it upon herself to answer. 'Oh, Miss Rosewarne doesn't flout the *law,* Penaluna. That's her great strength, you know.'

Johanna thought it an odd remark but let it pass. 'So, where were you?' she asked. 'Had you left Porthleven by then?'

He shook his head and grinned. 'But I'll tell 'ee this mistress – I heard they banging and bailing and cater-wauling for a half-hour. And if they hadn't made so much noise, they'd have heard the bottles a-shivering and a-clicking under their very feet. Now I won't say more'n that. I just come to express our thanks, like, in the traditional manner, as they say.'

Everyone laughed and told him he was a capital fellow, and Mrs Troy ordered two dozen for herself, and Johanna sent him to the kitchen with leave to eat and drink his fill – which he took full advantage of.

She pushed one bottle across to Liggat. 'Souvenir of Cornwall,' she said. 'Come back soon.'

He smiled. 'I think there's no doubt of that, Miss Rosewarne.'

And so the meal wound to its stately close. When the ladies withdrew to ease their stays and analyse the port and brandy drinkers directly, Mrs Troy said, 'He is not at all the sort of man I expected. Vulgar, of course – yet amusing and at times profound.'

'I had hoped to sell him this house,' Johanna confessed. 'But now . . .'

'Oh, persevere, persevere! He would enliven Helston society no end. Don't you think so, Miss Coad?'

Miss Coad, who had actually found the man's ramblings rather a bore, heartily agreed – 'though the sort of novels I like,' she added artlessly, 'are just for reading, you know.'

'But why would you sell this house, my dear?' Mrs Troy turned back to her hostess.

Johanna told them of the good news in Hal's letter that day.

'Ten thousand dollars?' Mrs Troy could always go to the heart of the matter. 'That would be what? Almost fifteen hundred pounds. Well, let us hope it is a *steady* mine, for it is certainly not spectacular. On the other hand, gold has one great advantage over tin in that its price cannot possibly fluctuate since it is its own measure of value.' She smiled.

Miss Coad begged leave to withdraw for a while.

Johanna took advantage of her absence to say, 'I must thank you for coming tonight, Mrs Troy. After my inexcusable discourtesy to you I had no right to expect it.'

Mrs Troy appeared surprised. It wasn't that she believed no apology was due, but she had not expected Johanna to offer it.'That was a difficult time for you,' she replied. 'I should have made more allowance.'

'May I ask what changed your mind?'

The woman smiled. 'People have cut you and snubbed you − and it's had not the slightest effect. It simply does not work with you as it does with other people. Hamill is the same. He . . .'

'Mrs Troy − pray forgive my interrupting you − but if this is leading back to your notion that Hamill and I should marry . . .'

She flapped away the idea. 'God forbid! No − it is a measure of my own progress in − how may I put it − in coming to terms with you? It is a measure of my own progress that I now find the idea of such a marriage as absurd as you always have.'

'Oh, not absurd. But improbable, I agree.'

'I was saying − people used to try to snub Hamill, but it never worked. Nowadays he's tolerated because *he* doesn't upset anything very much.'

'But who do I upset?' Johanna asked.

Mrs Troy laughed as if she thought the question was a joke.

'I mean, I know I upset people that time when I failed to return their calls − after Lady Nina died.'

'My dear girl, it's not *who* you upset but *what*. And the fact is, you upset the whole blessed applecart. People like you are more dangerous, in my view, than all those gun-waving revolutionaries who turned Europe upside down last year. They, thanks be to God, and to military might, are now safely behind bars. Either that or they're in government and mellowing as fast as they can get their hands on ready money. But you are still at liberty, quietly going about your business of undermining our very foundations.'

'I'm afraid all this sounds rather fanciful to me, Mrs Troy. Flattering though it is.'

'Flattering!' Mrs Troy put a clenched fist to her brow. And then, against her will, she laughed. 'Only you could possibly have said that. Never mind — I've rambled away quite enough for one day.'

'If it's any comfort to you,' Johanna concluded, 'I shall be leaving the district next April. I'm off to America to marry Hal Penrose — only I'll be obliged if you'd not mention it until I've found the occasion to break the news to my other friends. You are the first to know of it.'

Mrs Troy nodded; she looked as if it were no comfort at all to her. Miss Coad returned at that moment and the conversation reverted to small talk; but Johanna found her mind returning, again and again, to Mrs Troy's astonishing analysis of her character and situation. Why had she spoken like that? It was obviously something she had prepared — and yet that only deepened the mystery, for it was the last sort of thing one said to one's hostess at a dinner party. And it went nowhere toward explaining why she had swallowed her annoyance — her justifiable annoyance — and accepted tonight's invitation.

Johanna had the feeling she had missed something extremely obvious.

When the evening was done and her guests were taking their leave, Mrs Troy said, 'Do be sure to come out and see me, Miss Rosewarne — at your convenience. Don't wait for an invitation, and don't feel you have to confine yourself to when I'm At Home — just call by.'

Johanna was overwhelmed at this mark of esteem; and Miss Coad, she saw, could hardly believe her ears.

Was that it? Had the redoubtable Mrs Ramona Troy accepted this evening's invitation not to make some significant social gesture, not to signal that Johanna Rosewarne was once again *persona grata,* but simply to extend and invite a friendship?

If that were so, then she had laid aside her own principles and ignored those strict social conventions of which she was a leading arbiter in these parts; indeed, it would seem to indicate that she had tacitly accepted Johanna's view of things — notwithstanding all the fine words she had spoken out against it. It was, in a way, a conditional surrender. Johanna wondered what would follow next. And that was one further reason to be glad she was delaying her departure to America until next April.

Chapter Fifty-Eight

It was Christmas Eve, 1849. The Cardew children remembered the ritual from last year — only too well in James's case. He stole down to the linen press and borrowed a pillowslip to hang at the foot of their bed. Since last year's stocking had been filled until it threatened to burst, he had reasoned it out that only the size of the container had limited the generosity of Father Christmas.

When Johanna saw what he had done she took one of Hannah's baby socks, filled it to bursting with an apple, a new halfpenny, and three hazel nuts, and hid it in the linen press. In the pillowslip she left a note: 'Where I came from, there he went. What greed would have added, that he took away. Yet what life begrudges, he will give.'

She filled the other stocking for Hannah, who, when asked next morning what Father Christmas had left her, ignored the coins and nuts and sweetmeats scattered on and in and under and around her cot and held up the single stocking in the greatest delight.

James was quite good at his reading by now, though he needed Hilary's help in deciphering 'begrudges'. It did not take him long to find his way back to the press — where he burst into tears, empty pillowslip in one hand, bulging baby stocking in the other. But Christmas breakfast, with spiced, mulled ale, honey-cured ham, and porridge with cinnamon and almonds, soon bucked him up; and the size of the goose, which Mrs Machin was then flouring and covering over with bacon rashers, held him in awe.

'Miss Rosewarne,' he asked as they walked to church, 'what does life begrudge?'

'Oh, Jimmy — so many things. Where does one start? Why d'you ask?'

'I just wondered.'

'If you told me what's on your mind, perhaps I could give you a better answer.'

But he was not going to confess his shame to people who — he was sure — had no inkling of it.

Oddly enough, though, the sermon brought him within an ace of his answer. Canon Price, without once looking in Johanna's direction, preached on the redemption that is implicit in the birth of Christ. Johanna had attended matins there every Sunday since Greep's famous sermon against her; not the severest chill, nor even an abscess in a wisdom tooth, had been able to keep her away. This had led to a sort of cold tolerance toward her among the better-off in the congregation. The poorer members, because of her work with the doctor, had never put her outside their pale; but it was now that work, rather than the transgression Greep had castigated, that made her wealthy neighbours glad of the excuse to go on cutting her. Mrs Ramona Troy's example had not been followed generally; her gesture had been written off as eccentric — she was growing more and more like her grandson . . . always been something a bit odd about that family . . . old age has its privileges . . . and so on. Canon Price had obviously decided it was time for his bare tolerance to give way to something warmer.

He did not use the word 'begrudges,' but he did say, 'That which life on earth so rarely offers is freely given to us by God through the redeeming death of Jesus — namely: a second chance.'

The sentiment was close enough to the note left by Father Christmas that James decided to try his luck that very evening, and hang up a stocking of normal size. It says much for Johanna that, in all the unexpected turmoil of that night, she did not forget to honour the promise implied by a gentleman in a red dressing gown — a gentleman whose cotton-wool beard masked a face curiously like Tony Moore's.

When dinner was over, and Peggy Machin had gone to her daughter's over in Gweek for the rest of the holiday, taking little Betty Ferns, the scullery maid, with her, Tony and

Johanna settled by the fire to read aloud from Selina's revised manuscript, which they were at last permitted to see and even comment upon. Selina herself sat on the floor and listened with rapt attention. Hilary came and joined them when she had finished the washing up; she, too, was enthralled.

The tale was now called *Dozmary Tor* — a Cornish homage in the general direction of *Wuthering Heights*; and once the reader had accepted the basic improbability that a fairly prosperous and long-settled farming family from green and fertile Meneage would up sticks and set off in covered wagons to seek new pastures in the high, wild, cold, and thin-soiled wastes of Bodmin Moor, it was a cracking good tale. What Selina had always described as 'a minute and particular journal of one family's move to the New World!' had been transformed into an epic struggle between Good and Evil. Even to someone who had not read the first draft, it had quite obviously gained by the remodelling of its hero, John George. Apart from his new name — Tubal Starkman — he had acquired about a hundred pounds of solid muscle; dark, flashing eyes that stirred dark but imprecise thoughts in the heroine, Rosanna Faull; blood that throbbed darkly; and a dark, brooding side to his nature, with which his better half (colour unspecified) was at constant war. The New World was now nothing so literal as a continent over the waters; it was the life beyond the grave, where two poor, tormented souls, after a life-odyssey that carried them to the pit of despair, at last found peace.

The two alternate readers gabbled in their haste to reach the foot of each page and get on with the next. Just before midnight they arrived at the climax of the story: The tortured hero is dead and buried (on the shores of Dozmary Pool, for some unexplained reason), and Rosanna is safe at last in the arms of her new husband, the mild and kindly Arthur Sweetman, who has loved her since childhood; but the unquiet shade of Tubal Starkman will give her no rest; it calls to her from beyond the grave, tapping at her window through the twigs of trees that stir, 'strangely uneasy on a night without the slightest breeze . . .'

Johanna, who was no great reader at the best of times, and hadn't enjoyed a single spare moment these months past, since she had decided to plunge most of her inheritance into the new brewery, marvelled at it. 'Selina!' she said. 'Where *do* you get such ideas?'

'Don't stop!' her cousin cried eagerly, as caught up in the telling as they, though she must have read it twenty times by then.

Rosanna was just about to rise and catch a fatal chill in her nightdress on Dozmary shore, when there came a violent hammering at the front door of Lanfear House – the sort that any doctor's household knows and dreads.

'Oh, botheration!' Selina cried. 'Why do they have to come at just this minute?'

'On Christmas Day,' Johanna added.

The clock began its midnight chime. *'And* on Boxing Day, too,' Tony commented wearily as he rose to answer the summons.

Johanna came with him, carrying the lamp. 'It'll be Johnny Baker,' he said confidently. 'You wait – he'll say "Doctor, doctor, the missus'll burst if you don't come now."' That's what he said last time.'

'The sooner we get that midwife ...' Johanna began, before another bout of hammering drowned her voice.

Tony threw open the door to reveal, not Johnny Baker – indeed, not any member of their union – but Squire Pellew, carrying in his arms the limp and apparently lifeless body of his son Raymond. 'Oh, Doctor Moore, help him please? Do what you can for him. I think he's done for.'

Tony didn't even wait to ask questions. He was already walking back down the passage toward the kitchen. 'Bring him through,' he called over his shoulder. 'Jo – fetch the oilcloth and plenty of light.' To Selina and Hilary, who emerged from the drawing room as he passed, he said, 'Draw up the fire in the range and get some water boiling.'

Johanna stepped aside to let the squire pass. He moved so swiftly his cloak flew out behind him. She realized that it had until then concealed Mrs Pellew, pale, shrivelled, and seeming ten years older than when they had last spoken together. She was too distracted to remember to shut the door and Johanna, having delivered her, and the lamp, to the kitchen, had to go back and do it. She returned bearing two more lamps, from the dining room.

'Did you put the guard in front of the drawing room fire?' she asked Selina – who went at once to do so.

Tony was asking, 'And where precisely was this pain? No, no – don't touch, just hold your finger above it.'

Pellew complied.

Tony gave Johanna a bleak, grave glance. 'You know the little military bed in my room?' he asked.

She shook her head.

'Well, it's all folded up in the brassbound chest at the foot of my bed. Go and bring it down here, please.'

As she left she heard him explaining, 'It sounds like an appendicitis. I'm afraid only surgery can save him now.'

While she hunted for the bed her heart was weighed down with pity. Though there was little cause to spill much love between her and the Pellews, an appendicitis was the last thing even an outright enemy would wish on them; it was virtually a sentence of death.

The young man, who was in his mid-twenties, came round as they lifted him from the table so as to slip the low bed beneath him. He at once began to groan at the pain.

'Get him some brandy.' Tony said. 'Bring the whole bottle.'

Mrs Pellew tried to soothe him by stroking his brow, but any kind of touch seemed unbearable to him. Tony shook his head at her and she stopped. Johanna and Hilary, unbidden, started removing the young man's boots. Their eyes met and the girl gave a dour little smile; Johanna knew then that it was not the first time she had performed the service for Raymond Pellew. When the boots were off, they took a breeches leg each and waited for the nod from Tony. Mrs Pellew guessed their intention and turned to her husband. 'My dear,' she said sharply and nodded toward their son's feet.

Tony had meanwhile unlaced the man's breeches. 'Steady as she goes,' he told them.

'My dear!' Mrs Pellew repeated even more sharply.

He shot her a glance so furious that she held her tongue for a while.

Selina returned with the brandy and a cut-glass tumbler. 'I couldn't find the proper glasses,' she said – which, in that tense atmosphere, caused a small ripple of laughter. The young man, who was passing in and out of consciousness, was roused by it and gave another deep groan.

'Half and half with water,' Tony told Selina. He leaned over their patient and shouted: 'Drink some of this − hold his head up, ma'am, if you please − not quite so high. Now drink this. It'll take away the pain.'

The poor man took a swig or two and then choked. The effort of coughing caused so much pain that he passed out again.

'Quick,' Tony said.

Johanna and Hilary whipped down his long underpants. Mrs Pellew gave a little cry and, seizing up a teatowel, threw it where it would spare her son's embarrassment were he conscious.

'Will that be in your way, doctor?' Pellew asked through clenched teeth.

Tony gave him a grim smile and shook his head.

Johanna knew what needed to be done; she had assisted Tony at impromptu surgery before − though of a much less serious kind than this − in miners' homes and at the Temperance Hall. 'Bring the salmon kettle half-full of boiling water,' she told Hilary. Meanwhile she threw a blanket, which had been conveniently airing in front of the range to warm Hilary's bed later that night, over the unconscious man's legs − covering the teatowel in passing; onto it she began to unpack the scalpels, clamps, and other paraphernalia of the operating theatre. Tony was washing his hands at the sink.

He didn't even waste time drying them; they were still dripping wet as he picked up the scalpel and, before anyone could even draw breath, made a five-inch incision over where the appendix usually lies. The blood started vividly, almost too red to be natural.

'Clamps,' Tony said calmly.

Mrs Pellew gave out a gasp and nearly passed out. She reeled backwards and blundered into the door of the broom closet. She clutched a pile of maids' aprons draped on a nearby peg and ripped all their hanging loops. It was Johanna, not her husband, who went to her aid.

'Come and sit in the drawing room, my dear,' she coaxed. 'This is no proper place for you.'

653

The woman was too shocked to do anything but obey. As they left, Johanna said, 'Hilary − can you assist the doctor? You've done it before a couple of times, haven't you?'

'She'll be all right,' Tony assured her − only glad that Mrs Pellew was going.

Hilary, who had discovered at that first shout of scarlet blood that she was not in the least squeamish when the matter was as serious as this, nodded reassuringly.

Johanna helped Mrs Pellew along the passage and into the darkened drawing room. She thought of going next door for candles but decided instead to rake up the fire and throw on some small wood. Soon she had a merry blaze going, which did more to soothe the woman than all the candelabra in the house might have managed.

'A small glass of port?' Johanna suggested. 'I think we both could do with one.' And without waiting for a reply she went to the tantalus and poured two good glasses full.

'You are so kind,' Mrs Pellew said mechanically as she took it.

'Success to your son!' Johanna raised her glass encouragingly in the toast. 'It'll soon be done, you know. Dr Moore is one of the fastest surgeons in Cornwall − they all say so. Even though it isn't his main line of work. Your son's ordeal will soon be over.'

'So kind,' the woman repeated.

Her own words seemed to wake her up. For a moment she stared about her in consternation, having no idea where she was. The sight of Johanna brought it all back. She stared into her glass, took a good swig from it, breathed out the fiery afterglow, and went on. 'More than kind, in fact. When I think of the way we've ... what we ...' Tears started into her eyes.

'Now now,' Johanna told her, beginning to feel acutely embarrassed. 'There's no need to rake over all that. You have your principles and you didn't shrink from applying them. You have nothing to reproach yourself for in that.'

Mrs Pellew closed her eyes and shook her head.

Johanna went on, 'And, much as I have regretted the ending of our acquaintance − which I always hoped might ripen into friendship − I should not dream of using your present distress as a means to re-establish it.'

The woman stared at her. 'Did you?' she asked incredulously.

'Did I what?'

'Hope it might ripen into – as you said – friendship?'

'Yes, I did.'

The other shook her head in amazement.

'Why should that surprise you?' Johanna asked.

Selina poked her head around the door and said, 'It's going very well. Tony says to tell you.'

Mrs Pellew gave out a great sigh of relief.

'Thank him,' Johanna said. 'And do keep letting us know what's happening.'

In the easier atmosphere that followed this interruption, the two women sat awhile in silence, staring into the fire, and sipping their port.

'I don't understand,' Mrs Pellew said at length. 'You turned down a most marvellous offer from old Mrs Troy, and yet . . .'

'She told you that?'

The other nodded. 'She rather blurted it out that time we all offered you the pipe of peace and you simply ignored us. She regretted it at once, of course. But what I don't understand, you see, is that you turned her down and yet you hoped for my friendship.'

'But I see no possible connection between the two,' Johanna objected.

'My dear! Ask yourself – now you're older and let us hope wiser – what could I possibly have offered you that could in any way have matched that?'

Johanna gave a baffled laugh. 'But I just meant friendship, you know. Not friendship *for* anything. Just . . . well, what other word is there for it? Communion of minds . . . laughter . . . shared sorrow . . . friendship.'

Mrs Pellew stared as if she were trying to believe it but couldn't. 'With me?' she asked.

Johanna nodded. 'Is that so extraordinary?'

The whole notion seemed to leave the older woman in a daze.

Johanna started supplying her with excuses. 'Naturally, it was presumptuous on my part. You must enjoy that sort of companionship with so many already.'

'Stop!' Mrs Pellew cried out. She held her eyes closed a long moment. When she opened them they dwelled in her glass, which she then tossed back in one gulp. She passed it to Johanna for a refill, still not looking at her or saying anything.

Selina popped her head around the door again and said, 'Nearly done. It wasn't perforated, Tony says. I don't know what that may mean, but it's a good thing apparently.'

'There now, isn't that splendid?' Johanna passed her the refilled glass. 'Where will you take him for his convalescence? If Dr Moore says he can withstand the voyage, I'd recommend the Orient. I always regretted we didn't go on and visit Egypt – when we were in Petra, so close to it.' From Mrs Pellew's slightly amused gaze she became aware that her words could be seen as building up to an offer to accompany the invalid herself. 'One day,' she added hastily, 'perhaps I shall have the time to make the trip there myself. I know that if I were forced into it by convalescence, that is where I would choose to go, especially at this season, when even Italy and Spain are so inhospitable.'

Mrs Pellew took another good mouthful. Alcohol seemed to have no effect on her. Johanna began to wonder if she wasn't rather used to it. 'Did we do right?' the woman mused. 'Bringing him here?'

'Who is your usual doctor?'

'Perry, in Marazion. We delayed sending for him because of its being Christmas Day. The pain didn't start until after dinner and we all thought the boy had simply eaten too much – which he certainly had. Then, when we finally sent for Perry, he was dining with the St Aubyns on St Michael's Mount and cut off by the tide. They said they'd try to get a boat out but it could be an hour or so. And by then the poor boy looked as if he were dying, so I said carry him here.' She closed her eyes and sighed. 'Oh, there was battle royal about that, I can tell you. If anything happens to him now, Pellew will taunt me with it for the rest of my life.'

'Oh, surely . . .' Johanna mumbled, embarrassed at the revelation.

The woman took another sip and then stared at her intently. 'Tell me,' she said, 'if you'll pardon my utter frankness – though, as you were saying just now, we are not total strangers. Do you believe you have suffered, doing what you have done? Has it blighted your life the way people . . .' She shrugged, appealing for Johanna to grasp the unfinished thought.

Johanna said the words then: 'Having a baby out of wedlock? Have I suffered?' She closed her eyes and thought it over. 'No, in the long run I don't suppose I have. I didn't enjoy being preached at and I didn't enjoy it when Charley Vose put my bags out in the rain.'

'Nor when Lady Nina Brookes threw you out, I'm sure.'

'But she didn't. I put that tale about to protect her reputation.'

Mrs Pellew stared at her. 'Oh, Miss Rosewarne, you make me feel more ashamed by the minute. I'm doubly sorry I interrupted now. You were saying – you didn't think you'd suffered?'

'I learned who my true friends were. That was a great advantage, in fact. And I was freed from the restraints of gentility – so that I could get on with what I truly wished to do.'

The other woman nodded vigorously. 'And the little baby? A treasure and a darling, I'm sure?'

Johanna smiled. 'No horns. No tail.'

And then, apropos nothing, she said, 'Funny you should mention Charley Vose. Ever since the Ram closed down, Pellew has become impossible to be with. Tonight, for example . . .'

'Mrs Pellew,' Johanna interrupted. 'Please don't allow these alarming circumstances to prompt a confession you may later regret.'

Her face fell. She shrugged and stared into her glass, which was once again empty. 'Why should you be interested?' she asked bleakly. 'Much less wish to help. Where was I when *you* needed help.' A tear rolled down her cheek. 'Oh – everything's in such a mess!'

Johanna hastened to her side. 'I didn't mean that,' she assured her gently. 'If you think I can help in any way, I will – and gladly. But people in distress often reveal things they later bitterly regret even mentioning. I just wanted you to think before you spoke.'

While the woman dried her eyes, Johanna refilled her glass; oblivion seemed to be what she needed tonight.

As she replaced it in those limp hands, the question fell: 'All those things they whispered about the Ram — were they true? I couldn't believe it, you see. Not with you in charge. I still can't.'

As briefly as possible Johanna explained the complexities of the situation during her times there.

'And my husband . . . did he . . .' She raised her eyebrows hopefully.

'You must not ask me that, Mrs Pellew.'

'So he did!'

'Nor must you draw any conclusions from my refusal to answer. I've told you. I kept as far away as possible from what happened there, or who came and went. I tried to serve good food and good ale and to offer clean and convenient rooms to genuine travellers. The rest is between you and the Squire.'

'There is now nothing between me and the Squire. Our union has become a hollow sham. I keep my part of the bargain — I manage his house, entertain his guests, support his opinions, restore his pride when it is wounded, look after his wastrel son, smile through hours and hours and hours of tedious gossip because somewhere among it will be a crumb or two of use to him . . . I do all these things, as any woman would, in return for a little esteem, a little affection, a little recognition that these services are of some value. That is the bargain. That is what marriage is. But he has broken it.'

'By going — or so you believe — to Paradise Row?'

She shook her head almost angrily. 'Not a bit of it. If he sees anything in those vulgar trollops, let him take it. No. He has broken our bargain by robbing me of my own worth. I now face a lifetime of entertaining, supporting, managing . . . all those things I said . . . smiling bravely in public — playing my part as the Squire's lady. And when they have gone, when the door closes on the last of them, I turn and face an empty house where I am nobody. D'you understand now?'

Johanna nodded sympathetically, but inwardly she was filled with misgiving; for she believed she understood rather more about the Squire's lady than did the lady herself. Mrs

Pellew was now seeking to re-establish their friendship, not so much because she had mourned the loss of it, but in order to flaunt her — the notorious woman of West Penwith — before the squire. Their son's illness had given her a chance that might never be repeated, and she was now seizing it.

But what made it worse was the fact that — never mind the woman's motives — she, Johanna, was mightily tempted at the prospect of such patronage. It could certainly do her business no harm. Her smile broadened. 'Yes, indeed,' she said. 'I do understand — and sympathize. You may think me presumptuous for saying this — but, if you feel I may help in any way, I hope you'll not overlook it.'

'All sewn up and breathing nicely,' Selina called even as she was opening the door. 'Tony says he'll have to stay here. He can't be moved for several days.'

Johanna was about to offer Mrs Pellew a room in the house when she realized it would make her seem as if she were mistress here — in all senses of the word. So she asked Selina if she would mind Mrs Pellew staying. And to give her cousin time to absorb the shock (for Selina would not have considered even the meanest attic in the house to be at her disposal), she turned to the woman and asked, with a merry smile: 'The Squire can manage on his own for a week or two, I presume?'

'He'll just have to,' she replied with relish and turned to await Selina's decision; as if it were an inducement she added that her maids would come over from Skewjack Hall each day and would see to all the housework.

Selina had meanwhile come to the same conclusion as Johanna had earlier: to say either yes or no would cast her reputation in a most unfavourable light. 'The only person who can possibly answer to that,' she said frostily, 'is Dr Moore himself.'

Tony was, of course, only too delighted to offer Mrs Pellew whatever hospitality the house afforded. He asked the squire to help carry his son into the drawing room, which was already warm and where the fire could be kept going all night. 'We'll make a proper sick room for him in the morning,' he said.

He offered the man a drink but Mrs Pellew began reciting a list of the things she'd need if she was to stay here and help

659

nurse the patient. He repeated his thanks to Tony, for the umpteenth time, and made to leave. Johanna saw him to the door – and, in fact, out to his carriage, too.

'What was she saying to you in there?' he asked brusquely.

Johanna did not flare up, though she wanted to. Calmly she said, 'Those are not the first words I expected to hear from you.'

'Er ... quite.' He cleared his throat awkwardly. 'Yes. Owe you an apology. Said an unforgivable word. Deeply ashamed. All right?'

'It wasn't the *word*. Squire. The word itself is nothing. It was your intention in using it – the hurt you wished me to feel.'

'Hah! Never saw anyone look less hurt in my life.'

'No!' She glanced up at the coachman and saw that it was, once again, Jenkins. But for that particular audience she probably would not have said it: 'The only reason I wasn't hurt was that I was too fucking angry.'

Pellew stared at her as if she had bitten him. Then, greatly against his present mood, he laughed. 'Oh, Miss Rosewarne,' he said. 'What a loss you were! You should have stayed there.'

'Coming from the man who bent heaven and earth to have me dismissed, that has a richness all of its own.'

'I know!' He sighed angrily as he climbed up inside. 'Everything's just gone to pieces. Drive on, Jenkins.'

Chapter Fifty-Nine

During the lull Johanna remembered to honour the promise
Father Christmas had implied in his note to James. But it
was only a lull, for at three o'clock that same night she was
awakened by a hesitant tapping at her cottage window.
Thinking that some new crisis had developed with Raymond
Pellew, she leaped from the bed and hastened into her
dressing gown. 'I'm coming,' she called. The entire cottage
had only three rooms, 'two forth and one back', so she was
soon at the front door. 'Sorry,' she said as she pulled it open.
'Were you knocking a long time?' She assumed that
whoever it was had come to her window because hammering
at the door had proved vain.

'Oh, Miss Rosewarne,' cried a dark shape, coming toward
her. The voice was female.

'Who is it?' she asked, slightly alarmed, as she stepped
back.

'I thought you weren't home,' the woman went on.

Now she placed her. It was Diana Jewell. 'Come in,' she
said wearily. 'Just wait in the doorway there while I get a
light.'

'No.' The other said quickly.

Johanna hesitated. 'Why not? What is it you want, then?'

'I don't know.' The dark silhouette of her, which was all
Johanna could see, leaned against the doorjamb and she
burst into tears.

'Is it your mother? Has something happened to her?'

'No.' The tears did not stop.

'I thought you lived in Penzance. Have you walked out
from there?'

'Yes.' It was a ghost of a whisper, between her sobs.

'Then you must be hungry? There's no food here, I'm afraid. We'll have to go to the house.'

'No.'

'Something to drink, then. I have that. Come, let me guide you to the table.' She took her by the arm.

Immediately Diana winced and her crying redoubled. But now it was a howl of pain.

'What is it?' Johanna asked. There was no reply. 'Very well. I'm going to light a candle and see for myself.'

What the sudden light revealed almost caused Johanna to drop the candlestick. 'Dear God!' she cried. 'What has happened to you? Come away in now.' Again she touched her arm – and this time it was the merest touch, but still she winced. 'There too?' she asked. 'Were you attacked on the way?'

The girl shook her head, and her dress confirmed it; though it bore the marks of her walk, it was not torn or dishevelled.

'The doctor must have a look at you,' she decided.

'No!' Diana said at once.

'Yes! There's no question he must. Come over to the house.'

Reluctantly she straightened herself and, with Johanna shielding the candle flame so as to light their path, followed her across the yard to the kitchen door. Her weeping tailed off as they went.

Hilary, who was staying up to watch over young Pellew that night, was in the kitchen, making herself a fresh cup of tea. 'Di?' she asked in disbelieving alarm when she saw who was following Miss Rosewarne. The only answer was a dispirited, 'Lo.'

'Put that in the bigger pot and add more leaves,' Johanna told her. 'I'm going up to wake the doctor.' At the door she added, 'And get some more hot water on the go.'

Tony, by long practice, was alert at once. 'What is it?' he asked. 'Is our patient in difficulty?'

'We have a second one, I'm afraid.'

'Oh, our troubles come not single spies! One of the miners?' He slipped into his dressing gown.

'One of Widow Jewell's daughters. Diana. She's been

appallingly mistreated. I have the most awful premonition about it.'

He put an arm lightly around her shoulder as he steered her back to the door. 'You could be wrong. What is it?'

'I'd rather not say. Just have a look at her. I don't think it's only her face. It's all over. And she's *walked* out from Penzance like that!'

Tony's immediate reaction on seeing Diana was the same as hers had been, but he swiftly became professional again. 'Is there more?' he asked, taking up her hands and looking at her wrists, the only part of her that was not covered. 'Yes, I see. You'd better take your clothes off and let me have a look at you. Jo, go and get some blankets. Hilary – the lint and the borax powder.'

Diana began to whimper again. 'It won't hurt, will it?'

'And the laudanum,' Tony added. 'Leave your skirt for the moment. We'll just have a look at the top half first.'

Her chemise had to be bathed off her in places, where congealed blood had fastened it to her cuts. She was a mass of bruises from the crown of her head to her waist, with hardly an inch of unblemished skin. She gave out one or two shivery moans, but the laudanum was taking effect. He worked in silence, dressing her wounds while Johanna rubbed salve lightly over the bruises. She helped the girl into an old cotton shirt of Tony's, which had been put out for charity. Then they dealt with the rest of her.

'Not so bad,' said Tony, ignoring her backside for the moment. Below the knee she was hardly marked.

As he worked he began to talk – ostensibly to Johanna and Hilary. 'Write it down somewhere – one hundred and twenty-nine strokes, as near as I can count.'

'How ghoulish,' Johanna commented.

He nodded dourly. 'Last time I had to do this, it's all the police were really interested in. That's when I was in Plymouth. I was locum for the police surgeon that night. They brought in a young girl, about your age, Diana, who worked in a house in Union Street, kept by a bully called Sweeny. He used to set his girls what he called their "ambition" for the night – a sum of money they had to earn. And if they failed . . .' He nodded at Diana's cuts and bruises. 'Was that it?' he asked her. 'Has some bully like

Sweeny set up shop in Penzance?' He had almost finished now.

She shook her head and looked, not at him but at Johanna, who said, 'No — this was a customer, wasn't it?'

Diana nodded.

'You may say his name,' Johanna went on.

Diana stared at her, crestfallen.

'Go on,' Johanna said evenly.

'John Visick,' she whispered, as if it were a confession, or even a defeat for her.

Tony shot a startled glance at Johanna. 'You knew?' he inquired. 'Did she tell you before you . . .'

Johanna was shaking her head. 'What payment was worth this?' she asked.

'He never paid I a farthing,' Diana said bitterly. 'He locked the door . . . how he got a key, I don't know. The keys are never left out. Anyroad, he locked the door and put the bed agin it and then he started. He had a set o' withies stuck down his trousers. And I was screaming and yelling. And first they thought 'twas Angie Viggers and her usual, which she do do very realistic. Then someone remembered Angie do never work Christmas Day — being in the glee choir and that. So then they broke in.'

'And Mr Visick? He's now with the police, I presume.'

Diana laughed bitterly. 'He's too good a customer for that, sir.'

'There!' Tony finished the last dressing. 'Wrap that blanket round you and get up to bed. Take another spoon of the laudanum — and you'll be able to sleep on your front, I should think.' He looked at Hilary. 'She can go in your bed?'

Hilary nodded.

'You must tell the police then,' Johanna urged before Diana could leave.

The girl shook her head. 'The joke is, I didn't need to go in to work today. I do live out, like, and I only went in to help, what with so many girls gone home for Christmas and me not having no home. But Jenny sent us passage money for America, see? So I never needed to go in at all. You do know all about that, I suppose — the gold they found, and that?'

Johanna nodded. 'But your mother's trial is still . . .'

'Lawyer says if she'll turn queen's evidence, she can go free. Or just pay a fine for the misdemeanour.'

'Poor old Charley,' Johanna commented.

Diana sniffed. 'You only seen one side of he.'

Johanna sipped her tea, which had gone almost cold by now. 'Why did you come all the way out here, Diana?'

She made an awkward gesture. ''Cos we haven't enough put by for the fine. It'd be a lot, see.'

'And all your earnings have gone on fine clothes and liquor and fancy men who won't lift a finger to help you now.'

She hung her head. ''Tis all gone, anyroad.'

'Sell some clothes, then.'

'There's no time. Her case do come up day after Boxing Day — when's that?'

'Tomorrow.'

'Anyroad, if I sold every stitch, t'would never make a hundred pound — and that's what t'would be with the lawyer's fee and all.'

'I'll pay it,' Selina said from the doorway.

'Darling!' Johanna ran to her. 'I didn't want you to know.' She rounded on poor Diana. 'Now look what you've done! This was your intention, wasn't it! I believe you made this happen. You know what John Visick is like and you provoked him into it. I don't suppose you meant it to go as far as it did. But you thought you . . .'

'Johanna!' Tony cried.

'No, let me say it. You heard her yourself — not a penny to her name. Desperate to raise the fine and run off to America — so what does she do? Provokes poor Uncle John into whipping her like that because she thinks we'll shell out whatever is needed to keep him out of the courts. That's why you looked so disappointed when I told you to come out with his name.' She turned to Selina. 'You shan't pay her a penny. She's brought this on herself.'

'I can still make it bad for John Visick,' Diana snarled.

'You hear her!' Johanna turned on Tony. 'She's not sleeping here tonight.'

He stared at her icily. 'You go too far,' he said, 'This is not your house. I am the one who says who may and who may not stay. And as for Selina's money — it is her own. You have no right to say she shall not use it as she sees fit.'

'You!' Johanna sneered. 'You just make me sick. The wonderful, tolerant, kindly, patient Anthony Moore! The feeble, smug, complacent, weather-cock Anthony Moore is closer to the mark. You just look for any excuse to do nothing. But God — if no one else is going to the police, I am! Then you'll have no cause to submit to this slut's extortion!'

Selina dropped to her knees in front of her cousin and, throwing her arms about her waist, cried, 'Please don't, Jo. Let him be — please?'

Trapped, Johanna stared furiously at Tony.

'If you really wish to be helpful,' he said calmly, 'you can go out and saddle my horse.'

'And what are you going to do?' Surprise began to take the place of anger in her tone.

'First, I am going to look at my patient. Then I shall dress. And then I'll be away for a few hours. If there is any difficulty with young Pellew — which I doubt — one of you will have to go down the road for Dr MacIntyre.' He walked toward her, touching Diana gently as he passed. 'Bed for you, young maid. Show her the way, Hilary.' To Johanna as he passed he added, 'I hope to be back in time to apply fresh leeches. Why isn't my horse saddled yet?'

Five minutes later she led the creature out into the yard and held its head while he mounted up. 'Won't you tell me where you're going?' she asked.

'It's my affair,' he said coldly. But over his shoulder he called back, with just a hint of his former warmth, 'Sometimes one must speak to people in their own language. What did I say? A hundred and twenty-nine, was it?'

He returned just before seven, in time for a hearty Boxing Day breakfast, shared with a jubilant James who had just discovered his refilled stocking. Then he went to deal with the leeches; Johanna, who was sitting at the invalid's bedside and trying to feed Hannah — or rather battle with her for possession of the teaspoon — yielded the struggle to Hilary and assisted Tony, instead.

He greeted her quite normally, as if there had been no words between them earlier that night. She wanted to ask him outright where he had been — though she knew very well it could only have been to her uncle's house in Penzance. Even more, she wanted to ask him what he had done there – though of that she was less certain.

Pellew woke up the moment they turned down the blankets. He stared at them in bewilderment.

'Don't try to sit up,' Tony warned. 'How d'you feel?'

He closed his eyes and groaned. 'What have I done this time?'

'This time it was done to you, old chap. Lie still. I'm just going to apply fresh leeches.'

The old ones he had set to work last night, on each side of the suture, were gorged and bloated. They came off easily.

'I've never seen that done before,' Johanna commented. 'Not for a cut.'

'I don't usually bother with minor incisions, but I've noticed that where there's a deep surgical wound with massive oedema, the leeches seem to help.'

He was being uncharacteristically clumsy, she noticed. He asked her to apply the fresh, lean contingent for him. 'Why have you still got your gloves on?' she asked.

He smiled and offered them to her to pull off. She tried, but they wouldn't budge; then she saw how swollen his hands were inside them – and her questions were answered.

They helped Pellew with his ablutions, which so exhausted him he fell back to sleep at once. 'He can have all the stout he wants,' Tony told his mother, who had meanwhile risen and breakfasted, 'and a spoon or two of honey, but no hard food for a while.'

'Will you have to keep those gloves on all day?' Johanna asked as they shut the door behind them.

'Let's stick them in cold water and see what happens. Come out and work the pump.'

The water was crystal clear and ice cold. She filled one of the mashing tubs and brought it to him in the kitchen of her cottage. He winced as he lowered his hands into it. 'I'm sorry I was short with you last night,' he told her. 'We were all rather tired and on edge, I suppose.'

She butted his arm with her head, and left it touching him there. 'Oh, Tony, it's the other way round. The things I said to you.'

'No, you were right. My instinct was to go and deal with

your uncle more than a year ago — the moment I realized
those diaries were, indeed, yours. I only held back because I
feared I might kill him. Last night I was less personally . . . I
knew I could do it.'

She wanted to reach up and kiss him. She wanted to tell
him she loved him, which was true, in a way . . . and that she
had loved him for months past, which, as she was only now
beginning to realize, might also be the case.

'Oh, oh . . .' he began to chant, closing his eyes as if in
pain.

'What is it?' she asked, trying to pull his hands out of the
water. 'Are they hurting?'

'No.' He laughed. 'I met the postman on my way back. I
forgot. Will you ever forgive me?'

'Oh, is that all! Goodness, you gave me a fright. He'd
have been coming for his Christmas Box.'

'I know. I gave him five shillings.'

'Tony! Half a crown would have been plenty. Anyway,
why the fuss?'

'Because of what I forgot. Reach in my inside pocket there
and you'll find a letter from California.'

She fished it out and tilted it toward the growing daylight
to read the date. 'Posted only three days after his last,' she
commented. 'And they arrive a month apart. I hope it's not
bad news.'

'Open it.'

'It seems very short.' She half turned from him and broke
the seal with her nail. It was, indeed, brief.

My own dearest Johanna,
This is in the nature of a post-scriptum to my last, in
which I begged you to come out here with all haste. But
since talking with people here in Sacramento, including
many who have newly arrived, I have heard tales of the
most dreadful epidemics along the trail. A whole party,
thirty wagons, wiped out by cholera at Independence
Rock. Typhoid along the South Platte. And smallpox a
great scourge everywhere. With the agreement of my
fellow venturers, by the time you receive this I shall be on
my way through S. Calif. to scout a route there or via
Mexico for you and others of their families who wish to

join us here. I am to bring the whole party back. Jenny, for example, wishes her mother and sister to join us. The Collets' old folk, too. And even Frank has a cousin in Liverpool who might wish to go out. So, if all have the emigrant bug, we shall be quite a party. Expect me at any time, the earliest possible being February next or early March. Perhaps I may even pre-empt this letter and my last. How nerve-racking it all is!

In haste from, Yr ever-loving Hal.

PS – We shall be married with a splash! All Cornwall shall see that Hal Penrose is not the man to run from his obligations.

Chapter Sixty

Diana developed a mild fever and slept the clock around. It was left to Selina to go to the courthouse in Helston, pay the fine, and settle with Mrs Jewell's solicitors. Johanna, assuming the mother would want to be near her daughter, had arranged for her to lodge at the Lion and Lamb in Ashton; but the moment she was freed by the court she went straight down to the Anchor, telling Selina she'd be following later. Instead, she spent the night back in the lock-up, this time on a drunk and disorderly charge. She never came out to see Diana at all.

Johanna spent that first day after the holidays hard at work in the new brewery, up in St Clair Street; she had chosen the site because it had a good well, far enough from the sea never to risk contamination with salt. They were now busy installing a steam engine to power the mashing tubs and turn the many pumps that moved the liquors from one process to the next; she felt it was important to bring it in steam by the first day of the new decade. Even though it would pump nothing but plain water, while they adjusted the valves, tightened the glands, and checked all the plumbing for leaks — even so, the brewery would at last be *alive*.

Penzance was a small enough town for her to have little difficulty in discovering where Diana had lodged; on her way home she called there and collected a few things she thought the girl might need. She arrived back at Lanfear, later than usual and a little dispirited that the holidays should have been spoiled by such unwanted excitements. Selina was waiting for her. 'Hello,' she said bleakly.

670

'What's the matter?' Johanna asked. 'Trouble with the Widow?'

'Not with the business in court. Perhaps it was foolish to expect gratitude from that woman. Aren't they awful people! D'you think it's ... you know ... their trade which has made them like that?'

'Where is she now? In Ashton?'

'Not that I can talk,' Selina added. 'Did you go and see my father today?'

'No.'

'Are you going to?'

'No. I take it the Widow was let off with a fine?'

Selina nodded.

'Lord!' Johanna commented. 'When you think that children of nine are transported for stealing handkerchiefs — there's something very wrong. Did you see Charley Vose at all?'

'No. They expect him to plead guilty now they've got the Widow against him. She just made a beeline for the nearest pub. There's no sign of her coming out here. Oh, I say — Tony just told me. Isn't it marvellous about Hal!'

'Yes. Marvellous.'

'Golly, I'd expect more enthusiasm than that from people waiting to be hanged.'

Johanna smiled warily. 'I've almost forgotten what he's like, you know.'

'He's like Tubal Starkman.' She gave an impish smile.

'Yes, dear. I had noticed a certain passing resemblance. But I mean what he's really like. Also ...' She fell silent.

'Also what?' Selina prompted.

'Well, I feel ... this is going to sound dreadful, after all that's happened, and after all this time, too ... but I think I may actually be falling in love with Tony as well.' She spoke to her hands, loosely entwined upon the table. 'Not instead but as well! And I was so *certain* of Hal. All those months when everyone else was so beastly about him.' After a pause she added, 'I miss Nina more than I can say. D'you suppose she was right about Hal?'

She looked up at Selina then — only to find her staring back in horror.

'What's the matter?' she asked. 'What did I say?'

671

'How can you?' her cousin almost whispered.

'What? Saying that about Nina? But I do miss her.'

'No. The other thing. About you and Tony. You've felt nothing for him all this time, and now . . .'

'That's not true. We've been very close − as close as any two people could be without falling in love. That's what I think has happened now. Anyway − what's it to you? You live in ethereal realms far above all that sort of thing.'

'But you can't be in love with him,' Selina almost pleaded.

Johanna sighed. 'It's not something I wanted to happen.'

'Why can't you go on just being in love with Hal? You've borne his child. He's coming back across half the world to fetch you. A lot of girls would just swoon at the thought of it.'

'Too many − perhaps that's the trouble.'

'It never worried you before.'

Johanna nodded at the justice of that. 'Well, I don't feel noble about it − if that's any comfort to you. It is a kind of betrayal of Hal. But I can't help the way things are.'

After a pause Selina said, 'You only need to flutter one eyelash and he's your slave.'

'That's no longer true.' A thought struck her. 'Perhaps that's why I've changed. When he looked at me the other night, so full of anger and . . . well, it was almost contempt. And yet so restrained.' She shivered at the intensity of her memory. 'I thought all my insides were turning over.'

'And what are you going to write and tell Hal, eh? You always make such a point of how honest *he* is.'

'There'd be no purpose in writing now. He's probably already somewhere on the Atlantic.'

Selina rose and went to the door. A further thought struck her. 'By the way, what I really came over here to say was that Hilary needs her bed back tonight. We've moved Pellew up to Deirdre and Ethna's old room, with his mother in the other bed. So Diana Jewell had better come out here.'

'Oh no,' Johanna said firmly. 'She can go in Terence's old room.'

'It's full of rubbish.'

'One more bit won't be noticed then. Or what about the servants' attics?'

'The floorboards are still up for the new water pipes.

Honestly, she'll have to come out here.'

Johanna nodded glumly, admitting defeat without putting it in so many words.

'We changed her dressings after tea,' Selina added by way of consolation. 'Tony said she's healing wonderfully. So it won't be for long.'

After she had gone Johanna kindled a fire and sat staring at it, trying to empty her mind, trying to convince herself to do nothing about her feelings for Tony. They were still so new – could they not be nipped in the bud? Poor Selina, she was the one who really deserved someone like him, a good, strong, kindly man. Nina always said he was truly in love with Selina; all he needed was to forget his infatuation for her, Johanna, and he'd realize it himself.

She decided she wouldn't go over to the house this evening, except briefly to scavenge a meal from the larder. She'd give her cousin a clear run of it. Then she remembered that, since Christmas Day had fallen on Thursday, which was his usual day for the Redruth clinic, he had decided to go today, instead; and if he had many calls, he'd stay there overnight. So her generosity was of a very token kind.

Suddenly, with a stab of guilt, she remembered Hannah. She glanced at the clock. Too late. She'd be off to sleep by now. That was the first time she'd missed – or avoidably missed – the bedtime ritual. The thought only made her feel more gloomy. Fortunately, that little hedonist wouldn't have missed her mother in the slightest. Hilary was a wonderful friend, and nurse, and alternative mother to her.

She was just putting the guard in front of the fire when the girl herself appeared – carrying a tray full of delicious cold leftovers from Christmas, garnished with some sizzling-hot bubble and squeak. Also the last of the pudding. Also just a handful of mince pies to fill any odd little corners. Best of all, there was a new bottle of port left in that afternoon by everyone's favourite smuggler, Edward Penaluna.

'Here!' she cried as she hastened to take the tray from the girl. 'That must be pulling your arms off.'

'I'm all right – honest. Just move that chair.' Despite her avowal, she gave a great sigh of relief when she set down the tray.

'Bless you, dear,' Johanna said. 'I was just coming over to do that myself. How's the Beast?'

'She went off good as gold tonight. That means she'll wake up four o'clock and start giggling.'

'Bring her down here later, if you like. Tomorrow's Sunday. We can lie in until seven. You need your beauty sleep. Go on — sit down. Take the weight off your feet. Have a glass of port.'

Hilary stared at her. 'Can I?'

'Half and half with water.' She started tucking into the meal. Only then did she remember she had gone without luncheon. 'Tell me what horrors have happened today.'

Hilary sipped her port and smacked her lips grandly. 'Mrs Pellew had two bottles of sherry sent over from Skewjack.'

'Yes, I thought as much. Usually one locks the tantalus to keep the servants sober, not one's guests. How is she?'

'She isn't much affected by it, seemingly. And her son is healing proper handsome.'

'That's those leeches.'

'Mister says 'tis all that liquor he've put inside his skin. He's pickled from the middle out.'

'Has he recognized you yet?'

She smiled. 'He isn't certain.' She took another sip. 'And I shan't tell he.'

'I should think not. I'm sorry you have to face that daily reminder of what you must almost have forgotten by now. At least I hope you have. Are the maids from Skewjack being helpful?'

'A bit lawdy-daw.' She pulled a naughty-girl face. 'But I never seen the house so clean.'

'That's because you never saw it in *my* day,' Johanna told her with mock severity.

After a silence Hilary, avoiding her eye, asked, 'Is it true you and mister will go your ways soon?'

'Is that what he said?'

'I heard he tell Miss Selina about Mr Penrose coming back for to collect 'ee and all they others.'

Johanna could hear the anguish in the girl's question. Because she had never, until very recently, thought of her future as anything but joining Hal in America, she now realized how little thought she had given to the alternatives,

674

or even to the implications of leaving Lanfear and the unusual little family that had formed around it.

'Why? Would you like to come, too?' she asked. 'I'm sure you could — all four of you, if you'd prefer to stay together.'

Hilary shook her head and swallowed rather heavily.

Johanna laid down her knife and fork and, reaching across the table, took the girl's hand between both of hers. 'You don't want to leave mister?' she guessed.

Hilary nodded and blinked back her tears. 'Neither on 'ee.'

'Well, to tell you the truth. I'm no longer sure about leaving this place, either . . . leaving mister . . . leaving you. I simply don't know how things are going to work themselves out.'

Hilary smiled; the tear that at last rolled down her cheek was of joy. Johanna made to retrieve her hands but the girl clutched at her more tightly. She did, however, permit her fingers to snake forward and pluck the handkerchief from her cuff. Johanna raised it to dab at her cheek. 'It all seems so important to you now,' she went on. 'To have to leave us would be like the end of the world. I remember that feeling, you know — when my parents died and my aunt and uncle brought me here. That *was* the end of the world. And yet I can promise you this — three or four years from now some gawky young boy out there, someone you wouldn't look at twice if you saw him today, he's going to steal your heart away. And then you won't be able to leave us soon enough. That's the way of it, Hilary.'

'Is that why you was leaving Lanfear, ma'am?'

Johanna chuckled. 'No. Strangely enough, that may be why I'll stay — if we do stay.'

Selina and Hilary helped Diana across the yard shortly before nine. Unable to sit yet, she knelt on the hearth-rug and stretched her hands toward the fire.

'I hope you don't mind an early night,' Johanna warned her.

After a silence the girl replied, 'I'm sorry to be causing you this trouble now. You were right, of course. I did coax your uncle on. And he did go farther than what I planned.'

Johanna relented a little. 'Would you like a glass of port? No — I'll pour it, you stay there.'

675

Diana accepted it gratefully but she said, 'Only the one, mind. This was our ma's ruin — being so close to the Ram. She got fuddled in the end, see. And then, I don't know how it is, seemingly they men couldn't get satisfaction with the same caper week after week. Always wanting more ... different. And always worse.'

'I don't really wish to hear about it, Diana. You know my opinion of it all.'

The other sniffed heavily. 'Easy for some. I only got the one *commodity,* as they do call it.'

'Well, there it is. You have your opinion. I have mine. But I'm sorry for the pain you suffered. Plenty would say you deserved it, but I know what that pain is like — and the terror of enduring it. If you were my sworn enemy, I wouldn't wish it on you.'

There was a lengthy pause before Diana said, 'He kept calling I Johanna. "My little Johanna's been a wicked, wicked girl. A whip for a horse. A rod for a fool's back."'

'Proverbs Twenty-six!' Johanna closed her eyes and shuddered. The girl's mimicry of her uncle's accent and of the lascivious stress he always laid on those words brought it back with overwhelming immediacy.

'That's right,' Diana said in surprise. 'That's what he said.'

'Well — I repeat. I wouldn't have wished it on my worst enemy.'

Diana was silent again. Johanna could almost feel the dislike radiating from her. That little bit of seemingly idle speculation — 'He kept calling I Johanna' — and the look on her, which said, 'Isn't it funny and I wonder why he did it?' — that had been pure spite, just to annoy her. It probably wasn't even true.

Actually, it probably was.

'If you have no money, how will you live between now and when Mr Penrose comes?' Johanna asked.

'Mister Penrose! It wasn't no Mister Penrose as our Jenny whispered in his earhole, out Chynoweth woods.'

'If you like, I could advance you enough to get by without going back to the gay life again.'

'Gay!' Diana echoed ironically — not wishing to turn down the offer, but not wishing to put herself under any obligation, either.

676

'You needn't think of it as my money,' Johanna went on. 'I'm sure your sister would send it at once if only there was some way of doing so.'

The other gave a tight little nod and continued staring into the fire. Johanna smiled to herself. If that one had come out here to pick a delicate quarrel, this was obviously the way to head her off. She needed the money. 'In fact, I won't advance it out of my own account at all. Hal Penrose, being the sort of man he is, sent me twice what I needed for my fare – before he decided to come back himself and collect us. So that's Penrose Mine money – part of which must be Jenny's anyway, through her connection with Mr Ashburn.'

Diana turned and gave her a withering glance – or was it pitying? She felt her anger rising, but checked it. That was probably what the girl was trying to provoke. 'I've lodged it with Grylls's Bank in Helston. D'you want to draw a weekly allowance – knowing what your mother might do with a lump sum?'

This ruthless generosity won at last. Diana nodded and thanked her.

'I expect you're looking forward to leaving this country?' Johanna went on. 'It'll be a fresh start for both of you, as it was for Jenny.'

The other shook her head gravely. ''Twasn't hardly no fresh start for she.'

'What I mean is no one need know of your past. Surely you want to meet a decent young fellow and settle down and raise a family?'

She shrugged. 'Yes – and be Queen of England one day, too.'

'Why d'you say that? Surely it's not impossible – marrying, I mean. No one need ever know.'

'I'd know.'

'Ah.' Johanna was silent a moment and then said, 'You don't suppose you're the only person in the world with something to forget, do you?'

Diana said nothing.

'You either learn to accept it . . . do better in future . . . or it will surely poison your whole life. It must be very hard to see it now, especially after what's just happened to you . . .' She broke off suddenly.

677

Diana was curious enough to turn and ask her why.

Johanna stared at her a moment, sizing her up. 'When he used to flog me like that — well, never so badly as that, thanks to my aunt, but he used to draw blood — afterwards, I used to run away, up Godolphin Hill, just to be alone. And I tried to hate him. And hate my aunt, and Selina, and all my cousins. But I couldn't. D'you know why?'

'Oh, 'cos you were always some kind of a saint, I'm sure.'

Johanna laughed. 'Not a bit. I could tell myself how unfair they were, and how beastly they were towards me, and how I'd done nothing to deserve it ... And it was all true, I *knew* it was true, and I hated them for it. But in the end — I can't explain it — all my hatred used to fall off them and land on me. I was the one I ended up hating. I hated my thoughts, I hated my body — I was really glad when my aunt cut my hair off. I hated being imprisoned in here' — she tapped her brow — 'being forced to look out at the world through these eyes. I've often wondered ... I've never met anyone else who's been whipped like that ... has it had that effect on you?'

Diana knelt and stared at the fire a long time. Then, having forgotten to breathe, she heaved a great sigh and said, 'Yes.' After a little moment of breathlessness, she added, 'I never saw it, but it's true I turned on my back in bed this morning to *make* it hurt. I couldn't understand why.'

'I remember that exactly,' Johanna told her.

'I never thought much of myself anyway.'

'Well, it'll pass, Diana. I can promise you that. This feeling of worthlessness — it's not part of you. It's part of what happened. And as the memory of that fades, it will fade, too. But it's like a scab — the less you pick at it, the faster it will heal.'

They could hear Hilary and Selina coming across the yard, carrying Hannah's crib between them. Johanna rose to take over from her cousin, who said, 'Don't fuss. Just say where you want the little monster.'

'In there, beside my bed. Why all the blankets?'

'We aired them for Diana. Now is there anything else your ladyship requires?'

'Yes. You may remove my supper tray,' Johanna answered grandly.

678

Laughing, they went.

'We'd best think of turning in,' Johanna said when the two of them were alone again. 'You won't be cold with the fire in here. By the way, I hope you don't mind — I brought a few of your things out from Penzance, from your lodgings. They're in the box by your bed there.'

'I never told 'ee where I lived,' the girl responded as she walked on her knees to investigate.

'Well, let's just say you weren't hard to trace. I'm sorry if I did wrong.'

'No, no I'm glad you did. Thank 'ee.' There was a pause before she added, 'See this letter from our Jenny, did 'ee?'

'I saw the cover.'

'And read 'n?'

'Of course not.'

Diana stayed a further three days; then she left to go into Helston and take her mother in hand, to keep her dry and out of the lock-up until it was time for them to leave for America. Each evening before she left, Johanna sensed that the girl wished to tell her something. Time and again her conversation edged clumsily toward California, the mine, Hal, Frank Ashburn, Jenny, the future . . . but at the last minute her courage would desert her and whatever she had really wished to say remained unspoken amid a welter of platitudes and commonplaces.

When Johanna returned on the Wednesday, the day Diana left them, she found a note awaiting her. As she unfolded it, a second note fell out, which she then recognized as the letter from Jenny. Diana's note read:

Dear Miss Rosewarne,

You are a good Person and I have wronged You often in Thought, Word, and Dede. Yet You have done me grate Kindness, which I must now repay. When I come out to slepe in Your cottij the other nite I wished to taunt You with certin faxts relating to what is in Jenny's Letter. Now I must let You know same but out of Grattitude for I cannot see You deceved more and You so Good and Trustin.

Hopin You think no wuss of me but I do it out of Kindness to you and not out of Spyte.

Yr Freind, Diana Jewell.

And the letter from Jenny read:

Dear Sister,

What you write concerning our Mother's Addiction to the Bottle is bad. She always was a bit that way, as I well recall, but this is beyond all her Previous. It will surely end in her Ruin, and after all our bright Hopes!

It is no better here for me. The Letters I wrote previous were for the Benefit of Saint Rosewarne, not to let her know the true state of things betwixt Hal and me. This is not for her Sight so do not show it her. My Design has not prospered. My Belief was that as Hal is so Proud in his Prick and cannot contain himself where there is a Skirt to lift, I should make myself the Quencher of *his* Addiction until he could not think of his Bed without me. And so, starting Somewhere on the Atlantic until here in California, we have frolicked nightly, tapping his Cream. From the Start he said his only Love was Saint Rosewarne and that we were but each other's Bedwarmers, that I did It for my Pleasure equal with his, or any other selfish Purpose, which therefore rid him of Obligation to me for It. Yet I thought to bind him to me by his Lust and so turn it into Love.

But so it has not been. He has enjoyed me as often as he pleased, sometimes Twice and Thrice a day when the Storm raged and Naught else was possible. And it pleased me, too, I confess, I made no Complaint on that side. Yet in the Matter of Love I am no more forward with him than I was that Day I followed him from Sunny Corner. He frolics in my Open Sea but the name on the prow is Rosewarne.

Now he is going back Home to Cornwall and fetch her here and I have lost. I need not have sent you the Fare last Week, for he will bring enough and More. When he and she return here I will be gone I will let you know where but most likely Sacramento. We can start a good House here and make a grander Fortune than even the Gold Miners

680

we will fleece. Twenty Girls and never work ourselves except we like the Look of the Man. And the Work so easy in America, too! You will not credit it, but neither Party is required to remove any Cloathing. The man lies on his Back and, when decently (!) covered by her Skirts, looses his buttons and works his way upward into his Pleasure. All she must do is jig a Bit or wriggle. Their Preachers forbid their Wives to oblige them in this Fashion so that is all they want! Many a Gay Woman here I have spoken to who never yet saw a Man in all his Pride, only knew it from feeling it! They sit at their Needlework in Hotel Lobbies, all shy and quiet and Eyes downcast, and no Paint or Color. And the Men pick them out and pay Madame, who touches her Shoulder. Then she goes above and he after, never closer than a dozen paces. They need no Skill at all not even in Speach, so imagine, dearest Sister, what we may do with all those Tricks we know!

If Hal had paid like any other Man, I should now be £140 the Richer, so you may reckon the Tally of our Joys. I will take that from him somehow while he is gone — and let him dare lay Complaint for it when he returns!

Burn this. Do not let St Rosewarne see it like the Rest. Let her get well and truly Yoaked to him and grow fat with bearing his Childer. Then let her watch his Eyes go roving after every Bit of Parsley. Let her scent new Perfumes on his Cloathes. Let her find him strangely spent when she would jig with him abed. It is all I desire for her who has robbed me of the only Man I ever loved or truly wanted.

Yr Loving Sister, Jenny.

Chapter Sixty-One

Some weeks after his operation a slimmer, drier, and much healthier Raymond Pellew returned to Skewjack Hall. His mother went with him; but the following evening she was back. 'I seem to have mislaid a packet of embroidery needles,' she said. 'I wonder if by any chance?' It was the sort of errand you'd entrust to a fifteen-year-old maid.

When they were discovered and returned to her, she 'wondered if by any chance Miss Rosewarne were at home?'

Hilary pointed toward the cottage but warned, ''Tis the second Wednesday in the month, ma'am.'

'What does that mean?'

She sucked her tooth. 'Accounts.'

'Ah. Well. Perhaps I'll just pop my head around the door.'

Johanna was in the act of closing the huge daily ledger, with a very terminal thump, and heaving an obviously final sigh of relief; ten seconds earlier and she'd have been able to point to an open tome surrounded by a clutter of bills and invoices and say, 'I know you'll excuse me.' Instead she cried, 'Why, Mrs Pellew, how *nice* to see you — it's been such ages.'

'I just forgot these.' She held up her box of needles and smiled. Her eye fell on the port decanter. 'Actually, my dear,' she went on, 'the reason I came in person is I have a bit of news for you.'

Johanna started gathering up the papers. 'Do sit down,' she said. When the table was clear again, she threw another log on the fire.

Mrs Pellew took off her coat and scarf before she sat. She

682

watched as if Johanna's every movement were part of a ballet, designed to give pleasure. She gazed approvingly around the simply furnished room. 'If one only has the determination, you see, it *can* be done.' Her tone suggested it was the conclusion to an argument she had been waging with herself.

'What in particular?' Johanna asked, setting a modest glass of port before her.

'What *you've* done. Even down to simple things like putting a log on the fire. At Skewjack, I'd have rung for a servant. We are never without servants – d'you realize that?'

'Surely it's normal for people in your position?' Johanna sipped her glass with relish.

The Squire's wife did not touch hers. 'But you see what it means? It means we are hardly ever private.' She tapped her forehead. 'Not even in here. We are always on display. And the rooms we call "ours" – they are always on display, too. We fashion them for others. If this were my room, every shelf would be crowded with bric-à-brac. More work for servants!'

'But they give you pleasure, surely? I remember your showing me those lovely paperweights with coral scenes . . . and the Chinese fans . . . and that table top all made of birds' feathers from the Amazon jungles . . .'

'Stop!' she begged. At last she took a sip of port – and it was the merest sip, too. 'It's only since I stayed here, this past fortnight, that I've come to realize . . .' She couldn't think of the words for it; she merely waved her hand around her in a gesture that included the cottage, Johanna, and the life she led. 'This is where you derive it all – that inner certitude. You have that unquenchable determination to live your life the way . . .'

'I wish people would stop saying that,' Johanna interrupted. 'If only you knew how divided I feel at the moment.'

'You?' Mrs Pellew stared at her in disbelief.

Johanna immediately regretted her outburst. 'Oh,' she said vaguely, 'setting up a new business is never easy, you know. And the other brewers – who never imagined there could be so much trade with private houses, with people who are fond of good ale but who'd not be seen dead near a public house – they're all furious now.'

It was true, but it was not, of course, the reason for her discontent. Mrs Pellew suspected as much but let it pass for the moment. 'In that case,' she said, 'I don't know whether my little bit of news is welcome or not. You know that old scoundrel Vose was sentenced today?'

'Oh no, I hadn't heard. Poor man – I hardly dare ask how long...?'

'Ten years servitude in the penal colony in Australia. They say he was lucky not to get twenty.'

Johanna closed her eyes and shook her head. 'And Widow Jewell pays a small fine and goes free!' She smiled wanly. 'Well, thank you for coming to tell me.'

'Oh, but that wasn't my news. No, no – it's something much more practical than that. I don't know whether you were ever aware of the fact, but Vose had the Golden Ram under a fee-farm grant from the Skewjack estate. We are the ground landlords. Before he was convicted he sold the remainder back to us to help defray his legal expenses. The understanding was that if he got off with a fine, he'd have first option on a new lease, for a fixed term this time. Obviously that's all gone by the board now.'

'So you'll be inviting tenders?' Johanna guessed.

She gave a knowing smile. 'For some reason, my dear, the Squire is most keen that the lease should go to you. But, of course, being a man of business, he doesn't wish you to know of it. I say a fig for all that! You helped save our son's life. We should offer you a sensible but still favourable lease in return. It's the least we can do – assuming, naturally, that you're interested?'

Johanna sighed. 'I don't know, Mrs Pellew. It's extremely kind of you and don't think me insensitive to the fact. But an undertaking of that magnitude – on top of the burdens of building up the Penzance business – well, it would require careful thought.'

Mrs Pellew gave out a silvery peal of laughter. 'Now I *know* you'd give your eye teeth to get it! You are so like the Squire – that is precisely what he would say if acquiring the lease were the apple of his eye. You needn't worry, my dear. Pellew would boil me in oil if he knew I were telling you all this, so I'll carry no tales back with me.'

Johanna tried to suppress a smile. 'Very well. What next?'

'There is just one thing: He abhors the thought of doing business with a woman.'

Doing certain kinds of business ... Johanna made the correction to herself. 'A tentative inquiry from my solicitor?' she suggested. 'Not mentioning me by name? I presume he knows Coad acts for me – I mean, he'd put two and two together?'

She nodded. 'Once you've shown an interest, I don't think he'll prove difficult. But the first move must come from your side.'

Johanna nodded. 'Once again, I'm most grateful.'

Mrs Pellew gave an impish grin. 'You see how useful it can be at times – to belong to Society! One hears all sort of things to one's advantage, you know.'

Johanna felt like pointing out that if one had friends like Mrs Pellew and Mrs Ramona Troy, one could forego one's own subscription to that particular club, but, on the whole, thought better of it. She eyed the woman shrewdly. 'I still wonder why you've told me,' she said. 'It isn't just gratitude at your son's recovery, is it – or else you'd be telling Dr Moore something to his advantage rather than me.'

'As a matter of fact, I could. But I'll leave that to the Squire. He's always dismissed the doctor as a wild, anarchist revolutionary, a traitor to his class, and so on. What he saw during his visits here has moderated his views considerably. However, that's by the way.'

'Have you ever gone against his express wishes before?' Johanna risked asking.

The woman shook her head and took another small sip.

'If he finds out, he'll blame me,' Johanna added.

'I'm well aware of that, my dear. Don't worry, though. He won't – or not from me.'

'I don't wish to be the cause of any discord between others, you know. I am not an *example* – good or bad. I am just me, quietly going about my own business and wishing to upset no one.'

Mrs Pellew laughed.

When she had gone – leaving half her glass untouched –

Johanna sat and stared at the fire. What to do about Hal, and going to America, and all that, now? It had occurred to her that a brewery with a number of public houses exclusively tied to it was much stronger than one like hers, with a large but possibly fickle off-licence trade and no exclusive contract with any pub. If she hadn't been going to America soon, she'd have started sniffing around for new or expiring leases all over West Penwith. And now this opportunity – this *golden* opportunity! – had fallen into her lap. She couldn't ignore it. Yet every day she seemed to acquire more and more reasons for delaying her departure – reasons that helped her avoid thinking about the *real* issue: herself and Hal.

Would he mind her delaying just one more year? That would really put the business on its feet. She hated leaving something only half done.

There was a knock at the door. Probably Hilary with something to tell her about Hannah. 'Come in,' she called.

It was Tony, looking slightly apprehensive, followed by Selina, who had the air of a cat beside an empty aquarium. 'We have something to tell you,' she said archly.

'And I have something to tell you,' Johanna replied. 'But you first.'

Selina looked at Tony, who seemed surprised she should leave it to him. 'It must come from you,' she murmured.

He nodded – and then, it seemed, remembered to smile. He turned to Johanna and, looking somewhere over her left shoulder, said, 'Selina and I are getting married.'

'Soon,' Selina added.

Johanna could only sit and stare at them. 'I had no idea . . .' she said in a daze. 'No idea.'

'It is . . . sudden,' Tony admitted.

Johanna nodded. There must be a million things to say but none of them occurred to her.

'Aren't you happy?' Selina asked. 'For us, I mean.'

That was one of them. 'Yes! Of course – forgive me. It was such a . . .' She touched her heart, which she now felt beating away like a mad thing. 'Yes, I hope you'll be enormously happy – both of you. Sit down. Let's drink a little toast to it.'

Shivering like an aspen she rose and fetched a pair of

glasses, removing Mrs Pellew's at the same time. It was a shame to pour away such a good vintage; as soon as she was out in the kitchen she knocked it back. Its afterglow certainly helped steady her against this shock.

Well – there it was! Her mind made up for her.

'When did this happen?' she asked as she returned.

'This afternoon,' Selina replied.

'This evening,' Tony said simultaneously.

They turned to each other and laughed.

'That's love,' Johanna sighed.

Tony's eyes fell at her use of the word but Selina prattled on: 'Both, I suppose. I needed to go into Helston to get a draft for seventy-five pounds for Liggat – the advance on my novel. And Tony had to go in, too, to meet the new partner, so ...'

Johanna struck herself on the forehead. 'I completely forgot! Dr Sheridan! Aren't I terrible? What's he like?'

'Never mind that now,' Selina replied.

'Good man,' Tony slipped in. 'Settling in at the Lion and Lamb. Coming up here shortly.' He smiled at Selina. 'Sorry.'

'Anyway,' she continued. 'We started talking – talking and thinking – and we just never stopped, all the way. And then, after I'd been to the bank and posted the draft, the coach was delayed because of the storms, and we just went on talking ... and then we just seemed to find ourselves engaged.'

'I didn't actually pop the question until we got back,' Tony said, trying to justify his earlier reply without making it sound like a correction of her tale.

She hugged him and giggled. 'Darling! I'm a proper novelist now. I know that all the important things happen between the lines. You popped the question in every possible way this afternoon – short of actually putting it into words.'

He turned to Johanna, smiled, and shrugged.

'Well' – she raised her glass – 'once again, I wish you both the greatest happiness. Here's to marriage – we can all drink to that.'

She shouldn't have knocked back Mrs Pellew's glass, she thought. Then came the response, from far deeeper within her: why not?

'Anyway,' Selina went on, 'the thing is, it would hardly be proper now for me to go on sleeping under the same roof as Tony.'

'Why not?' Johanna asked at once.

'Well!' Selina laughed and blushed. 'Of course it wouldn't.'

'I never heard anything more absurd in my life. I wouldn't just sleep under the same *roof!*'

'Jo!' Selina was scandalized.

'Well, it's ridiculous to start worrying about the proprieties now.'

'It's not the proprieties,' Selina murmured in a tone that begged her cousin to stop talking about it. Her voice fell almost to a whisper as she added, 'It's what might ... happen.'

Johanna glanced toward Tony, who looked away at once. Then she lifted the port bottle and set it down, four square in front of Selina. 'Try that.'

Selina pushed it aside.

'So you and Dr Sheridan will have to change rooms?' Johanna suggested. 'You down in Ashton; him up here?'

They glanced at each other; that had plainly not occurred to either of them. 'He can have my room,' Selina said. 'But I was wondering if I could put up here for a bit?'

'No,' Johanna said at once.

Selina stared at her.

'No,' she repeated, retrieving the bottle. 'I value my isolation out here.' She poured herself another glass before offering it to Tony. He shook his head.

Selina just went on staring at her.

'When is it to be?' Johanna asked.

'We haven't set a time,' Tony replied.

'We haven't even discussed it yet. Can't I just stay tonight? You let Diana.'

'That was only under protest.'

Selina grinned. 'Can I stay under protest, then?'

Johanna threw up her hands. 'I suppose so. Just one night – if the very prospect of spending one more night in the same house as your *fiancé* is such anathema to you.'

Selina rose and skipped to the door. 'I'll get Hilary to help me across with my things.'

'Just your bedclothes and nightdress,' Johanna called after her.

In the silence that followed she turned her gaze to Tony. 'It'll be good,' he said evenly. 'We get on well together. She'll be a good companion to me, and I believe I know what she needs.'

'To whom it may concern! It sounds like a character for a good and loyal housekeeper.'

'Well, there's a lot of that in marriage, too.'

Johanna gave a despairing shake of her head. 'You haven't the first idea of what she needs.'

'I couldn't remain celibate for ever.'

She gave him a pitying look. 'And it doesn't strike you that this is a fairly drastic cure for that rather easily managed complaint?' Her eyes raked the ceiling beams: 'I know why she's done this!'

'To you everything is so simple,' he commented. 'If I decide to get married at last, having waited for − well, never mind that − but if I decide to get married, it's for one reason, according to you. And if Selina does, too, that also is for just one reason. Anyway, what has she done? You say you know why she's . . .'

'It's just because I blurted out . . . oh, what's it matter? I should have known − she's done it all our lives. The very night I walked into that house' − she jerked her head toward Lanfear − 'on the day of my father's funeral, she wanted the dress I was wearing. She did the same with me and Nina, too.'

'What are you saying, Jo?'

'It doesn't matter now.' She pulled herself together and smiled at him. 'It's just jealousy talking. Her happiness is here. Mine is how many thousand miles away on the Atlantic? I know when he's here there'll be no question of sleeping under separate roofs!'

Tony rose and went to the door. 'Good night,' he said, without so much as a backward glance.

Johanna toasted the empty space where he had stood, drained her glass, and poured herself another.

At five the following morning, a quarter of an hour before her usual time for rising, her head was throbbing and her mouth as dry as a biscuit barrel. But that wasn't what woke her — it was Selina, slipping into bed beside her. 'Jo?' she murmured.

'Mmmm?'

'I'm sorry.'

Johanna groaned and turned over.

'It's just that, when you started telling me that time about how you were falling in love with Tony, well . . .'

'You talk as if that was ages ago. It was only last week.'

'It was two weeks ago, actually.'

'It wasn't.'

'Was.'

'Wasn't.'

'Was, then! Anyway, I've been in love with him for ages.'

'Oh yes! I remember your telling me *last week!* A regular chatterbox you were — couldn't stop you talking about it!' She reached out and lit the candle, and then poured herself a glass of water.

'Perhaps I didn't know it then,' Selina admitted. 'Not consciously. But I've realized it since.'

'Yes and I wonder why? You didn't need to go into Helston at all today — or yesterday. I could have got a draft for you in Penzance — for a better rate than you, too.'

'You've still got Hal. I don't see what there is to complain about.'

Johanna lay on her back and stared at the ceiling. She still had Hal. 'You're not even ready for marriage,' she sneered. 'Look at you! Skulking out here because you're terrified *he'll* come creeping into your bed and . . . oh horrors! Eek! What's this nasty great unpleasant *thing,* my dear? Shouldn't I be wearing gloves?'

Selina had stopped breathing.

Johanna went on: 'What's he going to make of you when you finally overcome your terrors and force yourself under the same roof as him?'

She rose and went to the washstand. The southwest wind carried the smell of bacon and eggs. Thank God for Hilary! Thank God for someone in this place you could trust!

Selina just lay there with the tears rolling silently down her cheeks.

At the door, fully dressed, headache gone, ready once

again for everything the day could throw at her, Johanna paused. 'Last night I asked him why he's marrying you. He said he couldn't stay celibate for ever.' She laughed. 'What a shock *he's* got coming, eh?'

Chapter Sixty-Two

The clipper that brought Hal's letter from New York (and would have brought the man himself if there had been a berth to spare) docked at Liverpool in mid-March. He wrote that he would arrive in Falmouth aboard the good ship *Windrush* in the first half of April — earlier if the winds were favourable. From the moment the letter arrived Johanna sent down daily to the coastguard, asking whether the vessel had been sighted yet; they grew so weary of it that the man whose job was to tap out the telegraph to the harbour office in Falmouth, telling them of all eastbound sightings in Mount's Bay, promised that the moment the *Windrush* was logged and his message acknowledged he would sprint up to St Clair Street and she would be the first outside the service to know of it.

Day by day the tension mounted until she thought she could bear it no longer. All her hope of love and marriage was back where it started, with Hal. Word came at last on Saturday the 23rd of March, at eleven o'clock in the morning. The *Windrush* had been sighted off the Longships light some two hours earlier.

She ran from her office, still carrying her hat in her hand, leaped into her gig, and set her horse to the fastest pace she knew he could sustain. All the coastguard had been able to tell her was that the vessel was a three-masted brigantine. She did not even try looking for it until she was through Marazion and up the hill — a couple of hundred feet above sea level. Then, cursing the motion of the gig yet not wishing to halt it, even for a moment, she trained her binoculars upon the bay.

There were two ships of that general description. One was hull down, eight miles south of the Lizard, and heading straight for Falmouth; if she were the *Windrush,* Johanna had no hope of greeting her arrival. However, she was a little far out for a vessel sighted off the Longships less than three hours ago. Despite appearances she might not be heading to Falmouth at all; with this sou'easterly half-gale blowing, she could be on the port tack of a voyage to Brittany. The other three-master was much closer to shore, some six miles off St Michael's Mount with the wind scant on her starboard beam. Now if she were the *Windrush* ... there was just a chance. Her master must have misjudged the tidal drag in Mount's Bay for she had made too much leeway to round the Lizard on her present course. In a moment she'd have to wear ship and put the wind fair to port, running before it (but directly away from Falmouth) so as to acquire enough water to clear the point. By that time Johanna could be through Helston and out on the Falmouth turnpike.

For ten anxious minutes she watched the two vessels every time a gap in the hedge or a rise in the road gave her a chance. Then, as if they were in direct communication, their simultaneous movements confirmed her hopes and marked the nearer vessel as the *Windrush.* For a time or two she tried to make out Hal − or anyone − on board. She knew he'd be at the rails, training his glass on Lanfear. It gave her an idea.

At Germoe Cross she left the highway and took the back lane home, where she told Peter to change horses. She went indoors and threw some cold meat, bread and pickles into a hamper − plus a half-dozen bottles of ale − and shouted for Hilary. The girl came running.

'Listen and don't question,' Johanna told her. 'Go out to my cottage, find the dark-brown dress with the purple piping around the neck and put it up. Then go to your room − which used to be mine, if you recall − and wave out of the window as long as ... you'll spy a three-masted brigantine. She'll be six miles off Rinsey Head in about half an hour's time. Just wave to her until she's about half way between there and the Lizard. Understand?'

'What − wave all the time?'

'Not steadily. Once or twice a minute. Get one of mister's big white handkerchiefs.'

Hilary grinned. 'You going to deceive Mr Penrose, are 'ee? Make he think you'm here and then be there to greet he over to Falmouth?'

Johanna smiled at the thought. 'Yes. It hadn't struck me that way, but yes — it will give him a surprise. Put up one of my caps, to cover your hair.'

Selina came bouncing into the kitchen. 'Can I come too?' she asked. 'Please?'

'No,' Johanna told her curtly. 'Where's Tony?'

'Oh, please? I won't be in the way, honestly.'

'No. How many times?'

'Just as far as Helston then? I'll go and torment my brother. Tony's sulking. He refuses to discuss wallpapers. He says the present ones are quite adequate. Actually, he's taken Dr Sheridan over to Camborne- Redruth.'

'All right — but only to Helston mind.' Johanna was already halfway back to the gig. 'Come on. We don't have much time to spare. Tie your horse behind. You'll have to ride back.'

'Why can't Hal?'

'Selina, you are not coming to Falmouth. Get that firmly into your mind now. Anyway, Hal can't ride back because it's too far for someone who's been out of the saddle for three months.'

'Oh, hang it — I'll rent a hack in Falmouth. I mean Helston.'

Actually, they had plenty of time now, but one never knew. A horse could cast a shoe ... a tyre could split ... anything could happen, so it was best to have time in hand.

As soon as they were safely on their way Selina said, 'Actually, *ma chère cousine,* one must start thinking of your reputation again.'

'Don't be absurd.' She clucked the new horse into a trot.

'What's absurd? I think it would be most improper for you to drive back alone with Hal over Long Downs and Laity Moor.'

'Absurd,' Johanna repeated.

But Selina insisted. 'Wouldn't it be nice now to do everything properly? It would show the world you and Hal feel a decent respect for each other. People would notice it, you know, and their opinion of you would shoot up no end.'

Johanna besought the heavens. 'And they used to say *I* was sixpence short of a shilling.'

'Well, do whatever you like. It's all one to me. I've made Deirdre and Ethna's old room ready for him.'

'He'll sleep with me,' Johanna told her firmly. 'And tonight – at long long last – you are *definitely* going to have to stay at the Lion and Lamb.'

'Oh?' Selina whined, making three notes of the word.

'Why?' Johanna smiled sweetly. 'Did you hope to stay in the cottage and learn a thing or two?'

'Now who's being absurd?' Selina asked crossly.

After a minute or more of silence she returned to her theme. 'Seriously, Jo, if he's going to marry you by special licence, you won't have all that long to wait. And people would remember the way you behaved during that time. Don't you care what they'll say about you here after you've gone?'

'Of course I do. The difference between us is that I'd care even if they said, "Wasn't she good! She hardly let him touch her until the ring was on her finger!" Remarks like that would seem just as insufferable to me. It's none of their business if I sleep with Hal, and it's equally none if I don't.'

Then Selina found the knock-out argument. 'What you're saying is you're just going to throw yourself at him. He's been away two years, you know. Look at how you've changed in that time. He might have changed, too. All sorts of things might have happened. I thought you might be rather glad of a third party – at least on the journey home, until you find out what he's like nowadays. Still – it's up to you, as I say.'

It was a knock-out in the sense that Johanna made no reply to it at all.

After they had passed through Breage, she said, 'Still no date for your wedding, then?'

'Tony's so busy always. Besides, I'm not in any hurry now. I don't think he wants you here for it. He'll wait until you've definitely gone.'

'It would step around a lot of difficulties.'

'Have you found a buyer for the brewery yet? Or do they have to guess the name of Rumpelstiltskin as well?'

Johanna laughed. 'That young man who called yesterday,

Victor Berenson – he was the best to date. The best by far. Unfortunately he lacks capital. It gave me another idea, though: keep the brewery and put him in as manager with Tony and Terence on the board.'

'Tony won't have time,' Selina said at once.

'He'll just have to find it, then. Listen – ten percent of the brewery's profits go straight into the Medical Union. So it's very much in his interest to find time.'

'Anyway, tell me about Mr Berenson. What's he like?'

'He knows the trade inside out. Served his apprenticeship with Burton's. He believes . . .'

'Young? Old? Tall? Short? Dark? Fair?'

'Oh, I see. Er . . . young. Our sort of age – twenty-five, twenty-six. No capital, as I said. But he's sure Rosewarne could brew a pale ale for export. The advantage . . .'

'Jo!'

'What?'

'I don't give a fig for export ale or import ale or stale ale – or any kind of ale. Has Mr Berenson got a wall eye? Is he a hunchback? Why don't you describe him?'

'Because I was much more interested in his ideas. He's good looking, I suppose. Pleasant in his manner. I've always resisted the idea of brewing for export because the duties on malt are so stupid. The excise people assume you get four barrels of ale to each barrel of malt – which is impossible with a wort of specific gravity one-point-oh-four-two, you see. And yet that's the best wort to give an ale that will resist secondary fermentation in tropical climes. Instead you have to use one-point-oh-five-five or heavier.'

'I'm going to start screaming in a minute,' Selina warned.

'No – listen! It's interesting. The heavier malts are quite unsuitable for tropical ales, but the excise people refuse to change the law so that you only pay duty on the ale you actually brew.'

Selina began to hum 'Greensleeves'.

'But Berenson says he knows a way to do it – to brew for export using the proper malt and still reclaim the full five shillings on every barrel. He's shown me I'm still treating brewing as a cottage industry. The chemicals one can use nowadays are amazing!'

Selina stared at her balefully before she said, 'I simply

don't understand why you didn't marry the man on the spot. You are quite obviously intended for each other.'

They chatted on, more or less at cross purposes, until they reached the bottom of Sithney Common Hill; there Selina turned sharply to her. 'Aren't you going past Terence's office?'

Johanna shook her head. 'The incline is greater this way — and it's not all that much longer.' As an afterthought she added, 'I suppose there's something in what you say. You'd better come to Falmouth with me.'

Selina threw her arms around her and kissed her.

'But you'll hire a gig there, or a hack, and go ahead of us on the way home. Is that understood?'

'Perfectly. You're an angel.'

At the top of Wendron Street they saw Willy Kemp standing in the middle of the road; behind him the usual Saturday round-up of prisoners from local lock-ups was in progress. When he saw the gig was driven by Johanna, he came running to stop her. 'I expect you might like to wait a minute or two, Miss Rosewarne,' he suggested. 'I've an old friend of yours aboard.'

She glanced at the wagon and found herself staring straight into the eye of Charley Vose — or a pale, gaunt, collapsed version of the Charley she had known. He dipped his head to show he had seen her, but he could not even then raise a smile.

'Poor devil,' she murmured. He had an air of bewilderment about him, as if he were still wondering where it had all gone wrong. 'May I give him something?'

'What? Not money.'

'Something to eat, then? Or drink?' She remembered the ale. 'Why can't they just jump out? The creels aren't even shoulder high to most of them.'

'They're shackled to the floor. We aren't as stupid as some would have it. Talking of which — you weren't thinking of passing him a couple of bottles of Martell, were you? Pale brandy, very old, superior quality . . . just a whiff of salt water around the cork?'

She laughed. 'Something better than all your French muck.' And she pulled out a bottle of Rosewarne pale ale.

He took it and inspected it as if it might be a grenade. 'I'll see he gets it,' he said.

697

'Keep that for yourself,' she told him. 'What about a box of cheroots? Could I give him that, too?'

'Let's see it.'

'No. I'll have to go back into town and buy some. We'll catch you up — you're going to the prison hulks in Falmouth, I presume?'

He nodded and returned to supervise the shackling of the new intake. 'Thanks for the ale,' he called out as she began to face the gig back the way they had come.

'Trade sample,' she told him. 'I'd welcome a regular order from your station, you know.'

He waved ambiguously.

'What was all that about?' Selina asked. 'Have we got time to do this?'

'We'll just have to make time. I couldn't drive past Charley and say, "Here — have a bottle of my ale." He'd think I was rubbing salt in the wound. Actually — that gives me an idea.'

'What?'

'You'll see. I'll drop you off at the tobacconist and you can catch me up at the Angel. Get a box of cheroots — about a hundred — you know the size he used to smoke. Put it on my account.'

'I didn't know you smoked.'

'I don't, but where d'you think Peggy Machin's snuff comes from?'

Five minutes later Selina found her at the Angel, dropping half-sovereigns into an uncorked bottle of Rosewarne ale. '...eight ... nine ... ten,' she said. 'I don't think we dare risk more. Now, landlord — if you'd be so good as to recork it?'

Five minutes later they were back on the road, having lost the best part of half an hour. She began to regret the delay. But then, going up the hill to Trevenen, she got a brief glimpse of the bay and saw that the *Windrush* had once again drifted too close inshore to round the Lizard. 'She must be one mass of barnacles below the water line,' she commented. 'At this rate we'll have time for tea at Pearce's.' A less happy thought struck her. 'Poor Hilary! I didn't imagine they'd have to turn and run again. She'll be standing there waving for about two solid hours!'

She slowed down to conserve the horse's strength, knowing they would still overtake the lumbering old prison wagon somewhere before Half-way House. But it made better speed than she realized, for it was actually just past that landmark, on the rise to Dead Man's Corner, that they drew level. Charley was right at the front now and seemed not to notice their approach. There were two constables standing on the tailboard – liveried footmen to the sweepings of Cornwall's gaols. She passed the box of cheroots to the nearer of them. 'This is for one of the prisoners,' she said. 'I spoke to Inspector Kemp about it, but you'd better let him have a look.'

The man leaped down and sprinted forward. All the prisoners turned to see what the commotion was about and, once again, she found herself staring into the very face of misery. She urged her horse forward until she was level with the front of the wagon. 'All right to give him the ale?' she asked Willy Kemp.

He waved cheerfully and went on poking and prying into the box of cheroots.

'Here you are, Vose,' she called out as she handed the bottle across to him. 'That's the way to brew good ale! Drink it to the last bitter dregs and reflect on what might have been.'

He stared at her in horror, unable to believe she could be so cruel. He almost dashed it to the ground but the alarm in her eyes stayed him. She waited until Kemp passed the box back to the constable – when neither would be looking at her – before she repeated her words: 'To the last drop, Vose!' But this time there was a wink to go with it. And then, as if her apparent cruelty had been a joke, to prepare him for the real gift, she took the box from the constable and added, 'And if it tastes too bitter for you, sweeten it with one of these.'

He took the gift from her and almost laughed – the almost-laugh of a man who has almost forgotten how. There were tears in his eyes and he shook his head, trying to convey feelings for which there were only the rustiest of words.

She was passing beyond earshot when he called out, 'Mistress – is that a fact you got the Ram now?'

She held up a hand to acknowledge the truth of it. 'Come

back someday,' she shouted. 'There'll always be a room there for you.'

When they were well out ahead, Selina said, 'You're mad, you know. D'you realize you could go to gaol for what you've just done?'

Johanna grinned. 'I think not — certainly not with Willy Kemp in charge.'

'Why?' she asked in astonishment. 'What's he to you?'

'Oh — nothing these days, but ... er, we've had our moments.'

'Jo!' The astonishment turned to shock. 'How many men *have* you done it with then?'

'I don't mean that. For heaven's sake! I only mean we kissed. You remember the time they came searching for brandy? And I thought he'd find it, so I gave him a wink and went up into the hayloft.'

'But he didn't do it with you?'

Johanna shrugged.

'Or did he?' Selina persisted.

'Not exactly. He put his finger there, that was all.'

'All! My goodness! And you didn't stop him?'

'I thought he might come back another time and do it again — or go a bit further, perhaps.'

'And you'd have let him?'

'I might have. It all depends.'

'On what?'

'On how I felt. You can't plan these things.'

'Did you love him?'

'No, or only a tiny bit.' A thought struck her. 'Perhaps that's the best way to start — with someone you only love a tiny bit. Because you're not so ... bowled over by it. You can keep an eye on what's happening.'

After a thoughtful pause Selina repeated her original question but without its tendentious overtones: 'How many men have you done it with — go on, tell me?'

'Kissed? Quite a few.'

'No! You know what I mean. What's it like? Really, really like?'

'Oh, Selina! You're going to drive yourself mad. It's not for me to tell you what to do, but why don't you pick on some man you admire the look of — like me with Willy

Kemp — and just give him a bit of encouragement? If you're not head over heels in love with him, it doesn't matter, if it's awful, or just so-so — and you'll be in less danger of losing control.'

To Johanna's surprise, her cousin actually appeared to be thinking it over; but then she said, 'I missed my chance.'

'My dear, there are as many chances as there are men. They're ready for it at the drop of any eyelash.'

'No, I meant when ... after you left Liston Court and I was alone with Nina, she often tried to persuade me to — you're going to hate this. She used to say, "Let's dress up as common women and go up and try and get an evening's work with Widow Jewell!" It used to fascinate her — the idea of being one of those women.'

'Did she ever go alone?' Johanna asked.

'No. She said she'd only go if I did. And of course I'd sooner die that do that. She said I was a wet blanket. She said you'd have gone there with her if you hadn't been in that condition.' After a pause she asked, 'Is it true? Would you?'

'Perhaps if I were starving — or Hannah needed something and I had no money. I wouldn't say I'd sooner die. Life can be rather sweet.' She laughed. 'Especially on a day like this.'

Selina frowned and then remembered. 'Oh yes — Hal.'

They had by now passed through the Long Downs and were on the downhill run to Penryn at the head of the creek. 'She'll only just be rounding the Lizard now,' Johanna commented. 'Let's have tea at the Greenbank instead and then drive up to the castle and watch her come in across the bay.'

It was almost five by the time they reached the driveway up to Pendennis Castle. 'There she is!' Johanna cried at once, jigging up and down in her excitement.

The *Windrush* was at last living up to her name, running before the gale, overtaking the swell and buffeting it aside at every plunge, throwing up vast curtains of white water. She was carrying too much sail for that wind, but nothing that good seamanship couldn't manage. 'He's annoyed he had to luff twice back in Mount's Bay,' Johanna commented. 'If he hadn't been so eager to shave the Lizard, he could have been here an hour ago. Now he'll be too late for the porters and stevedores and there'll be an extra day's demurrage to pay.'

Selina looked at her in surprise. 'You know a lot about it suddenly.'

'Oh, Mr Berenson practically explained the entire shipping business to me yesterday.'

'Oh lord, I'm sorry I asked. Aren't you going to try to look for Hal?'

'Oh yes.' She raised the glasses to her eyes, but then almost immediately lowered them again and passed them to her cousin. 'No, I forgot — Hilary's idea of surprising him. Let's go back and wait down on the quay. He might spot us here.'

As they dropped out of sight behind the castle peninsula Selina said, 'I've never seen you like this — so scatterbrained.'

'Oh, I don't know if I'm standing or sitting. Feel my pulse.'

Selina tried but gave up. 'You haven't got one,' she said.

'It must be going too fast to register. Oh — this is torment. Why can't the ship be already tied up? Who put this stupid idea of getting here first into my head?'

'Oh, Mr Berenson, I'm sure.'

'He's there, Selina! Just behind us over the brow of the hill — you saw it. God, it's like a century ago I came back from saying our farewells in Redruth and wondering if I'd ever see him again — and crying every other step of the way back to Liston Court. And since then he's helped build a town in Iowa and I've had a baby and he's crossed that whole vast continent and started a proper mine and I've built a brewery and now he's come back all that way — just because I'm here. I can't believe it. Can you believe it?'

'Let me drive. That's twice you've put us on the footpath. Whoops! Three times.'

Johanna handed her the reins, still in a daze. 'There *was* a ship off Swanpool wasn't there — a three masted brigantine? We didn't just dream it?'

'Yes, there was a ship there. And no, we didn't dream it.'

'We didn't see the name though. It probably wasn't her.'

'She had two zephyrs carved on each side of her bowsprit. Could that *possibly* mean *Windrush?*'

'What's the smell? Am I imagining it? There's a . . .'

'Someone must be smoking a pipe behind one of these garden hedges. The smell, by the way, is called tobacco smoke.'

Johanna stared at her in bewilderment.

'Tobacco? A vegetable leaf of the tropics, brought to Europe by Sir Walter Raleigh.'

Johanna shook her head. 'It can't just be one man behind a hedge. It's everywhere. I can still smell it — can't you?'

Selina had to admit that she could. 'Gee up!' She gave her horse a tap with the whip. 'It must be a whole warehouse on fire. Wouldn't that be our luck! All ships forced out into Carrick Roads because of a fire!'

But as they drew near to the custom house, they saw the cause of it all. The excise men were burning contraband tobacco; a huge, square chimney at the corner of the building, made for the purpose, was belching great aromatic clouds of finest Virginia, which, in the whirlpool of air created in the lee of the peninsula, was milling around as if deliberately to tease and infuriate the populace.

They tethered the horse just beyond Killigrew Manor and gave him his nosebag to keep him happy. Johanna brought the glasses with her. The two cousins found a sheltered spot in a doorway, directly opposite the pipe-smoking chimney. They had not long to wait.

Within a few minutes the *Windrush* slipped between the two castles — Pendennis and St Mawes — and into the quieter waters of the Roads. Then the agony began all over again. The nearer she came to the custom-house quay, the more she had to turn, first across and then actually into the wind. The last half mile was at a veritable snail's pace.

'I still can't see him,' Johanna cried in anguish.

'You've been saying that ever since they came into view. Let me try.'

'Yes, but they're close enough now.'

'You've said that before, too. Come on — I'll bet I'll find him for you.'

'You won't. He's not there. Something's happened — I can feel it in my bones.'

Selina tugged at the leather carrying strap.

'In a minute,' Johanna promised. 'I bet I know what's

happened. He paid the captain to put him off in a long boat when they were still in Mount's Bay — to surprise us. They could have come in at Porthleven. Oh, Selina, what fools we've been! I'll bet he's laughing his head off at Lanfear this very minute. Come on — let's go back to the gig.'

Selina took the glasses from her and trained them on the ship, which was now making fast astern at the quayside.

'He's not there,' Johanna assured her. 'You're only wasting time. He'd be up on deck.'

'Got him!' Selina exclaimed triumphantly. 'He is on deck — but not the one you were searching.'

'Where? I looked everywhere.' She squinted hard at the ship, trying to sharpen her vision.

Selina passed her the glasses. 'Try looking at that little covered quarter-deck, or whatever it's called, right at the stern. But there's a bit of a mystery all the same.'

Johanna swung the glasses to where her cousin had indicated — and gave a laugh of triumph. She was just about to lower them and go running along the quay, shouting his name, when she froze.

Selina had obviously been waiting for the moment. 'Yes,' she said, 'how on earth did Diana Jewell get aboard?'

Chapter Sixty-Three

'What now?' asked Selina when Johanna had calmed down sufficiently to explain her understandable error. They had withdrawn once again into the concealment of the doorway.

'What would you do?' Johanna replied – vehemently, not as if she was interested in knowing.

'Tear him limb from limb? Pursue him with demons? Harry him into the grave and beyond . . .'

'And call him names, no doubt,' Johanna interrupted angrily. 'Like Tubal Starkman.'

'It's one way of coping.'

'I'm talking about in a real situation like this.'

'Ah, forgive me, but it didn't sound like a real question.' She gave the matter some cursory thought. 'I suppose I'd simply write finis to an inglorious page.'

'What – just turn about? Go away? Go back home?'

'Yes, simply cut him out of your life. But then I'm not in love with him, or' – she smiled to show she was joking – 'perhaps only a tiny bit.'

Johanna was too deep in her own thoughts to see the reference. 'The trouble is, buried inside that faithless body is a good man – a man worth fighting for.'

Selina's eyes gleamed in anticipation. 'You're going to fight then? Who – Jenny Jewell?'

She shook her head. 'There he is, coming down the gangway. No sign of her. Can you go and bring the gig round here?'

'And miss this? Not for words.'

Johanna put the glasses back to her eyes. 'You mean not for worlds,' she said, glad of the rare chance to correct her cousin on her own ground. Hal was not looking about him as if he expected a welcoming party. Arrived at the foot of the gangway he sent a porter off to get him a cab. He just stood there and waited, smiling at the world in general, sniffing the burning tobacco, and relishing the feeling of being on dry land after so many weeks afloat.

'I mean not for words,' Selina murmured.

There were a couple of dozen ladies of the town to greet the boat; two of them approached Hal, arm in arm. He took their hands in his, one in each, and had a brief, good-humoured conversation with them before he looked at his watch and shook his head. They drifted off. Another approached him. He took her by the hand, too, turned her around, slipped the other arm around her waist, and walked her two or three paces before he let her go and returned alone to the foot of the gangway. He had to touch them, Johanna thought.

Whatever it was he had said to the woman, it gave her plenty to smile about.

The porters started to raise a second gangway aft. 'Let's go and surprise him,' Johanna said grimly.

He saw them when they were still twenty paces off. 'Jo!' he cried out and came running to meet her.

She threw herself into his arms. 'Oh! Hal! Hal! I can't believe it – is it really you?' His greatcoat was open and she burrowed inside. There in the unforgotten warmth and aroma of him she felt herself drowning in forgiveness and oblivion. Rescuing that 'good man' was not going to be quite as straightforward as she had supposed.

Selina, standing a decent way off (for a keen observer of life), watched. Above Johanna's head his eyes were roving anxiously over the quayside. She could see the object of his search beginning to descend the second gangway, behind him and some way off to his right. His eyes met hers. 'Selina,' he cried in even greater surprise.

Johanna released him but kept hold of his hand.

'I didn't expect either of you,' he said, still quartering the quayside with his eyes. He turned back to Johanna. 'I could have sworn I spied you waving to me from Lanfear House. Oh, we had such a struggle in Mount's Bay!'

'We saw,' Johanna told him. 'That's why we raced over here.'

706

'Metaphorically speaking.' Selina held out her hand. 'Hello, Hal. You're looking well.'

'You too, my dear.' He took his hand away from Johanna so he could clasp hers in both of his. He leaned forward to kiss her, turning to Johanna and saying, 'She will soon be my step-sister-in-law. You'll permit it?'

'What's one more?' Johanna asked, giving him a dazzling smile. She had meanwhile spotted Jenny at the foot of the other gangway.

He straightened up and dropped Selina's hand. 'One more?' he echoed in bewilderment.

Rescue came in the shape of the porter with his cab. 'How did you come over here?' Hal asked the two of them.

'In my gig,' Johanna told him. 'Selina was going to ride back, but . . .'

'Oh, I can ride,' he volunteered. 'By the way, how's my other little darling? You haven't brought her with you? I'll bet she's . . .'

'Over there.' Johanna nodded toward the second gangway.

Mystified, he turned in that direction. She watched his face and then she said, 'I have a better idea. You could take your . . . friend' — she waved her little finger once again toward where Jenny was waiting — 'and your other baggage along to the livery at the Moor. Get all your farewells over and done with. And then we could hire another gig — they have an arrangement with the Angel. We'll be able to leave it there.' She was going into this superfluous detail to give him time to absorb the shock. 'Selina and I will meet you at the Moor, where she and you can exchange places. You come back with me, and she can go with whatsit.' She turned to her cousin. 'You'd prefer that, wouldn't you, darling — a bit of company on the way home?'

Hal stared at her, bewildered and uncertain. At length he inclined his head toward Jenny and said, 'It's not what you're probably thinking, you know.'

'Oh, darling!' She stroked his arm fondly. 'I'm quite used to that by now. See you at the Moor.'

She glanced back over her shoulder after they had gone about ten paces and gave him another warm smile; she thought she had never seen a man more irresolute.

'What are you going to tell him?' Selina asked in slightly awestruck tones. 'Lord, I wish we'd come in Nina's landau. I'd give anything to hear it.'

'It depends on what he's got to say for himself. All I know is that by the time we reach Lanfear, he's going to be in no doubt as to my opinion.'

'Try and remember it — what you tell him. Try and *burn* the words into your memory.'

'They'll surely be hot enough!' Johanna laughed.

'Tell me all later.'

They reached the gig. The nosebag was empty and the horse seemed glad to be relieved of it, eager to be moving again.

'You won't be idle yourself,' Johanna said as they set off toward the Moor. 'I'll bet Jenny has a tale to tell — which a skilled weaver of words might draw out of her almost without realizing it.'

'Yes!' Selina's eyes glowed at the prospect.

With Easter only a week away the moon was already bright, but they kindled the lamps on both gigs before they set off. Jenny did not once look at Johanna.

'Well,' Hal said ruefully as they started to climb the hill toward Greenbank, 'I can't say it's the homecoming I'd expected.'

'Not the one you planned, you mean?' Johanna said affably. 'Still, it's marvellous to see you back here, darling. All in one piece.'

Warily, he accepted her conversational lead until they reached the hilltop, where the houses peter out on the estuary side and there is a magnificent view over the river to Flushing and the rich, rolling landscape of the Fal. It was especially beautiful in the last light of the dying day, when all its colours were brought so close in tone that they jostled each other restlessly, mysteriously, caught in the very act of folding themselves into the dark.

'You and Cunningham were going to spoil all this with a railway once,' she commented. 'Whereabouts exactly were you intending to cross the river?'

'Look, if you're angry,' he said, 'just come out with it. Let's have it now. I hate this brittle pleasantry.'

'How is Cunningham, by the way?'

'Oh, he'll live to be a hundred. Did you hear me?'

'Yes.'

'Well?'

'Hal — if there's anything to "have out" as you put it, I rather think it's for you to begin.'

'Oh.'

'Don't you. We are talking about *liaisons,* aren't we?'

'Well . . . indeed.' He cleared his throat. 'I was hoping you were going to explain your, er, *liaison* with Charley Vose.'

She turned around, not to check on the others, who were dawdling some way behind, but toward the Roads, the outer harbour. He, meanwhile, was continuing, 'It's not the sort of thing I could write. I mean, a question that's meant in a perfectly straightforward manner can seem querulous and accusing to the other person. But I must say I was shocked when I heard . . .'

'If your captain hadn't tried to cut it so fine around Lizard Head, you'd have met poor Charley this afternoon. Did you happen to notice that prison hulk? It's too dark now but you passed within a chain's length of it on your way in.'

'Charley in gaol?' He was genuinely shocked.

She explained what had happened earlier that day. 'Poor old boy,' he said. 'It's half a year of hell, that voyage. You've probably saved his life. He'll have nothing left when he gets there, but at least he'll be alive.'

'Slow down a bit,' she said. 'Let the others get within hailing distance at least.'

After a pause he returned to the attack: 'It makes your working for him at the Ram even more foolhardy.'

'At least we're no longer calling it a *liaison.*'

'Why did you do it, darling?'

'I told you all that in my letter,' she said patiently. They had two hours' driving ahead of them, at least. Long before it was over he would run out of these little delaying complaints — and then he would have to address his own behaviour. She could wait.

'When you told me once,' she went on, 'about the fortune Charley Vose could command if only he took his brewing business seriously, I made that my ambition.'

'But didn't you realize how it would reflect on . . .'

'He annoyed me so much. I could do the housekeeping job in my sleep. There was no challenge there. But he was so idle! One week at a time — that's how he lived.'

'What was wrong with staying at Liston Court? Did you and Nina fall out before you left?'

'I'll tell you what was wrong — I mean, setting aside the fact that I could not have stayed beneath her roof without disgracing her — what was wrong was . . .'

'Yes, that's another thing I wanted to ask.'

'I was simply turning into a vegetable. We imagine we were brought up like gentlefolk, you and I, just because we know our manners and don't drop our aitches or use obvious provincialisms. But we haven't the first idea. To be able to enjoy idleness — to live in it like a bird takes to the air — the way Nina enjoyed it . . . that takes generations to acquire. Charley Vose could become a gentleman' — she snapped her fingers — 'like that! My cousin Terence has also discovered he's not cut out for it. He actually enjoys working now. Sometimes at Liston Court, when I faced yet another long summer afternoon on the lawn, stretched out in the shade of that great chestnut tree, waiting for my appetite to recover, I thought I would scream. I used to lounge out there, looking up at the windows and seeing Margaret and the maids, busy about the house, and it was all I could do to stop myself from springing up and joining them.'

She realized that if she went on like this, she could soon use up the whole journey. 'Next question?' she said merrily.

He winced. 'Don't put it like that. It's not an inquisition.'

'No, you're right.' She spoke as if accepting a rebuke. 'It's really just catching up on all the things we couldn't put in our letters, isn't it.'

'Yes,' he said dubiously.

'So shall we take turn and turn about?'

'Er, what d'you want to know?'

'No — don't let's make it question and answer. It's not an inquisition, as you say. You just tell me something you felt unable to write about for fear of its being misunderstood.'

When he did not immediately leap at the suggestion she added, 'Or try and put yourself in my position. Try and

710

imagine the sort of thing which I might feel calls for some explanation?'

There was another long pause, which this time she did not fill. 'Jenny Jewell,' he said at last.

'For example.'

Again he was silent.

'You can't think where to begin?' she suggested. 'I expect during your brief cab ride to the Moor she had time to tell you about her last letter to Diana? She probably also assured you that no power on earth could have induced Diana to show it to me.'

'But she did − is that what you're saying?'

'What Jenny doesn't know is that her mother was also threatened with transportation.'

'What − just for running a ... one of those houses? What's been happening to England while I've been away?'

'Not enough broad churchmen, my darling − they've all been busy emigrating.' She laughed at the words once they were out. 'Actually, that's closer to the truth than I realized. It is a kind of religion with you, isn't it.'

She remembered something Hilary had told her, in those first few days at Lanfear, immediately after her ordeal, when she had to talk and talk to get it out of her − a verbal extension of her need to vomit in the hedge. Among it all was an image of the Reverend Greep squirming all over her naked, terrified young body, murmuring, 'This is the temple where I worship ... these are the pillars of my temple, smooth as marble, my adorable little marble columns. And here comes mighty Samson − the only fellow powerful enough to thrust the pillars apart and enter in ... to paradise.'

It *was* a kind of religion with him − with lots of men. Why hadn't she realized it before? She shivered.

'Are you cold?' he was relieved to be able to ask.

'You could put an arm around me if it helps.'

He complied gladly, but his tone was flat when he next spoke: 'So. I suppose Diana did show you the letter after all.'

'Out of gratitude, she claimed. Selina and I helped her mother escape with a fine. You could go a bit faster now. I think I can hear them behind us.'

'Gratitude!' He gave a hollow laugh and flicked the horse back into a trot. 'Diana must hate me.'

'D'you think so?'

'Look at it from her point of veiw. I called on them that day and the next thing she knows, Jenny is gone — leaving the two of them to manage on their own. To her it must look as if I induced her to run away. She doesn't know what really happened.'

'Who does?'

'You're right.' He hung his head. 'I can only ask you to believe that I really did not intend to take up with her.'

'Again.'

'What d'you mean?'

'Weren't you and she couranting once?'

'Oh, I see.' There was a thoughtful silence before he went on. 'You've got to realize that before I met you, I never thought much of women at all. I mean ... they were just there. A fact of life like food in the shops, or horses in stables. Women were just *there*. And I never *thought* about them at all. I'd see a pretty face, or a figure that would set me itching to know more. And well, dash it — they always seemed willing enough, too. I mean I never forced myself on anybody. If they said no and meant it, and a lot of them say no and don't mean it, but if they meant it, I'd just tell myself there were plenty of others.'

'And there always were.'

'Yes. You were the first girl I never thought of in that way.' He hesitated and then went on. 'Well, if utter honesty is at the stake, you were the second. The first was Joan Ninian, but I didn't realize it until it was much too late.'

'Oh Hal!' She closed her eyes and hugged him tight. 'That baby! The one there was all the fuss over ...'

'... was mine. Yes.'

'And all that court case, and her name being dragged through the mud?'

'Yes. Don't go on! That's why I recognized it when it happened again with you. That's why I fought against it so bitterly. I didn't want to' — he laughed but it was near to despair — 'risk the same thing happening to you. I worshipped you, Jo. I still do. But I don't think I'm worthy to be within a thousand miles of you.'

'Oh my darling!' She leaned her head against his arm. 'How can you be so utterly . . .'

'No, don't stop me now,' he begged. 'Let me say it all.' He leaned his head down briefly to touch hers. 'When we said goodbye . . . d'you remember that morning?'

'Will I ever forget it?'

'Nor will I. I took three pictures away in my mind. Not one of them was you − deliberately − and yet they were all you. Because they were pictures of the world and you were all my world. One was a hawk, circling the sky. One was sunlight, striking against stone. And one was a lone pine tree.'

'I remember them!' she cried, and out of the darkness her mind's eye conjured the scene to the last detail.

'On that coach drive to Plymouth I made vows that were almost monastic. In fact, they *were* monastic. I promised myself to use my time in America to purge myself of all my old ways. So that I could begin, just begin, to be good enough to ask you to marry me.'

'But you already had.'

'I know. I was going to write . . . my first letter from Boston was going to tell you everything, all my past. I was going to say you were not to consider yourself bound by anything we had said or done. Of course, I didn't know about the baby then.' A memory struck him. In a different tone he said, 'I really did want to know, when I asked about her down by the ship.'

'She's fine. You'll love her.'

'I already do.'

'She thinks she's going to stay awake till you come. But she forgets how strong Mr Sandman is.'

'Mr Sandman!' It was a name, and a game, he hadn't heard it in years. 'Oh − all those nursery rhymes and things. I'll have to learn them all again.'

They drove on awhile in silent, happy contemplation of the prospect.

Then he sighed and resumed his confession. 'But, of course, I never wrote it. Before we were half-way over the Atlantic my resolve was shattered.'

'It must have been very fragile.'

'At two in the morning? After a month of celibacy? The

first month is always the worst — when you give up anything, I mean. And when a soft, willing girl comes creeping into your bunk at that hour and . . .'

'Yes! Very well, Hal — I do understand. I mean, I can see the problem without needing an actual picture to go with it.'

'Sorry. I shouldn't have given way — I know that.'

'But if it hadn't been for Jenny being there,' she asked 'd'you think you'd have kept them — your monastic vows?'

He could feel the tension in her grip as she waited for his reply. He hated himself more than ever now, but he had to say it: 'No, I'm afraid not, my darling. Even with Jenny beside me, there were still others.'

'You mean actually *beside* you?'

'I thought you didn't want pictures.'

She chuckled. At least he was honest. 'Tell me why,' she said. 'What is it that makes you . . .'

'D'you really not understand? Don't you remember those two nights we spent together? Wasn't that the greatest pleasure for you, too?'

'Yes.'

'That's one thing I've never fathomed about women. Where d'you keep that memory in between times? Haven't there been moments when you've longed for it again? And with me five thousand miles away, haven't you even considered other partners?'

She took time over her reply. 'Only when I . . . when I despaired of you,' she said.

'Oh, Jo!' He leaned his head against hers once more — and then stiffened. 'But you only *considered* it, I hope?'

'We seem to have strayed from your point, Hal.'

'Jo! Tell me — I must know.'

'What if I said I did more than "consider" it?'

'I'll kill him,' he replied at once. 'Who was it?'

'So it's all right with you if I kill that trollop back there?'

'She's not worth it. Anyway, it's different in my case.'

Johanna was glad of the dark — that she could not see his eyes and be persuaded by them. He was no more than an obstinate silhouette against the fitful lighting from the Ponsharden shipyard. She saw men suspended in mid-air, in little pools of lamplight, shaving ribs, reaming spars, and caulking the nearly completed vessels.

714

'You'd never give yourself lightly like that,' he went on. 'But she's a trollop, as you say. And I'm not worthy to touch the hem of your dress. So what I've given to her, or she's given to me, was worthless anyway. Two worthless people giving each other their trash − that's all it was. But you could yield nothing less than the costliest jewel. Gem, I mean.'

Johanna ignored the chance for irony. 'Well − there's a convenient argument,' she said bleakly. 'It kills three birds with one stone.'

'Three?'

'Past transgressions. Present offences. And all future amours.'

'Oh, darling − it would be so different if we were married. Why didn't we? We should have got married before I left. Then I'd never have succumbed to that one back there − not even if she'd come to my bed in the middle of the night. If I had been bound by the vows of marriage, to support my own feeble resolve, then it would have been different.'

Did he not remember his letter from Kanesville, she wondered? She knew it by heart, along with all the rest: 'From the moment I digested your news properly I have considered myself married to you, and you may take it that I already feel myself bound by every vow I shall one day make with you in person, as set forth in the Book of Common Prayer.'

'It will be different, Jo, my darling. This confession may kill two birds but not three. It is no augury for the future. When we are married, from that moment on, I shall never look at another woman.'

What it boiled down to, she told herself was: Would she prefer Hal, with all his faults . . . no, that made him sound dreadful. Would she prefer Hal, with his one lamentable (and perhaps incurable) fault − Hal being unfaithful, then guilt-ridden, then contrite . . . and then unfaithful all over again − would she still prefer him to any other man, whose ardent passion might be more easily governed because he had less of it in the first place?

Disappointed in her silence, he added, 'I'll tell you this, Jo − God preserve the happy innocence of any wife whose husband never outlived the curious schoolboy, the adventurous youth, the bachelor libertine.'

'Well, Hal,' she told him, 'you can remember *some* of your finer sentiments.'

But he seemed not to hear her. 'You've no idea of it,' he went on. 'It's such a shallow pleasure when there's no love to go with it. The hours and hours and hours of my life that I've wasted! And what was it all for? Once I stayed all night outside a girl's house. I didn't even know her name. All because I saw her getting undressed, and I was sure she'd seen me and was just doing it for my benefit. So I told myself it was my lucky day and she'd be out as soon as the house was asleep. And after two hours I was saying no, she wasn't going to appear and I was a fool. And that was one o'clock in the morning. And I was still saying it at four − by which time I had to leave, on account of a slight touch of pneumonia. It's slavery, Jo. All I want is for it to be over. Believe me, I'm cured of philandering now.'

When she still made no reply he asked, 'You didn't really go with any other man, did you? You were only saying that?'

It was, she supposed, the sort of choice every woman made in the end − men being what they are.

'Of course I didn't.' She laughed. 'Anyway, I know it's over − for you.'

'How?'

'Because if, after we're married, you ever go with another woman, I'll kill you.'

He thought it was his turn to laugh.

'I mean it, Hal,' she said evenly. 'Do be quite clear about this. To me, what we did before you left − making Hannah − was the most wonderful and precious thing in my life. If you ever tried to share it with another woman after you'd promised it exclusively to me, I would kill you for it.'

She smiled to herself; she had never before realized that you could actually *feel* a person going pale beside you in the dark.

He swallowed audibly. 'Tell me about Hannah,' he said.

And between Penryn and Helston she told him rather more than even the most devoted father who has not yet met his daughter could possibly wish to hear. But he had no wish to interrupt her and hear about the other subject, either.

When they arrived at the Angel they yielded up the hired gig. Johanna, speaking as if Jenny were a wayfarer they had lifted along the way, told her where Diana had found lodgings with their mother. The hotel porter carried down her bags. Johanna watched Hal watching her go; his eyes lingered on her and she knew he was getting used to the idea of *never again*. When he turned and found her eyes upon him, he gave her a sad little nod that — oddly enough — she found more convincing than all his earlier protestations. 'I'd better hire a hack,' he remarked, knowing the hills ahead were too much for the three of them in the gig.

As they began to climb Sithney Common Hill he cleared his throat and asked, with delicate emphasis, 'What are the arrangements for tonight?'

'Ah!' Selina said in tones of promise.

Johanna trod lightly on her instep. 'There's a guest room for you at Lanfear, if you wish — or you could put up down the road at the Lion and Lamb in Ashton. The beds there are extremely comfortable, they say.'

'Ah,' he said, 'Good. And you?'

'Selina and I sleep in the cottage — for the sake of propriety. Tony's alone in the house, except for the servants, of course.'

'I see — and he won't mind my staying in the house?'

'He'd be delighted. Oh, of course, there's Dr Sheridan too — he's the new partner — he's staying this week while he has the decorators in. So — the more the merrier.'

Peggy Machin, helped by Hilary, had prepared a marvellous dinner. Just before they arrived, the girl slipped back into the clothes she had been wearing while she waved from the window.

'So it was you!' Hal cried the moment he saw her. 'You little deceiver!'

She giggled and then glanced at Johanna to check she had not overstepped the mark. 'I thought my arms would drop off,' she said.

It was incredible, Johanna thought. They had never met. Hal was twice her age, though she was a big girl now. They exchanged one sentence each — and bang! There it was — swift as thought — that well known gleam in both their eyes. She gave the girl a hug. 'You poor thing! I had no idea she'd turn again before she left the bay.'

'I'd rather stick cabbage all day in the rain than stand waving a hankie out a window. I know that,' she said. Her eyes kept returning to Hal.

'Just for that you shall give me a kiss,' he told her, intending more to tease Johanna than be taken seriously.

Hilary's freckles turned dark brown but before anyone could stop her she flung her arms about him and gave him what he demanded. His astonished eyes found Johanna through a fringe of her fiery hair; desperately he turned so that the girl's lips were at least on his cheek. His wildly arched eyebrows signalled: *I never intended this — but see how it happens!*

'Here — you never shaved!' Hilary, now that she had taken what she wanted, pretended to a disgust that allowed her an easy exit. She pushed him away from her and rubbed her lips as if his stubble had skinned her.

Tony came in at that moment, with Dr Sheridan at his side. Introductions followed all round; he welcomed Hal with guarded bonhomie. 'I owe you an apology,' he murmured, taking Hal by surprise.

For reply he nodded toward Johanna. 'She'll assure you you don't, sir. And there's a baby upstairs will confirm it.'

'At all events, I'd be honoured if you'd accept the hospitality of this house while you are here in Cornwall!'

Hal bowed and said he would be delighted.

'Dinner in half an hour, then?' Tony told Hilary. He turned to Johanna. 'Shall she stay in that dress?'

'Yes, why not?' she replied. 'And eat with us, too. She'll even up the numbers — and if anyone's deserved it today, she has.'

'Before we dress,' Hal asked Johanna, 'could we just . . . ?' He pointed vaguely upstairs.

Johanna turned to Hilary. 'How is she?'

'Good as gold. She said "Where's Dada?" and went straight off.'

Johanna grasped Hal by the hand and led him upstairs. She took a lamp from the landing as they passed. 'This is the moment I dreamed of most,' he told her.

She squeezed his hand, 'Me, too.'

They stood side by side and stared down at their child, who lay flat on her stomach, her thumb all sucked to wrinkles and discarded an inch from her mouth. He squatted down beside the cot and blinked, and grinned ruefully, the helpless prisoner of an overwhelming emotion.

After a while he mastered himself and rose again. Johanna – unnecessarily – straightened the blanket before she joined him at the door. 'Never seen one before?' she asked.

He knew she didn't mean babies in general. 'There's only ever been one other – as far as I know.'

'Yes, I see him quite often in Penzance. They go walking on the Green. She's widowed now, you know. Quite well off, too.'

'Why are you trying to spoil it for me, Jo?' he asked.

She put down the lamp and flung herself into his embrace. 'Because' – her breath was hot in the narrow space between them – 'when I saw you with her just now . . . I . . . felt' – her voice began to crack – 'jealous.' She ended on a whisper. One more word and she'd break down.

He just stood there, like a rock, and held her until she was calm again.

The two cousins went over to the cottage to dress. 'Well?' Selina said eagerly.

'I could ask the same of you.'

'Oh, yes, I had a most illuminating conversation. Miss Jenny Jewell is actually quite a nice person, you know. Much superior to her sister. Apart from their looks, you'd never know they were twins.'

'All right. That's enough about her.'

'And Hal?'

Johanna shook her head. 'Where does one begin? I'm still in a turmoil about him. Most of the time I think he's the only man in the world I'll ever love or want. But even then I know, you see – I realize he has this flaw in him. You saw it yourself with Hilary just now. They'd never met each other in their lives – and hey presto! There it was. Of course, I know they were only being playful – but nevertheless, it was there. Being married to him would be a torture. And yet to see him married to someone else would be ten thousand times worse. What am I going to do, Selina?'

'Nothing in a hurry, I hope? Did he explain why . . . Jenny and all that?'

'Oh, endlessly. I had his whole life story — his slavery to women . . . standing outside houses and catching pneumonia . . . everything.'

'But he can't have been as vague as that — not all the way home.'

'Oh, what it all boiled down to is that around two o'clock in the morning he's got no resistance at all and any female who comes creeping into his room may have her way with him. Did you ever hear anything so feeble!'

On their way back to dinner Johanna noticed her cousin was carrying her nightdress and sponge bag. 'What's all this?' she asked.

'Oh,' Selina said archly. 'I feared I might feel a little *de trop,* you know? Remembering your homily on people minding their own business this morning.'

'Yes, well, I've changed my mind on that. I think you were right and I was wrong. So you can take those things back.'

Selina actually took two steps toward the cottage before she turned about once again. 'Actually,' she said, as if the thoughts were occurring to her as she spoke, 'with two guests in the house, my original objections do seem a little beside the point. And as it won't be long before I'm mistress there in my own right, perhaps I ought to move back at least while both of them are there.'

'Not on my account,' Johanna repeated. 'My door will be locked.'

'And it's unfair to leave all the responsibility to Hilary.'

Johanna laughed. 'Why? What could possibly happen?'

'You never know,' her cousin said vaguely. 'It could be anything.'

Chapter Sixty-Four

The attendance of Hal and Johanna, side by side, before the very pulpit from which she had been denounced as a notorious woman, was the sensation of that Sunday's worship. People who had not spoken to her since then were actually seen to give her a grave nod in passing; those who had never done more than nod gravely, now exchanged a courteous word or two; and Mrs Babcock, who had previously confined herself to courteous words in passing, asked if Johanna might find time to give a talk next week to the Helston Townswomen's Country Pursuits League on the dying art of home brewing and wine-making.

What annoyed Johanna most was that, notwithstanding the contempt these shifts in social acceptance aroused in her, she could still feel pleased to be their object. She even heard herself accepting Mrs Babcock's invitation; a few more nails in the coffin of home brewing would do Rosewarne's trade no harm.

Hal spent most of the service trying to convince himself that the church was not pitching and yawing on the waves; he remembered the same trouble in Boston. 'What on earth is a Country Pursuits League?' he asked as they drove back to Lanfear.

'It is absurdity upon absurdity,' Johanna told him. 'I mean, look at the size of Helston. A good pole vaulter could stand by the Town Hall and put himself in an open field within three leaps. And here are these women, shopkeepers' wives, mostly — superior artisan people — who have to form a league to encourage each other to visit that remote and dangerous territory. As to what they do, they keep bees

721

and press flowers and ...' She broke off and laughed at a sudden memory. 'Hamill Oliver gave them a talk last year on ancient Celtic harvesting customs, and it was just about that time of year, so suddenly all the mowies in West Penwith were full of bewildered agricultural workers being taught how to dance and chant by the wives of drapers, grocers, and pharmacists from Helston. Fortunately the Methodist minister frowned on it and so yet another "ancient custom" was nipped at its birth.'

Hal joined her laughter. 'And yet there *is* a sort of harvest ritual. I remember doing it at Nineveh years ago. "I'll have 'un, I'll have 'un ..." You must know that one? The Death of Gwydian, they call it.'

She shook her head. 'It's not in Old Cornish, so it can't be genuine. Actually, you ought to see Hamill while you're back. He and Tony probably saved Hannah's life between them, when she was born. Shall we go after lunch? He doesn't mind people just dropping in. In fact, you'd wait till doomsday for a proper invitation.'

But as it was Hal's first day back they decided to postpone such a visit and simply pass the day together as a family. 'Let's take Hannah down to Praa Sands,' Selina suggested.

'Ah!' Hal exclaimed. 'To see the sea again!'

'But Hannah adores it,' Johanna explained.

He yielded.

'You'll come too, won't you, Tony?'

He raised an eyebrow at Dr Sheridan, who said, 'If you'll excuse me, I'd rather like to pop back and take another look at that church while there's no one about.'

They went in the landau, with the Cardew children in the gig behind, taking the route the two cousins had shown Tony, a lifetime ago, or so it seemed. At the foot of Pentreath Hill they hobbled the horses and turned them loose to graze.

Peter Cardew had developed a passion for snakes and lizards. A bright, sunny day like this, when there was still a nip in the air, proved ideal for catching them barehanded. He had salvaged an old aquarium, once the pride and joy of cousin Terence, and set it up in the kitchen garden, where it housed his ever-changing collection of adders, grass snakes, slow worms, and sundry lizards. So that was Peter lost for the entire afternoon.

James and Iris were the civil engineers of the family. Huge rocks that would have defeated them at threepence a hundredweight, carried from the fields, were childs' play down on the sands – but no one dared suggest the result was mere childish play; by the end of the afternoon their dam penned back a sizable pool, deep enough for children to swim in had it been summer. Hilary, the eternal scavenger, had discovered – and had then been given – Selina's old sketch books. She made an artistic arrangement of bladder-wrack, dead crabs, bleached driftwood, and fragments of fishing net, which she then tried to draw.

Hannah, delighted to have tamed the new monster in her life – and such a big, booming, friendly monster, too – was now exploiting his support to go as far into the waves as she dared. The slope here, though steep by the standards of north-Cornish beaches, was much shallower than at Loe Bar; so that huge waves, which broke some twenty paces off, would sent vast sheets of black water and white foam hissing and sizzling up the incline; on the return run it would vanish into the sand, which was loose and yielding and almost quick beneath the feet. The merest trickle reached the sea to impede the successor wave in its equally fugitive assault on that all-absorbent slope.

When a wave vanished before it reached them, she said, 'Awwww.' When it wet their feet just a little, she counter-feited a scream of monstrous insincerity and stamped heavily into the puddled sand to make it seem deeper. And when every seventh wave (or so) threatened to bowl them over, first knocking and then plucking at their calves, she threw acting to the winds and screamed in earnest – always shouting at the sea, 'Againg! Againg!'

And Johanna sat above the tideline, out of the wind, which had gone round northwest, and came to terms with her jealousy of Hal and their daughter. He was like a new toy to the child; she had discovered she could twist him round her little finger and she was now testing the possibilities of the situation to destruction – his or hers, it was a toss-up.

At last there came a wave so big that he had to pluck her out of harm's way, hurting her shoulder with the suddenness of his movement. Then he overbalanced and fell backwards into the water, or the dying surge of it. She fell on top of him.

For a couple of seconds she hooted with laughter. Then the pain got through to her and, without even pausing for breath, turned the laugh into a howl. He tried to hug her back to happiness, but it was no good. The friendly, booming monster had shown her his ugly side and she was now inconsolable.

He turned helplessly to Johanna, who smiled at him — trying not to make it too triumphal — and held out her arms; from which shelter the child stared up at him for a moment or two, her eyes sullen with accusation, and then fell asleep.

Tony, who had been strolling backwards at Selina's side, saw the whole episode. 'What d'you think?' he asked. 'Are they right for each other?'

She turned around briefly. 'Jo's not certain. I feel sorry for him in a way. I mean, women do more or less throw themselves at him. He's not utterly to blame for the way he is.'

'But explaining it doesn't make it easier to accept — for her.'

'No, that's it exactly.'

He cleared his throat. 'Does he have that effect on you?'

'I should jolly well . . .' she began stoutly. Then, in a less willing tone: 'Perhaps, in a very . . .' Then, dismissively, 'I don't think it can be quite proper for you to ask such questions.'

'I was astonished at Hilary last night. I've never seen her like that before.'

'Hilary, my dear, is growing up. I've seen her looking at you in a rather speculative way before now.'

'Oh, really!'

'Really and truly. I'm coming to your rescue just in time.'

He took her arm and patted it affectionately. 'Nina always maintained they were wrong for each other.'

Selina nodded. 'She was usually right.'

She felt him go slightly tense as he asked, 'You know what she said about us?'

'Yes, I wondered if she ever told you.'

'Apparently she came to that conclusion the very first time we met, when I was telling her what a splendid young woman you are but how much I loved Johanna. And she realized that what I felt for Jo was mere infatuation, whereas my feelings for you were much deeper and more genuine.' He gave a single, self-deprecating laugh and added, 'She saw it at once and yet it's taken me all this time.'

Selina clung to him more tightly. 'I miss her so much,' she said. 'And d'you know what I miss most? We were talking about it only last night. What we both regret most is that we can't say thank you. She's changed our lives and there's nowhere to leave off this burden of gratitude. We both cried about her last night.'

'You had a very emotional day.'

After a silence she went on, 'To answer your question, I think Jo really does love Hal — and he certainly loves her. It's not that overwhelming passion — that heedless, thoughtless tumult we love to read about ...'

'And write about,' he interjected.

'Yes, it's not that. In a way it's much deeper and more true. More steadfast. She knows his faults. She knows that his easy way with other women is going to give her endless heartache — I mean, she has a very cool, sensible eye to all the difficulties ahead. And yet the rest of her is upside down, head over heels — all that.'

He said nothing.

'Don't you agree?' she prompted.

He shook his head. 'I wasn't really thinking of her feelings for him, I mean, I don't think they're so much in question. It's his for her that worry me. Does he know her at all? We've watched her change, day by day, so it's hard for us to appreciate the problem he's going to face.'

'But he's had her letters,' Selina objected. 'He knows more or less what's been going on.'

He clenched and unclenched his fists impatiently. 'It's not what she's done, it's what she's become. Listen — you remember the last time all three of us were down here? You and me walking like this, and that demure, reticent, rather lonely young woman back there. Remember?'

'Of course I remember.'

'Well, that's the young woman Hal Penrose left behind. Can you imagine *her* going round the lanes blowing an old post-horn and soliciting orders for *anything*? Or so deeply impressing her will upon the customers at the Ram — the squires and lords of the earth — that not one of them dared mention or even jest about his reason for being there? Or going back to that same pew in church, week after week, after being called all the foulest names the wit of man can devise against an erring woman, and forcing them, bit by bit, to accept her, not as a penitent — that would be easy — but as herself? Or taking up an absurd, casual dream like wanting to be a brewer, and actually making it come about?'

Selina said nothing; her pace dropped almost to a standstill.

Tony went on. 'Now we've seen it all happen, day by day. We've become accustomed to it. But poor Penrose has to experience all that in the space of a week or less. They'll be going in to the brewery tomorrow — and no doubt she'll make her usual half-dozen calls on the way. Have you ever been with her when she's drumming up trade?'

Selina nodded and pulled the kind of face that says, 'And I've just about got over it!'

'What's Hal going to make of that!' His laugh was not entirely kind. 'It's going to be an interesting supper tomorrow night. Thank heavens we know each other so well, my darling, and are past such difficulties!'

But all Selina could think of was Nina, standing with Tony by the Angel stables, listening to him talking about Johanna and realizing that the man loved her, Selina, instead. For now she found herself in an almost identical situation. The only difference was that Nina had got it precisely the wrong way around.

What to do about it was quite another matter.

Chapter Sixty-Five

When they set off again, up the hill past the Falmouth Packet, Hal's face was black as thunder. 'Do you have to engage in such banter?' he asked grimly.

'What banter?' she asked, genuinely taken back.

'All that innuendo. You know what he was hinting at.'

'But that's John Moyle.' She laughed at the absurdity of it. 'I've known him ever since he took over from old Morcom there. I sold him some of the first Vose's Ales — weaned him off Saunders Brewery in Penzance.'

'And that gives him the right to make all those intimate suggestions, does it? Is that what you're saying?'

'What *are* you talking about, darling? What intimate suggestions?'

'All that business about "getting in the right spirit," and "needing a bit of warmth," and "spring in the air" and so on.'

'But that's just friendly banter. It doesn't mean a thing. Good heavens, Hal, if that upsets you, what about the hours I've spent alone with him in the dark of his cellar? And dozens of others, too. And I've never had one of them take the slightest liberty.'

'Ye gods!' he cried.

But she was now in full fig. 'I think it helps, that banter. Charley Vose used to carry on like that all the time, with every woman he met, but it never led to anything. I think if a man can pass a remark or two — all right, a bit near the knuckle, I grant that — and if we can both have a little laugh at it, he feels he's a gay young dog at heart and he needn't do anything more about it (which most of them probably couldn't manage, anyway), and please can we get on with what we're really interested in, which is making money? That's how it works.'

When he said nothing she added, 'And it doesn't mean anything more than that.'

Still he was silent.

'Anyway, it won't be for much longer,' she added.

'You mean it's been going on most of the time I've been away?' he asked.

She paused before she said, 'It's called selling.'

'And you've been blowing that horn, too? Making a proper spectacle of yourself?'

Now it was she who said nothing. At Kenneggy, still in silence, she turned off the highway.

'What now?' he asked. 'Are we going up Goldsithney?'

'Yes,' she said, neglecting to add that the road also led past Skewjack Hall. At the top of the little rise leading down to the manor gates she once again put the post-horn to her lips and — by chance — blew one of the sweetest little phrases she had ever managed.

'You should have heard my earlier efforts,' she commented ruefully as she tucked the instrument back under her seat. 'Tony said he'd never hear a donkey in pain without at once thinking of Vose's Ales.'

'Did he now.'

'Are you going to be grumpy all day?'

'I can't say I think much of Dr Tony Moore. I pity poor Selina.'

'I don't see why.'

He laughed. 'Can't you picture it — the pair of them after they're married, going at it like rabbits once a month to be on the safe side and him saying to her, "I enjoy undressing you, my dear, for three principal reasons." I can just hear him.'

Unfortunately, so could Johanna. Hal's mimicry of Tony's voice was so accurate — and yet the sentiments so out of character — she could not help bursting into laughter. 'There's a cruel streak in you,' she told him. 'Actually, I think Tony will be perfect for her. Don't ever reveal I told you this, but she is petrified — absolutely petrified — of going with a man like that. She's fascinated by the idea of it

– I'm not saying she's prudish. Quite the opposite. But, in herself – physically, you know – she's just all nerves. And I think, if there's one man in all this world with the patience and kindliness and wisdom to help her overcome it, that man is Tony.'

She realized she was laying it on a mite thick, but she wanted him to stop denigrating Tony, and also – slightly below the level of her consciousness – she wanted to hurt Hal, just a little ... stick a pin in his pride. And praising Tony in that way, she suspected, would do the trick. To judge from his countenance, she was right.

Mrs Pellew came striding out in person to greet them. 'My dear Miss Rosewarne, you're in fine musical form today – and now I see why! Is this the great Mr Hannibal Penrose about whom we've all heard so much? Do come in.'

Hal recovered his composure at once and began to bask in her delight.

'No deliveries today, I'm afraid,' Johanna told her. 'Just orders.'

'And you shall have them,' she trilled as she led them indoors. A groom took the gig around to the yard. 'Ah, Mr Penrose, you have plucked the jewel from our crown!'

'Eh ... ma'am?' he responded. 'Ah, yes, I see.'

'And I trust you appreciate it.'

Twenty minutes later they were back on the road – a slightly more thoughtful Hal beside a Johanna very much restored in confidence.

She called on three more customers, two of them public houses, and gained substantial orders at each. There was the usual banter, the winks, the sly innuendoes – all without further comment from him.

'You've built up quite a trade in a very short time,' he commented as they left Long Rock, where she had made the last of her calls. Only Penzance Green now lay between them and the town proper.

'That was pure luck, Hal,' she told him. 'This is the perfect year for it. I think even last year, when I was drumming up trade for Charley Vose, I was just a trifle premature – though we did well enough, and at least I cut my teeth on it. But this year it's like looking for water when it's raining.'

'Your ale is good, too. There's no doubting that.'

'Of course it helps but . . .'

'The best I've tasted, here or in America.'

'Even so, word has somehow gone out ahead of me. I called on a tiny little alehouse in Wendron, the other day . . . Wendron! You know what it's like — two houses and a church. Never called on the man in my life before, though I knew him. John Stillgoe — d'you know him? His mother was a Richards from Drym. Her sister Ivy married that tailor who lived over to Copperhouses, next door to Margaret Tyzack's granny.'

'Oh yes — Blewitt, wasn't he called? No — Plunkett. He made the suit I wore to church yesterday, funnily enough.'

'Anyway, I had no real hopes of taking any orders there, but, bless me — the fellow had it already written out! "I was coming up your place next week if you hadn't called," he said. There must be some burr-old drinkers there, too, I can tell you. But you see what I mean — I've just been lucky and picked the perfect time.'

She had, too, for in the distance she spied the familiar figure of Joan Ninian — as was, taking her daily walk with her five-year-old son. It wasn't long before Hal recognized her, too. 'Oh, my God!' he murmured. He turned and looked at Johanna accusingly; then he smiled. 'No — even you couldn't have arranged this. More of your confounded luck!'

'Luck?' she asked.

'Yes — now you'll see me discomfited.'

Even at the time she thought it was a profoundly revealing little aside — a window opening onto his view of their relationship.

Joan recognized him when they were still a couple of dozen paces apart. She lifted up the little boy and murmured something in his ear. He stared at Hal in fascination.

'Shall I stop?' Johanna asked out of the side of her mouth.

'No,' Hal said out of the side of his.

When they were about to draw level he raised his hat and inclined his head toward her. She made a slight bow in

730

acknowledgement, but what Johanna remembered best, when it was over, was that knowing, forgiving, sadder-wiser, sardonic smile of hers, which never once wavered. It put her on Olympus and Hal somewhere in the foothills.

'There would have been no point,' Hal said as soon as they had passed. 'Is she still looking at us?'

Johanna turned. Of course the woman was still looking at them. Johanna smiled and she smiled back; it was as if a torch had passed from one to the other.

'Is she?'

'Yes. That's a handsome little boy. He'll break a few hearts when his time comes.'

'What did she say to him, I wonder?'

'Can't you guess?'

'There goes Public Enemy Number One?'

'Oh, Hal!' She put an arm briefly around him. 'I don't know which you enjoy more − seducing pretty women or lacerating yourself for it after. I can tell you exactly what she said to him. She said, "See that man there? Have a good long look at him. One day I'll tell you a funny thing about that fellow." That's all she said.'

He nodded at the likelihood of it and stared glumly at the road ahead. 'I must admit,' he responded after a while, 'of all the things she might have said − that makes it sound pretty final, doesn't it? It shows it's really over and done with.'

And there was another revealing remark, she realized. Most people would have known it was 'over and done with' years ago. The hope that kept him outside that unknown girl's window until he caught a chill was obviously a disease of his very soul. All those little 'slices of cut cake' that bestrewed his life like daisies in a lawn − something within him must still be hoping they had all been miraculously restored to their original, uncut condition in the meanwhile, so that they were all potentially still out there, waiting to be enjoyed all over again.

She drove up the full length of St Clair Street without once saying, 'That's my brewery.' They arrived at its gate, whose mighty arch bore the legend *Rosewarne* in letters two feet high, with him still seeking it somewhere ahead of them.

'If they were any bigger,' she told him in exasperation,

'they'd leap down and bite you.'

He saw them then but still hardly took them in. His lips actually spelled it out, like a child at his primer, before he turned to her in utter amazement, 'That?' he asked faintly.

'Now you see why I need to drum up so much trade.'

'But Jo — it's vast!'

'Oh, come on — it's not so very big.' Modestly she added, 'It's only the biggest in West Penwith.'

'I should think so. I had no idea!'

As they drove on through the gate he said to himself, but loud enough for her to hear, 'How dared I laugh at you?' And when they dismounted from the gig he turned to her and said, still marvelling, 'And you never complained! How you must have smarted at my sneers.'

Her grin almost touched her ears. 'Oh, how I wish Tony were here!'

His face fell.

'He asked me what I'd do if you disapproved of all this — which you did at the time. And I said when you saw it, you'd understand and withdraw your objections. And he sneered, "Oh, yes — I'd forgotten that well-known humility of the man." You could imitate him perfectly — go on, say it.'

He shook his head. 'I think I've heard enough of that man for one lifetime.'

And so it went all day until it was time to leave for home. He saw her going about the brewery — sampling, sniffing, inspecting — and he noticed how the workmen hung on her judgement. How decisive she was, too — yet with the ease of one who knows her business not with the besieged authority of the martinet. He read *The Brewer's and Maltster's Gazette,* which might as well have been printed in double Dutch for all that he gleaned from it, while she dictated letters to alternate secretaries, switching with ease from legal business to brewing machinery, and rattling it out like a steam engine. He accompanied her into the town and saw the respect with which she was greeted on every hand; and these were not folk simply after her money — their esteem, as it had been with Mrs Pellew, was heartfelt.

He thought the bank agent a bit patronizing, but then the fellow grew overconfident and made a minor slip or two, and she put him right with such tact and good humour; after that he treated her with proper respect.

And she, he realized, somehow compelled this behaviour from them — not by demanding it, still less by behaving as if it were her due, but by knowing her business and expecting everyone else to know theirs. Indeed, it went further than that. She knew her business because she loved it — not just the brewing but everything that went with it — making customers, joking with them, managing the accounts, dealing with the bank ... it was meat and drink to her. More, it was nectar and ambrosia.

For his sake they left early that afternoon; she knew he would want time to play with Hannah — who had, of course, entirely forgotten his monstrous behaviour within the hour. He was rather thoughtful all the way, which did not trouble her one bit — for now he understood the whole business from her point of view.

It was a merry dinner that evening at Lanfear. Tony flirted with Johanna and Hal did not seem to mind — indeed, he flirted with Selina, which Tony accepted with equanimity. Everyone had some cause for celebration. Johanna because Hal at last understood. Hal, ditto — though in a very different sense. Tony and Dr Sheridan because they had that day decided to enter into a full partnership in their somewhat novel practice. And Selina because she had at last reached a decision.

Much later that night, as the clock down in the hall struck two, she opened Hal's bedroom door without knocking — though her knees bid fair to do the office for her. She had changed her mind and put him in Terence's old room, at the far end of the house from the two doctors and even farther from the queen of light sleepers — Hilary — who was in Johanna's old room, by the new nursery, on the next floor up.

She stood beside his bed, shivering with more than the cold — though it was sharp enough — and staring down at his sleeping form. He was so big and powerful ... surely he would crush her?

Surely she would not mind.

One by one she loosened the buttons of her nightdress until it simply fell from her. The bright paschal moon fell across the wall beside her, just grazing her where she stood. In the looking glass she saw it lay a silver line down her shoulder, her breast, her hip . . . and there the shadow of the sill put the rest of her in mystery.

Her breasts sagged. She put her hands under them and lifted. Here, Hal — for you. She touched her nipples. A different shiver overlaid the first; there was a sweet sensation within her, hard to locate; her spine tingled.

'You'll catch cold,' he whispered.

Even without looking she could hear the smile in his words. She put a knee on his bed. He lifted the blankets and she saw that he slept naked. Manwarmth wreathed about her, engulfed her. He touched that knee and the sweetness began to gather into more definite places.

Then she was lying beside him and his fingers were in her hair. 'I have never . . .' she began.

'Ssssh,' he said. 'I know. Just lie there a while. There's no hurry.'

She closed her eyes and thought of all the words she had prepared for him — warnings, pleadings, special words for that ecstasy when he gave it her. They had all evaporated. And there were his fingers in her hair; raising gooseflesh in her scalp that trickled down to the very soles of her feet; they were telling her that fingers can say it all.

His mighty arm went about her and his other fingers joined the parliament. His nails raked the side of her breast, nearly reaching her nipple but always stopping short of contact there. At last, with a little moan that slipped her guard she turned herself into it. The sweetness intensified and spread.

Now both his hands were about her breasts, mighty hands with a touch like silk and softer than down. There was an awesome sinking feeling within her, like drowning. Drowning in that sweetness, which now spread to every part of her. Gently he took her hand and pushed it down upon himself.

There it was, then — not at all like she'd imagined it. Not smooth and evenly tapering but . . . full of differences, a tactile landscape to explore. While she satisfied her curiosity he did nothing but hug her. When she finished, his hands once again began to move — wider now, and deeper. Up and down her stomach, conjuring once again that sensation of drowning. Her breath became erratic.

'Selina,' he whispered. 'You are so beautiful.'

The disorder grew; now she was gasping for breath. There was the pressure of his hands upon her hips. He was lifting her — further onto him — right onto him. Panic gripped her. This was the moment. This was when that huge thing she had explored — all those parts and bits — somehow crammed inside her. But she knew she'd never manage it. He would hurt her — not because he meant to but because he'd think she was like all those other girls — like Jo — who had obviously managed it with ease, and delight, and come back for more.

In all her imaginings she had somehow never pictured this — how he'd sweat and try again and then curse her for leading him on and failing him.

'No?' she begged.

'No,' he assured her. 'I'm not going to try. Something else instead — and just as beautiful. You'll see.'

She half relaxed.

'Trust me, beautiful, beautiful Selina,' he went on whispering. 'We have all the time in the world. Days and nights and days and nights ... This is only the beginning.'

Without relaxing she found she had relaxed. She was lying upon him, her back on his chest, heads side by side, both staring up at the ceiling, and her thighs were lightly parted, and that thing was there against her but not inside. He put her hand upon the end of it and squeezed once, twice, until she took over. Then his hands once again began to caress her body freely, everywhere, as far as they could reach. He seemed to know exactly which part of her ached most for the touch of him; his hand was always there where her desire was at its peak.

His breath began to shiver but still he made no move that might panic her again; only his hands, endlessly straying over her flesh, turning it to velvet with the pile inside. And at last, when all her longing rose in one explosion of unimaginable ecstasy, his fingers found a place down there that made it go on and on until she begged him to stop.

For an eternity they lay there, relearning how to breathe.

'Will I have a baby now?' she asked.

'No.' He kissed her ear, making her shiver once more.

Later she asked, 'Will you be able to go inside next time?'

'Soon,' he promised. 'What does it matter when? Next time? Next week? Next month?'

'But it's no pleasure for you.'

'Oh, Selina!' He turned her over to lie face down upon him. She could hardly believe that so much gristle and bone and muscle could all belong to one man. 'That was one of the sweetest pleasures I have ever known. Did you think I was doing *you* a favour? You have taught me something tonight, something I hope you'll never let me forget.'

'I don't understand.' But actually, she didn't want to understand. She didn't care whether she understood or not. He had just said something — what it was she had already forgotten, but that didn't matter; forgetting was the whole point of it. Something he said had teased that last bit of dread from within her. Now she was content to lie upon him, remembering a sweetness she had never imagined could exist this side of paradise, and listening to his voice, wondering what all those words could mean.

But eventually some meaning filtered through. She heard him talking, again, about 'all the time in the world.'

'But Johanna?' she said.

'I am not going to marry Johanna.'

Selina froze. She repeated the words in her mind and then sat bolt upright.

He pulled her down upon him once more. 'She has gone from me. Beyond me. Nina was right. It would be a disaster. For both of us.'

'And for Hannah?'

'Even more for her.'

'I'm not going to marry Tony, either,' she said.

'I know.'

'How can you possibly know? I've only just realized it myself.'

'I could have told you the moment I saw you standing there tonight.'

'He loves Jo, you know. Still. I'm sure of it.'

It prompted an obvious question but he had sense enough not to ask it just yet. Instead he murmured, 'That's for him to work out.'

'First he's got to realize it. He's a deep man, you know. He seems so self-controlled — and on the surface he is — but inside him, things just burn. Johanna's never seen that side of him.'

'D'you suppose it would make a difference?' he asked. Then immediately he stopped his ears. 'No — I don't wish to know. We'd only be tempted to meddle — and that would be fatal. We have quite enough to be going on with as it is.'

'What'll we do now?'

He sighed. 'You'll go back to your bed and try to get some sleep. Somehow we'll get through tomorrow without giving anything away. And you'll come back here tomorrow night when you hear Tony start to snore.'

'He doesn't snore!'

Hal chuckled. 'I won't ask how you know.'

'Beast!' She thumped him on the chest with all her might. It had no observable effect whatever.

Chapter Sixty-Six

Johanna spent the day with Victor Berenson, the young brewmaster who had impressed her so much. She offered him the managership of the business, with the chance to work his way up into a full partnership over the next five years. It was a complicated proposal for his exact share of the firm would depend on its success under his management. She wanted 'success' defined in absolute terms – so much capital and so much turnover by such and such a date; he wanted to relate it to the rest of the industry, so that if the trade in general suffered but Rosewarne's emerged less scathed than the rest, he would be rewarded for it. They took most of the morning to work out a compromise. In the end she yielded rather more than she intended, but secretly she was still pleased. 'VB,' as he wished to be known, proved a tough, intelligent negotiator and a man who could keep his eye on the main issues, no matter how much she tried to obscure them; if he applied that talent to the business, it would grow even faster than she had hoped – in which case, she could hardly complain if he gained his share of it sooner than she might have wished. In any event it would never rise above forty-nine per cent, and they each had to give the other first refusal on selling out their portion. She was exhausted as she drove home, but it was the happy kind of exhaustion that follows a truly productive day.

Hal spent those same hours visiting old friends at various mines in the district. In passing – though it was, in fact, the whole point of the exercise – he made copious sketches of all the new machinery in sight; the latest in ore stamps, buddles, vanning tables, washes, calciners, and so on. He could get them all made up locally back in California, but it would save a lot of time and trial-and-error if he could go back with precise dimensions, thicknesses, eccentricities . . . He, too, came home happily exhausted, his head buzzing with plans and layouts for the Penrose Mine.

Selina passed the morning at Liston Court. She intended to reread some of the books Nina had found in Brookesy's locked cupboard after his death – *The Battles of Venus, Le Boudoir d'Amaranthe, Mons Veneris* . . . and so on. But after half an hour she could take no more of their coyness, their fascination with mechanics, and their complete failure to capture what had been, to her, the most sublime experience possible. In the end she wondered if the authors of these works (all hiding behind pseudonyms, of course, and all undoubtedly male even when they were writing *The Confessions of a Young Lady)* did not spend more time in reading one another than in practising the exercises they professed. What curiosity had compelled her to read, only last year, experience now urged her to reject.

Sadly she locked the books back in their lair and returned the key to its hiding place. She was just about to leave when she heard the front door open and close. She knew she had relocked it, so whoever it was must have a key.

'Who is it?' she called out.

'Selina? Is that you?' It was her brother.

She came out into the hall and gave him a kiss. 'What are you doing here?' she asked.

'I was about to ask the same of you.' He shivered. 'Aren't you cold? Let's light a fire.' He went past her into the library. 'No servants today? I came to finish the inventory Jo asked for. She wants to sell most of these books and some of the pictures.'

With skill he began to set the fire.

'Compiling an inventory is hardly work for an aspiring young lawyer.'

He shrugged. 'We're a pretty philistine family. Can't really blame her. Look at the way we always sneered at the Rosewarnes for their "artistic" pretensions. Have you seen the pater, by the way?' He struck a match and set the paper alight.

'Not for a few weeks. I meant to go into Penzance with Jo

this week, but it'll have to be after Easter now.'

'I ran into him yesterday. He's a changed man since Christmas. And the boarding house is actually making a better income than Wheal Venton did in the last five years.'

The fire took hold; the blaze was merry even though the warmth was not yet in it.

'Terence, what *did* Tony do that night? He won't talk about it, nor will Mama, and, of course, one daren't ask Papa. Whatever it was, it didn't leave a mark on him.'

'Not where you'd see it,' Terence agreed.

'You mean . . . .' Selina was unsure about following up the ambiguity.

'Did you know your Tony used to box for his school? And his medical school − Guy's, I think it was − when he was a student.'

He looked around for somewhere to wipe his hands. His eye fell on the curtains but Selina said no. She followed him out to the kitchen and pumped the water for him. 'Tony's never mentioned it,' she said.

'No. Apparently he nearly killed a man once, and he's never put up his fists since − except that night. The pater was dashed lucky. He's never discussed it with me, but whatever your *fiancé* did to him, it was skilfully managed and eminently effective.'

'There's a towel on the back of the door,' she told him.

They returned to the library, where the fire was now beginning to throw out a little warmth. 'You didn't say what brought you here,' he reminded her.

'Oh . . . I had an idea for a new book. I thought I'd find some peace and quiet here to try and set it all down.'

'Well, I shan't disturb you. Perhaps you can take me up to the Angel for luncheon?'

'We'll see.' She sat at the desk and took out some loose sheets of paper, wondering what on earth she was going to write on them.

'Actually,' he said, 'I've very nearly done. You wouldn't, er, know where the key to that cupboard might be? I tried all the ones on the chatelaine.'

Selina, whose immediate impulse was to deny all knowledge of it, thought a moment and then said, 'I seem to remember a key . . . ah . . . yes! Here it is.' And she handed it to him.

He hesitated.

'Well, go on,' she urged.

'I think I left the tap running in the kitchen,' he said, 'Would you be an angel and . . .'

'It was a pump, darling. I worked the handle – remember?'

'Oh . . . yes. Well – don't let me hold you back any longer.' He nodded toward the far side of the desk, where she had been sitting.

'No, I love secrets. I never knew that cupboard was kept locked.'

With infinite reluctance he knelt before the little door and inserted the key – which turned easily, of course. He opened the door a few inches and tried to peep inside.

'Boo!' she cried.

He started back in surprise and she pulled the door wide open.

'No!' he almost shouted.

She sat down and laughed. 'Terence! I'm teasing. Nina and I often sat down here all evening reading those books.'

He stared at them. The titles alone said it all. He turned to her, aghast.

'They're the funniest things ever,' she added.

He closed the door and locked it again, putting the key in his waistcoat pocket.

'Go on – I'll bet you're dying to read them yourself,' she accused.

He gave a reluctant smile. 'Not with you here. I must say – I'm shocked.'

'Oh, it's all right for you, is it – but not for me!'

He said nothing.

'Anyway,' she added, 'they're so unreal.'

He looked at her sharply. 'I dread to ask how you know that. I wouldn't believe it of Tony Moore.'

'And you'd be right.' After a pause she went on, 'I could write one that's ten times more truthful than anything in there. The real "confessions of a young lady"! Only this one was too clever by half.'

He pulled up a chair and sat beside her; taking her hand he said, 'D'you want to tell me?'

She nodded miserably. 'I can't think of anyone else.' She

looked vaguely about her. 'If only Nina were here.'

'Come and sit by the fire.'

She sat in Nina's favourite wingback; he reversed an armless chair and sat near her, straddling its seat and leaning against its rail.

Selina spoke in a faraway tone, as if this really were a tale about some completely fictitious heroine of hers. 'It's the story of a young woman of good breeding who, through a series of misunderstandings – mostly concerning her own nature, her aims in life . . . but also jealousy . . . anyway, for a whole variety of reasons she finds herself engaged to a man who doesn't love her.'

'He's the Hero?'

'I think he is – very much so. He *believes* he loves her, my Heroine, but really he's never got over his First Love – who is also part of the story. She, by the way, is engaged to . . . what shall we call him? The Other Man – Tubal Starkman, let's say. When my Heroine realizes her mistake she becomes desperate. For all sorts of reasons time is short so she must do something dramatic – to open the Hero's eyes to the fact that he doesn't truly love her.'

'Why not just tell him? Talk it over?'

'He wouldn't believe it. It wouldn't shake him enough. He's built a very convincing façade and it's going to take an emotional earthquake to . . . anyway, whose story is this? Mine or yours?'

'Yours I believe,' he said quietly.

'Yes. Very well. So – she has a brilliant idea. She can kill two birds with one stone. If she seduces Tubal Starkman and then makes sure both the Hero and his First Love know of it, their eyes will be opened, their mistaken engagements will be broken off, and the way becomes open for them to realize they never truly stopped loving each other.'

His eyes dwelled in hers. 'And what went wrong?' he asked.

She looked away. 'I'm only just working out that part of it. Those books there' – she gestured vaguely in the direction of the cupboard – 'are full of tales in which young virgins are ravished, almost violated, by skilful men, and then they find the activity so enjoyable that they fall deeply in love and become slaves of passion, or at least of the skilful men. Nina and I used to read them and get so angry. But the twist in my story is this. When my Heroine goes to seduce Tubal Starkman, he *doesn't* ravish her. He doesn't violate her. He doesn't even ... oh, what's the technical word? What d'you say in court?'

'Penetrate?'

'Yes — he doesn't even penetrate her. Instead he's just so ...' Tears began to press at her eyelids. 'So gentle ... and considerate and' — she closed her eyes and shivered at the memory — 'and so wonderful to her that she really and truly does fall in love with him. And now she knows it's love.' She began speaking more rapidly, to outstrip her urge to break down into tears. 'She's never felt like that before in her life. She isn't big enough to contain this new feeling. At any moment she fears it will tear her apart. You see the irony of her situation, Terence? She starts out thinking she's going to control all these events, but really, because she's a stupid, ignorant little virgin, she hasn't the first idea of the forces she's about to meddle with. And they just sweep her up and ... and make her an absolute prisoner — a slave! Yes, a slave, of all the things she thought she was going to control.'

She ran out of breath and had to pause.

'How does it all end?' he asked.

'I have no idea. That's what I was going to try and work out today.'

'But tell me — is she happy about it?'

Selina thought it over and then grinned broadly. 'Yes,' she said. 'Despite everything — all the pain she's going to cause ... I mean, she's got to be cruel to be kind — but despite all that, she is ecstatically, blissfully happy.'

'I think it could turn out all right then,' he said. 'In the end.'

Chapter Sixty-Seven

Hilary stirred. Selina cleared her throat a little louder and at last the girl came awake. 'Is anyone there?' she asked in a husky voice.

Selina gave a little tut of vexation. 'I'm sorry, child. I was trying not to wake you. I just thought I heard a noise up here, that's all.'

Hilary swung her legs out of bed.

'No, no.' Selina whispered urgently. 'Stay where you are. It can't have been anything – just my nerves. I've looked into the nursery. She's fast asleep. I'm terribly sorry – fussing over nothing like this. Just go back to sleep, eh?'

The girl put her legs back under the covers.

Selina gave her a conspiratorial smile. 'If you hear any sounds from the floor below, pay no attention. And whatever you do, don't . . . no – never mind. Forget I said anything about it. Good night, little one.'

'G'night, Miss Selina.' The moment Hilary was alone again, she got up, pulled on her dressing gown, and went into the nursery to see for herself.

Selina waited at the far end of the corridor until she saw the girl on her way back; only then did she set off down the servants' stairs to the floor below. Hilary was still too drowsy to grasp that something was amiss. In fact, she was back in bed before she realized how odd it was for Miss Selina to be using that particular way down. Her bedroom was close to the foot of the other stairs.

It was a moment or two more before the corollary struck her, when she remembered whose bedroom lay at the foot of the servants' stair. Once again she swung herself out into

744

the cold night and struggled into her dressing gown. She avoided the two creaking steps – which was more than Miss Selina had done – and arrived without a sound at Hal's bedroom door.

It was slightly ajar, she noticed – which was also odd. Earlier that night, when Hal had just entered his bedroom and she had slipped in after him to ask if he wanted a drink of hot milk – or 'anything else?' – he had been very firm, both in declining the offer and in closing the door behind her. Now she was beginning to understand why. The sounds from within – the rustling of bedclothes, sighs, small rhythmic movements – left little to be imagined.

Hesitantly she pushed the door slightly wider apart. What she saw made her blood boil; a mist of fiery anger rose about her, consuming everything except the last, immediate remnant of her caution. That at least persisted long enough to allow her to close the door in silence – or with such little noise that the two lovers, occupied as they were, would not hear her.

No words shaped her wrath as she stormed off along the passage; no discretion stayed her fingers as they grasped the handle of Tony's bedroom door; no heed could pen back the words she blurted out: 'If it please you, Dr Moore, sir, you'd best come see what's afoot.'

As always he came awake at once. 'Actually,' he said with a rueful laugh, tugging off his nightcap and tousling his hair with his fingers, 'it's really Dr Sheridan's night – but never mind now. Who is it?'

''Tisn't none of that, sir,' she assured him. ''Tis personal-like to you.'

'Eh?' His toes were groping for his slippers. She bent down and put them in the way. 'Thank you, Hilary. Now what is all this? Start from the beginning.'

She passed him his dressing gown. 'I can't say it, sir. Don't make I say it. Just come and see for yourself.'

'At least tell me where? I mean, do I put up my clothes or what?'

Reluctantly she muttered, ''Tis Mister Penrose's room, sir.'

'Ah.' He sat down on the bed. 'Listen, my dear. One may approve or one may disapprove, but what people do in private is really ...'

745

''Tisn't with Miss Rosewarne,' the girl blurted out. She watched his face fearfully, as if she believed he might strike her.

As he took in her words his lips compressed until his mouth almost vanished. There was a sudden hardness in his eyes. 'I see,' he said in a strange, clipped tone she had never heard from him before. 'Thank you, Hilary. You did quite right to come and speak of it. Now you may go back to your room and leave the rest to me.'

She needed no second bidding but raced upstairs — past her room, down the passage, until she stood at the head of the back stairs, fighting to breathe in silence.

She need not have hurried for it was some minutes before Dr Tony came. He must have got dressed, she thought, not daring to risk a peep. He certainly had his boots up — and he was certainly taking no pains to disguise his approach. Miss Selina must have heard it, too, for she gave a little squeak of alarm.

The door was flung open and Dr Tony's voice said, 'Get up, you.' Not roaring and bawling, but very quiet.

'Tony!' That was Miss Selina, shocked he should take that tone with her.

'I'm not talking to you,' he said. 'I'll deal with you later. It's that traitor I want.'

'Don't make a bigger fool of yourself than you already are, Moore.' That was Hal! Oh, why had she wasted her love on him?

'I'll give you five minutes, Penrose. I want you dressed and outside on the lawn in five minutes where I shall give you the thrashing of your life.'

Laughter. Hal again. Dr Tony must be mad to challenge he like that.

A mighty creaking of the bed. Hal getting up. Would he beat him there and then? His voice: 'Look at us, man — look at the difference in size. I'd kill you. I'm sorry about this but you'd already lost her, you know. She . . . ooofff!' Now he was struggling for breath. Coughing. Gasping.

'Now will you come out and fight?' Dr Tony must really be mad. She ought to go and waken Miss Rosewarne — she'd soon put a stop to this nonsense.

'Five minutes,' Dr Tony repeated. And there were his

746

boots going back along the passage ... and down the stairs. The front door opened and closed.

Hilary went back to the main stairway and crept down after him − but made for the kitchen when she reached the bottom.

By great good fortune Selina, who was then in her dressing gown and slippers, and helping Hal to dress, just happened to see her as she crossed the yard. She threw Hal's trousers at him and raced downstairs, leaving him even more bewildered than before.

She reached the cottage just as Hilary was launching into an explanation. Johanna was sitting up in bed struggling with a match that would not strike. She gave up and drew back the curtain, letting the moonlight flood the room.

'It's all right, Hilary dear, I'll explain,' Selina told her.

But the girl stood her ground, 'I should just think you'd done enough mischief for one night, miss.'

'You're quite right. I'm not going to try and shrug off my guilt. Jo − I've done a terrible thing. I can't expect you to forgive me. But there's no time for explanations now. You've got to come over and stop this nonsense.'

'What? At least tell me ...'

Hilary, realizing that Selina was, indeed, going to gloss over it with her talk of 'done a terrible thing,' and 'guilt' and 'you'll never forgive me,' blurted it out: 'That Hal Penrose and she − taking beef in bed together. Only now.'

'Beef?' Johanna asked, even as the meaning dawned on her.

'And Tony came and caught us' − Selina turned and stared at Hilary as she added − 'somehow. Now he's challenged Hal to a fight.'

Johanna gave a cry of alarm and stood up. 'Challenged Hal?' she cried. 'But he'll kill him. Oh, the fool!'

'That's what we were telling you. You've got to come and stop it. They'll listen to you.'

Johanna was already putting on her travelling greatcoat and boots. Hilary bent to tie them but she gave a little warning kick. 'No time for that. Where are they?'

'Tony said the front lawn.'

Moments later they were hurrying back across the courtyard. By the time they reached the side lawn, there could be no doubting that a fight was in progress. But the sound they heard made all three stop and stare at each other in bewilderment. For the voice that was saying, 'Ouch! ... Here! ... Oy!' was Hal's. And it was Tony who was saying, 'Give up? D'you give up?'

With mounting bewilderment the three of them crept forward until they were hard against the tracery of the pergola that made it possible to talk of a 'front' and 'side' lawn at all — for neither was much bigger than a good pocket handkerchief. Between the rustic woodwork and the black-spotted stems of last year's roses, they thus had a vantage that was better than the traditional 'ringside'. Had they not seen the fight, they would never have believed the way it went. They would have said — as many who heard of it later did say — that Hal had pulled his punches and done the only thing a gentleman could possibly have done, considering the circumstances of the challenge.

Tony, who yielded six inches in height, half as much in reach, and several stone in weight, was dancing around like a sprite — never still, never a target for more than a split second. It was just long enough for Hal to imagine he might get one in. But when he lunged, Tony had vanished, only to materialize again at his side and put a punishing blow between his ribs.

'D'ye give up?' he taunted, darting and weaving again, daring Hal to have another go.

'Damn you, Moore,' Hal muttered grimly. 'I'll wear you down yet.'

'We can't stop them now,' Johanna whispered.

The others did not disagree.

'Why aren't they hitting each other's faces?' Selina asked.

'They must have agreed it so,' Johanna replied, as mystified as her cousin. After more thought she added, 'Whoever won, they'd both be laughing stocks if they went around with their faces all cut and bruised.'

For ten more minutes it went on like that, Hal taking the most dreadful punishment, but always refusing to give his man best. And then Tony began to tire. He misjudged the edge of the lawn and stepped back into a small clump of berberis, whose thorns pricked deep.

'Oy!' he yelled.

And Hal, seeing his chance at last, stepped in and struck him a mighty hammer-blow that sent him reeling down the path. He recovered himself and soon returned to the fight. But from that moment on he had lost something of his waspish nimbleness. Though he still landed several blows that made Hal wince, he took almost as many in return.

At one moment each struck the other so hard that neither could continue. They just stood there, gleaming in the moonlight with the sweat pouring off them — despite the chill of the night — panting for all they were worth, and just hanging on the air.

'You caught me . . .' Hal began.

'Caught you — yes!' Tony gasped.

'No — caught me at the . . . worst time for a man.' He tried to laugh. 'I'd have killed you else.'

'I could have killed you.' Tony put up his guard again but Hal shook his head. 'What did you mean?' Tony went on fighting for breath. 'Lost her anyway?'

'Are those women watching us?'

Both men stared up at the windows and, of course, saw nothing. 'Good,' Hal said. 'She knows you don't' — he took one huge breath in an attempt to get ahead of his respiratory distress — 'you don't love her.'

'My God!' Tony, though still not recovered, put up his guard in earnest. 'I'm not going to discuss Selina with you!'

They resumed their fight but now both were visibly tiring. Tony was concentrating on one particular rib, where he had inflicted terrible damage earlier — in fact, he suspected he'd fractured it. Now he was desperate to finish the business quickly, even at the risk of a pneumothorax — a punctured lung; at least he knew how to treat that.

But Hal gained cunning as he lost in sheer strength. Not only was Tony unable to land a further blow there but, by tempting him to try, Hal led him into further errors — which he was quick to exploit. Soon they had fought each other to a second standstill.

'She's convinced you still love Jo,' Hal said, as if nothing had interrupted their previous conversation — and even though he had to gasp for every word.

Behind the pergola, Selina put her hand on her cousin's arm and squeezed it. Johanna frowned at her. Selina nodded and smiled, inclining her head toward the two battered men.

'I see!' Tony exclaimed, equally breathless again.

'See what?'

'Just an excuse. Because I love Jo . . . you free to . . . bed Selina. Clever!'

'Don't be stupid!' Hal roared. He stabbed at Tony and missed him by a foot.

'Stupid!' Tony echoed. He looked about them for something to lean on; for one petrifying moment the three behind the pergola were sure he had seen them.

'I love Selina!' Hal began to laugh. 'And you, my friend, are a fool.' The laugh turned into a cough.

Hal lumbered back into action. Or, rather, just stood there, guarding that one weak spot and letting Tony hit him wherever else he pleased. During their last break he had realized that his opponent's knuckles and wrists were hurting as badly as his own. The pain from every ligament forced him to pull each punch, however much he willed himself not to. The resulting blow was therefore little more than playful. Finally, when all that was left of Tony's skill was the ability to stand there, looking every inch a pugilist, with his fists raised high, and boxing shadows, Hal reached out and grabbed him by the forearms, holding him in a grip he could not shake.

'Against the rules,' Tony panted.

'A pox on the rules, man. I don't want to fight you any more. All right? You're too good for me. All right? You win. All right?'

'Dammit, I want to knock you down.'

Hal glanced at the moon – a brother lunatic – and, releasing his grip, offered Tony his jaw, side-on, an easy mark.

Tony hauled back his arm for a grand knock-out. Selina drew breath to shout no – and only just managed to stop herself when Tony gave a single, exhausted laugh and slumped where he stood.

To the amazement of the onlookers, Hal then put an arm around him and turned him toward the house; and Tony, to their even greater amazement, put his arm about Hal's shoulder – which he could just about manage without becoming too ridiculously lopsided – and walked in step with him, like a couple of chums at school.

'Let's cool off a bit,' Hal suggested, changing their direction toward the stone seat in front of the pergola.

The women, feeling sure of discovery now, stopped breathing. But the two men were only interested in retrieving their jackets, which they had slung carelessly on the seat. Moments later they were sprawled side by side, legs outstretched, heads thrown back, eyes closed, and with their backs to their audience, who were the width of the shrub border – a little over four feet – away.

'What did we prove?' Hal asked the sky. 'Except that you *are* more than a match for me. Where did you learn to box like that?'

'School. College. Why did you do it, Penrose? What gets into you?'

After some thought Hal said, 'Ask her. You wouldn't believe me anyway.'

'I don't know who I'd believe any more.'

'Tell me truthfully – do you love her?'

It was Tony's turn for thought. 'We could have had a very happy life together. Love can grow, you know.'

Hal turned to him and said, in something close to disgust, 'She asked for bread and you'd have given her stones.'

Silence fell between them. Johanna turned to Selina and nodded toward the back yard, raising her eyebrows questioningly. Selina shook her head vehemently.

Hal spoke again. 'Why are you so reluctant to admit you still love Johanna?'

'Hah!' Tony snorted. 'Suppose I do? You're the last person I'd admit it to. You may play the traitor as much as you wish ...'

'Traitor?' Hal felt his anger returning.

'Yes. You're a guest under my roof. You also happen to be engaged to Johanna, though it's obviously slipped your mind in the usual fashion.'

Hal began to laugh – mostly in disbelief. 'Are you saying that the only reason you won't admit it is because

I'm your guest and am supposed to be engaged to her?'

'It's not the only reason,' Tony answered defensively. 'There are others. For one thing – it's none of your damned business.'

'Oh, Moore – you are such a learned bloody fool. Even though you're too stiff-necked to admit it, you quite clearly still *are* in love with Jo. And that's all that matters to me.'

'All that matters? What d'you mean?'

'Because it sets Selina free. And it sets me free, too. We are both free of . . . you. Of obligation to you.'

'Bit sudden, don't you think?'

'Isn't it always? I don't know – I'm a stranger here myself.' After a pause he added, 'Anyway, you could hardly call it love at first sight.'

'Are you going to marry her?' Tony asked.

'That – to quote someone or other – is none of your damned business. But, as a favour, and because I've suddenly taken quite a liking to you – stubborn as you are – I'll tell you: I'd marry her tomorrow if she'd have me.'

'And what about Jo? She does love you, you know.'

'This is all wrong,' Johanna whispered in Selina's ear.

Selina dug her nails into her cousin's arm until it was all she could do not to cry out.

'Perhaps so,' Hal admitted. 'Just as I'm not saying I don't love her, too – in a way. But if we yoked ourselves to each other, I doubt we'd ever taste a single moment's happiness again. In her heart she knows it, too. But when it comes to stubbornness – to headstrong, perverse, obstinate, mulish inflexibility – she'll run circles round you. Even round you. So what I plan to do – during this time while I'm in Cornwall – is let her come to her own realization of it. Because no matter what anyone else tells her, it's only when she sees something for herself that she'll believe it. So. I'll thank you to say nothing of this – and I must somehow make it right with Selina, until Jo is convinced.' After a silence he prompted, 'Well?'

'And what about little Hannah?'

For a moment Hal seemed not to have heard him; then he replied. 'You'll see – when we say our farewells she'll whisper something in that child's ear. And I know exactly what it'll be. She'll say, "Take a good look at that man.

One day I'll tell you a funny thing about him".' His voice broke as he realized what Johanna had done.

Tony, who had no idea what he was referring to, nonetheless felt he had already trespassed too far.

'Well?' Hal recovered and repeated his prompting.

Tony sighed. 'I'll give you my answer in the morning. Here — I'd better look at that rib before you ... just sit still.'

He tapped Hal's rib cage, causing him to wince; he put his ear to Hal's mouth and made him breathe in and out as deeply as he could — and then was satisfied that the worst had not happened.

'You coming indoors?' Hal asked. 'I'll bet those women *were* watching. They won't know what to make of us, sitting here like this.'

Tony shook his head. 'I think I'll just go for a walk. Something seems to have given me a headache.' He held out his hand, which Hal shook rather gingerly.

Together they strolled back to the front door. And now Selina turned toward the back door, intending to beat them to it.

But Johanna pinched her sleeve and held her back. 'Hilary,' she whispered. 'Go in and make Mr Penrose a cup of tea.'

The girl needed no one to tell her twice; she skipped back indoors. Hal was her hero once again; she had always thought that Dr Tony and Miss Rosewarne were intended for each other — her true second mother and father.

'I don't know what to say,' Selina confessed when they were alone.

'That makes a change.' Johanna let her go.

'I keep doing things for one reason and then getting caught up in them for quite different reasons.'

'You'd better explain that. Come back to the cottage and have a drop of brandy.'

When they were indoors again she raked up the dying embers and put on more wood before she got out the bottle and glasses. Selina watched her and tried to think what to say.

'There.' Johanna placed a good measure before her.

The spirits did the usual miracle of revival. Selina

breathed out fire and smiled. 'You know why I fell in love with Tony, don't you.'

'It did seem quite sudden, after so many months.'

'It was because you told me you thought you were falling in love with him, too. And I thought to myself it was so unfair. You already had Hal − who we all knew adored you. And now there was Tony − and he'd come running if you just crooked a finger at him. And I just said, "why should she?"' She smiled feebly. 'And that's the only reason I fell for him. Of course, afterwards, I found out how good he is and then I thought I must be very lucky. I mean, I really did think I loved him then. Until last night with Hal.'

'*Last* night?' Johanna asked in surprise. She looked at the clock, thinking her cousin might just be being pedantic.

'No,' Selina said ruefully. 'It was last night *and* tonight.'

'I see. Go on − that's the part I thought you were going to explain first.'

Selina took another gulp of brandy. Johanna pointedly jammed the stopper in the bottle and put it back on the sideboard.

'You see, when Tony and I were walking along Praa last Sunday ... Did Nina ever tell you − no, never mind all that, now. Anyway, Tony was talking about Hal and you, and whether Hal appreciated you, whether he was good enough for you, whether he understood what a truly remarkable woman you are ...'

'How absurd,' Johanna erupted angrily.

'Oh, I agree.' Selina was straight-faced. 'He just went on and on and on. And I suddenly saw it − what it meant: he was still as much in love with you as ever.'

'Never mind that. Come to you and Hal.' Johanna relented and brought the brandy bottle back to the table.

But now Selina put her hand over the glass when she tried to refill it. 'You remember the first night you came to Lanfear?' she asked. 'How I took one look at you and bawled out that I wanted your dress?'

Johanna smiled. 'Only too well. But what has that to do with ...'

'And then, when you went to Liston Court, how I badgered Nina to take me to live there, too?'

'I didn't know that. Nina always said it was her idea.'

'But I put it in her mind. And then how I almost commandeered her when we went to the Holy Land? And I couldn't understand why it didn't upset you more ... and then you told us about the baby. Oh, I was so furious!'

'What − because you couldn't follow suit?'

'Yes! Who d'you think it was poured all that poison into Nina's ear against you?'

'No, Selina, I don't believe a word of this.'

'I didn't mean to, and I hated myself for it, but ...'

'Anyway, why are you going back over all this old ground now?'

'And taking Tony from you was all part of the same pattern. And only the other week − last week − I couldn't even let you meet Hal alone.'

'Jolly good thing, as it turned out.'

'That's not the point, Jo. Don't you see?'

'I wish I could see why you're telling me all this.'

'Because I want you to believe me − you more than anyone − I want you to believe me when I say that my going to Hal's bedroom last night had nothing to do with all that. I didn't think *that* much farther than my nose. I was in such a panic not to marry Tony − once I realized how much he still loves you. I knew that if I slept with Hal, Tony wouldn't even look at me again. And that was the only thought in my mind. I swear it!'

Johanna closed her eyes and murmured, 'Don't!'

'Why? I thought you wanted me to ...'

'It's not that. Oh, God − I've just remembered something I taunted Hal with. Yesterday.'

'What?'

'He made some sneering remark about Tony's probable capacity as a lover − in bed, I mean. So I told him − oh, darling, do forgive me? − I told him you were a little frightened of men in that way and that Tony was the ideal husband because he'd be so kind and gentle and considerate and understanding.'

Selina stared at her and then began to laugh. It came close to hysterics before Johanna reached across and shook her into a calmer mood. 'What's so funny?' she asked.

'It doesn't matter. I mean the reasons don't matter. It's

just one more twist. I went to Hal for one reason only — to put an end to everything between Tony and me. And he was so loving and gentle and wonderful to me that I fell in love with him — really in love, for the first time. You know the feeling, don't you.'

Johanna nodded.

'You can't mistake it.'

'But you can outgrow it. I've just managed it — at last.'

Selina, punctured for only a moment said, 'Well, it doesn't have to happen. Anyway, what I wanted you to know was that — despite all my past history of meanness and spite and jealousy towards you — I did not go to Hal simply to take him away from you ... even though that is the way it has turned out.'

'You didn't need to tell me that, darling.'

'I did.'

'No, I mean — even if that had been your intention, Hal would never have let you do it. If he loves you, as you heard him say, it's because he loves you — not because you trapped him into it. Look how long and hard poor little Jenny Jewell tried, and yet she never had the remotest chance. Hal is actually very faithful ...' Almost under her breath she added, '. . . to Hal.'

Selina shook her head pityingly. 'He'll be different now. You'll see. He's tired of all that philandering.'

Johanna yawned.

'Anyway,' her cousin went on, 'it saves me asking the one question that was uppermost in my mind.'

'Good.' Johanna stood up, put up her coat again, and went to the door.

'Where are you going?'

'To Tony, of course.'

'But he's gone for a walk. He could be anywhere by now.'

'I know exactly where he'll be.' She came back and took up the brandy bottle — then, for good measure, a spare blanket.

At the door she again turned and came back for another blanket. 'After all' — she smiled at her cousin — 'we're none of us getting any younger, are we.'

THE END

MALCOLM ROSS

**A rich West Country saga
in the bestselling tradition of POLDARK**

On a Far Wild Shore

Young, beautiful and newly widowed, Elizabeth Troy travels to her late husband's Cornish home hoping to find comfort in its fertile hills and valleys. But she is shocked to discover the vast, decaying acreage of Pallas is now solely her responsibility – a legacy as unexpected as it is unwelcome.

Elizabeth's plans for her inheritance provoke the bitter hostility of her sister-in-law, Morwenna, whose word has been law at Pallas for thirty years. To bring the troubled estate back to prosperity Elizabeth must look for help elsewhere. And there are many very willing to be more than a friend to the widow – David Troy, a poor relation whose sober exterior hides some disturbing secrets; Courtenay Rodda, the sensual newspaper proprietor; and James Troy, the rich and worldly wise American cousin who begins a thrilling but dangerous liaison with Elizabeth . . .

'The book is beautifully written, the characters depicted with a passionate realism that held me entranced. I simply loved it!' Patricia Wendorf, bestselling author of *Larksleve*.

FICTION   0-7472-3001-3   £2.95

More Compulsive Fiction from Headline:

LOUISE JAMES

GOLD ROUND THE EDGES

Eden Murray, seventeen years old and recently orphaned, returns to her native fishing village of Buckthorne to seek her roots and, she hopes, to discover a new, ready-made family. But she is surprised to find herself an unwelcome guest under the roof of her fanatical Uncle Caleb, and is shocked by the lustful advances of his son John. Yet Eden holds her head high and joins the fisher-lassies employed at the harbour, as skilled in the work as any of the Buckthorne girls.

Whenever she can she escapes to the arms of Lewis Ross, the only man she can trust. But her happiness is as fragile as the beautiful souvenir plate she found in Great Yarmouth — the one with the gold around the edges. Armed only with her youth and her passionate instinct for survival, Eden fights hard to win the man she loves and take her rightful place in the little village where she was born.

FICTION/SAGA 0 7472 3147 8 £2.99

GRACE THOMPSON

Dirty Nelly

A heartwarming story of Welsh village life
in the tradition of
Christine Marion Fraser's RHANNA

The little Welsh village of Hen Carw Parc –
the old deer park – seems to be an island of
rural tranquillity. But the inhabitants are a
lively and varied community – and none
more so than Nelly Luke, the cheerful
Cockney widow whose eccentric lifestyle
is the despair of her social-climbing
daughter Evie.

Yet Nelly's amiable warmth brings her
many friends – Kay, the young newly-wed
whose marriage is haunted by the all-too-
substantial ghost of her lost love; Amy, the
village postmistress, whose private life is
colourful indeed; the dignified Mrs French,
whose family cupboard contains several
unlooked-for skeletons.

Against the mounting excitement of the
Coronation summer, Nelly steers her
friends and family through storm and
sunshine alike . . .

FICTION/GENERAL   0 7472 3149 4   £2.99

More Compulsive Fiction from Headline:

JANICE YOUNG BROOKS
CINNAMON WHARF

by the
author of
CROWN SABLE

**For generations the masters of a vast
trading empire – bringing rare spices from
the four corners of the world to the
households of Europe – the Beecham
family is regarded as a model of prosperity
and self-worth. So George Beecham's
impulsive adoption of a foundling child is
all the more shocking in its
unexpectedness.**

**And Mary, the child George adopts, fits
uneasily into the leisured world of the
great house at Castlemere, finding its
luxury unimportant when set against the
exotic lure of the spice trade to which she
becomes heiress. But even great wealth
and the fascination of controlling the
centuries-old business cannot buy Mary
the one thing she craves – the love of her
sophisticated and unattainable cousin
Alex . . .**

**Also by Janice Young Brooks from Headline
CROWN SABLE**

FICTION/SAGA 0 7472 3203 2 £3.99

Headline books are available at your book-shop or newsagent, or can be ordered from the following address:

Headline Book Publishing PLC
Cash Sales Department
PO Box 11
Falmouth
Cornwall
TR10 9EN
England

UK customers please send cheque or postal order (no currency), allowing 60p for postage and packing for the first book, plus 25p for the second book and 15p for each additional book ordered up to a maximum charge of £1.90 in UK.

BFPO customers please allow 60p for postage and packing for the first book, plus 25p for the second book and 15p per copy for the next seven books, thereafter 9p per book.

Overseas and Eire customers please allow £1.25 for postage and packing for the first book, plus 75p for the second book and 28p for each subsequent book.